THE LABYRINTH OF OSIRIS

THE
LABYRINTH
OF OSIRIS

PAUL SUSSMAN

Atlantic Monthly Press
New York

First published in Great Britain in 2012 by Bantam Press
a division of Transworld Publishers
The Random House Group Limited, London

Printed in the United States of America

Published simultaneously in Canada

ISBN-13: 978-0-8021-2041-0

Atlantic Monthly Press
an imprint of Grove/Atlantic, Inc.
841 Broadway
New York, NY 10003

Distributed by Publishers Group West

www.groveatlantic.com

12 13 14 15   10 9 8 7 6 5 4 3 2 1

For Team Sussman – Alicky, Ezra, Jude and Layla.
With love, always.

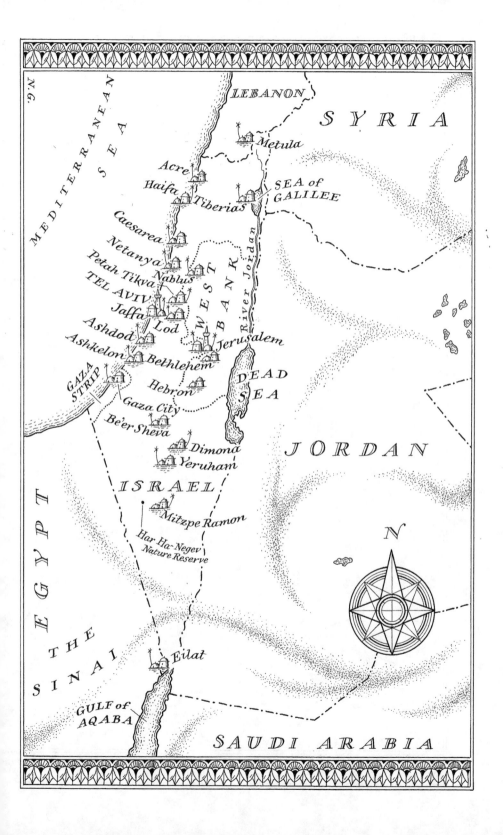

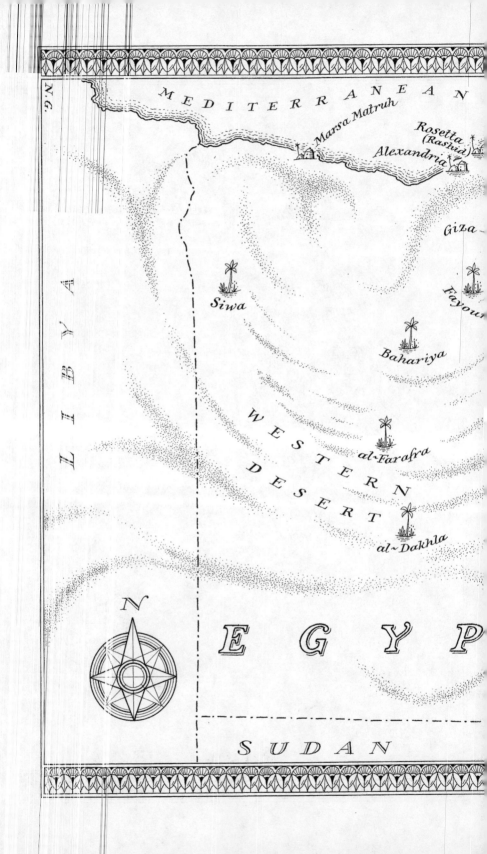

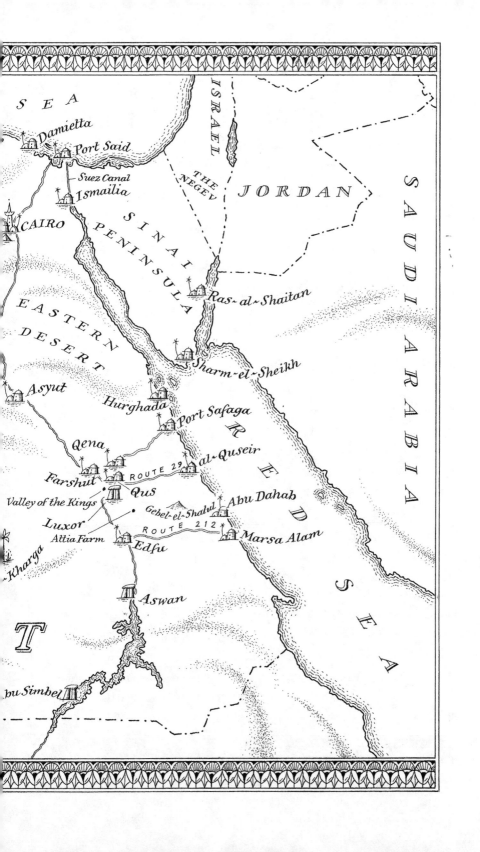

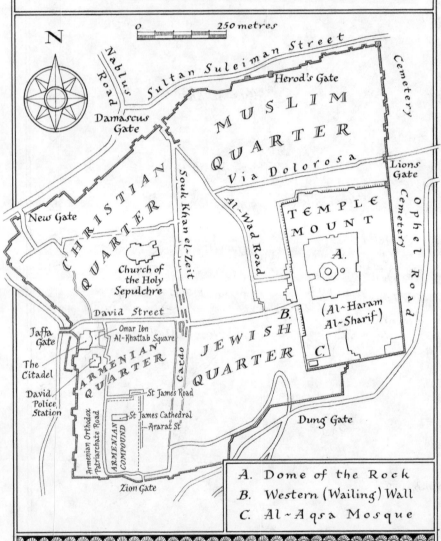

The OLD CITY of JERUSALEM

N

0   250 metres

Nablus Road

Sultan Suleiman Street

Herod's Gate

Cemetery

Damascus Gate

MUSLIM QUARTER

Via Dolorosa

Lions Gate

New Gate

CHRISTIAN QUARTER

Souk Khan el-Zeit

Al-Wad Road

TEMPLE MOUNT

A.

Ophel Road

Cemetery

Church of the Holy Sepulchre

(Al-Haram Al-Sharif)

David Street

B.

Jaffa Gate

Omar Ibn Al-Khattab Square

C.

The Citadel

ARMENIAN QUARTER

Cardo

JEWISH QUARTER

David Police Station

Armenian Orthodox Patriarchate Road

St James Road

ARMENIAN COMPOUND

St James Cathedral
Ararat St

Dung Gate

Zion Gate

A. Dome of the Rock
B. Western (Wailing) Wall
C. Al-Aqsa Mosque

PROLOGUE

LUXOR, EGYPT: THE WEST BANK OF THE NILE, 1931

Had the boy not decided to try a new fishing spot, he would never have heard the blind girl from the next village, nor seen the monster who attacked her.

Usually he fished a small inlet just beyond the giant reed banks, downriver of where the Nile ferry docked. Tonight, on a tip-off from his cousin Mehmet, who claimed to have seen shoals of giant *bulti* drifting in the shallows, the boy had gone upriver, past the outlying cane fields of Ba'irat, to a narrow sandbank screened from sight by a dense grove of *doum* palms. The place had a good feel to it, and he cast immediately. Barely had his hook hit the water when he heard the girl's voice. Faint but audible. '*La, minfadlak!*' No, please!

He lifted his head, listening, his line dragging in the pull of the current.

'Please, don't,' came the voice again. 'I'm scared.'

And then laughter. A man's laughter.

Laying down his rod, he climbed the mud bank fronting the river and moved into the palm grove. The voice had come from the grove's southern end and he angled in that direction, following a narrow dirt path, treading carefully so as not to make any noise or disturb the horned vipers that lurked in the undergrowth and whose bite was deadly.

'No,' came the voice again. 'In God's name, I beg you!'

More laughter. Cruel laughter. Teasing.

He stooped and picked up a rock, ready to defend himself if necessary, and continued forward, following the path as it curved through the centre of the grove and back towards the shoreline. He caught glimpses of the Nile to his left, slats of mercury shifting beyond the palm trunks, but of the girl and her attacker he could see nothing. Only when he reached the edge of the grove and the trees fell away did he finally get a clear view of the assault.

A broad track crossed in front of him, emerging from the cane fields to his right and running down to the river. A motorbike stood there. Beyond, clearly visible in the silvery moonlight, were two figures. One, by far the largest of the pair, was kneeling with his back to the boy. He wore Western dress -- trousers, boots, a dust-caked leather coat, even though the night was warm – and was holding down a much smaller figure in a *djellaba suda*. She didn't appear to be struggling, just lay as if frozen, her face hidden by her violator's sizeable frame.

'Please,' she groaned. 'Please don't hurt me.'

The boy wanted to shout out, but was afraid. Instead he crept forward and squatted behind an oleander bush, the rock still clasped in his hand. He could see the girl properly now and recognized her. Iman el-Badri, the blind girl from Shaykh Abd al-Qurna. The one they all laughed at because rather than doing the things girls ought to do – washing and cleaning and cooking – she instead spent her days in the old temples, tapping around with her stick and touching the carved picture writing, which people said she could understand simply by feel. Iman the witch, they called her. Iman the stupid.

Now, staring through the oleander leaves as the man pawed at her, the boy regretted his teasing, even though all of them had done it, even her own brothers.

'I'm scared,' she repeated. 'Please don't hurt me.'

'Not if you do as I say, my little one.'

They were the first words the man had spoken, or at least the first the boy had heard. His voice was gruff and guttural, his Arabic heavily accented. He laughed again, pulling off her headscarf and running a hand through her hair. She started sobbing.

Terrified as he was, the boy knew he had to do something. Sizing up the distance between himself and the figures in front of him, he pulled back his arm, ready to launch the rock at the rapist's head.

Before he could do so, the man suddenly came to his feet and turned, moonlight bathing his face.

The boy gasped. It was the face of a ghoul. The eyes weren't proper eyes, just small black holes; nothing where the nose should have been. There were no lips, just teeth, unnaturally large and white, like an animal's maw. The skin was translucently pale, the cheeks sunken, as

14

if recoiling in disgust from the grotesque image of which they formed a part.

The boy knew him now, for he had heard the rumours: a *hawaga*, a foreigner, who worked in the tombs and had only empty space where his face should have been. An evil spirit, people said, who prowled at night, and drank blood, and disappeared for weeks on end into the desert to commune with his fellow demons. The boy grimaced, fighting back the urge to scream.

'Allah protect me,' he murmured. 'Dear Allah, keep him away.'

For a moment he feared he had been heard, for the monster came forward a step and stared directly at the bush, his head cocked as if listening. Seconds passed, agonizing seconds. Then, with a low rasping chuckle, like the sound of a dog panting, the man walked to the motorbike. His victim clambered to her feet, still sobbing, although quieter now.

When he reached the bike the man pulled a bottle from the pocket of his coat, uncorked it with his teeth and swigged. He burped and swigged again, then returned the bottle to one pocket while removing something from the other. The boy could just make out straps and buckles and assumed it was a rider's cap. Rather than putting it on his head, the man gave the thing a shake and slap and lifted it to his face, bringing his hands around behind his head to thread the straps. It was a mask, a leather mask, covering his face from the forehead down to just above the chin, with holes for his eyes and mouth. Somehow it made him look even more grotesque than the deformities it was designed to cover, and the boy let out another low gasp of terror. Again the man stared in his direction, white eyes shifting behind the leather, peering out as though from inside a cave. Then, turning, he grasped the motorbike's handlebars and placed his foot on the kick-start.

'You tell no one about this,' he called to the girl, again speaking in Arabic. 'You understand? No one. It's our secret.'

He stamped down and the engine roared into life. He tweaked the throttle lever a couple of times, revving, then leant over and fumbled in one of the pannier bags slung across the back of the bike. Producing what looked like a packet or a small book – the boy couldn't be certain – he walked back to the girl, seized her *djellaba* and stuffed the object among the folds of black material. To the boy's disgust he then curled a hand behind her head and brought her face forward, pressing it against his own. She turned this way and that, seeming to gasp in disgust at the feel of the leather against her skin, before the man broke away and returned to his motorbike. He kicked up the front and rear stands, pulled on a pair of goggles, swung a leg over the seat and, with a final cry of 'Our little secret!', engaged the gear lever and roared off up the track, disappearing in a cloud of dust.

So terrified was the boy that it was several minutes before he dared move. Only when the sound of the engine had faded completely and the night was once again silent did he come to his feet. The girl had by now picked up her headscarf and retied her hair, mumbling to her-self, letting out strange keening sounds that the boy might have mistaken for laughter had he not seen what had just been done to her. He wanted to go over and tell her it was all right, that her ordeal was over, but sensed that it would only compound her shame to know that it had been witnessed. He stood where he was, therefore, watching as she felt in the grass for her stick and started tapping her way up the track away from the river. She went fifty metres, then suddenly stopped and turned, looking directly at him.

'*Salaam*,' she called, her free hand protectively clutching her *djellaba*. 'Is someone there?'

He held his breath. She called again, her sightless eyes straining, then continued on her way. He let her go, waiting till she rounded a bend and was lost among the cane plants. Then, making his way back through the palm grove, he picked up the path that ran alongside the Nile and broke into a sprint, his fishing rod forgotten. He knew exactly what needed to be done.

With its 488cc single-cylinder engine and 3-speed Sturmey Archer gearbox, the Royal Enfield Model J could reach a top speed of over sixty miles an hour. On the tarmac highways of Europe the man had had it up to almost seventy. Here in Egypt, where even the best roads were little more than glorified tracks, he rarely took it much beyond thirty. Tonight was different. Special. The alcohol and the euphoria made him reckless, and he pushed the speedometer up to forty-five, roaring north through the cane and maize fields, the Nile lost away to his right, the towering wave of the Theban massif tracking him to the left. He took frequent swigs from his whisky bottle and sang to him-self, tunelessly, always the same song.

'It's a long way to Tipperary,
It's a long way to go.
It's a long way to Tipperary,
To the sweetest girl I know!
Goodbye, Piccadilly,
Farewell, Leicester Square!
It's a long, long way to Tipperary,
But my heart's right here*!'*

Most of the west bank hamlets were deserted, ghost villages, their *fellaheen* inhabitants having long since gone to bed, their mud-brick dwellings as dark and silent as tombs. Only in Esba were there signs of life. There had been a *moulid* here earlier in the evening and a few late-night stragglers still lingered outside: a pair of old men sitting on a bench puffing *shisha* pipes; a group of children throwing stones at a camel; a sweet-seller trudging home with his empty cart. They looked up as the motorbike passed, eyeing its rider suspiciously. The sweet-seller shouted at him and one of the children held his index fingers up to his forehead in the sign of *al-shaitan*, the Devil. The man ignored them – he was used to such insults – and rode on, a pack of dogs chasing him out of the village.

'Mangy curs!' he cried, leaning round and snarling at them.

He came to a crossroads and turned left, heading west, directly towards the massif, its rearing bulk glowing a dull pewter colour in the moonlight. Tiny paths criss-crossed its face like white veins, some of them the same paths the ancient tomb-workers must have used to cross the hills over three millennia previously, on their way to the Wadi Biban al-Moluk, the Valley of the Kings. He had walked those paths many a time over the years, much to the bewilderment of the archaeologists and other Westerners out here, who couldn't understand why he didn't just take a donkey if he wanted to appreciate the views. Carter was the only one who really understood, and even he was starting to turn bourgeois. The adulation had gone to his head. He was assuming airs and graces. The stubbornness and the tempers the man could stand, but not the airs and graces. It was only a tomb, for God's sake. Fools, all of them. He'd show them. He *had* shown them, although they didn't know it yet.

He reached the Amenhotep Colossi and slowed, raising his bottle in mock toast, then sped up again, following the road as it swung north past the ruined mortuary temples ranged along the foot of the massif. Most were no more than shadowy jumbles of shattered blocks and mud-bricks, barely distinguishable from the surrounding landscape. Only those of Hatshepsut, Ramesses II and, further on, Seti I, retained any of their original grandeur, elderly courtesans still trading on memories of youthful beauty. And, of course, behind him, south, at Medinet Habu, the great temple of Ramesses III, his favourite in all of Egypt, where he had first glimpsed the blind girl and everything had changed.

I'll make her my own, he had thought at the time, spying on her from behind a pillar. *We'll be together for ever.*

And now they would be. For ever. It was what had kept him going through all those lonely months underground, the memory of her face, the small perfumed handkerchief he had taken with him. My little jewel, he called her. More radiant than all the gold in Egypt. And more precious. And now she was his. Oh happy day!

The road here was good, its dirt surface flattened and compacted by all the traffic the Tutankhamun discovery had brought to the area, and he pushed the Enfield up to fifty miles per hour, dust billowing behind him. Only as he came to Dra Abu el-Naga at the northern end of the massif – a scattering of mud-brick houses and animal pens perched on the slopes above the road – did he slow and pull over. To his left a pale ribbon of track wound away into the hills towards the Valley of the Kings. Directly ahead, at the top of a low brow, sat a single-storey villa with shuttered windows and a domed roof. He lifted his goggles and gazed at it, then drove on, motoring up to the front of the building where he cut the engine, removed the goggles and propped the bike against a palm trunk. Slapping the dust from his coat and boots, he took another long swig from the whisky bottle and marched across to the entrance, weaving slightly from the effect of the alcohol.

'Carter!' he bellowed, hammering on the door. 'Carter!'

No reply. He hammered again, then took a couple of steps back.

'I found it, Carter! You hear me? I found it!'

The building was silent and dark, no light visible behind the closed shutters.

'You said it didn't exist, but it does. Makes your little tomb look like a doll's house!'

Silence. He drained the last of the whisky and launched the bottle into the night, then stumbled around the outside of the building, banging on the shutters. When he reached the front again he gave a last hammer on the door – 'A bloody doll's house, Carter! Come with me and I'll show you something really impressive!' – before returning to his motorbike. He pulled on his goggles and slammed the kick-start.

'He was just a boy, Carter!' he yelled over the growl of the engine. 'A silly little rich boy. A thirty-foot corridor and four poxy rooms. I've found miles . . . you wouldn't believe it . . . miles!'

He waved a hand and drove off down the hill, missing the muffled shout that came from inside the house behind him: 'Bugger off, Pin-Cushion, you damn drunken Jew boy!'

Back on the road he headed south, back the way he had come. He was tired now and drove slower, no longer singing. He made a brief stop at Deir el-Medina to see how Bruyère and the French had been getting on at the ancient workers' village – such things always enthused more than tombs and pharaohs – and then at Medinet Habu. The temple looked spectacular in the moonlight, a magic silver city, not of this world. *A place of dreams*, he thought, standing inside the First Pylon, imagining the girl and all the things he would do with her. It made him laugh the way Carter and the others knew so little about him, thought he was one thing when in fact he was something entirely different. How shocked they would be to learn the truth!

'I'll show you,' he shouted. 'I'll show you all, you arrogant bastards!'

He let out a loud, barking laugh, then returned to his motorbike, and drove the short distance to his lodgings in Kom Lolah, relishing the prospect of his first proper night's sleep in twelve weeks. Parking the Enfield in the dirt alley behind the lodgings, he hunched over to unstrap the pannier bags. As he did so, something came at him from his left. He started to turn, only for an arm to lock around his neck, yanking him backwards. Hands grasped him, strong hands, lots of them, at least three men, although in the darkness and confusion he couldn't be sure.

'What the . . .'

'*Ya kalb!*' hissed a voice. 'We know what you've done to our sister. And now you're going to pay.'

Something heavy slammed against the back of his head. He slumped, flailed, was hit again and everything went black. His attackers dragged him out of the alley, heaved him on to the back of a donkey cart and covered him with a rug.

'How far?' asked one.

'A long way,' replied another. 'Let's go.'

They climbed on to the cart, whipped up the donkey and rattled away into the night. Behind them a faint groaning sound issued from beneath the rug, all but lost in the clatter of the wooden wheels.

1972

On the final day of their honeymoon on the Nile, Douglas Bowers treated his bride Alexandra to a surprise she would never forget, although not entirely in the way Douglas intended.

For two weeks they had cruised from Aswan up to Luxor, visiting what felt to Alexandra like every temple, ruin and fly-blown heap of ancient mud-brick in between, with barely a moment for her to do what she really wanted, which was to lounge in the sun sipping lemonade and reading a good romantic novel.

Their four days in Luxor had proved particularly arduous, with Douglas insisting on dawn starts so they could appreciate the sites before the arrival of coach-loads of what he ruefully described as 'hoi polloi'. Tutankhamun's tomb had proved vaguely interesting, if only because Alexandra had actually heard of Tutankhamun, but everything else had been deathly – an endless succession of claustrophobic burial chambers and hieroglyph-covered walls that would have left her cold had it not been so suffocatingly hot. Although she would never have said as much, as the end of the honeymoon approached Alexandra couldn't help but feel a twinge of relief that they would soon be on their way back to the monochrome normality of suburban south London.

But then, out of the blue, Douglas did something unexpected – something that reminded Alexandra what a kind, thoughtful person he was, and why she had married him in the first place.

It was their last morning. On Douglas's instructions they rose even earlier than usual, before night had resolved itself into dawn, and crossed the Nile. On the west bank a waiting taxi ferried them to the car park in front of the Temple of Hatshepsut, where two days previously Douglas had spent an entire afternoon taking measurements with the retractable tape he always carried with him. Alexandra envisaged a repeat performance and her heart sank. Rather than going into the temple, however, her husband directed her on to a narrow path that wound into the hills behind the monument. Up and up they trudged, the sky turning an ever-paler shade of grey above them, the Nile Valley dropping ever further below. Eventually, after over an hour of climbing, by which point Alexandra was starting to think that watching her spouse measuring blocks of stone might not have been so bad after all, they scrambled up a last steep incline and on to the summit of the Qurn – the pyramid-shaped peak that dominated the southern end of the Valley of the Kings. A picnic hamper was waiting for them.

'I had one of the bods from the hotel bring it up,' explained Douglas, opening the hamper and producing a half-bottle of chilled champagne. 'To be honest I'm surprised no one's nicked it.'

He poured two glasses, removed a red rose from the basket and went down on one knee in front of her.

'May your spirit live,' he intoned. 'May you spend millions of years, you who love Thebes, sitting with your face to the north wind, beholding happiness.'

It was so wonderfully romantic, so wholly unlike Douglas, that she burst into tears.

'Don't worry about the cost, old girl,' he chided. 'I got the champagne duty-free. Unbelievably cheap.'

They sat on a rock, sipped their drinks and watched the sunrise over the desert mountains, everything blissfully silent and still, the Nile cultivation a hazy blur of green far beneath, like a tiny model world. Once they had eaten breakfast they had a bit of a kiss, then packed up the hamper, left it where it was – 'Someone will come up and collect it,' explained Douglas – and started along the ridge path that ran off the back of the peak.

'According to that fellow in the hotel – you know the one, Rupert-whatever-his-name-was, pompous chap, big nostrils – if we stay on this path we can go right around the top of the plateau and come down near the entrance to the Valley of the Kings.'

Douglas waved his arm in a wide circle.

'Should only take an hour or so, and if we get a hoof on we'll easily be back in time for lunch.'

Alexandra had by now recovered from the climb, and although long walks over rugged terrain weren't really her thing, she was – thanks in no small part to the champagne – feeling adventurous, and dutifully fell into step behind her husband. The path was narrow and rocky and difficult in places, but like the gentleman he was, Douglas helped her over the hard parts, and to her surprise she found herself having rather a good time.

A real desert adventure, she thought. *Just wait till I tell Olivia and Flora!*

Further and further they went, deeper and deeper into the hills, the Nile now lost behind them, the landscape almost lunar in its desolation – just rocks and dust and a pale white sky. An hour went by, ninety minutes, and although Douglas had brought extra food and water in a knapsack, after two hours walking and with no end in sight, Alexandra was starting to tire. Her feet hurt, the heat had become uncomfortable and worst of all she needed the toilet.

'I'll turn my back,' offered Douglas when she alerted him to the situation.

'I'm not weeing in the open air,' she snapped, her mood not as good as it had been.

'For goodness' sake, it's not as if anyone's going to see you!'

'I'm not weeing in the open air,' she repeated. 'I want some privacy.'

'Well, either hold it in or go over there, behind that big rock. It's the best there is, old girl.'

Desperate, she did as her husband suggested, stomping thirty metres away and round the back of a large boulder that erupted from the gravelly desert surface like a giant mushroom. The ground sloped away steeply here, down into a small, funnel-shaped dell, but there was just enough flat space directly behind the rock for her to pull up her dress and squat.

'Don't listen,' she shouted.

There was a crunch of feet as Douglas moved further away, followed by the sound of whistling. Alexandra placed a hand against the boulder to support herself, and stared hard at the rock, trying to relax. The stone was yellow and dusty and scored with a curious matrix of scratch marks which after a moment she realized weren't scratch marks at all, but rather the faded remains of what seemed to be some sort of hieroglyphic text. She waddled backwards a little to get a better view, underpants stretching around her ankles. There was what looked like a hare, and a squiggly line, and a pair of arms, and other symbols she recognized from all the numerous monuments she'd been dragged around over the last couple of weeks.

'Darling,' she called, shuffling back another few inches, both her embarrassment and the need to pee momentarily forgotten. 'I think I've found—'

She got no further. Suddenly she lost her footing and was tumbling backwards down the sharp incline behind the rock, gravel and dust surging around her, her legs kicking frantically within their constrictive noose of knicker elastic. She hit the bottom of the slope, experienced a brief, curious sensation of crashing through a mass of twigs and branches, and then she was falling again, through open space this time, for what felt like an age, before she slammed into something soft and lost consciousness.

Up above, Douglas Bowers heard his bride's screams and came charging round the boulder.

'Oh my God!' he cried, scrambling down the slope towards the gaping hole at the bottom. 'Alexandra! Alexandra!'

A deep, rectangular shaft opened beneath his feet, cut vertically down into the white limestone, its walls smooth and neatly dressed, clearly man-made. At the bottom, almost twenty feet away, barely visible through the mist of dust with which the flue was choked, lay a tangled mass of twigs and branches that must once have plugged the shaft's opening. Of his wife he could see nothing. Only as the dust started to settle did he catch a shadowy glimpse of an arm, and then a shoe, and then the floral print of his wife's dress.

'Alexandra! Oh please, can you hear me! Alexandra!'

There was a long and terrible silence, the worst silence Douglas had ever known, and then a faint groan.

'Oh thank God! My darling! Can you breathe? Are you in pain?'

More groans.

'It's OK.' A groggy voice drifted up from below. 'I'm OK.'

'Don't move! I'll get help.'

'No, wait, let me . . .'

There was movement and a crack of twigs.

'There's some sort of . . . door.'

'What?'

'Down here at the bottom. It's like a . . .'

The cracking sound intensified.

'You're concussed, Alexandra. Just stay still. We'll have you out of there in no time!'

'I can see a little room. There's someone sitting . . .'

'Please, darling, you've hit your head, you're hallucinating.'

If she was, it was clearly very real to her because at that moment Alexandra Bowers started screaming hysterically, and nothing her husband could say or do would calm her down again.

'Oh God, get me out! Get me away from him! Please, get me away from him before he hurts me! Oh God! Oh God! Oh God!'

THE PRESENT

No one could say for sure where the causal chain that culminated in the collision actually started.

That the Nile barge was out of its lane was beyond question. Likewise the rowing skiff should never have been on the river, not after dark and with a leak in the hull, and certainly not with only one serviceable oar.

Such were the most obvious lineaments of the accident. Neither individually nor together, however, could they be said to have been the absolute cause. So many other random elements were required to transform a potentially dangerous situation into a tragic one.

Had a police motor launch not swung by and ordered the skiff back to shore, it might never have ended up directly in the barge's path. Had the barge's forward lookout not just bought a new radio, he would not have been absorbed in the Cairo football derby and might have raised the alarm sooner. Had the tanker bringing diesel to refuel the barge at the start of its journey not been delayed, it would have cast off on schedule and already been far to the north by the time the skiff and its occupants splashed out on to the water.

There were so many different links, the chain was so confused and tangled and multi-stranded, that in the final analysis it was impossible to isolate any single unique cause, nor to lay any firm and absolute blame.

Only two things could be said for certain.

First, that around 9.15 p.m. on a clear, cloudless night a terrible accident occurred on the Nile about a kilometre south of Luxor, witnessed by the crew of the police motor launch and an Egyptian family enjoying a moonlight picnic on the river's eastern shore.

Second, that in the aftermath of that accident the lives of those affected would never, ever be the same again.

PART 1

JERUSALEM, NINE MONTHS LATER

It's dark in here, like the inside of a cave, which is good. It means she can't see me. Not properly. I am just a shadowy outline to her. As she is to me.

When I followed her in through the door she turned and looked straight at me. For a moment I thought she might know who I was, even in the gloom, even with the hood pulled down low over my face. Her expression was not one of recognition. More of expectation. Of hope. She turned away almost immediately and took no more notice of me. A late evening worshipper, that's probably what she thinks.

Now I am watching her. There are windows set high in the walls and up in the dome, but they're dirty and anyway it's almost dark outside. What little light there is comes from one of the brass lamps hanging from the ceiling at the far end of the cathedral. Even that does little more than soften the murk in the immediate vicinity. She is standing almost directly beneath the lamp, in front of the carved wooden screen that separates the altar area from the rest of the church. I'm near the doorway, on one of the cushioned benches that run around the walls. Outside the rain is hissing on the courtyard flagstones. The weather isn't what I expected, but it's useful. It means I can keep myself wrapped up. I don't want my face to be seen. Not by her, not by anybody.

The drape covering the doorway suddenly lifts and thuds. She looks round, thinking someone has come in. Realizing it is just the wind, she turns forward, towards the icon-covered shrine behind the altar. Her travel bag sits on the carpet at her feet. The bag is a problem. Or rather the journey the bag implies is a problem. It limits my timeframe. She seems to be waiting for someone, and that's a problem too. One I can handle. Two is more complicated. I might have to improvise. I might have to do it sooner than planned.

She wanders over to one of the four giant pillars supporting the dome. A painting is hanging from the pillar, a huge painting inside a heavy gilt frame. I can't see what the picture is. I don't care what the picture is. I'm staring at her and thinking. Calculating. Should I do it sooner than planned? I can smell incense.

She looks at the painting, then moves back to the altar-screen and lifts her arm, examining her watch. I can feel the Glock in the pocket of my coat, but I worry that even with the rain the noise will be heard, will bring people running. Better to do it the other way. *How* isn't the issue. *When* is the issue. I'm supposed to find out what she knows, but with the bag and the possibility of her meeting someone . . .

She wanders off again. There are doors in the cathedral's side-wall, opening into what I think are small chapels, although it's too dark to be certain. She looks into each in turn, moving back towards me. Outside the nearest chapel an area of the carpeted floor is fenced off with a low wooden screen. She sits down on a bench inside the screen, barely visible. I grasp the wire, working everything through in my head, weighing the options. If only I wasn't supposed to interrogate her.

Now she's up again and coming towards me. I dip my head as if in prayer, keeping my face well hidden, staring down at my gloved hands. She walks right past, circling around the tiled walls back to the altar where she takes another look at her watch. Should I just keep following, see where she's going? Or do it now, while we're alone, while I've got the chance? I can't make the decision. Another few minutes pass. Then she picks up the travel bag, turns and heads for the door. As she comes level with me she stops.

'*Shalom.*'

I keep my eyes on the floor.

'*Ata medaber Ivrit?*'

I don't say anything. I don't want her to hear my voice. I feel tense suddenly.

'Do you speak English?'

I'm still looking at the floor. Very tense.

'Are you Armenian? I don't want to disturb you, but I'm looking for—'

I make the decision. Coming to my feet, I hit her hard underneath the jaw with the base of my palm. She staggers backwards. Even in the dark I can see blood bubbling from her mouth, a lot of blood, which makes me think the blow might have caused her to bite off the end of her tongue. It's a momentary thought. Almost immediately I am behind her and the garrotte is looped around her neck. I cross my wrists and yank hard on the toggles at each end of the wire, appreciating the grip they give me, the force I am able to exert on her windpipe. She is way bigger than me, but I have all the advantage. I kick away her legs and pull as hard as I can, arching my head back and holding her as she bucks and gurgles and claws at the wire. It lasts for less than thirty seconds, and then she goes limp. I keep pulling, making sure; absorbed in my work, not even thinking about the possibility of someone coming in and finding us, the wire biting deep into the flesh of her neck. Only when I am absolutely certain do I ease off and lower her to the floor. I feel elated.

I pause a moment to get my breath – I am breathing hard – then roll the wire into a neat loop, return it to my pocket and take a look through the door-drape into the courtyard. It is rain-swept and deserted. I allow the drape to drop, take out my pocket torch and play it across the carpet around the body. There are a few barely noticeable speckles, but most of the blood from her mouth seems to have been absorbed by her raincoat and jumper, which is good. I squeeze the sides of her jaw, opening the mouth. Although she has bitten deep into her tongue, it is still in one piece, which is also good. I feel in her pocket, find a handkerchief and stuff it in to prevent more mess. Then I shine the torch around the cathedral. I need to buy myself some time, can't have her being found just yet. I know where she lives and will go there afterwards, but for the moment I require somewhere secret. I dislike improvising, but hopefully it should all turn out OK.

* * *

Detective Arieh Ben-Roi of the Jerusalem Police narrowed his eyes and gazed into the murk, watching intently as the body was outlined to him. It seemed to be curled into a ball, and for a moment he couldn't be sure exactly what was what. Only slowly did the form become clear – head, torso, arms, legs. He shook his head, barely able to believe what he was looking at. Then he smiled and squeezed Sarah's hand.

'He's beautiful.'

'We don't know it is a "he" yet.'

'She's beautiful too.'

He craned forward, staring at the grainy image on the ultrasound screen. It was Sarah's third scan – their third scan – and even at twenty-four weeks he was still struggling to get to grips with the precise configuration of the baby (although he hadn't repeated his howler of the twelve-week scan when he had pointed out what he proudly assumed was an extremely large penis only to be told it was actually the baby's thigh bone).

'Is everything OK?' he asked the sonographer. 'Everything where it should be?'

'It all looks fine,' the girl assured him, sliding the scanner back and forth over the jellied parabola of Sarah's tummy. 'I just need Baby to turn so I can measure the spine.'

She squirted out more jelly and drove the scanner in just below the belly button. The image on the screen bulged and blurred as she struggled to get the angle she needed.

'Baby's being a bit stubborn today.'

'Wonder where he gets that from,' said Sarah.

'Or she,' put in Ben-Roi.

The operator continued probing, holding the scanner with one hand while with the other she manipulated the control pad beneath the screen, isolating still images of different parts of the foetus, taking readings and measurements.

'Heartbeat's good,' she said. 'Uterine blood flow's fine, the limbs are all within normal developmental—'

A blare of music interrupted her. Loud, electronic. 'Hava Nagila'.

'*Nu be'emet*, Arieh!' groaned Sarah. 'I told you to turn it off.'

Ben-Roi gave an apologetic shrug. Popping open a pouch on his belt, he pulled out his Nokia cell phone.

'He can never turn it off,' she sighed, addressing the sonographer, seeking sisterly support. 'Not even for his child's scan. Always it's on, night and day.'

'I'm a policeman, for God's sake.'

'You're a father, for God's sake!'

'Fine, I won't answer it. They can leave a message.'

Ben-Roi dangled the phone in his hand and allowed it to ring, making a show of leaning forward and staring at the screen. Sarah grunted. She'd seen it all before.

'Watch,' she whispered to the sonographer.

For five seconds Ben-Roi sat there, apparently absorbed in the ultrasound image. As the strains of 'Hava Nagila' continued to blast out, tinny and insistent, he started to tap his foot, then jiggle his arm, then shift around in his seat as if itching. Eventually, unable to stop himself, he glanced down at the phone, checking the incoming number. He was on his feet immediately.

'I've got to get this. It's the station.'

He moved across to the corner of the room and brought the phone up to his ear, accepting the call. Sarah rolled her eyes.

'Ten seconds.' She sighed. 'I'm amazed he lasted that long. It's only his baby, after all.'

The girl gave her a reassuring pat on the arm and resumed her examination. On the far side of the room Ben-Roi listened and talked, keeping his voice low. After a few moments he ended the call and slipped the Nokia back into its belt-holder.

'I'm sorry, Sarah, I have to go. Something's come up.'

'What's come up? Tell me, Arieh. What's so important that it can't wait five minutes till we've finished the scan?'

'Just something.'

'What? I want to know.'

Ben-Roi was pulling on his jacket.

'I'm not going to have an argument, Sarah. Not with you . . .'

He nodded towards her bare belly, the skin gleaming and slippery with ultrasound jelly, auburn wisps of pubic hair clearly visible within the opened V of her jeans front. The gesture seemed to rile her further.

'I appreciate your consideration,' she snapped, 'but I'm more than happy to argue like this. Now please enlighten me, what's so important that it takes precedence over the health of your baby?'

'Bubu's fine, she just said so.'

Ben-Roi flicked a hand towards the ultrasound operator, who was staring hard at the screen, trying to keep out of it.

'Thirty minutes, Arieh. That's all I ask of you. That for thirty minutes you forget about the force and give us your undivided attention. Is that too much?'

Ben-Roi could feel his temper rising, not least because he knew he was in the wrong. He held up hands, palms out, as much to tell himself to calm down as Sarah.

'I'm not going to argue,' he repeated. 'Something's come up and I'm needed. That's the end of it. I'll call you.'

He bent and kissed her head, threw a last look at the screen and crossed to the door. As he went out into the corridor he heard Sarah's voice behind him.

'He can't let go. It's why I had to end it. Even for thirty minutes. He just can't let go.'

He listened as the sonographer offered words of comfort, then pulled the door to.

Nothing in his life had ever brought him quite the degree of happiness he felt at the prospect of being a father. Nor, he reflected as he walked away, quite the degree of guilt.

Hadassah Hospital sat near the top of Mount Scopus, and the antenatal unit was in a suite near the top of the hospital. As he waited for the lift to take him down to the ground floor, Ben-Roi gazed out of a window, looking north across the Judaean Hills. In the distance he could just make out the drably uniform housing of the settlement suburbs of Pisgat Amir and Pisgat Ze'ev; closer were the equally drab, if more jumbled Palestinian tenements of Anata and the Shu'fat refugee camp. It was a forlorn landscape at the best of times: ugly swathes of housing interspersed with equally ugly swathes of hillside, rocky and rubbish strewn. Today it looked positively bleak, what with the curtains of rain drifting down from a leaden sky.

He glanced back at the lift, then out again, tracing the line of the Wall as it curled around Shu'fat and Anata, cutting them off from the rest of East Jerusalem. It was a subject that was guaranteed to get Sarah ranting, even more than his police work. 'An obscenity,' she called it. 'A shame on our nation. We might as well make them all wear yellow stars.'

Ben-Roi was inclined to agree, although not in such inflammatory terms. The Wall had reduced the number of bombings, no question, but at what cost? He knew a Palestinian garage owner, a mild-mannered man up in Ar-Ram. Every morning for twenty years he had walked the fifty metres from his house across the road to his garage, and every evening he had walked the fifty metres back again. Then the Wall had been built and suddenly there were six metres of vertical concrete separating him from his place of work. Now to get to his pumps he had to go round and through the Kalandia checkpoint, turning a thirty-second journey into a two-hour one. It was a story that was repeated the length of the barrier – farmers cut off from their fields, children from their schools, families divided. Go for the terrorists by all means, smash the bastards, but to punish a whole population? How much more anger did that generate? How much more hatred? And who was on the front line dealing with all that anger and hatred? Schmucks like him.

'Welcome to the promised land,' he muttered, turning as lift doors pinged open behind him.

Down in the car park he got into his white Toyota Corolla and drove out and down on to Hebrew University Road and then Derekh Ha-Shalom, back towards the Old City. The morning traffic was light and he reached the Jaffa Gate in ten minutes. Once through the gate, however, he found himself locked in a vice of stationary traffic. The municipality were upgrading the road system around the Citadel, reducing two lanes to one, clogging Omar Ibn al-Khattab Square and the top end of David Street. They'd already been at it for eighteen months and by all accounts had at least another year to go. Normally the traffic managed to get through, albeit at a crawl. Today a lorry was stuck trying to reverse out of Greek Catholic Patriarchate Street and no one was going anywhere.

'*Chara*,' muttered Ben-Roi. 'Shit.'

He sat tapping the wheel, staring ahead at a large hoarding carrying an artist's impression of what the new road layout would look like, accompanied by the logo: 'Barren Corporation: Proud to be sponsoring Jerusalem's future history.' Occasionally he pumped the horn, adding to the cacophony of irate hooting that already filled the air, and twice lowered the window and bellowed '*Yallah titkadem, maniak!*' at the truck driver. The rain hammered down, sending rivulets of muddy water streaming across the street from the roadworks.

He gave it five minutes, then lost patience. Retrieving his police light from the passenger footwell, he slapped it on to the roof, plugged the jack into its socket and hit the siren. That got things moving. The lorry driver shunted forward, the log-jam broke and Ben-Roi was able to drive the hundred metres round the corner to the David Police Station.

Kishle, as the station was generally known – the Turkish word for prison, the purpose it had served under Ottoman rule – was a long, two-storey building that dominated the southern end of the square, its grilled windows and stained, stone-block walls lending it an air of dour shabbiness. There was another Kishle up in Nazareth, widely considered the most beautiful police station in Israel. It was not an adjective Ben-Roi would have used to describe his own workplace.

The guard in the security post recognized him and retracted the electronic gate, waving him past. He drove through the arched entranceway and along the twenty-metre tunnel that cut through the middle of the building, emerging into the large compound at the rear. A stable block and horse exercise area occupied the compound's far end, with beside them a low, innocuous building that looked like a storehouse but in fact housed the city's bomb-disposal unit. All the rest of the space was taken up with parked cars and vans, a few with police number plates – red with the letter M for *Mishteret* – most with yellow civilian ones. Ben-Roi had a set of both, although he generally used the civilian ones. No point advertising he was a cop.

He slowed and swung into a space between a pair of Polaris Ranger ATVs. As he climbed out of the car someone held an umbrella over his head.

'*Toda*, Ben-Roi. You just won me fifty shekels.'

A paunchy, bearded man handed him a cup of Turkish coffee. Uri Pincas, a fellow detective.

'Feldman spotted you in the traffic jam,' he explained, his voice a gruff baritone. 'We had a little sweepstake on how long you'd last before you used the siren. I guessed right. Five minutes. You're getting patient in your old age.'

'I'll split it with you,' said Ben-Roi, taking the coffee and locking the car.

'The hell you will.'

They walked across the compound. Pincas held the umbrella over the both of them against the rain while Ben-Roi sipped from the Styrofoam cup. He might have been a sarcastic bastard, but his colleague certainly made a good coffee.

'So what's happening?' he asked. 'They said there was a body.'

'In the Armenian Cathedral. They're all down there now. The chief as well.'

Ben-Roi raised his eyebrows. It wasn't usual for the chief to get involved, not at this early stage.

'Who's the investigator?'

'Shalev.'

'Thank God for that. We might actually solve this one.'

They came to the tunnel that led into the compound. To their left a single-storey annexe ran off the back of the main building, the

36

control centre for the 300-odd security cameras that monitored the Old City.

'I'm in here,' said Pincas. 'See you when you get back.'

'Can I borrow the umbrella?'

'No.'

'You're inside!'

'I might go out.'

'*Ben zona*. Son-of-a-bitch.'

'But a dry son-of-a-bitch,' chuckled Pincas, grinning. 'Better get a move on, they're waiting for you.'

He walked towards the annexe's glass doors. When he reached them he turned. Suddenly his expression was serious.

'He garrotted her. The bastard garrotted the poor bitch.'

He fixed Ben-Roi with a hard, cold stare. He didn't say anything. He didn't need to. His meaning was perfectly clear. *We've got to catch this guy.* Their eyes held, then, with a nod, Pincas threw open the doors and disappeared into the building. Ben-Roi drained the last of the coffee.

'Welcome to the promised land,' he muttered, scrunching the Styrofoam cup and launching it towards the basketball hoop at the far end of the compound. It didn't even get close.

GOMA, DEMOCRATIC REPUBLIC OF CONGO

Jean-Michel Semblaire settled back into the brushed cotton of his hotel bed and reflected on a job well done.

It had been a trying fortnight. A renewed outbreak of rebel activity had closed Goma airport shortly after his arrival in the country, forcing him to kick his heels in Kinshasa for a week before he'd finally managed to get a flight east to the Rwandan border. Then there had been another four-day hiatus as his fixers hammered out the fine detail of the meeting, which had already taken the best part of three months to set up. Finally a Cessna ride out to the remote airstrip at Walikale, followed by a rattling two-hour drive through dense jungle, had brought him face to face with Jesus Ngande. The Butcher of Kivu, whose militias had turned mass-rape into a fine art and who, more important, controlled half the cassiterite and coltan mines in this part of the country.

After all the build-up, the meeting itself had lasted little more than an hour. Semblaire had handed the warlord a goodwill down-payment of $500,000 cash, there had been some rambling discussion of tonnages and how the ore would be moved north across the border into Uganda, and then Ngande had produced a bottle and proposed a toast to their new business partnership.

'*C'est quoi?*' Semblaire had asked, examining the reddish-purple liquid in his glass.

Ngande had beamed, the boy-soldiers around him collapsing into fits of doped-out giggling.

'*Sang,*' came the reply. Blood.

Semblaire had kept his cool.

'In France we prefer to shake hands.'

He chuckled at the memory. Lighting a Gitanes, he blew a smoke ring up towards the ceiling fan and stretched, enjoying the feel of the cotton sheets against his naked body. Although he had turned fifty this year, thanks to a careful diet, yoga and regular workouts with his personal trainer he had the physique of a man ten years younger. Maybe even fifteen. He felt good in himself. Strong, fit, confident. Even more so now that the meeting was done and he was on his way home.

Normally it would have been handled by someone lower down the company pecking-order. In this particular instance, with the Chinese clawing an ever-larger slice of Congo's mineral wealth, the board had asked him to come out and make the deal in person. Local representatives would handle everything from here – as one of the world's leading mineral traders they couldn't be seen to be associating with a mass-murderer – but for this initial contact the company had wanted to make an impression. Show Ngande they meant business. And Semblaire had been happy to do it. Not just because the potential profits were so immense, but because he liked a bit of adventure. Apartment in the 7th arrondissement, villa in Antibes, thirty-year marriage, three daughters – life, he sometimes thought, was just a little too comfortable. He needed the occasional frisson. And anyway, with the bodyguards the company had provided – five of them, ex-BFST, currently sunning themselves beside the pool now that the heavy stuff was over – he was never going to be in any danger.

From behind the bathroom's closed door came the hiss of a shower. Semblaire blew another smoke ring and touched his penis, recalling the pleasures of the previous night, thinking there was probably time for further fun and games before the flight back to Kinshasa. The morality of the thing never entered his mind. Or at least never troubled his mind. Any more than did the morality of doing business with a freak like Jesus Ngande. According to the UN, the man was responsible for the best part of a quarter of a million deaths, mainly women and children. With the money they were paying him – $5 million a year – that total would increase. But then Ngande controlled the mines. Other corporations, anxious to maintain the illusion of due diligence, sourced their material from middlemen who in turn sourced it from other middlemen in an extended relay of culpability-laundering that kept the ore's origins at a suitable distance. Anything up to ten exchanges between the slave mines of North Kivu and the markets of Europe, Asia and the US. And with each exchange the price per kilogram went up exponentially. Source the minerals direct, as they were doing, and you got them for a fraction of the price. Rape, mutilation, murder – they weren't pleasant things. But the money his company would be saving – and therefore making – was extremely pleasant. And frankly, who cared what blacks did to one another. Congo, after all, was a very long way from the boardrooms of Paris.

He finished his cigarette, swung off the bed and gave the bathroom door a quick rap to indicate he was ready to start again. Then he crossed to the French doors and tweaked open the curtains, looking out. In the distance rose the brooding bulk of the Nyiragongo volcano; below him ragged lawns ran down to the hotel swimming pool, where he could just make out his bodyguards, and a couple of other people. NGOs probably. Certainly not holidaymakers. No holidaymakers ever came here.

The NGOs amused him. Just like all those useless bleeding-heart, anti-corporate, anti-globalization idiots amused him. Prancing around with their laptops and mobile phones raging about Western exploitation of Third World resources. And yet without coltan and cassiterite there wouldn't be any laptops or mobile phones, and without corporations such as his there wouldn't be any coltan or cassiterite. Every e-mail and text they sent demanding justice, every call they made organizing another rally, every website they set up bemoaning human rights abuses – all were made possible by the very misery and exploitation they so vociferously condemned. It was laughable, utterly laughable. Or at least it would be if he bothered to give it a second thought.

Behind him the hiss of the shower slowed and stopped. Semblaire turned, glancing at his Rolex to check how much time he had. There was a knock at the door.

'*Merde*,' he muttered. Then, louder: '*Moment!*'

He swept a towelling robe off the floor, put it on and crossed the room.

'*Oui?*'

'*Garçon d'étage*,' came a voice. Room service.

He hadn't ordered anything, but he was in the hotel's most expensive villa and the management were forever sending over complimentary drinks and flowers and sweets, so he didn't think twice about clicking off the lock and opening the door.

A pistol jammed hard into his sternum. He started to speak but the woman holding the gun held a finger to her lips. Or rather to the lips of the latex Marilyn Monroe mask she was wearing. She backed Semblaire into the room. Three other figures followed – two male, one female – the last of them closing and bolting the door. All wore masks: Arnold Schwarzenegger, Elvis Presley, Angelina Jolie. They weren't African, that much he could tell from their bare arms and necks. Otherwise they gave nothing away. Were it not for the gun, the effect would have been comical.

'*Qu'est-ce vous voulez?*' he asked, trying to keep his voice calm. The woman with the pistol didn't answer, just pushed Semblaire back on to the bed. The one in the Elvis Presley mask went over and drew the curtains tight shut. Angelina Jolie knelt on the floor and clicked open the Samsonite briefcase she was carrying, removing a tripod and digital video camera. Arnold Schwarzenegger, a short, spindly man with tendrils of greasy hair poking out from beneath the neckline of his mask, walked round to the bedside table where Semblaire's MacBook was charging. He lifted the lid and turned it on. There was a chime and the screen went grey as the laptop booted.

'*Qu'est-ce que vous—*'

A hand whipped out and slapped Semblaire hard across the face.

'Shut up.'

The accent sounded American, with a hint of something else. Russian? Spanish? Israeli? Semblaire couldn't be sure. In front of him Angelina Jolie, who was darker than the other woman, extended the tripod's legs and placed it in the middle of the room, slotting the camera into the holding mechanism. She switched it on, opened out the viewfinder and angled the lens down so that it was aimed directly at the Frenchman's face. On the laptop a screensaver of Semblaire and his family came up, indicating the machine was fully booted.

'Password,' said Arnold Schwarzenegger, turning the MacBook round.

Semblaire hesitated. His first thought had been that this was a hold-up. They hadn't touched his wallet, however, which was lying in full view on the end of the bed, and their desire to get into his computer persuaded him this was something more sinister than plain robbery. There was a lot of stuff on there that neither he nor his company would have wanted . . .

'Password,' ordered the man again.

'Now,' snapped Marilyn Monroe, lifting the pistol and pressing it hard against Semblaire's temple. With no choice, he leant forward and started tapping. Schwarzenegger swung the MacBook round, slotted a USB stick into one of the ports and played a finger over the touchpad, exploring the hard drive. Semblaire was scared now, really scared.

'*Écoutez*,' he began, 'I don't know what you want from me—'

He was interrupted by a muted clatter from the bathroom. The intruders tensed, glancing at each other, the one with the gun tutting and shaking her head as if to say, 'We should have checked.' Schwarzenegger laid aside the laptop and slipped a Glock from the back of his jeans. Monroe and Jolie did the same, backing off and aiming at the door. The one in the Elvis Presley mask approached the bathroom and flattened himself against the wall beside the door. He paused, eyes flicking towards his colleagues, then reached out, turned the handle and threw the door open.

'*Oy vey*,' murmured Angelina.

A girl was standing inside, naked, her ebony skin still glistening from the shower she had just taken. Judging from her under-developed physique she couldn't have been much more than nine or ten. She was shaking, her eyes wide with terror.

There was a brief, horrified silence. Then Marilyn Monroe hurried across the room, ripping off her mask as she went, revealing a pale face and a tumble of reddish-brown hair. She snatched a towel from the bathroom rail and wrapped it around the child.

'It's OK,' she whispered, holding her. '*Ça va*. It's OK. It's over.'

She remained like that for a long time, calming and reassuring the girl, no one else moving or saying anything. Then, her cheeks flushed, she strode back into the room, went up to Semblaire and slammed the butt of her handgun hard against the side of his face, sending him sprawling backwards on the bed. He screamed and brought his hands up to defend himself. The other woman leapt over and grasped her companion's arm, trying to restrain her.

'*Lo*, Dinah!'

She tore her arm free and hit Semblaire again, and again, then grasped a handful of hair, yanked his head back and forced the Glock muzzle deep into his mouth, choking him.

'I'll kill you,' she howled, her face now stained a deep red, her cheeks wet with tears. 'I'll kill you, you vile animal. I'll blow your fucking head off.'

She was hysterical, unhinged. Only when the man in the Elvis mask came forward and wrapped an arm around her, gently but firmly drawing her away, did she begin to calm. The two of them spoke in low voices, in a language Semblaire didn't understand, although he was almost certain it was Hebrew. Then, trembling, she slipped the pistol back into her jeans. Returning to the bathroom, she helped the girl into the ragged pink dress that lay slung across the toilet seat. Taking her hand, she then led her to the main door, the child mute and acquiescent. She unbolted the door, swung it open and moved the girl through before turning back to Semblaire. He was curled on the bed groaning, his towelling bathrobe rucked up around his waist, its collar smeared with blood. For a moment she stared at him, faced twisted with loathing, then she spat in his direction.

'We are your nemesis,' she said, before stepping outside and closing the door behind her.

Once she was gone, Elvis Presley took a swift look through the garden doors to make sure Semblaire's bodyguards had not been attracted by the commotion. Satisfied, he returned to the bed and hoisted the Frenchman into a sitting position. His left cheek was swollen and puffy.

'*Elle a cassé ma mâchoire, la chienne,*' he mumbled, holding a hand up to his jaw.

The man didn't reply. Instead he took a couple of steps back and aimed his gun at Semblaire's head.

'You will look into the camera,' he instructed. 'You will state your name and the name of your company, and you will then explain exactly what it is you are doing here in Africa.'

He motioned for the camera to be switched on.

'Now start talking, you sick son-of-a-bitch.'

JERUSALEM

The Cathedral of St James sat at the heart of the city's Armenian Quarter, a two-hundred-metre walk from Kishle, along the high-walled canyon of Armenian Orthodox Patriarchate Road. Halfway there the rain really started hammering down, great driving sheets of it, forcing Ben-Roi to take shelter in the doorway of the Armenian Tavern. He cursed Pincas for denying him his umbrella, and pulled out his cell phone, taking the opportunity to call Sarah. To apologize.

It was strange the way life turned. How things never quite worked out the way you expected. A few years back he'd been engaged to be married. Then his fiancée Galia had been killed and his world had dropped into the abyss. He'd thought that was it, he was buried for ever, but against all expectations two people had pulled him out. Sarah was one of them.

Four years they'd been together. Good years. Wonderful years, particularly at the beginning. Galia would always be there, of course, but with Sarah his life had moved on. He'd healed. And not just on a personal level. His career too had got back on track. He'd been promoted to senior detective, won citations for his work on three separate investigations, rediscovered his passion for policing. His obsession with it.

Which is where the problems came. As any detective anywhere in the world will tell you, finding the balance between upholding the law and upholding a relationship is a tough thing to do. Doubly so in the pressure-cooker atmosphere of a city like Jerusalem. Trebly so in the Old City, where faith and fury, God and the Devil, crime and prayer were so closely entwined it was nigh-on impossible to prise them apart.

With only a couple of exceptions, all his colleagues had at least one divorce under their belt, usually more. Work and women – the two worlds just wouldn't be squared. How could you ease off on a drugs bust because your partner wants to have a cosy night in watching TV? How can you romance her in the evening when you've spent the day interviewing a serial rapist? How can you not answer the call to attend a corpse in a cathedral because you're looking at images of your unborn child? Where do you draw the line? *How* do you draw the line?

With Galia it had been a whirlwind romance, just a few months together before he'd proposed. There hadn't been time for the pressure to take its toll. With Sarah there had. She'd tried so hard, cut him so much slack, but there are only so many cancelled dinners you can deal with, only so much self-absorption.

The confrontations had grown ever more frequent, the distance between them ever wider, the resentment ever deeper. Eventually, inevitably, she'd ended it. They'd had a brief reconciliation – the sex, ironically, the best it had ever been – but his work had got in the way again and two weeks later she'd called a final time out.

'I love you, Arieh,' she'd said. 'But I can't live with only a fraction of you. You're never here. Even when you are here, your mind's somewhere else. It won't work. I need more.'

He'd moved out of their apartment, got on with his job, tried to persuade himself it was all for the best.

Five weeks after that she'd called to say she was pregnant.

'Is it mine?' he'd asked.

'No, it's Menachem Begin's. I froze a sperm sample before he died. Of course it's yours, *dafook*!'

He'd lost a lover and gained a child. Strange the way life turned.

Sarah's phone went straight to voicemail. He left a rambling message, saying he hoped everything had gone OK, was sorry to have ducked out early, would call later. Then, ringing off, he pressed himself back into the doorway and waited for the rain to ease.

Normally Armenian Orthodox Patriarchate Road was quiet. With the municipal roadworks closing the Jaffa Gate to outgoing traffic, vehicles wanting to exit the Old City now had to come this way down to the Zion or Dung Gates. The result: an endless stream of cars, taxis and No. 38 buses clogging the narrow thoroughfare and pushing whatever pedestrians there were up against the walls to either side of the street. A pair of *Haredim* bustled past, their heads down, plastic bags wrapped around their Homburg hats to keep them dry, and then a group of tourists, all wearing matching blue cagoules with the logo 'Holy Land Travel: Bringing You Closer to God' emblazoned on the back. They looked miserable. You didn't expect it to rain in the Holy

Land. Certainly not in June. It made God's city look distinctly uncelestial.

Eventually the downpour slowed and Ben-Roi continued on his way. He passed the Bulghourji Bar and went through a short 50-metre tunnel where he had to flatten himself against the wall to avoid being crushed by a 38 bus. At the other end, just past the Sandrouni Armenian Art Centre, an ornately arched doorway opened to the left, with above it a stone inscribed in Arabic, Armenian and Latin script: *Couvent Armenien St Jacques* read the only part Ben-Roi could decipher. Three regular policemen and a couple of green-uniformed border police stood guard underneath.

Ben-Roi flashed his ID and walked through the entrance, only the second time in his seven years with the Jerusalem Police he'd had cause to enter the compound. The Armenian community was a small, close-knit one and, in general, a lot less trouble than its Jewish and Muslim neighbours.

Inside the gateway, a vaulted passage ran away to his right. To his left was a glass-fronted concierge's office where three men in leather coats and flat-caps sat huddled around a CCTV monitor. Nava Schwartz, one of the Kishle camera experts, was standing behind them, leaning over towards the screen. When she saw Ben-Roi she waved and chopped a hand, indicating he should follow the passage and take the first opening on the left. It brought him into a small cobbled courtyard hemmed in by high walls, like a prison yard. The entrance to the cathedral was opposite, at the back of a deep, fenced cloister, its doorway cordoned off with a line of red-and-white police tape. Above, painted figures of Christ and the saints gazed into space, pointedly ignoring the cares of the world beneath.

There were more uniforms standing sentry around the door – all regulars, no border police – and, also, three handguns lined up on the pink marble paving: two Jericho 9mms and a Belgian FN. One of the constables must have noticed the quizzical expression on his face because she tapped her baton against the sign beside the door, which listed the various objects and activities prohibited inside the church. 'No guns or firearms' was the only one of the eight stipulations to which the word 'Absolutely' had been appended.

Normally police officers were not supposed to let their weapons out of their sight, but in this instance diplomacy seemed to have won the day. Ben-Roi doubted the same courtesy would have been extended had they been in an Arab place of worship. Then again, Armenians didn't have a habit of throwing rocks and taking pot-shots at you.

Unholstering his Jericho, he laid it with the others, switched off his mobile and stepped over the tape into the cathedral. It was dim in here, gloomy, even with the wooden doors thrown back and the entrance drape rolled up. Four giant pillars, thick as sequoia trunks, lumbered towards the domed roof high above; brass lamps hung everywhere, dozens of them, suspended from the ceiling by long chains, filling the air like an armada of miniature spaceships. There were gold and silver icons, and huge time-blackened oil paintings, and heavy carpets and intricately patterned blue and white wall tiles, the overall impression being less a place of worship than the interior of some vast, overstocked antiques emporium. He stood a moment getting his bearings, breathing the musky, incense-heavy air, watching as a sniffer dog and its handler worked the side-chapels to his left, then angled towards a doorway in the right-hand wall. From the room beyond came the strobe-like glare of camera flashes, and a hushed babble of voices.

'Kind of you to join us, Arieh.'

A balding, thickset man was standing just inside the door, his blue police jacket bearing the leaf and twin crowns insignia of a *Nitzav Mishneh* – Commander Moshe Gal, head of the David Police Station. He was flanked by his deputy, Chief Superintendent Yitzhak Baum, and First Sergeant Leah Shalev, a busty, broad-hipped woman in a blue uniform. Shalev nodded a greeting, Baum didn't.

'Sorry, sir,' said Ben-Roi, taking up position beside Shalev. 'I was over at Hadassah. The traffic . . .'

Gal waved a hand, dismissing the explanation as unnecessary.

'Everything OK with the baby?'

'Looking good, thank you, sir.'

'She's not,' said Baum, pointing.

They were in a long carpeted room, plainer and less ornate than the Aladdin's cave of the cathedral proper, its vaulted ceiling cracked and stained with mould. At one end was a stack of folding chairs; at the other a large, cloth-covered table serving as an altar. The front of the cloth had been lifted, revealing the space beneath. A couple of Crime Investigation Technicians in sterile gloves and white body suits were crawling around with tweezers and finds bags; another couple were dusting for prints. Bibi Kletzmann, the photographer from Russian

Yard, was on his knees snapping away with his Nikon D700, its flash illuminating the ample backside of Dr Avram Schmelling, the on-call pathologist, who was completely under the table.

The object of all this activity was not immediately clear. Only when Ben-Roi dropped to his haunches, balancing his elbows on his knees and leaning slightly to the side to get a better angle, did he see the body. Female, obese, lying on her back. She was illuminated by a police halogen lamp and looked old, or at least oldish – late middle age to judge by the greying hair, although it was hard to be sure because the body was six metres away and partially obscured by Schmelling's sizeable frame.

'Cleaner found her this morning,' said Leah Shalev. 'Lifted the cloth to hoover and . . .'

She flicked a hand towards the altar.

'Screamed the bloody place down, apparently. She's back at her house in the compound. One of the liaison girls is getting a statement.'

Ben-Roi nodded, watching as the pathologist shuffled himself round in the cramped confines beneath the table, probing at the body. A bear examining its dinner was the unpleasant image that came to mind.

'Do we know who she is?' he asked.

'No idea,' replied Shalev. 'There was no wallet or ID on her.'

'Not Bar Refaeli, that's for sure,' said Baum.

It was a tasteless joke and no one laughed. No one ever laughed at Baum's jokes. The man was an arsehole.

'One of the guys in the gatehouse thinks he saw her coming in around seven p.m. last night,' continued Shalev. 'He's being interviewed now. And the cleaner found her at eight this morning, so that at least gives us a rough time-frame.'

'Anything more definite?'

'Not at this stage. Schmelling's hedging his bets.'

'There's a surprise,' muttered Gal.

Ben-Roi looked for a moment longer, then stood.

'I saw CCTV as I was coming in.'

'They've got eyes all over the compound,' confirmed Shalev. 'They're sorting the relevant footage now. And I've got Pincas going through our cameras back at Kishle. Our man'll be on film somewhere. We'll get the bastard.'

'Reminds me of the Tel-Aviv *sherut*,' said Baum.

They all looked at him, waiting for the punchline.

'None come along for ages, and then you get two at the same time.'

The joke, such as it was, referred to the fact that after almost three years without a homicide within the walls of the Old City, suddenly, in the space of a fortnight, the Kishle team found themselves dealing with two. Ten days ago a *yeshiva* student had got himself stabbed in the gut down at the bottom end of Al-Wad in the Muslim Quarter. And now this.

'We're already overstretched,' said Baum. 'We might have to call in some guys from Russian Yard.'

'We can handle it,' growled the chief, looking at Shalev, who nodded. There was no love lost between the city's stations, especially Kishle and Russian Yard. It was bad enough they had to share the yard's photographer. Chief Gal wasn't about to start turning over his turf to their investigating team as well.

'I need to be getting back,' he said, glancing at his watch. 'Meeting at Safra Square. Lucky me.'

He zipped his jacket up to the neck. As well as his Commander's Insignia, there was a menorah-shaped gold pin on its left breast: the Presidential Award for Outstanding Service.

'I need a result on this, Leah,' he said. 'And quick. The press are going to be all over it. OK?'

'OK,' said Shalev.

He eyed her and Ben-Roi from beneath bushy brows. Then, with a last look towards the altar table, he stepped down into the cathedral, waving at Baum to follow.

'Keep me informed,' he called over his shoulder.

'Me too,' shouted Baum.

Ben-Roi and Shalev glanced at each other.

'*Maniak*,' they both said in unison.

For a couple of minutes they stood watching as the CITs methodically went about their business, then Ben-Roi asked if he could take a closer look at the body.

'Dressing-up box is over there,' said Shalev, pointing to an open case sitting on the floor at the far end of the room, beside the stack of chairs. Ben-Roi went over and pulled on shoe covers, body suit and gloves, then walked the length of the room and dropped to his knees beside the altar table.

'Knock knock.'

Schmelling gave a thumbs-up to indicate Ben-Roi could approach. You needed to be careful with Schmelling. He was notoriously protective of his crime scenes.

There was only about 70cm of head space beneath the table and Ben-Roi was a big man, long-limbed and broad-shouldered, unlike Schmelling, whose size was all in the waist and buttocks. Even crawling, it was a squeeze, his back scraping against the underside of the table.

'They should have got a smaller detective,' said Schmelling.

'They should have got a bloody midget,' retorted Ben-Roi, puffing. He reached the body, which was right up against the wall, and went down on his elbows, backside in the air. Schmelling shuffled round slightly to give him more room. There was a flash from Kletzmann's camera.

The victim was wearing a green canvas raincoat, jumper, slacks and sensible shoes, and up close looked even larger than she had done from the doorway. Huge breasts, bulging belly, heavy thighs – she must have weighed upwards of 100 kilos. Her eyes were partially open, the sclerae tinged a dull brown colour. A balled-up handkerchief, stiff with dried blood, protruded from her mouth; there was more blood caked across her chin, neck and the collar of her jumper. A yellowed indentation circled the lower part of the neck.

'Garrotted,' said Schmelling. 'With a wire, judging by the cleanness of the depression. We need to get her down to Abu Kabir for a proper examination, but it looks like whoever did this knew their business. See –' he indicated the ligature mark. 'We've got some parchmented abrasion and very minor linear abrasion, but there are no obvious congestive features and only limited petachial haemorrhaging.' He pointed to a faint scatter of reddish dots just beneath the eyes. 'All of which tells me the garrotte stayed in pretty much the same place throughout the killing, and with constant, heavy pressure. Given the size of the victim, and the fact that she was clearly struggling' – he touched his finger to a series of scratch marks around the neck, presumably where the woman had clawed at the garrotte – 'that takes a lot of strength and a lot of skill.'

He almost sounded impressed.

'Fuck me,' muttered Ben-Roi.

'Not her though.'

'Sorry?'

'Her clothes are all intact and there are no obvious signs of interference below decks.' He nodded towards the victim's groin area. 'Whatever else his motive was, I'd lay pretty good odds it wasn't sex. Or at least not the way you and I do it.'

Ben-Roi winced. The thought of Schmelling on the job was almost as distressing as the corpse itself.

'The handkerchief?' he asked.

'Again, I can't say anything definite till we get her in for autopsy, but there's some non-specific bruising around the underside of the chin which makes me think the killer probably hit her there and she bit her tongue. It definitely happened before the garrotting.'

Ben-Roi raised his eyebrows questioningly.

'There's too much blood for it to have happened after,' explained Schmelling. 'She still had pressure in the system.'

He made her sound like some sort of steam train.

'The sniffer dogs picked up blood traces between the cathedral and here,' he continued. 'So at this stage I'd hazard the chain of events was: he hit her, garrotted her, stuffed a handkerchief in her mouth, dragged her in here and hid her.'

'If you can just tell us who he is, we can sign the case off and all get home early.'

Schmelling chuckled. 'I just describe the crime, Detective. It's up to you to solve it.'

Kletzmann's camera flashed again. Ben-Roi brought up an arm and wiped it across his brow. It was hot under here with the halogen lamp and he was starting to sweat.

'Mind if I give her a quick pat down?'

'Be my guest.'

He shuffled a few inches forward and went through the victim's pockets. There were a couple of pens and a pack of paper tissues in the raincoat, but no wallet, keys, ID card, cell phone – none of the things you'd expect to find. The slacks proved slightly more useful, one of the pockets yielding a crumpled rectangle of paper that on closer examination turned out to be a library request slip. 'General Reading Room,' murmured Ben-Roi, repeating the words printed in red ink across the centre of the slip. He held it out to Schmelling.

'Say anything to you?'

The pathologist glanced at the slip and shook his head. Ben-Roi turned it over, then reached across, picked up one of Schmelling's plastic sample bags and dropped the form into it. He wiped his forehead again, took another look at the body, then crawled over to the sausage-shaped, brown leather holdall sitting just beyond the victim's feet.

'Is the bag hers?' he called to no one in particular.

'We're assuming so,' came Shalev's voice.

Ben-Roi asked if Kletzmann and the CITs had done their stuff on it and when they answered in the affirmative he grasped the handles and crawled out from beneath the table, pulling the bag with him. He stood, stretched the cramp out of his legs, laid the bag on top of the table and unzipped it. It was full of clothes, clean clothes, all jumbled up as if it had either been packed in a hurry or else someone had already gone through it. Ben-Roi guessed the latter. He rummaged around and pulled out a large white bra. Very large.

'Definitely her bag,' he called, holding it up.

'God Almighty, you could fit a pair of elephant's bollocks in that,' chuckled Kletzmann, taking a shot.

'Please, gentlemen, show a little respect. If not for the dead, then at least for a house of worship.'

A short, plump man was standing in the doorway, his beard white and neatly trimmed. He wore a black cassock, slippers, a circular velvet hat and, around his neck, a flat silver cross, its arms decorated with intricate floral patterning and opening into distinctive double tips. Ben-Roi vaguely recognized him from his one previous visit to the compound two years earlier. His Eminence something-or-other.

'Archbishop Armen Petrossian,' said the man as if reading his thoughts, his voice slow and husky, barely audible. 'A terrible business. Terrible.'

He walked across the room, his gait surprisingly sprightly for someone who must have been well into his sixties, if not older. When he reached the altar he bent and looked underneath, then straightened again and laid his hands on the table, head bowed.

'That such things should happen in a house of God,' he murmured. 'Such sacrilege. It is beyond understanding, beyond . . .'

He broke off, bringing a hand up to his forehead. There was a silence, then he turned towards Ben-Roi. His stare was unusually intense.

'We have met, I think.'

Ben-Roi was still holding the bra in his hand.

'Two years ago,' he said, stuffing the undergarment back in the bag. 'The seminary students.'

'Ah yes, of course.' The archbishop nodded. 'Not the Israel Police's finest hour. I hope in this case you will be able to show a little more –' he paused, choosing his words – 'balance.'

He made his way back across the room.

'Find whoever did this,' he said when he reached the door. 'I beg you, find them, and find them quickly. Before they bring any more misery into the world.'

He met Ben-Roi's eyes again, then turned and stepped down into the cathedral.

'Do you know who she is?' Ben-Roi called after him.

The archbishop was already walking away.

'I have no idea,' came his voice. 'But you can rest assured I will pray for her. Pray with all my heart.'

THE EASTERN DESERT, EGYPT

Inspector Yusuf Ezz el-Din Khalifa of the Luxor Police stared down at the dead water buffalo, its mouth choked with flies, its eyes dull and mucousy. *I know how you feel*, he thought.

'Three months it took me to dig that waterhole,' the buffalo's owner was saying. 'Three months with nothing but a shovel, a *touria* and my own sweat. Twenty metres through this shit –' he kicked at the rocky ground – 'and now it's poisoned. Useless. God have mercy on me!'

He sank to his knees, fists clenched, arms raised to the sky. A pitiful gesture from a broken man. Again the thought crossed Khalifa's mind: *I know how you feel*. And also: *We might have had a revolution, but for most of us life's still a bitch.*

He stood gazing at the muddy pool and the corpse slumped beside it, the only sounds the hum of flies and the farmer's sobs. Then, pulling out his Cleopatras, he dropped to his haunches and proffered the pack. The man swiped a *djellaba*-sleeve across his nose and took one of the cigarettes.

'*Shukran*,' he mumbled.

'*Afwan*,' replied Khalifa, lighting the cigarette and firing up another for himself. He took a drag, then reached over and slipped the pack into the man's pocket.

'Keep them,' he said.

'You don't have to . . .'

'Please, keep them. You're doing my lungs a favour.'

The man gave a weak smile. '*Shukran*,' he said again.

'*Afwan*,' repeated Khalifa.

They smoked in silence, the desert undulating all around them, barren and rock-strewn. It wasn't even mid-morning and the heat was already fierce, the landscape seeming to throb and shimmer as though gasping for breath. It was hot in Luxor, but at least the Nile breeze brought some small measure of relief. Here there was none. Just sun and sand and stone. A vast, open-air furnace where even the camel thorns and acacia bushes struggled for life.

'How long have you been out here?' Khalifa asked.

'Eighteen months,' replied the man, sniffing. 'My cousin was already here, a few kilometres –' he waved a hand to the north. 'He told us you could just about make a living. There's water if you dig deep enough. It comes out of the mountains.' He waved a hand again, east this time, further out into the desert, where a brownish blur of high *gebel* loomed on the horizon. As he did so, Khalifa noticed a small green cross tattooed on the upper side of his hand, just below the thumb joint, very faint. The man was a Copt.

'There are flash floods,' he was saying. 'The water soaks down through the rocks, forms underground channels. Deep. Run for miles. Like pipes. If you can get to them you can grow some corn and *bersiim*, support a few cattle. There's alabaster in the hills and I dig that as well, sell it to a guy from El-Shaghab. You can just about make a living. But now . . .'

He puffed on his cigarette and gave another sob. Khalifa reached out and squeezed his shoulder, then stood, shielding his eyes against the sun's glare.

The farm, such as it was, sat near the mouth of a broad *wadi*. There was a ramshackle dwelling – mud-brick and palm thatch – the water-hole and, lower down, a cluster of fields irrigated by channels running off the waterhole: one growing maize, one *bersiim*, one *molocchia*. Khalifa's deputy, Sergeant Mohammed Sariya, was standing down there, examining the withered crops. Beyond, a dusty track wound

53

away through the hills towards the Nile Valley forty kilometres to the west, a tenuous umbilical cord linking the farm to civilization.

'We're from Farshut originally,' said the man, pulling on his cigarette. 'Had to get out because of the violence. They hate Christians up there. The police never did anything. They never do anything unless you're rich. I wanted to give my family a better life, my kids. My cousin came here a few years ago, said it was OK, no one bothered him. So we came too. It's not much, but at least it's safe. And now they want to drive us away from here as well. God help us! What are we going to do? Please, God, help us!'

His sobs grew louder and he slumped forward, pressing his forehead into the dirt. Twenty metres away Khalifa could see the man's wife and three children standing in the door of their hut, watching. Two boys and a girl. The same as Khalifa's family. He stared at them, his mouth tightening fractionally as if he was trying to swallow something back. Then leaning down, he pulled the man upright and brushed the dust off his hair.

'Can we get some tea?'

The farmer nodded, struggling to recover himself. 'Of course. Forgive me, I should have offered. I'm not thinking straight. Come.'

He led the way over to the house and spoke to his wife. She disappeared inside while the two men sat on a bench against the wall, shaded by a corrugated-iron awning. The children remained where they were: barefoot, grubby-faced, watchful. There was a clank of pots, and then the sound of a running tap. Khalifa listened a moment to the hiss of splattering water, then frowned.

'You're still using the well?'

'No, no,' replied the farmer. 'That's just for irrigation and the buffalo. Our own water we pump up from Bir Hashfa.'

He pointed to a blue plastic hose that looped out of the ground nearby and ran around to the back of the house.

'The village has got a mains supply,' he explained. 'They bring it in from Luxor. I pay them to connect to it.'

'And these are the people you think have done this?'

Khalifa indicated the dead buffalo and yellowed crops.

'Of course they've done it. We're Christians, they're Muslims. They want us out.'

'It seems a lot of trouble to go to,' said Khalifa, swiping a fly away from his face. 'Coming all the way up here, poisoning your well and fields. They could have just cut your water supply and have done with it.'

The man shrugged.

'They hate us. When you hate, nothing is too much trouble. And anyway, if they'd stopped the water I'd have found somewhere else to get it from. Brought it up in bottles, if necessary. They know me. I'm not afraid of work.'

Khalifa finished his cigarette and ground the butt beneath his shoe.

'And you didn't see anyone?' he asked. 'Hear anything?'

The man shook his head. 'They must have done it at night. You can't stay awake all the time. Two, three days ago. That's when the buffalo started getting sick.'

'She'll get better, though, won't she, Daddy?'

The question came from the little girl. Leaning over, the man lifted her on to his knee. She was pretty, only about three or four, with large green eyes and a tangle of black hair. He wrapped his arms around her and rocked back and forth. The elder of the two boys stepped forward.

'I won't let them take our farm, Dad. I'll fight them.'

Khalifa smiled, more sad than amused. The boy reminded him of his own son, Ali. Not physically – he was too tall, his hair too short. But the defiance, the boyish bravado – that was pure Ali. He reached for his cigarettes only to remember he'd given them to the farmer. He didn't like to ask for one, not having made a gift of them, and so instead folded his hands in his lap and sat back against the wall of the house, watching as Mohammed Sariya came trudging up the track towards them. Despite the heat he was wearing a heavy jumper over his shirt. You could stick Sariya in an oven and he'd still be cold. Good old Mohammed. Some things never changed. Some people never changed. There was comfort in that.

There was a clinking sound and the man's wife emerged from the house carrying a tray: three glasses of tea, bowls of *torshi* and *termous* beans and a plate of pink sugar cake. Khalifa accepted the tea and took a handful of beans, but declined the cake. They were a poor family and he'd rather it was kept for the kids. Sariya came up and took a seat beside them, also accepting a glass of tea. He reached for the sugar cake, but Khalifa gave him a look and he diverted his hand towards the *torshi* bowl. They understood each other like that. Had always understood each other. Solid, dependable, on the level – had it not been for Sariya he probably wouldn't have got through those nightmarish first few weeks back at work.

'You're not going to do anything, are you?' said the farmer once his wife had returned indoors, taking the children with her. His tone was more resigned than accusing. The tone of a man who was used to being ill-treated and accepted it as the natural course of events. 'You're not going to arrest them.'

Khalifa stirred sugar into his tea and sipped, avoiding the question.

'My cousin said I shouldn't bother with the police. He didn't.'

Khalifa looked up, surprised. 'This happened to him as well?'

'Three months ago,' said the man. 'Four years he worked that farm. Turned the desert into a paradise. Fields, a well, goats, a vegetable garden – all ruined. I said to him, "Go to the police. This is not Farshut – they'll listen. They'll do something." But he wouldn't, said it was a waste of time. Moved out, took his family up to Asyut. Four years and all for nothing.'

He spat and fell silent. Khalifa and Sariya sipped their tea. From behind them, inside the house, came the sound of singing.

'Someone's got a good voice,' said Sariya.

'My son,' said the man. 'A new Karem Mahmoud. Maybe one day he will be famous and none of this will matter.'

He grunted and drained his glass. There was a silence, then: 'I won't leave. This is our home. They won't drive us out. I'll fight if I have to.'

'I hope it won't come to that,' said Khalifa.

The man looked across at him. 'You have a family?' he asked, his gaze searching, intense. 'A wife, children?'

Khalifa nodded.

'Would you protect them if they were in danger? Do whatever you had to do?'

Khalifa didn't answer.

'Would you?' pressed the man.

'Of course.'

'So, I'll fight if I have to. To protect my family, my children. It is a man's greatest duty. I might be poor, but I am still a man.'

He stood. Khalifa and Sariya did the same, finishing their tea and returning the glasses to the tray. The man called and his wife came out, the children too, the five of them standing together in the door-way of the house, arms around each other.

'I won't let them drive us away,' he repeated.

'No one's going to drive you anywhere,' said Khalifa. 'We'll go down to the village, speak to the headman. We'll sort this out. It'll be OK.'

The man shrugged, clearly not believing him.

'Trust me,' said Khalifa. 'It'll be OK.'

He looked at them, his eyes lingering on the eldest son, then thanked them for the tea and, with Sariya at his side, walked down to their car, a battered, dust-covered Daewoo. Sariya went to the driver door, Khalifa took the passenger side.

'I would,' said Sariya, climbing in and adjusting the mirror so he could look back at the family still standing in the doorway.

'Would what?'

'Do whatever I had to to protect my family. Even if it broke the law. Those poor kids.'

'It's a hard life,' acknowledged Khalifa.

Sariya re-angled the mirror and started the engine.

'I left a few pounds in the field,' he said. 'Underneath a rock. Hopefully one of the kids will find it.'

Khalifa looked over at him. 'You did?'

'Maybe they'll think it was left by a genie.'

Khalifa smiled. 'You make the world a better place, Mohammed.'

Sariya shrugged and put the car in gear.

'Someone's got to,' he said as they bumped off down the track. Beside him Khalifa rifled the glove compartment in search of a spare pack of cigarettes.

JERUSALEM

Once Schmelling had finished his preliminary examination of the body, it was bagged up and loaded into a Hashfela ambulance for the ride down to the National Centre for Forensic Medicine in Tel-Aviv – Abu Kabir as it was popularly known. Leah Shalev and Bibi Kletzmann headed back to the station. Ben-Roi hung around for another twenty minutes going through the woman's clothes and bag before he too got on his way, leaving the CITs to continue their fingertip examination of the chapel, a task that would most likely keep them occupied for the rest of the day.

'You want me to get some beers sent in?' he asked as he left the room.

57

'For God's sake, man, this is a crime scene!'

Ben-Roi smiled The CITs were renowned for two things: their obsessive attention to detail, and their complete lack of anything remotely approaching a sense of humour.

'*Blintzes?*' he called. '*Falafel?*'

'Piss off!'

Chuckling, he made his way back through the cathedral and out into the cloister, where he picked up his Jericho and slotted it into its holster. The rain had stopped and the sky was starting to clear, scattered streaks of blue now breaking up the cloud cover like sea-channels through Arctic ice. He stared up, breathing in the fresh air. Then, with a glance at his watch, returned to the glass-fronted office at the entrance to the compound. The three men in flat-caps were still sitting inside, grouped around their CCTV monitor. Nava Schwartz was still leaning over behind them. He put his head through the door.

'How's the footage coming?'

'Still running it off,' said Schwartz. 'They've got over thirty cameras around the compound so it could take another couple of hours.'

Ben-Roi stepped into the office and looked at the screen. A dozen images were displayed of various parts of the compound: courtyards, alleys, doors, staircases, tunnels – a city within a city, a world within a world. In one shot a group of young men in black robes were moving across the cobbles of a huge square. They disappeared from view, then reappeared in the shot of the vaulted passage in front of the office. Ben-Roi looked up as they trooped towards him and out of the gate, presumably heading for the seminary further down Armenian Orthodox Patriarchate.

'How many people live here?' he asked once they were gone.

'Within the compound itself, three or four hundred,' replied one of the flat-caps – a large man with a stubbled chin and nicotine-stained fingertips. 'Another few hundred in the streets around.'

'And this is the only way in and out?'

The man shook his head. 'There are five gates, although we only ever use two of them. One down there –' he waved a hand towards the south-west – 'for the schoolchildren. That's open between seven and four. And this one.'

'Which closes . . . ?'

'Ten p.m. sharp. After that no one can go in or out till morning.'

Ben-Roi looked at the heavy, iron-studded wooden door, then back at the screen. In the cathedral entrance one of the uniforms was talking to a priest in a black robe and pointed hood. They seemed to be arguing, the priest tugging at the line of police tape and gesticulating. Priests, monks, rabbis, imams – they got it in the neck from all of them. One of the joys of policing the world's holiest city.

'The cathedral closes at ten as well?' he asked.

'Usually it's only open for services. Six thirty to seven thirty in the morning and two forty-five to three forty-five in the afternoon.'

'Usually?'

'For the last month His Eminence Archbishop Petrossian has instructed that the doors should be left open until nine thirty.'

Ben-Roi frowned. 'Why is that?'

The man shrugged. 'So the faithful have more time for prayer.'

His tone was blank, displaying neither approval nor disapproval of the archbishop's edict.

Ben-Roi stared at the screen, watching as another priest in a pointed hood came into shot and joined the argument in front of the cathedral door. More policemen moved in to support their man, and the confrontation looked set to escalate. He wondered if he should go back and help defuse the situation, but decided he had enough crap on his plate as it was. Asking Schwartz to get the footage over to Kishle as quickly as possible, he made his way out of the compound and headed back towards the station, leaving the uniforms to deal with things as best they could. It was what they were trained for, after all.

The traffic on Armenian Orthodox Patriarchate seemed to have thinned out now that the rain had stopped and he covered a hundred metres before a large Bezeq telecommunications van forced him off the road and into the doorway of the Armenian Tavern, where he had sheltered earlier. Its door had been closed then. Now it was open. The Bezeq van passed and he moved back on to the street, only to glance at his watch, turn and enter the tavern. Leah Shalev had called a unit meeting for 11.15, which gave him thirty minutes. He might as well make use of them.

Inside, a stairway led down into a vaulted basement restaurant just below street level. Its décor, like that of the cathedral, was cluttered and ornate, with a tiled floor, icon-covered walls and brass lamps dangling from the ceiling. There were glass cabinets full of dusty jewellery – necklaces, bracelets, earrings – a pair of fake elephant tusks and, at the bottom of the stairs, a small bar, its shelves stocked with the usual array of Metaxa, Campari, Dubonnet and Jack Daniel's, as well as more exotic-looking bottles in the shape of elephants and horses and cats. As he reached the bottom of the stairs, a young man in jeans and an overly tight Tommy Hilfiger T-shirt emerged through the swing-doors of a kitchen area in the corner of the restaurant.

'Hey, Arieh,' he called.

'*Shalom*, George.'

They shook hands and the man showed Ben-Roi to a table beside the kitchen's serving hatch.

'Coffee?'

Ben-Roi nodded and the man relayed the order through the hatch. An elderly woman – George's mother – gave a sour smile and set about boiling water. George sat astride a chair opposite Ben-Roi and lit an Imperial cigarette, ignoring the no-smoking sign on the wall behind him. His prerogative, since his family owned the place.

The tavern, and George Aslanian, had come to occupy a special place in Ben-Roi's heart. In a past life it was where he and Galia had eaten on their first date. He'd been coming ever since, sometimes just for an Armenian coffee or a beer, sometimes for food as well – the *soujuk* and *kubbeh* were mouth-watering. He and Sarah had dined here often, which at first he had found unsettling, given the associations. After a few visits his unease had receded. Half of the Old City – half of Jerusalem – sparked memories of one sort or another and he couldn't just ring-fence those places as out of bounds. In a curious way it was actually appropriate that he and Sarah should come here – she was, after all, the only woman he had ever loved quite as much as Galia. And the *soujuk* and *kubbeh* really were addictive.

'You want something to eat?' asked George.

Ben-Roi had only managed a snatched breakfast and his stomach was rumbling. The sausages would take at least fifteen minutes to prepare, however, and he didn't have time.

'Coffee's fine,' he said. 'You heard what happened? In the cathedral?'

'Every Armenian in Jerusalem's heard about it,' said George, pulling on his cigarette. 'We heard about it before the police did. We're a close community.'

'Any thoughts?' asked Ben-Roi.

'What, like: do I know who did it?'

'That would be helpful.'

George blew a smoke ring. 'If I knew anything I'd tell you, Arieh. There's not an Armenian in Jerusalem who wouldn't tell you if they knew something. In the whole of Israel. To desecrate our cathedral like that.' He sighed and shook his head. 'We're in shock. All of us.'

There was a clatter on the stairs and a burly man descended, carrying a cardboard box full of what looked like bundles of spinach. George spoke to him in Armenian; the man deposited the box just inside the kitchen swing-doors and left.

'In shock,' repeated George once he was gone. 'In '67, during the fighting, there were people killed when a shell fell on the compound, but this . . . For everyone in our community, the cathedral is sacred. The centre of our world. It's –' he laid a hand over his heart – 'it's like it happened in our own home. Worse. Terrible.'

Despite his stern, slightly lugubrious features, George was, in general, a happy-go-lucky sort of guy. Ben-Roi had never seen him like this.

'I'm out of my depth here, George,' he said. '*Haredim*, Arabs – these I've got experience of. But the Armenian community – I've never really had any dealings with them. Apart from that thing a couple of years back.'

The tavern-owner looked puzzled.

'The seminary students,' prompted Ben-Roi.

'Ah yes.' George took another drag on his cigarette. 'Not the Israel Police's finest hour.'

It was the exact same phrase Archbishop Petrossian had employed. It had probably become standard usage, Ben-Roi thought, tagged on every time anyone in the Armenian community discussed that particular case. Not entirely without justification, although to be fair the blame lay more with the politicians than the police. As it always did. Get the politicians out of the way and everything would probably work a lot better.

What had happened was that a couple of seminary students over from Armenia had got into a fight with a group of *Haredi* teenagers from the Jewish Quarter. For months *Haredi* kids had been spitting at Armenian priests and students, and in this instance the students had retaliated. In a sensible world those involved would have got a stern talking to, a kick up the arse and that would have been the end of it.

61

But the Old City wasn't a sensible world. One of the *Haredi* kids had got his nose broken. The *frummers*, as was their wont, had demanded blood, and the Interior Ministry, as was *its* wont, had caved in. Result: the seminary students had been arrested, held and then deported. A ludicrous over-reaction, and one that had, not surprisingly, generated a lot of bad feeling among the students' fellow Armenians, not least because the *Haredi* kids had got off scot-free.

Baum had been the officer in charge of the whole thing, which had guaranteed a cock-up from the start. Ben-Roi had only played a minor role, conducting a couple of the early interviews, but he still felt tainted by association. Like the Wall, like the settlements, like so many things in this country, agendas set in offices and synagogues – and mosques and churches, for that matter – made the job of being a policeman extremely fucking difficult at times. Most of the time.

'Coffee.'

In front of him, the old woman had appeared in the serving hatch, a cup and saucer in each hand. George took them, laid them on the table and emptied a sachet of sugar into his. Ben-Roi emptied two.

'Like I say, I've not had many dealings with your community,' he resumed, sipping. 'As I'm sure you've heard, she was –' he made a garrotting motion around his neck. 'Probably some lone nutter, but we need to look at all the options.'

George didn't say anything, just stirred his coffee and puffed on his cigarette.

'Have you heard of any ... I don't know ... feuds within the community? Turf wars?'

No response.

'Vendettas?' pushed Ben-Roi. 'Any problems among the priests, the people who use the cathedral regularly? Grudges, grievances? Anything ... out of the ordinary?' He was scraping around, fumbling for leads. 'Anything, basically, that might give us some sort of steer on this?'

George lifted his coffee cup, slurped, and tamped his cigarette out in the dribble of dark liquid pooled at the bottom of his saucer.

'Listen, Arieh,' he said. 'We have our squabbles, like every community. Our bad apples, our troublemakers. Our priests get in fights with Greek Orthodox priests, this person dislikes that person, someone swindled someone else – these things happen, we're human. But let me tell you, unequivocally –' he looked up at Ben-Roi – 'no

Armenian would do something like this to another Armenian. And certainly not within our own cathedral. We're a family. We look out for each other, we protect each other. It just wouldn't happen. Whoever committed this crime, Arieh, I can guarantee you they're not Armenian. Guarantee it.'

He turned and spoke to his mother, who jabbered back at him before putting her face through the serving hatch.

'No Armenian,' she said. 'No Armenian do this.'

She scowled at Ben-Roi to make sure he'd got the point, then returned to her cooking. Ben-Roi finished his coffee.

'Well, at least that narrows the field,' he said.

There was a hubbub of voices and half a dozen people clumped down the stairs from the street above: tourists, elderly, American or English judging by their guidebooks. George went over to seat them and hand out menus. Soft music started playing through the restaurant's speaker system, although who had turned it on Ben-Roi couldn't see.

'You haven't heard anything about who the victim is?' he asked when George returned. 'Rumours on the grapevine?'

George shook his head. 'Not an Armenian, that's for sure. Or at least, not one from Jerusalem. Everyone here knows everyone else.'

'From outside Jerusalem?'

George shrugged. 'Possible.' He tapped out another cigarette and put it in his mouth, then thought better of it and laid it on the table.

'The person you should speak to is Archbishop Petrossian. He knows everyone and everything in our community. Not just Jerusalem, the whole of Israel.'

'Already saw him,' said Ben-Roi. 'Back in the cathedral. He said he didn't know anything.'

'Well, there's your answer. Petrossian knows more than the Patriarch and the other archbishops put together. More than the whole community put together. Nothing happens in our world that he doesn't know about.'

He looked round as if to make sure no one was listening, then leant forward. 'We call him the octopus. He's got tentacles everywhere. If he can't help you . . .' He threw up his hands, the gesture substituting for the words 'nobody can'. On the other side of the restaurant one of the tourists called 'Hello' and waved a menu, indicating they were ready to order.

'Sorry, Arieh, I've got to deal with this.'

'No problem. I should be getting back to the station.'

Ben-Roi stood and pulled out his wallet, but George motioned him to put it away.

'On the house.'

'You'll let me know if you hear anything?'

'Sure. And say hi to Sarah. Tell her we hope everything's OK with the—' he patted his stomach, and moved away to take the order. Ben-Roi started back up the stairs to the street, juggling a vague feeling of disappointment that he hadn't managed to land more information with a rather more distinct feeling of guilt that Sarah and the baby seemed to be more in other people's thoughts than his own. His child hadn't even been born yet and already he felt like the crappest father in the world.

About halfway down its length, just before it passes the entrance to the compound of St James, Armenian Orthodox Patriarchate Road runs through a tunnel. In the wall above that tunnel there is an arched window, its panes barred and grimy and criss-crossed with filigrees of withered creeper. It was from this vantage point that His Eminence Archbishop Armen Petrossian watched as Ben-Roi entered the Armenian Tavern. He was still watching twenty minutes later when the detective emerged and set off down the street towards the David Police Station.

Stroking his beard, the archbishop kept the tall, bear-like figure in his sight, tracking him as he strode down the street and rounded a bend into the top end of Omar Ibn al-Khattab Square. Only when he was completely lost to view did the archbishop turn from the window and make his way down to the compound's main gate. He nodded to the men in flat-caps sitting inside the concierge's office, and motioned one of them to join him. They moved a few metres along the vaulted passage leading into the compound, stopping beside a green baize notice board, out of earshot of both the office and the five Israeli policemen standing guard outside the gate. The archbishop looked around, then, leaning forward, whispered in the man's ear. The man nodded, patted his leather jacket and strode through the gateway out on to the street.

'God protect us,' murmured the archbishop, raising his hand and kissing the amethyst ring on his finger. 'And God forgive me.'

THE EASTERN DESERT, EGYPT

The village of Bir Hashfa was seven kilometres west of the farm, back towards the Nile Valley, clustered around the intersection of two dirt tracks: one running east–west from the mountains to the river, the other, broader, north–south, parallel to the Nile, linking Highways 29 and 212. As they approached, Khalifa checked his mobile and asked Sariya to pull over.

'I've got a signal,' he said. 'I need to give Zenab a call. Won't be a moment.'

He climbed out and crunched across the gravel, stopping ten metres away beside a rusted oil drum. He dialled, then, as he waited for his wife to answer, bent down, picked up a couple of Coke cans that were lying on the ground and placed them on top of the drum. Inside the car, Sariya smiled. The action typified his boss. He was a man who liked to bring order to things, keep them tidy, even in the middle of a desert. That's why he was such a good detective. The best. Still the best, even after everything that had happened.

Reaching for the pack of mints sitting on the dashboard, Sariya popped one in his mouth and sat back, watching Khalifa talk. He'd lost weight these last months. Khalifa, not Sariya, who'd actually put on a few kilos since his mother-in-law had come to live with them and taken over the cooking duties. Slim at the best of times, Khalifa now looked positively gaunt, his cheekbones even more prominent than they used to be, the cheeks themselves deeply sunken. His eyes, it struck Sariya, had also lost some of their old brightness; the bags beneath them had become heavier and darker. Although he would never have said as much, he worried about him. He thought the world of his boss.

In front of him Khalifa was pacing to and fro, patting the air with his hand as if to say: 'Calm down, it's OK.' Sariya crunched the mint and popped another one in his mouth, and then another. He was on to his fourth when Khalifa finally finished the call and came back to the car.

'Everything OK?' he asked.

Khalifa didn't answer, just climbed in and lit a cigarette from the pack he'd found on the drive down from the farm. Sariya knew better than to push the matter – if his boss wanted to talk, he'd talk; if he didn't, he wouldn't. Instead he started the engine and continued on to the village, which was five hundred metres away, beyond a scatter of olive groves and maize fields.

There were only about forty houses, most of them plastered mud-brick, although there were a couple of larger red-brick and concrete buildings as well – symbols of wealth and status, whatever that meant out here.

Sariya took them into the middle of the settlement and pulled up beside a whitewashed mosque. Friday prayers had just finished and men were emerging from the entrance, slipping on their shoes, squinting in the glare of the sun. Khalifa called a *sabah el-khir* and asked where they might find the village headman. There was mumbling and not a few unfriendly looks – in these out-of-the-way places strangers were always treated with a degree of suspicion, if not outright hostility – before they were directed, grudgingly, to one of the larger buildings at the far end of the hamlet.

'Cheery lot,' said Sariya as they moved off. 'Maybe I should send the mother-in-law here. They can all be miserable together.'

'Never disrespect your elders, Mohammed.'

'Even the fat bossy ones?'

'Especially the fat bossy ones.'

Khalifa looked across at him, a hint of the old sparkle in his eyes, then forward again.

'Watch the goose,' he said.

Sariya swerved around the bird, which had taken up position in the middle of the track and showed no sign of moving, and idled along to the end of the village, where he pulled up in front of the house. It was a two-storey affair, its brickwork uneven and shoddily pointed, iron rods sprouting from the corners of its flat roof in preparation for a further level that chances are would never be built. The wall around the front door had been rendered and painted with a colourful if clumsy mural – a car, a plane, a camel, the black cube of the Qa'ba in Mecca – indicating that the building's occupants had been on Hajj. Another symbol of wealth and social standing.

News must have travelled fast because a wizened old man in a white *djellaba* and *imma* was waiting for them in front of the door, a *shuma* clutched in his hand. With his stubble-covered cheeks, small eyes and pointed nose he looked distinctly like a rat.

'We don't get many police out here,' he said as Khalifa and Sariya got out of the car, his stare hard, bordering on hostile, his Saidee accent so thick it was barely understandable. 'We don't get *any* police out here.'

They hadn't mentioned who they were, but then they didn't need to. Egyptians, like all subjects of authoritarian states, have an instinctive radar when it comes to those tasked with upholding the law. An instinctive radar, and also an instinctive dislike.

'We keep ourselves to ourselves,' added the man, squinting at them.

For form's sake the two detectives showed their badges. There was an uncomfortable pause as the headman just stood there, eyes flicking from Khalifa to Sariya and back again. Then, hawking noisily and spitting in the dust, he led them into the house, shouting to someone to bring them tea.

It was cool inside, dark, sparsely furnished, the floors bare concrete overlaid with mats. The headman led them down a corridor, up a set of stairs and out on to the building's roof, the late morning heat once again enveloping them. Most of the space was taken up with a carpet of drying dates, but there was an awning on the far side with a table and chairs beneath. He led them over to it. The village spread beneath them, surrounded by fields and olive and citrus groves, although Sariya suspected they were up here less for the view than because the headman didn't want to entertain police inside his house. They sat and Khalifa lit a cigarette. He didn't offer the pack to their host.

'So?' asked the man, not bothering with preliminaries.

'I want to talk to you about the Attia family,' said Khalifa, waving his cigarette in a roughly easterly direction, back towards the farm in the hills. 'I believe you know them.'

The headman grunted. '*Meseehi-een*,' he said. 'Christians. Troublemakers.'

'How so?'

The man shrugged, avoiding the question. 'I hear their water's gone bad,' he said. 'Allah always punishes the *kufr*.'

'Mr Attia seems to think the punishing is being done by someone a little closer to home.'

'Attia can think what the hell he wants. When a perfectly good water source suddenly goes rotten for no reason, that's God's work. How else do you explain it?'

Khalifa drew on his cigarette and hunched forward. 'You don't like Christians?'

'God doesn't like Christians. It says so in the Holy Koran.'

Khalifa half opened his mouth as if to take issue with this, but seemed to think better of it and instead took another drag.

'What are your relations like with the Attias?' he asked.

'We don't have relations with the Attias. They keep themselves to themselves. And so do we.'

'They pipe their drinking water off your system.'

The headman made no response to this. Hardly surprising, given that the arrangement had most likely been made without the knowledge of the Luxor Water Company and was therefore illegal.

'How much do they pay you for it?' asked Khalifa.

'Enough.'

'More than enough, I expect.'

The headman bristled. 'It was them who approached us. If they don't like it they can go elsewhere. We're doing them a favour.'

Khalifa said nothing, just fixed the man with a cold stare and took another pull on his Cleopatra. A young woman appeared at the top of the stairs with a tray of tea. She waited, head bowed, until the headman waved her over, whereupon she laid the tray on the table and hurried away. Although she was wearing a loose headscarf and kept her face down, the bruising around her left eye was unmistakable.

'Your daughter?' asked Sariya.

'Wife,' replied the headman. 'Any other questions? Want to know when I last took a shit?'

The detectives exchanged a glance, Khalifa giving a barely perceptible shake of the head to indicate that Sariya should not rise to the insult. Somewhere below them a camel started honking.

'Apparently Mr Attia's cousin had problems with his water as well,' continued Khalifa. 'A couple of months back.'

'So I heard.'

'You have any problems with your water?'

'Not for the last forty years.'

'Before that?'

'Before that there was no village here.'

Khalifa nodded and stood. Taking his tea from the tray, he walked to the edge of the roof and looked out over the fields. Fifty metres away water was gushing from a pipe into a large concrete cistern from which it ran off into a network of irrigation channels. As well as maize, olives, oranges and *bersiim*, there were fields of *molocchia*, mulberries, melons, tobacco and what looked like guava – an island of green in the midst of a vast yellow ocean.

'You've done well here,' he said.

'We like to think so.'

'Plenty of water.'

The headman mumbled something inaudible.

'Mr Attia tells me it comes out of the mountains.'

'So the experts say. We just use it. We're farmers, not . . .' He frowned, searching for the right word.

'Geologists,' offered Sariya.

'Whatever,' said the headman. 'It's good water, there's a constant supply. You have to go down deep for it, but it's there. That's all we care about.'

'And you've not had any problems?' asked Khalifa.

'None. I just told you that.'

Khalifa looked out a moment longer, sipping his tea, then turned. 'So why do you think Mr Attia's water's gone bad?'

'I just told you that as well. Allah always punishes the unbelievers. It's His will.'

'And do you think anyone in the village may have taken it upon themselves to help God's will along a bit?'

The headman snorted and dropped his head back, launching a thick wad of spittle off the roof and down into the street below, his lips pulling back to reveal uneven rows of brown teeth, like lines of snapped twigs.

'Why don't you stop pissing around and just come out with it?' he said, eyes swivelling towards Khalifa. 'You're accusing us of poisoning their well.'

'Did you?'

'No we didn't. If we wanted them out, why the hell would we supply them with drinking water?'

It was the same point Khalifa had raised back at the farm.

'Maybe you're looking to up the supply,' he suggested, dragging off the last of his cigarette and flicking the butt in the same direction the spittle had just gone. 'Squeeze even more money out of them.'

The headman gave a dismissive grunt.

'Or maybe someone did it without you knowing?'

'I'm the headman. Nobody farts in this village without me knowing about it. Whatever's happened to those people, it's nothing to do with us. They've got their lives, we've got ours. It's not our problem. Anything else?'

There wasn't really. Khalifa threw out a few more questions, more, it seemed to Sariya, to show the headman they meant business than because he thought he was going to get anything useful out of him. Apparently Mr Attia's cousin had had a dispute with one of the villagers a couple of years back over the ownership of some pigeons, but the matter had been resolved to the satisfaction of both parties. And the village imam originally hailed from Farshut, like the Attias, although as far as the headman knew they had never crossed paths. That was about the sum of it. With the conversation going nowhere, the detectives drained their tea and ended the meeting.

'I'm going to be keeping a close eye on all this,' said Khalifa once they were back out on the street, turning to the headman and pinning him with a hard stare. 'A very close eye. If the Attias have any more problems, anything at all, I'll be back.'

'Bully for you,' said the headman.

They climbed into the car and Sariya started the engine.

'And for what it's worth,' said Khalifa, winding down the window, 'the Holy Koran specifically teaches respect for the *ahl el-kitab*, Jews and Christians.'

The headman shrugged and spat. 'If we need a new imam I'll be sure to contact you,' he said.

Khalifa eyed him, then nodded at his sergeant and they drove away.

'You think he's telling the truth?' asked Sariya once they were clear of the village and bumping along the track back to Luxor.

Khalifa shrugged. 'God knows. For those sort of people, lying's such a way of life, half the time even *they* don't know when they're telling the truth.'

He pulled out his cigarettes, then reconsidered, returned them to his pocket and instead took a mint from the pack on the dashboard.

'He's a wily old bugger, that's for sure. Certainly wasn't giving anything away. Whether there's anything *to* give away . . .' He folded his arms and sat back, sucking meditatively, staring out at the desolate landscape. 'Someone's got it in for those people,' he muttered, talking more to himself than his deputy. 'Someone wants them out of there.'

Beside him Sariya couldn't help smiling. A penniless peasant family with water problems out in the middle of butt-fuck nowhere, an area so remote it wasn't even clear which force had jurisdiction over it – every other detective in Luxor would have relegated the thing straight to the bottom of their in-pile, if not direct to the wastepaper bin. Only Khalifa would have taken it so seriously. Given it all the thought and attention he would a major case. Best cop in Luxor. In the whole of Egypt. And no one was going to tell Mohammed Sariya any different.

'You know what I feel like,' he said, dabbing the brakes as they approached a deep rut in the road, 'a big glass of iced *karkady*.'

Khalifa looked across at him, and then away. 'Ali's favourite drink,' he said.

Sariya wasn't sure how to respond to that and so just focused on the driving, taking them over the rut and picking up speed again, heading west, the rocky wilderness pressing in all around.

JERUSALEM

First Sergeant Leah Shalev's office was a cramped, windowless room on the ground floor of the David Police Station, one of half a dozen similarly cramped, windowless rooms on a corridor running off the station entrance tunnel. At 11.20 there were six of them in there for the initial case briefing, including Shalev herself, who was seated behind her desk and, as the investigator on the case, led the meeting.

The Investigator model was, so far as Ben-Roi was aware, unique to the Israel Police. In other forces, detectives were responsible not only for the actual investigating, but much of the time-consuming bureaucratic bullshit that went with it: budgets, form-filling, report-writing, departmental liaison. In Israel the two roles had been separated. While the detectives got on with the sharp-end job of asking the questions, doing the interviews, running the informers, the investigator's task was to oversee and coordinate the whole thing. It was the investigator who was first on the scene of any crime, who managed the *Tik Chakira* – the Case File – who apportioned jobs, shouldered the paperwork, kept the Attorney General's office up to speed. All the distracting crap, basically. It was an important, if unglamorous role, and was recognized as such – hierarchy-wise, investigators outranked detectives. Some of Ben-Roi's more *loh boger* – immature – colleagues, the detectives with an overdeveloped sense of their own importance,

71

thought it was *they* who should pull rank, but Ben-Roi wasn't bothered. Personally, he was just happy to be able to get on with his job unhindered by all the tedious administrative bollocks. As he liked to think of it, the investigator ran the case, but it was the detective who actually solved it.

'OK, guys,' said Shalev, slapping a hand on the table to get everyone's attention, 'let's get going.'

She used 'guys' literally – Leah Shalev was the only woman in the room. As well as Ben-Roi there were Uri Pincas, Amos Namir – a greyhaired Sephardi who had the distinction of being not only the longest-serving detective on the squad but also the grouchiest – and Sergeant Moshe Peres, who would be coordinating whatever uniformed support was needed.

All of these people knew each other, had worked together many times. The odd one out was a slim, boyish figure with circular glasses and a knitted blue *yarmulke* on his head, sitting slightly apart from everyone else in the corner of the room. The youngest person there by a good ten years, his name was Dov Zisky, something Ben-Roi had only discovered five minutes previously when Leah had introduced him to the group. He'd transferred over from Lod, apparently, where he'd only recently qualified as a detective, although he barely looked old enough to be out of school. Barely looked old enough even to be shaving.

'I'm assuming everyone's up to speed on the basics,' Shalev was saying. 'Unidentified female, garrotted, Armenian Cathedral.'

Nods all round. Zisky had taken a fancy-looking moleskin notebook from his pocket and was scribbling in it.

'Forensics have already sent the first samples over to Mount Scopus, so hopefully we'll have something by close of play today. Likewise the autopsy – I've told Abu Kabir to fast-track it.'

'Avram Schmelling couldn't fast-track his own piss,' muttered Namir.

Shalev ignored the comment.

'We need an ID on the victim. That's a priority. We also need to be thinking about what's driving this guy. The victim's wallet and personal effects seem to be missing, so was this first and foremost a robbery? Did he have some personal grudge against her? Did she just happen to be the one who got his blood up: wrong place, wrong time?'

'Religious angle?' asked Ben-Roi. 'She was in the middle of a cathedral, after all.'

'Possible,' replied Shalev, 'definitely possible. At this stage everything's in the frame. Whoever our man is—'

'Or woman.'

The voice was Zisky's. Soft, cultured, effeminate. The voice, thought Ben-Roi, of a screaming gayboy. Judging by the looks the guy was drawing, it was an assessment shared by his colleagues.

'The killer might be a woman,' Zisky added, glancing up from his notebook. 'We don't know it's a man. Not yet.'

Pincas and Peres were smirking. Amos Namir looked like he was about to blow a gasket.

'What the hell are you talking about? From what I heard the victim weighed over a hundred kilos. How the fuck's a woman—'

'It's a fair point,' said Shalev, motioning Namir to be quiet. 'At this stage we need to keep all our options open. So: whoever our man *or* woman is, there's a strong possibility they'll try it again. We need to move fast on this, gentlemen. Not easy, I know, with half the team working the student murder, but we'll have to make do.'

No one said anything. Resources at Kishle were always overstretched. It was a fact of life and they were used to it.

'How are we doing with the security cameras?' asked Moshe Peres.

There were over three hundred cameras bolted throughout the Old City, allowing the police to keep tabs on everything that was going on within the most hotly contested two square kilometres in the world. Whenever a crime was committed, any sort of crime, they were always the first port of call for any investigation.

'The one above the tunnel on Armenian Orthodox Patriarchate picked up the victim just before seven,' replied Pincas. 'There's someone behind her, but it's crapping with rain and you can't really see anything, even with blow-ups. Might be the killer, might not be.'

'What about the eyes on the corner of Armenian Orthodox and Zion Gate?' said Peres. 'They should cover the compound entrance.'

'Too far away,' replied Pincas. 'You can't see anything, particularly with the rain. We're trying to track the victim back, find out where and when she came into the Old City, but it's going to take time.'

'Compound cameras?' asked Shalev.

'They were still running off the footage when I left,' said Ben-Roi. 'Nava reckons it's going to take another couple of hours.'

Shalev nodded, fiddling with the insignia strip on her blue police jumper.

'OK, let's divvy this up. Uri, get back on our screens, see what you can find. I want to know everything there is to know about the victim's movements from the moment she entered the Old City. When the compound footage comes in, you and Schwartz can go through that as well. Who's duty sergeant in surveillance?'

'Talmon,' said Pincas.

'Tell him to give you a couple of his people. We need to get cracking on this.'

'Already asked. He says he hasn't got any spare bodies.'

'Well, tell him to find some spare bodies. Or else he can drag his sorry arse in here and answer to me.'

Ben-Roi smiled. They all smiled. Leah Shalev was generally laid-back, certainly compared to Yigal Dorfmann, the investigator on the *yeshiva* student murder, who was a Grade One interfering arsehole. When the mood took her, however, she could hard-nose with the best of them.

'I need uniforms going door-to-door through the compound and the whole Armenian Quarter,' she went on. 'Lots of uniforms. Moshe?'

'On it,' said Peres.

'Kletzmann's printing off photos now so you can take those with. And, Uri, if you can get any halfway decent stills off the cameras, those would be useful as well.'

Pincas nodded.

'Amos, you take old cases and cold cases. See if you can turn up anything similar. And get the word out among your informers.'

Namir nodded.

'Are you running any Armenians?'

'A couple.'

'Talk to them as well. You never know, someone might have heard something.'

'I just spoke with an Armenian guy I know,' said Ben-Roi, sitting forward. 'Owns the Tavern, got his ear to the ground. He said there's absolutely no way anyone from his community would have done something like this.'

Shalev pondered a moment.

'We still need to cover all the angles,' she said eventually. 'Even if there's not a direct Armenian link, it happened in their quarter and someone must know something. But you're right, we should keep an open mind.'

She lifted the cup of coffee sitting on her desk and sipped, her lipstick leaving a heavy red smudge around the Styrofoam rim. Normally Ben-Roi didn't give Leah Shalev's lipstick a second thought. This morning he couldn't help but be reminded of the blood caked around the woman's mouth.

'I guess I'm taking the victim,' he said, shaking his head to dispel the image.

'You are,' said Shalev. 'I want to know who she is, where she's from, what she was doing in the cathedral. Everything. And I want it an hour ago.'

She took another sip, looking around the room. Everyone was silent, ready to get going.

'Me?' asked Zisky. He was sitting forward like a dog waiting to be taken for a walk, his hands – soft, girl-like hands – clasped around his notebook.

'Me?' murmured Pincas, mimicking the young man's effeminate voice. Shalev shot him a warning look.

'For the moment, get over to the compound and ask some questions. Maybe talk with some of the priests. And have another go at the guy who was manning the gatehouse last night. He's given a statement but it's all pretty vague. When you've done that, you can come back here and partner Arieh.'

'No kissing,' murmured Pincas.

'Fuck off,' said Ben-Roi.

Behind the desk Shalev had come to her feet.

'OK, gentlemen, let's get to work. The press are going to go to town on this, so I want results. And quick.'

She clapped her hands and they all stood, chairs scraping on the linoleum floor. As they trooped out into the corridor, she called Ben-Roi back, indicating he should close the door.

'Thanks for the girlfriend,' he said, sitting down again.

Leah Shalev had a particular way of balling her fist when she was pissed off, and she did it now.

'Zip it, Arieh. I expect that sort of thing from Neanderthals like Pincas and Namir, but I was hoping for a bit better from you.'

'Oh come on, Leah. The guy's a raging nancy-boy. What the fuck's he doing in a front-line station like Kishle?'

'I seem to remember a few people asking the same question about me when I first came here,' said Shalev, thumping herself down in her chair.

It was true. The appointment of a female investigator at Kishle – the only female investigator in the whole of Jerusalem – had raised more than a few eyebrows, Ben-Roi's among them. 'Window-dressing,' he'd called her. 'A sop to the equal opportunities brigade.'

'That's different,' he said.

'Oh really?'

'This is a tough place dealing with tough people. *You* can hack it.'

'And he can't?'

'Look at him, for God's sake! He's a screaming—'

Shalev brought her fist down on the desk.

'Zip it!' she repeated. 'I've got a dead woman in the middle of a holy site, a psycho roaming the streets, no manpower, Commander Gal breathing down my neck – that's enough to deal with without a homo-phobic harassment suit landing on my desk as well. We don't even know if he is . . .'

'A *noshech kariot*?'

'Oh get a fucking life, Arieh. What he does or doesn't do outside the station is none of our business. Right now I need you people to work together on this one. All of you.'

Ben-Roi mumbled something.

'What?'

'Point taken.'

'I hope so, Arieh. I really hope so. Because we're seriously bloody stretched here.'

Ben-Roi resisted a quip about the same probably being true of Zisky's butthole.

'He's got good references from Lod,' Shalev continued, '*and* the academy. Some of the best references I've ever read. And he's keen – specifically requested a transfer up here so he could work at the sharp end. Given that Kishle doesn't exactly have a reputation for social broad-mindedness, that took some bottle.'

She primped her hair, swivelling back and forth in her chair.

'He also specifically requested the chance to work with you.'

Ben-Roi looked up.

'What the hell's that about?'

'Come on, Arieh. He's read about the Shamir case, the Mauristan fire when you saved that Arab girl. He admires you. God alone knows why, but he admires you. Give the kid a break, eh? Give him a bit of encouragement.'

'OK, OK,' said Ben-Roi, holding up his hands. 'We're bosom buddies.'

A pause, then: 'Although not in *that* sense.'

Despite herself, Shalev smiled. 'Get out of here, you *schmuck*. And get me some results.'

Ben-Roi stood and headed out of the office.

'And for your information,' she called after him, 'according to the academy, he was one of the best Krav Maga students they've ever had. He's a tough boy. And make sure you call Sarah! You can spare a couple of minutes, even on a murder case.'

He was already striding away down the corridor, and if he heard her he didn't acknowledge it.

Vancouver, Canada

Whenever he got drunk, Dewey McCabe thought about Denise Sanders in HR. And whenever he thought about Denise Sanders in HR he got sad and angry about her not wanting to go out with him. And whenever he got sad and angry he felt an irrational need for revenge.

This morning – it was past 2 a.m. – he was very drunk, and very sad and angry, and feeling particularly vengeful. Which is why, as he weaved his way back along Burrard Street after a seven-hour drinking session in Doonins Irish Pub on Nelson, he decided to stop by the office and do a shit on Denise Sanders' desk.

The plan started to unravel from the outset. He reached the concrete tower of the Deepwell Gas and Petroleum building OK. When he pushed at the revolving doors, however, they were locked, which of course he should have known they would be at 2 a.m. That meant he had to wave over one of the night guards to let him in, and although Dewey had a security pass, the guard was clearly suspicious, which he also should have expected, given that he was pissed as a skunk. For a moment he thought he had salvaged the situation by spinning the guard a line about how he needed to send an urgent e-mail, but when the guard took it upon himself to accompany Dewey into the lift, he accepted that on this particular occasion Denise Sanders' work station was going to remain disappointingly turd-free.

Not wanting to lose face he took the lift up to IT on the sixth floor and, with the guard still in tow, went over to his desk and switched on his computer.

'Sure must be an urgent e-mail,' said the guard, who wore a turban and was even fatter than Dewey.

'Un-huh,' replied Dewey, anxious to keep conversation to a minimum because he was slurring so badly.

There was a pause as the machine booted, then the screen went blue and his log-in box appeared. He entered his username and password – deweysbigcock69 – all the while trying to think of someone he could e-mail. For some reason the system wouldn't accept his details. Assuming he must have entered them wrong, he tried again. Same result.

'Problem, sir?' asked the guard, standing annoyingly close.

'No problem,' mumbled Dewey, trying, and failing, to get in for a third time.

He pondered, then shunted his chair and leant forward so as to block as much of the screen as he could. Typing quickly, he entered Denise Sanders' username and password, which he knew because he was one of the three people in the office with system administration rights and went into her account every day to see if she was e-mailing that cunt Kevin Speznik. He got in immediately.

Dewey was starting to sober up. Logging out of Sanders' account, he tried his own again. Still no joy. He typed in Kevin Speznik's details, which he also knew. Speznik's account was blocked as well, which was interesting because Speznik was one of the three administrators.

'Could you move back a bit?' he said, flapping a hand at the guard, who smelt of some kind of spice and was really starting to piss him off. 'There's something going on here and I need to . . .'

He tailed off, scratching his head and staring at the row of clocks on the opposite wall, each of which showed the time in one of the company's sixteen offices around the world. It was 2.22 in San Diego, 4.22 in Houston, 5.22 in New York. Way too early for anyone to be in. Or late, depending on which way you looked at it. 10.22 in London, though. Better. He paused, then picked up the phone and dialled, asking the London switchboard to put him through to Rishi Taverner in IT. Voicemail. Bollocks.

'Is there a problem, sir?' repeated the guard, whose spicy smell was still clearly detectable even though he had backed off a few paces. Dewey didn't answer. He called Frankfurt, where he also got a voice-mail, and then, working eastwards, Tel-Aviv. Their system administrator was on lunch.

'Does no one fucking work any more,' he muttered, checking his extensions list and tapping in the number for Delhi. Here he got through to a guy called Parvind, who spoke like someone out of one of those old black-and-white movies and told him that they too were experiencing administrator problems. Three further calls revealed a similar story in Kuala Lumpur, Hong Kong and Adelaide. Dewey's head was really starting to clear. He pulled out his mobile and scrolled through its contacts list to the number he wanted, then hit dial. His boss, Dale Springer. Home landline. It took eleven rings before Springer picked up.

'Yeah.'

The voice was thick and bleary, like it was coming from underwater.

'Dale, it's Dewey. I've been locked out.'

'Unh. What?'

'I've been locked out.'

A befuddled pause, then: 'Well, what the fuck am I supposed to do about it? Go sleep on a park bench. Jesus, what the hell—'

'Locked out of the system,' said Dewey, cutting him off. 'I'm in the office and I've been locked out of the system. So has Speznik. And so have the administrators in our other offices. Normal accounts seem to be OK. It's just those with admin rights.'

There was a silence, then a sound of sheets rustling as if someone was getting out of bed. When Springer spoke again he sounded much more awake.

'Diagnostic.'

His boss was always using dickhead words like that. He'd been watching too much *Star Trek*.

'Diagnostic,' said Springer, louder. And then, before Dewey could answer: 'We're being hacked.'

'Certainly looks like it.'

'Oh fuck.'

79

After that everything started moving fast. Very fast. Springer was in the office within twenty minutes – his pyjama bottoms sticking out from beneath his jeans – followed by a steady stream of management, including Alan Cummins, Deepwell's CEO. Dewey had been with the company eight years and had never got within a room's length of Cummins. Now, suddenly, he was leaning right over his shoulder.

'Get them out,' he snarled. 'Get them out now.'

'It's not as easy as that, sir,' said Springer. 'They seem to have got sole administration rights to the domain controller.'

'What the fuck does that mean?'

'Basically, they're God,' said Dewey, who was feeling amazingly clear-headed given how hammered he'd been less than an hour previously. 'They control the whole system. They can do what they want, go where they want, look at whatever they want.'

'Accounts? E-mails?'

'Everything.'

'*My* e-mails?'

Dewey nodded.

'Christ fucking Jesus!'

'They must have got hold of someone's login and used that to access the SAM file,' said Springer, sounding nerdishly impressed. 'Then all they've got to do is copy it, run a password recovery program . . .'

Alan Cummins had started breathing very hard.

'A dictionary attack, a Rainbow Table algorithm—'

Cummins slammed his fist down on the table, narrowly missing Dewey's keyboard.

'Shut up! Just shut up and get them out.'

'We can't get them out, sir,' said Dewey, who was rather enjoying himself, like he was in a sci-fi movie or something. Playing the hero. Bruce Willis. Or, better, Steven Seagal. 'They control the system. All we can do is shut the whole thing down.'

'Then do it!' yelled Cummins. 'If the environment brigade gets hold of a fraction of the—' He broke off, clenching and unclenching his fist.

'Sir, to shut the system down every single employee in every single office in every single city has to logout,' said Springer. 'Basically the company has to stop operating.'

Cummins pulled at his hair. 'We'll lose millions,' he groaned. 'Millions.'

There were a lot of people in the office now, all of them crowded around Dewey's desk, including the spicy security guard, who had stuck around for no obvious reason and was now standing just behind Cummins, his hand on his sidearm like some sort of half-arsed gunslinger. Everyone was silent.

'Sir?' asked Dewey.

Cummins was still tugging at his hair.

'Sir?'

A few more seconds passed, then the CEO of Deepwell Gas and Petroleum let out a pained sigh and dropped his hands.

'Do it,' he said. 'Close it down. All of it.'

Dewey reached for his phone. As he did so, the screen in front of him suddenly morphed from pale blue to brilliant red. There was a pause, then a flurry of white letters appeared, whirling around like leaves in a breeze before resolving themselves into five words that filled the entire screen: WELCOME TO THE NEMESIS AGENDA.

Despite himself, Dewey McCabe smiled. Whatever was going on here, it sure as hell beat laying a crap on Denise Sanders' mouse mat.

JERUSALEM

The Kishle detectives worked out of a dingy suite of ground-floor rooms on the opposite side of the station to Leah Shalev's office. They used to be up on the first floor, but a couple of years back the station had been reorganized and they'd been dumped down here, much to their collective annoyance.

The section was accessed by a low door at the back of the building, and Ben-Roi paused here to give Sarah another call. This time he got through. She was still pissed off with him for ducking out of the scan, although less so than she had been earlier and they were able to conduct a reasonably civil conversation, which made a change. The upshot was that all was well with the baby – 'Bubu', as they had nicknamed him or her – and another antenatal appointment had been scheduled in six weeks. He didn't bother writing down the date and time – Sarah would remind him of them at least once a week until the appointment came round.

'And please don't forget about tomorrow,' she said.

Tomorrow was Saturday, his day off, and he had promised to go over to her flat in Rehavia – what had used to be *their* flat – to decorate the baby's room.

'Of course I won't forget,' he said.

'Somehow your "of courses" don't fill me with confidence.'

Ben-Roi grunted, acknowledging that he was indeed an unreliable fuck-up. There was a silence, then Sarah spoke again, her voice softer suddenly, more intimate.

'There's lots of movement today. It feels like Bubu's turning cartwheels.'

Ben-Roi smiled, leaning back against one of the air-conditioning units bolted to the wall beside the detective-section door.

'The features were so clear on the scan,' she said. 'The nose, the eyes. I think he's going to be very handsome. Or she's going to be very beautiful.'

'Takes after their mother, thank God.'

There was an amused grunt at the other end of the line. For a moment he thought she was going to say something nice. If she had, he would have said something nice back. It was a while since they'd done that. As it was, she just told him to look after himself, not to forget about the decorating and rung off. He stared down at the phone and sighed. Although he put on a tough front – a typical *sabra*, as his sister never stopped reminding him – the truth was, he missed Sarah. And not just because she was carrying his child. Sometimes he wondered if they shouldn't give it another try. For a mad, fleeting instant he thought about buying some flowers, getting in the car and driving over to surprise her. It only lasted couple of seconds. Then, with a shake of the head as if to say 'Don't be so bloody ridiculous', he slipped his phone into its holder and headed into the office.

Give Bibi Kletzmann his due. When Ben-Roi got to his desk and turned on his computer, the photographer had already downloaded pictures of the dead woman on to the system. There were several dozen of them, from various different angles, plenty of face shots, not exactly pretty but then it wasn't a modelling competition. He chose one and copied it into a separate folder.

There were two other case-related items on his computer, sitting on the keyboard rather than cheering up the screen. One was a note from Dov Zisky giving his cell phone number – 'Just in case you need it.' The other was the plastic sample bag containing the library request slip he'd found in the victim's slacks pocket back in the cathedral. Pushing aside Zisky's note, Ben-Roi focused on the slip.

It would have been great if it had actually been filled in, since as well as the date, and the title and author of the publication they were requesting, readers were also required to provide their name. As it was, the form was blank, limiting its use as a lead. It still *was* a lead, though. Just about the only one they'd got at this stage, and Ben-Roi turned it back and forth in his hand, the voice of his mentor, old Commander Levi, echoing at the back of his head, as it always seemed to do at the start of an investigation. 'Building a case, Arieh, is like forging a chain,' he used to say. 'You start with a crime and a clue, and from there you join the links, one link to the next, one clue to the next, the chain getting longer and longer until eventually it leads you to your perpetrator. Forge a good chain, and you forge a good case.'

The library slip was the first link in the chain. Ben-Roi wondered where it was going to lead.

'Anyone any idea which library this is from?' he asked, holding the slip up.

There were two other detectives in the room: Yoni Zelba and Shimon Lutzisch, both working the *yeshiva* student stabbing. Lutzisch had never been near a library in his life. Zelba, on the other hand, was a serious bookworm and, coming over, he took the slip from Ben-Roi.

'National Library,' he said without hesitation. 'Over at Givat Ram.'

Ben-Roi nodded, took the slip back and Googled the library, getting the phone number. Once he'd got through to someone in Reader Services, he explained the situation and e-mailed over the jpeg of the dead woman, warning the man at the other end that it wasn't a pretty sight. Two minutes later he came back with a name: Rivka Kleinberg. Jewish Israeli by the sound of it. Certainly not Armenian. Ben-Roi scribbled it down. Second link.

'She's a journalist,' said the librarian, whose name was Asher Blum and who sounded distinctly shaken – not surprising, given the state of the body. 'Used the library quite a lot. I think she works for *Ha'aretz*.'

The name didn't ring any bells, but then Ben-Roi had always been more of a *Yedioth Ahronoth* man himself. He made another note. Third link.

'Do you have contact details?'

The librarian was able to give him Kleinberg's address, e-mail, home phone number and also date of birth – she had been fifty-seven. They had no record of a mobile phone – 'Although she definitely had one. We were always having to tell her to stop using it in the reading room' – and no details of next of kin.

'Do you know when she was last in?' asked Ben-Roi.

'She was definitely here last week,' said the man. 'I saw her up in General Reading, on the microfilm readers. I don't know if any of my colleagues have seen her more recently. I could ask around.'

'If you could,' said Ben-Roi. He doodled a moment, then: 'Any idea what she was looking at on the readers?'

Something from the library's newspaper archive, apparently, although what exactly the man couldn't say. Which was a shame. Small things like that had been known to open a case right up. Ben-Roi gave him his mobile number in case he thought of anything else, thanked him and rang off. Outside in the corridor Amos Namir was standing at the water cooler. Scribbling the victim's name and details on a separate sheet of paper, Ben-Roi waved him over and handed him the information. While Namir went to circulate it round the rest of the team, Ben-Roi put in a call to Natan Tirat, a journalist friend on *Ha'aretz*. The two of them had done their military service together – in the Golani Brigade – and had stayed in touch, developing a reciprocal arrangement whereby Ben-Roi slipped Tirat the odd story and Tirat tipped off Ben-Roi if he heard anything interesting on the grapevine, which he seemed to do at least once a week. 'We're just detectives with better grammar,' Tirat used to joke.

'Sure I know her,' he said when Ben-Roi put the name Rivka Kleinberg to him. 'Used to work here. Why do you ask?'

Ben-Roi hesitated. He knew Leah Shalev and Commander Gal were hoping for a bit more breathing space before the press got hold of the story. Then again, there was no question the press *would* get hold of it, and he figured it was better to give first bite to someone who was at least sensitive to the needs of a police investigation. He filled his friend in. Just the basics, enough to give him the picture.

'It was always on the cards, I suppose,' said Tirat when he'd finished. 'Rivka wasn't exactly popular.'

'How do you mean?'

'Well, she was a serious investigative journalist. And I mean *serious*. Turned up a lot of stuff a lot of people didn't want turned up. Made a whole load of enemies. Powerful enemies.'

Ben-Roi leant forward, interested. 'Any names?'

Tirat gave a hollow laugh. 'Where do you want me to start? Remember the Meltzer kickbacks scandal?'

How could Ben-Roi forget? It had dominated the headlines a few years back. A group of planning committee MPs had been pocketing bungs running into tens of millions of shekels from a consortium of Russian-backed construction companies. As far as he knew, the ring-leaders were still serving time in Maasiyahu.

'She broke that?'

'Certainly did. And the IDF shoot-to-kill story. The Hamas rape videos. The Likud funding scandal. That poisoned kiddie-food thing back in ... when was it? ... 2003. The list goes on. Palestinians, settlers, right-wing, left-wing, security services, politicians – she pissed off just about everyone it's possible to piss off. To be honest I'm surprised she lasted this long.'

'Any specific death threats?'

Again that hollow laugh. 'Only a couple a day. Switchboard used to log them. I think the record was twenty after an exposé she did on some dodgy *tzadik* over in Mea Sharim.'

Ben-Roi tapped his pen on the desk. He'd been hoping to narrow the field. From what Tirat was saying, it now seemed half of Israel and the Territories had a motive.

'You said she used to work there.'

'They showed her the door a couple of years back. Probably closer to three.'

'Reason?'

'Well, she was a nightmare to work with, for starters. Rude. Argumentative. Used to give the subs hell if they changed a single word of what she'd written. We're talking screaming here. Which was fine so long as she was producing the goods. But towards the end of her time ...'

'She stopped producing the goods?'

'It was more a case of her getting a bit ... conspiracy-happy.'

The click of a lighter echoed down the line followed by the sound of a deep inhalation – Tirat firing up one of his appropriately named News cigarettes.

'We've got this phrase in the business,' he continued after a pause. 'Shadow-chaser. Basically, it's a journalist who starts seeing plots and cover-ups everywhere. A story is never just a story – there always has to be something going on behind it. Some conspiracy. Something dodgy. You obviously need a bit of that if you're going to be any good as a journalist, and believe me, Rivka was bloody good, certainly when she was younger. But while most of us tend to start with the facts and see where they lead us, more and more Rivka was starting with the assumption she was going to uncover some earth-shattering intrigue and then scraping around for the facts to support that. She began coming up with some very weird ideas, did a couple of stories that landed us in some pretty hot legal water. I mean we all know Liebermann's a fucking arsehole, but I can't see even him presiding over a plot to blow up the *Haram al-Sharif*.'

From his experience of the Israeli extreme right-wing, Ben-Roi wasn't so sure about this, but he kept the thought to himself.

'Anyway, the powers that be decided she'd become a liability and gave her the boot. I was sorry to see her go. A lot of us were. She could be hard work, but when she was on the ball she was like a bloody Exocet. No one got to the heart of a story quite like Rivka Kleinberg. Totally fearless. Suicidally fearless, some would say.'

Ben-Roi was scribbling notes.

'Where did she go after she left?' he asked. 'To another paper?'

'No one would take her,' said Tirat. 'Certainly none of the big nationals. Too much baggage. Last I heard, she was working for some campaigning magazine down in Jaffa. You know the sort of thing – worthy, left-wing, circulation of ten.'

'Have you got a name?'

'Hang on.'

There was a babble of voices as Tirat asked around the office. It was over a minute before he came back on the line.

'It's called *Matzpun ha-Am*,' he said. 'Conscience of the Nation. Which makes me think my circulation estimate was a bit optimistic. Office on Rehov Olei Tziyon.'

He gave Ben-Roi an address and phone number, and also the name of the magazine's editor: Mordechai Yaron.

'And in case you're looking, I'm pretty certain she didn't have any next of kin. Parents committed suicide. Gassed themselves. Which was a bit of a sad fucking irony given that they were Holocaust survivors. She did an article on it. Probably why she was so screwed up herself.'

'Siblings? Partner?'

'Not that I ever heard of. I seem to remember she had a cat.'

Ben-Roi asked him to put out some feelers, see if he could come up with any more information. Then, deciding he had more than enough to be going on with, he drew the call to a close.

'Let me know if you think of anything else,' he said.

'And *you* let *me* know if there are any interesting developments.'

Ben-Roi thanked him and hung up. A minute later Tirat was back on the line.

'One thing that may or may not be relevant,' he said. 'Shortly after Rivka left, I remember chatting with Yossi Bellman, the deputy editor, and he told me that of all the death threats she got, there were only two that ever really seemed to rattle her. This is going back a few years so there's probably no connection, but . . .'

'Go on,' said Ben-Roi.

'One was from the Hebron settlers. She'd done an article on some vigilante squad they were running, used to go around at night kneecapping Arab kids. They got hold of her home address, started sending her jiffy bags full of bullets and rotten meat. That's Baruch Goldstein country so you have to take that sort of thing seriously.'

Ben-Roi was scribbling notes. 'The other one?'

'That was just after the Meltzer scandal. There were some seriously pissed-off Russians who'd forked out millions in bribes in the expectation of landing a load of building contracts which, thanks to Rivka's article, never materialized. *Russkaya Mafiya*, apparently. Word was they'd put out a contract of their own. On her. Completely freaked her apparently. That was, what, four years ago, so why they'd wait till now . . . like I say, there's probably no connection, but I thought it was worth mentioning anyway.'

He rang off, leaving Ben-Roi staring down at his pad. The chain was getting longer. And, it seemed, more complex.

LUXOR

It was past lunchtime when Khalifa and Sariya finally made it back to Luxor, coming into town from the east, on the airport road. As they waited at the lights at the junction of El-Karnak and Al-Mathari, Khalifa suddenly opened his door and got out.

'See you back at the station,' he said. 'There's someone I need to talk to.'

He slammed the door and set off along El-Karnak. After fifty metres he turned into what looked, from where Sariya was sitting, like a small sweet shop. He emerged a few minutes later clutching a paper bag, but by that point the lights had already switched from red to green and back again, and Mohammed Sariya was long gone.

Everything has changed. It was what Khalifa thought whenever he walked through the centre of town these days. *Nothing is what it used to be.*

Egypt had changed, of course, what with Mubarak going and the new government coming in. Long before the January Revolution had transformed the face of national politics, however, Luxor had already begun its own metamorphosis. Once an endearingly chaotic hotch-potch of dust-grimed buildings and traffic-choked streets, a testament to urban misplanning – or rather absence of planning – the town had for the last few years been in the throes of a radical facelift. The regional governor wanted clearance and modernization and that's what he was getting, no expense spared, no prisoners taken. Roads were being widened, fancy new traffic-control systems installed, old buildings flattened, new ones erected. The eight-storey pink monstrosity of the New Winter Palace had been torn down; Midan Hagag paved over; the Karnak esplanade remodelled; the entire Corniche el-Nil was being dug up, pedestrianized and dropped to the level of the river.

Most dramatic of all, a hundred-metre-wide swathe of town between Karnak in the north and Luxor Temple in the south – a distance of almost three kilometres – was being swept away to reveal the ceremonial, sphinx-lined avenue that had linked the temples in ancient times. Among the numerous buildings that had been sacrificed to clear this gaping chasm were two with a particular resonance for Khalifa: the old police station beside Luxor Temple, and the drab concrete apartment block where he and his family used to live.

The loss of the station was no great tragedy. He had, after all, dealt with some pretty unpleasant stuff there. The loss of his home, on the other hand, on top of everything else, was beyond heartbreaking. Sixteen years of memories and associations, laughter and tears, joy and pain – all obliterated in the stroke of a wrecking ball so that a bunch of overweight Westerners would have something pretty to photograph. Khalifa had always loved his country's heritage – if financial necessity had not pushed him into the police force he would almost certainly have ended up working for the Antiquities Service. Now, for the first time in his life, he found himself resenting that heritage. Thousands of people uprooted, thousands of lives turned upside down, and for what? A row of sphinxes that hadn't even been properly excavated and half of which were concrete replicas. It was madness. The madness of power. And as always in Egypt – as always everywhere – it was those without power who paid the price.

He turned down Sharia Tutankhamun, a narrow street running along the side of the Coptic Orthodox Church of Santa Maria. A hundred metres on, both street and church ended abruptly in an expanse of dusty, rubbish-strewn wasteground. To left and right the Avenue of Sphinxes ran away into the distance, a six-metre deep wound slashed through the heart of town like the trail of some enormous plane crash. This was one of several points along its length where the avenue had yet to be excavated, leaving a land-bridge allowing you to cross the trench. Khalifa walked over to Sharia Ahmes and made his way along to a ramshackle building with peeling paintwork, broken shutters and a Coptic cross above its door. A sign on the wall read: 'Good Samaritan Society for Handicapped Children'. He climbed the front steps and entered the building.

Inside, in the foyer, a young boy was sitting on a Dayun motorbike. Spindly-legged and hunchbacked, he was rocking back and forth, making a growling noise like the roar of an engine. Rifling in his paper bag, Khalifa produced a chocolate bar and handed it over.

'I'm looking for Demiana,' he said. 'Demiana Barakat.'

The boy contemplated the bar. Then, without saying anything, he slipped off the bike, took Khalifa's hand and led him through a door into a large sitting room. There were more children in here, some in wheelchairs, some playing on the floor, some sprawling listlessly on a sofa watching cartoons on an ancient black-and-white TV. A young man was sitting at a table spoon-feeding a baby who didn't have any arms.

'Can I help you?'

'I'm looking for Demiana.'

'In there.' The man nodded towards a door on the far side of the room.

Khalifa gave him the paper bag, indicated that its contents were to be distributed among the children, and went over to the door, the hunchbacked boy still clutching his hand. It was ajar and, giving it a tap, Khalifa pushed it open. A thin, angular woman with greying hair and a small gold cross around her neck was sitting inside, her elbows resting on a large, cluttered desk, her head in her hands. She looked up. Behind her gold-rimmed glasses, her eyes were red.

'Yusuf,' she said, forcing a smile across her face. 'What a lovely surprise.'

'Is this a bad moment?'

'Right now it's always a bad moment. Come in, come in.'

Removing her glasses, she wiped her eyes and waved Khalifa forward. The boy came with him.

'Helmi, why don't you go outside and play on your motorbike?'

Still the boy held on, and the woman was forced to come round the table and gently ease his hand away.

'Off you go, there's a good boy. Go and have an adventure.'

She kissed his head and led him back out into the sitting room, closing the door after him.

'What did you give him?' she asked as she returned to the desk.

'A chocolate bar.'

She smiled. 'He likes people who give him things. Gets attached to them. Please, sit. Can we get you tea? Coffee?'

'I'm fine, *shukran*,' said Khalifa, taking the chair in front of the desk. 'Sorry to intrude.'

'Don't be silly. It's good to see you. It's always good to see you. It's been too long.'

Khalifa and Demiana Barakat went way back. One of his first cases after being posted down to Luxor from his native Giza had involved the town's Coptic community, and Demiana had been roped in as a liaison figure. As well as running the Good Samaritan Society and half a dozen other charitable organizations, she sat on the municipal council and edited a small community newspaper. If anyone had a more in-depth knowledge of the Coptic world than Demiana Barakat, Khalifa had yet to meet them.

'How's Zenab doing?' she asked.

'Good,' he replied. 'Much better. She's . . .' He hesitated, not quite sure what else he could add. He couldn't think of anything and so just gave an inane nod and deflected the conversation. 'Any news on the church?'

'Still fighting it, although the result's a foregone conclusion. The question is when, not if.'

Like Khalifa's old home, like the old police station, like so many other buildings, the Church of Santa Maria was scheduled for demolition to make way for the Avenue of Sphinxes.

'At least this place is safe,' he said.

'Not for much longer.' She held up a sheet of paper. 'Letter from the governor's office. They're halving our funding. Which is as good as saying they're closing us down. They can find the money to dig a three-kilometre hole in the ground, but for helpless children . . .'

She removed her glasses and wiped her eyes again. 'That boy who brought you in. Helmi. He's been here his whole life. Some volunteers found him when he was just a baby. Parents had left him on a rubbish dump, would you believe. What's he going to do? Where's he going to go?' Her voice was starting to catch. 'It's just such a cruel world,' she murmured. 'Such a bloody cruel world. But then you know that, don't you, Yusuf?'

'Yes,' said Khalifa. 'I do.'

For a moment their eyes held. Then, drawing a deep breath, she laid the letter aside and placed her hands on the table, palms down, suddenly businesslike.

'Anyway, I'm sure you didn't come here to listen to my woes. What can I do for you?'

Khalifa shifted uncomfortably. After what she'd just told him it didn't seem particularly appropriate to be asking for her help, not with everything else she had on her plate. She saw what he was thinking and smiled.

'Come on, Yusuf. We've known each other long enough. Spit it out.'

'It's not that important,' he mumbled. 'It can—'

'Yusuf!'

'OK, OK. I wanted to pick your brains about the Coptic community.'

She clasped her hands on the desk. 'Pick away.'

'You've got your ear to the ground. Have you heard of any anti-Christian activity lately? Attacks, vandalism?'

'There are always attacks on Copts. You know that as well as I do. Only last week there was a guy up in Nag Hammadi—'

'Not in Middle Egypt,' he said, cutting her off. 'Around here. Around Luxor.'

Her eyes narrowed. 'Why? Has something happened?'

Khalifa told her about the farmer and his poisoned well.

'His cousin's water went bad as well,' he said. 'The farmer thinks it's someone from the next-door village, but the headman denies any knowledge. I was just wondering if it's a localized problem or part of a wider pattern.'

She sat back, fiddling with the small silver crucifix around her neck. Overhead an ancient ceiling fan flopped lazily around, doing almost nothing to dispel the heat in the room.

'I've not heard anything,' she said after a long pause. 'There's a lot of tension up north, as you know, but around here things have always been pretty quiet, thank God. There was that Shaykh who used to preach out in the villages, Omar whatever-his-name-was . . .'

'Abd-el Karim,' said Khalifa.

'That's the one. He was always whipping up trouble, although I seem to remember most of his preaching was anti-Semitic rather than anti-Christian. And there was that incident a couple of months back when the shoe-shine guy got thrown in the Nile. He was a Copt, although I think it was more to do with money than religion.'

She fell silent, fingering the cross. Outside the door a child had started crying, hoarse, racking sobs that seemed to shake the whole building.

'I really can't think of anything,' she said eventually. 'We're a minority community, so we're always on our guard, particularly after the Alexandria church bombing, and the Imbaba riots. But to date we've not had anything like the problems they have had up in places like Farshut. No violence, certainly. There are Muslims who don't want to mix with us, and people in my community who don't want to mix with Muslims, but in general everyone mucks along pretty well. The occasional unfriendly looks about as bad as it gets. That and having our church knocked down. But then they've been bulldozing mosques as well, so you can't really blame that on religious intolerance.'

'Just the idiots who run our town,' said Khalifa.

'Second that.'

There was a knock on the door. The young man Khalifa had seen earlier put his head into the room and told Demiana the Bank Misr people were due in a couple of minutes.

'We're applying for a loan,' she explained. 'I doubt we'll get it – we've been turned down by every other bank – but we have to try. I'm sorry, I'm going to have to cut this short.'

Khalifa waved a hand. 'I ought to get back to the station,' he said.

They stood and went out into the sitting area. The sobs were coming from the baby with no arms, who was now propped at the end of one of the sofas like a large broken doll. A girl, thought Khalifa, although he couldn't be sure. Going over, Demiana picked her up and held her to her breast. Almost immediately the crying gave way to muted whimpers. She rocked the child then handed her to the young man and led Khalifa out into the stairwell. The hunchbacked boy was back on the motorbike, his oversized mouth smeared with chocolate. When he saw them he climbed off and took Khalifa's hand again.

'Would you mind asking around?' said Khalifa as they crossed the foyer to the front door. 'See if anyone's heard anything.'

'Of course not. I'll let you know.'

They stopped in the doorway. Outside a sudden wind came up, filling the air with spirals of dust and grit.

'Good to see you, Demiana. And I'm sorry about your funding.'

'Don't worry about us,' she said. 'We'll get by. God'll make sure of that.'

Not so long ago Khalifa would have believed her. Now he wasn't so sure. His home wasn't the only thing to have crumbled these last few months.

'I'll e-mail a few people,' he said. 'See what I can do.'

'Thank you. And please tell Zenab we're thinking of her.' She hesitated, then took a step towards him. 'Yusuf, I wanted you to know . . .'

He held up a hand to quieten her. Wriggling his other hand free of the boy's grasp, he dropped to his haunches and clasped the child's deformed shoulders.

'Do you believe in magic, Helmi?'

No response.

'Shall I show you some?'

The boy gave the faintest of nods. Holding his gaze, Khalifa quietly removed the Mars bar he'd put in his pocket to eat on the way back to the station and brought it up behind the hunched back.

'*Abracadabra!*' he whispered, pretending to pull the bar from Helmi's ear.

The boy laughed in delight. He was still laughing as Khalifa stepped out of the house and set off down the street. It was, he thought, one of the saddest sounds he'd ever heard.

JERUSALEM

Ben-Roi put in three more calls before heading over to Rivka Kleinberg's apartment.

The first was to the office of *Matzpun ha-Am*, the magazine she had been working for down in Jaffa. He got an answerphone and left a message, leaving his mobile number and asking someone to come back to him as soon as possible.

The second call was a long shot, to El-Al. The travel bag they'd found in the cathedral suggested Kleinberg had either been on her way somewhere, or on her way back – going most like, since all the clothes in the bag had been clean. Among them he'd found an unopened pack of elastic compression stockings, which made it at least a reasonable bet her travels involved a plane – Ben-Roi's mother wouldn't dream of flying without her anti-embolism stockings. There were dozens of possible airlines, and they'd all have to be checked if his El-Al hunch didn't pay off, but as Israel's national carrier, it was the obvious place to start. He got through to someone at their head office, explained the situation and asked them to check their flight lists for a Rivka Kleinberg.

The final call was to Dov Zisky. His number went through to voicemail.

'Zisky, it's Ben-Roi. We've got ID for our victim – I need you to chase up her e-mail, landline and mobile. I've left all the details on your desk.'

He hesitated, wondering if he should say something else, give the kid a bit of encouragement, like Leah Shalev had asked him to. It wasn't his style and with a curt 'See you later' he started to hang up, only to bring the phone to his ear again.

'Also, while you're in the compound, do me a favour and drop in on Archbishop Petrossian. Armen Petrossian. I spoke to him earlier and he says he doesn't know anything, but it's always worth another go. I'll be interested to see what you can get out of him.'

Again he hesitated, then, with a muttered 'Good luck' hung up, grabbed his jacket and got on his way.

Kleinberg's apartment was in a block on the corner of Ha-Eshkol and Ha-Amonim, a stone's throw from the multi-coloured bustle of the Mahane Yehuda Shuk. Blagging a lift with a patrol car that was heading in that direction, Ben-Roi got out just before the market and made his way into the covered arcades. This being Friday the place was rammed, everyone rushing to stock up before *Shabbat* came in: fruit, vegetables, meat, fish, olives, cheese, *challah, halva* – every stall was walled round with a jostling press of shoppers, a fair proportion of them black-suited *Haredim*. The place had been bombed three times over the years and still the crowds came back. And why not – best fresh produce in Jerusalem.

He stopped off at a baker's and bought a couple of *burekas* and *sofganiot*, then pushed through the market and out the other side. By the time he'd reached the apartment block at the bottom of Ha-Eshkol – a nondescript three-storey building with plant-covered balconies and a café on the ground floor – the food was gone and his stomach had stopped rumbling.

There was an intercom panel on the wall beside the block's steel and glass door, beneath a *mezuzah* the size of a Havana cigar. Wiping his hands on his jeans, Ben-Roi stepped up to it. Some buzzers had names, other didn't. No Rivka Kleinberg. He pressed the button marked 'Davidovich – Caretaker'.

'*Ken.*'

The voice was a man's. Elderly by the sound of it.

'Mr Davidovich?'

'*Ken.*'

'*Shalom*. My name's Detective Arieh Ben-Roi of the Jerusalem—'

'Finally you get here!'

'Sorry?'

'Four days ago I called. *She'elohim ya'a zora* – God help us, if this is how the police operate no wonder the country's going down the shit-hole.'

Ben-Roi had no idea what he was talking about.

'I'm here about Mrs Rivka Kleinberg.'

'I know you are, you don't have to tell me!' The man sounded exasperated. 'Wait there, I'll let you in.'

The intercom clicked off. There was the sound of a door opening and footsteps shuffling along a hallway, followed by a rattle of locks. The front door swung back and Ben-Roi found himself looking down at a small, balding man in a cardigan, carpet slippers and white *yarmulke*. For some reason he was wearing a 'Vote Shas' badge, even though there was no election pending.

'So what took you so long?' he snapped.

'I think there must be some mistake,' said Ben-Roi. 'I'm here because of—'

'The threats. I know. It was *me* who called *you*, remember. *Oy vey!*'

Ben-Roi was playing catch up. 'Someone threatened Mrs Kleinberg?'

'What?'

'You called the police because someone threatened Mrs Kleinberg?'

'What the hell are you talking about, *dafook*! Kleinberg threatened me! Said she was going to have me killed, the mad bitch! I'm the caretaker, I have to keep this place clean. Her cat shits on the landing, I have every right to complain. Bang in the middle of the floor, it was. A shit the size of my fist! If I had a gun I'd have—'

'Mrs Kleinberg was murdered last night,' said Ben-Roi.

That shut him up.

'Her body was discovered this morning. We've only just found out her address.'

The man stood there blinking, shuffling from foot to foot.

'Size of my fist,' was all he managed to say. 'Right in the middle of the landing.'

Ben-Roi explained that he needed to take a look round the victim's flat. Grumbling, the caretaker shuffled off to fetch the master keys. When he'd got them he pressed a push-button light-timer on the wall and led Ben-Roi upstairs.

'She was a difficult woman,' he said as they climbed. 'No disrespect, and I'm sorry for what's happened to her, but she was a difficult woman. Residents aren't even supposed to have pets, it's against the lease. But I turned a blind eye. Just keep it in your flat, I said to her. Keep it inside and I won't say anything. But she doesn't and it shits on the landing. And when I remonstrate she flies into a fury! My God, what a fury! The mouth on that woman! "Effing this, Effing that! You keep out of my effing business!" Shame on her. Vile woman, disgusting. No disrespect.'

They reached the top floor. Davidovich pressed another light-timer and crossed to a door at the far end of the landing, slowing en route to point out to Ben-Roi the precise spot where Kleinberg's cat had done its business.

'Size of my bloody fist it was,' he muttered.

The door had a spy-hole and two locks, both mortise, one in the middle, one further up. The caretaker fumbled a key into the top lock, realized it was the wrong one, tried another, started to turn it.

'Hang on.'

Ben-Roi grasped the caretaker's hand and moved him back a step.

Something had caught his eye. On the floor. A fragment of matchstick, less than a centimetre long, lying on the tiles at the base of the door, up against the frame. He stooped and picked it up. It could be nothing. Then again, from what Natan Tirat had told him, Kleinberg had clearly had reason to be paranoid. And the match-in-the-door trick was a classic paranoiac's ruse. Wedge a small fragment of match between door and frame when you go out. If the door is opened the match drops and you know someone's been in there.

'Have you opened this door in the last twenty-four hours?'

'Are you crazy?' cried the caretaker. 'After the way she talked to me? I haven't been anywhere near the bloody woman!'

'Anyone else got keys?'

'I sincerely doubt it. I had enough trouble getting these ones off her. "Mrs Kleinberg," I told her, "I'm the caretaker, it's in the lease, I have to have a spare set of keys in case there's a fire or a gas leak or a pipe . . ."'

Ben-Roi wasn't listening. There had been no keys on the victim's body. Which meant if someone *had* accessed the flat there was a strong possibility . . .

He pulled out his mobile and called Leah Shalev, told her to get forensics over to the flat ASAP. And some uniforms to statement the block's residents. When he'd rung off, he took the keys from the caretaker and opened the door himself, taking care not to touch anything. As he swung it back a smell of dirty washing and fouled cat litter wafted out on to the landing.

'*Oy vey*,' muttered Mr Davidovich.

A corridor ran off in front of them, lino-floored and gloomy, with half-open doors to either side and, at the end, what looked like a living room. An overweight tortoiseshell cat with a bell round its neck was sitting in the middle of the corridor. It stared at them, then disappeared into the living room with a loud tinkling.

'That's the shitter,' said Mr Davidovich, scowling.

There was a light switch on the wall and, pulling a handkerchief from his pocket, Ben-Roi dabbed it on. He ran his eyes back and forth. Then, thanking the caretaker for his help, stepped inside and closed the door. Out on the landing Mr Davidovich could be heard grumbling about cats and leases and how the country was going down the shit-hole.

The immediate thing that struck Ben-Roi was the level of security in the flat. In addition to the spy-hole and two mortise locks, there were, on this side of the door, a chain, two bolts – top and bottom – and, standing ready on a shelf by the door, a canister of mace spray. Kleinberg had clearly been a frightened woman.

He moved along the corridor, nudging doors open with his foot. The place was a mess, a real pigsty. Untidy owner mess, he thought, rather than the disorder left by someone having ransacked the flat, although he couldn't be certain. There were plates of half-eaten cat food in the kitchen, a turd-filled cat-litter tray in the bathroom, clothes all over the floor of one bedroom and stacks of cardboard boxes in another.

The living room – which doubled as a study – was particularly chaotic, every available inch of space heaped with teetering mounds of papers and books and magazines and newspapers. 'Like a bloody Exocet' was how Natan Tirat had described Kleinberg's journalism skills. The same, it seemed, could be said of her housekeeping. It would take him days to sift through all this. Weeks. A whole team of them weeks.

'*Zayn*,' he muttered as he surveyed the mayhem. Fuck.

A glass-paned door with a cat-flap in it gave out on to a balcony, where the tortoiseshell was now lying curled on a reclining chair. Beside the door was a desk. He stepped over to it. Heaps of photocopies and newspaper cuttings, a leather-backed blotter, a Rolodex, two dictionaries and a thesaurus, a ceramic cup full of biros. Also, a printer and a modem. No computer. Ben-Roi squatted and looked under the table. He could see none of the cabling you'd expect with a desktop hard drive, which suggested Kleinberg had worked off a laptop. He had a quick scout around the flat but couldn't find one. Possibly it was buried somewhere and he'd missed it. Possibly it was at the menders. Or possibly the killer had taken it, either from here or from Kleinberg's bag in the cathedral. Instinct told him it had been taken, although there was no way of knowing for sure.

He took out his pen and, using the butt-end, poked around the paperwork on the desk, making sure he didn't actually touch anything. There were quite a few printouts about the Armenian community and the Cathedral of St James, which was obviously relevant, although it all seemed to be fairly generalized information. Also, a lot of stuff on prostitution and the Israeli sex industry, including several booklets on the subject from something called the Hotline for Migrant Workers. There were copies of *Matzpun ha-Am*, the magazine Kleinberg worked for; an atlas bookmarked at a map of Romania; individual fold-out maps of Israel and Egypt; numerous random cuttings on everything from computer hacking to British military decorations, the psychology of child abuse to gold smelting (three of them on that particular subject). It all seemed totally haphazard, without theme or connection. If there were clues he had no idea what they were or how to interpret them. Like looking for a needle in a haystack. Worse: like looking for a needle in a haystack when you don't actually know what a needle looks like.

'*Zayn*,' he repeated.

He spent thirty minutes sniffing around the rest of the room with its floor-to-ceiling bookshelves and filing cabinets crammed to overflowing with more papers and cuttings. Then, having barely scratched the surface, he moved into the bedroom. Unmade bed, clothes all over the floor, half a dozen pill bottles on the chest of drawers, a childlike painting of a woman with long blonde hair sellotaped to the wall, watercolour, on pale blue paper.

On the bedside table there were three photographs, all in Perspex holders, the only photos he'd yet seen in the flat. He bent down for a closer look.

One was a group shot of some twenty young women, all smiling broadly at the camera, all dressed in military fatigues and bush hats – presumably doing their national service. Rivka Kleinberg was standing at the left of the group, arm thrown around the shoulder of an attractive woman in sunglasses – a much younger version of Kleinberg, although still recognizable from her heavy-boned frame and curly hair. On the back was a dedication: 'To darling Rivka – Happy Days!'

Next along was a black-and-white shot of a young man and woman, standing hand in hand with their backs to the sea. There was something dead-eyed about them, haunted – a look he'd seen in many Holocaust survivors. Kleinberg's parents, he assumed.

The third picture was of a young girl. Only about eight or nine, she was smiling broadly, her auburn hair done up in pigtails, her pale face dotted with freckles. On the back, in neat child's writing, English rather than Hebrew, was some sort of nonsense rhyme or doggerel:

> *Sally, Carrie, Mary-Jane,*
> *Lizzy, Anna, what's in a name?*
> *Hannah, Amber, Stella, Lee,*
> *Keep me hid, let no one see,*
> *Jenny, Penny, Alice, Sue,*
> *But only Rachel's really true.*

Ben-Roi glanced up at the painting on the wall, then back down at the photo. Something about the two images felt distinctly out of place in the flat, not things that fitted with the Rivka Kleinberg he'd been hearing about. Maybe it would be worth looking into them at some point, trying to find out who the girl was. They didn't seem to have any immediate relevance to the investigation, however, and after gazing at the photo for a while, he resumed his trawl of the apartment.

He got his first break in the kitchen. In the bin. It was a pedal model and, more for the hell of it than because he expected to find anything useful, he dabbed it open with the toe of his trainer. It was three-quarters full of rubbish: Coke cans, an Elite coffee jar, a crumpled Mr Zol carrier bag, empty cat-food tins. And, also, a used Egged bus ticket. So far he'd been careful not to actually touch anything, not wanting to leave prints or physical traces before the forensics guys got here. Curiosity now got the better of him. Pulling the ticket out, he unfolded it. It was dated five days ago, four before Kleinberg's murder – a return to Mitzpe Ramon, a dead-end town down in the middle of the Negev. Significant? He had no idea, although something told him it was. He stared at the ticket, then folded it and slipped it into his pocket.

He took the spare room last. It gave him the answer to something that had been nagging him since he'd looked round the living room – the absence of notebooks.

Every journalist he'd ever met had notebooks. Not just for immediate use, but old notebooks as well – like detectives, there was always a need to back-check or cross-reference information that had been gathered at an earlier date. Natan Tirat had an apartment full of the things – Ben-Roi remembered him almost breaking up with his wife after she threw a load out during her spring cleaning.

He hadn't seen a single one in Kleinberg's work area. Turned out it was because they were all filed in the spare room's cardboard boxes. Neatly filed, in marked contrast to the chaos that reigned throughout the rest of the flat. Three decades-worth. Her entire career, by the look of it. Hundreds of them, all labelled with the dates of the period covered by the notes inside – in both Hebrew and English, for some reason – all sorted chronologically and boxed up by year so that if you wanted to find, say, the research notes for an article written in April 1999, you would know immediately where to go. Early on she had used all manner of different types of pad – A4, A5, lined, unlined, spiral-bound, stitched. For the last two decades she had favoured the same black A4 book, hard-covered and wide-lined.

There was potentially useful information here, no question, but it was going to take a lot of work to prise it out. Not just because there were so many of the things, but because all the writing in them was in shorthand. It would have to be done, but for the moment what was troubling Ben-Roi was not so much what was here as what wasn't. Search as he did, he couldn't find any notepads or books covering the last three months. He flicked through every box, and re-examined the living room and bedroom, but there was nothing. It was as if her journalistic life had come to an abrupt halt twelve weeks ago.

His mentor, old Commander Levi, the one who had come up with the chain analogy to describe the building of an investigation, had bequeathed another gem of policing wisdom to Ben-Roi: the 'bellyaches'. The bellyaches were the feeling you got when something wasn't quite right about a case, didn't fit with the overall narrative of the crime. A garrotted corpse in the middle of cathedral wasn't right, of course, but the bellyaches weren't about crimes per se. They were about anomalies within crimes. And the absence of notebooks was an anomaly.

As with the missing laptop, there were possible explanations. His gut instinct, though, was that the notebooks had been taken by Kleinberg's killer. And that was a bellyache, a serious bellyache, because a killer who stole shorthand notebooks fitted a wholly different pattern to one who garrotted a woman and stole her wallet, keys, mobile and laptop. It was a disconnect. It just didn't mesh. He leant against the window frame and stared out over the rooftops, thinking. He was still there fifteen minutes later when the forensics team pitched up.

He hung around for another half hour, wandering through the flat while the CITs got down to business in the living room. He didn't find anything obviously useful and eventually he left them to it and headed for the front door. He was already out on the landing when one of the forensics – a girl – called after him:

'I don't know if this is anything.'

He backtracked. She was standing in front of Kleinberg's desk, pointing down at the leather-backed blotter. When Ben-Roi had gone over the desk before, the blotter had been all but buried in papers, but these had now been cleared aside.

At first he couldn't see what she was pointing at – apart from a couple of biro marks and a smudge of black ink, the blotter was blank. Only when he bent down and examined it more closely did he see faint traces of lettering indented into the soft white paper, echoes of things Kleinberg must have been writing on a separate sheet. Most of the words were too faint and overwritten to make out clearly. One, however, was more deeply indented than the others, rendering it easier to decipher. Repeated over and over again, it appeared in at least eight different places across the blotter: *Vosgi*.

'It's like she was really pressing the pen down,' said the girl. 'You know, like when you've got something on your mind, when it's really bugging you.'

Vosgi.

'Mean anything to you?' asked Ben-Roi.

She shook her head. 'You?'

Ben-Roi shook his. It certainly wasn't Hebrew. Pulling out his notebook, he wrote the word down. He stared at it a moment. Then, with a shrug, pocketed the book and made for the front door.

'And see if you can find a home for the cat,' he called over his shoulder.

LUXOR

Khalifa only knew three rich people.

One was a childhood friend who had made good in the dotcom industry; one a millionaire American novelist with whom he had struck up a loose friendship after she had visited Luxor to research a detective series based on the Luxor Police (ludicrous idea). The third was his brother-in-law Hosni.

Walking back through the centre of town after his meeting with Demiana Barakat, he stepped into an internet café and composed e-mails to the first two, explaining his friend's funding problems and asking if there was any way they could help. He didn't feel comfortable doing it – he was a proud man and it wasn't in his nature to ask for assistance, especially financial assistance. He couldn't get the image of the hunchbacked boy out of his head, however, and felt he had to do something.

Hosni he didn't bother with. Vice-President of the largest edible oils company in Egypt, his brother-in-law was widely known to be tighter than the masonry joins of the Great Pyramid.

He sent the mails, left the café and wandered down on to the Corniche el-Nil, trying to decide if he should head over to the new police station in El-Awamaia – a swish new building to which they'd all re-located after the old station had been demolished – or simply go home.

In the end he did neither. His boss, Chief Inspector Abdul ibn-Hassani, was scheduled to give one of his interminable 'modernizing' lectures that afternoon – 'New Egypt, new Luxor, new station, new force!' as he was wont to put it – which frankly Khalifa could do without. Back home, Zenab's sister Sama – Hosni's wife – had flown in from Cairo for the day, and the prospect of listening to her nattering about make-up and shopping and the latest high-society gossip was even less inviting than one of the chief's homilies.

Instead he hopped on a motorboat over the Nile, took a service taxi up to Deir el-Medina and climbed to his 'thinking seat' in the cliffs around the midriff of the Qurn.

It was where he always came when he wanted to be on his own, completely on his own, just him and his thoughts, away from everyone and everything. A rock ledge at the base of a shallow cleft, about halfway up the mountain, it afforded spectacular views out across the Valley of the Kings and away northwards into the distance where Nile, farmland and desert gradually merged into a dull featureless haze. He'd discovered it years ago, when he'd first arrived in Luxor, and had been coming up here on and off ever since, especially these last months, when he had felt in particular need of the calm and solitude it provided.

It was a strenuous climb, doubly so in the afternoon heat, and he was breathing heavily by the time he eventually reached the seat. Scrambling up the dusty scree slope at its foot, he swung himself on to the ledge and settled back into the shade of the cleft, folding his arms and gazing out, heart thudding.

Things were changing on this side of the Nile too, just as they were back in Luxor town. Not as fast, perhaps, or as dramatically, but changing nonetheless. The ramshackle mud-brick dwellings of Old Qurna, which used to cluster like a fungus around the foothills of the Theban massif, had all been bulldozed, their inhabitants moved out to a characterless housing estate up north at El-Tarif (he could just make it out in the distance – tightly regimented rows of apartment blocks, more like military barracks than homes). The massif itself, which not so very long ago had looked pretty much exactly as it must have done in pharaonic times, was now dotted with a collection of ugly concrete guard posts, complete with generators and radio masts and floodlights. Down below, bang in the middle of the Valley of the Kings, the finishing touches were being put to a huge new museum and visitor centre. Funded by some American multinational and two years in the building, it was due to open in a couple of weeks, which had got Chief Hassani into a right flap – apparently half the government were coming down for the inauguration ceremony.

Everything Khalifa knew, all the familiar places and views and points of reference, were morphing into something different. And he was morphing with them. Could feel it. The Yusuf Khalifa who sixteen years ago had laughed with carefree delight when he first discovered the seat, was not the Yusuf Khalifa who was sitting up here now.

Everyone changes with time, of course, but there is an essence that remains the same. A bedrock. Khalifa felt as if his bedrock had shifted and cracked. There were moments these days when he barely recognized himself. The dark moods, the sudden, inexplicable flares of anger, the corroding sense of powerlessness and frustration and guilt.

He never used to be like this. In the past, whatever hardships life had thrown his way – and there had been plenty of them – he had always got on with things, refused to allow the unfairness of the world to unbalance him. But these days ... Their demolished home, the Attias' poisoned well, Demiana's funding, the little boy on the motorbike: things he would once have coped with emotionally, life's everyday cruelties, now seemed to drive ever deeper splits into his already broken foundations. Everything was falling apart. More than once he'd wondered if it was why he'd started coming up here so frequently. Not for the peace and the silence and the head space, but for the simple relief of feeling something solid around him.

He unscrewed the top of the Baraka water bottle he'd bought on the way over and took a swig, then lit a cigarette and nestled himself back even further into the shade of the cleft. In front of him and slightly to the left he could just make out the mud-brick remains on top of the Hill of Thoth; to his right lay the tumbled ruins of the 'way station', where the ancient tomb-workers had stopped off on their daily walk to and from the Valley of the Kings. A sort of ancient clocking-in post. The rock faces around here were covered with the workers' graffiti, dozens upon dozens of inscriptions marking a brief, fleeting moment in lives that had been every bit as real as his own and were now completely lost to history.

One such graffito was right there beside his head: a trio of cartouches – Horemheb, Ramesses I, Seti I – scored into the yellow limestone by someone styling himself 'The scribe of Amun, Pay, son of Ipu'. A circled number accompanied them – 817a – left by Czech Egyptologist Jaroslav Černý, who had recorded the inscriptions back in the 1950s.

Khalifa had often wondered about this son of Ipu. Who was he? What sort of person? Had he had brothers and sisters? A wife and children? Grandchildren? Had he been happy or sad? Strong or weak? Healthy or sick? Lived long or died young? So many questions. So much lost. An entire life reduced to nothing more than a few scratch marks on a limestone rock face.

It was something that had struck him more and more of late – the transience of things. The meaninglessness. Once Pay had been a living, breathing human being, just like him. His life had been a story, full of drama and emotion and relationships and change. He had been a baby, and then a boy, and then a man, and then, maybe, a husband and father. He had been so much. His story had been so rich. And then, suddenly, the story was over, and all that was left was this tiny fragment scored into the rock. Fragments, that's all that was ever left. And however many fragments you gathered, however many words and sentences and paragraphs, you could never know the whole story. Never fully know that person. Certainly never bring them back. They were gone and that was it.

Taking a drag on his cigarette, he pulled out his wallet. There was a plastic pocket inside, and inside the pocket a photo: Khalifa, his wife Zenab, and their three children: Batah, Ali, little Yusuf – Team Khalifa as they jokingly called themselves. It had been taken at this very spot a couple of years back – they had all bundled together and Khalifa had held the camera out in front of them, which explained why the angle was slightly askew. They were all laughing, particularly Khalifa, who had Ali on his lap and was only just managing to keep his balance. A second after the shutter clicked he had slipped, and he and Ali had gone sliding down the scree slope beneath the seat, which had made them laugh even more.

There'd been so much laughter.

He gazed at the picture. Then, touching it to his lips, he put it away, sat back and stared out at the barren vistas all around.

JERUSALEM

When Ben-Roi got back to Kishle, Dov Zisky was sitting in the office bent over a desk like some sort of *Talmid hakham*. Yoni Zelba and Shimon Lutzisch had both gone out so it was just the two of them.

'Any progress?' he asked, throwing off his jacket and sitting down at his own desk.

'Not really,' replied Zisky. 'Six across is a bugger.'

Ben-Roi opened his mouth, about to ask why the fuck the boy was doing crosswords when they had a murder to solve. Then, realizing it was a joke, he gave an amused grunt. The kid might sound like Dana

International, but fair play to him, at least he had a sense of humour. You needed that in the Israel Police Force. Without a sense of humour you ended up a grumbling, embittered bore like Amos Namir. And that wasn't a good place to be.

'So where are we at?'

Zisky swung round in his chair and opened his moleskin notebook.

'I've tracked down the victim's mobile account. She's with Pelephone. They're doing a breakdown of all her calls over the last six months. Same with her Bezeq landline and Gmail account. Everyone's shutting down for *Shabbat* so it's not going to be till Sunday at the earliest.'

Ben-Roi grumbled, but didn't push the matter. It was how things worked in this part of the world – even murder investigations took a day of rest.

'What about the compound?' he asked, eyes running over the headlines of the *Yedioth Ahronoth* he'd bought on the way back from Kleinberg's flat: government corruption scandal, peace talks deadlock, Hapo-el Tel-Aviv hammered in the Champions League. Same old, same old. 'Anything useful from there?'

'Not much,' said Zisky. 'The duty concierge from last night couldn't really add anything to the statement he's already given. The victim came through the gate about seven p.m. He thinks someone may have come in behind her, but he was on the phone to his wife so he wasn't really paying attention. He certainly can't give any sort of description. Hopefully we'll get something more detailed from the compound cameras.'

'Hopefully,' said Ben-Roi.

'He did mention he'd seen her before.'

Ben-Roi looked up.

'So did several other people. Seems she's been visiting the compound quite a lot over the last two or three weeks.'

Ben-Roi folded the paper and sat back, interested. 'Tell me more.'

'Well, the guy from last night reckoned she'd been in at least twice before. And there's another concierge who says he's clocked her four or five times. There's also a priest, name of . . .'

He consulted his notebook, trying to find the name. Ben-Roi waved a hand to indicate it didn't matter.

'Anyway, he said she'd sat in on a few services, morning and afternoon. He thought she might have been waiting for someone, but none of the people I spoke to could remember seeing her with anyone. The uniforms are still doing door to door – they might come up with something.'

Ben-Roi nodded, drumming his fingers on the desk.

'I also spoke to Archbishop Petrossian,' said Zisky.

'And?'

'He only gave me fifteen minutes so it wasn't exactly an in-depth interview. Said he couldn't believe anyone from his own community would do something like that, but otherwise there wasn't anything he could tell me.'

'Did you believe him?'

Zisky shrugged. 'He was definitely upset by the whole thing. You could see it in his eyes. I got the feeling . . .'

'He was lying?'

'More that . . . there was something else going on with him. Something he wasn't saying. It was nothing definite. Just an intuition.'

A *lady's intuition*, thought Ben-Roi. He kept it to himself.

'Does he have an alibi?'

'Said he was in his private apartments all evening. We haven't found anyone to corroborate that yet.' He reached up and fiddled with one of the clips keeping his *yarmulke* in place. 'I could do a bit of digging, if you want. Pull out a bit of background.'

'Do that. And while you're at it, see what you can find out about this.'

Ben-Roi fumbled in his pocket and threw the Egged bus ticket he had found in Kleinberg's flat on to the desk. Zisky came over and picked it up, bringing a vague smell of aftershave with him.

'Kleinberg used it five days ago,' said Ben-Roi. 'To Mitzpe Ramon. I'd be interested to know what our victim was doing out in the middle of the Negev.'

Zisky examined the ticket.

'Also,' said Ben-Roi, rather enjoying having someone to dump stuff on, 'can you find out what this word means?'

He opened his notebook, turned it and, sitting forward, flattened it on the desk, pointing at the word they'd found indented on Kleinberg's blotter: *Vosgi*. Zisky leant over to look, his cheek almost touching Ben-Roi's. The smell of aftershave suddenly grew stronger.

'Sorry, boys, not interrupting anything, am I?'

Uri Pincas had appeared in the doorway. Ben-Roi sat back sharply.

'Don't you ever fucking knock, Pincas?'

His colleague smirked and puckered his lips, making the shape of a kiss. Ben-Roi scowled.

'What do you want?'

'Just come over to let you know the camera material's ready. We're viewing in five minutes. Hopefully that'll give you both time to . . . you know, freshen up.'

'*Shak li b'tahat*, Pincas!' Kiss my arse.

'I'll join the queue. See you over in the annexe.'

He winked, puckered another kiss and disappeared into the corridor.

'And if you've finished with my Yahonathan Gatro CD, I'd like it back,' he called.

'Prick!' Ben-Roi bellowed.

If Zisky had picked up on any of this – and it would have been hard not to – he showed no sign of it. He just scribbled *Vosgi* in his notebook and went quietly back to his desk. Ben-Roi wondered if he should say something, but Zisky was already lifting his phone and dialling. Instead he went out and used the toilet, then poured himself a cup of water from the cooler in the corridor. He filled another cup for Zisky and went back into the room.

'Gold.'

'Sorry?'

'*Vosgi*. It means gold. In Armenian. Gold, golden.'

Bloody hell, the kid moved fast. He'd only been out of the room a couple of minutes.

'Right,' said Ben-Roi. 'Thanks.'

Zisky nodded and took the cup of water. 'Would you mind if I left a bit early?' he asked. 'I need to pick up some things for *Shabbat*.'

'Sure,' said Ben-Roi. 'No problem.'

He hovered a moment, then, with a repeated 'Right', made for the door.

'Oh, and sir?'

Ben-Roi swung round.

'If you're into Yahonathan Gatro I've got all his albums – I'll happily burn you some copies. I've got plenty of Ivri Leder and Judy Garland as well.'

Zisky flashed a smile and turned back to his desk. Despite himself, Ben-Roi smiled too. He was starting to warm to the kid.

Pincas and Nava Schwartz had put together a 17-minute DVD featuring all the relevant footage they could come up with from the night of Kleinberg's murder, both from police cameras and those in the Armenian compound.

They viewed it in a glass-walled side-room off the station's main camera control centre. Everyone from the morning's case briefing was there bar Zisky, whose place was taken by Chief Superintendent Yitzhak Baum. Baum always sat in on the camera viewings. More often than not they threw up the clue that helped crack the investigation, and he liked to be in on the glory.

Today he was disappointed. They all were.

Police cameras were able to track Kleinberg from the moment she alighted from a bus just outside the Jaffa Gate through to the tunnel in the middle of Armenian Orthodox Patriarchate Road. The CCTV in the Armenian compound then picked her up as she came through the compound's front gate and followed her through to the cathedral entrance.

All the way, the same figure was walking about 30 metres behind her. He entered the cathedral just after her, and emerged thirty-six minutes later. He then retraced his steps through the Old City and disappeared along the Jaffa Road.

That it was the killer no one was in any doubt. Unfortunately he was swathed in a hooded coat against the rain, and even with enhancement and close-ups, his face remained resolutely hidden. He had been on the bus with Kleinberg, was of medium build and had deliberately followed her through the Old City into the cathedral – that was about as much as they got. They couldn't even be certain if it was a he.

They watched the footage through three times, the mood in the room increasingly deflated, and were just starting on a fourth viewing when Ben-Roi's mobile went off.

El-Al. They'd gone through their records and found a match.

On the night of her death, Rivka Kleinberg had been booked on the 11 p.m. flight to Alexandria in Egypt.

'Personally I'd go for a five.'

Sir Charles Montgomery smiled. A sly, patronizing smile – not quite wide enough to appear rude, but more than sufficient to show that not only did he disagree, but that he was right to disagree. He took a nip from his hip flask and slid a Callaway Graphite 6 Iron from his golfing bag.

'It can be so difficult to judge accurately,' he said, his tone indicating that he thought quite the opposite. 'You never really know till you've made the shot.'

He took a couple of practice swings, eyeing the green 140 yards away, the smoothness of his action belying his sixty-eight years. Then, planting his white-and-tan Footjoy Classics a metre apart, he let fly, shielding his eyes as he tracked the ball's trajectory. It seemed to hang in the air for an age before eventually it descended and plopped on to the incline at the rear of the green. It sat a moment, then, slowly, rolled back towards the flag, stopping about two metres away. Montgomery gave a satisfied nod and slid the iron back into its slot, acknowledging the 'bravos' of his fellow players.

'Breeze must have given it an extra push,' he said with glaringly false modesty.

He was having a good round. An excellent round. Just as he was having a good retirement. An excellent retirement.

A couple of years back, what with all the unpleasantness on the subcontinent, things hadn't been looking quite so rosy. Corroded blanketing valve, faulty monitoring system, hydrogen sulphide cloud, thousands of blistered wog-wallahs. For a while it had looked like it was going to cause as much of a stink as Bhopal and the Trafigura thing, which wouldn't have been at all good for the company. Or for him personally, given that it had been his decision as CEO to delay installing the up-to-date safety systems that had long been standard in their plants in Europe and the US.

No, it hadn't looked good at all. For a few months he'd really sweated, especially when reports started coming through of miscarriages and birth defects, babies born blind and malformed and retarded. Blind, retarded babies, especially Third World ones, never played well in the press.

Fortunately, the situation had resolved itself to everyone's satisfaction. Sizeable payments to various government bigwigs had smoothed things at the Indian end, while a truly wonderful firm of City lawyers had employed all manner of clever legal ruses to keep the thing out of the British papers. They hadn't even had to compensate the victims, although for appearance's sake they'd made modest donations to some local charities. Very modest donations.

When he'd retired last year Charles Montgomery had done so with a generous pension package and a Knighthood of the Realm for services to industry. After cashing in his share options, he'd even made it on to the *Sunday Times* Rich List, albeit towards the lower end of richness. Life was good. And when life was good, so was his game. His handicap had improved no end these last few months. Which was rather more than could be said for those Indian babies.

Tory MP Tristan Beak took his shot, bunkering five metres short of the green. The quartet of players then set off down the fairway, pulling their trolleys behind them. As well as Montgomery and Beak there was Sir Harry Shore, a senior member of the judiciary, and Brian Cahill, a crude but spectacularly wealthy Australian hedge-fund manager. Gas leak or no gas leak, Sir Charles Montgomery still moved in the highest circles.

They covered thirty metres, then Shore, who was slightly ahead, slowed and raised his arm.

'What's that idiot doing?' he asked, pointing.

The green backed on to woodland. A figure – from this distance it was hard to tell if it was a man or woman – had emerged from the wall of trees and rhododendron bushes and was now standing on the green beside the flag. They seemed to be holding some sort of sign or placard.

'Get off,' shouted Shore. 'Away with you. This hole's in play!'

The figure didn't move, just lifted the sign or placard or whatever it was up into the air. There was something written on it, although it was too far to see precisely what. Another figure – this one definitely a woman – pushed out of the woods. She seemed to have a placard as well.

'Clear off!' shouted Montgomery, waving an arm. 'This is a private—!'

His mobile went off. Still gesticulating, he pulled the phone from his plaid golfing trousers and held it to his ear, too distracted to check the incoming number.

'Yes,' he snapped.

'Charles Montgomery?'

The voice was a man's. Unfamiliar.

'Yes.'

'*Sir* Charles Montgomery?'

'Yes, yes. Who is this?'

Two more figures had now appeared on the green. And there seemed to be more coming. A whole crowd of them.

'Fuck off!' bellowed Tristan Beak MP. 'You'll damage the grass.'

'Do you have access to the internet, Sir Charles?'

'What? Who is this? How did you get this—'

'Because if you do, there's a website you really should check out. It's called www.thenemesisagenda.org.'

The man gave the address slowly, spelling it out.

'There are some lovely pictures of you,' he added. 'And lots of details about your company's work in Gujarat.'

Montgomery's face had already assumed a reddish tinge. Now it darkened towards purple.

'Who the hell is this?' he shouted. 'What do you want? I'm in the middle of a golf course.'

'I know you are,' said the voice. 'I'm looking right at you. Nice trousers, you sick fucking baby-killer.'

The line went dead. At the same moment the crowd on the green, which now numbered upwards of twenty people, with more coming – men and women, old and young – started chanting, their voices carrying across the otherwise sedate expanse of Wetterdean Grange Private Members Golf Club:

'Gujarat! Gujarat! Gujarat!'

They started moving towards the four golfers, the slogans on their placards gradually coming into focus: 'BABY-KILLER', 'JUSTICE FOR THE CHILDREN', 'WWW.THE NEMESISAGENDA.ORG', 'HAPPY RETIREMENT, SIR CHARLES'.

Montgomery hesitated, his broad, meaty face registering both abject fury and growing alarm. Then, turning, he started back towards the clubhouse as fast as his legs would carry him, his colleagues trailing in his wake.

'Gujarat! Gujarat! Gujarat!'

Suddenly his comfortable retirement was looking rather less assured.

JERUSALEM

As Friday afternoon progresses and *Shabbat* draws in, the streets of Jerusalem steadily empty. By late afternoon the centre of the city is all but deserted.

The same, in microcosm, happened in the David Police Station. When Ben-Roi dropped into Leah Shalev's office just after 5.30, they were the only two people left in the Kishle Investigations Department.

Shalev made them both coffee and Ben-Roi ran through the day's developments: the *Ha'aretz* threats, the missing notebooks, Kleinberg's visits to the Armenian compound, the El-Al flight to Egypt. And, also, the *vosgi* thing, which for no reason he could put his finger on, he sensed was important.

Shalev listened in silence, sipping from her Maccabi Tel-Aviv basketball mug, her lipstick, as it always did, leaving a red smudge around the rim. On-duty officers weren't supposed to wear make-up, but Leah Shalev bucked the rules. Lipstick, nail varnish, eyeshadow – Ben-Roi had never been able to work out if she did it simply because she wanted to look good, or to wind up the likes of Baum and Dorfmann, who didn't think women had any place in Investigations. If it was the former, she didn't quite pull it off. If the latter, it more than had the desired effect.

'Thoughts?' she asked when he'd finished going through it all.

Ben-Roi shrugged. 'Botched robbery. Lone psycho. Mafia hit. Personal grudge. Combination of any of the above. Take your pick. They're all in the frame.'

'Which would you go for?'

It was a game they often played at the beginning of an investigation, Shalev daring him to stick his neck out and make a call. Usually he was happy to oblige. With this case, even at such an early stage, there already seemed to be so many permutations and contradictions he was reluctant to be drawn.

'Come on, Arieh,' she said, sensing his reticence. 'Take a punt.'

114

'It's tied up with her journalism,' he said after a pause, not entirely answering the question. 'I'd lay odds on that. Given that her notebooks for the last three months seem to be missing, I'd guess it's something to do with a piece she'd been working on recently.'

'Unless our man's trying to muddy the waters,' said Shalev. 'Throw us off the scent.'

Ben-Roi acknowledged it was a fair point.

'What about her editor?' Shalev asked.

'Still hasn't come back to me. I've left four messages.'

'Only four? Not like you to be so restrained.'

'Not like you to make such good coffee.'

They both smiled. Despite his initial suspicion of her, he'd grown to like Leah Shalev. A lot. And not just because she was good at her job. She was one of the few people in the force he'd actually consider calling a friend.

'Any news from the autopsy?' he asked.

She shook her head. 'I spoke to Schmelling just before you came in. They found a hair on the victim's clothes which they've sent off for DNA analysis, see if they can match it to anything we've got on the database. And there was definitely no sexual interference. Apart from that and an estimated time of death between seven and nine p.m. – which we already knew from the camera footage – nothing. Oh yes, she had piles. The worst case Schmelling has ever seen, apparently.'

'Nice. Forensics?'

She threw up her hands to indicate 'Nothing'.

'Neighbours?'

'So far we've only managed to interview five of the flats – everyone else is out.'

'And?'

Up went the hands again. 'It's a craptangle,' she said. 'No question about it. A real craptangle.'

Like Ben-Roi with his bellyaches, Leah Shalev had her own unique policing idiom. She glanced at her watch, then finished her coffee and stood.

'I've got to get going. Craptangle or no craptangle, the Shalev household still has to eat.' She started gathering up her stuff.

'Kids OK?' asked Ben-Roi, also standing.

'Fine, although Deborah isn't speaking to me. A slight contretemps about her choice of boyfriend.'

Ben-Roi smiled. He had it all to look forward to. 'Benny?'

'Good. He's got a show over in Ein Karem and there's talk of him exhibiting in the US.'

In contrast to his wife's line of work, Benny Shalev was an artist. A well-respected one. Their marriage was one of the few police relationships Ben-Roi knew of that had managed to withstand the stresses of one partner being in the force. Leah and Benny Shalev were about as solid as it was possible to get. Although he would never have admitted it, even to himself, whenever he saw them together Ben-Roi felt a certain wistfulness, a regret for what might have been. Sometimes he really did miss Sarah. A lot of the time. Most of the time.

'You with Sarah for *Shabbat*?' asked Shalev, as if reading his thoughts.

'She's at her folks.'

'You want to come to ours? You're welcome.'

'Thanks, Leah, but I'm promised elsewhere.'

'Sure?'

'Sure.'

They left the office and went out into the yard at the back of the station. Shalev's Skoda Octavia was parked at the far end, beside the horse exercise enclosure. Ben-Roi walked her over to it.

'I want to keep Namir on the olds and colds,' she said as they went, reverting to case talk. 'And also the Armenian angle. Pincas can follow up the Russian and Hebron settler threats, see if he can make any links. He speaks Russian, and I know he's running at least one settler informer.'

'Me?' asked Ben-Roi.

He put on a camp voice, imitating Dov Zisky's question from the morning briefing. Shalev shot him a withering look.

'Stay on Kleinberg. I want to know what she was writing about, who she was pissing off, why she was on her way to Egypt and why she was visiting the Armenian compound so often.'

They reached the car and Shalev clicked it open.

'How's it going with Zisky, by the way?' she asked.

'Great. We're moving in together next week.'

'*Mazel tov.*'

She dropped her bag into the back seat, climbed in and slammed the door. Away to their left a Polaris Ranger ATV chugged into the yard, the only vehicle capable of negotiating the steep, stepped streets of the Old City. Shalev waited for it to park up, then started the engine.

'You're off tomorrow, right?'

Ben-Roi nodded. 'Decorating at Sarah's,' he said. 'If you want I could—'

'I want you to do your decorating. Although if it's anything like your police work I dread to think what it'll look like. See you Sunday.'

She flicked a salute, put the car in gear and idled towards the station entrance tunnel. Halfway across the yard she stopped and lowered the electric window. Ben-Roi came up to her. She was staring face forward, hands grasped around the wheel.

'I can't explain it, Arieh,' she said, her tone suddenly serious. Thoughtful. 'But I've got a bad feeling about this case. Have had from the start.'

'That'll be because a woman got garrotted in the middle of a cathedral.'

She didn't smile. 'It just feels like it's going to lead somewhere . . .'

'Bad?'

She shifted her eyes to meet his. 'Be careful, Arieh. Be careful and keep me informed. OK?'

In five years of working together, Leah Shalev had never spoken to him like this. Ben-Roi found it curiously unsettling.

'OK?' she repeated.

'Sure,' he said. 'OK.'

She nodded, wished him *Gut Shabbas* and drove off out of the station. It started drizzling again.

LUXOR

'Daddy, we're watching Merry Poppings!'

Khalifa had barely opened the front door of their apartment when his youngest son Yusuf came bursting out of the living room and leapt into his arms. The boy gave him a fierce hug, kissed him on the lips, then wriggled free and charged off back down the corridor. Khalifa smiled, shook his head and closed the door. For a moment he stood there, the bunch of lilies he'd bought on the way back from the Qurn dangling in his hand, his eyes roving around as if to reassure himself this was definitely where he lived. Then, with a sigh, he went after the boy.

They'd been in the apartment six months. When his old block had been demolished, all the other residents had been relocated to a hideous concrete development ten kilometres out of town, up near the Nile road bridge. In an uncharacteristic show of helpfulness, his boss Chief Hassani had pulled some strings and got the Khalifas a place in El-Awamaia, just round the corner from the new police station.

It was larger than their old flat, and more convenient for work, and had a mosque and school right on the doorstep. It was even fitted with air-conditioning, a source of endless fascination to Yusuf, who was for-ever turning the system up to full blast and then building camps in which to shelter from the cold.

Despite the added amenities, Khalifa had never warmed to the place. And not just because of Yusuf's air-conditioning experiments. Even after all these months he still felt like a stranger in his own home.

Partly it was the neighbours. There was a nice old lady who lived on the floor below, and the family in the adjoining apartment were decent enough even if they did insist on having their TV on full volume 24/7. But there was none of the closeness there had been in the old block, none of the sense of community that comes with living in a place for sixteen years. In the old apartment they had belonged. Here they didn't. Every time he came home Khalifa was struck by the same sense of isolation. Of having got off the bus at the wrong stop.

Worse than that was the soullessness of the place. There were no memories or connections here. No feelings. Nothing to anchor them. Losing their old apartment had been like losing a swathe of their past. Even with all their stuff in it the new flat felt . . . empty.

Furniture you could bring with you. Associations, he had dis-covered, were strictly non-transferable.

He popped his head round the door of his oldest son Ali's room, as he always did when he came in, then continued into the kitchen, where his daughter Batah was preparing dinner.

'Good day?' he asked, wrapping his arms around her and kissing her forehead.

'Wonderful,' she replied, returning the embrace. 'Auntie Sama was here.'

'That must have been exciting.'

'It certainly was. She told us all about the shopping trip Uncle Hosni's just taken her on to Dubai. *All* about it.'

The sarcasm was subtle, but unmistakable. Khalifa smiled and flicked her nose. She was seventeen now, and so like Zenab when she'd been younger. In looks – slim, long dark hair, huge eyes – but also in her sense of humour.

'How is she?' he asked.

'OK. She's watching . . .'

Batah dipped her head towards the far end of the flat. Khalifa nodded, kissed her again and headed down the corridor into the living room where Zenab was curled on the couch with Yusuf in her arms. They were watching Ali's *Mary Poppins* DVD, humming along to the rousing strains of 'Let's Go Fly a Kite'. Or, as the Egyptian subtitles rendered it: 'We're sending our kite into the sky.'

Laying the flowers beside his wife, he circled his arms around her shoulders and kissed her head.

'Everything OK?'

She reached up and touched his hand, but kept her eyes on the screen.

'I'm off tomorrow. How about we spend some time with our boy?'

She squeezed his hand again, but still didn't look up. He stood where he was a moment, breathing in the scent of her hair. Then, with a whispered 'I love you', he returned to the kitchen to help Batah with the dinner.

'You don't need to,' she said as he pulled a knife from the drawer and took up position beside her.

'Come on, you know how I love chopping. At least allow me that little pleasure.'

She gave him a playful nudge and got on with slicing potatoes. For a moment Khalifa's gaze lingered on the fist-sized chunk of concrete sitting on the windowsill, its upper surface embedded with miniature tiles – a fragment of the fountain he'd built in the hallway of their old flat. A solitary souvenir of happier times. Then, refocusing, he began chopping onions. In the living room the *Mary Poppins* DVD played itself out, and then started over again.

Ben-Roi had lied to Leah Shalev. He wasn't promised anywhere for Friday night dinner. Instead, the day finished, he got in his car and headed home alone. There were places he could have gone, plenty of them – although he'd never been especially *frumm*, it was unusual for him to miss *Shabbat*. Tonight he was tired and not in the mood for socializing. Do some reading, maybe watch *Eretz Nehederet*, get an early night. There was a lot of stuff churning round in his head and he didn't feel like other people's company. Or God's, for that matter.

As he motored out of the station and down towards the Zion Gate – the only car on the streets at that time – he called Sarah on the hands-free.

'Everything OK?' he asked.

'Pretty much as it was when we last spoke.'

'Bubu?'

'Hang on.'

In the background he heard whispering.

'Great,' she replied. 'Just gearing up for some gymnastics.'

He chuckled. Things like that, the silly things – it was why he'd fallen in love with her in the first place. Head over heels in love.

'Your folks well?' he asked.

'Fine. Yours?'

'I'm about to call them.'

'Give them my love. And don't forget . . .'

'About decorating tomorrow. Don't worry, I've had it tattooed on my forehead. As soon as I shave in the morning I'll be reminded.'

She laughed. An infectious, girlish laugh. The laugh of someone who is genuinely amused. It was a great sound.

'*Shabbat Shalom*, Sarah.'

'You too, Arieh. *Shabbat Shalom*. See you tomorrow.'

There was a silence, as if both were waiting for the other to say something else. Then, with a repeated *Shabbat Shalom*, they both rang off.

He reached the Zion Gate and manoeuvred his way through, appreciating the smoothness of the Toyota's power-steering, the ease with which it negotiated the gate's cramped dog-leg. He'd only had the car a couple of months, after his beloved BMW had finally given up the ghost, and he was still getting used to having a vehicle whose controls actually did what they were supposed to. The BMW, for all its character, had been a truculent bugger. Lovable, but truculent. How he liked to think of himself in many ways. And now he was driving a Toyota Corolla. There was a metaphor in there somewhere.

Outside the gate, he turned right on to Ma'ale Ha-Shalom and headed downhill round the side of Mount Zion, the roof and bell tower of the Dormition Abbey flitting in and out of sight through the cypress trees above him. He called his parents back home on the family farm to wish them *Gut Shabbas*, then his grandmother in the nursing home – 'Are you eating, Arieh? Please God, tell me you're eating?' – and then his sister Chava, at whose flat he had first met Sarah, and who spent most of the conversation telling him what an idiot he was to have split up with her.

Finally, as he drove up Keren Ha-Yesod and turned into Rehavia, past the Women in Black protesters who always stood on the corner, he put in a call to Gilda Milan. His former mother-in-law. *Almost* mother-in-law. Her daughter Galia had been killed before she and Ben-Roi had made it underneath the *Huppah*.

'So are you back with Sarah yet?' she asked the moment she heard his voice.

'*Shabbat Shalom* to you too, Gilda.'

'Well, are you?'

'Not when I last checked.'

'Idiot.'

Ben-Roi smiled wearily. 'That's the second time I've been called that in the last five minutes.'

'Why not? It's the truth.'

Gilda Milan was nothing if not direct. Nothing if not courageous either. Not only had she lost her only child in a terrorist bombing, but four years back her husband Yehuda had died in the same manner while speaking at a peace rally outside the Damascus Gate. Lesser people would have been sunk by just one of those tragedies. Gilda Milan had sat *shivah* for the two people she loved most in the world, and yet remained defiantly buoyant. With Yasmina Marsoudi, wife of the Palestinian politician who had been killed alongside Yehuda, she now travelled the world promoting the cause of peace. Outside Israel and the Territories the two women were feted. Here, their voices fell on deaf ears. These days people were more concerned about paying the rent and getting food on the table than they were with the

Palestinian situation. The days of hope, it seemed, were past. These were the days of resignation. Yet still Gilda Milan refused to be bowed. She was, Ben-Roi thought, everything that was good about his country. Even if she did give him a hard time about Sarah.

They chatted until he pulled up in front of his apartment block, whereupon they wished each other *Gut Shabbas* and rang off. He locked the car and headed inside.

After he'd split with Sarah he'd slept for a month on a friend's sofa over in Givat Sha'ul. It hadn't been a happy arrangement. Partly because the sofa was a foot too short for his sizeable frame, mainly because Shmuel and his girlfriend had been frequent and extremely noisy love-makers. After four weeks of nightly grunting and shrieking, by which point both the friendship and Ben-Roi's sanity had been stretched to snapping point, he'd packed his bag and moved into a shabby one-bedroom apartment in a block on Ha-Ramban. It was a shoebox of a place and the rent gouged a chunk out of his 12,000-shekel monthly police wage, but at least he could get a proper night's sleep. More important, it was just down the road from Sarah's place on Ibn Ezra and directly opposite the kiddies' playground where she'd be walking their baby once he or she arrived. Which offered some small consolation for the fact that he wouldn't actually be living with them.

Once inside, he took a shower, pulled on some clean clothes and opened the sliding doors on to the thin rectangle of dusty concrete that masqueraded as a balcony. In the twenty minutes since he had left the station the rain had stopped and the clouds had broken up, leaving a deep azure sky blushed with hints of pink and green. A beautiful Jerusalem evening. The sort of evening that made you forget all the other shit that happened in the city. He fetched a Goldstar from the fridge – he didn't drink much any more, but what the hell, it had been a long day – shunted an armchair over to the doorway and propped his feet on the balcony rails. For a while he just sat there listening to the silence, breathing in the smells of jasmine and wet leaves, gazing out towards the sails of the Rehavia windmill. Then, reaching down, he picked up the book that was lying on the carpet just inside the sliding doors. *Shalom, Baby: 101 Tips on How to Be a Good Dad.*

He opened it and started to read, swigging from the bottle. His mind was elsewhere, however, and after only a couple of minutes, he put the book down.

Garrotted corpse. Flight to Egypt. Missing notebooks. *Vosgi*. Thoughts of impending fatherhood receded as the case once again filled his mind.

* * *

The family comes first. Always. That's what we were raised to believe. You serve the family. Whatever is required, wherever, whenever. No questions asked. No doubts entertained. It supports you, you support it. The family is everything.

I've done my duty over the years. Here, there and everywhere. A lot of travelling, a lot of mess cleansed. That's how I think of it – cleansing mess. I've always been a neat sort of person.

The family has other resources, of course. Abundant resources. But some messes require particular attention. Personal attention. Someone who belongs to the family. Who is *of* the family, has the family's well-being at heart. Someone, above all, who can be trusted.

It's a big responsibility, trust. A heavy weight. Normally I wear it lightly, don't give it a second thought. I've grown up with it, after all. Have had it drummed into me from my earliest years. I do what I'm told to do and that's the end of the matter.

Only in this instance I do feel the weight. Safe in my routine, life back to normal, everything tidy and ordered and in its place, I can't stop thinking about the cathedral. Did I act too quickly? Did I leave loose ends? Should I have waited?

It ought to have been neat, like all the others. Go to her flat, find out what she knows, cleanse her, cleanse the evidence, leave. Simple. Like all the others.

Except that when I arrive at the flat she's coming out of the front door. With her travel bag. People everywhere. Eyes, witnesses. So I have no choice but to follow. On to the bus. Off the bus. Through the Old City. Into the cathedral. And all the time I'm thinking about the travel bag. Thinking if I should do it sooner than planned, while I've got the opportunity. Trying to make the decision.

Now I fear I made the wrong decision. The mess is gone, that's for sure. So are the laptop and the notebooks. Others are dealing with the technical issues. But there are loose ends. Too many loose ends. The photo, for instance. Should I have taken that? Should I have just fired the whole flat? Should I have kept following her? Should I, should I, should I?

I haven't spoken of these doubts. The family don't ask, I don't tell.

But they're there. Gnawing at me. Distracting me. None of the other missions distract me. I don't even think about them. But Jerusalem, the cathedral . . .

I fear I may have let the family down. Not done what I was supposed to do. That there's trouble coming, and that I have brought it. Please God, don't let me have brought trouble on the family. The family is everything to me. Without the family I am nothing.

And so I hope. And wait. And get on with my duties as best I can.

One curious thing: her hair smelt of almonds. Just like my mother's.

JERUSALEM

When his cell phone rang mid-morning, Ben-Roi was still fast asleep, sprawled face-down on his bed like some oversized starfish.

He'd eventually turned in at 2 a.m., having spent most of the evening surfing the net looking for stuff on Rivka Kleinberg. There was plenty to be found, all of it confirming what Natan Tirat had already told him. Kleinberg had been widely admired, particularly early in her career when she had received a succession of awards for her investigative work, including two Journalist of the Year gongs, one for an article on Israeli destruction of Palestinian olive groves, the other for a piece on the politicization of water resources in the West Bank.

Widely admired, but even more widely reviled. Tirat had mentioned a few of the groups she'd upset over the years, and the web threw up a whole load more: feminists, farmers, Mossad, Hamas, the Israel Police, the Palestinian Police, big industry – the list went on and on. Everyone, it seemed, had a gripe against Rivka Kleinberg. When he'd eventually flopped into bed his head had been buzzing and he'd fallen into a restless, troubled sleep, dreaming of a baby being mauled by cats in a cobweb-filled cathedral and, for some reason, a body washing up on a shore.

He lay now with his face jammed into the pillow, groggy and grumpy, his mobile blaring out its 'Hava Nagila' ringtone from the bedside table. He was tempted to let it go to voicemail, but then the thought struck him it might be Sarah, perhaps there was something wrong. Groaning, he reached over and grabbed the handset. It wasn't

Sarah's number on the display. He hesitated, again tempted to leave it. Then, accepting he wasn't going to get back to sleep and so might as well talk to whoever wanted to talk to him, he rolled on to his back and answered the call.

'*Shalom.*'

'Detective Ben-Roi?'

'*Ken.*'

'Mordechai Yaron.'

For a moment he couldn't place the name. Then it came to him. Rivka Kleinberg's editor. He swung himself on to the side of the bed, his mind rapidly clearing. 'I've been trying to get in touch with you.'

'I know. I'm sorry. I'm out of town. I only just picked up your messages.'

The voice was low and gruff. Educated. Difficult to guess his age. Sixty, maybe.

'I'm up in Haifa,' he added. 'Our daughter just had a baby. We're up here for the *Bris.*'

'*Mazel tov,*' said Ben-Roi.

He gave it a couple of beats, feeling a curious need to separate the news of a birth from that of a murder, then explained what had happened. Yaron interjected the odd '*Elohim adirim*' and '*Zikhrona livrakha*' but otherwise listened in silence.

'I'll get the first train down,' he said when Ben-Roi had finished. 'We were due home tomorrow anyway, but I can cut the trip short.'

Ben-Roi told him not to bother. 'Tomorrow's fine. I'm tied up today anyway. What time are you back?'

'Mid-morning.'

They arranged to meet at the *Matzpun ha-Am* office at twelve.

'One quick question while I've got you on the line,' said Ben-Roi, standing and padding through into the kitchen. 'Can you tell me what Mrs Kleinberg was working on?'

'Most recently, a piece on sex-trafficking,' replied Yaron. 'You know, girls smuggled into Israel, forced to work as prostitutes. Slavery, basically. Very distressing. She'd been on it for over a month.'

Ben-Roi recalled the desk in Rivka Kleinberg's flat, all the cuttings on prostitution and the sex industry. That would explain it. He reached down a jar of Elite coffee from the overhead cupboard and switched on the kettle.

'Before that?' he asked.

'She did a big piece on the collapse of the Israeli Left and something on American funding of extremist settlers. Before *that* . . . let me think . . . oh yes, an exposé on domestic violence in the Palestinian Territories. She spent two months on that one. Rivka certainly never stinted on her research.'

Ben-Roi spooned coffee into a mug and glanced at his watch. Ten o'clock. He'd said he'd be at Sarah's at eleven to start the decorating and didn't want to be late. He'd got everything he needed for the moment and so thanked Yaron, confirmed their meeting and rang off. He ate a swift breakfast, shaved, dressed and headed out of the flat, leaving all thoughts of the case behind. This was a no-work day. A day for Sarah and the baby.

Outside, yesterday's rain was a distant memory: the sky was clear, the sun out, the atmosphere warm and sultry. He stood a moment breathing in the air, then set off on the five-minute walk to Sarah's, whistling tunelessly. He felt good. He was going to be early. First time ever. Let the trumpets sound!

'Hava Nagila' blasted out again.

'*Shalom.*'

'Detective Ben-Roi?'

'*Ken.*'

'Sorry to disturb you on *Shabbat*. It's Asher Blum.'

For the second time that morning the name sounded familiar, and for the second time that morning it took Ben-Roi a moment to place it. Then he remembered. The librarian from the National Library, the one who'd ID'd Rivka Kleinberg.

They'd found something, Blum told him. Something that might be important. Could he come over?

Ben-Roi stood a moment, eyes flicking up the road to the junction with Ibn-Ezra, where Sarah lived, and down the road to his Toyota.

'I'll be right there,' he said, and jogged back towards his car.

The Armenian Patriarchate of Jerusalem is headed by a quartet of archbishops. One of the four serves as supreme patriarch, the other three each have their own separate spheres of duty.

Archbishop Armen Petrossian was responsible for Church administration, a position that – with His Beatitude the Patriarch in failing health – placed Petrossian in de facto control of the entire community. Or, as he preferred to think of it, in de facto control of the family.

The family was not as extensive as it had once been. In its heyday it numbered upwards of 25,000 people. Now, what with the Arab–Israeli wars and the economic situation, the number had dwindled to just a few thousand. Australia, America, Europe – this was where the young people saw their future, not Israel.

Even a diminished flock brought with it duties, however, and His Eminence was nothing if not dutiful. They were his children, all of them, and if the vow of celibacy had precluded him from siring his own offspring, he still looked on himself as a father. To succour and shield, to nurture and protect – these were the responsibilities of fatherhood. And it was with these responsibilities in mind that he left the compound this morning and, throwing frequent glances over his shoulder to ensure he wasn't being followed, made his way down into the Old City.

Although the compound formed the bulk of the Armenian Quarter, around its walls were spun a filigree of narrow streets and alleys that formed the quarter's outer strands, dividing it from the Jewish sector to the east. The archbishop navigated this maze at something just short of a trot, stopping every fifty metres and swinging round before hurrying on his way. High walls rose to either side, echoing canyons of pale Jerusalem stone, with every now and then a grey steel door, each one accompanied by a plaque bearing the name of the family who resided within: Hacopian, Nalbandian, Belian, Bedevian, Sandrouni. There were Armenian flags, and posters commemorating the genocide of 1915 – the Jews, they reminded anyone who bothered to stop and read, did not have a monopoly on suffering. There were no people about, however. Of all the Old City quarters, the Armenian was by far the quietest.

He continued down to the bottom end of Ararat Street, where, with a final look back, he slipped into a narrow alley. At the far end was a door with above it a plaque carrying the name Saharkian. He pressed the video intercom. There was a pause, then the sound of bolts being drawn. Many bolts. The door opened. A man was standing inside with a pistol in his hand. Behind him were two more men, both holding shotguns. The archbishop gave a satisfied nod.

'Secure?'

'Secure,' the men replied in unison.

Petrossian raised a hand in blessing, turned and hurried back along the alley. From behind came the slam of a door and the clack of bolts sliding into place.

A rectangular, modernist affair set in the grounds of the Hebrew University's Givat Ram campus, the National Library of Israel looked like a large concrete sandwich.

Asher Blum, head of Reader Services, looked like a caricature. Beanpole thin, with thick spectacles, pudding-bowl haircut and jeans that were at least an inch too short for him, he ticked every librarian stereotype you could think of.

'We're closed on *Shabbat*,' he explained as he let Ben-Roi into the building. 'We only came in today to catch up on some book-stacking. I told Naomi what had happened and she mentioned the notes. She wasn't in yesterday which is why I haven't contacted you sooner.'

He waved Ben-Roi through the glass doors, locked them and led the way upstairs to a large open-plan mezzanine area. Reading rooms opened off to either side; a stained-glass window – a triptych of windows – took up the entire wall at the head of the stairs. Its coloured panels seemed to burn in the morning sunlight, casting pools of red, green and blue across the carpeted floor.

'The Mordechai Ardon windows,' explained Blum. 'Our pride and joy.'

Ben-Roi gave what he hoped was an appreciative nod and checked his watch. 10.56. He was going to be a bit late, but then Sarah would expect that. He still had some leeway.

They crossed the landing and pushed through a door marked General Reading Room. It gave into a high-ceilinged, softly lit space with desks, book stacks and grimy, aluminium-framed windows look-ing out on to a drab internal courtyard. Just inside the door was an L-shaped wooden counter, with behind it a second librarian, this one far from stereotypical: brunette, attractive, with a stud in her nose and wearing a slightly-too-tight Kings of Leon T-shirt.

'Naomi Adler,' said Blum, introducing her. 'She was duty librarian the last time Mrs Kleinberg was here.'

Ben-Roi shook her hand, trying to keep his eyes off the girl's chest.

'Apparently you've found something?' he said.

The girl nodded and, reaching beneath the counter, produced a crumpled sheet of A4.

'Mrs Kleinberg left it beside the microfilm readers,' she explained, handing the sheet across. 'I knew it was hers because I recognized the writing. She was always leaving stuff lying around.'

'This was when?'

'Last Friday. In the morning.'

A week before Kleinberg's murder.

'You asked what she'd been looking at on the readers,' put in Asher Blum. 'We thought it might be important.'

Ben-Roi examined the sheet. There were, in his experience, pieces of evidence that leapt right out at you, screamed: 'Look at me! I'll solve the crime!' And there were pieces of evidence that didn't. This fell squarely in the latter camp.

It was a list. Of newspapers. Four of them. Just the title and date of publication. One was the *Jerusalem Post* for 22 October 2010; the other three were *The Times* – 9 December 2005; 17 May 1972; 16 September 1931.

'She was looking at these?' asked Ben-Roi.

The girl nodded.

'Do you know *what* she was looking at, exactly?'

'She was definitely reading something on the business pages of *The Times*. I was helping someone set up on the machine beside hers and could see over her shoulder. I think it was that one.'

She touched a finger to the 9 December 2005 listing.

'She was making notes,' she added. 'A lot of notes.'

'The other three papers?'

The girl shook her head.

He looked back down at the list, then at his watch. 11.02. He really ought to be going, could follow this up another time. Then again, a few more minutes wouldn't make any difference. He hesitated, professional interest wrestling with personal obligation. Professional interest won out.

'Can we take a look?'

'Sure.'

The librarian came out from behind the counter and led him over to a row of metal cabinets ranged along the wall at one end of the room. Asher Blum left them to it, busying himself stacking books on to a trolley.

The cabinets were labelled with the names of half a dozen newspapers, some English, some Hebrew: *Ha'aretz, Ma'ariv, Yedioth*

Ahronoth, The Jerusalem Post, The Times, The New York Times. Taking the list from Ben-Roi, the girl ran her eyes up and down, then started opening drawers. Each was filled with neatly arranged rows of cardboard boxes, each box labelled with the publication dates covered by the microfilm inside. She picked out the relevant ones, carried them over to the nearby reading machines and sat down. Ben-Roi took up position behind her.

'Where do you want to start?' she asked.

'I guess with the paper you saw her looking at. Do you remember the page?'

'Not off the top of my head. I probably would if I saw it again.'

She switched the machine on. Opening one of the boxes, she removed its roll of film, loaded it on to the runners and wound it on to bring up the first page image. She made sure the image was centred and focused, then fast-forwarded, pages flying by across the projection plate in an indecipherable blur of grey type, the room echoing to the puttering rush of spooling tape. She located the right edition – Friday, 9 December 2005 – then slowed the reel right down, winding through the pages one by one in search of the section she'd seen Rivka Kleinberg reading. Headlines and parts of headlines rolled past – 'Hospitals may ban treatment for smokers and drinkers', 'Blair attempts to isolate . . .' '. . . lost her legs to walk down the aisle', '. . . dies peacefully at 113' – before she eventually stopped on page 66. She gazed down a moment, then nodded.

'This is it,' she said. 'I recognize the photo. How's your English?'

'Good.'

'In that case I'll leave you to it and set up the other reels. Save a bit of time.'

She pointed out the forward and rewind buttons, then moved to the adjacent machine and started loading up the next film. Ben-Roi sat down and stared at the page in front of him.

There was a picture of a man he'd never heard of called Jack Grubman, and a half-page advert for – appropriately – a collection of crime fiction audio books. Only three articles. One on the Indian economy, one about an investor dispute at some banking conglomerate and one about gold-mining.

Gold. *Vosgi.*

He leant forward and started to read.

Romania gives Barren gold green-light

Bucharest – US minerals and petrochemicals giant Barren Corporation has been granted a 30-year licence to develop the Drăgeş gold mine in the western Apuseni Mountains. Barbados-registered Barren Corp. will hold a 95% stake in the mine, with the remaining 5% held by state-owned Minvest Deva.

Known since Roman times, the Drăgeş deposit is still estimated to hold 30–40 million ounces of refractory gold, at a uniquely high concentration of 35 grams per tonne.

In a ground-breaking industry move, the licence was granted only after Barren offered legally binding guarantees concerning pollution management and environmental protection. The process of extracting gold from ore results in significant levels of toxic waste, and the Romanian government are anxious to avoid a repeat of the 2000 Baia Mare disaster when a tailings lake burst its dam and polluted much of the upper Danube basin. While the terms of the Drăgeş concession permit fast-decomposing toxic material to be disposed of locally, Barren have undertaken to transfer all non-degradable residue to processing facilities in the US for immobilization and landfill.

'We take our environmental responsibilities extremely seriously,' commented Barren CEO Mark Roberts. 'At Drăgeş we are delighted to usher in a new era of cooperation between the mining industry and green interests.'

When fully operational the mine is expected to produce 1.5 million ounces of gold annually. Gold is currently priced at $525 per ounce.

Ben-Roi reached the end and sat back, puzzled. There was no question this was what Kleinberg had been looking at. Not just because of the gold/*vosgi* connection, but because among the confusion of papers on the desk in her apartment there had, he seemed to remember, been several things on gold smelting, and also an atlas bookmarked at a map of Romania. *Why* she had been looking at it was a different matter. According to her editor, Kleinberg had been working on an article about sex-trafficking at the time of her death. How that linked with a gold-mining operation in Europe Ben-Roi couldn't begin to imagine, although the name Barren did seem to ring a vague bell. He scratched his head, trying to remember where he'd heard it before. He couldn't pin it down and after scribbling a couple of notes he decided to move on.

Next up – already loaded and ready to go – was *The Jerusalem Post*. Friday, 22 October 2010 edition. Front page mostly taken up with articles on *ha-matzav*, the current political situation, with a small picture piece on chess and, in the bottom right-hand corner, an advert praising Rabbi Meir Kahane – 'the truest, most noble Jewish leader of our generation'. He shook his head, torn between black amusement at the sheer stupidity of it, and annoyance that a dickhead like that should get front-page coverage in a major national. Then, dismissing it, he pressed the forward button and started working his way through the paper.

It took him less than a minute to make a link. Page 4. News In Brief. Barren again.

Tel-Aviv office break-in
The Ramat Hachayal offices of US multinational Barren Corporation were broken into on Wednesday night. An anti-capitalist group styling itself The Nemesis Agenda held security guards at gunpoint, removed paperwork and hacked into company computer systems. Anyone with information is asked to contact the Israel Police on (03) 555-2211.

He remembered now where he'd come across the name Barren. Yesterday, when he'd been stuck in traffic inside the Jaffa Gate. There'd been a hoarding with an artist's impression of what the area would look like once all the roadworks were finished. Its strapline had read: 'Barren Corporation: Proud to be sponsoring Jerusalem's future history.'

Why Rivka Kleinberg should have been interested in the company or a break-in at their offices he had no idea – as with the gold-mining article, there was no obvious cross-over with the story she had apparently been working on. He quickly went through the rest of the paper to see if anything else struck a chord. It didn't, and having again scribbled a few notes, he shifted to the next machine along. *The Times*, 17 May 1972. Front-page photo of a man in hand-cuffs, accompanied by the headline: 'Mr Wallace, now off critical list, heading for big victory in the Maryland primary.'

So far things had moved along reasonably swiftly. Now they slowed to a crawl. Although only twenty-eight pages long, the paper was crammed from one end to the other with a dense thicket of text: news stories, features, op-eds, letters, reviews, births, marriages, obituaries, classified ads, all in a type so small it made his eyes swim and his head ache. For a moment he thought he'd found what he wanted on page 7 where there was a big piece on the opening of a new hydro-electric dam in Romania. It had an Israeli angle as well: a couple of paragraphs at the end described how Romanian President Ceauşescu had recently held a meeting with Golda Meir to discuss the Palestinian situation. Romania and Israel. Clear links. Something, however, some gut instinct, told him that they were only coincidental and it was not this that Rivka Kleinberg had been looking at. He read the article through a couple of times, then moved on.

In the end he spent the best part of an hour on the paper, laboriously ploughing through articles on everything from the assassination attempt on Alabama Governor George Wallace to the Vietnam War, from industrial unrest in the UK to the population boom in Japan, from a woman who had given birth to eight pairs of twins in Iran to another woman who had fallen down a hole in Egypt. Naomi Adler and Asher Blum wandered around the room returning books to shelves, then went out to get some lunch, then came back and still Ben-Roi sat there, oblivious to them, oblivious to the time, oblivious to everything except the text in front of him. Jerusalem, he had once heard, had the highest per capita concentration of eye problems in the world due to all the *yeshiva* students who did nothing but pore from dawn to dusk over the fine print of Jewish holy texts. The more he read, the more Ben-Roi suspected it was a statistic to which he'd soon be adding. And still he could find nothing that might explain why Rivka Kleinberg should have been interested in that particular publication.

Eventually he reached the end of the paper and, defeated, gave up the search, accepting that whatever Kleinberg had been looking at, he wasn't going to find it. He changed chairs yet again and focused on the last of the papers on Kleinberg's list: *The Times* – 16 September 1931.

To his dismay, the articles here were even more crammed, and the text even smaller than the 1972 edition. The first three pages didn't even carry articles, just eye-wateringly minute lists of births, marriages, deaths and classified adverts. Rather than go through it all with a fine-tooth comb, as he had the previous paper, he decided to skim, skating from page to page in the hope that something would leap out at him.

And it did. Finally. On page 12. Imperial and Foreign News. A short three-line story wedged between pieces about floods in China and a hurricane in Belize. It was so brief he had already looked over it and moved on when something suddenly clicked and he went back.

Englishman missing
(From our own correspondent)
Cairo, September 15
Mr Samuel Pinsker, a mining engineer of Salford, Manchester, is reported missing from the town of Luxor. The search continues.

He was tired and had a headache and it took a moment for him to remember where he'd seen the name before. Then it came to him. Standing, he went back to the previous reading machine and the previous *Times*, 17 May 1972. The last page of the paper was still displayed. He rewound the reel. Back to page 2, then forward, searching. He went through pages 3, 4, 5, 6 and 7, then doubled back, eventually cornering his quarry in the bottom right-hand corner of page 5. The story about the woman falling down a hole in Egypt. He hunched forward, reading:

A lucky escape
Luxor, Egypt, May 16 – A British woman enjoyed a lucky escape after falling into a remote shaft tomb during a honeymoon stay in Luxor. The accident happened while Alexandra Bowers was walking with her husband in the hills around the Valley of the Kings. Despite falling 20 feet, Mrs Bowers suffered nothing more serious than a fractured wrist and bruising. Someone else had not been so lucky. While at the bottom of the shaft, Mrs. Bowers discovered the body of a man, perfectly preserved in the dry desert conditions. Although a formal identification has yet to be made, the body is believed that of Samuel Pinsker, a British engineer who went missing over forty years ago and is believed to have fallen into the shaft while exploring the Theban Hills. Mr. and Mrs. Bowers have now returned to the United Kingdom.

He read through it three times, went over and reread the earlier story, then sat back, rubbing his eyes. A mining engineer disappears in Egypt, an American multinational opens a gold mine in Romania, their offices are broken into in Israel, Rivka Kleinberg is interested in all these things, Rivka Kleinberg gets garrotted. There were threads here. Threads and connections, a whole spider's web's worth. It all linked somehow, formed a pattern. Work out the links, understand the pattern, and you solved the crime. Simple. Like doing a jigsaw. Except that this particular puzzle seemed to have a thousand different pieces and no clue as to what the overall picture actually looked like.

It was, to use Leah Shalev's phrase, a craptangle. The mother of all craptangles. And the more he thought about it, the more confusing it seemed and the more his head hurt.

He groaned and stretched out his legs, staring distractedly at a wall clock on the far side of the reading room. 1.20.

A moment later Asher Blum and Naomi Adler looked up, startled, as a cry of 'Oh shit!' shattered the silence.

When Ben-Roi ran out into the campus car park, he was in such a hurry to get into his Toyota and over to Sarah's place that he didn't notice the university athletics track 200 metres away, let alone bother looking at it. Had he looked, he would have seen a lone figure jogging around the track's perimeter. And had he waited until that figure reached the nearest point on its circuit he would have recognized it as his fellow detective Dov Zisky.

Zisky often came down here after Saturday morning *shul*. There were rabbis who said you shouldn't run on *Shabbat*, that it was a day of rest and exercising was contrary to the law, but Zisky had always had his own take on the faith. Had his own take on most things. He was dutiful, but not to the point of slavishness. And anyway, the *Tanach* enjoined *oleg Shabbat* – the pleasure of the Sabbath – and keeping fit gave him pleasure. Ergo it was OK. *Ha-Shem*, he imagined, probably had bigger things on His mind.

He speeded up and sprinted for a hundred metres, then slowed and threw out some punches, loosening his arms. He knew what people saw when they looked at him, what they thought. That he was weak. Effete. A pushover. Appearances can be deceptive. He didn't make a big thing of it, always tried to side-step confrontation, but when the situation arose, he could more than take care of himself. People had learnt that over the years. People like Gershmann at the Police Academy. Normally Zisky shrugged off the gayboy taunts – he'd been getting them for long enough – but sometimes he could be pushed too far and would launch in. Apparently Gershmann had used to do a bit of modelling in his spare time. Not any more. Now he'd have a crooked nose for the rest of his life.

He broke into a sprint again, then dropped to the grass at the side of the track and started doing press-ups, really pumping them out, enjoying the pull on the muscles of his arm and chest. As he jacked up and down, a silver *Magen David* flopped out of the top of his sweatshirt and he was forced to stop in order to tuck it back in. It had belonged to his mother and he didn't want it getting damaged. He ensured it was safely stowed, finished the press-ups, rolled on to his back for a round of sit-ups and hit the track again.

She'd died a couple of years ago, his mum, although it still only seemed like yesterday. Cancer. Lymph, lungs and stomach. Everything, basically. A week before the end, emaciated, all her beautiful golden hair lost from the chemotherapy, she'd insisted on leaving hospital to attend his police graduation. Her brother had been a policeman, had died in the line of duty, and now her son had got his badge as well. She'd wept with pride. And Zisky had wept too. Not in front of her, but later, back in the academy building. That's when Gershmann had found him and started in with the gayboy stuff. Six foot two and 90 kilos, but Zisky had taken him to pieces. Ignorant shit.

He increased his speed, holding it at just short of a sprint, his trainers beating out a rhythmic thud on the track surface, the cold pendulum of his mother's *Magen David* sliding back and forth across his sweat-drenched sternum.

He thought about his mother a lot. A cliché, he knew, the gay man who loves his mum, but that's how it was. She'd been a good woman. Strong. Had kept the family together through some tough times. At the end he'd sat holding her hand and stroking her bald head and she'd made him promise to be a good son and brother to his father and siblings. And, also, to be a good policeman. To always try to do the right thing and bring the wrongdoers to justice.

Which was why, after he'd showered and had a bite to eat, he would be heading over to Rivka Kleinberg's apartment for a poke around. Because he wanted to do the right thing. Bring the wrongdoers to justice. The faithful weren't supposed to work on the Sabbath, any more than they were supposed to jog or do sit-ups or practise Krav Maga moves. But then Dov Zisky had never been one to stick slavishly to the rules. He had his own take on things.

It was something he'd inherited from his mother.

Ben-Roi still had keys to Sarah's flat – their split had not been so acrimonious that she had demanded them back. When there was no response to his knocks, and with her cell going straight to voicemail, he let himself in.

Unlike Galia, who had had a fiery temper, Sarah was not someone who was quick to anger. She'd speak her mind, certainly, and if she was annoyed she'd let you know it. In general, though, she was a calm, laid-back sort of person. Remarkably so, given some of the shit he'd shovelled her way over the years. It was one of the things that had drawn him to her in the first place. One of the many things. Just as it was one of the things he missed about her. One of the many things.

Today she *was* angry. Very angry. So much so she wasn't even there when he got into the flat. Instead she'd left a pile of decorating equipment heaped on the hall floor – paint pots, brushes, tool box, packaged shelving units – with on top of them a note, devastating in its curtness. *Gone to Deborah's. Get on with it.*

Which is what he did for the rest of the day, the joy of preparing for the arrival of his firstborn tainted by the knowledge that his firstborn's mother thought he was a complete arsehole.

HOUSTON, TEXAS

William Barren stared down the boardroom table – a runway-sized length of highly polished red maple – and wished he hadn't done quite such a large line of coke before coming into the meeting.

He'd actually only cut himself a small one – a thin, inch-long sliver of Bolivia's finest, neatly marshalled with the edge of his Amex Black. A little pick-me-up to keep him on his toes after a heavy night (why did they always hold board meetings on a Saturday?).

Once the line was arranged, however, sitting there on his office desk like an emaciated threadworm, it had looked so insubstantial, so wholly inadequate for the hour of corporate tedium ahead, that rather than snorting it he had instead reopened the wrap and chivvied out another heap of crystalline powder, crunching it with the corner of his Amex and adding it to what was already there. Even that had seemed insufficient, and he'd ended up scraping off the wrap's entire remaining contents – the best part of a third of a gram – and sweeping them into a ridge the size of his little finger. He had hoovered it with a single practised snort, using the silver coke pipe he'd had specially made for the purpose. Then, licking the wrap and swiping an arm across the table to remove any evidence, he had taken the lift up to the boardroom feeling seriously fucking good about himself.

Now, twenty minutes later, he was regretting it. His heart was thudding, he couldn't stop grinding his teeth and his thoughts were careering around his head at such a frantic speed, and from such unexpected directions, that he could barely catch hold of them. Instead he just sat there at the head of the table jiggling his leg and gurning inanely as the other board members blahed on about leveraged buy-outs and offshore trust restructuring and the Egyptian gas field tender, which, if it came off, was going to dwarf anything the corporation had done to date and push it right up there behind Cargills in the Forbes private companies list.

They despised him, he knew that. All of them, particularly Mark Roberts, the CEO. Thought he was an embarrassment. A lightweight. Not one of them. Was only on the board because he was great-grandson of the revered Joe Barren, whose tiny gold-prospecting concession up in the Sierra Nevada had spawned the multi-billion-dollar empire that was Barren Corporation. A humble, God-fearing teetotaller – born, according to family legend, in a one-room log cabin – Joe could never have imagined that three generations on his little business venture would have ballooned into a mining and petro-chemicals colossus with interests across six continents and a direct line into the White House. Nor, for that matter, that his great-grandson would be sitting in the company boardroom coked off his head having spent most of the night romping with a mother-and-daughter hooker combo to celebrate wheedling his way out of yet another drink-driving rap (drink-driving – talk about the tip of the fucking iceberg!).

Yes, they despised him. Mark Roberts, Jim Slane, Hilary Rickham, Andy Rogerson – William ran his eyes round the table and felt disapproval burning off every one of the twelve board members ranged along its length. Most of all he could feel it emanating from the video conference screen at the far end of the table, where his father's bloated, grizzled face hovered in mid-air like some sort of monstrous bumble bee.

If Joe Barren had started the company, and his son George expanded it, it was Nathaniel Barren – old Joe's grandson, William's dad – who had transformed it into the behemoth it was today. It was Nathaniel who had diversified into oil and gas; Nathaniel who had taken the business global with subsidiaries everywhere from Russia to Israel, China to Brazil; Nathaniel who had cultivated the political links and spun the threads of obligation that had

138

drawn governments around the world into the Barren web.

Nathaniel *was* Barren Corporation, and although age and ill-health had recently forced him to take a step back after almost four decades at the helm, even now, as non-executive chairman, he still called the shots.

Not for much longer, though. Not if William had anything to do with it. The old man was ailing, losing his touch, and William was more than ready to step up to the plate. He might have a taste for coke, cars and hookers – lesbian hookers preferably, rough-trade, two of them straddling each other while he filmed them with one hand and jacked himself off with the other – but that didn't mean he was stupid. Far from it. He'd been spinning a few webs of his own these last few years. Nice, tight little webs. He had connections, people in high and useful places. Inside people. Looking around the table he counted at least seven of the twelve who'd side with him when the time came. Because if they despised him, they feared him a whole lot more. Like Michael Corleone in *The Godfather*, William Barren would soon be settling family business. All family business. And woe betide anyone who got in his way.

'Something amusing you, Billy-Boy?'

An ursine growl issued from the conferencing screen. It filled the room, snapping William from his reverie. Just as they could see him, a small camera on top of the screen relayed the boardroom and its members to Nathaniel Barren, who these days rarely left the family mansion over in River Oaks. He was staring directly down the table, straight at his son.

'Something amusing you?' he repeated, his swollen basketball of a face radiating disapproval.

'No, sir,' stammered William, the words tumbling out of his mouth like dice down a craps table, which they always seemed to do when he'd taken coke. 'Nothing.'

'But you're grinning, Billy-Boy. People don't grin unless they're amused. Please, share it with us.'

William hadn't even been aware he *was* grinning. He squeezed his mouth taut and shifted uncomfortably as thirteen pairs of eyes bored into him. Like when he'd been a kid and the old man had humiliated him in front of the servants, made him feel like an imbecile. A loser. But he wasn't an imbecile. And he certainly wasn't a loser. He was a winner. And soon he'd be—

'Billy-Boy?'

That gruff, menacing voice. Orson Wells without the bonhomie. The voice of William's nightmares.

'I guess I must have been thinking about the Egyptian tender,' he mumbled, fighting to rein in the coke surges, to keep his tone slow and measured. He over-compensated, ended up sounding like Forrest Gump. 'If we get the deal it'll . . . take us to another level. Really put Barren on the map.'

His father stared at him from out of the video screen, a cobra eyeing a racoon. Or rather a rhino eyeing . . . whatever the hell it was rhinos eyed. This was the pivotal moment. The moment of agony. The moment that even now, aged thirty-three and vice-chair of a $50-billion-dollar-turnover multinational, still made William want to shit his pants. Would the old man go for him? Take him apart and flay him like he'd been doing for as long as he could remember? Or would he ease off and let the matter drop. William's leg hammered up and down. The other board members sat in transfixed silence. Tension lasered from one end of the table to the other. The seconds ticked by.

'Barren's already on the map,' said his father eventually, just at the point where William was about to start screaming. 'All over the map.'

The old man gave it another moment, really cranking things up, stretching his son another couple of notches on the rack. Then, with a satisfied grunt, he settled back into his chair.

'Hell, we own the goddamn map!'

Laughter rippled around the room and the tension dissipated. William laughed loudest of all.

'Too frickin' right!' he cried, clapping his hands. 'It's our goddamn map! We're all over it like flies on shit!'

It was a stupid comment, his relief and the coke getting the better of him. He regretted it immediately as around the table the smiles gave way to embarrassed coughs. Fortunately his father didn't seem to notice. Lifting a plastic oxygen mask to his face, he took a deep, rasping breath – Christ, how William would have loved to fill that mask with sarin gas, watch the old bastard choke! – and waved the meeting on. CFO Jim Slane started number-crunching, his droning, nasal voice filling the room, draining it of life and colour.

William rested his elbows on the table and clasped his hands, sitting as still as he could, trying to look intense and focused, sinking back into himself. They thought he didn't understand any of it, but he did.

Knew the business inside out and back to front. The figures, the angles, the deals, the sub-deals. Everything, even the stuff his dad didn't think he knew. It was *them* who didn't understand *him* – how clever he was, how determined, how ruthless. Just like Michael Corleone. Soon he'd be settling the family business. He had plans. He had friends. He had backup. There was going to be a bloodletting, and when it was over he'd be in control. Complete control.

LUXOR

With its grand latticed façade and cavernous marble-floored foyer, the new police station in El-Awamaia was a profoundly ugly building with delusions of architectural grandeur.

Locals referred to it as *El-bandar*, 'the hub'.

Those who worked there called it variously the mosque, the castle, the wedding cake and Hassani's Folly.

Arriving on Sunday morning after his day off, Khalifa pushed through the dusty glass entrance doors, nodded a greeting to the desk sergeant and trudged upstairs to his office on the fourth floor. In the old station he'd always made a point of being at his desk by 8 a.m. at the latest – whatever else Chief Hassani had been able to fault him for, timekeeping had never been on the list. Since the move, he'd allowed things to slip. Now he was rarely in before nine, and this morning it was pushing ten when he eventually reached the top of the stairs and walked into his office.

'Evening,' said Ibrahim Fathi, the detective with whom he shared the room. *El-homaar*, as everyone called him: the donkey.

Khalifa ignored the sarcasm and plonked himself down behind his desk. He turned on his computer and lit a Cleopatra.

'Any messages?'

'None that I've taken,' replied Fathi, pulling out a comb and running it through his heavily oiled hair.

'Is Sariya in?'

'Been and gone. Another motorboat's had its diesel siphoned out. Third one this week. He's down on the Corniche talking to the owner.'

Khalifa drew a lungful of smoke. There was no point in him going

141

down to the river as well – Sariya was more than capable of dealing with things on his own. He therefore made a quick call home – he'd only left ten minutes ago, but he liked to keep in touch, make sure Zenab was OK – and started flicking through the files on his desk. The Tutotel nightclub stabbing was coming to trial in a couple of weeks, but he'd already submitted his report and there was nothing more for him to do other than show up in court and give his evidence. The dope-dealing thing in the souk still needed looking into, and he should probably drop into Karnak at some point, check out the reports he'd been hearing of thefts from the *talatat* storage magazine. In the past he would have been straight down there. This morning he decided it could wait. The souk as well. As was so often the case these days, he just wasn't in the mood. He thought about giving Demiana Barakat a call, chasing up their conversation of the day before yesterday, but if she'd heard anything she would have called herself, so again he decided to leave it. Instead he continued to thumb through the notes with one hand while with the other he logged on to the internet and brought up one of the chat rooms he'd taken to visiting of late. Not to actually chat himself – he was way too self-conscious, even under an assumed name – but rather to read what other people were saying. People in the same boat as him. It helped a little to know he wasn't alone.

The site loaded and he leant forward, ready to read. As he did so his mobile went off. Well, well – Demiana.

'*Sabah el-khir, sahbitee,*' he said, his eyes still locked on the screen. 'I was just thinking of calling you. Everything OK?'

'Fine,' she replied. 'Listen, I'm about to go into church so it's just a quick one. I wanted to pass on some information that might be relevant to what we were discussing the day before yesterday.'

Khalifa stared at the page for a moment longer – another post from Gemal in Ismaliya, who even after two years was still struggling to come to terms with the loss of his wife – then turned away, affording his friend his full attention.

'I'm listening,' he said.

'After we spoke I put the word out to see if anyone had heard of any incidents like the ones you described,' she continued. 'You know, wells being poisoned, people driven off their farms. No one had. Or at least not in the area you were describing. But then this morning I was talking to Marcos who runs the bookshop here and he mentioned something that did sound similar. It happened ages ago and in a completely different location, so it's probably not connected, but I thought I'd let you know anyway.'

'Go on.'

'Have you heard of Deir el-Zeitun?'

Khalifa hadn't.

'It's a monastery, tiny place, way out in the middle of the Eastern Desert. There's hardly anything there, just a couple of buildings, an artesian well and an old olive grove, which is where the monastery gets its name from. St Pachomius himself was supposed to have planted it, which is probably wishful thinking, given that Pachomius lived in the fourth century. The trees were certainly old, though, a good few hundred years at least. Anyway, about three or four years ago they all suddenly died. Every one of them. The monastery vegetable garden too. Just shrivelled up and withered away.'

There was a loud crunching on the other side of the room as Ibrahim Fathi helped himself to a handful of *torshi* from the bag he always seemed to have on his desk. Khalifa turned round further, trying to block out the sound.

'The grove was irrigated with water from the well?' he asked.

She gave an affirmative 'un-huh'.

'The garden too,' she said. 'The monks' drinking water comes in by tanker so they weren't affected. Just the trees and the vegetables.'

Khalifa pondered. Then, drilling out his cigarette, he stood and walked over to the large map on the wall behind Ibrahim Fathi's desk. The Eastern Desert showed as a blank expanse of pale yellow sandwiched between the Red Sea and the slim green bow of the Nile Valley. Highways crossed from west to east like the rungs of a ladder, but otherwise there was nothing. Just sand, rock and mountains.

'This monastery is where, exactly?' he asked.

'About midway between Luxor and Abu Dahab on the coast. A little west of Gebel el-Shalul.'

Khalifa traced a finger across the paper, locating the *gebel*. The monastery wasn't marked, but if it were small it wouldn't be. He moved his finger further west, locating Bir Hashfa, the village near the Attia farm. It was almost forty kilometres away, which on the face of it looked too far for there to be any obvious link between the incidents. And yet, and yet . . .

'Are the monks still there?' he asked.

'They moved out. Apparently there's some legend the monastery would only survive as long as its olive trees. When the grove died, they packed up and abandoned the place. There were only a handful of them anyway.'

'Had they had any trouble before that?'

Not so far as she was aware.

'Been threatened in any way?'

'It's the middle of nowhere. Hardly anyone even knew they were there. It might as well be the moon.'

'And you've not heard of anything else in the area?'

'I don't think there *is* anything else in the area. Like I say, it's the middle of nowhere.'

There was a sound of whispering in the background.

'I'm sorry, Yusuf, the service is about to start, I'm going to have to go.'

'Of course. Thanks for letting me know. If you hear anything else . . .'

She rang off. Khalifa stared at the map, scanning the rectangle of desert between Highways 29 and 212, then returned to his desk. The Attia well, Mr Attia's cousin, and now Deir el-Zeitun. Three poisoned water sources, all of them Coptic. One could be bad luck, two even, but three – even with so much distance between them, that suggested a pattern. He lit another cigarette and gazed at his computer screen. Abdul-hassan43, another chat-room regular, had posted a series of verses from the Holy Koran. And also a poem about how there was no shame in crying. He read half of it, then closed the site, lifted his land-line and dialled Chief Hassani's extension.

On the far side of the room there was a loud crunching as Ibrahim Fathi helped himself to another fistful of *torshi*.

ROAD TO TEL-AVIV

When they had talked the previous morning, Mordechai Yaron had offered to come up to Jerusalem to speak to Ben-Roi, save him the trouble of an hour's drive down to Tel-Aviv. Ben-Roi had told him it was no trouble at all. Like an overbearing mother, Jerusalem could get to you sometimes. Sometimes you needed to escape for a while. Clear your head.

Which was what he was doing this morning, driving out of the city along the meandering sweep of Route 1, down through the Judaean Hills towards the coastal plain, the sky a dome of pristine blue above, the warm air buffeting his arm through the open window. Not so long ago the city suburbs had come to an abrupt halt just beyond Romema. Now they seemed to go on and on, creeping inexorably out across the landscape like some ever-expanding algae, smothering the world in concrete. Building, always so much building. If they carried on at this rate there wouldn't be any land left.

Only when he was out past Mevaseret Zion, ten kilometres from the centre, did the houses and apartment blocks finally relent and the hills revert to their natural state. Rocky, tree-scattered slopes leapt and rolled as if breathing a sigh of relief. Ben-Roi breathed easier too. He increased his speed and switched on *Kol Ha-Derekh*, Voice of the Road. Alicia Keys pumped out of the speakers. 'Empire State of Mind'. He smiled. One of Sarah's favourite songs.

They were just about back on an even keel after his late show the previous day, although it had taken a lot of work to claw his way back into her good books – or at least out of her bad ones. He'd ended up staying at her flat till past midnight decorating the baby room, and had returned this morning to finish the job off. The upshot was that the room looked great, she'd made him *blintzes* for breakfast – a sure sign a thaw was under way – and he had done nothing whatsoever to follow up the newspaper articles he'd found in the library.

Which was annoying, because the more he'd thought about it – and eleven hours of sandpapering, painting and putting up shelves had given him plenty of time to think – the stronger the feeling had become that, for reasons he couldn't yet fathom, the stories the articles were telling were central to understanding the story of Rivka Kleinberg's murder. Gold, Egypt, mining, Barren Corporation. The elements had kept turning over in his head, rolling around like the tumblers of a safe. Get the sequence right and the combination would click and the case suddenly open up. Fail to do so and it would remain resolutely closed, however hard you hammered at it.

There had been one interesting development. Very interesting. Back in Jerusalem, kicking his heels in the traffic jam that always seemed to stack up behind the lights on Sderot Ben Tsvi, he'd taken a call from Dov Zisky. Kleinberg's landline, mobile and e-mail providers had all got back to him first thing. All, apparently, with the same story. They were unable to provide a breakdown of the victim's calls and mails for the last two quarters because her records were blank. Before that, everything was logged and itemized as normal. From the start of the year, however, all her communication details appeared to have been wiped. They were looking into it, but at this stage the only explanations they could offer were either a computer error at their end – which seemed an impossible coincidence, three separate systems malfunctioning and Rivka Kleinberg the only customer affected – or, more likely, that someone had hacked into their networks and tampered with her account.

'I've spoken to a friend of mine,' Zisky had said, 'works in cyber security. He says that communications companies are normally pretty on the ball when it comes to network protection. They're not that easy to hack. This is someone who knew what they were doing.'

Which threw up two immediate possibilities. Computer crime in Israel, like just about every other area of organized crime, was dominated by the *Russkaya Mafiya*. The same *Russkaya Mafiya* who had, according to his journalist friend Natan Tirat, issued a specific death threat against Kleinberg a few years back. And the anti-capitalist group in the *Jerusalem Post* article he'd read yesterday, the Nemesis Agenda, they too had apparently engaged in a bit of hacking. Coincidence? Connection?

There was digging to do. A lot more digging. It would have to wait, though. This morning he wanted to focus on Kleinberg's journalism. The investigation was only a couple of days old and already he felt himself floundering in a soup of disconnected information. Now it was time to get down to specifics. To start isolating individual strands. He pushed the speedometer up past 120km/hour as 'Empire State of Mind' gave way to the more insistent, driveable beat of the Stones' 'Sympathy for the Devil'. One of *his* favourite songs. Jerusalem dropped away behind him, the flat green sheet of the coastal plain opened up in front. It felt good to be heading west.

The old Palestinian port of Jaffa – *Urs al-Bahr*, the Bride of the Sea – occupies a promontory that swells like a comma from the southern end of the Tel-Aviv coastline. Once a city in its own right, it was long ago swallowed up by the larger conurbation to the north, its Arab population pushed out into the suburbs of Ajami and Jabaliya, its decaying Ottoman and Mandate-era buildings taken over by new Israeli owners.

The office of *Matzpun ha-Am* was in one such building: a shabby two-storey affair on Rehov Olei Tsyon, bang in the middle of the Shuk ha-Pishpeshim flea market.

Arriving shortly before midday, Ben-Roi parked round the corner and slapped on his red police number plates to stop the Toyota being ticketed. He then made his way through the colourful crush of antique, textile, bric-a-brac and *falafel* stalls and up to the building's entrance. Mordechai Yaron buzzed him in.

'You found it OK?' he called from the first-floor landing as Ben-Roi climbed the staircase.

'No problem. I used to live in Tel-Aviv. Came down this way quite a lot. It hasn't changed.'

'Trust me, the rents have. What Irgun did to the Arabs, the landlords are doing to us tenants. Another rise and we'll all be driven out.'

Ben-Roi reached the landing and the two men shook hands. Squat and balding, with jug ears and a high-domed forehead framed by tufts of white hair, the editor bore a striking resemblance to David Ben-Gurion. Or would have done were it not for his clothes: sandals, baggy shorts and a Gush Shalom T-shirt. Aged hippy rather than founding father.

'You want coffee?' he asked, ushering Ben-Roi through a door into the office. 'Or something stronger?'

'Coffee's fine.'

Yaron waved him into an armchair and busied himself with a kettle. The room smelt of stale pipe smoke, and was cramped and cluttered: bare wooden floor, desk, bookcases, ancient photocopier in one corner. The open windows looked north towards the Bloomfield Football Stadium and skyscrapers of central Tel-Aviv; the walls were hung with framed posters publicizing, among other things, a Hadash rally, a vigil for Mordechai Vanunu and a performance of Shmuel Hasfari's play *Hametz*.

'She's been in all the papers,' chattered Yaron as he spooned coffee into a mug, his back to Ben-Roi. 'Inside pages. You'd think the murder of one of this country's finest journalists would make the headlines, but apparently the Mayor of Jerusalem's sex life's more important.'

Ben-Roi hadn't looked at the press. It seemed their fears of a media feeding frenzy had proved unfounded. For the moment at least.

'*Ha'aretz* gave her a nice obituary,' added the old man. 'Which was the least they could do, given the number of exclusives she broke for them. Poor Rivka. Terrible business. I still can't believe it.' He sighed and shook his head. 'She was a good woman. Hard work, but a good woman. And a bloody good journalist. *Zikhrona livrakha.*'

The kettle came to the boil – it must already have been hot because it had been on for less than a minute – and Yaron filled the mug.

'Afraid I haven't got any milk.'

'Sugar?'

'That I can do.'

'Two, please.'

Yaron ladled in a couple of spoonfuls and handed the coffee to Ben-Roi along with a copy of *Matzpun ha-Am.*

'This month's edition,' he said. 'Just to give you an idea of what we're about. There's a piece by Rivka on the collapse of the Israeli Left. You won't read a better analysis of why this country's politically fucked.'

He went over to the desk and sat down. Ben-Roi stared at the magazine's front cover. It carried an outline of the map of Israel, drawn in such a way that the country resembled a funnel, with an opening at its southernmost point. A jumble of words – Labor, Meretz, Peace Now, Pluralism, Tolerance, Democracy, Sanity – were sliding through the funnel and out the bottom into a large trash can. The headline read: 'Hope Goes South'.

'Good graphic, don't you think? Designed it myself.'

'It's certainly . . . provocative.'

'You interested in politics?'

Ben-Roi shrugged. Sometimes he was, sometimes he wasn't. Not today, certainly. The editor read his expression and didn't pursue the matter.

'The Left's dead,' was all he said. 'Has been since we invited a million bloody Russians to make *aliya*. They've pulled this country so far right even Ze'ev Jabotinsky must be turning in his grave.'

He tutted, picked up a pipe and started cramming it with tobacco from a creased leather pouch.

'Anyway, that's by the by. Please, tell me how I can help.'

Ben-Roi sipped his coffee, which tasted like sweetened washing-up

148

water, and shuffled his chair around so he was facing Yaron directly.

'I want to talk about Mrs Kleinberg's journalism,' he began, laying the magazine on the floor and flipping open his notebook. 'When we spoke yesterday you said she was writing a piece on prostitution.'

'*Forced* prostitution,' Yaron corrected. 'Sex-trafficking. There's a difference. Although I know plenty of people who'd argue all prostitution is coercion, certainly from an economic standpoint.'

'Do you know any details?' asked Ben-Roi. 'What exactly she was writing?'

'Well, the original idea was to use trafficking as a way into a broader polemical piece,' said Yaron, pressing more tobacco into the pipe's bowl and tamping it down with his thumb. 'State-of-the-nation thing, sex-slavery as a metaphor for the moral disintegration of Israeli society. But Rivka being Rivka, that soon went by the wayside.'

He produced a lighter and hovered it over the bowl, his lips making a dry popping sound as he puffed it into life, his face momentarily blurring behind a veil of blue-grey smoke.

'First she decided she wanted to concentrate more on the human interest angle,' he said. 'Lose the wider socio-political context and focus on the girls themselves. Give them a voice. Let them tell their own stories. Then it started morphing into a big investigative thing about the actual mechanics of trafficking: how it's organized, how the girls are moved around, who runs the industry. It was only supposed to be a thousand-worder, but it kept getting bigger and bigger and the deadline kept slipping.'

He shook his head, wafting a hand to dispel the smoke.

'Typical Rivka. I remember right at the start of her career, when we were both working for a small arts magazine up in Haifa – that's how we met, incidentally, back in the seventies – she got sent out to do a piece on Druze textile weavers. Ended up filing four thousand words on Golda Meir and the betrayal of Jewish feminism.'

He smiled and took another pull on his pipe.

'That's how she was. Always going off on tangents. And then tangents on tangents. One idea would lead to another and you'd end up with an article that was weeks late and bore no resemblance whatsoever to the original brief. That's why she got the heave-ho from *Ha'aretz*.'

'A contact of mine told me it was because she'd got a bit –' Ben-Roi consulted his notes, looking for Tirat's precise wording – 'conspiracy-happy. Paranoid.'

149

Yaron grunted.

'The way this country's going, she was right to be. In my experience, when Rivka saw smoke, there was usually fire somewhere not too far away.'

He dropped his head back, puckered his lips and popped out a ragged smoke ring. Outside someone was shouting '*Shkadim! Almonds!*' over and over, a street vendor trying to attract customers.

'She *was* difficult,' said Yaron after a pause. 'More and more so as she got older. Exasperating at times, particularly if you were trying to edit her. But she was a bloody good journalist. You just had to handle her right. Which basically meant letting her get on with it and keeping your fingers crossed she'd deliver something eventually. Which to be fair she always did.'

'And you don't know details,' said Ben-Roi, repeating his question of a moment earlier, drawing the conversation back to Kleinberg's article. 'What *exactly* she was writing? Who she was talking to?'

'I know she did some interviews over in Petah Tikvah. There's a shelter there for trafficked girls. Only one of its kind in the country, apparently. Other than that . . .' He shrugged. 'Like I say, I tended to just let her get on with it.'

'Do you know the name of the shelter?'

'Hofesh, I think. Yes, Hofesh. The Freedom Shelter.'

Ben-Roi scribbled a note.

'Did Mrs Kleinberg intimate she'd received any threats as a result of this article? That she was in any danger?'

'Not that she ever told me,' said Yaron. 'But then she didn't tell me a lot. She tended to play her cards quite close to her chest.'

'Did she *ever* get threats?'

He gave a humourless snort. 'She probably would have if anybody actually bothered to read the magazine. Before Rabin got shot we were selling 180,000 copies a month. Now we're down to 2,000. We can't give them away. No one's interested any more. Rest in Peace the Left. Rest in Peace the whole bloody country.'

He took another long draw on his pipe, sending melancholy curlicues of smoke drifting from the corners of his mouth. Outside the cries of the almond vendor had been joined by those of someone selling grapes and dates: '*Anavim! Tamar!*' Ben-Roi slurped his coffee, which tasted less bad the more of it he drank.

'When did you last see Mrs Kleinberg?' he asked.

'*Saw* her about six weeks back. She came down to Tel-Aviv and we had lunch. Little Palestinian-owned restaurant over in Dakar. Lovely place. I last *spoke* to her eight days ago when she called to ask for another deadline extension. Said she'd turned up something interesting and needed a bit more time to look into it.'

Ben-Roi's eyes narrowed. 'Did she say what it was?'

'Well, usually when Rivka said she'd turned up something interesting it was shorthand for "I'm about to take the article in a completely different direction". I would have asked more about it, but our daughter had just gone into labour and I had other things on my mind. Obviously if I'd known that was the last time we'd speak, I'd have paid a bit more attention.'

He sighed, lifted the lighter and started to run the flame over the pipe bowl again. Ben-Roi looked down at his notes. He was thinking about the newspaper articles Kleinberg had been researching six days before her murder. Those had been a different direction.

'Does the word *vosgi* mean anything to you?' he asked. 'It's the Armenian word for gold.'

Yaron pondered, then shook his head.

'Barren Corporation?'

'I've heard the name. Some American multinational, isn't it?'

'Mrs Kleinberg seemed to be interested in them. In a gold mine they were operating in Romania.'

Yaron raised his eyebrows. It was clearly news to him.

'Did she mention *anything* about gold or gold-mining?'

'Not that I recall.'

'What about Egypt? The night she died she was booked on a return flight to Alexandria.'

Again the editor's eyebrows lifted in surprise. 'She certainly never said anything to me. She did a piece on smugglers' tunnels a while back – you know, Palestinians breaking the Gaza blockade, sneaking supplies in from Sinai. But that was over a year ago.'

'Could she have been going there on holiday?'

'Rivka? To Egypt? I sincerely doubt it. She wasn't really the holidaying kind. And anyway, she never had any money.'

Ben-Roi tapped his pen on the pad. 'Samuel Pinsker?' he tried. 'Have you ever heard of him?'

'Leon Pinsker I've heard of. The nineteenth-century Zionist?'

'*Samuel* Pinsker. British mining engineer.'

'Him I don't know.'

'The Armenian community? Did she ever discuss that?' ·

No.

'The Armenian compound? The St James Cathedral?'

No and No.

'What about the anti-capitalist movement? Did that interest her?'

Yaron gave him an 'is-that-a-serious-question' look. 'Of course it did. It interests all of us. Capitalism's screwed the world. How can you *not* be anti a system that leaves two and a half billion people living on less than $2 a day and concentrates 85 per cent of global wealth—'

'The Nemesis Agenda?' cut in Ben-Roi, not wanting to get dragged into a political lecture. 'Did that name ever crop up? They're an anti-capitalist group, go around breaking into offices, hacking into—'

'Computers,' said Yaron, cutting Ben-Roi off in his turn. 'Yes, I know them.' He paused, examining his pipe, then added: 'And yes, the name did crop up.'

Ben-Roi sat forward. Finally, a bite. 'Recently?'

Yaron shook his head. 'Two, three years ago, when Rivka first started writing for us. She suggested doing a piece on them. Said she had an in with the group, might be able to wangle an interview with one of their people. Which would have been quite a scoop, given that so far as I'm aware they've never talked to the press.'

He sat a moment. Then, leaning over, he typed something into the Toshiba laptop sitting on the desk beside him, his plump, wrinkled fingers clattering over the keypad with surprising speed and dexterity. When he was done he turned the screen and beckoned Ben-Roi over to take a look.

'Interesting crowd,' he said as the detective stood and crossed the room. 'Sort of an extreme form of these whistle-blowing websites. Wikileaks with menaces. They've certainly had an impact. The multi-nationals are shitting themselves, apparently.'

Ben-Roi rested his palms on the table and leant down, looking at the screen. It carried the homepage of a website titled www. thenemesisagenda.org. Functional rather than stylish, it was topped with the headline: 'The Nemesis Agenda – Working to expose the crimes of global capitalism.' The A of 'Agenda' had been manipulated to resemble a skull. There was an e-mail address – tellus @nemesisagenda – a menu-bar with click-through options such as

Targets, Archive, Video, News, Take Action, Who Are We? and various black-and-white images of devastated landscapes, emaciated children, scarred bodies and weeping women. The centre of the page was dominated by a video player, stilled on the badly swollen face of a man in a bloodied towelling robe. The accompanying title read: 'Monsieur Semblaire's Congo Confession.'

Ben-Roi took all this in at a glance, then dragged the cursor up to 'Who Are We?' and clicked. A new page loaded, blank save for five words: *Wouldn't you like to know.* He only just had time to read it before the letters seemed to burst into flames. There was a fierce crackling sound and the screen blazed red before abruptly reverting to the homepage. He looked up. Yaron's eyes were twinkling mischievously.

'The times certainly are a-changing,' he chuckled. 'In my day, if you wanted to protest you went on a march or distributed some leaflets. Maybe staged a sit-in or sprayed some graffiti if you were feeling really angry. These people, they're more like Mossad. They abseil into offices, hack into computers, interrogate executives at gunpoint, film it, then post it all on the web. Radicalism for the twenty-first century.'

He laid his pipe in an ashtray and sat back.

'And good for them, I say. These multinationals get away with murder. Literally. They steal, exploit, dump, pollute, cheat, tax evade, cosy up to some of the most grotesque regimes on the planet. There's nothing they wouldn't do to turn a profit, no abuse too immoral, no trick too dirty. And because most of it goes on in countries that are too weak or poor or corrupt to stand up to them, they're never held accountable. But the moment their grubby little secrets are exposed on the internet –' he waved a hand at the laptop. 'The web's not just the great democratizer of our time, it's the great court of justice. The information gets picked up by the public, goes . . . what's the word . . . virulent?'

'Viral.'

'Exactly. Suddenly the whole world knows what they're doing and all hell breaks loose. Their offices get picketed, their executives harassed, their computer systems are targeted by other hackers, their image goes into freefall, their share price collapses . . .' He gave a satisfied nod. 'I've never been one for mob rule, but you can't help but feel a certain schadenfreude when you see the bastards getting a bit of their own medicine. The name says it all – Nemesis,

Goddess of Vengeance. Take a look round the site. It speaks for itself.'

He retrieved his pipe and puffed it into life again. Ben-Roi was staring at the swollen-faced man in the video box, wondering how on earth any of this fitted in with Rivka Kleinberg's murder.

'They're Israeli, this group?' he asked.

'My understanding is they have different cells in different countries. That's how these sort of organizations tend to work – a loose collective rather than a single homogenous entity. To be honest, I don't know a great deal about them. I don't think anyone does. That's why it was such a coup to get an interview with one of their people. Or would have been if it had actually come off.'

'It didn't?'

'Rivka's contact got cold feet at the last minute. It was all set up, apparently, but when she went to do the interview –' he made a slicing motion with his hand. 'I have to confess, part of me did wonder if she actually *had* a contact. I mean, these Nemesis people have never spoken to anyone else so why the hell they should suddenly decide to open up to a no-circulation outfit like ours . . .'

He blew another smoke ring and folded his arms.

'She wouldn't admit it, but getting the sack from *Ha'aretz* really hit Rivka, knocked her confidence. The thought did cross my mind that maybe she was just trying to . . . you know . . . prove she still had it in her. Could still get the big stories. She didn't have to prove anything to *me*, but perhaps she needed to make *herself* think . . .' He shrugged. 'Who knows? Maybe I'm being unfair. She certainly didn't make a big song and dance about it. Just said she had an in with the group, might be able to get one of them to talk, but when she went down to Mitzpe Ramon for the meeting . . .'

Ben-Roi's attention had been starting to drift. At the mention of Mitzpe Ramon his head jerked up. The destination on the bus ticket Kleinberg had used four days before her murder. For the first time since the interview had started he felt a buzz of adrenaline. The buzz he always got when he thought he might be on to something.

'Do you know who this contact was?' he asked, leaning forward over the table.

'I seem to remember Rivka saying it was some old friend,' replied Yaron, eyes registering surprise at the sudden urgency in Ben-Roi's voice. 'Apart from that . . .' He shrugged helplessly. 'Rivka was notoriously protective of her sources. All I know is that she schlepped all the way down into the Negev only for the contact to tell her they didn't want to do the interview after all. And that was the end of the matter.'

Ben-Roi's mind was clicking, like a switchboard trying to make connections. 'Did Mrs Kleinberg mention this person recently?'

'Not to me. Why?'

Ben-Roi told him about the bus ticket. Yaron could provide no explanation.

'Any idea why she might have wanted to get back in touch with them?'

'None whatsoever.'

'Did she know anyone else in Mitzpe Ramon?'

'God knows. I don't think so. But then she didn't tell me everything.'

'What about the Nemesis Agenda? Did that ever come up again?'

Yaron shook his head.

'Did she say anything about them breaking into an office in Tel-Aviv?'

Another shake.

'Barren Corporation?'

And another.

Ben-Roi pushed and pushed, went all round the subject trying to get a handle on it. The editor could add nothing to what he'd already told him and in the end Ben-Roi was forced to let the matter drop. It was important, he could sense it, another crucial element in cracking the Enigma code of Rivka Kleinberg's murder. Unfortunately, like all the other crucial elements he'd turned up so far, it took him no nearer to understanding, let alone solving the case. On the contrary, it only seemed to add an extra layer of complexity to an already fiendishly difficult algorithm. Three years ago Rivka Kleinberg had been interested in the Nemesis Agenda. Then, a few days before her murder, the group had suddenly popped up on her radar again. That was about as much as he could say. Which wasn't really much at all.

The two of them talked for another thirty minutes, but nothing else of obvious use emerged and eventually Ben-Roi called it a day and brought the interview to a close. Yaron went back on the internet and tracked down a number for the Hofesh Shelter. Then, sliding half a dozen copies of his magazine into a plastic bag and presenting the bag to Ben-Roi, he escorted the detective downstairs to the street.

'It's funny,' he said as they descended, 'but talking to you has made me realize how little I actually knew Rivka. Forty years we were friends and yet there are whole swathes of her life that are a complete blank to me. She very much kept things compartmentalized. Broke her world down into different boxes, kept all the boxes separate. I was in the journalism and politics box. You want to know what she thought about the Oslo Accords, Kadima, Peres, Netanyahu – that I can tell you. But there was a whole other side of her that I was never privy to. You know, in all the time I knew her I never once saw the inside of her home.' He shook his head.'Maybe I wasn't as close a friend as I thought I was.'

They reached the ground floor and Yaron opened the front door.

'If you're interested in a subscription I'll do you a good deal,' he said.

'I'll get back to you,' said Ben-Roi. 'Right at the moment I've got other things . . .'

'Of course, of course. I'm not trying to convert you. Just to get you to engage. No one in this country seems to engage any more. It's like we've lost the will to think.'

They shook hands and Ben-Roi stepped out on to the street. He was about to walk away when Yaron reached out and took his arm.

'Rivka was a good person, Detective. She could be appalling when the mood took her, but at heart she was a good person. Justice meant a lot to her, sticking up for the underdog, helping people in trouble. She'd call you every name under the sun for changing a single word of her copy, and then empty her purse for some crack-addicted beggar she'd found on the street. She had an instinctive empathy for people who were in pain. Probably because she was in so much of it herself. She cared. She really cared. Please, do everything you can for her.'

He held Ben-Roi's eyes a moment, then, with a nod, released his arm and disappeared back into the building. Ben-Roi started walking. He gave it a hundred metres, then dumped the magazines in a bin. Engagement was going to have to wait. He had a murder to solve.

'Oh for fuck's sake, Khalifa, spare me another of your crackpot conspiracy theories! You're a dreamer – always have been, always will be! A bloody dreamer!'

That's what Chief Inspector Abdul ibn-Hassani would have said not so long ago if Khalifa had come to him with news of a plot to drive Copts out of the Eastern Desert.

The two of them had never got on, not since Khalifa had first been posted to Luxor. A fractious, bullying, unimaginative man, the chief had never trusted his subordinate's more freeform approach to police work, his preparedness to go with gut instinct over the strict letter of the rule book. For his part, Khalifa had always been irked by his boss's assumption that the way to get the best out of his men was to intimidate and shout at them, by his obsession with procedure, above all by the fact that his priorities seemed to lie less with the actual solving of cases than with ensuring they were solved in a manner that conformed unerringly to the manual of Egyptian policing.

It wasn't an entirely fair assessment – for all his narrow-mindedness, Hassani knew a good detective when he saw one, and had, albeit reluctantly, cut Khalifa a fair degree of slack over the years. Despite that, their relationship had never been comfortable, and if anything was guaranteed to get the chief's back up, it was having to listen to his underling's far-fetched tales of conspiracy and intrigue. A stern dressing-down and a homily on the need to stick to the facts and keep your imagination in check was his usual reaction, progressing to a full-on explosion if Khalifa refused to let the matter drop.

That had been then. These days, since his return from extended leave, Khalifa had noticed a distinct mellowing in Hassani's manner. He had reined in his temper, cut right back on his use of expletives – always a major part of any verbal encounter between the two of them – and even taken to calling him Yusuf, an uncharacteristically informal mode of address traditionally reserved for the chief's small coterie of toadies and favourites.

All of which, well meant as it doubtless was, only served to increase Khalifa's sense of dislocation. Of things not being as they ought to be. Like his old apartment, like his beloved Luxor before they'd driven a three-kilometre trench through the middle of it, like his wife Zenab's laughter, Chief Hassani's foul-tempered belligerence had been one of the constants of his existence. And now, just when he needed their settling effect the most, those constants seemed to have evaporated, leaving him exposed and floundering.

Sitting in Hassani's office this afternoon, going through the story of the poisoned wells, part of him yearned for his boss to revert to type and launch into one of his extended you're-a-fucking-dreamer-Khalifa rants. Instead he listened patiently, if a little twitchily, as Khalifa outlined the situation. Then, rather than hammering his fist on the table and telling him what a clueless idiot he was, he sat back, drummed his meaty fingers on the edge of the desk and jutted out his lower jaw, something he always did when he was trying to convey an impression of deep thought.

'Interesting,' he said. 'Very interesting.'

'I know the incidents are a long way apart,' said Khalifa. 'Or at least the monastery is a long way from the two farms.'

'Forty kilometres, wasn't it?'

'Probably closer to thirty.'

'And the olive trees died . . . ?'

'Three or four years ago. I know it all seems a bit tenuous, but even so . . . Three Coptic wells all poisoned, all *roughly* in the same vicinity. It would seem to suggest . . . there does seem to be some . . .'

He trailed off, waiting for Hassani to interject a comment. He didn't, just sat there in silence, fingers drumming, jaw pushed out, eyebrows – thick, bushy eyebrows that ran into one another like a pair of colliding trains – crunched up into an expectant frown. In the past, the chief's habit of shooting down his opinions the moment he expressed them had only served to reassure Khalifa those opinions were probably correct. In an unsettling reversal of normal practice, Hassani's silence now left him wondering if maybe he was reading too much into the situation.

'It just seemed strange,' he said, a hint of doubt creeping into his voice. 'More than a coincidence. The water supply at Bir Hashfa, the village near the Attia farm, that hasn't been affected. Just the three Coptic wells.'

Hassani clasped his hands and leant his head slightly to one side, his face framed by a rectangular shadow on the wall behind where a picture of Hosni Mubarak had once hung. He'd had it taken down the moment it was clear the president was a busted flush. Despite his hulking frame, the chief always blew with the prevailing wind.

158

'Of course, strictly speaking, none of these places falls within our direct jurisdiction,' he said after a silence. 'Certainly not Deir el-Limoon.'

'Zeitun,' corrected Khalifa.

'Exactly. But let's leave that for the moment.' He gave a theatrical push of the hand, as if moving something out of the way. 'And let's also leave aside the fact that wells do sometimes go bad of their own accord. They do, don't they? Go bad of their own accord?'

Khalifa acknowledged that it had been known to happen.

'What you're suggesting is that someone's going around the Eastern Desert deliberately poisoning Coptic waterholes.'

Khalifa nodded.

'Or rather, four years ago they poisoned one waterhole, and now over the last couple of months they've poisoned another two.'

Khalifa nodded again, with rather less conviction. 'I know it all seems a bit tenuous,' he repeated.

Hassani smiled and shook his head as if to say, 'Not at all.' The expression was forced, and his eyes gave him away. The eyes said: *You're damned right it's tenuous.*

'So who do you think these mysterious well-poisoners might be?' he asked, his voice sliding half a notch higher as he struggled to keep his tone reasonable.

Khalifa pulled out his cigarettes. He didn't open the packet, just turned it over in his hands.

'At first I thought it must be someone from Bir Hashfa,' he said. 'That's certainly who Mr Attia seems to think is responsible. But with the monastery being so far away –' he rotated the pack a couple of times – 'Muslim Brotherhood, maybe.'

'In the middle of the Eastern Desert!' Hassani's voice rose, then fell again as he brought it back under control. 'Come on, Khalifa . . . Yusuf . . . The Brothers are city-boys. Slum rats.'

'Salafists, then. They're out-of-towners.'

Hassani looked far from convinced.

'Well *someone*'s got a religious axe to grind,' said Khalifa. 'I can't see any other possible explanation. If it was just Mr Attia and his cousin who were affected, that might be a local grudge, or a family vendetta. But when you factor in the monastery – why else would someone travel a hundred kilometres into the middle of nowhere to foul a water source that's only used by a couple of monks? It's fanaticism, it has to be. Either that or there's some oddball out there who gets his kicks creeping around the desert poisoning random wells just for the hell of it.'

'Or the wells went bad of their own accord and it's just a coincidence they're all owned by Copts.'

Khalifa flicked the pack round another few times, then returned it to his pocket without removing a cigarette. He felt muddled suddenly. Wasn't sure what he thought any more. 'I've just got a feeling there's something wrong,' he mumbled lamely. 'That there's something going on and we ought to look into it.'

Few things irked Hassani more than being told someone had a feeling about something – 'Women and poofs have feelings; policemen have evidence,' was one of his most frequently deployed put-downs. To his credit, he didn't use it now, although the tautness of his mouth suggested he would dearly have loved to. Instead he heaved himself up and walked across to the window.

His office – the penthouse, as they called it – was on the top floor of the station, a palatial, marble-floored space that seemed to dwarf everyone and everything inside it. When they'd moved here six months ago, its windows had offered spectacular views across town to the Nile and the Theban massif beyond. That was before the Interior Ministry building behind had decided to go up an extra two storeys. Now when he looked out, Chief Hassani was confronted with a blank wall of concrete peppered with air-conditioning units. The more aesthetically minded would probably have been disappointed. Hassani barely noticed. Pretty scenery had never been of much interest to him.

He stared out at the non-view, his back to Khalifa, the stitching of his jacket seeming to strain under the pressure of his broad fighter's shoulders. Then, cracking his knuckles, he turned.

'I'll be honest, Khalifa . . . Yusuf . . . this isn't a great time to be bringing me something like this. I'm not saying you were wrong to bring it, or that your concerns aren't valid. It's just that we've got a lot on our plate at the moment without stirring the possibility of some marauding religious nut-job into the soup.'

For a fleeting moment his eyes crunched up and his head dropped as he tried to work out whether the soup metaphor worked or not. He gave it the benefit of the doubt and came forward a step, jerking a thumb over his shoulder towards the window behind him.

'This new museum visitor centre thing in the Valley of the Kings –

the inauguration ceremony's less than a fortnight away and, let me tell you, it's using up a lot of resources. A *lot* of resources. The minister's coming down, the American ambassador, the head of the company who funded the bloody place. I've got forty-nine separate dignitaries to move from the airport to the West Bank and then I've got to guarantee protection once they're there. Do you know how many men it's going to take to shut down and ring-fence the entire valley? Hundreds! Sharp-shooters, special forces, police, army . . .'

A small green vein had started to pulsate beneath his right eye, a sure sign he was getting worked up. With a considerable effort of will he reined himself in, raising his hands and lowering them as if to push down a rising tide of panic and ire.

'What I'm saying is that we're under a lot of pressure here and it's perhaps not the best time to be launching a full-scale investigation into the possibility that a couple of wells that may or may not be within our jurisdiction may or may not have been poisoned by someone who may or may not be a fundamentalist head-banger. Do you see what I'm getting at? Any other time I'd be happy to accommodate you, but right now . . .'

He broke off, bringing up his hand and gently massaging the pulsing vein. Khalifa stared down at the floor. In the old days, if he'd had a suspicion about something he'd have stood his ground, argued the point with Hassani till he'd got what he wanted. Today he could summon neither the energy nor the conviction that he actually *had* a point. Maybe the chief was right. Maybe the wells *had* gone bad for natural reasons and the fact that they were all Coptic-owned was just a coincidence. Maybe he'd allowed his pity for Mr Attia to cloud his judgement. He used to be so sure of his instincts. Now he wasn't sure of anything any more. Not for the first time these last few months, the thought struck him that he wasn't half the detective he used to be. Not even a quarter of the detective.

'Can we at least put a couple of uniforms on the Attia farm?' he asked, pulling out his cigarettes and turning them over in his hand again. 'Just to keep an eye on things.'

Hassani seemed surprised by this, as if he had been expecting his subordinate to put up more of a fight. He stared at Khalifa, waiting to see if he was going to ask for anything else. When no request was forthcoming, he gave a satisfied nod and stomped back to his desk.

'Why not?' he said, sitting down and clasping his hands, looking more relaxed than he had since the conversation had started. 'I'll tell you what, let's call it three uniforms, just to be on the safe side.'

'I think two's probably enough.'

'No, no,' insisted Hassani, all cheery bonhomie now that it was clear he wasn't actually going to have to do anything. 'You have concerns, and I'm listening to those concerns. We'll send three men out to the farm to keep a watching brief, and once this damned Valley of the Kings thing is out of the way, we'll review the situation. If indeed there is a situation. And if you think it needs reviewing. OK?'

'OK,' mumbled Khalifa. 'Thank you.'

'On the contrary, thank *you*. You were quite right to bring this to my attention.'

He smiled, an expression that on his particular face looked wholly out of place, as if someone had drawn it on as a joke.

'Anything else?' he asked.

'No, sir.'

'Sure?'

'Sure.'

'Right. Well, thanks for coming in. And keep up the good work.'

It was less a compliment than a dismissal. Khalifa stood and walked to the door, his footfall sounding unnaturally loud on the marble floor. As he stepped out into the corridor Hassani called after him.

'Give my regards to Zubaidah.'

'Zenab.'

'Exactly. Tell her she's in our thoughts.'

The chief held the smile a few seconds longer, then let it go and looked down at his desk.

Khalifa pulled the door to. As it clicked shut he heard Hassani muttering to himself. 'Stupid fucking dreamer.'

Just like old times. Strangely, it didn't make him feel any better.

TEL-AVIV

The moment he got back to his car, Ben-Roi called the Hofesh Shelter, spoke with its director and arranged to come straight over to interview her. Petah Tikvah, the drab satellite town where the shelter was located, was only ten kilometres north-east of Tel-Aviv, and shouldn't have been more than a fifteen-minute drive, double that with traffic. Today, the Tel-Aviv ring-road was bumper to bumper, and even with his police light slapped on to the roof it still took him the best part of an hour to get there.

Which at least gave him the chance to put in a call to Dov Zisky to see if there had been any progress on the bus ticket from Rivka Kleinberg's flat.

There hadn't.

'I've sent her picture down to the station in Mitzpe Ramon,' said Zisky. 'They're circulating it, but haven't come up with anything yet. I've also been on to Egged on the off-chance one of their drivers might remember her. There are only four of them who run that route, but inevitably the one we need to speak to is away on leave. They've been trying to contact him, but he still hasn't been in touch.'

'Keep on it, will you?' said Ben-Roi. 'It's important. Maybe very important.'

He filled Zisky in on his conversation with Mordechai Yaron. And, also, the articles Kleinberg had been reading in the library.

'You want me to look into this Nemesis group?' Zisky asked when Ben-Roi had finished. 'My friend who works in cyber security, the one I mentioned this morning – he might know something.'

'Why not? And while you're about it, see if you can pull out some background on Barren Corporation. In particular, anything you can find about a gold mine they're operating in Romania. I've got a contact on *Ha'aretz*, you can give him a call if you like. He covers some business stuff, might be able to give you a steer.'

He passed on Natan Tirat's details, the barely audible whisper of pen on paper drifting down the line as Zisky scribbled a note.

'Anything else happening?' asked Ben-Roi.

'Forensics came in an hour ago. They drew a blank on the hair from the victim's clothes. They're pretty certain it came from a woman because of its length, but there was no DNA match.'

Ben-Roi wasn't surprised. It was by no means certain the hair even came from Kleinberg's killer, and if it did, it was still a long shot they'd have a match on file. Their murderer, he sensed – had sensed from the outset – was not going to be someone who was already known to them. The fact that it was a woman's hair was mildly interesting, but it didn't take them anywhere and for the moment he simply filed it at the back of his mind and moved on.

'Any joy with Kleinberg's neighbours?' he asked.

'There's still a couple we haven't managed to speak to. None of the others saw or heard anything.'

A fractional pause, then: 'One lady did mention a smell.'

'Smell?'

'Soap or perfume or something. "Musky" – I think that's the word she used. Said she'd lived in the block for thirty years and she'd never smelt it before. Just the night of Kleinberg's murder. Detective Pincas came in and told me about it. Said I might want to follow it up.'

Ben-Roi's mouth tightened into an annoyed pucker. He knew exactly what Pincas had been implying, and was sure Zisky did too: *soap, perfume, job for the gayboy.* Forty-eight hours ago he'd been making the same quips himself. Now, having got to know the kid slightly better, he found the joke less amusing.

'You tell Detective Pincas from me he's a fat shit and can follow it up himself,' he growled. 'Got that?'

'Got it.'

He couldn't be sure, but he thought he caught a hint of gratitude in Zisky's voice.

'Anything else?'

There wasn't, really. Both Pincas and Amos Namir were still waiting on their informants; Namir had turned up nothing in the old cases and cold cases.

'Although I did find out something about Archbishop Petrossian.'

There were so many other disparate strands winding around inside his head Ben-Roi had completely forgotten about the archbishop.

'Surprise me,' he said.

'It turns out his apartments have their own private street door. Opens on to St James' Road. Which means he can get in and out of the compound—'

'Without anyone seeing him.' Ben-Roi finished the sentence. He draped an arm out of the window and drummed his fingers on the Toyota's door. He knew for a fact there weren't any police cameras on St James. And aside from around the Kotel, there were none in the Jewish Quarter, which was where St James ended up. (Palestinian joke: The Jews got the land, the water, the borders and the airspace, but at least we got the cameras.) So in theory Petrossian could get out of the compound, down through the Jewish Quarter and out of the Old City and no one would be any the wiser.

'You say he doesn't have an alibi for the night of the murder?' he asked.

'Not that we've been able to corroborate. He claims he was in his apartments all night, but we haven't found anyone who can confirm that.'

Ben-Roi thought a moment, the Toyota's metalwork echoing to the thud of his fingertips.

'Do me a favour, take this to Leah Shalev,' he said eventually. 'It needs following up and you've already got enough on your plate. For the moment I want you to concentrate on the stuff we've already discussed: Mitzpe Ramon, Nemesis, Barren. I should be back late afternoon. See what you can dig up by then.'

He rang off, staring down the lines of stationary traffic towards the distant glittering towers of Ramat Gan. Thirty seconds passed, then, pulling out his mobile, he thumbed a text: 'Gd wrk, Zisky.'

He hesitated, then changed Zisky to Dov, pressed send and banged on his police siren. Less because he thought it would get the traffic moving than to show the world he was still a tough cop and wasn't going soft in his old age.

LUXOR

After his meeting with Hassani, Khalifa tried to push the whole well-poisoning thing out of his mind. Maybe there was something going on, maybe there wasn't – either way, there wasn't a lot more he could do about it. He went back to his office and made arrangements for a couple of uniforms to be posted out to the Attia farm. Then, it now being his lunch break, he took himself over to the police shooting range for an hour of what Corporal Ahmed Mehti – the moustachioed, crew-cut giant who for as long as anyone could remember had run the range – euphemistically referred to as 'bullet meditation'.

When he wanted to think about things, really think about them, Khalifa would head over to the West Bank and climb to his 'thinking seat' at the base of the Qurn. When he *didn't* want to think about things, really didn't want to think about them, he would go shooting. He'd been top marksman in his year at the Cairo police college and had always kept his hand in. Lately he'd been visiting the range more and more often, welcoming the focus it gave him, the chance to push all his problems aside and, if only for a few moments, narrow his world down to the thin slit of a Lee-Enfield .303 rifle sight.

The range was an indoor one – a sweltering concrete bunker out on the desert margins beyond the eastern edge of town. He'd called ahead to say he was coming and Corporal Mehti had everything set up – ear-protectors, paper target in the shape of a charging soldier, box of five-round stripper clips, even a glass of tea. Khalifa was the only person there at that time, which was how he liked it, and having signed for his Enfield he went out on to the range and got down to business. His first shot nudged fractionally wide, the second was too high, but after that everything else was spot on, the room echoing to the rhythmic crunch of the rifle bolt and the sharp crack of exploding cordite as he punched round after round into the target's face and torso, each hit taking him a little further away from himself. A couple of times he had to shake his head to dispel the image of Zenab lying slumped and dead-eyed in the hospital emergency unit; and, once, the sound of Mr Attia's voice back on his farm in the Eastern Desert: *I'll fight if I have to. To protect my family, my children. It is a man's greatest duty.*

Other than that, his mind was mercifully blank. When he left forty minutes later he had emptied twelve ten-round magazines, reduced five targets to tatters and felt a whole lot calmer. Bullet meditation indeed.

PETAH TIKVAH

Maya Hillel, the director of the Hofesh Shelter for Trafficked Women, was disconcertingly attractive. Late twenties, slim, with huge grey eyes and an unruly tumble of black hair that cascaded across her shoulders like a rush of dark water, she looked more like a model than a social worker. Given the nature of the job she was doing, Ben-Roi knew it was perverse of him to be viewing her in those terms, but he couldn't help it. He was a man, and that's how men thought. Attractive was attractive. End of.

She met him outside the shelter – an innocuous whitewashed

building in a street of dusty *shikunim* five minutes from the town centre – and led him through a heavy steel gate into a paved forecourt.

'We have to be careful,' she explained, indicating the gate, the uniformed guard manning it, the security fence surrounding the building. 'We get a lot of pimps coming down here trying to lure the girls away. There's one across the street now.'

Ben-Roi glanced over his shoulder, but the gate had already swung shut.

'You want me to have a word?'

'Not worth it. He'll just clear off and come back again as soon as you've gone. The way he sees it, we've got his property and he wants it returned. Thanks for the offer, though.'

She waved him round the side of the building and through an open door into a tiled foyer area. An empty kitchen opened off to the left; on the walls were a selection of trafficking awareness posters, including one depicting a dozen naked women curled up and packaged on a polystyrene tray like a row chicken drumsticks. 'Fresh Meat' read the label. Ben-Roi stared at it, then fell in behind Hillel as she started up a staircase.

'How many girls have you got here?' he asked as they climbed, trying to keep his eyes off her backside.

'Fourteen,' she replied. 'Most of them are out at work at the moment, which is why it's quiet. We arrange jobs for them – waitressing, cleaning, that sort of thing. We've actually got space for thirty-five, but referrals have gone down the last couple of years. When we opened in 2004 we had over a hundred girls coming through the doors. This year there's only been twenty.'

'Glad to hear things are improving.'

'That's one way of reading it, I suppose. Personally I'd argue it's because the police are no longer prioritizing the problem and fewer girls are being rescued.'

She reached the first-floor landing and looked round at him, holding his eyes a moment before continuing upwards.

'Things *are* better than they were a decade ago, I'll give you that,' she went on. 'Back in the nineties we were getting two, three thousand girls a year being trafficked into the country. Now it's into the hundreds. It's still a problem, though. And you guys aren't allocating the sort of resources you were a few years ago. Mainly, to be fair, because the politicians aren't allocating the resources. The

Interior Ministry doesn't give a shit. Saving *goy* prostitutes isn't exactly a vote winner.'

They reached the second-floor landing. Corridors ran off to left and right lined with closed doors. In a room directly in front of them a girl in a baggy velour tracksuit was standing on a set of scales while a plump, middle-aged woman noted her weight on a clipboard. The woman nodded a greeting; the girl stared blank-faced. Painfully thin, with hollow cheeks, lank hair and a faintly yellowish tinge to her skin, she looked like a death camp survivor.

'Everything OK, Anja?' Hillel called over to her.

The girl gave a limp shrug.

'She's doing brilliantly,' chipped in the woman cheerfully. 'Up half a pound.'

'That's great,' said Hillel. 'Really great.'

She diverted into the room and gave the girl a reassuring rub on the back, then led Ben-Roi up a final set of stairs to the top floor.

'Moldovan,' she explained, dropping her voice so it wouldn't carry. 'Police picked her up in a raid down in Eilat a few weeks ago. I've seen some bad cases in my time, but she was –' she stopped, looking back down the stairs. 'Tuberculosis, hepatitis, just about every STD you care to mention bar HIV – and that's nothing compared to the damage up here.'

She tapped the side of her head.

'She's been granted a work permit so she can stay in the country for a year to rehabilitate, but she's refusing to testify, so once the year's up she'll be deported. And when she's back in Moldova she'll be targeted by the people who brought her here in the first place and re-trafficked. It's how these things work. Heartbreaking. She's still only nineteen.'

Ben-Roi's eyebrows lifted. He'd pegged the girl's age at closer to thirty.

'Can't she get compassionate residency?'

'Oh do me a favour! When was a non-Jew ever granted humanitarian status in this country? No, the best she can hope for is to find someone who wants to marry her. Which knowing the sort of men who are attracted to ex-prostitutes isn't going to make her life a whole lot better.'

She sighed, turned and carried on up to the head of the stairs, which came out into a large open-plan office space. Three more women were sitting here behind desks, staff, Ben-Roi guessed from their age and appearance. Aside from the security guard at the front gate, he had yet to see another man in the place. Hardly surprising after what he'd just been hearing.

Asking one of the women to bring them coffee, Hillel led him through into a smaller, private office with a sloping ceiling and a large picture window looking out over the Petah Tikvah rooftops. She waved him into a chair and heaved herself up on to the desk in front of him, swinging her legs.

'So,' she said. 'Rivka Kleinberg. What can I tell you?'

For a moment Ben-Roi's eyes lingered on the framed photos hanging above the desk – Hillel shaking hands with Hillary Clinton, Hillel receiving some sort of award from Shimon Peres, Hillel with what he assumed must be her husband and daughter, which surprised him – for some reason he hadn't thought of her as having a family. Then he pulled out his notebook and got down to business.

'Her editor tells me Mrs Kleinberg visited the shelter,' he began, flipping through to a blank page.

Hillel nodded. 'She called up about four weeks ago. Said she was doing a piece on trafficking, asked if she could come down and have a look around.'

A beat, then: 'You think that was why she was killed? Because of the article?'

Ben-Roi gave a non-committal shrug. 'At this stage we're keeping an open mind.'

'It wouldn't surprise me,' she said. 'Trafficking's big business, as I'm sure you're aware. And the guys who run it don't like having the boat rocked. Particularly the Russians – they control eighty per cent of the trade and they're not the sort of people who appreciate having their affairs looked into.'

Ben-Roi stared down at the pad. *Russkaya Mafiya* again. They seemed to be featuring a lot in this case. He made a note to pass it on to Pincas, who was covering the Russian angle.

'So she visited the shelter,' he continued, 'talked with you.'

'Correct.'

'About?'

'A whole load of stuff: where the girls come from, how they're brought into Israel, what happens to them when they're here, what's being done about it. She spent an entire day with us, and then we spoke again on the phone a week later. Not the most socially adjusted

169

person I've ever met, but she clearly cared about what we're doing. And she was wonderful with the girls. Genuinely compassionate.'

Ben-Roi recalled Mordechai Yaron's parting words: *Rivka had an instinctive empathy for people who were in pain. Probably because she was in so much of it herself.*

'Was there anything in particular she wanted to discuss? Any specific angle she was coming from?'

'We talked a lot about what the government's doing to tackle the problem,' she said, pulling an elastic hairband from the pocket of her shirt and stretching it with her fingers. 'Or rather not doing. I mean, until recently we weren't even meeting the *minimum* US State Department standard for combating trafficking. Attitude-wise, most of our politicians are still stuck in the dark ages. Most police as well, frankly. They seem to think that being locked up in a brothel and forced to have sex with twenty men a day is some sort of conscious career choice.'

Ben-Roi shifted uncomfortably. He'd done a brief stint in Vice himself, when he was just out of Police Academy, and he knew exactly the mindset she was describing. He pressed on, not wanting to get bogged down in the subject.

'Anything else?' he asked. 'Any other areas Mrs Kleinberg seemed particularly interested in?'

'We spent quite a lot of time on the demographics of trafficking,' she said, still working the band. 'Where the girls come from, the fact that we're seeing more and more Israeli girls being forced into the business, picking up the slack now that there aren't as many foreign girls to go around. And she wanted to know all about the punters, especially the ultra-Orthodox ones. They're a big market. The brothels are full of them on Fridays, getting their kicks before *Shabbat* comes in.'

She gave a shiver of distaste.

'She also asked a lot of questions about trafficking routes,' she added, sweeping her hair back and tying it with the band. 'Particularly the one through Egypt.'

Ben-Roi's eyes flicked up. Egypt again. Like the *Russkaya Mafiya*, it seemed to be dotted all over this case. He started to ask for more information, but was interrupted by a knock on the door. One of the women he had seen outside came in with a tray of coffee and biscuits. He waited for her to put it down, hand Hillel a letter and leave, then picked up the conversation.

170

'This Egypt route,' he said. 'A lot of girls are coming in that way?'

'Not as many as a decade ago,' replied Hillel, stirring her coffee. 'Then it was by far the main smuggling channel. After the crackdown in the early 2000s the traffickers left it alone for a while, found other ways of getting the girls in. Fake passports, false marriage documents, that sort of thing. They're clever like that, always adapting, keeping one step ahead.'

'But now the route's open again?'

'Well, it's hard to get precise statistics, but there's a lot of anecdotal evidence to suggest that's the case. There was a big Tel-Aviv pimp, a guy called Genady Kremenko – apparently he brought most of his girls in that way.'

Ben-Roi recognized the name. 'Arrested a couple of months back?'

'That's the one. There was a rather unpleasant joke doing the rounds about Moses bringing the Israelites out of Egypt and Kremenko bringing the girls. Not a nice man. But then none of them are.'

Ben-Roi spooned sugar into his own coffee and stirred. 'Do you know if they are ever taken through Alexandria?' he asked, thinking of the El-Al flight Kleinberg had been booked on the night of her murder.

'It's usually Cairo or Sharm el-Sheik. They get flown in from Eastern Europe, Russia, Uzbekistan, and are then moved up through the Sinai and across the border by Bedouin.'

'And Mrs Kleinberg wanted to know about all this?'

'Not so much the first time she visited the shelter. We touched on it, but not in any great detail. It was when she called a week later that she really started asking questions.'

'And you told her . . . ?'

'Pretty much what I've just told you. The pimps have overseas recruiters who target the girls and fly them down to Egypt, and then a network of Bedouin who take them across the Sinai and up into the Negev. That's about as much as I know. I'm a social worker, not a cop.'

She blew on her coffee and sipped, cupping the mug in her hands. Ben-Roi stared down at his notepad. Mitzpe Ramon was in the Negev, only twenty kilometres from the Egyptian border. And Rivka Kleinberg had taken a bus to Mitzpe Ramon four days before her murder. Just as she'd gone there three years ago for the abortive

171

Nemesis Agenda interview. So: another aspect of the case that seemed to be repeating itself, winking at him like some sort of pulsing homing beacon. *Russkaya Mafiya*, Egypt, the Negev. He tapped his pen on the chair arm, shuffling the pieces of the jigsaw, trying to shunt them into some sort of coherent picture. None of it seemed to fit together, none of the links to connect, and with Hillel kicking her legs waiting for the next question, he scribbled a note, let it go and moved on.

'You said Mrs Kleinberg spoke to some of the girls?'

'Three of them,' she replied. 'Lola, Sofia and Maria.'

'You sat in?'

'I did with Lola and Sofia. We have to be careful with strangers – a lot of the girls are extremely fragile, not comfortable around people they don't know. But Rivka was fantastic with them. Really gentle, really caring. It was extraordinary how they opened up.'

She took another sip of her coffee. Ben-Roi reached for a biscuit and crammed it in his mouth, the closest he was going to get to lunch.

'What did they talk about?' he asked, crunching, his voice thick with Digestive.

'Their experiences, basically. The sort of stuff I've just been describing.'

He rolled a hand, indicating she should tell him more. She crossed her legs, balancing her mug on one knee.

'Lola's Uzbek,' she said. 'She answered an advert back home for a waitressing job, ended up getting sold to a pimp up in Haifa. The usual story – everything seems fine till they're actually in the country, then they have their passports taken, get raped to break them in and put to work eighteen hours a day in a brothel. She was here for five years before she got rescued.'

'Did she come in through Egypt?'

Hillel shook her head. 'Flew into Ben-Gurion on a work visa. Sofia did, though. She's Ukrainian. Boyfriend said he could get her a job in Israel, except of course he wasn't a boyfriend, he was a recruiter. They target girls like her. Vulnerable, poor, abusive background, low self-esteem – it's the classic profile.'

'And she was trafficked through Sinai?'

Hillel nodded. 'Had a terrible time crossing the desert, poor girl. They all do, of course, but her experiences were particularly bad. Gang raped. Anally raped. Saw one of the other girls getting her kneecaps blown off for trying to escape. I don't even want to think about it.'

Ben-Roi was reaching for another biscuit. He withdrew his hand, his appetite suddenly gone.

'Are they here now, these girls?' he asked.

'Out at work,' replied Hillel. 'Like I said, we find them jobs. All menial, but it's still an important part of their rehabilitation. Helps them build self-respect, interact with people in a way that isn't predicated on abuse. Sofia shelf-stacks in an AM-PM. Lola does cleaning.'

'The other one?' asked Ben-Roi, glancing down at his pad for the name. 'Maria.'

There was a pause. When she answered, Hillel's voice was quieter than it had been. 'Maria's not with us any more.'

'She was deported?'

'She . . . disappeared.'

Ben-Roi looked up. 'Ran away?'

'Either that or her pimp came and took her. We're praying she ran away.'

Although her demeanour remained businesslike it was clear she was upset by the situation.

'Her visa was about to expire,' she went on, 'and the ministry had just turned down her request for an extension, so that could well have acted as a trigger. She was absolutely terrified of being sent home. Was convinced she'd be re-trafficked. Or worse.'

She didn't expand on what 'worse' meant. Didn't need to.

'This was recently?' he asked.

'A few weeks ago. Just after Rivka's visit to the shelter. Maria went into work one morning, never came back. That's about all we know. We've got people on the ground looking for her, and the police have obviously been informed, but so far . . .'

She drew a breath and shook her head. For the first time Ben-Roi noticed that the roots of some of her hairs were going grey.

'And Mrs Kleinberg interviewed this girl?'

'It wasn't quite as formal as that. They definitely talked. Painted as well.'

His forehead rucked. 'Painted?'

'It's something we encourage the girls to do,' she explained. 'Drawing, painting, sculpture. Helps them express themselves, get stuff out in the open they might not otherwise want to talk about.

We've got a small art room and we found Maria in there when I was giving Rivka a tour of the house. I got called away to deal with something, left Rivka with her, and when I came back the two of them were sitting side by side painting together.'

An image from Kleinberg's apartment flashed into Ben-Roi's mind. 'Blonde hair?'

'Sorry?'

'A woman with blonde hair. On blue paper.'

Her eyes screwed up in surprise. 'How did you . . .'

'The picture was in Mrs Kleinberg's flat.'

'Right,' she said. 'Well, that would figure. She asked Maria if she could keep it, took it away with her.'

Ben-Roi's trainer had started tapping on the floor, slow and rhythmic, an involuntary motion that always seemed to kick in when he sensed the conversation might be heading somewhere interesting.

'So you got back, they were painting together . . .'

Hillel nodded. 'And then when I suggested Rivka and I carry on with the tour she asked if Maria would take her round instead. And Maria agreed. Which surprised me because she was extremely withdrawn, rarely talked to anybody, even our specialist counsellors.'

'But she did to Mrs Kleinberg?'

'It certainly looked like it. I saw them out of the window at one point, sitting down in the yard, and they were holding hands and chatting. They spent well over an hour together.'

She flicked a stray hair out of her eyes.

'It happens like that sometimes. Something clicks for no obvious reason. A girl who's barely ever said a word suddenly pours out her heart to a complete stranger. There just seemed to be something in Rivka's manner that helped her open up.'

Again Mordechai Yaron's parting words echoed in Ben-Roi's head: *Rivka had an instinctive empathy for people who were in pain.*

'And you've no idea what they talked about?'

'None at all, I'm afraid. Maria didn't say anything about it afterwards and it wasn't my place to ask. It was a private conversation and we respect that here. To be honest, I was just happy to see her connecting with someone. She was terribly traumatized, had a lot of bad stuff inside. Needed to let some of it go.'

'Did Mrs Kleinberg say anything?'

'Not really. Just that Maria had shared some of her experiences and that it broke her heart someone so young should have gone through what she'd gone through. Maria clearly made an impression on her. That's why she called back a week later. To ask if she could come down and talk with her again. Ask some more questions.'

She was silent a moment, her fingertips flicking against the table, her head tilting slightly as though she was thinking, then: 'Actually, she said she needed to talk to her *urgently*. Wouldn't say what about. Just that she really needed to see her again. She was very concerned when I told her Maria had gone missing.'

The speed of Ben-Roi's foot-tapping increased fractionally.

'And this was when she started asking about the Egypt route?'

There was another brief silence as Hillel worked through the chronology, then she nodded.

'Did Maria come in through Egypt?'

'We never found out for sure,' she said, slipping off the desk and going round to sit in the swivel chair behind it. 'She refused to talk about it. Like a lot of the girls, she was suffering from a form of post-traumatic stress, had built a barrier in her mind between the present and the past in an effort to block out what had happened to her. We got a few details of her early life, but in terms of her trafficking experiences all we ever discovered was that she had been working out of an apartment down in Neve Sha'anan, and that she'd been in Turkey at some point. Which suggests she was either flown in, or shipped through Cyprus into Haifa or Ashdod.'

She sat back, running a finger to and fro along the edge of the desk.

'That woman, by the way, the one with blonde hair – she was always drawing her. The only thing she ever did draw. We never found out who she was.'

Ben-Roi made a mental note to take another look at the picture in Kleinberg's flat.

'You wouldn't happen to know *who* trafficked her?' he asked. 'Who her pimp was?'

She shook her head. 'Like I said, we just deal with the damage, not the people who cause it.'

'And there's been no word of her? No indication of where she might have gone?'

'None at all. We thought she might have drifted back to Neve Sha'anan. It happens with runaways – they gravitate towards the places they know, even if it means getting pulled back into the brothels. But no one's seen anything of her down there.'

'Do you have a photo?'

'Sure.'

She reached down and switched on her computer.

'Her real name's almost certainly not Maria, by the way. The girls always take a different name, helps distance themselves from what they're being made to do. Allows them to think it's someone else who's doing it, not the real them.'

She sat back, waiting for the machine to boot. Ben-Roi drained his coffee, which was now cold, then stood and wandered over to the window.

Outside everything was quiet and still and peaceful, bathed in the benign honey-glow of the sinking afternoon sun, a million miles from the world they'd been talking about. He gazed out over the ranks of dusty *shikunim*, then dropped his eyes to the pavement opposite. A ratty, greasy-haired man was standing there, leaning against the bole of a sycamore tree, staring across the street at the front of the shelter. The pimp Hillel had mentioned earlier. He was tempted to open the window and yell at him to fuck off, but decided the message would be more effective delivered face to face. Maybe accompanied by a little slap to drive the message home. He'd never liked pimps. Did so even less after everything he'd just heard. He stared at him, scowling, then dropped his eyes to the yard at the front of the shelter. There was a wooden picnic bench with a couple of ashtrays on it, a swing-seat, a clothes line and, in the corner, a Barbie scooter and a plastic pedal tractor. He hadn't noticed them when they'd come in.

'You've got kids here?' he asked, surprised.

'Five of them,' came her voice behind him. 'They're out at school.'

'The mothers are –' he was about to say hookers, but stopped himself, realizing the word wasn't appropriate – 'staying here?'

'Sure.'

'The fathers?'

'Pimps, clients.' Her tone was offhand. 'Not the ideal family dynamic but that's the way it goes. When the girls are rescued the kids obviously come with.'

She continued clicking, searching for the picture. Ben-Roi gazed down at the toys. As a cop you developed a thick skin, a filtering mechanism that caught the really bad stuff before it got into your system. Every now and then, despite your best efforts, things slipped through. This was one of those occasions. The toys disturbed him more than everything else he'd heard at the shelter. More than everything else on the case so far. There was just something so desperately sad about them, about the helpless, damaged little lives they represented, ruined before they'd even started. He felt a lump rising in his throat, and with it a sudden urge to contact Sarah, let her know how much he loved her and the baby. He actually pulled out his mobile, but then Hillel called him over and the moment was gone. He stared down for a few seconds longer, then pushed the thought from his mind, returned the mobile to its pouch and crossed to the desk.

'This is her,' said Hillel, angling the screen towards him.

He leant forward, looking at the photo. It was a headshot, cropped a little too tightly just below the chin – a pale, solemn-faced girl with long black hair, full lips and enormous brown eyes. Young. Very young. She was staring straight into the camera, her expression at once both intense and curiously blank.

'Can you print this off?' he asked.

'Sure. We've got another one – do you want that as well?'

'Why not.'

She circled the mouse, double clicked. There was a pause, then a second photo appeared, also a headshot although less severely cropped than the previous image so that the girl's neck and T-shirt were now visible.

Earlier that day, questioning Mordechai Yaron at his office in Jaffa, Ben-Roi had felt a buzz of adrenaline at the news Rivka Kleinberg had visited Mitzpe Ramon for her abortive Nemesis Agenda interview. He felt a similar buzz now, although much, much stronger. More of a jolt. A sharp electric jolt of recognition. Not at the girl's physical appearance, but rather at what she was wearing round her neck.

'This girl,' he said, reaching out and touching a finger to the cross lying against her sternum – the flat silver cross with intricately patterned arms, each opening into a distinctive double tip. 'Do you know where she was from originally?'

The answer came simultaneously, from both of them.

'Armenia.'

It was the thing that had been troubling him from the outset – the lack of any apparent link between the scene of Kleinberg's murder and every other lead the case had thrown up. Now, it seemed, he had the link. There was still a long way to go, but for the first time he felt he was starting to move forward.

177

'. . . only remains to clear away those final houses and you will enjoy a spectacular view from here where we now stand all the way to Luxor Temple, a distance of no less than two thousand seven hundred metres. One thousand three hundred and fifty individual sphinxes! I do not exaggerate, ladies and gentlemen, when I say that Sphinxes Avenue is truly the Eighth Wonder of the Ancient World.'

The tour guide pointed his sunshade theatrically to the south, out though the Tenth Pylon of Karnak Temple to where a sad huddle of mud-brick houses was being attacked on all sides by a ring of earth-moving machinery – the battered remnants of a ragtag army making its final, hopeless stand against a far more powerful invading force. There was a dull click and bleep as his tour group took pictures.

'What about the people who live there?' asked a large, sunburned woman in an 'I Love King Tut!' T-shirt. 'What's going to happen to them?'

'Oh, for them it is very good,' laughed the guide. 'Not only do they receive compensation, but also beautiful new apartments, all mod-cons, much nicer than their old homes. I wish my house was being knocked down!' He raised his arms to the sky. 'Please, God, knock my house down so I can have a new kitchen and toilet with flush!'

The group tittered. They liked their guide. He was informative and polite, but also slightly buffoonish. The perfect Egyptian.

'But seriously,' he continued, 'I can tell you as a fact that these people are happy to move so that this ancient wonder can be revealed. In Egypt we are very proud of our history. And very proud to share our history. That is why the avenue has been excavated in record time – so we can share it with the whole world. Our past is your past. Just as my heart is your heart!'

He winked at the sunburned woman, raising another laugh from the group. A little bit of clownish innuendo – they liked that as well. He started into an explanation of how the avenue dated from the reign of Pharaoh Nectanebo I and was used during the famous Opet festival, but Khalifa didn't listen to any more. Lighting a cigarette, he moved out of the shade beneath the pylon – where he had been standing when the group arrived – and started back towards the centre of the temple complex. Part of him wondered if he shouldn't have said something; told them that his own home had been demolished to make way for the avenue, and he was most assuredly *not* happy about it. But what was the point? They'd paid good money to come out here, and didn't want to be troubled with his problems. Egypt's past might have been their past, but its present was of no concern to them whatsoever. Pharaohs and queens, tombs and hieroglyphs – that's what they were interested in. Not a two-bit detective whose world had collapsed around him in ruins. That was just . . . boring. Irrelevant.

He passed through the Ninth, Eighth and Seventh Pylons, and into the broad paved expanse of the Cachette Court. A crowd of children were having their photograph taken at the feet of the Middle Kingdom statues fronting the Seventh Pylon; a man was sitting cross-legged on the ground sketching the copy of Merenptah's 'Israel' stela – the only text ever found in Egypt to mention the name Israel. Although the afternoon was pushing on and the shadows lengthening, the temperature was still into the high thirties – a dense, smothering blanket of heat only partially eased by the occasional wafts of breeze coming east off the Nile.

He'd spent most of the afternoon down here, after his lunch-hour excursion to the police rifle range. Some *talatat* blocks had gone missing from the secure magazine at the back of the complex – a couple of them carrying Akhenaten cartouches – and he'd been taking statements from all those with access to the store. He would put out some feelers, do the rounds of known antiquities dealers, but he didn't hold out much hope of recovering the blocks. They could have been stolen months ago, years even – the magazine was rarely inspected, and it had only been by chance the blocks' absence had been noticed. By now they were almost certainly gracing the mantelpiece of some millionaire collector on the other side of the world. Like the tour guide said, Egypt's history was everyone's history. Even if you had to steal to get a piece of it.

Dragging on his cigarette, he angled through the doorway in the court's north-western corner and into the towering column forest of the Great Hypostyle Hall. A few hours ago the place had been all but empty, the unbearable mid-afternoon heat driving the tourists back to the sanctuary of their air-conditioned hotels. Now they were flooding back and the hall was rammed. He eased past a crowd of Japanese tourists – or were they Chinese? he could never tell – and made his way towards the Second Pylon and the temple exit. Halfway across the hall, he suddenly slowed and stopped, as if struck by a thought.

He frowned, checked his watch, then, with a muttered 'Dammit', turned and retraced his steps. Back through the hall, out of the Third Pylon this time, past the rearing spike of the obelisk of Tuthmosis I, the Fourth Pylon, Hatshepsut's obelisk, and so round into the vast, palm-dotted open space of the Sacred Lake enclosure. A gently rippling rectangle of murky green water stretched away in front of him, with beside it an awning-covered refreshments area and, at its far end, the ugly concrete grandstand from which tourists watched the nightly *Son et Lumière* show. A small rowing boat was sitting right in the middle of the lake, its gunwale dipped almost to the level of the surface as a plump, bespectacled man in overly tight blue overalls and a woollen hat leant over the side and held something into the water.

'Thought you might be here,' murmured Khalifa.

He waited as the man pulled out a large test tube, sealed it and stowed it in a box at the bow of the boat. Then, tamping his cigarette out on the bole of a palm tree and flicking the butt into a bin, he came forward on to the stone quay beside the lake.

'*Salaam!*' he called.

The man looked up, squinting behind his thick spectacles. For a moment he looked confused, then broke into a broad smile.

'Yusuf!'

'How are you, Omar?'

'I'm in the middle of a lake sampling polluted water – couldn't be happier! You want to come out? It's a lovely day for rowing.'

'Not in that, thanks. It looks unstable enough with one person in it.'

'Nonsense!' the man cried, standing and rocking the boat from side to side. 'Look at that! Safe as the Nile ferry.'

He rocked harder to emphasize the point, only to lose his balance and lurch forward. The boat tipped dangerously to one side, sloshing water over the gunwale, soaking his feet and ankles.

'*Khara!*' Shit!

Khalifa smiled. 'Fancy a Coke?'

'A change of clothes would be more useful,' muttered the man, slapping at his sodden overalls. 'Go on then. I'll meet you at the steps.'

He gave the overalls another slap, pulled off his gloves and manoeuvred himself backwards on to the boat's seat.

'Actually, make it a Sprite,' he called, dropping the oars into the water and starting to row. 'And I wouldn't say no to a Snickers either. I've been out here for two hours.'

Khalifa raised an arm in acknowledgement and went into the café. He pulled a Coke, a Sprite and, in the absence of any Snickers bars, a Kit Kat from the upright fridge, then joined the queue at the till, taking up position behind a young Egyptian couple. By the time he'd paid and returned to the lake, his friend had reached the far end, tethered the boat and climbed the steps up to the quayside.

'Forgive me, Yusuf,' he said as Khalifa approached, holding up his hands apologetically. 'That thing with the boat, I didn't think. It was a stupid . . .'

Khalifa threw him the Sprite, the gesture saying no offence had been taken and no apology was necessary. The Kit Kat followed and the two of them embraced, the man kissing Khalifa once on each cheek.

'How's Zenab doing?' he asked as they sat down on the quayside, legs dangling against the lake's stone-block retaining wall.

'Better every day,' replied Khalifa, not entirely truthfully. 'Rasha?'

'Good, although she's overworked at the moment. They're short-staffed and she's having to do double shifts. Can barely keep her eyes open, poor girl. Last night she didn't get in till past midnight.'

Rasha al-Zahwi, Omar's wife, was a paediatrician at Luxor General. Omar worked as a site analyst for the Luxor Water and Wastewater Company, with a special responsibility for water management around ancient monuments, which was how his and Khalifa's paths had crossed. Over a decade ago now. They'd used to socialize a lot. Less so this last year.

'How's it looking?' asked Khalifa, opening his Coke and nodding towards the surface of the lake.

'Crap,' replied Omar. 'Literally. All the vibration from the earth moving they've been doing for the Avenue – it's fractured the sewage main at this end of town. There's piss and shit draining into the groundwater and then getting pumped into the lake whenever they top it up. I've been monitoring it for a month now and it's been getting steadily worse.'

'I can't smell anything.'

'Trust me, you will in a couple of weeks. No one's going to be able to go near it, the thing'll stink so bad. They're going to have to drain the whole enclosure and refill it from the Nile. Oh bloody fuck it!'

A geyser of Sprite had erupted from his can as he pulled the tab, spraying all over his hands and overalls. He held the can away from him and pulled off his woollen hat.

'I was dry till you came along,' he grumbled, wiping the hat across his sodden overalls.

Khalifa shot him a mock-apologetic look and sipped his own drink. Behind them whistles started blowing, alerting visitors that it was closing time and they should start moving towards the temple exit. From further away came the rhythmic clank and thwack of piledrivers, the predominant backing-track to life in Luxor over the last couple of years.

'Are you testing the water on site?' asked Khalifa after a pause, swiping a fly away from his face and taking another swig of Coke. Omar shook his head.

'We send the samples up to a lab in Assyut. We used to have an arrangement with the hospital lab, but there's been so much testing needed since they started all this bloody building work, the hospital couldn't cope any more.'

Khalifa kicked his legs for a moment, then: 'Can I ask a favour?'

'You can ask.'

'I've been getting reports of wells going bad out in the Eastern Desert and I need some advice.'

He outlined the situation – Mr Attia, his cousin, Deir el-Zeitun – which, despite his best efforts to put it out of his mind, had continued to nag at him. There was something wrong, something going on, and even if he wasn't half the detective he used to be, he was still enough of one to want answers when faced with a pattern of events that had no obvious explanation.

'Could it be natural?' he asked when he'd finished going through the story. 'The wells going bad of their own accord?'

Omar took a thoughtful glug of his Sprite. 'I very much doubt it. Wells dry up, for sure, and they go bad too, although when they do it's almost invariably because of industrial pollution. Or occasionally sewage contamination like we're getting here. But you say these are in the middle of the Eastern Desert?'

Khalifa nodded.

'Then that's much harder to explain. I'm assuming there's no heavy industry nearby – cement factories, paper mills, that sort of thing?'

'Not that I'm aware of.'

'It certainly sounds suspicious. Very occasionally water sources go off because of subterranean movement, but we're talking big movement, earthquake size, and that's something we'd have heard about. And the fact that all the wells are Coptic-owned . . .'

He took another sip of his Sprite, then put the can down and started unwrapping his Kit Kat, methodically running a thumbnail down the foil between each ridge of chocolate.

'You want me to look into it?' he asked, snapping off a finger and handing it to Khalifa. 'Take some samples and have the water analysed?'

'Would you mind?'

'Of course not. You've got me interested now.'

'I could go out and get the samples myself, if that would help.'

'It's easier if I do it. Gives me a chance to look at the terrain, see if there's any obvious geological explanation. It might take a few days.'

'Whenever. There's no hurry. I'll pay for your petrol.'

Omar waved the offer away. 'I owe you for the Kit Kat and Sprite,' he said. 'Call it quits.'

'That doesn't seem very fair.'

'This is Egypt. Nothing's fair. Like you getting one finger and me getting three.'

He winked at Khalifa and crammed the remainder of the Kit Kat in his mouth.

'Even with Mubarak gone, there's still so much injustice,' he said, munching cheerfully. 'It's heartbreaking.'

Khalifa smiled and they fell silent, gazing out across the lake while behind them the whistles continued to blow, although less frequently now as the tourists got the message and drained out of the temple complex and into their waiting coaches. Khalifa finished his Coke, ate his Kit Kat finger and lit a Cleopatra, his eyes lingering on a patch of empty sky out beyond the towering rectangle of the Tenth Pylon. This time last year that same patch of sky had framed his old apartment building, one of a row of drab concrete rectangles that had risen above the north end of town like a line of weathered tombstones. Whenever he'd visited Karnak in the old days he'd always made a point of wandering out to the pylon and calling home on his mobile, getting whoever was there to lean out of the living-room window and wave at him. A childish game of which none of them had ever tired, particularly Ali, who on one memorable occasion had once hung a large sheet out of the window on which he'd painted the words 'We love you, Dad'. He wished he'd taken a photo. There were so many things he wished he'd photographed. And now they were gone for ever, replaced by empty sky and a trench full of sphinxes. Progress? It certainly didn't feel like it to him.

'I should be getting back to work,' said Omar, draining the last of his Sprite and clambering to his feet. 'I've still got some samples to take and I don't think they'd appreciate me splashing around during the Sound and Light show.'

'I don't know,' said Khalifa, also standing, 'They might think you were part of the display. Amun parading on his *manjet* barque.'

'In overalls and a beanie hat? Interesting interpretation.'

They laughed. Or at least Omar did. Khalifa just smiled.

'I'll try and get out to the wells in the next few days,' said Omar. 'Can you send me details?'

'I'll e-mail them as soon as I'm back in the office.'

'I'll tell the lab it's urgent, so should have something for you by the end of the week.'

Khalifa thanked him. 'One other thing. I'm pretty certain the farm at Bir Hashfa's piping its drinking water illegally. They're poor people – do me a favour and keep it to yourself.'

'Our little secret,' said Omar, giving his nose a conspiratorial tap.

He embraced Khalifa, pulled away, laid his hands on the detective's shoulders. 'You OK?'

'Never better.'

Omar's hands tightened. 'You OK?' he repeated.

This time Khalifa hesitated before answering.

'I'll live,' he said eventually.

'You do that, my friend. You live long and healthy. And the same for Zenab and the kids.'

He held Khalifa's gaze, then gave his hair an affectionate ruffle, pulled on his woollen hat and returned to his boat.

'I'll let you know as soon as I've got the results,' he called, clambering on board and untying the tether rope. 'I'll be interested to see them myself. Don't be a stranger.'

He pushed off, sat, and heaved on the oars, propelling the dinghy back out across the water. Khalifa watched him for a moment, then looked out past the Tenth Pylon again to where his old apartment block used to be. Up and down the tectonic split of the avenue you'd find people looking in exactly the same way, gazing forlornly into space as if willing their old home to miraculously reappear. Like mourners beside a grave. Half of Luxor, it seemed to Khalifa, was in mourning for the way things had been. He shook his head, picked up the two drinks cans and made for the exit. Sometimes it was just so hard to let go.

TEL-AVIV

Outside the Hofesh Shelter, Ben-Roi crossed the road to have words with the pimp standing on the opposite pavement. The man saw him coming and legged it. Ben-Roi chased him for half a block, then gave up. He'd almost certainly be back, as Hillel had said, but at least he'd given him something to think about. Then again, maybe not. Guys like him didn't really think. Just did what they did without awareness of meaning or consequences. Certainly no emotional connection. He'd hide round the corner, wait for Ben-Roi to leave, then resume his vigil untroubled, like a fox returning to a dustbin. Feral, basically. And nothing Ben-Roi did or said was going to change that. The eternal dance of law-keepers and law-breakers. Not for the first time he wondered why the hell he bothered.

He hung around for a few minutes, making his presence felt. Then, with a bellowed, 'I'll be seeing you, loser!' returned to his car. He dropped the photos Hillel had printed off for him on the passenger seat, called Zisky, filled him in on what he'd found out.

'You think that's why Kleinberg was visiting the Armenian compound?' Zisky asked when he'd finished. 'Because she was looking for this girl?'

'Or meeting her,' said Ben-Roi. 'Either way, it's the best lead we've got. The shelter's e-mailing pictures across now. Do me a favour and get some uniforms to circulate them around the compound, see if anyone recognizes her. I'm going to take a spin back to Neve Sha'anan on the off-chance someone's seen the girl down there. Any joy with the Nemesis thing?'

'I've spoken to my friend and he's given me some background,' said

Zisky. 'I've also dug up some stuff on Barren Corporation that might be relevant. You want to hook up this evening?'

'Why not. You drink?'

'Only champagne.'

Ben-Roi was wising up to Zisky's humour and let out a rumbling chuckle.

'The tab's on you then. There's a bar at the Old City end of Jaffa Street. Putin's.'

'Know it.'

'Meet you there at nine?'

'It's a date.'

Ben-Roi ended the call, made a second one. To Sarah this time. Back in the shelter, gazing out of the window at the sad collection of toys down in the yard, he'd experienced an uncharacteristic rush of emotion, a sudden, urgent desire to tell her how much he still loved her. He *did* love her – desperately, if he was honest with himself – but the inclination to open up about it had gone. Instead, when she came on the line, he kept the conversation chatty and brief, asking after the baby, suggesting they meet for lunch the following day, side-stepping her questions about what he was doing in Tel-Aviv. Not because he thought she couldn't deal with it – she was a tough cookie, strong – but because there were some parts of his life he wanted to keep fenced off from other parts. Rape, violence, abuse – those weren't the sort of things he wished to share with the mother of his child. They talked for a couple of minutes, agreed a time and place for lunch the next day, rang off.

Once she was gone Ben-Roi sat a moment, then picked up one of the photos from the passenger seat, the headshot. He held it against the steering wheel. The girl's huge, almond-shaped eyes stared up at him, empty and yet at the same time strangely forceful, their irises so brown they were almost black. She wasn't conventionally beautiful – her nose was a little too flat, her eyebrows too heavy – but there was definitely something about her that drew you, something in the inter-play of vulnerability and toughness, damage and strength. It was almost as if two different faces with two different expressions had been superimposed on each other – one that of a victim, the other a survivor's.

She was the key to the case. He'd felt it the moment he'd first seen her. The point around which everything else revolved. The thread that bound it all together.

He gazed at her for almost a minute. Then, laying the photo aside, he started the engine and headed back into the Tel-Aviv haystack in search of a needle called Maria.

If Israel was the Promised Land, Neve Sha'anan was the place where the promise got broken. A seedy, grubby, run-down wedge of Tel-Aviv sandwiched between the city's old and new bus stations, the district had long been a magnet for immigrants, drunks, drug-addicts and sex-workers. Some people called it colourful. A melting pot. To Ben-Roi it just looked like a shit-hole.

It was gone six when he arrived and parked up on Saloman Street, beside the abandoned, weed-covered expanse of the old garage. He sat a moment staring across the road at a group of *schwartzes* hanging around in a bar doorway. Then, grabbing the headshot photo, he locked the car, pulled on his jacket and went walkabout.

The area was starting to come to life, its pulse seeming to quicken. On Neve Sha'anan itself, the pedestrianized drag of soiled, decaying tenements that formed the district's backbone, discordant blasts of noise filled the evening air: music; television sets; the clang and bleep of gaming arcades; the Babel-chatter of Oriental women as they crowded around the fruit and vegetable stalls. There were rubbish-jammed alleyways, and neon-lit bars, and swirls of graffiti demanding an end to immigration and a return to the Torah and death to Islamic scum. Drunks and heroin-shooters lurked in doorways like creatures in their lairs; there was a lingering odour of trash and fish, and fast food. And, also, something more intangible: poverty, hardship, violence waiting to happen. Tourist-brochure material it most certainly wasn't. This was the underbelly. Israel's foetid basement, where all the junk got dumped.

Ben-Roi walked the length of the drag, past the liquor stores and laundromats and stalls selling fake designer watches, showing the photo to passers-by, hoping against hope someone might have sighted the girl. A couple of street-hawkers thought they vaguely recognized her, but couldn't remember from where or when or indeed if it was actually the same person; an elderly woman in a brightly lit shop sell-ing Christian paraphernalia – crosses and plastic Jesuses and bottled water from the River Jordan – was more definite that she'd seen her. It had been a long time ago, though, certainly not recently. One man said he'd *like* to see her, show her a good time; another, a *meshugganah*

Haredi with wild eyes and crusty, dreadlock-like *pe'ot* hanging almost to the level of his chest, was adamant that the girl was an evil spirit sent by *Ha-Satan* to tempt the faithful. Given that he was barefoot and had a cardboard sign round his neck proclaiming they were all going to *Gehinnom*, Ben-Roi didn't take him too seriously. No one could offer any concrete information.

He worked his way to the bottom of the street and stopped at the grim, garbage-filled throat of the Levinsky underpass. Although the tunnel was gated off, he could see shadowy figures down there, indeterminate hummocks of humanity looming in the darkness: crack-heads, piss-heads, booby-cases. If someone was desperate, really desperate, needed shelter for the night, it was the sort of place they might take refuge. In the light of day he might have considered hopping the gate and going down, passing the photo around, asking if anyone recognized it. He sure as hell wasn't going to do it now, not in the dark and with his Jericho locked up in the secure box underneath his car seat. He was foolhardy, but not that foolhardy. It would be a waste of time anyway – most of them were too spaced to even register they were being shown a photo, let alone remember if they had seen the person in it. Instead, after staring down for a while, his nostrils recoiling at the odour of rubbish and sour piss, he gave Neve Sha'anan a second pass, then branched out into the parallel streets: Hagdud Haivri, Yesod Hamaala, Fin, Saloman.

When he'd been stationed in Tel-Aviv a decade ago there had been wall-to-wall hookers along these streets. They'd cleaned it up a bit since then, but it was still palpably a red-light district: sex shops, 'Pip' shows, boarded shop fronts with micro-skirted women standing in their doorways, louch and jaded. Pimps as well. Leaning against lamp-posts, hanging around on corners, they stuck out a mile with their watchful faces and beady, calculating eyes. Lowlifes, every one of them. Scumbags. Although when all was said and done they were only feeding a demand. The punters were as much a part of the equation. And while it was easy to despise the pimps and the traffickers, the clients didn't pigeonhole quite so comfortably. Half of his friends had been with a prostitute at one time or another. All of his work colleagues probably, excepting Leah Shalev. Himself too, once, years ago, when he'd been doing his national service up on the Lebanese border. He and Natan Tirat had got hammered one night on cheap whisky, gone to a brothel in Metulla, got themselves a blowjob from a surly, large-breasted woman called ... he couldn't even remember what she was called. It had been a laugh at the time, a sort of rite of passage, and if subsequently he'd felt a bit embarrassed about it, and had certainly never said anything to Sarah, it had never caused him any particular angst.

Tonight, wandering around, he was more troubled by the memory. He was fairly certain the woman hadn't been trafficked, or at least not from abroad, but all the same, he couldn't imagine her life had been a particularly happy one. And a pair of drunken conscripts waiting in line to stick their cocks in her mouth couldn't have done much to improve it. He glanced at the photo in his hand, wondering what sort of things the girl had been forced to do – *knowing* what sort of things – and feeling sickened by it. Culpable as well, in an abstract sort of way. He'd paid money into the industry, after all. Availed himself of its services. Fed the beast. If it wasn't for users like him there wouldn't be an industry, just as there'd be no sweat shops were it not for the fashionistas wanting to wear cheap designer clothes, and no drugs wars without the otherwise oh-so-respectable weekend coke-snorters. They were all exploiters in their own way, all users and abusers, and if the pimps and traffickers were the obvious face of exploitation, the circle of responsibility spread a lot wider than that. He didn't dwell on the thought. Metulla had been a long time ago, a one-off that he had no intention of ever repeating. Right now he just needed to find the girl and solve a murder. Reflections on the ethics of supply and demand in the sex industry were for another day.

He turned on to Hagdud Haivri, past the anomalously named Kingdom of Pork butcher on the corner and along to a couple of hookers standing post a few doors down. One, a peroxide blonde in jeans and boob-tube, had the washed-out complexion and bruised, striated arms of a long-time smack-addict; the other was older, middle-aged, brunette, wearing a tight black dress and stilettos. Healthier looking, although that wasn't saying much. Both Israeli, by the look of it. He flashed his badge and held out the photo.

'You know this girl?' he said, not bothering with preliminaries. 'Used to work around here?'

The blonde shook her head.

'Try looking at the picture.'

Her eyes rolled down, then up again. 'No.'

'Sure?'

'If you're hunting young meat I know where you can find it, but it'll cost you. Real young, if you're interested.'

Ben-Roi ignored the comment, angled the photo to the other woman.

'How about you? Recognize her?'

The woman reached out and took the picture, dragging on the Marlboro she was holding. Although she was carrying weight around her middle, and was wearing too much mascara, you could see she had been attractive once. Still was, in a weary, fractured sort of way. No obvious signs of drug use, which made him wonder how she'd ended up down here. Maybe debt, maybe an abusive relationship, maybe one of a hundred reasons. Hell, maybe she even enjoyed it, although that was the least likely scenario. They all had their different stories. Their own private staircase down into the underworld.

'Well?' he asked.

Her eyes darted up from the photo, then back. 'Why are you asking?'

'Police business. Come on, you either recognize her or you don't.'

She took another drag. Her hand, he noticed, was trembling. Maybe she was doing drugs after all.

'Can't help you,' she said, returning the photo.

'Sure?'

'Can't help you,' she repeated, firmer.

Ben-Roi scanned her face, trying to work out if she was holding something back. She just stood there pulling on her cigarette, hand shaking, not meeting his gaze, and after a moment he accepted he wasn't going to get anything more and moved on. The blonde's voice echoed behind him, shrill and taunting.

'Real young meat if you're interested, darling. Fresh off the lorry! You come back any time, Mr Policeman!'

He could still hear her laughter as he turned the corner at the bottom of the street.

He wandered around for another hour, stopping into the bars and sex shops and strip joints, talking to the prostitutes and the pimps. A few punters as well – furtive, hunched figures sliding guiltily out of the doors that gave straight off the pavement into dingy, cell-like rooms with a bed and a sink in them. A couple of Eastern Europeans on Fin remembered Maria from when she used to work the area, but could tell him nothing about her, certainly not where she might be now. A doorman outside the VIP Sex Bar on Saloman also recognized her, with the added detail that she had appeared in a couple of internet porn shoots. Other than that, he drew a complete blank. No one else remembered the girl, no one else knew anything about her. Or at least no one was admitting to it, which was the same thing. At eight, having trawled the district from end to end and back again, and aware that he needed to be heading up to Jerusalem for his meet with Dov Zisky, he called time and returned to the car. It had always been a long shot. Hopefully they'd have more luck back at the Armenian compound.

He removed the Toyota's red police number plates and dumped them in the boot, then got in. For a moment he sat there, worn out suddenly, oppressed by everything he'd heard and seen over the course of the day. Maybe he should cancel the meet, just go home and crash. He was anxious to know what Zisky had found out about Barren and Nemesis, however, and anyway, he could use a cold beer. He gave himself a few seconds. Then, with a roll of the neck, he started the engine and was just putting the car into gear when there was a sharp tap on the window. He tensed, startled, then relaxed as a face loomed beside him. The brunette from Hagdud Haivri. He lowered the window and she bent down, making a show of sticking out her backside, a street-walker propositioning a client.

'Why are you asking about her?' Her body language might have been seductive, but her voice was tight, urgent. 'Maria,' she hissed. 'What's happened to her?'

Ben-Roi neutralled the gears and cut the engine, leaning back slightly and turning in his seat to face her.

'I thought you said you didn't—'

'I know what I said!' She threw a nervous glance over her shoulder. 'You think I'm going to let the whole world hear me talking to the police? That sort of thing doesn't go down too well in this part of town. Now what's happened to her? I thought she was out of it. In a hostel.'

'She ran away. A couple of weeks ago. We thought she might have come—'

'Back here?' She let out a low throaty sound, part laugh, more disbelieving choke. 'Are you fucking kidding me? After what she went through? She wouldn't show her face round here in a million years.'

'You were friends with her?'

She gave an impatient flick of the hand. 'No one has friends in this business! It's as much as you can do to keep your own head above water.'

She looked round again, anxiously scanning the street, then pushed her head further into the car, coming so close Ben-Roi could smell the cigarettes on her breath, see the individual crow's feet around her eyes.

'Our paths crossed a few times,' she said. 'They had us doing . . . you know . . .'

'What?'

'For God's sake! Films, private shows. You need me to spell it out?'

He didn't, knew exactly what she was talking about. Mature and young, mother and daughter, teacher's pet.

'She was just a child, for God's sake. It's bad enough at my age, but for someone like that . . .'

She bit her lip, her luridly painted fingers curling around the doorframe, her face a study in humiliation.

'I didn't want to do it. Neither of us did. But if that's what they tell you to do . . . It's not like you can just pass on the job. Know what I'm saying?'

Again, he did. Perfectly. This wasn't a business renowned for respecting the rights of its employees.

'Do you know who was pimping her?'

She shook her head. 'They just used to bring her along to wherever we were . . . doing it. Studios, clubs, private houses. She always had a couple of minders with her. She was so scared. *So* scared. I tried to help her, make it a bit easier, but how do you make something like that easier?'

Her eyes flicked up and down again, unable to meet his gaze. Her hands were clenched so tight around the door that her knuckles had turned white.

'She cried once. Just lay there crying with me on top of her. Stag party it was, soldiers. They loved it. Animals!'

Images and sounds flashed through Ben-Roi's mind, the sort of stuff he'd seen on the internet. He shook his head, trying to get rid of them.

'Do you have any idea where she is now?'

'A long way away, if she knows what's good for her. Listen, I need to get back, I've already been away too long. I just thought you might know something, wanted to make sure she hadn't been . . .'

'What?'

'What do you fucking think? They pulled a girl out of the Yarkon only last week. They'd cut off her ears and tied dumbbells to her feet. That's what happens to girls who get away. There was a journalist woman down here asking questions a few weeks back, I was frightened the same thing might have happened to Maria. Now I've got to go.'

She started to straighten, but Ben-Roi grabbed her wrist.

'She was fat, this journalist, greying hair?'

She hesitated, then gave a wary half-nod.

'Her name was Rivka Kleinberg. She was murdered three days ago. In Jerusalem. In the Armenian Cathedral. We think she was there looking for Maria. Or possibly meeting her. I need to find Maria, urgently. If there's anything you can tell me, anything at all . . .'

For a moment the woman stood there, her eyes darting back and forth, as though she was processing what she'd just heard, trying to figure out what it meant, how it might affect her. Then, yanking her wrist free, she stepped away from the car.

'I can't help you,' she said. 'I don't know anything. Now I've got to—'

'Iris!'

She froze rigid as a voice rang out from across the street. Ben-Roi flicked a look in the side-mirror. A man was approaching along the opposite pavement: burly, flat-cap, leather jacket, some sort of mastiff or pit bull terrier dragging furiously at the dog lead in his hand.

'Oh God,' she whispered, her jaw tight, her eyes bulging with fear. 'Please, go! Go now! If he sees me with a cop . . .'

'What's going on, Iris?' shouted the man. 'Who are you talking to?'

'Just trying to drum up some business,' she called, trying, and failing, to mask the terror in her voice. 'It's been a slow night.'

'So what's all the chatter? He either wants it or he doesn't.'

'Go,' she hissed under her breath. 'In the name of God, just go. He'll kill me!'

The pimp was crossing the road thirty metres back, the dog snarling, its paws clawing furiously at the tarmac in its eagerness to reach her. Ben-Roi wondered if he should get out and flash his badge, tell the man to back off, but he knew it would only bring the woman trouble. If not now, later.

'At least give me something,' he growled, starting the engine, his eyes jinking from the woman to the mirror and back again. 'You must know something.'

'I don't! God Almighty, he's going to—'

'Is he trying to knock you down, Iris?' The pimp had speeded his step, was now less than twenty metres away, near enough for Ben-Roi to see the stubble on his face and the individual spikes on the dog's chunky leather collar. 'You fucking tell him the price is the price! You hear me? The price is the price!'

'Please,' she groaned, her voice now demented with terror, 'I'm begging you, just—'

'Not till you give me something!'

For a fraction of a second she remained frozen. Then, with the pimp now only ten metres back, she stepped up to the car, leant in and whispered hurriedly in Ben-Roi's ear.

'Now piss off out of here,' she hissed underneath her breath, backing away again. Then, louder, for the benefit of the pimp:

'Well fuck you, you bastard!'

Assuming someone had insulted one of his charges, the man let out a furious bellow and made a dash for the car. Ben-Roi's eyes met the woman's, only for an instant, then, with a nod, he slammed the Toyota into gear and lurched forward, the whole vehicle shuddering as the dog slammed itself into the rear bumper. He picked up speed, glanced in the rear-view mirror. The dog was scuttling behind him, its lead trailing along the street; the pimp was standing beside the woman, one arm wrapped protectively around her shoulders while with the other he furiously punched the air and yelled insults that Ben-Roi couldn't make out over the roar of the car's engine. He looked just long enough to make sure the woman was OK, which she seemed to be – or as OK as was possible, given the world she inhabited – then dropped his eyes forward again. He reached the end of Saloman, turned on to Harkevet and from there on to the Ayalon freeway back towards Jerusalem. He was driving on automatic, barely noticing what he was doing. All he could think of were the words the woman had whispered to him:

Her real name was Vosgi.

HOUSTON, TEXAS

William Barren swung his Porsche Carrera GT through the gates of the family estate and let rip a brief, satisfying burst of speed along the tarmac drive. The V10, 612 brake horsepower engine catapulted him up to 100km per hour in a matter of seconds. Almost immediately he eased back, dropping the speed right down as the drive started its curve round to the turreted granite bulk of the family mansion, which even in the morning sunshine still managed to look malign and gloomy. Not for nothing was the place called Darklands.

He checked the dashboard clock – a little before 10.20 – and pulled over, underneath one of the giant bur oaks with which the drive was lined. He'd been summoned for 10.30, and his father didn't like people arriving early. Didn't like them arriving late either. Didn't like them arriving any time other than on the dot, exactly when he'd told them to get there. As a kid William had tried so hard to get it right. Somehow he'd never managed to do it, had always ended up being a few moments to either side of the allotted hour. Sometimes early in his eagerness to prove himself, sometimes late because he'd got so worked up about the whole thing he'd gone into a sort of stress-induced trance and lost track of what he was doing. Never on the nail. And then it would be another scolding. Another growling, finger-wagging lecture on how a child who couldn't stick to the clock would grow into an adult who couldn't stick to anything, and an adult who couldn't stick to anything was destined for failure and ignominy and uselessness. Even now, a grown man, he was still haunted by those lectures. *You're not what I was hoping for, William. You've not got what it takes. Others have, but not you, I'm afraid.* Well, he *did* have what it took. And soon the old man would be finding that out for himself. He might not have been the favoured one, the love and attention might all have gone elsewhere, but William was the one who was going to come out on top in the end. Soon. Very soon.

Not today, though. Today he just wanted to be on time.

He cut himself out a quick line on top of a CD case. He snorted it, then opened the case and slotted the CD into the deck. Eminem, *Bully*. Bumping the volume up, he settled back, banging the base of his fist against the steering wheel in time to the beat, mouthing the words. *I ain't bowing to no motherfucking bully.* Too right. You're going to bow to *me*, old man, bow right down on those gross, fat, swollen, elephant knees of yours. Bow, bow, bow. He hammered his fist harder, the whole car shaking to the rhythm of his hatred. Bow, bow, bow.

He threw another glance at the clock.

Delusional Personality Disorder, that had been one shrink's assessment. There'd been quite a few of them over the years. Shrinks, analysts, counsellors, head-doctors. All had come up with their own variations and interpretations, their own gobbledygook terminologies. The one he'd seen four years back after his mother had died, the woman with the whore's lips and the big nipples, had come right out and told him he was a borderline sociopath, although that might have had something to do with him following her home after one of their sessions and asking if he could go down on her (to which, funnily enough, she'd said yes – despite, or perhaps because of his demons he'd always been attractive to the opposite sex. That and the fact he hailed from a family of billionaires).

Yes, there'd been a lot of therapy. A lot of sitting around in soothing armchairs in pleasantly decorated offices while Dr this and Dr that questioned him about his childhood and his family and the drugs and the hookers and how he felt about his mum getting charred to a cinder like that.

Her, they always asked a lot about *her*.

And through all of it, two decades and more of questions and answers and evasions and occasional collapses into hysterical, howling floods of piteous weeping at his inability to live up to his pa's expectations, to be the heir the old man doted upon and loved – a dozen different shrinks in a dozen different offices and not a one of them had told him anything he didn't already know. Namely, that his father was the root of all his problems. The poisoned cesspit from which all his troubles exuded. How he loathed him! Worshipped him as well, of course, in the way you worship a wrathful Old Testament deity who scares the living shit out of you and yet at the same time whose beneficence you desperately crave. Loathed him a whole lot more, though. His father had fucked up his life. Had fucked up all their lives (that night in the cupboard, listening, *Please don't, it hurts, it hurts*) and so long as his father was around, the fuck-up would continue. Just as the moment his father was gone, everything would be OK. Like in that Shakespeare play they'd studied before he'd been kicked out of school, the one about Prince Hal and his father the king, where the prince had been a complete fucking wastrel until the king had got ill and died and Hal had assumed the throne and put all his wild days behind him. Blossomed into a great man. *He* was going to blossom into a great man. Was already a great man, if only his father would get the hell out of the way and let him prove it. Not long now. Soon he'd be settling family business. And unlike Prince Hal he wouldn't be affecting any touching reconciliations with Daddy before assuming rule of the kingdom. On the contrary, once Daddy was six feet under he'd be putting on his tap shoes and dancing on his fucking grave.

He took yet another look at the clock and realized with a jolt that it was almost 10.30. Cursing, he killed the Eminem, started the engine and sped along the drive, the bur oaks blurring past to either side as he roared round the curve and up to the front of the house. He skidded to a halt, took the steps two at a time up to the door, checked his watch: 10.30 on the dot. With a triumphant bark of laughter he reached out and pressed the polished brass bell-nipple, holding it down for way longer than was necessary, the chime clanging angrily through the house, leaving no one inside in any doubt that not only was he there, but he was there on time. Right on the money.

'Good morning, Master William.'

Stephen, his father's manservant, had opened the door and was standing in front of him: ramrod straight, black suit, vague smell of pomade, shoes so intensely polished their caps gave off a dim reflection of the ceiling above. He gave a deferential nod and stepped aside, ushering William into the house.

'I trust you are well, sir,' he crooned, closing the door after them, his voice soft and sibilant, giving no hint of age or character.

'Fine and dandy, thank you, Stephen. Although I'll be a whole lot better in twenty minutes when I'm on my way out of here.'

William flashed a grin to which he received no visible reaction, the butler's pale, thin-lipped face a study in controlled neutrality. He'd always been like that, for as long as William could remember. As a child he'd harboured a fantasy that the man was actually a robot and that if you undid the screws behind his ears you could ease his face off to reveal the circuitboard beneath. Maybe reprogram him, make him do some fun things. Like rape his father. Or drag him down to the ornamental lake at the rear of the house and drown him, put them all out of their misery. A couple of times he'd actually tried to do it – climbed on to a chair and felt around the margins of that pale, expressionless mask, working his fingers underneath the oiled hairline in the hope of finding a button or a catch or a switch, some means of getting inside and assuming mastery. And Stephen had let him do it, played along with the game. William had always been grateful for that – the passive acquiescence to the fantasies of a young child. Despite the rigidly formal façade, Stephen was one of the good guys. Recognized the potential to which his own father was so wilfully blind. One day he'd reward him for that. The king never forgot those who showed him loyalty in exile. Just as he never forgot those who'd sent him into exile in the first place.

'In the library?' he asked.

'He is indeed, sir. Let me show you up.'

The manservant led him across the hallway – all gloomy oak panelling, leaded window panes and heavy brass door furnishings, more like a coffin than a home – and on to the grand staircase. Portraits tracked them as they climbed, gazing out from the wall with the studied impassivity of those who do not wish to reveal anything of themselves beyond their physical appearance, and do even that reluctantly: his great-grandfather, the family patriarch, thin as a pick-axe and hard as iron; his grandfather, stooped, moustachioed, a gun dog at his feet and a cigar in his hand; his own father, monstrous, bearded, snake-eyed, radiating malevolence, or so it had always seemed to William. There were others, grim-faced figures accompanying them all the way up to the first-floor landing, uncles and great-uncles, some of whom he dimly remembered, most of whom were complete strangers to him. And then more along the panelled corridor leading into the west wing of the house, women this time, the Barren matriarchs: wives and sisters, aunts and daughters. All carried the same weary, slightly disappointed expression, as though even with all the jewellery and fine clothes and elevated social standing, their lives hadn't turned out quite as happily as they had expected or hoped.

Right at the very end of the passage, beside the door to the library, the last painting in line and the only one illuminated with its own small hooded lamp, was William's mother. Blonde-haired, sad-eyed, painfully thin. She'd been a good woman in her own way, had done her best to protect and shield, but ultimately there was no standing up to the malign piledriver that was Nathaniel Barren. She had wilted, like all the Barren women wilted. William threw the picture a cursory glance, but didn't allow his eyes or thoughts to linger on it. His mother couldn't help him now, any more than she'd been able to help him as he was growing up. He was on his own.

'Here we are, sir.'

Not entirely on his own. There was always Stephen.

'Thank you, Stephen. I'll take it from here.'

'As you wish, sir.'

The manservant gave a polite tilt of the head, turned and walked back the way they had come, his feet moving soundlessly along the carpeted corridor as though they weren't actually making contact with the ground. William watched him go – good man, Stephen, reliable – then squared up to the library door, his stomach tightening, as it always did when he stood on this spot, his hand instinctively slipping into his pocket and playing with the coke wrap. He resisted the temptation to backtrack to the toilet for a top-up toot. Afterwards, maybe, but for the moment he wanted to keep his wits about him. He could do that with drugs, take them or leave them. He was in control. Strong. Never forget that, he told himself. *You are in control. You are strong.*

He drew a breath and knocked.

'Enter.'

The command came like a rumble of distant thunder. William hesitated, steeling himself – *You are in control. You are strong* – then opened the door.

His father was sitting behind his desk on the far side of the library, hulking, white-haired, dressed in a heavy tweed suit. Although the room was huge, double height with a domed ceiling and a gallery running round the upper level, Nathaniel Barren nonetheless dominated it, his huge frame blocking the light from the windows behind the desk, his entire being seeming to permeate every corner of the space like a dark mist. Even at this distance William could smell his aftershave – heavy, sour, like overheated machinery – and hear the pained rasp of his breathing.

'You're late,' he growled, his voice deep and unyielding, subterranean, the sort of sound rock might make if it could talk.

'I don't believe I am, sir.'

'Don't contradict me. You're late.'

The old man laid an elbow on the table and tapped his watch. William toyed with the idea of fighting his corner, insisting that he had arrived spot on 10.30 as instructed, but it wasn't worth it. He'd never won an argument with his father in his life and wouldn't be doing so today. No one ever won arguments with his father. If Nathaniel Barren said the earth was flat and the moon was made of cheese, that's the way it was, there was no gainsaying the man. Instead William stood in silence, the last of the coke buzz humming around the margins of his brain, reassuring himself he was in control, he was strong, waiting until his father made a beckoning motion with his finger and he was able to come forward. There were two chairs in front of the desk – ornate, antique chairs with curving backs and worn silk seats – and again he waited for a signal. It didn't come and so he remained standing. A clock ticked on the mantelpiece, his father's lungs rasped. Rather than disturbing the silence both sounds seemed only to intensify it, rendering the atmosphere even denser and more oppressive. Suffocating. Every time William came here he felt like he was being buried alive.

You are in control. You are strong.

'How are you feeling, Father?' he asked.

'I'm feeling fine, thank you.'

There was no reciprocal inquiry as to the state of William's health. He shuffled his feet, tried to block out the clock's hollow metronomic slap, which had already started to drill into his skull. Maybe he should have had that top-up toot after all. There was an awkward pause, then:

'I thought the board meeting went well.'

'Did you?'

'Jim did a good job on the finances.'

His father pinned him with a withering stare, a stare that said, 'What the hell would you know about it?'

Everything, actually, you vile, bloated cunt.

His father looked away, shuffling papers on his desk. The clock ticked, his father wheezed, books pressed in all around: hundreds upon hundreds of volumes, thousands of them, their spines arranged in neat, serried ranks from one end of the room to the other and from floor to ceiling. They gave the place an unpleasantly leathery, segmented feel, like the interior of some monstrous, ossified stomach cavity. So far as William was aware, none of them had ever actually been opened, let alone read. They had been purchased by his grandfather as a job lot and were there simply for show, to create an illusion of depth and intellect. The Barrens didn't have much time for learning or culture. Money, that's what they had time for. Money and control. In that, at least, William was very much heir to the family tradition.

'I was talking to Hilary after the meeting,' he began, doing his best to keep his voice level. 'She thinks the Egypt tender could—'

His father cut him off with a sweep of the hand. Lifting a document from the desk, he held it up, moving it back and forth in front of William, something distinctly accusatory in the motion, as though he were a lawyer brandishing a damning piece of evidence.

'You want to tell me what this is about?'

The reason for the summons. No chatty preamble. Straight to business. Pretty much what he'd been expecting.

You are in control. You are strong.

'They were some ideas I had about the future of the company, Pa. Ways of moving it forward, taking us up to the next level. Thought you and the board might be interested. I've highlighted some possible—'

'You think the corporation needs ideas?'

William bit his lip. He'd known the document would spark a confrontation, had been readying himself for it, but now that he was here, in the eye of the storm . . .

'A business always needs ideas, Pa. What's that word the Nips use? *Kaizen.* Continual improvement.'

His father shifted in his seat, his bulk rising up like a wave about to slam on to a beach.

'You think the corporation needs *improvement?*'

You're fucking right it does, William thought. *Sure we're big, but we're unwieldy as well. Too many arms, too much going on, too much ballast. Other companies are tightening and streamlining, adapting, refocusing. We're just resting on our laurels. The tides are changing and we're not going with them. In a few years we'll be overtaken, beached. Get your hands off the tiller, old man. Time for a new captain. I'm* the future of Barren.

He remained silent.

'Ideas,' his father intoned, leafing through the document, his voice a rasping basso-profondo. 'Improvement.' He was shaking his head, his heavy-lidded eyes bright with ridicule.

'They're just thoughts, Pa,' said William, struggling to hold his nerve. 'I'm concerned we're pinning too many hopes on the Egyptian gas tender. If it doesn't come off—'

'It'll come off.'

'There's been a change of regime over there—'

'You're an expert in geo-politics now?'

'All I'm saying—'

His father let out a contemptuous snarl, reached an arm across his chest and hurled the document at William's head. It missed and fluttered away behind him, crashing to the carpet like a dead bird.

'I didn't put you on the board to have ideas, boy! I put you there to do what I tell you and only what I tell you. You think you know how to run this company better than me? Know better than I do what's good for it?'

William resisted the temptation to shout, *Yes I fucking do!*

'Forty years I've run Barren. I *am* Barren! I made it what it is today, and now suddenly my drug-snorting, whore-mongering wastrel of a son thinks he can waltz in and lecture me . . .'

The old man started coughing, rocking back and forth, the diseased honeycomb of his lungs buckling under the weight of his fury, his face turning a deep shade of purple. *Maybe he'll just choke himself to death right here and now*, thought William, *save us all a lot of trouble.* 'Whore-mongering wastrel!' The old man started in again, jabbing a trembling finger at William. 'Trying to tell me my business. To turn the board against me. Ideas – you've never had a single worthwhile goddamn . . .'

The tirade faltered as he was overcome by a renewed fit of coughing. He dragged a handkerchief from his pocket and held it to his mouth, then grabbed the plastic mask from the desk beside him and clamped it to his face, frantically drawing oxygen up the tube from the tank on the floor, eyes blazing like globs of molten iron. William forced himself to meet his father's gaze, to hold it, although, my God, it was hard, took every ounce of will he possessed. He managed it for a few seconds, then, feeling he'd just about made his point, shown he wasn't going to be intimidated (although he *was* intimidated, wanted to piss and shit his pants he felt so threatened), he turned and walked over to the document on the floor. Bending, he picked it up and smoothed down the crumpled pages, the rasping grate of his father's breathing pushing at his back like a predator gathering itself to pounce.

Once, as a child, years ago, when his mum had still been alive and *she* had still been around, William had drawn up a family tree. It had been a beautiful, intricate thing, modelled on one of the bur oaks that lined the mansion's front drive, the names of all the different family members hanging like acorns from its spreading branches. He had spent almost a month working on it, getting it just right, making sure he didn't leave anyone out, the names of the family's central male bloodline – his great-grandfather, grandfather, father and he himself – running down the trunk and highlighted in gold to emphasize their position at the very core of the family. He'd framed it with his own hands, helped by Arnold the gardener, who was good at stuff like that, and presented it to his father on his fiftieth birthday, confident that this would be the thing that opened the old man's heart, persuaded him that he, William, was a worthy successor to the family name. His father had given it only the most cursory of glances before putting it aside. 'I'm not sure *your* name should be in gold,' had been his only comment.

William thought of that family tree now as he looked down at the document in his hand. Twenty-five years ago he'd been crushed by his father's ingratitude. Today, having long ago abandoned any hope of gaining the old man's good favour, he was more sanguine about his reaction. He'd neither been looking for nor expecting approval. Rather, the document had been about throwing down a gauntlet. Putting his head above the parapet and alerting not just the old man, but the board as well that he was ready to start flexing his muscles. And his father knew it. Hence his fury. With a sudden thrill of understanding it struck William that his pa was frightened of *him*. The old bull elephant raging at the appearance of a younger, healthier rival in the heart of the jungle.

He turned, holding the thought, ready for the denouement.

'I want more control, Pa,' he said, unable to hide the tremor in his voice. 'I've asked you before, and now I'm asking you again. You can't go on for ever. It's time to start handing over the reins. I'm ready.'

His father's eyes burned fiercer than ever, the transparent rubber of the oxygen mask misting as he panted into it.

'Never,' he croaked.

'It's time, Pa. It was time a while ago.'

For a moment the old man just glared at him, his chest heaving. Then, slowly, deliberately, he lowered his oxygen mask, his eyes never leaving William, his monstrous weight looming at him across the desk like a boulder about to topple. The ticking of the clock seemed to deepen as though picking up and amplifying the tension in the room.

'It'll never be time!' Nathaniel Barren snarled, raising a baseball-glove-sized hand and slamming it down on the desk's leather surface. 'Do you understand me, boy? You will never lead Barren Corporation. Not now, not ever. You haven't got it in you. Never have, never will. And the sooner you get used to that idea, the better.'

He clamped the mask back to his face, heaving for breath. William stood silent in front of him. He'd always known it would be a waste of time, that his father would never yield, but he'd needed to bring it to a head. Assure himself the path he was taking was the only one open to him. He'd wanted to leave it a bit longer, move a few more pieces into place, but after the coked-up idiot he'd made of himself in the board meeting he felt a need to assert himself. Hence the document. And hence this meeting. The start of the endgame. He felt curiously light-headed. *You* are *strong. You* are *in control.* He stood a moment longer, forcing himself to hold his father's furious gaze. Then, with a nod, he turned, walked across to the door and opened it. As he stepped out into the corridor he looked back.

'She's dead, Pa,' he said. 'Dead and gone and she ain't coming back. It's only me now. I'm Barren. And that's an idea *you'd* better start getting used to.'

His father's voice thundered across the room as he closed the door. 'Over my dead body!'

'My thoughts exactly,' murmured William.

Outside the door he leant a moment against the panelled wall, breathing heavily, gathering himself, then walked back through the mansion and down the grand staircase, past the sombre faces of his ancestors. Stephen was waiting at the bottom.

'I trust your meeting went well, sir.'

'Pretty much as expected, Stephen. Pretty much as expected.'

The butler made no response to this, just stood impassively. William threw a glance back up the stairs, thinking of the day his own portrait would hang there, taking its rightful place in the Barren roll of honour. At the head of the Barren roll of honour. Then, clapping Stephen on the shoulder, he went out to his car and sped off down the drive. He hadn't touched the coke. Some highs just came naturally.

On the drive back up to Jerusalem, foot to the floor so as not to be late for his meeting with Dov Zisky, Ben-Roi put in an urgent call to George Aslanian at the Armenian Tavern. Yes, George confirmed, the Armenian word for gold, *vosgi*, could indeed be employed as a proper noun, as well as a regular noun or adjective.

'It's like . . . what's a Hebrew example? . . . *Chaim* or *Ilan*. They can be used as names, or as the words for "life" and "tree". Same principle.'

Which left Ben-Roi with a quandary. If the word Rivka Kleinberg had left indented all over the desk blotter in her apartment was actually a name rather than a specific reference to gold, then maybe the whole Barren/Romanian-gold-mine thing was a complete red herring. And if Barren was a red herring, maybe the Nemesis Agenda angle was too. Maybe half the leads he'd been chasing weren't leads at all. For a panicky moment he saw his entire case, or what little there was of it, unravelling in front of his eyes.

It passed swiftly. As he spooled back over the evidence, the dark, rocky mass of the Judaean Hills slowly closing in around him as the road curved and climbed, he saw there were still more than enough connections to suggest he was on the right track, even without the *vosgi* one. The photocopied articles on gold-smelting he'd found on Kleinberg's desk; the atlas bookmarked at a map of Romania; that British mining engineer who'd fallen down a hole in Egypt. *How the hell did that fit in?* Half a dozen signposts to reassure him.

As a rule, detectives distrust coincidences. In this instance, Ben-Roi concluded he *was* dealing with a coincidence. An unlikely one, certainly, but a coincidence nonetheless. Rivka Kleinberg had been interested in a trafficked Armenian prostitute whose name translated as 'gold', and at the same time, either because of something that prostitute had told her, or for a completely different reason, she had also been interested in a gold-mining operation run by Barren Corporation. The only other interpretation was that he *was* on completely the wrong track, and all the *other* connections were coincidental. And if there's one thing a detective hates more than a single coincidence, it's a collection of them.

By the time he came into Jerusalem and turned on to the ring road towards the Old City, he'd gone over and over it all and was satisfied he was on solid ground. He hadn't moved forward but, much to his relief, he hadn't gone backwards either.

One thing was for sure – he'd certainly earned a cold beer.

Putin's Pub was right at the eastern end of Jaffa Street, within sight of the Old City walls. A long, narrow space with a bar down one side, booths along the other and a back room with a dancefloor and projection screen, it used to be called Champs. A few years back, new owners had come on board and given the place a Russian-themed makeover: new name, new décor, new choice of beers and spirits. Despite the facelift, the place retained a general air of retro seediness, and, also, a general lack of clientele. In all the years he'd been coming here, Ben-Roi had never once seen it more than half full, and when he walked in tonight – fifteen minutes late – there were only six people present. An attractive middle-aged woman sitting on a stool chatting to the barman, two younger women in one of the booths and, in the other, Dov Zisky and a muscular, tanned man sporting a tight white T-shirt and diamond ear-stud. Ben-Roi bought himself a bottle of Tuborg and slipped into the seat beside them.

'Joel Regev,' said Zisky, introducing his companion. 'My computer-expert friend. Thought he might as well come along and talk to you direct.'

Ben-Roi shook hands with the man, who had the grip of a body-builder and looked about as far from the stereotypical computer geek as you could possibly get. He and Zisky were cradling bottles of Staropramen and sitting almost leg to leg, which made Ben-Roi think maybe they were more than just friends. They didn't say anything, and Ben-Roi didn't ask.

'Dov tells me you work in cyber security,' he began, glugging a mouthful of Tuborg.

Regev nodded, sipped from his own bottle. His biceps were huge, the left one decorated with a tattoo: a dagger with a rose curling round it.

'We advise companies on network protection,' he explained. 'Malware intrusion, hacking, that sort of thing. We also do some computer forensics work for you guys. We're advising Russian Yard on a cyber-fraud case at the moment.'

His voice was deep, masculine, the polar opposite of Zisky's effeminate drawl. For a moment Ben-Roi found himself staring at the two of them, wondering about the dynamic of their relationship. If indeed it was a relationship. Across the table Zisky's mouth tweaked into a barely discernible smile as if he could read the drift of his thoughts and was amused by them. Ben-Roi took another swig of his beer – nice and cold, refreshing – and made a show of focusing his attention on Regev.

'Dov said you knew something about a group called the Nemesis Agenda.'

'A bit,' replied Regev. 'What I've picked up from contacts and on the net. We actually did some consulting for one of their victims about six months back, big defence and security contractor down in Be'er Sheva. Nemesis had hacked their system, infected it with a virus that melted every hard drive on their network. Shut them down for the best part of a month.'

He glanced at Zisky, thumb flicking at the lip of his Staropramen bottle.

'I probably shouldn't be saying this, but at the time I couldn't help thinking good luck to them. According to the Nemesis website, the company was doing business with some pretty unpleasant regimes, supplying them with landmines, interrogation management systems' – he lifted his hands and flicked inverted commas in the air – 'for which, read torture equipment. I can't say I felt particularly good about myself helping to get them back up and running again, but then what do I know? I'm just a lowly computer nerd.'

Ben-Roi sensed movement beneath the table, thought Zisky might have been giving his friend a reassuring pat on the thigh. He couldn't be sure, and didn't try to look, although again, he caught a flicker of amusement on Zisky's face.

'I've printed some stuff off the web that might be helpful,' continued Regev. 'A couple of articles, a few chat-room threads –' he nudged Zisky, who produced a manila envelope and handed it to Ben-Roi – 'but to be honest, most of it's just supposition. Hard facts about the Agenda are pretty thin on the ground. It's what makes them so interesting. No one really knows anything about them. They're not like, say, Wikileaks, where it's common knowledge who's behind it. The guys who run Nemesis are shadows, completely invisible.'

Ben-Roi opened the envelope and had a quick flick through the sheaf of papers inside. 'So what *do* we know?'

'Well, they're good,' said Regev. 'You could start with that. The authorities have been trying to pin them down for years now – we're talking some of the best cyber-brains in the business – but the Agenda have always managed to keep one step ahead. The only real lead anyone's got is their website, and they've been extremely clever about keeping that out of reach. They host on offshore servers, proxy servers, ping servers, mirror off different servers, switch servers the moment anyone starts getting close to them. They also seem to be using some pretty sophisticated anonymizing technology.'

He clocked the bewildered look on Ben-Roi's face and laughed.

'Ignore the geek-spiel,' he said, waving a hand. 'All you really need to know is that no one's ever managed to shut the Nemesis website down. And no one's ever managed to get behind the website to the people who are actually running it. These guys are seriously tech savvy.'

'And they're targeting multinationals, big business?'

Regev nodded. 'Specifically multinationals involved in dodgy dealings. Third World exploitation, illegal polluting, corporate malpractice. Organizations with skeletons in the closet, basically. Nemesis gather the evidence, put it out there on the web, the public pick it up, the press . . . Trust me, it's caused a lot of companies a lot of problems. Big problems.'

Pretty much the picture Mordechai Yaron had painted earlier that day.

'Apparently they have different cells in different countries,' said Ben-Roi.

'That's one theory,' acknowledged Regev, 'although so far as I'm aware no one's ever proved it conclusively. We're pretty certain they started out in the US – there are various small, rather complex technological indicators to suggest that's the case. I won't bore you with all the details – there's some stuff about it in there.' He tapped the envelope.

'And there does appear to be an Israel connection,' he went on. 'Several of the people who've been targeted by the group claim they were using Hebrew words, and there seems to have been a disproportionate number of incidents on Israeli soil. It's not exactly definitive, but it would suggest they've got a presence here. Whether it's a cell, or a splinter group, or the original people simply relocated' – he shrugged – 'there's no way of saying. Nor whether they've got

208

people in other countries. They've got a contact e-mail on their web-site – routed round a dozen different ghost addresses on a dozen different servers, so again effectively untraceable – which would suggest that at least some of their information is coming from insider tip-offs. And the fact that everything gets channelled through a single website points to some sort of centrally organized structure. How it's organized, though, and who's organizing it, and how many people are part of it, and where they're based . . .'

He gave another shrug and downed the remainder of his beer. Ben-Roi asked if he could get him another, but Regev held a hand over the top of his bottle, as did Zisky. From the room at the back came the muted babble of football commentary, highlights of that evening's Haifa derby, Maccabi versus Hapo-el. Ben-Roi was a Maccabi man and would have liked to catch the game, but for the moment he zoned it out and focused on the discussion in hand.

'I was talking to someone this morning and he was saying these Nemesis people aren't just hackers. Apparently they're breaking and entering, using weapons, physical violence. More like Mossad than whistle-blowers, was how he described it.'

Regev smiled. 'That's possibly a slight exaggeration. It's not like they're going around assassinating people. Or at least not that I've ever heard of. But yes, they are ruthless. Violent, too, when the mood takes them. In that sense they've definitely upped the ante over the last few years.'

Ben-Roi's eyes narrowed. 'How do you mean?'

'Well, when they first came on the scene about six, seven years ago, they *were* just hacking. And launching the occasional virus attack. All cyber stuff, basically. But then – I think it was about three or four years ago – they firebombed an office in Tel-Aviv, some big multinational, the first time they'd ever done anything like that. No one was actually hurt but it was still a big departure. And from that point on their tactics have definitely been a lot more . . . confrontational: forced entry, sabotage, kidnapping executives, forcing them to make filmed confessions. There's a rather gruesome one on their site at the moment. Some French guy whose company was involved in shady dealings down in the Congo. It's only been up twenty-four hours and apparently there's already been a mass protest outside the company's head office in Paris and half a dozen cyber attacks on their computer network. That's the sort of impact the Agenda has.'

He sat back and folded his arms, glancing over at the next-door booth where the two women had erupted into peals of laughter. He was silent a moment, then looked back at Ben-Roi.

'Interestingly, the change in tactics does seem to have coincided with the appearance of this Israeli cell,' he said, 'splinter group, faction, whatever you want to call them. They seem to be the ones who are behind most, if not all, of the violent direct action; who've shifted Nemesis from a purely cyber-based organization to something more like a full-on guerrilla outfit. Or terrorist outfit, depending on your viewpoint.'

'Any idea why the shift?' This from Zisky, his first contribution to the conversation.

'No one really knows for sure,' replied Regev, 'although there's been some pretty intense web chatter on the subject. I've included some of it in the printouts.'

He tapped the envelope again.

'Majority opinion seems to be that certain people within Nemesis wanted to take a more hardline approach and, for reasons best known to themselves, relocated to Israel to do it. They've stayed within the Nemesis fold to the extent that they've continued feeding material into the website, but alongside that have got on with pursuing their own more militant agenda. A sort of agenda within the Agenda, if you like. It seems a reasonable explanation. Certainly more reasonable than that of the conspiracy theorists who argue it's all an elaborate plot to discredit Nemesis cooked up by the security services and/or a cabal of multinationals. I really can't see that one scanning at all.'

Another peal of laughter rang out from the next-door seat. In the room at the back of the bar the football commentary became more animated, and there was a sudden roar of cheering, presumably as one of the sides scored. Ben-Roi dipped his head, trying to catch who it was. Hapo-el. Shit. He listened a moment, then again zoned it out.

'This Israeli lot,' he said, turning his attention back to Regev. 'You haven't come across any mention of them being linked to Mitzpe Ramon, have you?'

Regev shook his head. 'Dov told me you thought there might be a connection. If there is, I've certainly never heard about it.' He flicked at the top of his bottle. 'Although there *does* seem to be a connection with a company called Barren Corporation. Dov said you were interested in them as well.'

Ben-Roi sat forward. 'What sort of connection?'

'Well, Nemesis seem to have a bit of a thing for Barren,' said Regev. 'Or *against* Barren. I did a quick breakdown . . . hang on –' he opened the manila envelope and flicked through its contents, pulling out a sheet of A4.

'These are all the instances in which Nemesis have targeted Barren. Or at least all the *reported* instances. As you can see, there're quite a few of them. Way more than any other company, so far as I can make out.'

Ben-Roi stared down at the sheet, counted off nineteen separate incidents, stretching back seven years.

'They were one of the first companies Nemesis ever cyber-attacked,' continued Regev, 'and they seem to have been going for them on and off ever since, particularly over the last few years, since this Israeli group have come on the scene. That bombing I told you about in Tel-Aviv, the first time Nemesis had ever done anything violent . . .'

'Barren?'

Regev nodded. 'They've also broken into their offices, sabotaged a couple of their installations . . . it's almost like they've got a vendetta against them. More than almost like – they clearly *have* got a vendetta against them.'

'Any idea why?' asked Zisky.

'Again, there's a fair bit of chat-room speculation on the subject,' replied Regev. 'Everything from a disgruntled employee throwing in his lot with Nemesis to a rival multinational somehow using Nemesis to undermine their competitors. None of it really stacks up. My own guess, and it *is* just a guess, is that Nemesis are pissed off because they can't actually get anything on Barren. The worst they ever seem to have uncovered about them were some health and safety failings in one of their operations in Australia. Hardly earth-shattering. It's like Barren's the one that got away, and they've never forgiven them for that. Taken it as some sort of personal insult.' He shrugged. 'Then again, maybe I'm talking complete bullshit. Like I said – when it comes to the Nemesis Agenda, there are a lot of theories out there, but almost nothing by way of hard fact. For all we know, the whole thing could be run by a bunch of Martians.'

Ben-Roi smiled. Regev tilted his head and murmured something to Zisky, which Ben-Roi didn't catch, then glanced at his watch, a huge silver Tag Heuer that looked more like something off an aircraft instrument panel than a timepiece.

'I should probably be getting off,' he said.

'Sure I can't get you another one?'

'Better not. I've got an early start tomorrow.'

He gave Zisky a quick squeeze on the shoulder and stood. Ben-Roi slid out of the booth to let him pass. The two of them shook hands.

'I'll have an ask around,' said Regev. 'Let Dov know if anything else comes to mind.'

'Appreciated,' said Ben-Roi. 'And thanks for the printouts.'

Regev waved a hand, started to turn, then swung back. 'Listen, it's none of my business, but Dov mentioned this was to do with that woman in the cathedral. Don't worry, he didn't give me any details . . .'

Ben-Roi shook his head to show he didn't really care if Zisky had.

'For what it's worth, I really can't see Nemesis being involved in something like that. I'm certainly not condoning their methods, but to date they've never targeted anyone who didn't . . .'

'Deserve it?'

Regev grunted. 'I just think they have a very specific remit. And murdering female journalists doesn't really fit the profile. It's only an opinion and, like I said, I'm a computer geek, so what the hell do I know? I just thought I'd mention it. Don't keep him out too late. He needs his beauty sleep.'

He winked at Zisky, nodded at Ben-Roi and left.

Ben-Roi bought another round.

'Nice guy,' he said, sliding back into his place and handing Zisky the Jack Daniel's he'd requested.

'Certainly is,' acknowledged Zisky, accepting the drink and moving over to make more room.

'Really nice.'

Zisky didn't rise to that, just sipped his bourbon and gave another of those knowing half-smiles. Ben-Roi thought about pushing the conversation, trying to find out more – if Regev had been a woman he would certainly have pressed for details, engaged Zisky in some risqué banter. In this instance it didn't seem appropriate. Instead he took a swig of his beer and filled him in on the *vosgi* situation. The kid's smile faded.

'I'm sorry,' he said. 'I should have—'

Ben-Roi waved a hand. 'It happens. If I had a shekel for every time I'd got the wrong end of the stick, I'd have enough shekels to . . .'

'Buy a better stick?'

Ben-Roi smiled, laid an arm across the top of the seat. He'd been tired when he first arrived at the bar. The Tuborg had sharpened him up, given him a second wind.

'You said you'd found some stuff on Barren?'

Zisky produced a second manila envelope. It was bulging with papers. Not for the first time, Ben-Roi had to take his hat off to the kid's efficiency. There was enough material here to keep him up all night.

'I'm afraid I didn't have time to do a full report,' said Zisky, pulling a set of stapled sheets from the envelope and handing them over. 'I've done some bullet points which might help.'

Hats off again. Ben-Roi ran his eyes down the sheet. 'You want to give me the highlights?'

'Well, the company's big. Fifty-billion-dollar turnover, offices round the world, several dozen subsidiaries, interests in everything from oil drilling to gold-mining to biofuels. Secretive as well. Doesn't welcome publicity. Head honcho's a guy called Nathaniel Barren . . .'

He fumbled in the envelope and produced an image – a huge, glowering, bearded man in a tweed suit.

'He's been chairman for the last forty years. Bit of a hard nut, by all accounts, although it seems he's not in great health now. Son's a loose cannon, apparently.'

Another image came out, this one of a younger man, blond-haired and handsome, his mouth curled into something midway between a smile and a sneer.

'Had a few run-ins with the law. Drugs, assault – reportedly tried to throttle a hooker a few years back. Father had to pull a lot of strings to get him off the rap. It's all in there.' Zisky touched a finger to one of the bullet points.

'Anything about that Romanian mine?'

'All above board, apparently. Barren have been running it since 2005 and there hasn't been any controversy. Good relations with the Romanian government and the local community. *And* the green lobby – seems they've done some deal to recycle the worst of the waste back in the States, which means there haven't been any of the usual run-ins with environmental groups. Everyone's happy, basically.'

Ben-Roi sucked on his beer. Again, the thought struck him: Maybe I *have* got it wrong. Maybe it *is* all a red herring.

'There *were* a couple of things that jumped out at me,' continued Zisky.

'Go on.'

'A big Israel link, for one. Barren have got interests all over the country: stakes in a potash mine down on the Dead Sea, an offshore gas field up by Haifa, a big diamond cutting operation in Tel-Aviv. Political influence, too. I spoke to your friend on *Ha'aretz*, and he told me Barren are a major donor to Kadima, Likud *and* Yisrael Beiteinu. That gives them a lot of leverage. "One of the untouchables" was how he described them.'

He glanced up as a group of young men came in through the door, laughing and chatting. They spread along the bar and ordered pints of Kasteel.

'There's a personal angle as well,' he added, turning back to Ben-Roi. 'Seems Nathaniel Barren's wife was Israeli. Died a few years back. Car smash. He's never got over it, apparently.'

Ben-Roi sipped and pondered, again trying to compute how any of this might link in with Kleinberg's murder, again failing to come up with any obvious explanation. At the bar the attractive middle-aged woman had turned slightly on her stool, assessing the new arrivals. A cougar eyeing potential prey. One of the men, spotty and pale-faced, smiled at her and raised a hand in greeting. *Out of your depth, son*, thought Ben-Roi. He watched a moment, amused by the tableau, then:

'What was the other thing?'

'Sorry?'

Zisky, too, was analysing the dynamic at the bar.

'You said a couple of things leapt out at you.'

'Right, yes. Well, Barren have got an Egypt connection as well. According to your friend, they've cultivated some pretty close business and political links there over the years. They've got an office in Cairo, interests in several mining operations. Seems they're currently tendering for the rights to some big gas field out in the Sahara. Apparently if it comes off it'll be one of the biggest deals they've ever done. *The* biggest deal. Seems this Nathaniel Barren's staking his reputation on it.'

At the bar, the men had got their drinks and started trooping off to

214

the back room to watch the football. The spotty guy said something to the middle-aged woman, but she just shrugged and turned her back on him, not interested. Ben-Roi felt sorry for him. It had been the same story when he'd been that age.

'You didn't come across anything about sex-trafficking, did you?' he asked.

'What, like are Barren involved in it?'

Zisky's tone pretty much answered the question. Whatever other pies Barren had its fingers in, illicit prostitution was unlikely to be one of them. Ben-Roi took another punt.

'How about a guy called Samuel Pinsker?'

Zisky looked like he recognized the name. 'Remind me.'

'British mining engineer. Fell down a hole in Luxor. Kleinberg was reading about him in one of those articles I told you about.'

'Right. No, he didn't crop up.' He rolled the last half centimetre of bourbon around the bottom of his glass. 'Although Luxor did.'

Ben-Roi sat forward, motioned for Zisky to tell him more.

'Well, it seems Barren have been pouring a lot of money into the country lately, funding quite a few social projects. All to do with that Saharan gas field tender I mentioned.'

'Bribery?'

'Your friend Natan Tirat called it "profile raising", but I guess it comes down to the same thing. Anyway, one of the projects is a big museum in Luxor, in the Valley of the Kings. Barren have paid for the whole thing, apparently, laid out a good few million on it. Seems Nathaniel Barren himself is coming over for the opening. I guess it's a link of sorts, although I can't exactly see the relevance.'

He shrugged, gave his Jack Daniel's another swirl and downed it. Ben-Roi did the same with his Tuborg. In the back room the men had started singing a Green Apes supporters' anthem – badly out of tune, but at least they were rooting for the right team. The girls in the neighbouring booth stood and left, still giggling; a moment later the attractive middle-aged woman did the same, leaving just them and the barman in the front room.

'Another one?' asked Zisky.

Ben-Roi glanced at his watch – past ten – and shook his head.

'I think that's enough for one night. We can go through it all in more detail tomorrow. Like your friend said, young chap like you needs your beauty sleep.'

Zisky rolled his eyes in a mock patronized look, but didn't argue. He slid from the seat and pulled on his jacket.

'Next round's on me.'

'I'll keep you to that. And thanks for the notes. Great work.'

Zisky's eyes twinkled, as though he was pleased by the comment. He didn't say anything, just nodded, flicked a salute and headed down the bar.

'Give my best to Joel,' Ben-Roi called after him.

He got a finger in response, which made him grin. The kid was OK, was becoming one of the team.

Once he was gone, Ben-Roi changed his mind and bought himself a nightcap, a Jameson's on ice. He popped his head into the back room to check the football score – still one–nil to Hapo-el – then settled back into his seat and texted Sarah, wishing her and the baby goodnight. He got one straight back, wishing him the same, followed almost immediately by a second reply, this one addressed 'To Daddy' and signed 'Bubuxx'. He smiled. Throwing a glance at the barman to make sure he wasn't looking, he lifted the mobile to his lips and kissed it.

'And you think *Zisky's* gay,' he muttered, pocketing the phone and stretching out his legs. 'Get any softer and you'll turn into a fucking marshmallow!'

He chuckled, sipped the Jameson's and circled his glass on the tabletop, gazing distractedly at a framed print on the wall, retro-Soviet, advertising cigarettes. Some piped music came on, Dire Straits, 'Brothers in Arms'. The thick, smoky guitar intro weaved through the room like drifting mist. His thoughts picked up the rhythm and went with it, floating this way and that, first to Sarah and the baby, then the spotty guy trying to chat up the woman at the bar, then to Zisky and Regev, then, inevitably, to the case.

This was always his best thinking time, right at the end of the day, when his body was gearing down and his head starting to unclutter, and he allowed his mind to go where it wanted, not pushing things, just kicking back and letting his thoughts meander, weaving randomly through everything he'd discovered tonight, today, over the last couple of days, seeing where they took him.

And where they took him, over and over again, like a visitor always drawn back to the same pictures in a gallery, were to two particular aspects of the investigation.

The girl Maria/Vosgi. She was the person on which it all hinged, absolutely no doubt about it. And, also, Egypt. That was the *place* on which it all hinged. Equally no doubt. Barren, Nemesis, Pinsker, Kleinberg's flight to Alexandria, the Sinai route used by the sex-traffickers – every thread seemed to intersect with Egypt at some point, all roads seemed to lead there. Egypt was where the answers were. Maybe *the* answer.

He took another sip of his whiskey and slid his gaze from the print to the barman, tracking him as he moved along the counter dabbing at stains with a J-cloth. Their eyes met and the man made a pouring motion, asking if Ben-Roi wanted a top-up. He raised a hand in thank you and shook his head. From the back room came a shout of 'We've *all* shagged your girlfriend, Joni!' followed by a burst of raucous laughter; Knopfler's guitar hummed and growled; ice cubes clinked as Ben-Roi rolled them around his glass.

Egypt. There were some things he could follow up himself, or else get Zisky to look into. Calls that could be made, information gathered, background checked. You could only do so much over the phone, e-mail and internet, however. What the case really needed was some-one chasing things on the ground. Someone with a knowledge of the country and its language. And that meant putting in a request to National Police Headquarters, from whom official clearance was required for any dealings with foreign authorities, particularly Arab ones. And official clearance could take days. A lot of days, knowing the glacial speed at which the National Police bureaucracy moved. He'd get on to them first thing, set the wheels in motion, but for the moment it looked as if Egypt, important as it clearly was, would have to sit on the back burner.

He sighed and lifted his glass, ready to drain off the last of the Jameson's and head home, weary now, the day catching up with him. As he did so his eyes crunched, as if he had been struck by a thought. Because of course there was another option. Someone who *was* on the ground. An old contact of his. An old *friend*. They'd worked together a while back, on that extraordinary Hannah Schlegel case, had stayed in touch, although it had been a while since they'd last spoken, twelve months or more, which is why he hadn't thought of him immediately. He glanced at his watch – late, but not too late – and, almost without realizing he was doing it, pulled out his cell phone.

Four years ago, languishing in the abyss after the death of his fiancée Galia, convinced the rest of his days would be lived in darkness and grief, two people had come along and shown him the way back up to daylight. Sarah had been one. The other . . .

He brought up his contacts list and scrolled through until he came to the Ks. There was only one name there. He smiled when he saw it. It had been way too long, would be good to hear his voice again.

He checked his watch a second time, then moved his thumb across and pressed the dial button.

LUXOR

Khalifa was on the roof of his apartment block when his mobile went off, sitting on an upturned crate gazing out across the twinkling Luxor nightscape.

He came up here most nights, once he'd got Zenab off to sleep. He would hold her hand, and stroke her long black hair, and sing tunelessly to her until eventually her breathing settled and her body relaxed, and the tight, anxious line of her mouth softened and curled – not so much into a smile, more an expression of relief that the waking was over and she could once again lose herself in the nothingness of slumber. Later the nightmares would come, jagged shards of memory scratching at her subconscious, turning sleep into as much of a torment as wakefulness. For a couple of hours she would be at peace, however, swaddled in a blanket of dreamless oblivion, and he could come up here for some peace of his own, secure in the knowledge that their bedroom window was directly beneath him and if she called out he would hear her and be down in a matter of seconds.

He liked the roof. It was the one part of their new home for which he had come to feel any degree of affinity, particularly at night. By day Luxor could be a dull, monochrome place, the harsh sunlight bleaching away the town's colour, amplifying its drabness. With darkness, paradoxically, the colour returned: the bright, translucent green of the mosque minarets, the icy striplight-white of the cafés and shops, the garish neon of five-star hotels, a thousand tiny spatters of orange and yellow from the windows and streetlamps and car headlights.

Night transformed the town, cancelling out all the characterless concrete and crumbling architecture, reducing everything to primary colours: clean and bright and simple. Sitting on his crate and gazing out always soothed Khalifa, in the same way that climbing the Qurn and shooting on the police rifle range soothed him. Allowed him to feel, if not better about things, at least not so painfully aware of them.

But now his mobile was ringing and the spell was broken.

He snapped to his feet and fumbled the phone from his pocket, a pulse of anxiety shooting from his chest down to his gut, as it always did these days when he received an unexpected call at an unusual hour. For a brief moment scenarios flashed through his head, dreadful scenarios: sirens, hospitals, running feet, piteous howling. Then he saw the caller's name and his breathing eased. He sat back down and stared at the phone, rubbing his temple with thumb and forefinger. There was a time he would have been glad of the call, delighted. He owed the man his life, after all; they'd been through a lot together. Tonight his immediate reaction was annoyance that the caller should have rung so late and scared him like that. Annoyance and, also, a dull, weary dread that he was going to have to go through it all again, tell yet another person what had happened and how everything had gone so wrong for him and his family. Relive the whole thing. And then there'd be the embarrassed silence at the other end of the line, the fumbling for words, the blurted I'm-so-sorry-if-there's-anything-I-can-dos – the reminder, if Khalifa ever needed a reminder, that he had become someone indelibly marked with tragedy. That whatever else he had done and would do in his life, it was this that now defined him.

He dangled the phone, its trill echoing through the hot Luxor night, unable to bring himself to answer, thinking he'd just let it go to voice-mail. But then to do so would simply be putting off the inevitable. He couldn't avoid him for ever, would have to talk to him some time. And he *had* saved his life, that night four years ago, in Germany, when he'd carried him out of the burning mine. He owed him. Whatever his own personal problems, Khalifa took the debts of friend-ship seriously.

'Dammit,' he muttered.

He allowed the mobile to ring a couple more times, steeling him-self, staring across at the Elnas Mosque, the slim spike of its minaret seeming to spear the moon like a needle puncturing a duck egg.

Then, just at the point when the phone was about to click over to voicemail, he drew a breath, pressed answer and held the handset up to his ear.

'Hello, my friend,' he said quietly.

JERUSALEM

The moment he heard Khalifa's voice, Ben-Roi broke into a broad smile and held up his glass as if toasting the Egyptian.

'Hello to you too, you cheeky Muslim cunt!'

It was how they always greeted each other, with a cheery insult to their respective cultures, a nod to the first time they had met, when they had argued and very nearly come to blows. Traditionally Khalifa would respond by calling Ben-Roi an 'arrogant Jew bastard'. On this occasion he merely gave a low *hrumph* to acknowledge the joke and asked Ben-Roi how he was doing.

'Great, fantastic. You?'

'Fine, thank you.'

'I didn't wake you up, did I?'

Khalifa assured him he hadn't.

'What's it been? A year?'

'At least,' replied Khalifa.

'Time flies.'

'It certainly does.'

'God knows where it goes.'

Khalifa mumbled something Ben-Roi didn't catch. He couldn't be sure, but he got the impression the Egyptian was slightly out of sorts. Softly spoken at the best of times, tonight he sounded positively subdued. Ben-Roi wondered if maybe he should have left the call till tomorrow.

'How's Zenab?' he asked, deciding he might as well push on with the conversation now he'd started it.

'She's . . . OK.' The reply was hesitant, evasive almost. 'Sarah?'

'We split up.'

There was a fractional pause.

'I'm sorry. When?'

'A few months ago.'

220

'I am so sorry.'

'Me too. All my fault, of course. I'm an arsehole.'

Ben-Roi thought Khalifa might pick up on this, throw out some witty riposte, but he didn't say anything. There was another pause, awkward – the Egyptian definitely seemed out of sorts. Away to Ben-Roi's right the bar door banged open and the two young women who had left fifteen minutes ago came back in, arms round each other's shoulders. He watched them as they tottered up to the bar and ordered vodka-Cokes, then:

'Hey, I've got some news.'

The click of a lighter echoed down the line, followed by the sound of inhaling breath.

'Don't tell me: you made peace with the Palestinians?'

That was more like it! That was the Khalifa he knew and loved!

'Even better!' laughed Ben-Roi. 'Certainly more incredible.'

He let the comment hang, building things up, then: 'Sarah's pregnant. I'm going to be a father!'

He said it loud, relishing the announcement. So loud that the barman and the two young women heard him. The barman gave a thumbs-up; the women clapped and shouted *Mazel tov*. From Khalifa there was nothing.

'I'm going to be a father,' repeated Ben-Roi, thinking the Egyptian hadn't heard him.

'*Mabruk*,' said Khalifa. 'I am very happy for you.'

He didn't sound it, his tone flat and expressionless, which surprised Ben-Roi. Needled him, in fact. Khalifa was one of the few people he hadn't yet told – just about the only person – and he'd been looking forward to his reaction, had had it in the back of his mind from the moment he'd decided to call him. The lack of reaction was . . . insulting almost. OK, it had been over a year since they had last been in touch – four since they had seen each other face to face – and Khalifa clearly wasn't in the best of moods, but even so he would have expected at least some enthusiasm on his part. Fatherhood was a big thing, after all, something to celebrate. And Khalifa wasn't celebrating. Ben-Roi wondered if maybe he didn't approve of the domestic set-up, of him having a child out of wedlock. Yes, that must be it. Different cultures, different ways of doing things.

'Obviously me and Sarah not being together any more makes things a bit more complicated,' he acknowledged, tackling the issue head on, 'but we're still close, and, trust me, whatever happens I'm going to be there for her and the baby. And who knows, once he arrives – actually we don't know it *is* a he yet, although between you and me I've got a feeling it's going to be a boy . . . Anyway, babies change things, you know that, so maybe once he or she arrives Sarah and I might give it another try, see if we can patch things up, you know, start over, the three of us together . . .'

He was rambling. Shouldn't have had the Jameson's, not on an empty stomach.

'The point is, I'm not going to be one of these absentee fathers,' he continued. 'I'm in for the long haul. The fact that me and Sarah aren't living together won't affect anything. This baby's going to have the best home in the world and the most loving parents. I'm so excited, Khalifa. *So* excited. I'm going to be a father!'

He could feel his voice starting to crack, his eyes welling up. Definitely shouldn't have had the Jameson's.

'*Mabruk*,' repeated Khalifa. 'I am very happy for you. For both of you.'

The same blank tone, the same absence of emotion. Ben-Roi's jaw tightened. *Miserable bastard*, he thought. *Here I am pouring out my heart and you can't even make the effort to sound like you mean what you're saying. Maybe it* is *against Muslim principles, but you could at least pretend for the sake of friendship. A fine state of affairs when I get more of a reaction from a barman and a pair of pissed-up dolly birds than from someone whose life I saved.*

'Listen, maybe it wasn't a good idea to call so late,' he said, unable to hide the annoyance in his voice. 'There was something I wanted to ask you, to do with a case I'm working on, but this obviously isn't the right—'

'No, no, please, it's fine. If there is something I can do for you . . .'

The man sounded borderline spaced, completely disconnected, like he was on drugs. Perhaps he *was* on drugs, thought Ben-Roi. Was ill or something. Maybe *that* was the explanation.

'You OK, Khalifa?'

Silence.

'You OK?' he repeated. 'You don't seem . . . I mean, I don't want to make a big thing of it, but I'm about to have a baby and I get the impression you're not particularly pleased for me. Not even particularly interested.'

There was another soft rasp as the Egyptian pulled on his cigarette. When he spoke again he sounded genuinely apologetic.

'Forgive me, my friend. I *am* interested. And happy for you. *Really* happy. To have a child is a wonderful thing. It's just that . . .'

Another rasp, another exhalation. Ben-Roi's annoyance gave way to a vague rumble of concern.

'Just that what?'

In the back room the football commentary was ramping up again, accompanied by shouts of 'Go, Katan!' and 'Cross it!'

'Just that what, Khalifa? Is something wrong?'

Glasses clinked at the bar, accompanied by a renewed explosion of giggling. Dire Straits seemed somehow to have morphed into Britney Spears's 'Toxic'.

'Khalifa?'

'Cross it, fuck sake!'

'Khalifa?'

'Actually yes, something is wrong. Something . . .'

A muffled choke echoed down the line, which Ben-Roi might have taken for a sob had it not been for all the ambient racket. The rumble of concern grew stronger.

'What's happened? Tell me, Khalifa.'

There was yet another pause – it was like the conversation was on some sort of time delay – then the Egyptian started to explain, something about a boat, an accident. His voice was lost in a sudden, deafening eruption of cheering from the back room as Maccabi Haifa finally got the ball in the net and brought the scores level. Ben-Roi held a hand over one ear and ducked his head down almost to the level of the tabletop, trying to block out the noise.

'I'm sorry, I missed that. What did you . . . ?'

Everyone was bellowing and shouting, even the girls.

'Khalifa, I'm sorry, I can't—'

One of the young men came leaping down the steps into the bar and charged the length of the room pumping his fists in the air. Another followed, and then another, the three of them doing an impromptu conga, which made the girls scream with delight. Ben-Roi waved a hand, trying to get them all to quieten down, but to no avail. With no sign of the celebrations diminishing, he told Khalifa to hang on, stood and went outside, pulling the door to behind him.

Suddenly everything went very quiet.

'That's better,' he said, pacing down the deserted street. 'It was all kicking off in there, I couldn't hear a bloody thing. Now what were you saying? What's happened?'

This time Khalifa's voice came through loud and clear. It stopped Ben-Roi in his tracks.

'My son died. There was an accident on the Nile and my son Ali was killed. I've lost my little boy. Oh God, Ben-Roi, I've lost my little boy.'

LUXOR

Even now, almost a year on, Khalifa wasn't even close to coming to terms with what had happened. Couldn't imagine a time when he ever would come to terms with it. He'd lost his eldest son, his golden boy. How could you ever rest easy with that weighing on your heart?

They'd been at it for months apparently, ever since they'd found the skiff abandoned in a reed bank. Ali and a group of his friends, invincible fourteen-year-olds on the lookout for fun and adventure. They had patched the boat up, filched one oar from a felucca-yard down by Karnak, fabricated another from some old scrap wood, started taking it out on the Nile. Nothing too daring at first: a splash up and down the eastern shoreline, a hop across the narrow channel to Banana Island where they would build camps and eat sweets and smoke pilfered cigarettes. All perfectly harmless.

As time had gone on, however, they had grown bolder. Once they had persuaded a motorboat owner to tow them all the way up to the Nile road bridge so they could drift the ten kilometres back downriver; another time they had paddled around to the far side of Banana Island and out to the buoys marking sand bars to the west of the island.

On the night of the tragedy, six of them, including Ali, had set off on their greatest adventure yet, a voyage right the way across the river to the far shore and back again.

It had been planned meticulously. For weeks they had been hoarding food and drinks and cigarettes to sustain them on their epic journey; on the chosen night each boy had claimed to be going to a sleepover at one of the other boys' so as not to arouse parental suspicion. They had rendezvoused after dark at a small inlet well south of Luxor, loaded the boat, taken a vow of eternal friendship in case of shipwreck or enemy attack – a playful gesture that in the event had proved agonizingly prescient.

And then they had pushed off, feeling like the greatest explorers that had ever lived. No lifejackets, of course, but then they could all swim, so why would they need them?

They had suffered an early setback when, barely on to the river, the boat had sprung a leak. They should have turned back immediately, but they had been anticipating the adventure for so long, were so excited and pumped up about the whole thing, that they had ploughed on regardless, two of the boys bailing with plastic pots while the others propelled the boat with the oars plus a pair of wooden planks they had pressed into service to give them extra momentum.

After the unpromising start, things had got back on track and, with the leak under control and the Nile flowing slow and calm, they had made it all the way out to the middle of the river without further mishap.

Then, however, everything had started to unravel.

In the first of the series of random events that would combine to shunt an innocuous situation inexorably towards tragedy, a police motor launch, patrolling well south of its normal remit, had spotted the skiff, swung past and ordered them back to land.

The other boys had been all for waiting for the launch to disappear and continuing their adventure. Ali – son of a policeman – had insisted they comply with the order. (How many times had Khalifa berated himself for not teaching his boy to be more disrespectful of authority?)

And so they had turned – with disappointed groans and much playful ribbing of Mr Goody-two-shoes-always-do-what-I'm-told – and started back the way they had come. Only to discover that the current, which had been perfectly manageable on the way out, was for some reason much more aggressive in the opposite direction.

'It was like the river didn't want to let us get back to shore,' recalled the one boy to have survived the tragedy, and from whose testimony the story had slowly been pieced together. 'The current kept pulling us north and pushing us back towards the middle. Every inch was a fight.'

The makeshift oar had snapped in half; one of the wooden rowing planks had been dropped and swept off into the night. The leak had rapidly worsened, shipping water faster than the bailers could empty it. By the time they had dragged themselves half the distance back to the east bank, the skiff was effectively unmanoeuvrable and the boys were all exhausted.

Which was when they spotted the barge.

At first they weren't alarmed. It was a long way away, well over a kilometre, a distant black scratch on the moon-silvered surface of the river, and although it seemed to be heading directly for them, well out of the normal shipping channel over by the western shore, none of them doubted that its forward lookout would spot them in time and signal an adjustment in course.

The adjustment never came. As the current swept them north, and the barge held its relentless line south, the boys started to grow worried, and then scared. They began shouting and waving their arms, trying to warn the barge away, at the same time furiously splashing at the water in an effort to claw themselves out of its path.

To no avail. The skiff swept downriver, the barge ploughed up, the two of them locked into a seemingly irreversible trajectory, the distance between them growing narrower by the second.

'Like two trains running towards each other on the same track,' was how one eyewitness on the shore described it.

'We just sort of froze,' said the survivor. 'We could see the barge getting closer, but it was like it was all happening in slow motion, in a dream. I remember Ali shouting we should all jump overboard, but we couldn't move. Right up to the last minute we thought they'd see us and change course.'

Eventually the barge's forward lookout did spot the skiff, alerted by a horn blast from the police motor launch which had come back to make sure the boys had done what they were told. The lookout had screamed at the wheelman who had frantically spun the rudder in an effort to avert collision, but by then it was way too late, less than a hundred metres now separating the skiff and the towering scalpel of the barge's prow.

According to one of the river police, at the last moment the boys had all stood and wrapped their arms around each other, as if by sheer force of friendship they might hold a thousand tonnes of metal at bay (to his dying day that image would haunt Khalifa, six terrified children bonded in a final, hopeless embrace).

And then, like a sledgehammer pulverizing a matchbox, the barge had hit.

Four of the boys were killed instantly, sucked under the water and cut to shreds by the vessel's giant propellers (only two recognizable bodies were ever found). A fifth managed by some miracle to thrash his way clear of the scene and was rescued by the police motor launch, so traumatized that for a week after the disaster he wouldn't speak a single word.

A sixth boy had also lived – Ali. His unconscious, waterlogged body had been spotted thirty minutes after the accident by the police launch, tangled face-down in a raft of *ward-i-nil*. He was plucked from the river and rushed ashore to Luxor General, where he was recognized by Rasha al-Zahwi, the paediatrician wife of Khalifa's friend Omar, who was covering the late shift in the hospital's emergency unit. It was she who had called the Khalifas to tell them what had happened.

When they arrived at the hospital and saw their boy on the life support – ashen-faced, wire-covered, an intubation pipe protruding from his mouth like some monstrous worm – Zenab had collapsed. Khalifa had helped her up and got her on to a chair at the head of the bed, assuring her it was all going to be OK even though he had known instinctively it wasn't. Then, not caring what anyone thought of him, oblivious to the doctors and nurses bustling all around, he had climbed on to the bed beside his boy and held him, telling him how much he loved him, pleading with him to stay with them, pleading with Allah to be merciful, humming 'Let's Go Fly A Kite' from *Mary Poppins*, which even at the age of fourteen was still Ali's favourite DVD.

For six days and six nights they had held vigil, not once leaving their son's bedside. There was never any hope. He'd been under the water for too long. His heart might have continued to beat, but his brain, according to the doctors, was to all intents and purposes dead. He never regained consciousness; Allah in His infinite wisdom chose, on this occasion, not to grant a miracle. The six days were, in a sense, simply an extended leave-taking.

On the seventh day they had agreed to let him go.

Khalifa had insisted that he should be the one to do it – it was too personal a thing, too intimate to entrust to a stranger. They had kissed Ali, and held him close, and told him over and over again how much they loved him, how much joy he'd brought them, how he would always be a part of their lives. Then, each of them clasping one of his hands, both weeping uncontrollably, they had said a final goodbye and Khalifa had leant across and switched off the life support.

Fourteen years before he had watched his son coming into the world – delivered at home in the bedroom of the apartment that would in a month's time be demolished so tourists would have something interesting to photograph.

Now he watched him taking his leave of it, his boy's beautiful, precious, irreplaceable life slowly fading to a monotonal flatline on the screen of the hospital heart monitor.

The agony of it was indescribable, the sorrow beyond any sorrow he had ever thought it possible to experience.

Zenab had never recovered. She had barely spoken a word since, just spent her days looking through photo albums and watching Ali's *Mary Poppins* DVD and dusting the room they had made for him in their new apartment. Even now, nine months on, she still woke every morning with the same bereft howl of 'I miss him!'

Khalifa had taken an extended leave of absence to nurse her through the worst of it, and, also, to be there for Batah and Yusuf, who had both been devastated by the loss of their brother (although with the resilience of youth they had swiftly assimilated the loss and got on with their lives). In an uncharacteristic display of decency, Chief Hassani had not only swung them the new apartment, but had also insisted Khalifa be paid a full wage while he was away, which had at least made things easier on a practical level. Khalifa still wasn't sure whether to feel gratitude for the gesture, or resentment at the fact he was now such a pitiful figure even a renowned tough-nut like the chief felt sorry for him.

In the early days – blank, grey, disbelieving days, like a monochrome dream from which he could never wake – all he had been able to think about were the times he had scolded Ali; the occasions, too numerous to count, when he had not been the father he would have liked to be.

As the days slipped into weeks and the weeks into months, happier memories had come back to him. The rag-tag games of football they used to play; family holidays by the sea at Hurghada; the day he and Ali had been given a private tour of the closed tombs in the Valley of the Kings by his Egyptologist friend Ginger; visits to the Luxor McDonald's, which if Khalifa was honest with himself had given the boy more pleasure than all the monuments of Egypt put together. So many happy memories. A whole lifetime's worth.

Not enough, though, to absolve Khalifa of the guilt he felt that the last words he had ever spoken to his son had been words of admonishment for not doing his homework.

Nor to block out the image that lived with him day and night of his boy flailing frantically beneath the waters of the Nile – alone, frightened, dying.

Nor, of course, to ever bring Ali back. For all their worth, memories did not have the power to raise the dead.

He was buried in a small plot on a headland overlooking the Nile, not far from the inlet where he and his friends had set out that night on their great expedition. It was a beautiful spot, with flame trees and hibiscus bushes, and wonderful views across the river to the Theban massif and the desert beyond. Khalifa liked to think that from his final resting place his son could look out and, in his own special way, dream of adventure.

No formal inquiry was ever held into the accident, no action ever taken against the barge's captain or owners. One of the largest transport companies in Egypt, they were not the sort of people you went up against. Some facts of life even a revolution didn't change.

JERUSALEM

'Oh dear God, Khalifa, I'm so sorry.'

Ben-Roi paced along the street to a bench and sat down, hunching forward.

'I'm so desperately sorry,' he repeated. 'For your loss, and also for going on about . . . you know, Sarah and me, the baby . . .'

'You have no need to apologize, my friend. If anything it is me who should be saying sorry. For . . . how do you say . . . dampening your wonderful news. I am happy for you. Truly happy.'

Ben-Roi stared down at his trainers, trying to think of something appropriate to say, feeling like the biggest shit in the world for misreading Khalifa. He wasn't good in these sorts of situation, always managed to come out with the wrong thing. In the end he just said sorry again and asked if there was anything he could do to help.

'You are very kind, but no, we are OK.'

'You want me to get on a plane, come over?'

'Thank you, but it is not necessary.'

Ben-Roi leant to the side and rested his elbow on the arm of the bench. He found himself thinking about his own loss, when his fiancée Galia had been killed in the bomb blast, five years ago now. How the kindness and sympathy and words of condolence had some-how only made the whole thing worse, served to emphasize the enormity of the tragedy that had befallen him. Nothing, he knew from experience – no words, no cards, no prayers, no flowers – could help ease the pain of these situations. You were on your own, just had to ride it out. Grief, when all was said and done, was a profoundly solitary business.

'I'm here if you need me,' he said lamely.

'Thank you. You are a good friend.'

They fell silent. Not the awkward silence of a few moments ago, rather the silence of two people who cherish each other's company and are secure enough in their relationship not to need to talk if they haven't got anything specific to say. An elderly *Haredi* man shuffled past, his walking stick clacking on the pavement; a moment later there was a low whoosh and one of the new Jerusalem trams hove into view further down Jaffa, coming his way, its sleek silver and glass body looking somehow out of place against the crumbling Mandate-era buildings. Old and new, past and present, ancient and modern – in Jerusalem everything seemed to bleed into everything else. Literally.

'You wanted to ask me something,' said Khalifa eventually.

'Sorry?'

'About a case you were working on.'

'Oh right. Yes.'

Ben-Roi had completely lost track of why he had called. After what he'd just heard, it seemed totally irrelevant. Inappropriate, too, to be ask-ing the Egyptian for help what with everything else he was having to deal with. He could go through official channels, palm it off on someone else. It would slow things down a bit, but that was no great disaster. Even he accepted there were times you had to ease off (shame he hadn't realized that when he'd been with Sarah).

'Forget it,' he said.

'Come on, Ben-Roi.'

'No, honestly, forget it. It was nothing. Just an excuse to get in touch.'

'Sure?'

'Sure.'

There was another pause – the whoosh of the tram growing steadily louder as it swept along the tracks towards Ben-Roi – then Khalifa said he ought to be going.

'I don't like to leave Zenab for too long,' he explained.

'Of course, I understand. Please give her all my best wishes. And again, I'm so very sorry about Ali.'

'Thank you, my friend.'

'We should try not to leave it so long.'

'Absolutely.'

A hesitation, then Khalifa added: 'It's good to hear your voice, you arrogant Jew bastard.'

Ben-Roi smiled. 'Yours too, you cheeky Muslim you-know-what.'

They promised to stay in touch, said their goodbyes and Ben-Roi started to lower his phone ready to ring off, only to suddenly slam it to his ear again.

'Khalifa!'

Four years ago, when he had been down in the abyss, still poleaxed with grief at his fiancée's death, the Egyptian had got him involved in the Hannah Schlegel investigation, and through that involvement Ben-Roi had found renewed strength and purpose, begun the slow climb to recovery. The situations were different, of course, but maybe, it struck him, just maybe he could return the favour. He doubted it would do much good – to lose a child, dear God, how deep an abyss must that plunge you into? – but if nothing else it might provide Khalifa with a brief distraction. He sure as hell couldn't think of any other practical way of helping his friend.

'There is something you might be able to help me with,' he said.

'Of course. Anything.'

Barren, Nemesis, the Sinai route, Kleinberg's flight to Alexandria – all those Egypt links could be followed up in other ways. There was one thread, however, that seemed tailor-made for Khalifa.

'Have you ever heard of a guy called Samuel Pinsker?' he asked.

Khalifa hadn't.

'He was a British mining engineer. Disappeared from Luxor some time in the early twentieth century. His body was discovered in a tomb in 1972.'

'I'm intrigued.'

'Me too. He seems to connect with a murder case I'm working on,

231

although how or why I've no idea. I thought maybe, what with you being in Luxor . . .'

'I could do a little exploring.'

'If you've got too much on your plate . . .'

'No, no, I'm happy to help. Can you send me some details?'

'I'll e-mail them first thing. For God's sake don't waste too much time on it, just enough to . . .'

'Solve your case for you?'

Ben-Roi chuckled. 'Exactly.'

He was silent for a few seconds, gazing down towards the Old City, its monumental stone-block walls glowing orange in the light of the floodlamps that lined them. Then, hit by a sudden rush of affection for his old friend, he blurted: 'How about this, eh, Khalifa? You and me working together again. The A-Team. Just like old times!'

The Egyptian's response was less buoyant. 'Nothing will ever be like old times, my friend. They are gone for ever. I'll get back to you as soon as I have something.'

And with that he rang off.

PART 2

FIVE DAYS LATER

You take care of the small things and the big things will take care of themselves.

That is what my parents taught me. I still live by the same rule. I am getting on with things – the small things, the daily routines – and trusting that the issues surrounding the cathedral cleansing will sort themselves out. As they seem to be doing. There have been no phone calls, no unexpected arrivals, no troublesome contact from outsiders. The dust appears to be settling. Normally I dislike settled dust, but in this instance it is something to be welcomed.

My parents influenced me greatly. Continue to do so, each in their own separate ways, for good and for ill. I hear their voices often. Smell their smells, too. I have always possessed a keen sense of odour, and the scent of my elders lives sharp in my memory. That is why, in the cathedral, contrary to normal practice, I lay with the fat woman a while, beneath the table, after I had dragged her under there. I turned off my pocket torch and curled beside her in the dark, holding her hand, pressing my face against hers, breathing in the delicious almondy scent of her hair. It was almost as if my mother was back with me, which I found reassuring. Although responsibility for the family has long been mine and mine alone, I still need reassurance at times. Need to know I am serving to the best of my ability.

I need it more than ever at present, what with the decision I am being required to make. The big decision – bigger by far than the one I took in the cathedral, when I performed the cleansing sooner than planned. A decision upon which the whole future of the family rests.

Get it right and the future is secure. Get it wrong . . .

In a sense, of course, I have already made my choice, but I still find myself troubling about it. Wondering what my parents would have

235

done in my position. They placed the family above all things, as I do, but even so – to act within the circle: that is unheard of. Such are the dilemmas of duty. It is not merely about obeying. It is about deciding *whom* to obey. And for what reason.

Tradition has not prepared me for such challenges. There is no comfort in precedent. I call to my forebears, but they do not answer. I am alone. I know what must be done, for the well-being of the line, but still I am troubled.

Although on one aspect at least I am settled. If and when I do act, it won't be with the garrotte. In this instance, even greater discretion than usual is required.

Now, however, I must get on. I have things to attend to. Routine things. Small things. The big ones, hopefully, will take care of themselves.

THE NEGEV DESERT, ISRAEL

The runner moved swiftly, traversing the moonlit desert with panther-like agility. Every now and then he stopped and scanned the rocky slopes, listening. Then he moved on, angling towards the steep, flat-topped hill that dominated the landscape. He came to the base of the hill, stopped again, for longer this time, catching his breath, then climbed swiftly to the summit, the barely audible hiss of trainer on gravel the only indicator of his progress. At the top he slid a Glock 17 from his knapsack and tracked to the summit's far edge, gun held in front of him, eyes jerking left and right.

The ground dropped away abruptly here, stepping down in a series of broad rock-shelves to the tarmacked thread of Route 40 below. His target was sitting on the uppermost shelf, her head tilted back, her eyes closed, a pair of iPod headphones drilled into her ears.

For a moment the man stared down at her, the crown of her head just a few centimetres from his shoe-tips, the tinny echo of music just audible through the headphones. Then, grinning, he bent and scooped a fistful of gravel in his free hand. He aimed the Glock and extended his arm, ready to start dribbling the gravel down on to her hair.

The woman moved so swiftly his brain didn't even have time to register she *was* moving. One moment she was sitting there below him. The next she had launched to her feet and spun, in the same movement somehow sweeping the phones out of her ears. He tried to scramble backwards out of her way, but she had already locked a vice-like grip round his wrist. With her other hand she snatched at his jumper and yanked him forward off the lip of the summit. For a brief, surreal instant he felt himself being guided through the air like some sort of circus acrobat before he was slammed down on to his back – hard enough to wind him, not so hard as to cause any real damage. A foot pinned his right wrist, a second Glock appeared out of nowhere and hovered an inch above the bridge of his nose. From the dangling earphones came the muffled pulse of music – Pink Floyd: 'Breathe'.

'You want something?'

It was a few seconds before he was able to do what the music was telling him. When he did manage to get enough air into his lungs to speak, his voice was throaty and hoarse.

'Thought I had you that time.'

'You didn't.'

'So I noticed.'

For a moment he lay staring up at her, her face pale and intense, a faint smile playing across her lips. Then, raising his free hand, he slid it across her cheek and round to the nape of her neck. She allowed it to sit for a couple of seconds before gently brushing the hand away and backing off.

'Don't you ever give up, Gidi?'

'Don't you ever give *in*, Dinah?'

'Not tonight, lover-boy.'

He laughed at that. 'God, you're sexy. I've got a hard-on for you from here to Haifa.'

She gave a weary tut. Gideon was always trying it on with her, had been for the four years she'd known him. Just as he was always trying to catch her out when she came up here for a bit of head space. He meant no harm by it, and she took no offence. Gidi was a good man. The best. It's just that good men weren't really her thing.

She clicked off the iPod and dropped it into the knapsack resting against the back of the shelf, followed by the Glock. Gidi heaved himself into a sitting position, rubbing his wrist.

'How did you know I was there?'

'Caught your aftershave.'

He grunted. 'Beaten up for smelling nice.'

She slid the knapsack on to her shoulders and held out a hand. He grasped it and she yanked him to his feet.

'Race you back?' she said.

'I reckon I'll sit out here a while. Smoke a joint, watch the stars, deal with the rejection. It's a beautiful night.'

He was still clasping her hand.

'Stay with me, Dinah. No funny business. Just sit with me. The cathedral thing . . . at least allow me to hold you.'

She stood facing him, making no move to break his grip. The moon-light seemed to amplify the fineness of her features, the delicate cheekbones, the large, sad eyes. A few seconds passed. Then, squeez-ing his hand, she leant forward and kissed him on the cheek.

'I'll see you back at the compound.'

And with that she was gone, leaping down the rock steps towards the highway beneath.

'From here to Haifa!' he called after her.

'Stick an ice pack on it!' her voice drifted back.

When she reached the flat she skirted the hill and picked up the track that led off Route 40 and out across the desert, the only sounds the crunch of her feet and the distant melancholy howling of a hyena. The track ran straight for a few hundred metres, bordered with boulders and the occasional flaccid cactus, then dipped through a narrow cleft and dog-legged sharp right. Ahead, just over two kilometres away, gleaming in the moonlight, sat a huddle of buildings: domed roofs, whitewashed walls, like a scatter of sugar-cubes. She increased her pace.

They'd been out here for three years. In the early days, the four of them had operated from her apartment in Tel-Aviv. There had been too many eyes, too many opportunities for their comings and goings to attract unwanted attention, especially as their missions had grown more daring, the heat on them more intense. They'd decamped to a rambling villa on the outskirts of Be'er Sheva. Then, wanting still more privacy, out here.

Back in the 1960s the place had been a thriving, if remote, *moshav*. It had long ago been abandoned, its buildings taken over by scorpions and salamanders, its vegetable plots lost beneath a blanket of dust and weeds. They'd picked up the lease, knocked it into shape, installed solar panels for electricity, a satellite system for phone and internet. They wouldn't stay here for ever. Rule One in this business: never put down roots, always be ready to move at the drop of a hat. For the moment, though, it suited their needs perfectly.

She'd paid for it all, as she did for everything. She didn't tell them how, they didn't ask. Rule Two: no unnecessary questions. The four of them were close, a family, but there were still parts of her life she needed to keep private. They didn't even know her real name. Which was exactly how it was going to stay. The past was the past.

She reached the compound in under eight minutes, sprinting the final four hundred metres. Tamar's light was off – she must have turned in early. Faz, to judge by the ghostly grey flickers emanating from its window, was in the tech room, as he always was, hunched in front of one of the screens trawling the nether regions of cyberspace. Faz was the black sheep – Arab-Israeli, surly, introverted. He was also a tech genius, one of the best hackers in the business, so the fact that he rarely said anything was irrelevant. They all served in their own way. He could hack, and plant a virus, and use a gun. That was all that mattered. At the end of the day, none of them were in it for the conversation.

She leant up against a wall by one of the 4x4s and stretched out her calves, drawing air into her lungs, then crossed to the tech room and stuck her head round the door. Faz was sitting with his back to her, eyes glued to the screen, his head haloed with cigarette smoke.

'Anything?'

He extended an arm and jabbed a thumb towards the floor, like a Roman emperor signalling the termination of a gladiator's life. It had been the same for the last six days, ever since news of the murder had broken and they'd hacked the Israel Police mainframe to keep tabs on the investigation. Whatever else they were doing, the dickheads in blue certainly weren't getting any closer to the perpetrator.

'Barren?'

Another thumbs down.

'Sure?'

'Yes.'

That was as much as you were ever going to get from Faz. She told him to keep on it, backed out and crossed the yard to her own room where she stripped and went through into the shower. Pulling the curtain closed, she turned the taps and stepped straight underneath the showerhead, not waiting for the water to run warm, dropping her head back and allowing the jets to play across her face and breasts. A minute went by. Then she suddenly tensed and swung as behind her a figure loomed through the curtain's opaque plastic. Instinctively her fists came up to fight him away, then dropped at the sound of Tamar's voice.

'It's only me. The door was unlocked.'

She reached out and drew aside the curtain, doing nothing to hide her naked body. Tamar was standing on the other side: lithe, dark-skinned, hair cropped short, baggy white T-shirt falling to just above her knees.

'You OK?' Tamar asked gently.

Dinah nodded.

'I'm worried about you.'

'I'm fine.'

'Really?'

'Really.'

They stood looking at each other, water continuing to cascade down Dinah's head and back, splashing out on to the bathroom's tiled floor. Then, smiling, she took a step to the side. Tamar reached down and lifted the T-shirt over her head, revealing small firm breasts and wisps of dark pubic hair. She came into the shower and the two women embraced.

'We'll get them, Dinah. I promise you, we'll get them.'

She said nothing, just pulled the curtain closed with one hand while with the other she stroked her companion's hair and drew her close.

Neither woman clocked the camera in the extractor vent above the shower. Nor would they have done even if they'd been looking directly at it. It was too well concealed. Like all the other cameras. The watcher watched, and no one was any the wiser.

BETWEEN LUXOR AND QENA, EGYPT

Yusuf Khalifa pulled on his Cleopatra and gazed out of the window as the train clanked its way slowly northwards. Mud-brick villages drifted past, fields of maize and sugar cane, a butcher's kiosk hung with a morbid bunting of tripe and severed sheep's heads. At one point the train juddered to a halt and he found himself staring at a group of boys playing on a makeshift raft in the middle of an irrigation canal. He stiffened, fighting the urge to push his head through the window and scream at them to get off the water. It was a struggle – every reminder was a struggle – and he breathed a sigh of relief when the train jolted forward and the scene slipped away behind him. He dragged on the last of his cigarette and ground the butt out beneath his heel, taking care not to disturb the elderly man performing his noonday *salat* on the carriage floor in front of him.

There had been no further developments at the Attia farm. He was still waiting on his friend Omar for the results of the water analysis, but he was increasingly coming round to the opinion that Chief Hassani had been right and the whole thing was a wild-goose chase. He'd put out a few feelers on the missing Karnak *talatat* blocks, and chased up the stories of a dope-dealing ring operating out of the Luxor souk, which had turned out to be just that – stories. Otherwise his desk had been clear, and with the chief and most of the rest of the station obsessing about the museum opening in the Valley of the Kings, he'd been free to do some digging for Ben-Roi without anyone paying him any undue attention.

And unexpectedly interesting that digging had proved to be.

The Israeli had sent him over a basic outline of the case, including a possible connection with a company called Barren Corporation. The same Barren Corporation who were responsible for the new Valley of the Kings museum, which was a very curious coincidence.

Samuel Pinsker was a completely new name to him. Ben-Roi had provided links to a handful of internet references, but they had offered little beyond the fact that Pinsker was British, had been involved in archaeological work in the Theban Necropolis, had gone missing in 1931 and had suffered from some sort of chronic facial disfigurement. Even the dramatic discovery of his corpse in 1972, at the bottom of a remote shaft tomb way out in the western massif, seemed to have attracted only passing interest, most of it focused on lurid supposition as to the lonely, lingering death its owner must have endured. He had lived and worked in Egypt, and met his end in the hills above the Valley of the Kings – beyond that Khalifa could find no obvious tie-in with the case details Ben-Roi had furnished.

Egyptian police records had proved more informative. And, also, more intriguing.

The fact that there even *were* extant records had been a surprise. It had all happened a long time ago – a very long time, in the case of Pinsker's disappearance – and Khalifa had half expected whatever case notes had once existed to have long since been lost or destroyed. Fortunately the Egyptian police's fixation not simply with creating paperwork, but with hoarding it – usually so irksome to Khalifa – had in this instance worked in his favour. It had taken him a while to track down what he needed, but he'd eventually run it to ground the day before yesterday. Two batches of notes – one relating to the finding of Pinsker's body, the other to his original disappearance – the pair of them bound together with string and tucked away on a shelf in a government storage facility down in Esna.

Moving carefully so as not to disturb the man praying on the floor, Khalifa lifted the plastic bag at his feet and pulled out the files.

The one from 1972 was by far the larger of the pair. Half of it was taken up with a wad of black-and-white photographs: of the tomb – a deep shaft with a simple rock-cut burial chamber opening off the bottom, of Pinsker's mummified body in situ, of the body on a mortuary slab. There was a pathologist's report, a detective's report, statements from the couple who had discovered the corpse, even a report by a Dr Geoffrey Reeves, an expert in Theban tomb architecture, analysing the dimensions and cutting of the tomb and concluding it dated from the New Kingdom, almost certainly Eighteenth Dynasty. At the bottom of the pile, the last item in the folder, was a letter from a Mrs Yahudiya Aslani of the Egypt Jewish Welfare Committee. It agreed, in the absence of living relatives, to accept charge of Pinsker's body for burial in Cairo's Bassatine Cemetery. 'Although unfortunately, due to financial constraints, we are unable to provide a headstone.'

The 1931 file – a real history piece, its eighty-year-old contents yellowed with age – was much sparser. Despite that, it was the one that had immediately drawn Khalifa's attention.

There were statements from a number of people who'd known and associated with Pinsker, the longest and most detailed of them from a woman named Ommsaid Gumsan, the owner of the room Pinsker had been renting in Kom Lolah.

On the night of his disappearance, the Englishman had apparently only just returned to Luxor after an absence of almost three months – he often did that, she explained, disappeared for weeks on end before suddenly turning up again out of the blue, which was why she always insisted on rent in advance. She had heard his motorbike pulling up in the alley at the back of the house some time in the early hours. He hadn't actually entered the building, and there had been no sign of him the following morning, although his motorbike had still been there, its rear panniers half unstrapped. Used to his erratic comings and goings, she would normally have paid it no mind. This morning, for reasons she couldn't explain, she had had a presentiment of tragedy. She had spoken to her brother, who in turn had contacted the police. End of statement.

The other testimonies were briefer and less informative, although one man – a Mohammed el-Badri of Shaykh Abd al-Qurna – claimed to have seen Pinsker walking up into the hills swigging from a bottle, drunk as a skunk apparently. There was a photograph of the Englishman's motorbike, a copy of a poster asking anyone with information to contact either the police or their village headman, a telegram from British High Commissioner Sir Percy Loraine urging the Luxor authorities to do everything in their power to locate Mr Pinsker.

All of which was perfectly interesting. The document that had really got Khalifa's pulse racing, however, had been hidden away in a pocket right at the back of the file. A handwritten two-page letter from one of Pinsker's archaeological colleagues, it had been accompanied by a thumbnail sketch of the missing man – a simple yet compelling image of a leather-coated figure with its face hidden behind some sort of mask – and signed with a name that, unlike Pinsker's, was extremely familiar to Khalifa: Howard Carter.

Opening the file, he removed the letter and for the tenth time read through it, shuffling sideways as the elderly passenger finished his prayers and resumed his seat beside him.

Elwat el-Diban
Luxor
September 14, 1931

Dear Cptn. Suleiman,

Further to your enquiries concerning Mr. Samuel Pinsker, the following recollections may be of some assistance.

On the night of Mr. Pinsker's disappearance, September 12, I had retired early following dinner with Mssrs. Newberry, Lucas, Callender and Burton.

Shortly before ten I was awakened by the sound of a motorbike approaching from the direction of Dra Abu el-Naga. Shortly thereafter there was a knock at my front door, accompanied by Mr. Pinsker's voice. He appeared to be the worse for drink and was shouting incoherently, some tommyrot to the effect of 'I've found it, Carter', and 'It's miles long.' The disturbance continued for several minutes, whereupon I called for him to leave and he departed. We did not communicate face to face.

Mr. Pinsker has been known to me for three years, and last year worked for a period with myself and Mr. Callender in reconsolidating the entrance to the tomb of Tutankhamun. I believe he has also advised Mr. Winlock at Deir el-Bahri, and Monsieur Chevrier at Karnak.

Although I did not appreciate being woken in that manner, I bear Mr. Pinsker no ill-will, and trust he will be found in good time, and in good health.

Should I be able to offer any further assistance etc.

Yours Faithfully,

Howard Carter.

'*Tazkara.*'

Without looking up, Khalifa pulled out his police badge and flipped it open. The ticket inspector looked at it, grunted and moved on, leaving Khalifa staring down at the document, oblivious to the suspicious stares his badge had drawn from the surrounding passengers.

An original Carter letter – you didn't come across those every day, especially one accompanied by a sketch in the great archaeologist's hand. The references to other contemporary excavators made it doubly interesting, offering as it did a fleeting glimpse back into the golden age of Egyptian exploration and discovery. When Khalifa had alerted the curator of Carter House on the West Bank to the find, the man had practically leapt down the phone at him, so anxious was he to get his hands on it.

More than the letter's historical significance, however, what really intrigued Khalifa were the words Pinsker had shouted during his visit to Carter's residence on the night of his disappearance. *I've found it, Carter. It's miles long.* What did that mean? What was 'it'?

His immediate thought was that maybe Pinsker was referring to the tomb in which he had met his end – a hitherto unknown Eighteenth Dynasty shaft burial, even an empty one, would certainly have been cause for excitement. Perhaps Pinsker had found the shaft, descended to Carter's house to boast of his discovery, then gone back up into the hills and, drunk, fallen into the hole. But then the Englishman had described the mysterious thing or place as 'miles long', which certainly didn't tally with the modest single-chamber tomb of the police photographs. Drunken exaggeration? Possible, although again, 'miles long' seemed a strangely inappropriate choice of hyperbole. Khalifa had raised the issue with the curator of Carter House, but the man wasn't able to help him – he hadn't even heard of Samuel Pinsker. His old friend and mentor Professor Mohammed al-Habibi at the Cairo Museum *had* heard of him, but could shed no more light on the mystery. And Carter himself had been dead since 1939, so he wasn't going to be offering any explanation.

I've found it, Carter. It's miles long.

Was 'it' the tie-in with Ben-Roi's case? The reason the dead journalist had been interested in Samuel Pinsker? Or just another wild-goose chase, like the whole Coptic well-poisoning scenario? He had no idea. There were other people he needed to talk to. Mary Dufresne, for one. She knew everything there was to know about that period.

That was going to have to wait, however. For the moment, he had other things on his mind. Giving the letter a final once-over, he slid it carefully back into its pocket, closed and tied the 1931 file and opened the one from 1972.

The letter about the Bassatine Cemetery had obviously caught his eye – if Pinsker had been Jewish that at least provided some vague link with Israel. It wasn't that that was bugging him, however. He pulled out the wad of photographs and flicked through them until he came to one of the bottom of the tomb shaft: a dusty rectangle of chiselled stone half buried beneath a tangle of branches and twigs.

Branches and twigs. The branches and twigs didn't make sense.

Which was why he was on his way to Qena. Because if the players from 1931 were all long dead and buried, some of those from 1972 were still around. Including Ibrahim Sadeq, former chief of the Luxor Police, and the man who had headed up the investigation into the discovery of Samuel Pinsker's mummified corpse. Sadeq might be able to give him some answers.

He stared at the photo. Then, as the train rumbled past the smoking hulk of the Qena Paper Factory, returned it to the file and sat back. Further down the carriage a vendor was pushing his way through the crush of passengers, hefting a tray piled with strips of sugar cane, calling out for custom. A suited man waved him over, bought a piece, handed it to a boy sitting beside him. His son, Khalifa guessed, from the way the man curled an arm round the boy's shoulders and drew him close. The boy snuggled against his father, crunched into the stem and held it up for the man to take a bite, the two of them blissfully unaware of the stupendous importance of such transient interactions. Khalifa watched them a moment, then wiped his eyes and looked away.

Every reminder was just such a struggle.

BETWEEN JERUSALEM AND TEL-AVIV

Ben-Roi too was on the move, by car in his case, west again on Route 1, down through the Judaean Hills towards the coastal plain and the sea.

It had been a frustrating five days.

To say the investigation had stalled would be overly pessimistic, but it wasn't exactly powering forward either. Inching, more like. And now that the press had got their teeth into the story – their initial reticence had turned out to be a temporary reprieve, the calm before the storm – the pressure to score a conviction had gone off the scale. Leah Shalev was being called in for twice-daily briefings with Commander Gal and Chief Superintendent Baum – not a comfortable experience, given that she had precious little to brief them on. Two days ago Baum had gone so far as to suggest she wasn't up to such a high-profile case and maybe he should take over the running himself. To his credit Gal had stood by his investigator, although his support had come with a qualification: 'I need movement on this, Leah, and I need it soon. You've got a week. If we're still no closer by then we're going to have to review the situation.'

All of which made for a fractious working atmosphere. Doubly so with the second Old City murder case – the *yeshiva* student stabbing – also treading water. In his nine years at the station, Ben-Roi had never known Kishle to feel so tense. The place was like a boiler about to explode. Frankly, he was glad to get away for the day.

He pumped the horn and pulled out to overtake an IDF road transporter ferrying a pair of Merkava tanks down to the coast. Once he was round it, he swung back into the middle lane, put in a quick call to Sarah on the hands-free – she'd been sick in the night, he wanted to make sure she was OK – and took a slurp of the tepid coffee he'd brought at a Paz station a few miles back. On *Kol Ha-Derekh*, Pulp's 'She's Dead' gave way to some American singer called Susan Tedeschi with a number entitled 'Looking for Answers'. For God's sake, even the bloody radio was on his case!

They were still pursuing a three-track investigation. Uri Pincas remained on the Russian and Hebron settler angle, his remit now widened to include all the other death threats Kleinberg had received over the years as a result of her journalism. Amos Namir continued to beaver away on the Armenian side of things, as well as getting the word out about the girl Vosgi, who obviously tied in with the Armenian stuff. Neither man was getting anywhere fast. Neither man was getting anywhere, period.

For his part, Ben-Roi was still picking his way through the tangled thicket of leads and counter-leads thrown up by Kleinberg's more recent journalism. Sex-trafficking, Egypt, Barren, the Nemesis Agenda – all the pieces were still in play, although what exactly they were doing on the board, and how, if at all, they related to one another, he was no closer to finding out.

To be fair, there had been *some* progress. Dov Zisky, who seemed to be more indispensable as each day went by, had turned up a couple of very interesting little nuggets.

One concerned Rivka Kleinberg's planned trip to Egypt. Not only had she been booked on to a flight to Alexandria on the night of her murder, but, it transpired, she also had a reservation at a budget hotel in Rosetta, a small town sixty kilometres down the coast from Alexandria. What she intended doing there remained a mystery, but whatever it was, she clearly wasn't expecting it to take long. The reservation was only for a single night, after which she was booked on a return flight to Tel-Aviv.

The other nugget involved the ubiquitous Barren Corporation. Zisky had done some more background digging and managed to turn up an Armenian connection, albeit an old one. Back in the 1980s, through a subsidiary named YGE – Yerevan Gold Exploration – Barren had held a controlling stake in a large open-pit gold mine in the east of the country, on the border with Azerbaijan. Licensing disputes with the Armenian government had caused Barren to offload the company in 1991, but it was still an intriguing and potentially important link.

There had been a couple of other developments, including – and again, this had come courtesy of Zisky, who'd spotted it on the net – another Nemesis Agenda targeting of Barren, this one a hacking attack on the company's computer network.

By far the most promising new lead, however, was one Ben-Roi himself had turned up – somewhat to his relief, since Zisky seemed to have been making most of the running over the last few days.

During his meeting with Maya Hillel at the Hofesh Shelter, she'd mentioned a pimp named Genady Kremenko. A Ukrainian-born immigrant, Kremenko – along with his wife and two sons – had run one of the biggest prostitution rings in Tel-Aviv, using girls trafficked in from Egypt through the Sinai. According to Hillel, Rivka Kleinberg had shown a particular interest in that route, and since Kremenko had by all accounts exercised a virtual monopoly on it, Ben-Roi had decided to take a closer look at him.

Kremenko had been arrested a couple of months back and was currently on remand in Abu Kabir, a detention facility just round the corner from the National Centre for Forensic Medicine in south Tel-Aviv. Ben-Roi had been on to the anti-trafficking unit of Organized Crime and they'd forwarded him copies of everything they had on the man, which was a fair bit. He'd been pimping almost a hundred girls apparently, Eastern Europeans for the most part, although lately he'd been moving increasingly into Orientals and Africans. He had them working in twos or threes out of apartments scattered around the city – including several in Neve Sha'anan – their services advertised via the internet and business cards left in call boxes and on car windscreens, their every move watched over by a network of minders, maids and sub-pimps. Such was the level of fear he inspired that despite the numbers involved, and guarantees of protection, Organized Crime had been unable to find a single girl willing to testify against Kremenko, which was why, even with a mass of circumstantial evidence, the Attorney General's office had decided the best hope of securing a conviction lay with tax-evasion and money-laundering charges rather than trafficking and living off immoral earnings.

On Kremenko's Sinai operation, which was what Ben-Roi was really interested in, the files contained almost nothing. The girls had been recruited in their native countries, sent to Egypt, moved across the border by Bedouin. Pretty much what Hillel had already told him.

It had looked like a dead end. Then, however, one of those strokes of luck on which an entire case can turn. Ben-Roi had a contact in Abu Kabir, a warder who'd been at police college with him before transferring over into the prison service. Warders always had their ear to the ground, and, just on the off-chance, Ben-Roi had got in touch, filled the man in, asked if he knew anything that might be useful.

And lo and behold he did.

Eighteen days ago, it turned out, Genady Kremenko had had a visitor. A female visitor. Her name was Rivka Kleinberg.

So that's where he was going now. Down to Abu Kabir for a chat with the man they called the Schoolmaster on account of the age of some of the girls he was pimping. Throwing a quick glance at the pile of Toys R Us bags on the passenger seat, Ben-Roi swung out to overtake another tank transporter and pushed the speedometer up past 120km per hour. He only had an hour with Kremenko and didn't want to be late.

QENA, EGYPT

Unlike Luxor, sixty kilometres to the south, the town of Qena – perched on the bend in the Nile to which it gave its name – made few concessions to foreign visitors. There were no upmarket hotels, no restaurants serving fish and chips and full English breakfasts, all the signs were in Arabic. This was a town that received few tourists, and those that did come – usually to visit the Hathor Temple across the Nile at Dendera – were closely policed. Back in the 1990s, Al-Gama'a al-Islamiyya had launched a number of attacks in the area, and no one was taking any chances.

Ibrahim Sadeq lived in a river-front block five minutes from the town centre. The interview hadn't been easy to arrange – the former police chief guarded his privacy, didn't welcome visitors. He had seemed intrigued by Khalifa's request to discuss the Pinsker case, however, and after a bit of to-ing and fro-ing had relented and granted him an audience, on condition it was kept short. Khalifa phoned ahead the moment he got off the train, and was buzzed into the block within seconds of pressing its intercom. Sadeq was waiting for him outside the door of his apartment – a tall, thin Saidee with close-cropped grey hair, cold eyes and bad teeth. The two men shook hands, exchanged the usual pleasantries and went inside.

Sadeq had been before Khalifa's time. He'd met him twice, briefly, at official functions, but had never really spoken to him. He knew him through reputation, though. Sadeq was a hard man. Not hard like Chief Hassani and Ehab Ali Mahfouz, Hassani's immediate predecessor. Their hardness was all physical, in their fists. Sadeq was more of a thinker: a schemer and a manipulator. Where Hassani and Mahfouz would think nothing of rolling up their sleeves and wading into a suspect, Sadeq had preferred to lurk in the shadows, tweaking the strings while others got their hands dirty. Everyone had feared him, police and civilians alike. Under Sadeq, so the rumours went, the state torturers had never been so busy.

He led Khalifa through into the living room – spartan, neat, functional – where they were served tea by a well-dressed woman Khalifa assumed must be Sadeq's wife. Once she was gone, the former chief settled back in his chair and crossed his legs, balancing his tea glass on his knee. The room hummed with the low whisper of air-conditioning; from the kitchen came the intermittent crackle of an electric fly-killer. Khalifa found the sound disconcerting. Electricity, he'd heard, had been one of Sadeq's favoured methods of interrogation.

'So, Inspector, you've come about the man with no face.'

No small talk, straight to the point, the faintest hint of emphasis on the 'Inspector', just to remind Khalifa of his correct place in the hierarchy. He was going to have to tread carefully. Even in retirement, Sadeq wasn't someone you wanted to cross.

'You were in charge of the investigation,' Khalifa began, pulling out the later of the two police files from the plastic bag at his feet. 'I just wanted to clarify a couple of things.'

'Forty years after the event?'

'A friend mentioned the case. I thought I'd take a look. Just personal interest.'

He thought it best to keep Ben-Roi out of it. Sadeq's brother, he'd heard, had been taken prisoner by the Israelis during the 1973 Ramadan War and he couldn't see him being particularly well disposed towards assisting in one of their investigations, even indirectly. The Saidee stared at him, something faintly reptilian about his gaze, the way his eyes didn't seem to blink. For a moment it looked as if he was going to push for more details. To Khalifa's relief, he laid aside his tea and extended a hand.

'Show.'

Khalifa leant forward and passed the file across. Sadeq slipped on a pair of glasses and opened the folder.

'Been a while since I saw these,' he murmured, leafing through the file's contents. 'My first case after I made senior inspector. Memorable introduction.'

He pulled out a photo and held it up to the light. Pinsker's body was sitting propped in the rear corner of the tomb chamber, mummified in the dry desert heat, the head thrown back, the skin dry and un-naturally taut, as if his skeleton had been bound in dirty white wrapping paper. In one hand he held a leather mask with straps and buckles attached to it; where his face should have been, there was just a sort of blank space, smooth save for two small eye-holes, a lipless slit of a mouth and, in the middle, a slight creasing that hinted at a nose.

'Handsome chap,' grunted Sadeq, returning the image to the folder. 'I've seen some bad deaths in my time, but this one . . . I take it you looked at the autopsy report.'

Khalifa had indeed. It had made gruesome reading. As well as breaking both legs, right arm and three ribs in his fall down the shaft, Pinsker had also sustained a ruptured spleen and severe lacerations to the rear of his skull. Despite his injuries he had somehow survived the drop, as evidenced by the fact that he had dragged himself into the chamber and fashioned rough splints for his shattered limbs and a compress for his head. Although the age and desiccated state of the body had made definitive assessment impossible, the pathologist estimated the Englishman had lived for at least two to three days before eventually succumbing to a combination of dehydration, blood loss and internal trauma. A painless end it most certainly hadn't been.

Sadeq closed the file and removed his glasses.

'So what is it you wish to clarify?'

'It was mainly to do with the woman's statement,' replied Khalifa, reaching across and taking the folder back. 'The *ingileezaya*, Mrs –' he flipped through the notes to find the name – 'Bowers. There was something that didn't make sense to me.'

Sadeq picked up his tea glass, sipped, motioned for Khalifa to continue.

'Well, according to her account, she was walking in the hills with her husband, stopped to –' he consulted the notes again, looking for the precise wording – '"do what a lady has to do", which I presume means—'

'Take a piss.'

'Exactly. She lost her footing, slipped, rolled backwards down a slope and into the shaft.' He looked up at Sadeq, who gave a slight tilt of the head to indicate the chronology was correct. 'She also said that she hadn't noticed the shaft before because it was covered with branches.'

This time Sadeq didn't nod, just stared at Khalifa, the faintest hint of a smile lifting the corners of his lips.

'It was you who took her statement, right? The day of the accident, after she'd been helicoptered over to Luxor General.'

'That is my recollection.'

'I know it was a long time ago, but you don't remember how she was, do you? Did she seem concussed, confused . . . ?'

'She was a *hawaga*. In my experience they're all confused.'

Khalifa smiled at the joke. 'What I'm getting at—'

'I know exactly what you're getting at.' Sadeq's lips lifted a couple of notches further, the smile becoming more pronounced, as if he understood where Khalifa was going with this and was enjoying the ride. 'And no, the woman didn't seem at all confused. On the contrary, given that she'd only recently fallen down a twenty-foot hole and found a dead man at the bottom, she was remarkably lucid.'

'And she was definite about the branches? That they were covering the shaft.'

'Oh very definite. *Extremely* definite.'

'That's what I don't understand. If the branches were at the top of the shaft—'

He got no further. Sadeq's hand came up, motioning him to be silent. The former chief was smiling broadly now, although his eyes were steely, an unnerving disconnect, as if part of him was humouring Khalifa, another part warning him. From the kitchen came a muffled crackle as another fly immolated itself. There was a pause, then:

'They said you were sharp.'

'I'm sorry?'

'Hassani, Mahfouz. Others I've spoken to. One of the sharpest on the force, apparently. See things other people don't.'

He laid aside his tea glass and placed his hands on the arms of the chair, curling his fingers round the wooden arm-ends which were fashioned into the shape of scarab beetles. His thumbnails, Khalifa noticed, were much longer than those of his other fingers, as though he was deliberately growing them.

'Insubordinate as well, I'm told. Not something you'd have got away with in my day. In my day *no one* was insubordinate.'

His smile tightened, his eyes grew colder. Khalifa shifted in his seat, not sure where this was leading, wondering if perhaps he had made a mistake coming here. Things might be changing in Egypt, but you still had to watch yourself, particularly around scorpions like Sadeq. There was another uncomfortable silence. Then, to his surprise, the former chief lifted his hands and slowly clapped them, as if applauding.

'Well spotted, Inspector. Even the professor who did the study of the tomb didn't clock the problem with the branches. But I did. And now you have too. Very sharp.'

He replaced his hands on the chair arms, his left index finger tapping up and down. From the entrance hall came a muted click as the front door opened and then closed, presumably as his wife went out.

'As soon as the *ingileezaya* told me about the branches I knew there was something wrong. My first thought, as yours seems to have been, was that she was confused, hadn't remembered correctly. But she was adamant about it. The branches had been covering the shaft. Which meant that they'd got there *after* Pinsker had fallen in, otherwise he would have dislodged them. And since there are no trees within ten kilometres of the site, someone must have deliberately carried them up and put them there. There were possible explanations, but the obvious one was that someone didn't want either the tomb or Pinsker to be found. And the obvious explanation for *that* was that . . .'

'Pinsker's fall wasn't an accident.'

Sadeq gave another slow handclap. Ben-Roi's query, it seemed, was turning out to be rather less routine than either of them had expected.

'There was nothing about this in your report,' said Khalifa.

'In the circumstances I thought it better to keep the narrative simple.'

'But a man had been murdered.'

'That's one way of looking at it.'

'There's another way?'

'There's always another way of looking at things, Inspector. If there's one lesson I learnt in forty years on the force, it's that nothing is ever clear-cut.'

He took another sip of his tea, eyes locked on Khalifa as if daring him to pursue the point. Khalifa had dealt with people like Sadeq before – had been dealing with them his whole career – and knew there were times to push, times to keep quiet. This was a time to keep quiet. For a moment they sat in silence, Khalifa shuffling his feet, Sadeq sipping his tea. Then, with a nod, the former chief drained his glass and put it down.

'Personal interest, you say?'

'Yes, sir.'

'Sure?' He fixed Khalifa with a hard stare.

'Sure.'

'In that case I see no reason to keep you in the dark. It was a long time ago, after all. And in its own way justice *was* served.'

He indicated the plastic bag at Khalifa's feet.

'I'm assuming that's the file on Pinsker's disappearance?'

Khalifa acknowledged that it was. Sadeq motioned for him to pass it across.

'We ID'd Pinsker's body pretty quickly,' he said, sliding his spectacles back on and leafing through the folder's contents. 'He wasn't carrying any personal documents, but people don't easily forget a face like that. There were a good few *Qurnawis* who still remembered him, even after forty years. Once we had a name, it was a simple matter to dig out the case notes relating to his disappearance. And once we'd dug out the case notes, it didn't take long to get to the bottom of things.'

He removed a sheet from the file, held it out. It was the statement from the man who claimed to have seen a drunken Pinsker walking up into the Theban hills. Mohammed el-Badri of Shaykh Abd al-Qurna.

'I knew the el-Badris,' said Sadeq. 'Bad lot, troublemakers. Old Mohammed was still around, we pulled him in, put the screws on him. He was tough, but spilled eventually. They always do.'

He slid the sheet back into the folder.

'Turns out Pinsker raped their sister. Girl called Iman. Blind, not even twenty. Dragged her down to the river, battered her, took his pleasure. She struggled, apparently, tried to fight him off, but he was too strong. I wouldn't trust the el-Badris as far as I could spit them, but Mohammed had an eyewitness to corroborate the story. Local guy, respectable. He'd been a kid at the time, was out fishing the night it happened, heard the girl crying, saw the whole thing. He told the el-Badris about it, Mohammed and his two brothers . . . well, this was 1931, people hadn't forgotten Danishaway. And you know what the *fellaheen* are like. Proud. Do things their own way.'

He removed his spectacles, folded them, placed them on the coffee table beside his empty glass.

'I disapprove of vigilante justice,' he said. 'If it had happened on my watch I might have dealt with it differently, but this was forty years after the event. Two of the three brothers were dead, Mohammed was into his seventies and not long off dying, Pinsker had no living relatives, or at least none that we could find. It served nobody's purposes to start opening up old wounds. It was bad enough the girl had been violated. Why go reminding the whole world of her shame? Better just to let things lie. I had the old man beaten to teach him a lesson, and left it at that. Case closed. Which is how it's going to stay.'

He contemplated the folder, then snapped it shut and held it out.

'I trust that clarifies things.'

Khalifa leant across and took the file. He felt curiously unmoved by the story. The rape was obviously shocking – the girl had been the same age as his own daughter Batah. And blind to boot. But of Pinsker's fate . . . A year ago he would have been horrified by what had happened to him. Lynch mobs, people taking the law into their own hands – these were things from which he'd always instinctively recoiled, however grotesque the crime. These days his moral compass seemed less fixed. The man had died a terrible death, but then he'd done a terrible thing. Like Sadeq said, it wasn't clear-cut. Nothing was clear-cut any more. There was no certainty about anything, no black and white. Life had become . . . impenetrably grey.

He shuffled the folders on his lap, his thoughts turning to how, if at all, any of this related to a woman getting strangled in a church in Al-Quds. He could see no obvious link: two murders, eighty years apart, different nationalities, different countries.

'There was no suggestion of a religious element to the killing, was there?' he asked, fumbling for a connection. 'Pinsker being Jewish and all.'

Sadeq eyed him. 'A girl was beaten, raped, very nearly killed. A *blind* girl. I would have thought that was enough of a motive without bringing religion into it. And anyway, this was before the *naqba*. We didn't mind Jews so much in those days.'

There was a click as the front door opened again, accompanied by a rustle of shopping bags. Sadeq glanced up, then at his watch. He clearly believed they'd covered everything that needed to be covered and it was now time to bring the discussion to a close.

'You don't know what happened to Pinsker's personal belongings, do you?' asked Khalifa, trying to scrape whatever he could before he was shown the door.

Sadeq gave an impatient grunt. 'As far as I recall everything we found in the tomb was buried with Pinsker up in Cairo. There wasn't much. Just his clothes and that mask thing.'

'No documents of any sort? Papers? Letters?'

The older man's fingers started drumming on the scarab-shaped arm-ends. Whatever tether he'd granted Khalifa was fast starting to strain.

'No documents,' he replied curtly. 'Now if you don't mind . . .'

'And his things from 1931? You've no idea what happened to those?'

Sadeq's fingers ceased drumming, curled tightly round the scarabs.

'I have no idea at all. Dumped in the Nile, for all I know. It was eighty years ago and it's not relevant.'

'More tea?' His wife's voice echoed from the kitchen.

'That won't be necessary,' called Sadeq. 'We were just finishing. Weren't we?'

It was a statement rather than a question. End of tether. Khalifa nodded, thanked the old man for his time and, returning the folders to the plastic bag, stood. Sadeq led him out into the hallway.

'For personal interest you seem to be taking this thing very seriously, Inspector,' he said as they reached the front door. 'I've no objection to officers using their initiative, but initiative needs to be deployed *advisedly*. Maybe I'll have a chat with Hassani. Get him to give you some proper work.'

He opened the door and Khalifa went out on to the landing. He'd overstepped the mark, he could feel it, shouldn't chance things any further. People like Sadeq could turn unpleasant. Very unpleasant.

'One last question.'

Sadeq glared.

'In the 1931 folder there was a letter, from Howard Carter, the archaeologist. Apparently on the night of his murder Pinsker told Carter he'd found something. Some object or place that was "miles long". Does that mean anything to you?'

He fully expected the old man to lose his temper. He didn't. Instead, unexpectedly, he reached out and laid a hand on Khalifa's shoulder.

'I heard about your tragedy, Inspector. Please accept my sincere condolences. I do hope your family are well. And *remain* well.'

The way he said it sounded more like a warning than a good wish.

'And to answer your question, the Carter letter means nothing whatsoever to me. Now if you don't mind, it's time for my lunch. Have a safe journey home. We won't be seeing each other again.'

He squeezed Khalifa's shoulder, the fingers really digging in, then, with a nod, stepped back and slammed the door in his face. From within the flat came a muted crackle as another fly grilled itself against the electric insect-killer.

TEL-AVIV

Ben-Roi made two quick detours before heading down to Abu Kabir for his interview with über-pimp Genady Kremenko.

The first was to the Hofesh Shelter in Petah Tikvah, to drop off the playthings he'd purchased from the Jerusalem Toys R Us. He didn't make a big deal of it, just left the bags with the gatehouse guard and asked him to make sure they got to the shelter kids. The man wanted to call up to Maya Hillel, but Ben-Roi said he was in a hurry and got on his way. Didn't want the woman thinking he was trying to impress her. Or, worse, that he was some sort of softie.

The second detour was to central Tel-Aviv to pick up Dov Zisky. He was in town for the weekend staying with friends, and had asked if he could sit in on the interview, which was fine by Ben-Roi, although why the kid would want to waste his day off mixing with a sleazeball like Kremenko was anyone's guess.

He was waiting outside the Grand Beach Hotel on Nordau, leaning against a lamppost dressed in skinny jeans, tight white T-shirt, sandals and Ray-bans. Ben-Roi pulled into the kerb and threw open the Toyota's passenger door.

'You go to *shul* looking like that?' he asked as Zisky climbed in, bringing with him a waft of aftershave.

'Sure I do.'

'You smell like a rent-boy.'

'Well, they do say perfume is pleasing to the nose of the Lord.' He slammed the door and handed Ben-Roi a paper bag. 'Lunch.'

Ben-Roi sniffed the bag and grinned.

'And they also say *latkes* are pleasing to the nose of your boss. Good boy.'

He removed one of the patties, bit into it and swung round the corner on to Ha-Yarkon. For a moment they drove in silence, then:

'You smell a lot of rent-boys, then?' asked Zisky.

The two men looked at each other and burst out laughing.

Abu Kabir Detention Facility – aka The Jaffa Hilton – was at the south end of town, just round the corner from the National Centre for Forensic Medicine, where Rivka Kleinberg's body had been autopsied. An imposing three-storey block with grilled windows and a large observation tower in one corner, it was surrounded by a white-washed perimeter wall topped with chain-link fencing. Some sensitive soul had had the idea of dotting the wall with terracotta sculptures to try to brighten the place up a bit. Waste of time and money, in Ben-Roi's opinion. A prison was a prison, and short of removing the wall – and the bars and the doors as well – you weren't ever going to make it feel cheerful.

They parked up in the lot beside the facility's retractable steel gates and presented themselves at the main security window. The duty guard buzzed them in and put a call over to the main building to announce their arrival. A couple of minutes later another guard appeared and led them through into the compound.

'Adam Heber not around?' asked Ben-Roi as they crossed a concrete forecourt, referring to his warder friend.

'He's on nights at the moment,' replied the guard. 'Sends his best. Says he hopes you have a fun visit.'

'I'm sure it'll be thrilling,' grunted Ben-Roi.

They reached the main prison block and passed out of the sunlight into the gloomy interior. There was paperwork to fill in, after which the warder led them down a corridor, across an internal courtyard shaded by an overhead mesh, and into another wing. There was the sound of radios and chattering voices and, from somewhere above them, the clatter of a tin pot being banged against bars. No people they could see. Like all prisons Ben-Roi had ever been in, he had the unnerving feeling it wasn't actual humans who were making the noises but rather the building itself.

'You're in here,' said the guard, eventually stopping in front of a door and slotting a key into its lock. 'I'll go fetch the prisoner. His solicitor's already in there.'

He opened the door and stood back, waving them through into the room beyond: lino floor, barred window set high in the wall, wooden table with a water jug, paper cups and ashtray. A tall, middle-aged woman was facing them across the table, smartly dressed, something tight and pinched about her face, as though the features had all been squeezed into too little space. The detectives sat down.

'It was only supposed to be an informal chat,' said Ben-Roi as behind them the door closed and the lock clicked. 'He didn't need legal counsel.'

'My client prefers to keep everything above board.'

'Shame he didn't do the same with his business dealings.'

The woman tutted and folded her hands. No wedding ring, Ben-Roi noticed. One of those career junkies so focused on getting scumbags like Kremenko off the hook she didn't have time for a family. That or a dyke. Either way, he didn't like her. Didn't like any of her sort. Arrogant, slippery types who went home each day glad in the knowledge they'd made the police look like idiots and helped another paedo back on to the streets. Stupid bitch.

'I trust we can keep this civil,' she said. 'It's my daughter's birthday and I'd like to get home in a reasonably good mood.'

OK, wrong on that score.

'So here are the ground rules,' continued the woman. 'My client has agreed to answer whatever questions you have, and to offer whatever help he can in your investigation. In return, we would ask you to limit your questions to the agreed remit and, since Mr Kremenko has not been officially named as a suspect in your case, nor convicted of any other crime, to treat him with respect and courtesy.'

'Should I change his nappy as well?'

'Grow up, Detective. And do it quickly or this interview's stopping right here.'

Fuck you, he thought.

'This is?' She nodded towards Zisky. Ben-Roi made the introductions.

'The interview request was only for yourself.'

'He's just sitting in. I want to show him the ropes. Teach him the importance of respect and courtesy.'

She smiled at that, although there was a sourness to the expression.

'OK, I'll allow it.' She scribbled Zisky's details on her pad. 'I'll be recording the conversation –' she produced a Dictaphone and laid it on the table – 'which will constitute a legally admissible record should you decide to go off remit. I'll also be keeping a close eye on the time. I believe we agreed on sixty minutes.'

'You believe right.'

'Let's keep it to that.'

Preliminaries over, she sat back and folded her arms. From somewhere outside the room came the distant echo of music. Ben-Roi resisted the temptation to ask if she wanted to dance.

A couple of minutes went by, then there was a slap of footsteps in the corridor and the click of key in lock. The door swung open again and the subject of the interview entered the room. The solicitor stood; the two detectives remained seated.

Pimps and traffickers come in many different shapes and sizes, and from many different demographics, but if ever there was a stereotype, Genady Kremenko was it. A bulky, overweight man with a balding head, jowly face and pink, fleshy eyes, he combined cheery avuncularity with an undercurrent of brooding menace. He sported an array of heavy gold jewellery – neck-chain, bracelet, signet rings – and, rather to Ben-Roi's annoyance, since they were *his* team, a green and white Maccabi Haifa shirt. Prominently displayed on his forearm was a tattoo of a girl with her legs spread, the limbs, torso and head done in green ink, the vulva graphically highlighted in pink.

'Well, this is cosy, isn't it,' he chuckled, his Hebrew leavened with a thick Eastern European accent. 'Always a pleasure to welcome our brave boys in blue. Particularly such pretty ones.'

He grinned at Zisky, who to his credit didn't react.

'I'd give you both a hug, but unfortunately . . .' He held up his hands, which were cuffed.

'I don't think those will be necessary in here,' said his solicitor.

The guard looked at Ben-Roi, who nodded. The cuffs were undone.

'Can't blame them,' laughed Kremenko, rubbing his wrists and rolling his hands. 'You only have to look at me to see I'm a trained killer. A couple of years back I took out a whole tank regiment with a single fart.' He blew a raspberry and guffawed.

'I think we'd better get started,' said the solicitor primly.

The guard indicated a button on the wall which they could press if they needed anything, then left them to it, locking the door behind him. Kremenko sauntered round the table and took the seat beside his lawyer.

'Shall I buzz for champagne?' he asked, nodding at the wall button and letting out another guffaw.

Ignoring the comment, the solicitor checked her watch, then leant forward, turned on the Dictaphone and slid it across the table so it was positioned midway between Kremenko and Ben-Roi. She gave the location, date, time and names of those present in the room, then sat back and indicated that the interview could start.

'Just for the record I'd like to say the younger of the two detectives has really beautiful skin,' sniggered Kremenko.

Zisky smiled and crossed his legs, unperturbed. Ben-Roi laid the folder he'd brought with him on the table and got to work.

'Mr Kremenko, you recently—'

'Genady, please. We're all friends here.'

'You recently received a visit from a journalist named Rivka Kleinberg.'

'Did I?'

'Yes, you did.'

'If you say so. I seem to have become awfully forgetful these days. Something about the air in this place. Dulls the brain.'

Ben-Roi's jaw tightened. This was going to be hard work.

'Let me try and jog your memory, *Genady*. On May thirtieth, Mrs Kleinberg contacted *Shabas* with a request to visit you. That request was put to you, you agreed.'

'Without my knowledge,' cut in the solicitor.

'The reason for the visit was stated as "personal". Mrs Kleinberg attended the jail on the afternoon of June sixth when, between the hours of 13.30 and 14.05, you were alone with her in this room.'

'Not shagging, I can assure you of that,' grunted Kremenko.

'You remember now?'

'Suddenly I do. Big fat pushy bitch with massive –' he cupped his hands in front of his chest. 'Not a pleasant sight. I must have blocked it out.'

Beside him his solicitor sat poker-faced.

'Well, now that you've unblocked it,' said Ben-Roi, 'do you want to tell me what Mrs Kleinberg was doing here?'

Kremenko shrugged. 'Impression I got was that she was lonely. You know how it is: fat, unfuckable, getting on in life. I think she wanted some company. Saw my face in the paper, thought I looked a friendly sort of guy, decided maybe I was someone she could have a chat with.'

Ben-Roi played along, let him have his little joke.

'And what exactly was it you chatted about?'

Kremenko folded his arms and sat back, gazing thoughtfully at the ceiling.

'Now let me think. The weather certainly came up – it's been unseasonably hot, don't you think – and I seem to remember there was some political discussion: municipal elections, *ha-matzav*, whether Tzipi Livni takes it up the arse . . .'

Beside him his solicitor stiffened and blushed. Kremenko noted her embarrassment and grinned.

'Only kidding. We didn't really talk about that.'

'You don't say,' muttered Ben-Roi.

Slipping a hand underneath the shoulder of his football shirt, Kremenko pulled out a pack of Marlboro. He removed one with his teeth, took a lighter from the pack and, leaning his elbows on the table, lit the cigarette.

'OK, enough pissing around, let's get down to it,' he said, exhaling a dense billow of smoke towards Zisky, who wafted it away with a flick of the hand. 'This woman says she wants to come in and talk to me. I don't know her from Adam, but think why the hell not. You get bored in here, welcome any sort of distraction. Who knows, she might have been a looker, worth a wank. Which of course she wasn't. Built like a fucking Space Hopper. Very disappointing.'

He exhaled another waft of smoke, forcing Zisky to move his chair back a few inches.

'Sorry, darling.'

'And what did Mrs Kleinberg want to talk to you about?' asked Ben-Roi, putting his earlier question again.

'This and that.'

'This and that being . . .?'

'My business, the girls—'

The solicitor dived in. 'I think in the current circumstances we ought to steer clear . . .'

Kremenko extended a finger, quietening her. A small gesture, barely noticeable, but one that spoke volumes to Ben-Roi. This was a man who was used to being obeyed, especially by women.

'Relax,' he said. 'I'm here to help these gentlemen. I've nothing to hide, nothing to be ashamed of.'

He sat back and took another long suck on his Marlboro, holding it right at the bottom of the filter in the way that all lags seem to do. Beside him the woman folded her hands and stared across the table, tight-lipped.

'They've got it all wrong, you see,' said Kremenko. 'The police, the papers. They say I'm a pimp, a trafficker, but I don't even know what those words mean. I'm a businessman, plain and simple. A landlord. The only crime I've committed, and this I do hold my hands up to –' he raised his hands theatrically – 'is the sin of being too kind. These young girls, they come to Israel, they don't know anyone, don't speak the language. I help them out – fix cheap accommodation, lend them a bit of cash when they're short, get them back on their feet.'

'From what I've heard, it's more a case of getting them *off* their feet and *on to* their backs,' shot Ben-Roi.

Again, the solicitor was straight in. 'Any more cheap gags like that and this conversation—'

'Easy, tiger!' laughed Kremenko, waving her quiet. 'He was only joshing. Can't take offence every time someone makes a little joke. Can we, eh, Bambi?'

This last line to Zisky, who yet again let it roll over him. Credit to the kid for keeping his cool. If it had been Ben-Roi on the receiving end he'd have decked Kremenko by now.

'And this is what you told Mrs Kleinberg?' he asked.

'Exactly. I said to her, these girls, I'm like a father to them. How was I to know they were up to all sorts of naughtiness behind my back? Take it from me, I'm the victim here. Victim of my own trusting nature.'

He shook his head, all mock outrage. Ben-Roi flicked a glance at Zisky, then at the solicitor, whose expression remained resolutely neutral, even though it was obvious her client was talking horseshit. He wondered if it troubled her, defending a turd like Kremenko. Probably not. The law is impartial, she would argue, everyone is entitled to a fair defence. She might not have liked the man, but to her way of thinking, she was serving a higher cause. To Ben-Roi's way of thinking, she was as much of a whore as the girls Kremenko had been pimping. More of one – at least she had a choice in the matter.

'Tell me about the Egypt route,' he said.

'What's that, then?' Feigned outrage gave way to feigned bewilderment.

'The route the girls are trafficked into Israel – across the Sinai, up into the Negev.'

'I wouldn't know anything about it.'

'They say you run it.'

Kremenko shrugged. 'People say all sorts of things. They say you lot are a bunch of cunts but that doesn't mean you've got a clit on your head and piss blood every month.'

The solicitor winced. If Ben-Roi had been less frustrated by Kremenko's stonewalling he'd have found her discomfort amusing.

'Did Mrs Kleinberg talk about Egypt?'

'Might have. If she did, I'd have told her the same as I've just told you.'

'Which is?'

'That I don't fucking know anything!'

The pimp gave an impatient flick of the wrist, bling rattling. Ben-Roi rewound.

'Let's go back to the girls,' he said. 'Did Mrs Kleinberg ask about any of them in particular. Mention any names?'

'Not that I recall.'

'Maria? Did that name come up?'

Kremenko scrunched his eyes as if pondering, then shook his head.

'Vosgi?'

Another shake. 'Like I said to the fat woman, I've got a lot of tenants, I don't remember what all of them are called.'

'Maybe you'd remember a face.' Ben-Roi opened the folder, slid out the photo of Vosgi and laid it on the table in front of Kremenko. 'Was this one of your *tenants*?'

The solicitor caught the sarcasm and shot Ben-Roi a warning look.

Kremenko either didn't notice, or chose not to rise to it. He picked up the photo, made a show of staring at it.

'Never seen her before,' he replied after an extravagant pause, handing the photo back.

'Sure.'

'Sure as I've got a hole in my arse.'

'She's Armenian. Went missing from a shelter a few weeks ago.'

Ben-Roi threw it out to see if he got a reaction. He didn't. Kremenko just stared at him, his eyes puffed and pink and vaguely amused. He tried to read what was going on behind the eyes, to push inside, but the shutters were firmly down and he got nothing, not even a glimpse. Kremenko began to chuckle.

'You're fishing, Detective. Fishing with a broken rod in an empty pond and wondering why the fuck you're not getting any bites.'

Clunky metaphor, not that far off the truth. The pimp sucked away the last of his cigarette and, leaning forward, ground the butt out in the ashtray.

'I'll tell you what, I'm going to help you,' he said. 'You seem like a nice couple –' another wink at Zisky – 'and I'm an amenable chap, always anxious to please. So here's the score.'

He sat back again and folded his arms, man-boobs squeezing out beneath his elbows, the tattooed vulva on his forearm seeming to gape at Ben-Roi like an inflamed eye.

'Hand on heart, I didn't like the Kleinberg woman. I agreed to meet her, gave her the time of day, and by way of thanks she was a rude, pushy, mannerless bitch. Asked all sorts of out-of-order questions, made all manner of unpleasant insinuations about my personal and professional life. In the end I'm afraid I lost patience and told her to go fuck herself, which was frankly more than anyone else was ever going to do. In short, and I make no bones about this, we didn't hit it off. But if you're asking me – and I suspect this is what you *are* asking me in your own roundabout way – whether I had anything to do with the woman's murder . . .'

His solicitor started to protest, saying this wasn't germane to the interview, but again Kremenko waved her quiet.

'*If* that's what you're asking me, then I can tell you, again hand on heart, Jew-boy's honour, that no, I didn't. And if you're going to suggest otherwise, you'd better have some seriously fucking good evidence to back it up, or this charming lady beside me is going to come down on you like a hundred tons of the thickest shit that ever dropped out of a human butthole.'

He eyeballed the two detectives, fists clenched, the jokey charade parting like a curtain to reveal the true nature of the man behind: hard, brutal, thuggish. And then, as suddenly as the storm had blown up, it dissipated and Kremenko was all smiles again.

'Right, now we've sorted that out, let's get back to business.' He beamed and reached for the water jug. 'Refreshments, anyone?'

The interview continued for another forty minutes, but Ben-Roi was only going through the motions. He didn't expect Kremenko to tell him anything, and the man lived up to expectations. He was closed up as tight as a clam, batting away the detective's questions with the glib insouciance of someone who has spent his entire life playing cat and mouse with the law and was more than confident of his abilities to give his pursuer the run-around. He was obviously lying about his pimping and trafficking activities, and he had equally obviously lied about them to Rivka Kleinberg. The issue was less *what* she'd got out of him as what she'd *hoped* to get out of him. And again and again Ben-Roi came back to the same point – the girl was the key to it all. Kleinberg had applied to visit Kremenko the day after she'd heard of Vosgi's disappearance, and whatever information she'd been trying to prise from him, Ben-Roi was certain it was tied up with the missing Armenian. Had Vosgi been one of Kremenko's girls? Had Kremenko's people snatched her, maybe to stop her testifying against his operation? Had Kleinberg got too close to the truth and been bumped off as well? It was a feasible scenario – the most feasible scenario he'd yet come up with – albeit one that left a bundle of loose ends and unanswered questions. Over and over he steered the interview back in that direction, pressing Kremenko, showing him the girl's photo, trying to open up a chink in his armour. To no avail. Maybe at a later date he'd go in harder, get Kremenko up to Kishle, really turn the screws, but even then he doubted it would have any effect. Like the man said, he was fishing – plenty of supposition, fuck-all hard evidence. And Kremenko knew it. As the interview drew towards its conclusion he bore the look of a man who'd had a thoroughly enjoyable afternoon.

Spot on the sixty-minute mark – not a second over – the solicitor called time. Clicking off the Dictaphone, she stood, crossed to the wall

266

buzzer and rang for the guard. Kremenko lounged back and laid his arm across the top of his counsel's empty chair.

'It's been a real pleasure, gentlemen,' he grinned. 'Or rather, ladies and *gentleman*.'

Another of those teasing looks at Zisky.

'If there's anything else I can help you with, please don't hesitate to get in touch. I'll be residing here for another few weeks, after which I expect to be back home again.'

He threw a glance at the solicitor, who wore the expression of someone who'd spent the last hour sitting on a cactus. She took a step back towards her chair, saw the position of Kremenko's arm, remained standing. There was an uneasy silence, then the sound of approaching footsteps. Ben-Roi and Zisky stood, the lock clicked and the door swung open. Different guard this time.

'You go carefully,' said Kremenko, lifting a meaty, ring-covered hand and wiggling the fingers in farewell. 'Don't be strangers.'

Ben-Roi tried to come up with some caustic parting shot, something that would at least allow him to leave with his dignity intact, but couldn't think of anything and, with a nod at Zisky, the two detectives made for the door. As they reached it, the guard stepping aside to let them through, Zisky suddenly swung back into the room.

'Genady, what exactly is it you were doing for Barren Corporation?'

It was a punt to nowhere, like Ben-Roi's earlier one about Vosgi coming from Armenia. Unlike Ben-Roi's attempt, this one seemed to catch Kremenko unawares. It was only for the briefest of instants, just a second or two, but something about the widening of the pimp's eyes, the slight tightening of his lips, showed the question had slipped under his guard and touched a nerve. He recovered himself almost immediately.

'Oh I do like her,' he chuckled. 'Feisty little thing. And so pretty. If I *was* a pimp – which as we all know I'm not – I reckon she'd do some pretty good business for me.'

Grinning at Zisky, he lifted his arm, licked a fingertip and rubbed it up and down the tattooed vagina. It was all bravado. He was rattled. No question about it. Seriously rattled.

As they left the cell and headed back through the prison, Ben-Roi wrapped an arm round Zisky's shoulders.

'Good boy,' he said.

EGYPT

It was mid-afternoon when Khalifa arrived back in Luxor. At this hour most of the town's population had been driven indoors by the heat, and the streets were unnaturally quiet and still. A group of old men were playing *siga* beside the dried-up fountain on the roundabout in front of the station, *shaals* draped over their heads against the sun. A caleche clopped its desultory way up and down Sharia al-Mahatta on the off-chance of picking up some custom. Otherwise the place was dead. He bought himself a carton of Easy Mouzoo – mango flavour – and, sitting on the station steps, made a couple of calls. Home first, to check on Zenab – she'd had an even worse night than usual and was currently asleep, watched over by Batah. Then to Mohammed Sariya at police headquarters. Chief Hassani was on the warpath apparently, screaming the place down about a rash of anonymous fly-posters that had appeared across town accusing the force of incompetence and corruption. Khalifa's absence hadn't even been noticed, let alone queried. Sadeq, it seemed, had not acted on his parting threat to contact Hassani. Yet.

'Do me a favour, Mohammed,' he said while he had him on the line. 'If you get a moment, could you check up on a family from Old Qurna? Name of El-Badri. If any of them are still around they'd have been moved up to El-Tarif when the village got bulldozed.'

'Anything in particular you want to know?' asked Sariya.

'This is going back a while, but there were three brothers and a sister. One of the brothers called Mohammed, the sister Iman. They're all long dead, but I'd be interested to know if there are any surviving relatives. No great urgency. Just when you've got the time.'

Sariya said he'd get on the case and Khalifa rang off. For a minute he sat sipping his juice, watching as a Travco tourist coach lumbered its way round the roundabout, its occupants looking pale-faced and bored. Then, draining the carton and launching it into a bin, he stood and set off for the West Bank and the Valley of the Kings. If some anonymous fly-poster had had the decency to provide a distraction, he might as well take advantage of it.

'Valley of the Kings' is a misnomer. The ancient necropolis is neither the exclusive preserve of kings – it was also the final resting place of queens, princes, princesses, nobles and royal pets – nor is it a single valley. Rather, it comprises two branching *wadis*: the better-known East Valley, where are to be found all the main royal tombs including that of Tutankhamun, and the broader West Valley, or Valley of the Baboons, a much more desolate and less frequently visited burial corridor that splits from its more celebrated neighbour close to the latter's entrance and heads off on its own meandering course into the hills.

Having crossed the river, Khalifa hitched a lift up to the coach park at the juncture of the two valleys. He stood a moment gazing at the huge hoarding that had been erected at the side of the road to publicize the new museum up in the East Valley. 'Barren Corporation', proclaimed the strapline. 'Honouring Egypt's Past, Promoting Egypt's Future'. Then, flicking away his cigarette, he set off into the western branch of the necropolis.

In contrast to the perpetual tourist crush in its sister valley, this one was lifeless and deserted, a stark avenue of blinding-white limestone hemmed in by towering cliffs and heavy with the dense, smothering silence of the desert. There was a ramshackle caretaker's residence on a bluff near the valley mouth and, a little further along its course, a more substantial domed building that had once been home to Egyptologist John Romer. Other than that, and a pair of corroded metal signs pointing out the tombs of Amenhotep lll and Akhenaten, there was nothing. Just rock, and dust, and the occasional swift skimming across the cliff faces. Had an ancient Egyptian been walking alongside Khalifa, they would have noticed little difference from how the valley had looked and felt in their own day.

It took him the best part of forty minutes to walk the *wadi*'s length, the heat slowing his pace. Eventually, just as he was starting to think that maybe he should have waited for a cooler part of the day, the track curved to the right and petered out in a deep natural amphitheatre curtained by rearing walls of rock. There was a wooden rest shelter, and, beside it, the entrance to the tomb of the Eighteenth-Dynasty vizier-turned-pharaoh Ay. A dusty Jawa motorbike was propped nearby, which was a relief – he would have hated to come all this way for no reason.

Descending the steps to the tomb's open doorway, he put his head inside and called down the steeply sloping passage.

'Professor Dufresne!'

No response.

'Professor Dufresne! Are you there?'

Another silence. Then, from below, disembodied, like a voice from the underworld:

'Yusuf Khalifa, if I've told you once, I've told you a thousand times, it's Mary!'

Khalifa smiled. 'Yes, Professor.'

There was a faint echo of climbing footsteps and a head appeared far beneath, everything below the neck hidden by the corridor's acute slope.

'What the hell are you doing out here?'

'I wanted to ask you a question.'

'Sure must be an important one.'

'Shall I come down?'

'No, I was about to come up for air anyway. You thirsty?'

'Very.'

'You're in luck. I've got a flask of cold *seer limoon*.'

Good old Mary Dufresne.

'Give me a moment,' she called, and disappeared back down the passage. Khalifa returned to the shade of the rest shelter. A few minutes went by, then there was some movement to his left and a figure emerged from the tomb entrance – tall, grey-haired, dressed in jeans, khaki shirt and with a white linen *shaal* wrapped around her neck. She gave a cheery wave and strode up the slope towards him, moving with surprising speed given that she must now be pushing ninety. Khalifa stood and the two of them shook hands.

'How are you, you lovely man?'

'I am well, *hamdulillah*. You?'

'Pretty damn good, for an old crock. Zenab?'

'She is . . . OK.'

The woman held his eyes. Then, sensing that he didn't wish to pursue the line of conversation, gave his arm a friendly rub and lifted the flask she was holding.

'Drink?'

'I thought you would never ask.'

They sat and, unscrewing the flask's lid, she poured him a cup and handed it over. She poured one for herself and they toasted each other.

'Good to see you, Yusuf.'

'You too, *ya doctora*.'

She shot him a look.

'Mary,' he corrected, overriding his natural tendency to formality when addressing his elders and betters. She gave an approving nod and sipped her lemon.

Mary Dufresne – *ya doctora amrekanaya* as she was known to everyone in Luxor – was a throwback. The last surviving link to a golden age of Egyptian archaeology. Her father, Alan Dufresne, had been a conservator at the Met and had come out in the late 1920s to work with the great Herbert Winlock. He'd brought his wife and daughter with him, and, apart from a brief stint back at Harvard studying for her doctorate, Mary had been here ever since. Winlock, Howard Carter, Flinders Petrie, John Pendlebury, Muhammad Goneim – she'd known them all. An exalted band of which she herself was a deserving member. Mary Dufresne was, by popular acclamation, the greatest archaeological draughtsman ever to have worked in Egypt. Even the notoriously arrogant Zahi Hawass was said to be in awe of her.

'So how's the work going?' asked Khalifa, draining his lemon in one gulp and accepting a refill.

'Slowly,' she replied. 'Which is how it should be going. The world's getting way too fast for my liking.'

For the last decade Mary had been producing scale drawings of every painting and inscription in the West Valley. She'd been in the tomb of Ay for three of those ten years.

'Looks like you needed that,' she said as he again drained the cup in one long gulp.

'It was a longer walk than I remembered.'

'It's like that in the summer. When the weather starts to cool it gets a lot shorter. Come December you could hop it.'

She smiled and filled his cup for a third time.

'So what's this mysterious question you wanted to ask?'

Khalifa took another appreciative sip – Mary made her own lemonade and managed to get just the right balance between the bitterness of the lemons and the sweetness of the cane sugar. Then, wiping his mouth, he laid the cup aside.

'It's about a man called Samuel Pinsker,' he said. 'An Englishman. Used to work out here. I was wondering if by any chance you remembered him.'

'Samuel Pinsker.' She drew the name out as if getting a feel for the sound of it. 'My God, that's a blast from the past.'

'You do remember him?'

'Vaguely. He disappeared when I was just a kid. They found his body back in the seventies. Fell down a shaft tomb up on the high *gebel.*'

Khalifa had already decided to keep the fact that Pinsker had been murdered to himself. Like Chief Sadeq had said, some narratives are best kept simple. Instead, he asked if she could remember anything about the man.

'He spooked me, I certainly remember that,' she said, swishing a hand to scatter the flies that were darting around the rim of her cup. 'He used to wear this mask thing: little bitty eye-holes and a slit for a mouth. Made him look like some sort of . . . I don't know, monster or ghoul or something.'

She gave another flick of her hand, finished her lemonade and screwed the cup back on to the flask.

'Samuel Pinsker,' she repeated. 'What on earth makes you ask about him?'

'The name cropped up in a case a friend of mine is working on. I said I'd try and find out a bit about him.'

He fired up a cigarette.

'My friend's Israeli,' he added.

Dufresne's eyebrows lifted in surprise.

'How the hell does Samuel Pinsker relate to a police case in Israel?'

'I was hoping you could tell me.'

She shook her head. 'I'm sorry, Yusuf, I don't think I'm going to be much help here. I like to think I'm not going senile yet, but eighty years is a hell of a long time. I was only, what, six or seven when he went missing. Things tend to blur and fade.'

She pushed a hair out of her eye and sat back, crossing her legs and rearranging the *shaal* around her neck.

'I do remember him roaring around on his motorbike,' she said after a pause, 'and also scaring the shit out of me in a temple once, excuse the language. No idea which temple it was, or what I was doing there. I just remember him coming out at me from behind a pillar. I had nightmares about it for weeks.'

'Did he hurt you?' asked Khalifa, thinking about the girl Pinsker had raped.

'What, like molest me?'

Khalifa shrugged.

'Certainly not that I recall. I just remember him suddenly appearing, me screaming and running away, and him following me in that horrible mask of his.'

She dipped her head, thinking, then looked up again, her expression apologetic.

'That's about it, I'm afraid. To be honest, I can't even be sure if it actually happened like that. You know how memories twist themselves, get all tangled up. Watch out there.'

She motioned to the concrete bench where a large hornet had landed right beside Khalifa's hand. It meandered about, then wafted itself up on to the rim of his cup. He prodded it away with the tip of his cigarette, drank the remaining lemonade and, standing, took the cup outside the shelter and placed it on a rock. The hornet followed.

'Max knew him,' she said as Khalifa resumed his seat.

'Max?'

'Legrange. French archaeologist. Pottery genius. Worked with Bruyère and Černý at Deir el-Medina.'

'Never heard of him.'

'Before your time, young man. Dead now, of course. They all are. Only me left of that vintage.'

She sighed and for a moment her gaze drifted away down the valley, her mind seeming to cross over into a different time-frame. It only lasted a few seconds and then she was back in the conversation.

'Just after they found the body, I remember having tea with Max and him talking about Pinsker, what he'd been like. Didn't have much good to say about the man. Heavy drinker, apparently, always arguing with people. Got in a fight with some *Qurnawis* once, laid one of them out cold.'

Again Khalifa thought of the girl who'd been raped. She'd been from Qurna too. He could feel Pinsker coming into focus. The facial deformity obviously set him apart, but character-wise he sounded like a stereotype: the violent, boorish, superior Englishman who claimed a stake in Egypt's heritage and yet for whom Egyptians themselves were a subordinate race, there to be patronized and abused and violated. A typical old-school colonial.

'Carter liked him, apparently,' Dufresne was saying. 'Which I guess would figure, what with Howard himself having a bit of a temper. You know he once got sacked from the Antiquities Service for walloping a French tourist at Saqqara?'

273

Khalifa hadn't heard that story.

'Anything else?' he asked, trying to tease out some link with Ben-Roi's case.

'Well, I can't remember the conversation verbatim,' said Dufresne. 'Forty years is still a long time ago.'

She dipped her head, pondering.

'I do seem to recall him mentioning Pinsker was an extremely skilled engineer, did a lot of work shoring up monuments here and over on the East Bank. Oh yeah, and that he had a habit of disappearing into the desert for weeks on end.'

Khalifa was bending to tamp out his cigarette on the shelter's concrete floor. He looked up at this. Pinsker's landlady in Kom Lolah had said much the same in the statement she'd given to police after the Englishman's disappearance, although there had been no mention of a desert.

'Did your friend say which desert?' he asked, straightening again, interested.

'Eastern, I think. Yes, definitely the Eastern Desert.'

'Do you know what Pinsker was doing out there?'

She shook her head, unable to answer. Khalifa's mind was turning, cogs taking up the bite of other cogs. The night of his murder Samuel Pinsker comes back from another mysterious trip out into the middle of nowhere, gets drunk, rapes a girl, then staggers over to Howard Carter's house and boasts of finding something that was 'miles long'. The scenario was leading him somewhere, he could feel it, although whether that somewhere had anything to do with Ben-Roi's case was another matter entirely. It was certainly intriguing.

'Did you ever hear of Samuel Pinsker finding something?' he asked.

'How do you mean, finding something?'

'I don't know, a tomb maybe, a . . .' He tried to think of anything else that might warrant the description 'miles long'. A discovery Pinsker would have wanted to boast about. Nothing obvious came to mind. Even a tomb didn't really seem to fit the bill. 'Something big,' he said lamely.

Dufresne gave him a quizzical look, not understanding what he was driving at. By way of explanation he pulled the 1931 file out of his plastic bag, removed the Carter letter and handed it to her. She read through it, her eyes widening in surprise.

'How extraordinary,' she said when she came to the end. 'I can almost hear Howard's voice. "Tommyrot" – he was always using that expression.'

'Does it mean anything to you? That bit about –' Khalifa leant over and pointed to the relevant lines.

'Nothing at all, I'm afraid. I'm as much in the dark as you. It's certainly a mystery.'

She started to hand the letter back. Before Khalifa could take it, she suddenly withdrew the sheet and read through it again. Something about her demeanour as she did so, the way her eyes kept flicking off to the side as if reaching for a distant memory, hinted that some connection had suddenly suggested itself.

'No,' she murmured. 'It couldn't be.'

'What?'

'It was years later. Completely different context. Although it *was* Howard. And the language was certainly similar.'

She seemed to be talking more to herself than to Khalifa. For a brief moment he wondered if perhaps her age was finally catching up with her, her mental faculties starting to scramble. Then she looked at him and it was clear her mind was as lucid as it had ever been.

'What?' he asked again.

'Well, I really don't want to be confusing the issue. And it's almost certainly not connected, but . . .' She looked down at the letter again, then leant back against one of the posts supporting the shelter's roof. 'It was just something I overheard. About eight years after Pinsker disappeared. It stuck with me, and reading this, that line, "I found it, Carter", kind of brought it to mind. Like I say, it's probably something completely different, but –' She broke off, shaking her head.

'Do you want to tell me?'

'Sure. It's actually one of the handful of things from that period I remember quite clearly. Probably because it was the last time we saw Howard alive.'

She was silent for a few seconds, gathering her thoughts.

'It was three or four months before he died. Which would have put it, what, end of 1938, beginning 1939. He was living back in London then, but he used to winter in Luxor, and often came over for dinner with us. I always got sent upstairs, but like most kids I'd creep out on to the landing, try to eavesdrop on what the grown-ups were saying. I can't recall exactly who was there -- my father and Howard, certainly, maybe Herbie Winlock and Walt Hauser . . .'

She paused, thinking, then waved her hand.

'It doesn't matter. The point is, there was a big argument and Howard started shouting. He was always irascible and got worse towards the end, what with the Hodgkin's Disease. I've no idea what they were actually arguing about, but I do remember Howard shouting very loudly, "He did *not* find it. The whole thing is tommyrot. A myth. You can dig up the whole damned Eastern Desert and it won't be there, for the simple reason that the Labyrinth never existed."'

Khalifa frowned. 'Labby-rin?'

The word was unfamiliar to him.

'*Mahata*,' she translated.

'What does it mean?'

'I honestly couldn't say. The only labyrinth I've ever heard of is the Amenemhat pyramid complex, but that's over at Hawwara in the Fayoum. And anyway, Petrie had discovered that at the end of the 1880s.'

She scanned the letter again, then handed it back.

'That's it?' asked Khalifa, returning the sheet to the folder. 'You can't remember anything more?'

'Afraid not.'

'You've no idea who they were talking about? Who the "he" was?'

'I'm sorry, Yusuf. It's just that little fragment. Maybe it *was* about Petrie and Hawwara, and Howard just got his deserts mixed up, East for West. Maybe *I've* got the deserts mixed up – it was eighty years ago, after all. Memory plays tricks. It just struck me there was a similarity in tone. And the mention of the Eastern Desert . . .'

She gave an apologetic shrug. Khalifa hunched over and worked the folder back into the plastic bag. There'd been a moment when he'd thought she was going to tell him something illuminating. Instead she just seemed to have clouded the issue even further. Samuel Pinsker claimed to have found something 'miles long', possibly out in a desert somewhere. Someone else, who may or may not have been Pinsker, claimed to have found a labyrinth, possibly out in the Eastern Desert. Both claims were vague; neither seemed to have any obvious relevance to the case Ben-Roi was working on. It was, to coin one of Chief Hassani's favourite phrases, like playing *tawla* in a pair of buffalo turd goggles.

His perplexity must have registered in his expression, because Dufresne reached out and squeezed his arm.

276

'There *is* one person you could speak to,' she said.

He looked up.

'English guy. Digby Girling. Funny man, chubby, looks like a balloon. A few years back – actually more than a few years – he wrote a book on bit-players in the Tutankhamun excavation. I'm pretty certain Pinsker was mentioned. Digby might know something more.'

'Do you know how I can get hold of him?'

'Well, he's based in England – London, Birkbeck, I think – but at this time of year you'll probably catch him guest-lecturing on one of the Nile cruisers.'

Khalifa made a mental note, then looked at his watch. It was later than he'd thought.

'I ought to be getting back. I don't like to . . . you know . . . Zenab.'

She gave his arm another squeeze.

'I understand, Yusuf. I'm sorry I couldn't have been more help.'

'You've been extremely helpful.'

'At least I got you rehydrated,' she smiled, tapping the lemonade flask. 'Can I give you a lift down to Dra Abu el-Naga?'

She nodded towards her motorbike. Khalifa declined the offer, not wanting to inconvenience her, but she insisted, saying that she needed to go down that way anyway to pick up some things. A blatant lie, but the prospect of trudging all the way back down the valley in the blazing afternoon heat persuaded Khalifa to swallow his pride and accept the lift.

'Thank you,' he said.

'Thank *you*. It's not often these days I get to cruise around with a handsome young man riding pillion.'

She returned the lemonade flask to the tomb, locked its entrance gate and the two of them chugged off along the *wadi* and on to the tarmac road that curved down through the hills from the Valley of the Kings to the verdant plain of the cultivation below. Rather than dropping him at Dra Abu el-Naga, she continued all the way on to the river, a diversion to which he offered only token resistance. It felt good to have the wind in his face.

They said their goodbyes on the Gezira waterfront, he paid his fifty piastres, boarded the local ferry and rumbled his way over to the East Bank, all the while thinking about Samuel Pinsker, and the crime he had committed, and the lonely death he had endured, and the mysterious object or place he claimed to have found. Only when the ferry had docked on the far shore, and he had disembarked in the jostling press of passengers, and was climbing the steps up on to the Nile-front Corniche, did he suddenly stiffen and stop dead in his tracks.

For the first time in nine months he had been on the water and not thought about his son Ali. He swung back to the river, shocked, uncertain whether he ought to be feeling relieved at the momentary distraction from grief, or horrified at the idea that his boy was beginning to slip away from him.

TEL-AVIV

Having dropped Zisky off in central Tel-Aviv, Ben-Roi put in a call to his journalist friend Natan Tirat to see if he fancied hooking up for a drink. The ulterior motif being to pick his brains about Barren Corporation. Tirat was on a deadline – some fascinating story about a black hole in the IDF pension fund – but said he'd be finished in an hour if Ben-Roi was OK to hang around. He had no pressing reason to be back in Jerusalem, so said that was fine and they agreed to meet for a beer in a bar they both knew on Dizengoff.

He put in a second call to Sarah, left a message on her voicemail. Then, with time to kill, he parked up in a side-street off Ha-Yarkon and took himself for a walk along the seafront.

The Corniche was bustling, as it always was on Saturdays – walkers and joggers and cyclists and rollerbladers; rammed cafés; a row of couples playing *matkot* behind the Sheraton Moriah, the thwack of balls on bats audible for a hundred metres in either direction. There was music, and a crowd of people practising salsa moves, and down on the beach rows of sunbathers in costumes so skimpy they might as well have just gone naked. It didn't just feel like a different city from Jerusalem, but a different world – so much more relaxed and easy-going, so much less intense and up itself. In Jerusalem there was always a weight on your shoulders – of religion, of history, of the irreconcilable politics of the Palestinian situation. Here on the coast the burden was lifted, it almost felt like Israel was a normal country. Not for the first time he wondered why the hell he'd ever moved away.

He bought himself an ice cream – double scoop, strawberry and pistachio – and wandered south along the promenade, the sea to his right, the towering façades of the beachfront hotels forming an un-broken wall of concrete to his left. He thought maybe he'd go all the way down to Clore Park, give his legs a good stretch, but in the end only made it to the ziggurat-like hulk of the Opera Tower before he ran out of steam. He stood a while listening to a string quartet giving an impromptu concert underneath a palm tree. Then, crunching away the last of his ice-cream cone, he turned and wandered back the way he had come. His thoughts turned with him, away from random mus-ings on Tel-Aviv, Sarah and the baby, the direction his life was taking, back to the Kleinberg case. Thanks to Zisky's parting shot in the prison, it was clear there was some interface between Genady Kremenko and Barren Corporation, although what the hell that inter-face was was anyone's guess. And Kremenko's involvement in the sex trade obviously linked him with Vosgi, who in turn provided a connec-tion with the Armenian side of things. So far so good. But what about the Nemesis Agenda and Kleinberg's unexplained trip down to Mitzpe Ramon? Had Nemesis turned up something that was relevant to the article Kleinberg was researching at the time of her murder? Had Kleinberg gone to *them* with something? At a push, it could just about be made to fit, albeit in a not entirely satisfactory manner. So: Barren, Kremenko, trafficking, Vosgi, Armenian Cathedral, Nemesis – all potentially linkable, with a couple of the links weak at best.

The problem element was the articles Kleinberg had been looking at about gold-mining and Samuel Pinsker. The gold-mining piece obviously linked to Barren and, in a very tenuous way, to Samuel Pinsker, who apparently had been a mining engineer. And Pinsker connected with Egypt, which was a trafficking hub. Despite that, the two stories felt jarringly out of place, inexplicable diversions from the main thrust of Kleinberg's work.

Pinsker in particular was giving him a bellyache. Experience had taught him that every case throws up at least one rogue element, one piece of the jigsaw that simply refuses to slot with the rest of the picture. Pinsker was that piece. The Englishman felt like part of a completely different picture altogether. He'd been hoping Khalifa would turn up something, but five days had gone by and he'd heard nothing from the Egyptian. Which left him in a delicate situation. He badly needed to get to grips with the Pinsker angle, but at the same time didn't want to be pressuring Khalifa for an update, not with

279

everything else the man was having to contend with at the moment. He'd already called once, left a message, hadn't heard back, didn't like the idea of hassling him. Yet he couldn't wait indefinitely. He had a murder to solve, and Samuel Pinsker somehow tied in with that murder. Should he bite the bullet and call again? Should he start making his own enquiries, get Zisky to do a bit of ferreting? He was still trying to decide when his cell phone went off.

Well, well. Khalifa. Jew and Muslim so in tune!

'I was just thinking about you,' he said, waving away a vendor who was trying to flog him a sunhat.

'Not bad things, I hope,' said Khalifa.

'Nothing but sunshine and love, my friend.'

If Khalifa was amused by the comment he didn't show it. He apologized for not having called sooner, explained that he'd wanted to talk to a couple of people before getting back to Ben-Roi, then launched into an extended summary of what he'd unearthed so far: the rape, the revenge murder, the Howard Carter letter, the mysterious discovery Pinsker claimed to have made shortly before his death which may or may not have had something to do with a labyrinth. If Ben-Roi had been hoping for a dramatic shedding of light, he was sorely disappointed. Not for the first time on this case.

'What do you make of it?' he asked when Khalifa had finished.

'I don't really know,' replied the Egyptian. 'The labyrinth thing is intriguing, but whether it's what your murder victim was interested in—'

He broke off, shouting angrily in Arabic to someone at his end of the line.

'Sorry, kids about to run across the road,' he explained. 'Foolish. They ought to look before they cross.'

Ben-Roi started to smile, then didn't, realizing the resonance such things must have for his friend. Instead he asked Khalifa if he thought there might be any connection between the two murders: Luxor 1931, Jerusalem the present. The Egyptian gave a muted *hrumph*, the verbal equivalent of throwing his hands up in the air.

'I can't see an obvious one. Apart from the two victims being Jewish. Even that seems . . . how do you say? . . . flimsy, given that the murders are eighty years apart. But then I don't know all the details of your case so maybe I'm missing something.'

It was a fair point. Ben-Roi had only furnished the most basic overview of the situation. Partly because the powers that be would have taken a seriously dim view of him going behind their backs and spilling a load of confidential case information to a third party, particularly an Arab third party. Mainly because he hadn't wanted to pull Khalifa in too deep, look like he was taking advantage of their friendship.

But then without pulling Khalifa in, it was possible connections were being missed. Vital connections.

He hesitated, trying to balance out the imperative to find answers with a reluctance to pressure his old friend. It was Khalifa who resolved the dilemma.

'Can you send me more information?' he asked.

'Do you *want* me to send you more information?'

'Why not? Anything to further the cause of Arab–Israeli relations.'

This time Ben-Roi did smile.

'I'll get something over to you tomorrow,' he said. 'I'd appreciate it if it stayed between the two of us.'

'Of course. I will make an appeal on state television, but apart from that it is our secret.'

Ben-Roi smiled again. Despite everything he'd gone through, the old Khalifa was still there. Bruised, but still there.

'I do have one possible lead,' continued the Egyptian. 'An English academic. Apparently he's done some research into Pinsker, might be able to fill in a few gaps. He's lecturing on a Nile cruiser at the moment, but I've checked the itinerary and his boat docks in Luxor tomorrow afternoon. I'll go and have a word, see what he can tell me.'

'Appreciated,' said Ben-Roi.

'No problem.'

'Really appreciated.'

'Really no problem.'

There didn't seem to be anything else to say, not about the case at least, and they fell silent. Ben-Roi wandered along the seafront; in Luxor, Khalifa stood gazing at the family portraits in the window of the Fujifilm shop on the corner of Al-Medina and El-Mahdy. They couldn't explain it, but both felt curiously reluctant to end the call.

'How's Zenab?'

'How's Sarah?'

They spoke at the same time. Apologized at the same time too.

'You first,' said Ben-Roi. 'How is Zenab?'

'She is fine,' Khalifa replied. A brief silence, then: 'Actually that's not true. She's not fine at all. She doesn't sleep well, has nightmares, wakes up crying. Ali's death hit her hard. Hit us both hard.'

Ben-Roi tried to think of something comforting to say, couldn't come up with anything that didn't sound unbearably glib.

'I'm sorry,' he mumbled.

'It is as it is,' said Khalifa. 'We cope.'

One of the pictures in the Fujifilm window was of a young boy, about Ali's age, staring stern-faced into the camera. Khalifa gazed at it, then continued on his way down Sharia al-Madina al-Minawra.

'Sarah?' he asked. 'She is well, I hope?'

'Good,' said Ben-Roi. In fact she'd been sick the previous night, but it somehow seemed insignificant compared to what the Khalifas were having to deal with and he didn't bother mentioning it.

'The baby?'

'Also good. Thank you for asking.'

They lapsed back into silence, each appreciating the other's presence, neither feeling the need to vocalize that appreciation. Khalifa trudged homeward past the Puddleduck English Restaurant and the Luxor Security Directorate Building; Ben-Roi stopped by the Crowne Plaza hotel and watched the Saturday afternoon dancers: two dozen couples, old and young, good and bad, moving to the music blaring from a large ghetto blaster. When he'd come this way before they'd been doing some sort of salsa. Now the accompanying music had changed to a waltz.

'What's that I can hear?' asked Khalifa.

Ben-Roi explained.

'I like this,' said the Egyptian. 'People dancing in the street. We don't do things like that in Egypt, apart from the Zikr dancers. And revolutions. We always dance during revolutions.'

'I hate dancing,' said Ben-Roi. 'You'd get more rhythm out of an elephant.'

Khalifa chuckled at that. Not much of one, but a chuckle nonetheless.

'Zenab used to dance all the time,' he said after another silence. 'In our old apartment. I'd come back from the station and she'd have an Amr Diab cassette playing at full volume and be jumping around all over the place. She used to love dancing. Not any more, sadly.'

Again Ben-Roi tried to dredge up some appropriate comment, something that would acknowledge Khalifa's situation without sounding trite or mawkish. Sarah would have known exactly what to say. She had an instinctive feel for stuff like that, always seemed to come up with the right words. It was a gift that, despite his best intentions, Ben-Roi didn't possess. He fumbled a moment, then, feeling he had to say something, came out with, 'One day she'll dance again.' Even as he said it, he knew it sounded stupefyingly crass, like the title of some shit ballad. Should have just stayed *schtum*.

'*Inshallah*,' was Khalifa's only response.

They stayed on the line for a while longer, talking about nothing much in particular, Ben-Roi wincing inwardly at the dance line, trying to think of something more appropriate, some way of showing Khalifa how much he cared. It was only after they'd rung off and he was wandering round the city marina, gazing distractedly at the yachts and motor launches, feeling like the most useless friend in the world, that the name suddenly came to him. He let it sit a while, getting a feel for it, then called Sarah, asked what she thought.

'I think it's a wonderful idea,' she said. 'But what if it's a girl?'

He didn't have an answer to that. Had a hunch he wouldn't need one. Deep down he knew it was going to be a boy. He just knew it.

THE NEGEV

She'd read all the online chat and speculation, the convoluted theorizing about who they were and how exactly they linked into Nemesis. All of it was bullshit. There had been no internal power struggle within Nemesis, no breakaway group, certainly no agent-provocateuring by spooks or dodgy multinationals. The simple truth was that she'd e-mailed the Nemesis website urging a more radical engagement, and the people behind the website had got in touch and told her to go for it. A brief flurry of contact, and the Nemesis Agenda's militant wing was born. Even now, she was surprised by how straightforward it had all been.

There was more to it than that, of course. It wasn't like she'd just e-mailed them on a whim; woken up one morning and thought, *Let's go fuck the system.* There had been groundwork. Years of it. First in the States, after she'd escaped, drifting from one protest group to the next – anti-capitalists, anti-globalizers, communists, anarchists, radical environmentalists – marching and chanting and banner-waving and rioting, burying her past, rebuilding her identity.

Then, later, in Israel, where she had fled after the crash and where her anger had ratcheted up to a whole different level. Her shame too, although she knew she had nothing to feel ashamed about. It wasn't like she'd asked for it. None of it was her fault.

It was in Israel that she'd hooked up with Tamar – they'd met in a police van after being arrested at a demo – and, through Tamar, Gidi and Faz. Shared ideology had obviously been part of the draw. More than their beliefs, though, it was their personalities that had brought them together, the fact that all were driven by an ulterior motive, something more intimate than simply a desire to stick a spanner in the works of the capitalist meat-grinder. Faz, the Arab-Israeli whose entire life had been an assault course of discrimination and disenfranchisement; Gidi, the IDF conscript who'd been vilified for blowing the whistle on army atrocities in Gaza; Tamar, the daughter of ultra-Orthodox *Haredi* parents who had been shamed and ostracized for her sexuality. Each projected on to the wider canvas of global injustice something of their own internal landscape. Each, like her, had their secret demons. Each, like her, was searching for exorcism.

Most important, each, like her, had come to the conclusion that the traditional lines of protest – the marches and rallies and sit-ins and petitions – were a complete fucking waste of time. This was a war, and ultimately wars could only be won with violence.

So they'd started working together. Small operations at first – an office break-in here, an arson attack there. Then, more complex missions. A pipeline sabotage in Nigeria; a munitions factory bombing in France; the kidnapping and mock execution of a leading American food speculator whose trades had made millions for his Wall Street investment bank while condemning a similar number of human beings to starvation in Africa and India. Taking the fight to the enemy.

They worked well together, made a good team, tight: Faz at his computer gathering the inside information; Tamar sorting the logistics; Gidi sourcing the weapons.

And her? She was the brains, the mastermind of the group. Even collectives have to have a leader, and she was very definitely the leader.

It was she who chose the missions, she who planned everything out right down to the finest detail, she who had realized early on that the missions alone were never going to be enough. For every target they hit, there were a thousand more that deserved to be hit and weren't. Their reach was too small. A drop in the ocean. Because ultimately it wasn't about the violence per se. It was about the ripples that violence caused, the wider momentum it generated. And they weren't generating momentum.

Which was why she'd proposed throwing in their lot with the Nemesis Agenda. Piggybacking the Nemesis website to attract the sort of global attention they could never achieve on their own, however many executives they terrorized, however many installations they blew up. Initially the others had been sceptical, but she'd pushed the idea, insisted that Nemesis already had a profile and a following, that in alliance they could really start changing things. It had taken some persuasion, but eventually she'd won the day.

They'd filmed themselves firebombing the multinational's office in Tel-Aviv as a calling card, sent it into the website's secure mailbox, suggested joining forces. For a month they'd heard nothing. Then, one evening, she and Faz had been sitting in front of his computer and the screen had suddenly blanked out. Before Faz could determine what was wrong a small dot had appeared in the centre of the screen. It had slowly expanded and spread before forming into letters: OFFER ACCEPTED. WE FIGHT TOGETHER.

Connection made. Simple as that.

Who Nemesis actually were she'd never found out. A couple of geeks in a darkened room somewhere? An intricate worldwide matrix of activists? It was anyone's guess, although looking back she suspected that whoever they were, they'd had her in their sights for a while. From the moment she'd got involved in the movement she'd had the feeling she was being watched. Still got it sometimes, even out here in the middle of the desert. She tried not to let it bother her. She was in, that was all that mattered. Serving the cause to the best of her ability. Punishing those who needed to be punished. Abusing the abusers.

After that initial ice-breaking, contact was kept to a minimum. They ran their missions, channelled the stuff back to Nemesis, it went up on the website. That was about the extent of it. Her crew concentrated on the direct action side of things, the Nemesis people took care of the cyber side, although Nemesis would sometimes feed them leads and suggestions, and thanks to Faz's tech skills they weren't averse to launching the odd cyber attack of their own. It wasn't like there was a rulebook or anything. They were all fighting the same fight.

In only one respect were spheres of activity clearly demarcated. Barren Corporation was hers. It was something she'd insisted on right from the outset. Nemesis laid off Barren. If the company was going to be fried, she was going to be the one to do it. Because at the end of the day, that's what it was all about. The *only* thing it was about. It was their cyber-attacks on Barren that had brought the Nemesis Agenda to her attention in the first place. It was Barren that occupied her, day and night, especially after the cathedral. Everything was rooted in Barren, all roads led there. Barren was *her* ulterior motive. Always had been, always would be.

'Shit!'

She slammed on the brakes. The Land Cruiser lurched and skidded on the hot tarmac. She'd been so wrapped up in her thoughts that she had overshot the gap in the fence. Muttering, she reversed the car around and backtracked. A kilometre north along Route 10 she braked again and pulled off the road, bumping across gravel and up to the barbed-wire tube that marked the border. On this side, Israel and the Negev. On the other, Egypt and the Sinai. The government were in the process of erecting a less permeable barrier to hold back the drug and people smugglers – 215km of surveillance posts and electrified fencing stretching all the way from Gaza down to Eilat. They'd yet to start work on these remote middle sections, however, and for the moment you could still slip across without too much trouble. Normally she'd have brought the others with her, but for this mission she was on her own. Where Barren was concerned, she often flew solo.

She got out and surveyed the landscape. It might as well have been Mars for all the signs of human life. She gave it a minute, then went over to the fence and heaved aside the wire tube at the point where they'd cut it. She took the Land Cruiser through, attached the Egyptian number plates, repositioned the fence, sped off. It was the best part of 400 kilometres to Cairo and she wanted to be there and back before dawn.

'Do you think Barren Corporation might be involved in sex-trafficking?'

Natan Tirat damn nearly spat out his Goldstar.

'Is that some sort of joke?'

Ben-Roi's expression suggested he wasn't sure whether it was or not.

'I know it seems unlikely . . .'

'It's more than unlikely, it's completely fucking surreal.'

Tirat rocked back on his chair, dangling his Goldstar bottle in his hand.

'I mean, come on, Arieh. This is a company with . . . what, a forty, fifty-billion-dollar turnover. Ten billion profit at a conservative estimate. Probably closer to twenty. And you're suggesting they're topping that up with a sideline in illegal prostitution. Seriously, can you see that scanning?'

Ben-Roi admitted that he couldn't. Had never be able to see it scanning, not from the moment Barren and sex-trafficking had first announced themselves as part of the same equation.

'It would make a good story, mind,' continued Tirat. 'A *great* story. "Global Minerals Giant in Holy Land Pimping Scandal".'

He ran a hand through the air as if tracing an invisible newspaper headline.

'Scoop like that could make my career. Sort me out for life.'

Ben-Roi told him not to get his hopes up and swigged his Tuborg. They were sitting at a pavement table outside a bar on Dizengoff, the oldest people there by a good decade. Around them trendy young things in designer clothes were sipping designer drinks, chatting and laughing, making the most of the early evening sun before heading off for a night in the clubs. He was only in his thirties, but the surroundings made him feel like he was already over the hill. Although not as over it as Tirat, whose sizeable paunch, leather waistcoat and greying hair done up in a ponytail made him look like a relic of a not particularly successful 1970s rock band.

'Have you heard of Barren being involved in *anything* dodgy?' he asked.

Tirat's eyes had drifted to a girl at the next-door table, her cleavage bulging from the top of her low-cut dress. Ben-Roi had to repeat the question to get his attention.

'Your colleague asked me the same thing when he called the other day,' replied Tirat, reluctantly pulling his gaze round.

'And?'

'And nothing. Or at least nothing anyone's ever been able to pin on them. I mean, they're a global multinational so I'd be surprised if they weren't up to *something*. They all are. A bit of creative accounting, some environmental corner-cutting, off-the-record briefings against their competitors . . . like I told your friend, these companies are in it to make money, not win prizes for being the class nice guy.'

He drained his Goldstar in two long glugs and placed the bottle on the table beside the one he'd already finished.

'Good lad you've got there, by the way,' he added. 'Intelligent. You should hold on to him. Might actually help you solve some cases.'

He lit a cigarette and scrunched a handful of salted almonds from the bowl on the table, his eyes momentarily flicking back to the girl in the low-cut dress.

'There's no question that Barren *are* secretive.' he went on, his gaze returning to Ben-Roi. 'Even by multinational standards. They keep a tight rein on their image, don't welcome questions. And being a private corporation, they're obviously not open to the sort of in-depth scrutiny they would be if they were stock-listed. So who knows, maybe they *have* got a few nasties lurking in the closet. But honestly, Arieh, I can't see them being involved in something like sex-trafficking. Or murder, for that matter, which is where I'm guessing this is leading.'

He raised his eyebrows at Ben-Roi, who didn't respond to the prompt, just took another sip of his beer. A pair of female soldiers ambled passed, Givati Brigade, feet in sandals, M-16s hanging off their backs. In Jerusalem soldiers were part of the visual fabric. Here they stood out more. Ben-Roi watched them a moment, then picked up the conversation.

'Apparently Barren have got political clout,' he said, changing tack. 'Friends in high places.'

Tirat acknowledged that was the case. 'It's not exactly unusual. All these big multinationals have got an in to the corridors of power. Although Barren do seem to be particularly well connected. Bottom line is: money buys influence. And Barren have got money. A lot of it. From what I hear, they're bankrolling half the Knesset. Half of Congress too, if you believe the stories.'

He funnelled the almonds into his mouth, chewed, dragged on his cigarette. Ben-Roi bounced the Tuborg bottle on his knee, casting around for some sort of angle.

'Do you know anything about their dealings in Egypt?'

Tirat didn't, beyond what he'd already told Dov Zisky.

'What about the head honcho? His wife was Israeli, right?'

Tirat nodded, clawed another fistful of nuts.

'They met at some embassy event in Washington. She worked in Cultural Affairs. Apparently he sent her flowers every day for a year till she agreed to marry him. She died in a car smash a while back. He's never got over it, by all accounts.'

'The son? Dov tells me he's a bit of a bad boy.'

'And some,' grunted Tirat. 'Skag habit, violent temper, beating up on prossies – classic gossip-column material. Although to be fair I've also heard he's a lot sharper than people give him credit for and the high jinx are all just a front.'

He rattled the almonds in his hand.

'Truth is, he's an unknown quantity. They all are, frankly. There's a lot of speculation and hearsay, but when it comes to hard facts about the Barrens ... If they're secretive about their business dealings, it's nothing compared to how they are about their personal lives. Hardly anyone even knew there *was* a son till he suddenly popped up on the company board ten years ago. Schooled under a false name, kept well out of the limelight – the sort of money they've got, it doesn't just bring influence. Buys you a lot of privacy as well.'

He gave the almonds another shake, then dropped his head back and siphoned them into his mouth, munching vigorously.

'He comes to Israel a lot, if that's any use.'

Ben-Roi cocked his head. 'On business?'

'If you call snorting coke and shagging hookers business. Keeps a penthouse over in Park Heights. Party central, if the rumours are anything to go by.'

Ben-Roi pondered this, wondering if maybe there *was* a link between Barren and sex-trafficking. Genady Kremenko sources prostitutes for the heir to the empire; Rivka Kleinberg finds out about it and threatens to expose him; Barren Junior comes up to Jerusalem, follows Kleinberg to the cathedral, confronts her, loses his temper ... again, it was one of those scenarios that matched some parts of the case, didn't match others. Whichever way he moved the carpet, he could never seem to get it to fit perfectly.

'There was one little mystery you might be interested in,' said Tirat, sleeving salt speckles off his lips.

Not another one, thought Ben-Roi. 'Go on.'

'It's to do with the car crash. The one that killed Nathaniel Barren's wife.'

'What about it?'

'Well, the coroner's verdict was death by misadventure. A tragic accident.'

'So?'

'So it left a lot of questions unanswered.'

'Such as?'

Tirat sucked on his cigarette.

'Such as why a recently serviced car driving on open road in broad daylight should suddenly swerve for no obvious reason and smack head-on into a telegraph pole.'

He finished the cigarette and flicked the butt into the gutter.

'Your round, I believe.'

CAIRO

Having let himself into the Gezira apartment the company was renting for him, Chad Perks went straight through the living room and out on to the balcony. He leant on the balustrade, gazed across the Nile, farted loudly and, as he did at least a dozen times a day, thought: *Fuck me, life's sweet.*

Regional Director, Barren North Africa possibly suggested more than it actually involved. All the hard deal-brokering was managed directly out of Houston. His role was more in the line of public relations. As head of the Cairo office, he met with the Egyptian bigwigs, took them for expensive dinners – like the one tonight at Justine – paid the people who needed to get paid, flew down to Luxor every month to check on the progress of the new museum, which was now less than a week away from inauguration. Barren's face on the ground, basically. And, also, Barren's eyes and ears. With so much riding on the Saharan gas field tender, the company was anxious to keep tabs on the country's political mood – especially since Mubarak had been given the heave-ho – and Chad Perks was nothing if not good at keeping tabs on things. If and when the concession was granted, his role, he liked to think, would have been every bit as important as that of the people who actually hammered out the details of the contract. A fact reflected in the mouth-watering performance bonus he was set to receive once the deal was finally signed off.

Generous ex-pat wage, nice fat pension pot, luxury Nile-front apartment, impressive-sounding if slightly overblown title – *yup*, Chad thought, *life sure as hell is sweet*.

Or at least it was till he felt someone come up behind him, throw a cord round his neck and yank him backwards away from the balcony rail and off his feet.

Chad Perks had many admirable attributes, but bravery was not among them. He kicked and struggled for a moment, more out of instinct than any innate desire to battle his assailant, then went limp. He caught a brief, blurred glimpse of the Ramses Hilton on the far side of the river, and also a vague, musky waft of some sort of scent or antiperspirant – funny the things you registered when you were being throttled. Then suddenly he was face down on the living-room carpet and the cord wasn't there any more. He curled himself into a ball, coughing and choking and desperately trying to put together the Arabic for 'Please don't hurt me' (languages, like bravery, had never been Chad's strong suit).

He needn't have worried. When his attacker spoke, it was in English. The fact that the voice was a woman's gave him a momentary glimmer of hope. The feel of a pistol against his temple snatched it away.

'I want to know what your company's doing here in Egypt,' the voice snarled. '*Exactly* what you're doing. And if you try and bullshit me, I'll blow your fucking head off.'

Chad assured her he had no intention of doing anything other than cooperating fully.

'Right. Start talking.'

Chad started talking.

On Sunday morning Ben-Roi got up early. He banged out a four-page breakdown of all the key points of the case and e-mailed it to Khalifa. Then, just for the hell of it, he went on the internet and Googled the car accident that had killed Nathaniel Barren's wife. There wasn't much that Natan Tirat hadn't already told him. Her car had come off a road north of Houston, smashed into a telegraph pole, she had died instantly. One eyewitness claimed to have seen another person in the vehicle shortly before the crash, but no one else had been able to corroborate that, and a detailed investigation had concluded the accident was just that – accidental. After surfing for forty minutes he decided the whole thing was a red herring – there seemed to be a whole shoal of them swimming round this case – and shut his computer down. He called Dov Zisky to say he was going to be late, brought a bunch of roses from the flower stand opposite his apartment and walked over to Sarah's.

'What's this in aid of?' she asked when she opened the door to him.

'I felt like seeing you.'

He swept the flowers out from behind his back.

'I've been so tied up with work . . . I thought we could have breakfast and then I'd drive you over to the school.'

'I'm not due in till midday.'

'Great. We can spend the morning together.'

She eyed him suspiciously.

'This isn't like you, Arieh.'

'What's not like me?'

'Taking a morning off in the middle of an investigation. There's something going on.' Her tone was more teasing than confrontational. 'Come on, 'fess up. You've done something. Or you want something.'

'I just want to spend some time with you and Bubu. I've missed you both.'

Which was the truth. Something about this case – the whole sex-trafficking thing, Khalifa losing his son like that – seemed to be striking an unusually deep chord with him. Last night, when he'd got back from Tel-Aviv, he'd just lain in bed thinking about Sarah and the baby, wishing they were there beside him, chiding himself for the fact they weren't. Normally the way it went, particularly with an investigation as intense as this, the case dragged you away from the people you loved most. This one seemed to be pushing him back towards them. More and more he was thinking that they really ought to give it another go. *He* ought to give it another go. It was him who'd screwed the whole thing up, after all.

'Are you going to take these?'

'Of course. Thank you. They're beautiful.'

She accepted the flowers.

'I've got something else,' he said. 'Watch this.'

Pulling out his mobile phone, he wafted it in front of her, like a magician setting up a trick. With a flourish, he arced a finger through the air and pushed the off button, soundtracking the gesture with a loud 'Ta-Na!' She burst out laughing and wrapped her arms around him, the baby-bump pushing against his stomach, which felt fantastic.

'I thought the chief rabbi would be eating prawn cocktail before I ever saw you do that,' she joked.

'Well, there you go. Miracles do happen. Can I make you breakfast?'

'Yes please.'

Which is what he did, his Spanish omelettes mutating into scrambled eggs, his toast setting off the kitchen smoke alarm. She joshed him about his culinary ineptitude, drawing some sharp retaliatory comments about biting the hand that feeds you – fun banter, light-hearted. The sort of banter they had used to engage in all the time and that had been markedly absent this last year. God, she looked good.

Once they'd eaten – out on the balcony, the atmosphere curiously charged, like they were on a first date or something – he performed his second miracle of the morning by doing the washing up.

'Who on earth is this domestic god?' she asked in mock amazement.

'Nothing to do with me. You must have an intruder in the house. Better call 100.'

More laughter. The best sound in the world.

Afterwards she lay on the sofa so he could press a hand on her belly and feel his child going through what felt like a particularly vigorous Pilates routine. Then, at her suggestion, they took themselves down to Mamilla Mall to shop for baby clothes. Ben-Roi loathed shopping, rated it somewhere alongside doing his tax return. He put a brave face on it, glad just to be spending time with her, even if spending time did mean kicking his heels for two hours while she worked her way through an endless succession of babygros and miniature Crocs.

'Sure you're not bored?' she kept asking.

'Not at all,' he kept lying.

And then, suddenly, it was midday and he was driving her round the Old City walls and down to the play scheme she ran in Silwan – an Arab neighbourhood crowded on to the hillside to the south of the Old City. The scheme was experimental, tried to integrate Israeli and Palestinian kids by encouraging them to have fun together. Four years ago it had catered to upwards of thirty children. Now the number had dropped to less than a dozen, which said just about everything that needed to be said about the peace process.

'What's going on with the settlers?' he asked as they turned off Ma'ale Ha-Shalom on to the steep slope of Wadi Hilwah.

'What do you think's going on? Same shit as usual.'

A group of settlers – ultra-Orthodox, American-funded, as most of them were – had bought up the house next door to the school, and had been causing trouble from the off.

'The other day one of them lobbed a bag of piss into the play-ground,' she said. 'Damn near hit one of the kids. A *Jewish* kid!' She shook her head in disgust. 'Although credit where credit's due. Last week a group of *shebab* firebombed our minibus.'

This was all news to Ben-Roi. He'd been so wrapped up in his own work he hadn't even asked about hers.

'At least you've given the nut-jobs something to agree on,' he joked, a weak line that didn't even raise a smile.

'To be honest, I don't think we're going to be able to carry on much longer,' she said. 'There was a time when it looked like it was going to work, but the way things are going these days . . .'

She rubbed her temples.

'I tell you, Arieh, the lunatics are taking over the asylum. Have already taken it over. On both sides of the line. I sometimes wonder if this is a country I want my kid to grow up in.'

Ben-Roi slowed the car and took her hand.

'Our kid's going to have the best home in the world, Sarah. The hap-piest home, and the safest. I promise you that. With all my heart.'

She squeezed his hand, leant over and kissed his cheek.

'I love you, Arieh. You drive me nuts, but I love you. Now come on, I'm going to be late.'

He ruffled her hair and they continued down the hill to the school – a drab concrete compound with grilled windows and a graffiti-covered steel gate. He helped her out of the car and they crossed to the entrance, ignoring the neighbouring building with the giant white-and-blue Israel flag fluttering from its roof. Sarah pressed the school entrance buzzer.

'Thanks for a great morning.'

'Thank *you*.'

'We should do it again.'

'We certainly should.'

'The toast was delicious.'

'Screw you.'

They laughed and clasped hands. He wanted to say more, go deeper; tell her how special she was, how much she meant to him, how more than anything in the world he wanted their future to be a shared one. Before he could speak the gate swung open. Sarah rolled her eyes – maybe she'd been thinking the same things.

'Call me,' she said.

'Of course.'

She kissed him on the nose, touched her belly gently against his and, with a whispered 'Bye, Dad', stepped into the compound. A quick wave and the gate clanged shut. Ben-Roi stared at it, thinking how much easier life would be if he just had a normal job, something that wasn't forever clogging up his system with death and violence and misery. Then, with a shake of the head, he pulled out his mobile, switched it on and trudged back to the car. As he came up to it, a series of bleeps alerted him to missed calls and messages. A lot of missed calls and messages. Way more than normal. Frowning, he accessed his voicemail and leaned on the car roof, listening.

Inside the compound Sarah was walking across the play area with her colleague Rivka, telling her what a fun morning she'd had, how maybe, just maybe, she and Ben-Roi might try and make another go of it. Suddenly a familiar voice roared out on the far side of the compound wall.

'Oh no, no, no, you ignorant fuck! What are you doing?'

Her smile faded.

'Good while it lasted,' she sighed.

Ben-Roi drove like a madman, foot to the floor, siren blaring, police light strobing frantically on the Toyota's roof. He made it back to

Kishle in five minutes. Omar Ibn al-Khattab was jammed – several hundred Armenians chanting, shouting, hurling insults at the line of uniforms who'd been deployed to keep them back from the front of the station. All of it watched over by a crush of journalists, photographers and TV news crews. Pretty much what he'd been expecting, given that Archbishop Armen Petrossian had just been arrested on suspicion of murdering Rivka Kleinberg.

He nudged the Toyota up to the station's security gate, flashed his badge, barrelled through into the car park at the rear of the building. He'd called ahead and Zisky was waiting for him.

'This is Baum's doing, isn't it!' he yelled, scrambling out of the car. 'It's Baum who's behind this!'

'He pulled rank on Sergeant Shalev,' confirmed Zisky. 'Says he's got enough evidence to charge.'

'What evidence, for God's sake?'

Zisky didn't know details, just that the chief superintendent was claiming to have a watertight case.

'About as watertight as the bloody Titanic, knowing Baum's track record! Where's Leah?'

Apparently she'd been sent home to cool down. Had flipped out when she'd heard what was going on. Ben-Roi slammed a fist on to the Toyota's roof, then started across the compound, Zisky trailing in his wake.

'Chief Gal?'

'Across town briefing the ministry.'

'What a God-all-mighty bloody cock-up! The one community that actually behaves itself and he's got them out there rioting. In full view of the press! Imbecile!'

Ben-Roi reached the entrance to the detectives' suite, stormed inside. Uri Pincas, Amos Namir and Sergeant Moshe Peres were all sitting around with their feet up on the desks. They seemed to think it was a done deal.

'Nice of you to—'

'Where's Baum?' snapped Ben-Roi, cutting Pincas off mid-flow.

'—join us,' continued Pincas, finishing the sentence. 'Upstairs. Fielding calls from the press.'

'I'll bet he bloody is,' growled Ben-Roi, turning on his heel, hurrying back out into the car park and round into the station entrance tunnel. At its far end the crowd was pushing right up against the security gates, their cries filling the air, the line of uniforms struggling to keep them back. Ben-Roi swung right into a low doorway and started up a set of stairs.

'You want me to come with?' asked Zisky, still tagging along behind.

Ben-Roi wheeled. 'What I want you to do is to get out there and find a guy called George Aslanian. Owns the Armenian Tavern, everyone knows him. Tell him I'm on the case and see if he can do something to calm this lot down. OK?'

'OK.'

'And take a couple of plods with you. I wouldn't want anything happening to that peachy little face of yours.'

He gave the kid a pat on the cheek, wheeled again and clattered on up to the top of the stairs, taking them two at a time.

Chief Superintendent Yitzhak Baum was in his office, sitting behind his desk talking on the phone. A short, pudgy man in a neatly pressed uniform, the leaf and star insignia of a *sgan nitzav* gleaming on his shoulders, Baum had always exuded an air of prim self-satisfaction, and that was amplified this morning as he held forth on how he really couldn't give any comment beyond the fact that at this stage they weren't looking for anyone else in connection with Rivka Kleinberg's murder. Ben-Roi stomped across the room and jabbed a thumb-tip on the phone's on–off toggle, cutting the line.

'What the hell are you doing?' Baum's voice was an outraged squeal. 'That was the *Jerusalem Post* I was talking to.'

'Fuck the *Jerusalem Post*,' snapped Ben-Roi, leaning across the desk right into his superior's face. 'What's going on?'

It took Baum a moment to get his voice, his fleshy mouth twisting and contorting as he fought to bring his anger under control.

'What's going on, *Detective* Ben-Roi, is that I'm solving a murder. Which is a shit sight more than you've been doing for the last ten days.'

'Petrossian!' Ben-Roi's tone was incredulous. 'A seventy-year-old priest! How do you figure that one out?'

'How I figure it is by a time-honoured process of gathering evidence and following where it leads!'

'Oh spare me the clever stuff, Baum!'

'And you show me a bit of respect, Ben-Roi!'

'Fuck you!'

'Fuck *you*!'

297

Baum was on his feet now, the two men eyeballing each other. A young police constable stuck her head into the room, asked what all the noise was about.

'Piss off!' bellowed Baum.

He charged across the office, slammed the door, returned to his desk.

'You want to watch yourself, Ben-Roi,' he snarled. 'Speaking to me like that! You seriously want to watch yourself or I'll have you on a charge.'

'I'm trembling!'

'So you should be! You're a disgrace. You and that jumped-up tart of an investigator—'

'Don't you dare—!'

'Don't *you* dare!'

'*Maniak!*'

'Watch your language!'

'*Maniak!*'

It rumbled on for a while longer, back and forth, shouts and insults, until eventually they'd blown themselves out and fell silent, both of them panting heavily, the yells of the Armenian protesters barging in from outside. Ten seconds passed, then Baum sat back down. Ben-Roi lifted his hands and took a step away from the desk.

'Does Chief Gal know about this?'

'Of course he knows about it. You think I'd act behind his back? I showed him the evidence, he cleared it, signed off on the warrant.'

Ben-Roi shook his head. Chief Gal was no fool – if he'd authorized the arrest it was almost certainly because Baum had made the case sound stronger than it actually was.

'So what is this evidence? This *watertight* evidence.'

Baum settled back in his chair, chest puffing out. 'He's got form.'

'Petrossian?'

'Attacked a Greek Orthodox priest in the Holy Sepulchre. Damn nearly strangled him. Totally lost the plot.'

'This was . . . ?'

'2004.'

Ben-Roi let out a dismissive bark of laughter. 'Serial offender then.'

Baum bristled, but didn't rise to the sarcasm.

'There's more.'

'Do tell.'

'Back in the seventies he got caught cooking the cathedral books. He was in charge of the finances, was siphoning money off the accounts and reinvesting in dodgy bonds. The bonds went bad, damned nearly bankrupted the Church. *Ha'aretz* did a big exposé.'

Ben-Roi could barely believe what he was hearing. 'This is somehow relevant?'

'It certainly is.'

Baum's chest puffed out further.

'The journalist who did the exposé was a young trainee on her first major story. Name of . . .'

'Rivka Kleinberg.'

Ben-Roi finished the sentence. Baum smirked, as if he'd somehow scored a point.

'Namir turned it up. Good detective, Amos. *Thorough.*'

He let that hang a moment, then pushed on.

'Courtesy of Kleinberg, Petrossian got sent back to Armenia in disgrace, had to spend three years atoning for his sins doing outreach work in the arse-end of nowhere. Lost any chance he might ever have had of making Patriarch. Which to my thinking gives him a pretty damned good motive.'

'Thirty-five years after the event!' Ben-Roi was shaking his head. 'Come on, Baum, even by your standards it's thin. It's thin as cat's piss.'

'Piece by piece, Ben-Roi. That's how it works. Piece by piece, building up the case. And let me give you another piece. Petrossian lied about where he was the night of the murder.'

Ben-Roi opened his mouth, then shut it again. This sounded more damning. Baum saw that he had him on the back foot and his smirk widened.

'He says he was in his private apartments when Kleinberg was killed. Thanks to some sterling work by your little gayboy friend, we know those apartments have a private street door. And we've now got footage of Petrossian going walkabout in the Armenian Quarter when he claims to have been tucked up in bed.'

Ben-Roi ought to have thumped him for the gayboy comment, but for the moment let it go.

'What footage? There aren't any cameras in the Armenian Quarter.'

'No *police* cameras. But that store on the corner of Ararat and St

James, Sammy's, they've got a security video above the door. Namir took a look at it on the off-chance. Like I say, good detective Namir. Thorough. And what do you think he found? Crystal-clear images of your sweet little archbishop marching down Ararat at 6.04 p.m. on the night of the murder, and back up it again at 8.46. Which puts him bang in the frame, Ben-Roi. Right slap-bang in the middle of it.'

He was on a roll now, enjoying himself.

'We've got dodgy character, clear motive, false alibi.' He counted them off on his fingers. Soft, dumpling fingers that had never once come close to anything approaching hard work. 'And in case there's still any doubt in your mind, we've also got a confession.'

Again Ben-Roi's mouth opened, again it shut without anything coming out. Baum gave a satisfied nod, aware that he had the upper hand now. Lifting a sheet of paper from the desk, he read from it. Slowly, savouring the words.

'Her death's on my conscience. It's me who's culpable. It's me who killed her.'

He looked up at Ben-Roi, then read it through again, driving the point home.

'Obviously I'm missing some hidden meaning here, but for the life of me I can't see what it is. Perhaps you can help me out.'

The sarcasm was heavy, taunting.

'He said this to you?'

'To one of the other archbishops. One of Namir's informers over-heard it, passed it on.'

'So not a formal confession at all.'

Baum didn't answer that, just sat back and folded his arms, swivelling on his executive chair. He was in the driving seat now and knew it.

'This so pisses you off, doesn't it?'

Ben-Roi didn't say anything, just glared at him.

'*So* pisses you off. The great *balash*, winner of three citations for excellence in police work. Always gets to the bottom of a case. And this time round you're out on the sidelines. Someone else has solved it and all your sorry little leads turn out to have been just so much shit in the pan. God, that must pain you.'

'What pains me,' snapped Ben-Roi, 'is that you've fucked off the entire Armenian community and damned nearly started a riot for a case that any half-competent defence attorney's going to tear to shreds the moment he gets his hands on it. It's all circumstantial, Baum – you've got nothing, nothing that ties Petrossian directly to the crime.'

Baum stopped swivelling and leant forward over the desk.

'We'll get it, Detective. Trust me, we'll get it. Petrossian's our man, and if he didn't strangle her himself, he sure as hell knows who did. Forensics are working his apartments as we speak. Me and Namir are about to go in and put the screws on him. And you –' he jabbed a finger belligerently – 'I want you down at your desk filling in the blanks.'

'I'm sitting in on the interview.'

'You can sit on my fucking face!' cried Baum, pausing fractionally as he realized the insult didn't work the way he intended before launching in again.

'You've always been an uppity cunt, Ben-Roi, and I'm not standing for it any more. This is our line of inquiry, and you're going to stick to it. Understand? Or so help me God I'll have you busted straight down to *shoter* and stuck out doing guard duty on the most god-forsaken settlement I can find. Now get downstairs and get on it. That's a direct order.'

Ben-Roi stared at him, making no effort to disguise his loathing, then turned for the door. When he reached it, he swung round.

'You know what all this reminds me of?'

Baum's eyebrows lifted.

'The omelettes I cooked this morning.'

Baum looked confused.

'Egg,' explained Ben-Roi. 'A great big bubbling heap of egg. And it's heading straight for your face, *sir*. You've got the wrong man and if I were you I'd have a towel ready because when all this shakes down, you're going to have a hell of a lot of mess to clear up.'

He stepped out of the door, stepped straight back in again.

'And just for the record, you ever speak about my partner like that again and I'll deck you. Same goes for Leah Shalev. *Maniak*.'

He was halfway down the stairs before Baum could think of any suitable response.

The *Eye of Horus* docked midway through the afternoon, one of a convoy of cruisers that had come up from Aswan and manoeuvred themselves into the shore like a troupe of synchronized swimmers, lashing up three-abreast.

Khalifa was standing on the quayside waiting. The moment the gangplanks were lowered, he climbed aboard and went in search of Dr Digby Girling, the man Mary Dufresne had suggested might know something about the mysterious Samuel Pinsker. He eventually tracked him down in a lounge at the bow of the cruiser, delivering a talk on ancient Egyptian cosmetics to a group of middle-aged women. Khalifa hovered at the back of the room until the lecture was finished and the audience had started to disperse, then went forward, introduced himself and explained why he was there.

'A detective!' boomed Girling, his voice a fruity bellow. 'How wonderfully intriguing! Has a crime been committed?'

In a manner of speaking, allowed Khalifa. He couldn't go into details.

'Of course not, of course not. Mum's the word!'

The Englishman gave his nose a conspiratorial tap. Mary Dufresne had likened him to a balloon. To Khalifa he looked more like a pear. An over-ripe pear done up in a white linen suit, bow tie and sandals.

'Should we talk here?' he asked. 'Or would you prefer to repair to the poop?'

Wherever he was most comfortable, said Khalifa.

'Poop it is then. They've got Intermediate Belly-dancing in twenty minutes and I wouldn't want us to be disturbed. A real-life detective! Gosh, I feel like I'm in an episode of *Morse!*'

He gathered up his lecture notes, plonked a large straw sunhat on his head and, with a flamboyant wave to what was left of his audience, set off across the room.

'Don't forget tonight, Dr Digby!' one of the women called.

'I shall be a veritable Solomon,' cried Girling. 'Fair, but very, *very* firm!'

Another theatrical flourish and they were out of the lounge and heading up a set of carpeted stairs, the women's giggles echoing behind them.

'Sunday night Mummy competition,' explained the Englishman as they climbed. 'Thirty inebriated divorcees parading around swathed in rolls of lavatory tissue. And to me falls the honour of choosing the victor. Oh the shame of it!'

He gave a sorrowful shake of the head and continued to the top of the stairs and out on to the ship's upper deck. There was a small pool at one end, surrounded by bathers on sunloungers. At the other was an awning with beneath it a cluster of plastic chairs. The cruiser was moored in the outermost row of boats, and for a moment the Englishman's gaze lingered dreamily on the distant hazy humpback of the Theban massif. Then, with a clap of the hands, he took them over to the awning, lowered himself into a chair and waved Khalifa into the one beside him.'

'So, Inspector,' he said. 'Samuel Pinsker. I do hope I can be of some assistance.'

He wasn't the only one. After an interminable station meeting in which Chief Hassani had banged on for an hour and a half about the forthcoming Valley of the Kings museum inauguration – now just four days away – Khalifa had spent what was left of the morning following up the detailed case notes Ben-Roi had sent over. A call to the Rosetta hotel where Rivka Kleinberg had booked a room had revealed nothing beyond what they'd already told Ben-Roi's people. Serious Crime in Alexandria knew of no link between Rosetta and sex-trafficking, computer hacking or indeed any other form of organized crime other than the occasional case of illegal lobster fishing. Barren's Saharan gas field tender, if it came off, would, according to a contact of Khalifa's on *Al-Masry al-Youm*, be one of the biggest deals the Egyptian government had ever done with a foreign firm. Again, though, there was no obvious tie-in with a murder in Jerusalem. In short, he'd added precisely zilch to what the Israelis already knew. If he was going to help Ben-Roi with his case – and the more he'd delved into it, the more Khalifa had felt impelled to help – it was all down to finding out why Rivka Kleinberg had been interested in Samuel Pinsker. And finding that out, it seemed, was all down to this meeting with Digby Girling. So, yes, there was a lot riding on the conversation.

'I'm told you've done some research on Pinsker,' he kicked off.

'For a modest monograph I wrote a few years back,' confirmed the Englishman. '*All The Boy King's Men – Forgotten Members of the Tutankhamun Excavation Team*. Sold a princely twenty-six copies in the Petrie Museum bookshop. A veritable bestseller by Egyptological standards. Pinsker featured because of his work landscaping the entrance to the tomb. If you please, Salah!'

This to a white-jacketed waiter who was patrolling beside the pool. The man approached and asked what he could get them. Khalifa held up a hand to indicate he didn't require anything. Girling ordered a Pimm's.

'Always pick up a few bottles in duty-free,' he confided. 'Ahmed at the bar's a dab hand at mixing it. Plenty of mint, that's the secret.'

He winked, whipped out a handkerchief and began patting at his forehead, which in the two minutes they'd been out of the ship's air-conditioned interior had become drenched in sweat. Khalifa lit a cigarette and was about to pick up the conversation when Girling did the job for him.

'Interesting chap, our Samuel,' he said. 'He only figured briefly in the book, but I ended up doing quite a lot of research on him. Completely forgotten now, of course, but in his time he was quite an important figure. I've often thought of knocking my notes up into another book.'

He gave his forehead a final dab, removed his sunhat and began to fan himself with it.

'He was an engineer by trade. A Mancunian Jewish mining engineer, to be precise, which I can't imagine is a particularly extensive demographic. Originally came to Egypt to install a winching system in a phosphate mine over near Kharga and ended up staying on, advising some of the archaeological missions in Luxor. It was Pinsker who first realized the importance of properly ventilating the deeper tombs in the valley. If it hadn't been for him, there'd be no decoration left by now. Not that it would bother that lot too much.'

He tilted his head towards the pool, where two bikini-clad women were sitting on the shoulders of two overweight men, screaming with laughter as they squirted each other with water pistols.

'The siren call of *Femina britannica*,' sighed Girling, rolling his eyes and shuffling his chair further round so as to put the pool out of his sightline. Over his shoulder the broad emerald avenue of the Nile glittered in the afternoon sun, and for a brief moment Khalifa found himself staring at a barge ploughing its way upriver over by the western shore, its prow tearing a deep frothing gash through the water. Before he could sink too deep into his reverie, Girling's voice boomed out again.

304

'– in a Manchester slum, you know. Son of an illiterate Yiddish-speaking cobbler. Overcame the most appalling penury and religious discrimination to get himself qualified as an engineer. A quite brilliant man, by all accounts, although a difficult one. Big chip on his shoulder, strong socialist principles, which obviously set him at odds with most of the other colonials out here. He was always getting into scraps with people, was notoriously free with his, you know . . .'

He made a boxing motion with his fists. Khalifa recalled the story Mary Dufresne had told him, about Pinsker attacking a man from Qurna.

'Yes, there does seem to have been some sort of fracas,' Girling acknowledged when Khalifa mentioned the incident. 'I never found out the precise details, just that Pinsker took umbrage at something the man said and beat the living daylights out of him. Caused a lot of bad blood, apparently, although to be fair to Pinsker it was out of character. According to most accounts he was extremely respectful of the native Egyptians. Probably something to do with the old, you know –' He tipped a hand in front of his mouth as though drinking. 'That or his face. His appearance was a very touchy subject.'

'I was going to ask about that,' said Khalifa. 'His face was . . . how do you say? . . . a born deformity?'

'Birth defect?' Girling shook his head. 'No, no, the disfigurement came much later. He was actually quite a handsome young man, if the few early photos we've got of him are anything to go by. Dark eyes, strong Semitic features. The face was gas.'

Khalifa didn't understand.

'Mustard gas,' explained the Englishman. 'First World War. Battle of Passchendaele. Pinsker was a sapper. He was leading a team digging underneath the German lines, the Boche cottoned on to it, sunk a counter-shaft, pumped a load of gas into the British tunnel. Burnt the poor bastards alive. Pinsker risked his life trying to plug the breach so the others could get out. Won a Victoria Cross for his trouble, although he suffered for it to the end of his days. He was in constant pain, apparently. Needed booze and morphine just to be able to function. A tragic figure, in many ways.'

Khalifa doubted the girl Pinsker raped would have seen it like that. He kept the thought to himself, not wanting to get bogged down in the details of the rape. Instead, pulling a photocopy from his pocket, he turned the conversation to the aspect of Pinsker's story that really interested him: the Howard Carter letter.

'I don't suppose this means anything to you, does it?' he asked, handing the photocopy across.

Girling returned his hat to his head, slipped on a pair of half-moon spectacles and read through the letter. His eyes widened the further he went.

'Where on earth did you lay your hands on this?' he asked when he reached the end, looking up.

'It was in an old police file. I only discovered it a couple of days ago.'

'I wish I'd known about it. I could have included it in my monograph. Extraordinary. Absolutely extraordinary.'

'Have you any idea what it means? That bit about finding something.'

'Well, obviously I can't be a hundred per cent sure,' said Girling, perusing the letter again, 'but all things considered, I'd hazard good money he was referring to the Labyrinth of Osiris.'

The conviction with which he said this caught Khalifa off balance. He hadn't been anticipating such a direct answer, had been expecting to have to put in more spadework. He edged forward, an expectant tingle chasing up his spine, everything that had been said up to that point forgotten.

'What is this Laby-rin?'

'Labyrin-*th*,' corrected Girling. 'One of two ancient Egyptian marvels upon which the Greeks conferred the name. The other, of course, being the Amenemhat lll mortuary complex at Hawwara. Although in my opinion the Osiris Labyrinth is by far the more interesting of the pair.'

'It's a tomb, this Laby-rin?'

'No, no, no.' Girling's jowls wobbled as he shook his head. 'It was a mine. *The* mine, actually. Principal gold source for the pharaohs of the New Kingdom.'

The tingle grew a whole lot stronger. According to the notes Ben-Roi had sent over, Rivka Kleinberg had been reading up on gold mines.

'I've never even heard of it,' said Khalifa.

'Well, you probably wouldn't have unless you had a particular interest in ancient Egyptian material technology. To be honest I didn't know much about it myself till it cropped up in the research I was doing into Pinsker and I did some background reading on the subject. Put all the other gold mines in the shade, apparently. The Tutankhamun treasures, the Tell Basta hoard, the Ahhotep jewellery, the Djehuty burial – take a look at any of those and there's a good chance you're looking at gold mined from the Labyrinth. A veritable underground city, if you believe Herodotus.'

'And Pinsker was looking for this mine?'

'Certainly was,' said Girling. 'It seems to have become something of an obsession of his. I've no idea where he first heard about it, but pretty much from the moment he arrived in Egypt he was heading off on forays into the Eastern Desert trying to track it down. Which I suppose would figure, what with him being a mining engineer and all. There's a letter of his in the Bracken Archive in Manchester – Joseph Bracken being a 1920s union activist, an old wartime chum of Pinsker's – in which he goes on and on about the thing, about how amazing it would be to find it. Not so much because of the gold angle, but for the light the mine might shed on ancient working practices. In an age when every other bugger in Egypt was looking for pharaohs and treasure, Samuel Pinsker just wanted to know about the proletariat. A true disciple of Marx. Aha, the cavalry approaches!'

The waiter came up to them, balancing a tray on the tips of his fingers. He offloaded Girling's Pimm's and, although he hadn't asked for it, a glass of iced water for Khalifa.

'Bottoms up!' trilled the Englishman, hoisting his drink to his lips and downing a third of it in one gulp, his fleshy throat wobbling and swelling like a pelican's. Khalifa sipped his water, glad of it now that it was in his hand. There was a silence, then:

'*So deep are its shafts, so numerous its galleries, so bewildering its complexity, that to step through its doorway is to be lost entirely and Daedalus himself would be confounded.*'

Girling took another hefty gulp and settled the glass on the curve of his belly.

'That's how Herodotus describes the Labyrinth,' he said. 'Or at least it's a paraphrase of Herodotus – I can't remember the passage verbatim. Apparently the place was so rich in gold you could slice chunks of it off the wall with a knife as though you were carving meat, and when you emerged into the sunlight – assuming you ever *did* emerge – your hair would be glittering as though it was on fire because of all the gold dust. Never one for understatement, our Herodotus.'

He chuckled and swirled a sprig of mint around what was left of the Pimm's. Khalifa dragged off the last of his cigarette.

'Of course it was only the Greeks who referred to it as a labyrinth,' Girling added. 'The Egyptians had no such concept. They knew it by the slightly more prosaic title *shemut net wesir* – the Passages of Osiris. Osiris obviously being the God of the Underworld.'

Shemut net wesir did ring a bell, although only a vague one. Despite his fascination with his country's past, ancient mining wasn't an area of that past to which Khalifa had ever devoted much thought.

'Herodotus is our only source for this mine?' he asked.

'No, no, it's referenced in a number of different places,' replied Girling, giving the mint sprig another swirl before pulling it out of the glass, leaning forward and slurping at it. 'I certainly can't claim to be an authority on the subject, but there's definitely a passage about it in Diodorus Siculus. Describes how at its height the mine was being worked by upwards of ten thousand slave labourers and producing enough gold to outbalance an elephant on a set of scales. And I seem to remember there were some Agatharchides fragments as well. Plus the ancient Egyptian sources, which being ancient Egyptian sources are rather more cryptic and open to interpretation.'

He dropped the mint back in his glass, drained the last of the Pimm's and, pulling out his handkerchief again, dabbed at his shirt and trousers, which were dotted with dribble marks. From the poolside a woman's voice rang out demanding to know where Janine had put the Ambre Solaire. Out on the Nile a tourist launch was approaching, a sign on its roof bearing the not entirely inappropriate name *New Titanic*.

'Of course there *are* those who poo-poo the whole thing,' said Girling, again starting in without any prompt on Khalifa's part. 'Claim it's all a myth. A sort of Egyptian Eldorado. Carter, for one, always dismissed the idea, although he tended to dismiss anything that might have overshadowed his own discovery. The texts are surprisingly consistent though, certainly by ancient standards, and I believe some new inscriptions have been turned up recently that add to the evidence. The obvious stumbling block being that no one's ever actually found the damn thing. And now it seems someone has. Or at least did.' He brandished the letter. 'Extraordinary. Absolutely extraordinary.'

'Do you think he was telling the truth?' asked Khalifa.

'I don't see any reason why he'd lie about it. He was a brash northerner, not really given to flights of fantasy. If he said he found it, I'd take that at face value. Absolutely extraordinary. Would you mind if I took a copy of this?'

'Please, keep it,' said Khalifa. 'I've got the original in my office.'

'Much obliged. I really do think I should get working on that thing on Pinsker. Seems he's even more interesting than I thought. A sort of Egyptological Mallory.'

Khalifa didn't get the reference and didn't pursue it. His mind was drifting, trying to work through the angles of why an Israeli journalist doing an article on sex-trafficking should have been interested in the discovery of an ancient Egyptian gold mine. It wasn't his business to do so, it was Ben-Roi's investigation, but he couldn't help himself. Something about the case had hooked him. Hooked him in a way that nothing had done since . . .

'Do we know anything else about this mine?'

'Hmmn?' Girling was reading the letter again, lost in his own thoughts.

'The mine. Do we know anything else about it?'

'Well, like I say, it's not really my specialist field.' The Englishman folded the letter and slipped it into his shirt pocket. 'Always been more of a Graeco-Romanist myself. It was definitely big – all the sources agree on that. The daddy of all ancient Egyptian mines. And it seems to have been in use throughout the New Kingdom. Five-hundred-odd years' worth of burrowing and tunnelling – if you think that even the deepest tombs in the Valley of the Kings only took about twenty years to dig, that gives you some idea of the possible scale of the place. All mined out in ancient times, of course, but even so, it would still be a huge discovery.'

'And it was somewhere in the Eastern Desert,' said Khalifa.

'That's where the sources seem to place it. Most ancient gold works were in that part of the world. There or in Nubia. Which of course comes from *nub*, the ancient Egyptian word for gold.'

He pulled out his handkerchief and started dabbing at his forehead again.

'The people you should really be talking to are the Raissoulis,' he said. 'They've been tramping around that corner of Egypt for the last twenty years, know everything there is to know about ancient mining.'

Again, the name rang a vague bell with Khalifa.

'Brother and sister?'

'Exactly. Remarkable pair. Those new inscriptions I mentioned – I'm pretty certain it was the Raissoulis who turned them up. They're the ones you need to speak to if you want to know more about the Labyrinth. Based at Cairo University, I believe.'

Khalifa made a mental note to get in touch with them. He threw out a few more questions, but Girling could add nothing to what he'd already told him, and with the Englishman starting to sneak glances at his watch, Khalifa thanked him for his help and brought the interview to a close.

'I do hope I'm not rushing you,' said Girling apologetically. 'It's just that I'm due to take a group over to the Avenue of the Sphinxes at five and time's starting to get a little tight.'

Khalifa told him not to worry, he had everything he needed.

'Jolly well done on the avenue, by the way,' added Girling, levering himself out of his chair. 'A remarkable achievement. Totally transformed the town. As a Luxorite you must be very proud.'

Khalifa didn't respond to that, just gulped down his water and stood himself. For a brief instant his gaze snagged on a huge raft of *ward-i-nil* drifting down the centre of the river, a grey heron standing proud in the middle of it like a boatman guiding his craft.

Then, with a shake of the head, he fell into step beside the Englishman.

'There was one other thing,' he said as the two of them walked back across the deck. 'When you were researching Pinsker, you didn't come across any link between him and Israel, did you?'

The Englishman's brows knitted. 'Can't immediately think of one. Israel didn't even exist in Pinsker's time. It was British Mandate Palestine in those days. Or was it UN Mandate Palestine? I can never remember. Either way, I'm pretty certain Pinsker never went there. He was actually rather sceptical about the whole Zionist thing. Although he *was* in Egypt, so it's not impossible he popped up that way for a visit. If he did, I never heard about it.'

He reached the door into the ship, started to step through, then turned.

'Hang on, there was a family member who moved out there. Sometime in the late thirties. A cousin or something. Very distant. Stayed a couple of years, then got disillusioned and went back to England. Can't remember her name.'

He thought a moment, then gave an apologetic shrug and stepped inside. Khalifa stood where he was, watching as the clump of *ward-i-nil* drifted north on its journey to the sea, rotating slowly in the pull of the current. Then, firing up another Cleopatra, he followed Girling into the ship.

'I must say it sounds an intriguing case,' came the Englishman's voice from the stairs ahead. 'Ancient gold mines, disappearing archaeologists, mysteries in the Holy Land – sounds like the plot of a novel. I'd love to know what it's all about.'

Khalifa pulled on his cigarette. 'That makes two of us,' he muttered.

JERUSALEM

Seven o'clock saw Ben-Roi and Leah Shalev sitting on the balcony of her apartment in Ramat Denya, sipping wine and gazing out at a fiery, blood-red sunset. From behind them came the muted clatter of pots as Shalev's husband Benny busied himself with dinner. A small dog eyed them from the far corner of the balcony, a snuffling heap of hair that went by the unlikely name of Gorgeous.

'So what do you make of it all?' she asked.

'The words "complete fucking balls-up" come to mind.'

'That's certainly one way of describing it.'

She propped her feet on the balcony rail and pushed, pivoting on the back legs of her chair. Apparently she'd screamed the station down when they'd brought Petrossian in that morning. Now she was back to her normal self – calm, collected, focused.

'The old man's certainly got questions to answer,' she said. 'He lied about his alibi. And the phone call doesn't look good.'

The call was a new development. Amos Namir had spent the afternoon going through the archbishop's phone records, and lo and behold he'd turned up an incoming from Kleinberg's mobile. Three weeks before her death. Five-minute conversation.

'When we saw him in the cathedral he claimed he didn't know Kleinberg.'

'We hadn't identified her then.'

'It's still a direct link to the victim,' she said. 'And her name's been all over the papers. He could have come forward. He's dodgy. No question about it.'

'You sound like you're agreeing with Baum.'

'The day I agree with Yitzhak Baum's the day I hand in my badge. But Petrossian's not on the level. And right at the moment he's the strongest suspect we've got. The *only* suspect.'

Ben-Roi propped his own feet on the rail and took a sip of his wine. Barkan Chardonnay. Not his thing at all, but the Shalevs had been out of beer, and after everything else that had gone down that day, he'd needed a drink.

'He's an old man, Leah. You said it yourself.'

'So suddenly there's an age qualification? Amon Herzig wasn't exactly a spring chicken.'

Herzig had been the first murder case they'd worked on together. Wife-killer. Front-page news. He'd been eighty-three.

'Petrossian didn't do it,' insisted Ben-Roi. 'You know that as well as I do. Whatever else he's got going on – and he clearly *has* got something else going on – there's no way he garrotted Rivka Kleinberg.'

'So he knows who did and he's protecting them.'

That was slightly more feasible, although Ben-Roi still couldn't see it.

'It doesn't stack up, Leah. It just doesn't stack up.'

'So what does stack up?' She looked across at him. 'Tell me, Arieh, please. Because with the best will in the world, we're ten days into this and you've not come up with any better suggestions.'

Fair point. Sex-trafficking, Vosgi, Barren, Egypt, Nemesis, Samuel Pinsker – in the end they were all just random brushstrokes, crossing over in places but never in such a way as to produce anything approaching a coherent picture. He was on the right track, he could feel it – feel it with every policing cell in his body – but being on the right track and having a viable case were two very different things.

'I'm getting there,' he said lamely.

'I'm delighted for you. Unfortunately getting there's not going to cut any ice with Baum. He wants Petrossian. And he's standing at the head of a long queue.'

He frowned. 'Meaning?'

'Meaning the archbishop hasn't exactly endeared himself over the years. He's made some pretty inflammatory comments about the settlements, the Gaza blockade, city corruption. He's got enemies in high places. A lot of enemies.'

'You're saying they're going to pin it on him?'

'What I'm saying is there are a lot of influential people who wouldn't mind seeing him taken down a peg or two. We still abide by the rule of law in this country – just – and if the evidence isn't there they're not going to risk sending it to trial. But there's a lot of pressure to find that evidence. And the archbishop isn't doing himself any favours.'

Ben-Roi dropped his head back and rubbed his temples. It had been a long day. Another one.

'What's Chief Gal saying?' he asked.

'Not very much. Right now it's Baum's show.'

'Is he going to hold him?'

Shalev shrugged. 'The chief superintendent hasn't deigned to take me into his confidence, but my guess is that unless he turns up something rock solid he won't apply for an extension – the protests aren't good publicity. He'll keep him in for the full twenty-four, just to prove a point, then put him under house arrest.'

'I need to talk to him.'

Something about the way her mouth curled told Ben-Roi that wasn't going to be easy. Baum was guarding his golden goose. He dropped his feet and shunted his chair round so he was facing her directly.

'It's about the girl, Leah. Vosgi. She's the key. I don't know how and I don't know why, but Vosgi's the key. And something tells me Petrossian knows more about her than he's letting on. I need to talk to him.'

From the kitchen Benny Shalev's voice rang out, announcing that dinner was ready. His wife glanced over her shoulder, then dropped an arm and clicked her fingers. The dog came pattering along the balcony and leapt into her lap, making appreciative snuffling noises as she scratched behind its ears. For a moment she just sat there. Then, lifting the dog, she planted a kiss on its nose.

'I'll see what I can do,' she said. 'I can't promise anything more than that. And you need to tread carefully. *Very* carefully. Baum's a spineless little prick, but he's in with the right people. He can make a lot of trouble. Don't go rubbing him up the wrong way. OK?'

Ben-Roi gave an amused grunt. 'From what Zisky told me about this morning, you need to take a bit of your own advice.'

'That was this morning,' said Shalev. 'Tomorrow morning I'm going in and kissing the chief superintendent's arse. I've worked hard to get where I am and I'm not about to throw it all away.'

'Even if it means getting the wrong man.'

She didn't respond to that. Instead, lowering the dog to the floor, she drained her wine and stood. Ben-Roi did the same and they went back into the flat. Benny Shalev was bustling out of the kitchen with a large pot, followed by his youngest daughter Malka holding a pile of plates.

'You staying, Arieh?' he called. 'There's more than enough to go round.'

Ben-Roi thanked him, but said he needed to be getting on his way.

'I'm taking Sarah out for dinner. I cooked her breakfast and feel I ought to make up for it.'

They slapped hands and Leah showed him to the front door.

'Stay on it,' she said as he stepped out on to the landing and hit the light-timer. 'I'll cover you, try to give you some space. But keep your head down. And tread carefully. I've got a bad feeling about this case.'

'You said that before.'

'I know. And the feeling's getting worse.'

She hesitated. Then, coming up on tiptoe, she gave him a peck on the cheek. Five years they'd worked together, and she'd never done anything like that. The gesture seemed to take her as much by surprise as it did him. She blushed, and with a muttered, 'Watch yourself, Arieh,' closed the door. Ben-Roi only made it halfway down the stairs before the light-timer clicked off, plunging him into darkness.

LUXOR

Straight after his meeting with Digby Girling, Khalifa had put in a call to Cairo University, hoping to find out some more about the Labyrinth of Osiris. The woman he'd spoken to – a secretary in the archaeology department – had confirmed that brother-and-sister team Hassan and Salma Raissouli were indeed the country's foremost authorities on ancient gold-mining. Unfortunately they were currently doing fieldwork out in the middle of the Sinai and weren't due back in Cairo for another three weeks. Khalifa had told her it was urgent and she'd agreed to try to contact them on their satellite phone, although she'd warned him communication was notoriously sporadic and it could be days before he got a response. He'd left it with her, gone home, helped Batah with dinner, got Yusuf to bed, then, seized by a sudden urge to experience what it was like to be a normal couple again, pulled Zenab out for an evening stroll around Luxor.

They hardly ever went out any more. Before Ali had died they'd done it all the time: across the river for dinner with Mahmoud at the Tutankhamun; into the souk for coffee and a *shisha*; down to Karnak for a nocturnal ramble around the deserted temple complex (one of the perks of having a police pass). These days it was as much as he could do to get her from one end of the flat to the other. Tonight, as she always did, she'd said she didn't want to go, couldn't face it, but he'd badgered her, and eventually she'd relented, sensing it was important to him. And to her too, in a way. So they'd linked arms and wandered back along Medina al-Minawra towards the centre of town, not really saying anything, threading through the evening crowds, stopping for a while to watch the revellers at a huge outdoor wedding before ending up in a small café opposite the Medina Club pleasure garden. Which was where they were sitting now.

'More tea?' he asked.

'Thank you, no.'

Her voice was so quiet these days, barely audible.

'A puff?'

He proffered the mouthpiece of the *shisha* he was smoking. She shook her head.

'It's *tufah*.'

Another shake.

'You used to love *tufah*.'

A shrug this time. A donkey cart piled with gas canisters clattered past in front of them.

'Maybe we should think about getting back,' she said.

'We've only just come out.'

'I don't like to leave the kids. You know how Yusuf wakes up, gets . . .'

Khalifa wrapped an arm round her shoulders. 'The kids are fine,

315

Zenab. Batah's a big girl, she's more than capable of minding her brother for a couple of hours. She'll call if she needs us.'

He patted the mobile in his shirt pocket.

'Let's take some time for ourselves, eh? Try to enjoy the evening.'

It seemed like she was going to argue. Then, with a weak nod, she reached up a hand and linked her fingers into his.

'You're right,' she said. 'It's good for us to be out. It's just that . . .' She bit her lip.

'I know,' he said, drawing her close. 'Believe me, Zenab, I know. But we have to try and get on with things.'

He squeezed her hand and puffed the *shisha*, exhaling a slow stream of apple-scented tobacco smoke. From the tables around them came the babble of conversation and the clack of dominoes; in the pleasure garden across the street, children were yelling as they bounced on giant trampolines and flew down slides.

'Hey, Mohammed Sariya told me a good one the other day,' he said, trying to lighten the mood, draw her out of herself. 'Mubarak, Gadaffi, Ben Ali and a camel are all in a balloon together, and a storm suddenly blows up—'

The mobile went off. Zenab stiffened.

'It's OK,' he said. 'It's OK.'

Laying aside the mouthpiece, he pulled the phone from his pocket. It wasn't their home number. Wasn't any number he recognized. He showed her the display to reassure her, then answered. A blare of static crackled into his ear.

'Hello?'

More static.

'Hello?'

Nothing. Wrong number. Or one of those automated cold calls trying to sell him something. He gave it a third try, and still getting no response was about to ring off when suddenly:

'. . . to us about gold-mining. Said it was urgent.'

The voice – a woman's – came through loud and clear, the static receding to a vague background hiss. Khalifa unwound his arm from Zenab's shoulder.

'Miss Raissouli?'

'Please, call me Salma.'

'And I'm Hassan.' A man's voice echoed down the line. 'Sorry it's taken a while to get back to you.'

On the contrary, said Khalifa, he hadn't been expecting to hear from them so soon.

'Normally we keep the phone switched off,' came the woman's voice again.

'To conserve the battery,' put in the man.

'But we needed to arrange a food drop –'

'– which is how we picked up the message from Yasmina at the faculty.'

They seemed to talk interchangeably, the line of conversation passing seamlessly from one to the other and back again. Khalifa pictured the two of them sitting side by side holding the handset between them, each leaning into it in turn to have their say.

'So how can we help you?' they both asked simultaneously.

Covering the phone, he turned to Zenab.

'I'm sorry,' he said, 'I need to speak to these people. Do you mind?'

She waved a hand, indicating that he should continue with the call.

'Sure? I could ask them to call back.'

She shook her head and again motioned him to carry on. He felt bad about it, knew he should defer the conversation, but hopefully it wouldn't take long, and he really did want to know about that gold mine. He touched her forearm, mouthed that he'd be quick, then swivelled away from her and filled the Raissoulis in on the situation. Not the murder – just the Samuel Pinsker stuff. When he told them about the Howard Carter letter one of them gasped and the other whistled – it was hard to tell which was doing which.

'There've long been rumours that someone had tracked it down,' said Salma, 'but to be honest I didn't believe them. I've never even heard of this Pinsker man.'

'But you have heard of the Labyrinth?'

'Absolutely. It's one of the few ancient gold mines to have been known by a specific name rather than simply the generic *bia*.'

'The ancient word for a mine,' put in her brother.

After the initial interference, the line was crystal clear. Hard to believe he was talking to people out in the middle of the desert.

'And the mine definitely existed?' asked Khalifa.

'Oh yes,' said Salma. 'The Greek historians all mention it, although admittedly they were writing five hundred years later –'

'Closer to a thousand with Diodorus,' chipped in her brother.

'– but there are a good few contemporary references as well. Including a couple of inscriptions we ourselves turned up.'

Digby Girling had mentioned something to that effect. Khalifa threw a look back at Zenab – she was sitting with her hands in her lap, gazing at the revellers in the pleasure garden across the street – then asked for more information.

'One was a graffito near the bottom end of the Wadi el-Shaghab.'

Hassan again. 'The language is slightly obscure –'

'When is it ever clear?' his sister's voice echoed from the background.

'– but basically it records the passing of a gold convoy from the mine down to the Nile Valley. Probably left by one of the soldiers guarding the convoy. There's a Ramesses VII cartouche –'

'Or possibly Ramesses IX.'

'– which suggests that even at the very end of the New Kingdom the mine was still going strong.'

Over the way a chorus of screams erupted as a giant hydraulic fun-wheel levered itself into the air and started spinning. Khalifa clamped a hand over his ear to block out the sound.

'The other inscription?'

'That one's on a cliff face above the Wadi Mineh,' said Salma. 'We only found it last year so it's not even published yet. It's particularly interesting because to date it's the earliest known reference to the mine.'

'Early Eighteenth Dynasty,' came her brother's voice. 'Reign of Tuthmosis ll.'

'Again the language is pretty garbled,' said Salma, 'but so far as we can make out it's some kind of a royal proclamation announcing the mine's re-dedication. If you hang on a moment I'll –'

There was a rustling of pages being turned, presumably as she consulted a notebook.

'Here we go.' She started reading. '*The mine-land of gold that was revealed to my father and that was in the domain of Hathor is now in the domain of Osiris, and the gold is His, and it is He who has ownership of its many ways so that it shall now be spoken of as the* shemut net wesir – *Passages of Osiris.*'

A muted slap as the notebook, or whatever it was, was closed.

'Obviously there are a number of possible interpretations,' she continued, 'but what we think it's saying –'

'Are *sure* it's saying –' chipped in her brother.

'– is that a mine that was started in the reign of Tuthmosis 1 –'

'Or possibly Amenhotep 1 –'

'– has now gone so deep that patronage of it has passed from Hathor, the traditional Egyptian deity of mining, to Osiris, God of the Underworld. Which if we're right is absolutely extraordinary. I mean, most ancient Egyptian gold works were nothing more than open-cast trenches. Even the ones that did go underground never went further than a few dozen metres.'

'And this is right at the beginning of the mine's life, remember,' came in her brother. 'It's got another – what? – four hundred years of digging to go. Even allowing for periods when it wasn't being worked, the potential size of the thing still beggars belief. No wonder they also referred to it as *bia we aa en nub*.'

'The greatest of all gold mines,' translated Salma.

Khalifa fumbled for the mouthpiece of his *shisha* and took a puff. Interesting as all this was, he was still struggling to trace any clear line between a three-thousand-year-old gold mine and a woman getting garrotted in a church in Jerusalem. Sure, Barren Corporation were involved in gold-mining. And in his experience gold and violence were never that far apart. Even so, it all seemed pretty tenuous. Doubly so when you factored in the sex-trafficking angle. He took another puff, checked on Zenab – she was still staring straight ahead, lost in her own thoughts – then asked the obvious question:

'And the mine was definitely exhausted in ancient times?'

There was some whispering, then:

'It's a slightly moot point,' said Salma Raissouli.

Not quite the unequivocal answer he'd been anticipating.

'How do you mean, moot?'

'Well, Herodotus is very clear about it,' came Hassan's voice. 'He says the mine was abandoned at the end of the New Kingdom because all the gold had been dug out. But then Diodorus Siculus, who seems to have been working from a different source to Herodotus –'

'And on this particular subject is generally considered to be the more reliable of the two –' cut in his sister.

'– Diodorus merely says that the whereabouts of the mine was forgotten in the chaos at the end of the New Kingdom. The implication being that it wasn't exhausted, just lost. There are certainly no

319

contemporary references to it being worked after the end of the Twentieth Dynasty—'

'Although there *is* a Late Period papyrus that describes an expedition to try and locate the mine again,' said Salma. 'Which they obviously wouldn't have launched unless they'd believed there was still something there worth mining. Unfortunately the expedition got lost in the desert and they all died of thirst so they never got the chance to find out.'

'The simple fact is, nobody knows.' Hassan again. 'Personally, I lean towards Herodotus. Salma, being my sister, takes the opposing view. It's impossible to say for sure.'

'And will be until someone actually finds the mine,' added Salma.

'Which Samuel Pinsker seems to have done,' murmured Khalifa, taking another thoughtful pull on his *shisha*. Beside him a young man came up and started tweezering glowing charcoals on to the pipe's foil, replacing the original ones, which were starting to burn out. Khalifa barely even noticed him. He was getting another of those tingles in his spine. Not strong, but definitely there. He shuffled forward on his seat.

'Apparently Herodotus says something about the mine being so rich in gold you could –'

'– slice it off the wall with a knife.' Hassan finished the sentence for him.

'Any truth in that?'

Laughter. From both of them.

'You obviously don't know much about gold-mining,' said Salma.

Khalifa acknowledged that that was certainly the case.

'It's a good story, but total fantasy,' said Hassan. 'The Egyptians extracted most of their gold from seams of auriferous quartz – basically white quartz with minute flecks of gold locked inside it. To get at the gold they had to hack chunks of quartz out of the hillside, then crush it to a powder and then wash the powder through with water to extract the precious stuff. So not quite as simple as Herodotus suggests. Diodorus Siculus gets much closer to the reality.'

'Although there's no question the ancient deposits *were* uniquely rich,' put in Salma, 'and all the sources agree that the Osiris deposit was the richest of them all. So maybe there's a germ of truth in Herodotus. Analyses we've done of ancient slag heaps suggests that even the poorer mines were getting fifty or even sixty grams of gold per ton of ore, which is about double what the most productive modern mines achieve. And the purity was exceptional. As much as twenty-three or even twenty-four carats.'

The technical terms went over Khalifa's head, but he got the gist. The tingle was still there, nagging its way up and down his spine. Something was coming out of all this, he could sense it. Coalescing. Trying to reveal itself. Whether that something had any relevance to Ben-Roi's case – that was a different matter.

'And all we can say for sure about the mine's location is that it was out in the Eastern Desert somewhere?'

'We can probably narrow it down slightly,' replied Salma. 'The two *wadis* where we found the inscriptions – El-Shaghab and Mineh – both seem to have been used as primary routes to the mine, El-Shaghab from the west and Mineh from the north. And there are a couple of other graffiti that mention it over at Bir el-Gindi. So triangulating those three would put the mine somewhere in the central uplands of the desert. Which is still a very big area –'

'And an extremely remote one,' added Hassan. 'Might as well be the moon for all the signs of life.'

Khalifa seemed to remember someone else using that analogy recently. He couldn't recall the precise context and didn't waste time trying to do so. Instead:

'Would it be valuable, this mine? If someone did find it?'

The question popped out of his mouth almost of its own accord. The unspoken corollary being: valuable enough to kill for?

'I suppose that all depends on how you define value,' said Hassan. 'Archaeologically it would be an amazing discovery. Particularly if the mine had retained any sort of integrity and not collapsed in on itself.'

'I was thinking more in financial terms,' said Khalifa. 'Assuming there was still gold down there.'

'Well, that's a very big assumption,' said Hassan. 'Whatever Diodorus might imply, I really can't see there being anything left of the original deposits. Not after five centuries of continuous mining.'

'But if there was?'

'Then yes, of course it would be valuable. I mean, gold's gold. People covet it.'

'Although there's a bit more to it than that,' interjected Salma. 'Like we said before, it's not simply a matter of marching out there with a pickaxe and hacking a load of gold off the walls. It's a complex process

321

extracting the gold from the ore, and given the extreme remoteness of the area, you'd be needing to do it on an industrial scale to make the whole thing economically viable. Which the pharaohs could obviously do because they had an army of slave labour at their disposal. These days there are a few more overheads. So to answer your question, yes, it would be valuable, but not to your average Joe on the street. It's only really the government, or else a large mining conglomerate, that could deploy the resources necessary to actually realize the value.'

A conglomerate like Barren Corporation, thought Khalifa.

He sat back, blowing tendrils of smoke out of his nostrils, sifting through it all, sensing he was on to something, but still struggling to make the leap from a gold mine in Egypt to a corpse in Israel via a sex-trafficking industry straddling both countries. A few moments passed. Then, aware that the Raissoulis were waiting on him, and so was his wife, and that ultimately it wasn't his responsibility to make the leap anyway, merely to do what he could to help Ben-Roi get across, he thanked the brother and sister for their help, said he'd be in touch if he needed anything more and ended the call. He gave himself another couple of seconds, allowing the interview to settle in his mind, then turned.

'I'm sorry that took so . . .'

Zenab's seat was empty. He looked around, assuming she must have gone into the café to get something, or perhaps to look in the window of one of the neighbouring shops. No sign of her. He stood, running his eyes up and down the street, trying to pick her out in the crowds, concern rapidly giving way to alarm.

'Zenab,' he called. Then, louder: 'Zenab!'

Someone touched his wrist. He swung, thinking it was her, but it was the man at the next table.

'Over there,' said the man, pointing across the way. Khalifa followed the line of the man's finger. She was standing up against the railings surrounding the pleasure garden, gazing through at the children inside, her hands clasping the bars as though she was looking out of a prison cell.

'Oh Zenab,' he murmured. 'Oh my darling.'

Throwing some money on the table, he jogged across to her. Her shoulders were heaving. He wrapped an arm round her and gently pulled her back and away, cursing himself for not having kept a closer watch.

'It's OK,' he said. 'I'm here now.'

She swung into him and buried her face in his chest, sobbing uncontrollably.

'I miss him, Yusuf. Oh God, I miss him. I just can't bear the silence.'

The town was alive with sound – laughter, music, the blare of car horns, the clatter of carts – but he knew exactly what she meant. Without Ali, there would always be a corner of their lives that was unnaturally quiet, like a deserted house.

'It's OK,' he repeated, holding her tight, ignoring the looks of passers-by, the mutters of those who disapproved of such public displays of closeness between a man and a woman. 'We'll get through this. I promise you, Zenab, we'll get through this.'

They stood for a while, locked together, oblivious to the crowds eddying around them, closed off in their own private world of grief. Then, taking her hand tight in his, he led her home, his conversation with the Raissoulis utterly forgotten.

THE NEGEV

Since childhood she'd been alert to noises in the night, and the moment she heard the unfamiliar footfall outside – too heavy for Tamar; too slow and lumbering for either Gidi or Faz – she was wide awake and reaching beneath her pillow for the Glock. The footsteps stopped, started again, came right up to the door. She could hear breathing – low, feral, like some sort of prowling animal – then the handle started to turn. She levelled the Glock, sighting down the barrel. One turn, testing the lock, then another, harder, more insistent. The lock gave on the third turn and the door began to open, heavy oak panels easing back with a creak of unoiled hinges.

'Get away,' she hissed, finger tightening around the trigger. 'I'll kill you. Get away.'

'I just want to talk.'

'You never want to talk! Get away! Get away!'

'Don't make me force you, Rachel.'

She yanked the trigger. It stuck. She tried again, and again, acid rising in her throat, her heart thudding so hard she thought it was going to crash right through her ribcage. The Glock wouldn't fire. She kicked out, flailed her arms. He was on the bed now. A hand pushed beneath the cover, started to work her legs open.

'Oh no, please don't . . .'

'Sssshhh.'

'You're hurting me. Please, stop, you're hurting . . .'

'But I've paid. All that money.'

'It hurts. It hurts.'

'Sssshhh.'

'Stop! It hurts. You're tearing . . . Oh God, please don't . . .'

She jerked awake.

For a moment she lay there, the scene so vivid in her mind that it was only slowly she was able to transition from dream to reality. Then, struggling into a sitting position, she fumbled on the bedside lamp and drew her knees up to her chest, sobbing.

It was always the same dream. Night after night. The details varied – sometimes he came into the room, sometimes he'd already be there; sometimes she'd recognize him, sometimes it would be a stranger. The essence of it, though – the breathing, the weight, the sickening shock of penetration: that never changed. Hadn't changed for as long as she could remember. Every night she went to sleep pleading for a different movie. Every night her subconscious played out the same unbearable rape flick. With her as the star. She wiped her eyes and pressed her legs tight together, her vagina aching even though nothing had actually happened down there.

Several minutes went by. Slowly her sobs subsided, her heartbeat eased. She looked at the clock. 2.17 a.m. She thought about going into Tamar's room, curling up beside her, seeking shelter in the warmth of her body, but she was awake now, knew she wouldn't be able to settle. Instead, leaning across, she swung the laptop off the bedside table and switched it on. A screensaver of a tall glass-and-steel building came up, its windows glinting in the sunlight – Barren Corporation headquarters in Houston. She entered the log-in she'd extracted from Chad Perks and recommenced her trawl through the hard drive, searching for something, anything that might be considered incriminating. That could help skewer the company. The ache between her legs subsided as her entire being focused in on the mission.

'You're lying.'

'I'm sorry if I give that impression.'

'You know who the girl is.'

'I'm afraid I don't.'

'You know *where* she is.'

'Again, I'm afraid . . .'

'And Rivka Kleinberg thought the same thing. That's why she called you three weeks before she was murdered.'

'Sadly I can't recall the details of the conversation.'

'Sadly I don't believe you.'

'I'm sorry for that.'

'Where's the girl?'

'I couldn't tell you.'

'Why did you lie about your alibi?'

'I merely forgot to mention that I went for a walk.'

'Why did you say you were guilty of Rivka Kleinberg's murder?'

'I said I was *culpable* of her murder. It was me who ordered the late opening of the cathedral, after all. Had I not done so, she would not have been killed in there.'

'I don't believe you.'

'You're entitled to your opinion.'

'You're hiding something.'

'If you say so.'

'You're afraid of something.'

'We're all afraid of something, Detective.'

'Where's the girl?'

'I couldn't tell you.'

'You're lying.'

'I'm sorry if I give that impression.'

Ben-Roi's fist clenched in frustration. It had been the same for the last forty minutes, like a tape on endless repeat – round and round, back and forth, to and fro, getting nowhere. The same for the last twenty-two hours, by all accounts. The archbishop wasn't saying anything, wasn't admitting to anything, and with forensics drawing a blank in his private apartments, Baum's case was drooping like a flaccid cock. Which is why he'd finally relented and granted Ben-Roi his interview. A last, desperate throw of the dice before the twenty-four-hour holding period expired and a ton of egg slammed into his face. If Ben-Roi was frustrated, it was nothing to what his beloved chief superintendent must have been feeling at that current moment.

He glanced at his watch – 8.40 a.m. – stood and walked up and down the cell a few times, stretching his legs, clearing his head. The archbishop sat in meditative silence, a faint smile playing across his lips. Not cocky or mocking, like the smiles you got from career scumbags like Genady Kremenko. This was a different sort of expression – calm, stoic, assured. Pious almost. The smile of someone who believes they are doing the right thing and is more than happy to suffer whatever consequences that belief might bring with it. A martyr's smile, it struck Ben-Roi. And if he knew one thing about martyrs it was that they never broke, however hard you hammered at them. He returned to the table, sat down, picked up the photo of Vosgi.

'OK, let's go through it again. Do you know this girl?'

'I'm afraid I don't.'

'Why are you lying?'

'I'm not lying.'

'What are you afraid of?'

'As I said, we're all afraid of something, Detective.'

And so on and so on, same questions, same evasions for another thirty minutes until eventually he gave up, accepting that he was banging his head against a brick wall. Whatever the archbishop knew, it was locked inside him and no amount of poking and prying was going to force it out. Ben-Roi stood, went over to the cell door, smacked on the metal to get someone to open it. The archbishop remained where he was, his hands clasped in front of him, his ring of office glowing purple in the cell's harsh lighting. Still with that smile on his face.

'You know, right at the beginning of this case a friend of mine told me that nothing happens in the compound without you knowing about it –' said Ben-Roi as he waited for the door to be opened.

The archbishop gazed up at him.

'– He was wrong. I don't think you have the least idea who killed Rivka Kleinberg. And I sure as hell don't think you did it yourself.'

'I'm gratified to hear it.'

'But you do know what's happened to the girl,' continued Ben-Roi.

326

'And by withholding that information you're not only obstructing a police inquiry, you're allowing a killer to walk free. Possibly to kill again. Does that sit easy with your conscience, Your Eminence?'

Although the smile remained, there was the faintest movement in Petrossian's eyes, a fractional tightening of the irises. It might have been a flicker of doubt, it might have been nothing more than the reaction to a speck of dust. Either way, it was gone almost immediately.

'In my experience, matters of conscience are never as simple as they seem,' said the archbishop. 'They invariably throw up dilemmas and unintended consequences. The man who gives his life fighting a corrupt regime leaves behind a family who are then persecuted by that regime. The believer who burns at the stake for his religion sets an example of suffering that others feel compelled to follow. Conscience is a tricksy master, Detective. In this instance, however, so far as it possibly can be, mine is clear. Now if you wouldn't mind, I would beg a few moments to pray.'

Behind Ben-Roi the cell door opened. He stood a moment watching as the old man lowered his head and started to murmur, then stepped out of the cell.

'Well?'

Chief Superintendent Baum was waiting for him at the end of the corridor, pasty-faced and fretting. Ben-Roi shook his head, provoking an eruption of expletives and wall-kicking. A small consolation for the fact that the interview had been a complete waste of time.

LUXOR

When Khalifa arrived at the police station on Monday morning, a visitor was waiting for him in the foyer – Omar al-Zahwi. The two friends exchanged *sabah el-khirs* and embraced.

'Rasha well?' asked Khalifa, waving at one of the constables to bring them tea and leading Omar on to the stairs.

'Good, thanks. Zenab?'

'Better every day.'

For the first time in nine months, Khalifa was able to say it without feeling he was telling an outright lie. He'd feared the incident last night – the tears outside the pleasure garden – would set his wife back. Instead, it seemed to have provoked some sort of shift within her. This morning she'd risen before everyone else and prepared breakfast – something she hadn't done for a long time – and had then insisted on being the one to walk Yusuf to school. The grief was still palpably there – shadowing her eyes, etched into her face, dulling her voice – but alongside it there was a suggestion of purpose that Khalifa hadn't seen before. When he'd set off on the ten-minute walk to the police station, he'd felt better than he had done in ages.

'I'm guessing business rather than social,' he said as the two men climbed.

'Extraordinary powers of deduction,' quipped his friend, brandishing the briefcase and rolled-up map he was holding.

'The water test results?'

'The very same. Sorry to have kept you waiting.'

The apology was unnecessary. Since he'd started looking into the Samuel Pinsker story, the curious case of the Coptic well poisonings had receded to the very back of Khalifa's mind. There'd been no reports of further incidents, all was quiet out at the Attia farm. So far as it *was* still on his radar, he'd all but settled into the view that the whole thing was a storm in a tea glass.

'You're going to tell me they went bad naturally, aren't you?' he said.

'Nothing of the sort,' replied Omar. 'The wells were poisoned, no question. All seven of them.'

'Three,' corrected Khalifa.

'Seven. I did some trawling around and on top of the ones you gave me, I turned up another four that had also been affected.'

Khalifa stopped. Suddenly it was the Labyrinth of Osiris that had receded.

'You sure about this?'

'Absolutely. And those are just the ones that have been reported. There could well be more. No pun intended. You know – well, *well . . .*'

Khalifa ignored the joke.

'All Coptic?'

'Four of them are.'

'According to my maths that leaves another three.'

'On the ball as ever, *sahebi.*'

'And?'

'Those are Muslim-owned. One's a Bedouin watering hole over near Bir el-Gindi, one a smallholding down towards Barramiya, and the other one . . . I can't remember precisely where that was – I've got the details in here.'

He lifted his briefcase. Khalifa's mind was clicking, trying to adjust itself to a picture that appeared to be showing something very different from what he had initially imagined it to be showing.

'It's been interesting,' said Omar. 'Very interesting. Important, actually. I think we should talk. Shall we . . .'

He motioned up the stairs. Khalifa led the way up to the fourth floor and along the corridor to his office, only to find Ibrahim Fathi sitting in there with his feet on the desk, crunching *torshi* and chatting on the phone. The neighbouring room was free and they went in there instead.

'I've done a brief summary of the situation,' said Omar, once the door was closed, opening his case and handing over a stapled bunch of papers. 'Preliminary Report on Regionalized Hydro-geological Anomalies in the Sahara al-Sharqiya' read the title page. 'But it's probably easiest if I just talk you through the whole thing. If you wouldn't mind clearing a space there.'

He started unrolling the map while Khalifa made room for it on a nearby desk, helping his friend to flatten it out and weighing the corners with, respectively, a mug, an ashtray, a hole puncher and *The Complete Manual of Egyptian Policing* – the first time in twenty years Khalifa had ever found a use for the last. Unlike the map on the wall in Khalifa's office, which showed the whole of Egypt, this one covered just a small segment of the country: the rectangle of desert framed by the Nile to the west, the Red Sea to the east and Routes 29 and 212 north and south. Within the confused filigree of *wadis*, tracks, *gebel* and contour lines, seven small crosses had been marked in red ink. The poisoned wells, presumably. Khalifa lit a Cleopatra and the two men bowed over the desk.

'I'll try to keep this short and not bore you with a lecture –' began Omar.

'*Hamdulillah.*'

'– but before I get on to the wells –' he indicated the seven crosses – 'it's probably worth giving a bit of context so you at least understand what the hell I'm talking about.'

Khalifa dragged on his cigarette and motioned his friend to continue.

'So: the central Eastern Desert.' Omar slapped a palm on to the middle of the map. 'Geologically this sits on the edge of what's known as the Nubian Sandstone Aquifer – basically a vast subterranean sheet of water-permeated, semi-porous sandstone sandwiched between, and cut through by, layers of non-porous rock: basalt, granite, clay, that sort of thing. A "confined aquifer" as we refer to it in the business, meaning the water is locked underground.'

Khalifa took another drag. Whatever else he was getting out of helping Ben-Roi, it was certainly proving educational.

'The water itself is for the most part non-replenishable fossil water,' his friend went on. 'Which is to say, water that drained into the rock tens, if not hundreds of thousands of years ago and has been down there ever since. There's a limited amount of hydraulic conductivity due to gravity changes and atmospheric pressure differences – I won't go into the physics of it all –'

'*Hamdulillah*,' repeated Khalifa, who was already starting to get lost.

'– but to all intents and purposes the water is static. It doesn't move, it doesn't go anywhere, it's not recharged, it doesn't dissipate. It just sits down there in the pores of the sandstone, boxed in by the aforementioned non-porous layers. Imagine a sponge encased in watertight concrete and you get a rough idea.'

Through the wall Khalifa could hear Ibrahim Fathi talking on the phone, although thankfully the *torshi*-crunching remained out of earshot. It was a sound Khalifa had always found irritating, and he was having enough trouble keeping up with things without extra distractions.

'Virtually every well in the Eastern Desert,' continued Omar, 'and the Western Desert too, for that matter, is drilled down into this static water system. The depth of the wells obviously varies from place to place depending on the proximity of the aquifer to the surface – anything from twenty metres to two kilometres – but the basic principle is always the same. To reuse the sponge analogy, it's like pushing a straw through the concrete into the sponge and sucking out the water.'

He paused a moment to allow Khalifa to absorb this, then:

'There are, however, some rare and rather interesting exceptions.'

Something about his intonation made Khalifa prick up his ears at this.

330

'How do you mean, exceptions?'

'Well, in certain places the geology of the aquifer system is much more confused,' explained Omar. 'The non-porous bulkheads break down, the sandstone itself is fragmented, intercuts with seams of heavily fractured limestone – again, I won't bore you with all the hydro-geological detail. All you really need to know is that deep underground there are fault-lines zigzagging through the aquifer. Cracks, basically. Most of the time they're just a few hundred metres long, but occasionally they run for kilometres, or even tens of kilometres. Almost like subterranean pipes.'

There was a knock on the door and the constable from downstairs came into the room, bringing the tea Khalifa had requested. Omar waited for him to deposit his tray and leave, then picked up the thread.

'The extra space in these cracks obviously allows for increased water movement,' he said, spooning three sugars into his glass and stirring. 'We're not talking gushing underground rivers or anything, but the water does travel, in a way it doesn't in most other parts of the aquifer. Slowly, usually, a few dozen metres a year at most. If the crack is on an acute gradient, however, or if anywhere along its length pre-cipitative water from flash floods is able to penetrate, the movement can be considerably more pronounced. They did an experiment last year down at Gebel Hammata where they introduced dye into one of the cracks shortly before a flood and it was carried almost five kilometres in as many months.'

'Fascinating,' murmured Khalifa, wondering where on earth all this was leading. Omar saw what he was thinking and held up a finger, indicating that he should be patient, that the point was coming.

'It's only recently that people have started looking at these fault-lines in any sort of detail,' he said. 'Mainly because we haven't had the necessary technology. But there's now a team up at Helwan University who are using aerial remote sensing to try to map the cracks, or at least the major ones. And as luck would have it, one of the areas they've been surveying is the one we're interested in.' He gave the map another slap. 'Just on a hunch, I got in touch and passed on the coordinates of the poisoned waterholes. And what do you think they found?'

'All on fault-lines?' hazarded Khalifa.

'Exactly. All of the seven wells happen to have been dug down into hydro-conductive cracks. The water they're drawing is *moving* water. Keep that thought in your head –' he tapped Khalifa's temple – 'and now look at the distribution of the wells.'

He indicated the seven red crosses again.

'At first glance it all seems totally random, doesn't it? Just a scatter of wells without any obvious linking pattern. Factor in *when* they were poisoned, however, and a pattern does emerge. The earliest reported incident was here, at Deir el-Zeitun.'

He touched the cross nearest to the centre of the map, marking the monastery Demiana Barakat had told Khalifa about.

'And the most recent one here.' He touched the cross marking the position of the Attia farm. 'And from here –' Deir el-Zeitun – 'to here –' Attia farm – 'the poisonings form a clear dating sequence. Basically, the further they move from the central highlands, the later they get.'

A finger of ash was starting to build up on the end of Khalifa's Cleopatra. He didn't notice it. Out of nowhere the tingle in his spine had returned.

'Now there are various ways of rationalizing that pattern,' continued Omar. 'Conceivably it's just a coincidence. Or possibly, for reasons best known to themselves, someone's planned a campaign of well poisonings starting with the remotest ones first. For me, though, the obvious explanation – the *only* real explanation –- is that the wells aren't being poisoned from above ground, but from below. And whatever is causing the poisoning is somehow getting into the aquifer here –' he rapped a knuckle bang in the middle of the map, on the contour ripples of the Gebel el-Shalul – 'and percolating outwards and downwards along the hydro-conductive fault-lines.'

The ash on the end of Khalifa's cigarette snapped, raining down on to the map. He brushed it away. The tingle was getting stronger. Much stronger.

'All of which brings us neatly round to the water analysis,' said Omar, reaching over and picking up his report, which Khalifa had left on the neighbouring desk. 'It took a bit of time, and I had to call in a few favours, but I managed to get samples from all seven wells. The results came in yesterday. As I was expecting, all the wells were poisoned by the same thing, give or take some slight variations in specific concentrations. *What* they were poisoned by, however, came as a bit of a surprise.'

He opened the report, flicked through, started to read:

'Trace levels of mercury. Elevated levels of selenium, fluoride and chloride. Off-the-scale levels of –' He glanced across at Khalifa. '– arsenic.'

Khalifa gawped. 'Someone's dumping arsenic in the water?'

'It certainly looks that way. Although the interesting thing isn't so much the arsenic itself as finding it in combination with those other elements. This is getting way out of my field, but I've spoken to some people I know, and the consensus seems to be that we're dealing with the residue of an off-gas precipitate from a sulphur roaster.'

The gawp rearranged itself into a bewildered glaze. 'What the hell does that mean?'

'I had to ask the same thing,' said Omar, laughing. 'Apparently it's a stage in the process of separating ore from rock. It's used in various forms of metal extraction – copper, zinc, lead. Although in this case the high levels of arsenic point more towards the leftovers from—'

'Gold-mining.'

Khalifa finished the sentence. The tingle was gone. In its place a hard, throbbing drum-beat deep in the pit of his stomach. He stared at the map, at the highlands of the central desert, then squashed his Cleopatra into the ashtray holding down the map's south-east corner.

'Would you excuse me a moment, Omar?' he said. 'I've got a couple of urgent calls to make.'

JERUSALEM

Midway through the morning Archbishop Petrossian was returned to house arrest in the Armenian compound. The crowds in Omar Ibn al-Khattab dispersed, the journalists packed up, Baum got a roasting from Chief Gal for his handling of the whole thing. Ben-Roi and Zisky went back to their office and had just sat down to talk through their next move when their phones went off. Simultaneously. Zisky crossed the office and picked up his landline; Ben-Roi swivelled in his chair and answered his mobile. Khalifa. None of the usual pleasantries.

'I think I might be on to something.'

He filled Ben-Roi in – Pinsker, the Labyrinth, the possibility the mine might still be viable, the poisoned wells. Ben-Roi scribbled the odd note to himself, but for the most part just sat listening, his expression registering first interest, then amazement, then, with the news about the wells, disbelief.

'It has to be a coincidence,' he said when Khalifa had finished. 'My case, your case, same case – no, no, no, I don't buy it. It's too neat. Way too neat.'

'That's what I thought,' said Khalifa. 'I mean, it's not like Pinsker's mine is the only one in the Eastern Desert. But when I followed it up with the Ministry of Petroleum and Mineral Resources, they told me there are no other gold mines operating anywhere near that area. The nearest ones are at Sukari Hill and Hamash, which are down past Marsa Alam. Over two hundred kilometres away.'

On the other side of the room Ben-Roi could hear Zisky's voice – something about a bus, an unscheduled stop. He was way too engrossed in what Khalifa was saying to pay it any mind.

'I still don't buy it,' he said. 'There has to be another explanation.'

'What do you make of this, then?' said Khalifa. 'While I had her on the phone I asked the woman at the ministry to check if there had *ever* been any mining in that region. There hasn't. Or at least not in modern times. The only thing she could find was a lapsed exploration concession from fifteen years ago for a company called Prospecto Egypt. They spent eighteen months surveying in precisely that part of the desert.'

'So?'

'So, Prospecto are a subsidiary of Barren Corporation.'

Ben-Roi chewed his lip. In front of him Dov Zisky had stood and gone over to the map of Israel on the wall.

'So what are you suggesting?' he asked. 'That Barren found this mine, have been working it on the quiet?'

'I'm not suggesting anything. I'm just giving you the facts. Although that does seem to be where the facts are leading. Concession licences aren't cheap, after all. Barren would save themselves a lot of money working the mine illegally. And then if your journalist woman somehow found out about it, threatened to blow the whistle . . .'

Zisky called over, but Ben-Roi held up a hand to show he was busy. Funny, he thought – a week ago he'd asked Khalifa to do a bit of digging out on the margin of his case, now the Egyptian seemed to be solving it for him. He ran the scenario through his head, trying to match it with all the other clues they'd turned up. He had no idea whether it was feasible for someone to operate a gold mine in secret, although from what Khalifa had said the location was extremely remote, so maybe it *was* possible. Leave that aside for the moment. A lot of other pieces fitted. The newspaper articles, Pinsker, Barren, Egypt. The Nemesis Agenda too, if Kleinberg had been approaching them in the hope they'd picked up something about the mine in one of their hacking attacks. Or maybe she'd been going to tip them off. Either way it worked, just about. The problem element now was Vosgi and the sex-trafficking thing. How on earth did that relate to an illegal gold mine in the middle of the Egyptian desert? It didn't – or at least not in any way that he could immediately fathom. As before, he felt like he'd shunted the carpet to fit one side of the room only to leave an unsightly gap at the other. Try as he did, he could never seem to cover the whole floor.

'Ben-Roi?' Khalifa's voice echoed down the line.

'Sorry,' he said. 'I was just going through it all. Listen, I owe you big time for this, my friend. Really big time. We'll follow it up and I'll let you know how—'

Before he could say 'it all turns out', Khalifa jumped in.

'I'll see what else I can turn up,' he said. 'It might be remote, but even so I can't believe they could be running a mine out there without *someone* knowing about it. Someone must have seen or heard something.'

Ben-Roi told the Egyptian he'd already done more than enough, but Khalifa insisted, and in the end Ben-Roi thought, *What the hell, if he wants to help out, who am I to dissuade him? Maybe in a way it's helping him too. Like the Hannah Schlegel case helped me.* Which was, after all, the reason he'd got Khalifa involved in the first place.

They agreed to keep in touch and Khalifa rang off. Ben-Roi sat a moment, drumming and swivelling on his chair, mulling it all over. Then, standing, he crossed to Zisky's desk.

'Sorry about that, Dov. Some interesting developments in Egypt. What have you got?'

'The driver came back to me,' said Zisky.

Ben-Roi's brain was still half in the conversation with Khalifa, and it took him a couple of seconds to get what the kid meant. Of course. The Egged ticket. From the bin in Kleinberg's flat. Return to Mitzpe Ramon. The bus driver had been away on holiday.

'And?'

'And I think we might be on to something.'

The second time someone had used the phrase in the space of fifteen minutes. Things were looking up.

'Go on.'

'The man recognized Kleinberg's picture straight away. Said she'd been on his bus a few times.'

'What's a few?'

'Eight or nine in the last three years. Always a day return – he took her down, then back again on a later run.'

'I suppose it's too much to hope that he knew what she was doing in Mitzpe Ramon?'

'That's the interesting thing. She never actually went to Mitzpe. Or at least not all the way. She used to get off ten kilometres short of town. Then get picked up from the same spot for the return journey.'

He stood and waved Ben-Roi over to the wall map.

'Here,' he said, touching a finger to the north–south line of Route 40. It was the middle of nowhere, just desert and, beneath his fingertip, the intersection with a small secondary road running west towards the Har Ha-Negev Nature Reserve. And from there on to . . . the Egyptian border. Ben-Roi stared, cogs whirring inside his head. Then, reaching up, he started to pull the map from its Blu-Tack mounts.

'Do me a favour, Dov. Two favours actually. See what you can dig up about a company called Prospecto Egypt – they're a subsidiary of Barren, did some surveying out in the Egyptian desert a while back. And contact the Barren office down in Tel-Aviv. Tell them we're conducting a murder inquiry and want to speak to someone who knows about the company's involvement in Egypt. Someone high up – not a pen-pusher. See if you can sort something for later today or tomorrow morning. It's about time we found out what these people have got to say for themselves.'

'What are you going to do?' asked Zisky.

'Me?' Ben-Roi got the map down and folded it. 'I'm off for a nice little drive in the country.'

HOUSTON

Two in the morning Houston time and William Barren was wide awake. Not coked awake – he was putting all that behind him. No, this was clear-headed awake. Energized awake. The sort of awake he felt most nights these days as his plans all started to come together. He gazed out across the Houston nightscape, all twinkling towers and distant slashes of traffic, like something out of *Blade Runner*, wondering if he could be bothered to head up to the rooftop pool for a swim, or maybe down to the cardio suite to burn off some of the energy on the treadmills. Instead, swinging himself off the bed, he unleashed a flurry of karate chops towards the window, then padded through into the study and sat at his desk.

Earlier, he'd taken Barbara for dinner out at the country club. Increasingly he'd been thinking Barbara was probably the one. She was dull as hell, and sexually unadventurous to the point of catatonia (the first, and only, time he'd tried to sodomize her she'd screamed like a stuck pig and burst into tears). She looked good, though, and knew how to hold herself in a social situation, and hailed from thoroughbred WASP stock – just the sort of wife you needed as head of one of the country's leading multinationals. He'd get her checked, make sure she was fertile, could carry on the line, then propose next year, once all the company stuff had settled down. Or maybe the year after. With marriage, like all business decisions, you had to prioritize.

He eased back and propped his feet on the corner of the desk. Its surface was covered in paperwork – files, reports, spreadsheets, analysis: the Barren behemoth stripped down to its constituent parts. He picked up a sheet at random – figures for the proposed buy-into of a Canadian biofuels company – then threw it down again, not in the mood for number-crunching. On the computer screen the webcam was still playing – dingy room in Eastern Europe, girls being given a bad time – but he wasn't in the mood for that either. He ran a hand through his hair, flexed his abs, then, with a glance at his Rolex, he lifted the phone and dialled. Five rings, and the call was answered.

'Did I wake you?' he asked.

Yes, but it's not a problem, a soft voice assured him.

'You OK to talk?'

Perfectly OK.

'I just wanted to touch base, see if you'd thought any more about that thing we were discussing.'

Yes, came the voice, there had been more thought. A lot more thought. And a decision. William was right. It would have to be done. To secure the future. Assure continuity.

William smiled.

'I knew you'd understand. You're one of family, after all. We've got to help each other.'

Indeed.

'I've been thinking we should combine it with the Egypt thing. Keep it all at arm's length. Fewer questions that way.'

A very good idea.

'We're on, then?'

On.

William said he'd be in touch, told the person at the other end to keep their head down and rang off. For a moment he sat drumming his fingers on the desk. Then, heaving himself to his feet, he headed back to the bedroom for his towel and trunks. Maybe he'd have that swim after all.

ISRAEL

Mitzpe Ramon was 160 kilometres south of Jerusalem, a three-hour drive when you factored in traffic and speed limits.

Ben-Roi did it in just over two.

For the first 80 kilometres he sounded his siren, clearing a way through the busier roads down to Be'er Sheva. Then, when he was past Be'er and out into the blank rocky nothingness of the Negev, he yanked out the siren jack and pushed his foot to the floor. By midday he had reached the intersection where the Egged bus driver used to drop off and pick up Rivka Kleinberg. He pulled over, got out, stretched his legs, gazed around.

The place had looked desolate on the office map, and looked even more so now that he was actually standing here. There was the empty two-lane ribbon of Route 40; the secondary branch road heading off to the west; and three metal signs: a distance marker showing 10 kilometres to Mitzpe, a tourist hoarding for the Har Ha-Negev Nature

Reserve, a warning about stray camels. Otherwise, nothing. The sun beat down, the desert stretched out, five metres away a decomposing goat carcass gave off a vague waft of putrefaction. The erratic buzzing of flies was the only sound in the otherwise all-enveloping silence.

He scanned the landscape, not entirely sure what he was hoping to achieve by coming all the way down here, just sensing that whatever it was Kleinberg had been doing, he was more likely to find out about it by being here in person rather than trying to follow it up from his desk. Then, going round and opening the Toyota's boot, he pulled out a pair of binoculars. Clambering on to the car's bonnet, he scanned again, the metalwork creaking beneath his Timberlands as he slowly rotated through 360 degrees. The bins afforded him a more detailed view of what he'd already been looking at: rock, dust, hills, gullies and the odd forlorn clump of knotgrass. Not a human in sight.

He gave it a couple of turns, taking in the full desert panorama, then focused in on the curving thread of the westbound road. It was the thing that had leapt off the map at him when Zisky had first pointed out this spot back at the station; and it still struck him as the most likely reason for Kleinberg having alighted at this particular point. Had she been meeting someone who had slipped across the border from Egypt? Had she been intending to slip the other way *into* Egypt? Or had she got off here for a completely different reason and the proximity of the border was purely coincidental? Whatever the case, it was tied up with the Nemesis Agenda, no question about that. Three years ago she'd come down this way to meet a contact within the Agenda. And from what the Egged driver had said, she'd been coming down on and off ever since.

'But why this particular spot?' he murmured. 'Why here? What were you doing?'

He traced the line of the road from its junction with 40 to the point where it disappeared behind a rocky ridge in the far distance, scouring it with the bins, back and forth along its length as if the tarmac itself might yield the answers for which he was searching. No answers came and after ten minutes he gave up. He hopped off the bonnet and returned the binoculars to the boot. Ducking into the car, he removed the bottle of Neviot water and bumper pack of Doritos he'd bought from a service station on his way out of Jerusalem. He took a glug of the water, opened the Doritos, started munching. He'd got through a quarter of the pack before he heard the faint growl of an approaching vehicle, the first to come that way since he'd stopped. He dropped the Doritos and water on to the passenger seat, picked up the photo he'd brought of Rivka Kleinberg and stepped out on to the road.

The vehicle was a tanker, still a long way off, heading south from Be'er Sheva, its outline wobbling and bulging in the heat haze. He watched it for almost a minute, its approach tediously slow. Then, when it had closed to within five hundred metres, he ducked back into the car, turned the ignition key and jacked in the flashing roof light. There was a distant hiss of brakes and the tanker slowed, juddering to a halt ten metres up the highway. Ben-Roi walked over and motioned the driver to lower his window.

'I was inspected three weeks ago,' said the man, a cigarette dipping up and down in the corner of his mouth. 'Got the paperwork here if you want to check.'

Ben-Roi told him that wouldn't be necessary.

'You come this way often?' he asked.

'Twice a week. Ashdod to Mitzpe Ramon, then back via Yerukham and Dimona.'

'You ever see this woman?' Ben-Roi handed the photo up. The driver examined it, then passed it back, shaking his head.

'She would have been standing here. Like she was waiting for someone.'

'Never seen her before.'

'Sure?'

'Sure.'

'OK, on your way.'

Ben-Roi stepped back and jerked a thumb down the highway.

'And put that cigarette out!' he called as the driver started to move off. 'You're driving a bloody oil tanker!'

The man grumbled, flicked the cigarette on to the hard shoulder and picked up speed. Ben-Roi returned to his car and dived back into the Doritos.

He flagged down a further fourteen vehicles over the next ninety minutes, including a pick-up truck full of Bedouin, a military bus from the Ramon Air Force Base and an Audi R drop-top driven by one of the fattest men he'd ever seen accompanied by two of the most attractive women – an object lesson, if ever there was one, in the seductive allure of hard cash.

A couple of people recognized Rivka Kleinberg from her photo in the papers; none of them had ever seen her in person and certainly not at this remote spot. As the Audi sped off into the distance, music pumping, the women's hair whipping behind them in the wind, Ben-Roi accepted he was wasting his time. He'd follow the branch road west to the Egyptian border, see if anything caught his eye; cut back to Mitzpe Ramon to have a word with the local police; then head home. Some you won, some you lost. It had been worth a try.

He had a final sweep round with the binoculars, took a piss at the roadside and climbed back into the Toyota. Far away to the south another car was approaching, a distant white blob juddering in the watery heat. He hesitated, wondering if he ought to give it one last go. Then, deciding it wasn't worth it, that he had to call it quits some time and it might as well be now, he slammed the door, clunked on his seat-belt, unplugged the roof light and started to move off. Almost immediately he had a change of heart and stopped again. He neutralled the gears, re-jacked the light and unbelted himself.

'Sixteenth time lucky,' he muttered, grabbing the Kleinberg photo and climbing out.

The car was moving fast and in the fifteen seconds since he'd first spotted it, had broken from the heat mirage and come into much sharper focus. SUV, by the look of it. He stepped on to the road. The vehicle was really bombing along, eating up the distance between them. At four hundred metres he held up a hand, but the vehicle showed no sign of slowing. Three hundred went by, two hundred, and he was about to step back off the road when the driver suddenly braked. Hard. There was hiss of rubber, a faint puff of smoke from beneath the rear wheels and the car – a Toyota Land Cruiser – came to a halt on the hard shoulder with five metres to spare. Same occupant dynamic as the Audi – male driver, two female passengers, although in this case the man was slim and handsome. Ben-Roi walked over to his window and flashed his badge.

'If I'd had a speed gun you'd be out of a licence,' he said.

'Sorry,' said the man. 'I was miles away.'

'Not the best place to be when you're going that fast.'

'Sorry,' repeated the man.

Ben-Roi placed a hand on the roof and dipped his head, looking into the car. The woman in the front was slightly built with short-cropped dark hair, the outline of her breasts clearly visible through the material of her T-shirt. The one in the back had auburn hair done up in a bun and long, toned legs canted against the back of the driver's seat. Both, he couldn't help notice, were attractive, although not in the same way as the Audi driver's companions. They'd been bimbos, had sex written all over them. These two were more understated, had . . . attitude.

'You from round here?' he asked, addressing himself to the man.

'Tel-Aviv. We've been down in Eilat for a few days.'

Lucky you, thought Ben-Roi.

'You come down this way often?'

'Every couple of months, maybe.'

Ben-Roi's eyes flicked towards the woman in the back seat, then he handed in the photo.

'I don't suppose any of you have ever seen her around here?'

They looked at the image, the woman in the back dropping her feet and leaning forward.

'I have,' she said.

Ben-Roi's head came down further, right into the window.

'Around here?'

'No, in the paper. She's that woman who got killed in Jerusalem.'

She had an accent. Slight, but definitely there. American, he guessed, or possibly British. Intense grey eyes, a scatter of freckles across her nose – seriously attractive.

'But you've never seen her in this part of the world?' he repeated.

She shook her head.

'You?'

Shakes from the other two.

'Was she from round here?' asked the man, returning the photo.

'Just following up some leads.'

'Well, I hope you get him,' said the auburn head, sitting back and propping her legs up again. Ben-Roi's eyes lingered on her, something nagging at the back of his mind. He couldn't put his finger on it, and after hovering a moment, he thanked them for their time, straightened and stepped away from the car.

'And watch your speed,' he said. 'Not every cop's as forgiving as I am.'

The man smiled, flicked a salute and pulled away. Ben-Roi watched them go, staring at the head silhouetted in the rear window, the nag still there. Then, with a shrug, he went back to his car, got in and swung off 40 on to the smaller road heading west towards the

Egyptian border. He'd covered almost a kilometre when the words suddenly came out of his mouth: *Sally, Carrie, Mary-Jane.*

For a moment he looked confused, as though it had been someone else speaking. Then, with a bellow of 'For fuck's sake!', he slammed on the brakes. Dropping open the glove compartment, he pulled out his Jericho, then spun the car and roared off back the way he had come, siren blaring.

Gidi kept the speed down till the cop's car had disappeared from the rear-view mirror, then floored the accelerator. In the back seat, Dinah craned around, staring back along the road, watching for any sign of pursuit.

'I think we're OK,' said Gidi.

'We're not OK. The way he was looking at me . . .'

She swung back, pulled out her satellite mobile – terrestrials didn't work out here – thumbed in a number. Three rings, then:

'Faz, start shutting everything down. We might be on the move.'

She rang off, bent and pulled a Glock from her knapsack. In the front Tamar did the same. Gidi pushed the speedometer up past 160, taking them round a series of long sweeping bends before slowing sharply and skidding to a halt on the hard shoulder. Tamar already had the door open. Leaping out, she sprinted on to the hill overlooking the highway. Gidi screeched round the corner on to the track out to their compound; Dinah clambered into the front and thumbed her phone again, lurching back and forth as the Land Cruiser jolted over the uneven terrain. Six rings this time, then Tamar's voice:

'Almost there.' The sound of feet scrambling on rock, rasping breath. 'OK, I'm up.'

'And?'

'Can't see him.'

The Land Cruiser hit a rut and slewed, slamming her against the window. She threw the Glock on to the back seat, transferred the mobile to her left hand and grasped the door's grab handle to steady herself.

'Anything?'

'Nothing.'

Another ferocious lurch as they slammed into a dip, then skidded round the track's tight dog-leg. Gidi fought the wheel, got them straight, raced towards the cluster of domed buildings in the distance.

'Still can't see him,' came Tamar's voice. 'I think he might have . . . hang on, I can hear . . .'

'What?'

Silence.

'What, Tamar?'

'Siren! He's coming.'

'Shit!'

Dinah chopped a hand, urging Gidi to up the speed. From the hill-top Tamar kept up a running commentary.

'He's about two kilometres back . . . coming fast. Very fast. On the curve now . . . about a kilometre . . . really motoring. Underneath me . . . past! He missed the turn-off! He's carrying on north.'

They reached the compound and skidded to a halt beside the open computer room. Inside, Faz was furiously unplugging cables and box-ing up hard drives. Gidi ran in to help. Dinah remained by the Land Cruiser, mobile to her ear, Glock dangling in her hand. At the very edge of hearing she thought she could just catch the siren's wail.

'Talk to me, Tamar,' she said.

'He's still going.'

'How far?'

'About a kilometre. He's on the climb to the ridge.'

'Same speed?'

'Looks like it.'

'Now?'

'Still climbing.'

A silence, then:

'He's at the top and . . . over. Can't see him any more.'

Dinah clicked her fingers. Gidi and Faz stopped what they were doing and came outside. The three of them stood waiting, eyeing each other nervously. Thirty seconds ticked by.

'Tamar?'

'No sign of him.'

'Give it another minute.'

She did.

'Nothing. We're OK. He's gone.'

Dinah nodded to Gidi and Faz and they all let out a breath.

'No, he's not! He's coming back!'

'Fuck!'

The other two crowded in. She held up the phone so they could all hear what was going on.

'He's coming down off the ridge,' came Tamar's voice. 'Fast. On the flat now . . . less than a kilometre . . . five hundred metres . . . He's past the turn-off. Slowing. Stopped. He's . . . hang on . . . what's he doing? Reversing! He's on the track. We're busted!'

'Watch the road,' said Dinah. 'Let us know if he's got friends. Keep your head down.'

She rang off and pocketed the phone. Faz had already ducked back into the tech room. Gidi was rummaging inside the Land Cruiser. He emerged holding a mini-Uzi.

'You ready for this?' she asked.

He slammed in a clip. 'Ready.'

'OK, let's do what we have to.'

They banged fists and melted away among the buildings as the siren wail drew closer.

Ben-Roi dropped his speed right down, following the track away from the highway and out into the desert, steering with his left hand, the Jericho held ready in his right. After 400 metres the track dipped through a narrow cleft, then veered sharp right. Ahead, two kilometres away, he could make out a huddle of buildings, white against the drab yellow-brown of the desert. He stopped, cut the siren, fetched the binoculars, took a look.

The Land Cruiser was there, parked in front of one of the buildings, its driver door wide open. A second was sitting in the shade beneath a lean-to on the side of the same building. There were four other buildings, some solar panels, a large satellite dish, what looked like a vegetable plot. No signs of life.

He scanned the surrounding desert, then zoomed back in on the compound, as if hoping to catch someone unawares. Nothing. They'd either cleared out or were hiding. Probably the latter. He clicked his tongue, running through the options. There were at least three of them, possibly more. Almost certainly armed. And from what he'd heard of the Nemesis Agenda – and he had no doubt these people *were* the Nemesis Agenda – dangerous. Very dangerous. Better to call in backup. He threw the bins in the car, pulled out his cell. No signal. Same with the car phone. Shit. So: either head back to the highway, try to flag someone down, get them to run for the cavalry.

Or go in alone, which was a completely fucking crazy thing to do.

He went in alone.

He took it even slower than before, staying in second gear, idling along the track, stopping every few hundred metres to give the buildings another sweep with the bins, his Jericho at the ready. He saw nobody, nobody came at him. A hundred metres shy of the compound he stopped and got out. Total silence, not even the buzz of a fly.

'Hello!'

Nothing.

'Hello!'

The heat smothered his voice, dulling and thickening it, as if he was shouting into a blanket. He started forward, boots crunching on gravel, tracking the Jericho left and right in front of him.

'I saw your photo in her flat!' he yelled. 'Rivka Kleinberg's flat. You were just a girl. Took me a while to realize it was you, but I never forget a face.'

Nothing. No sound, no movement. He reached the Land Cruiser. Flattening himself against it, he glanced inside. The keys were still in the ignition. He paused. Then, dropping to his haunches, he skyed the Jericho and loosed off a single shot. No reaction. Maybe they *had* legged it. Or were hiding out in the desert somewhere, watching, waiting.

'She came to see you!' he bellowed. 'Four days before she was killed. She's been coming down here regularly. Why?'

Silence.

'Was she helping you? Is that it? Was Rivka Kleinberg part of the Nemesis Agenda?'

Still nothing. Absolute quiet, absolute still, like the entire world had been freeze-famed inside a vacuum jar. He blinked away a bead of sweat, stood, rolled around the car and hit the wall of the nearest building. The door was open. He checked the car beneath the lean-to, then, on the count of three, ducked through the door. There was computer stuff scattered everywhere – screens, hard drives, wires, modems, like someone was packing up in a hurry. He ran his eyes around, then stepped back out. The doors of the other four buildings were closed. He took them one by one, working his way round the central yard. The first three were unlocked – simple rooms, spartan, empty. The last door held firm. He looked around, then kicked it in, the entire frame coming away from the wall in a shower of broken plaster.

The interior was cool and dim, the blinds down against the sunlight, a vague smell of antiperspirant hanging in the air. There was a bed, a wardrobe, a bedside table and, through a door, a bathroom. He checked the bathroom, put his head back out into the yard, then crossed to the bedside table. A laptop was sitting there charging, the screen on. A moving screensaver ranged up and down the front of a tall glass-and-steel building framed against a bright blue sky. At the bottom of the building, gleaming above the entrance, a row of gold letters spelt out the name 'Barren Corporation'. He stared at it, then sat on the bed and tried the table's drawer. Locked. He yanked, but it wouldn't give. Another yank, then, losing patience, he leant back, aimed and shot the lock off. He slid the drawer out and rifled its contents. There were a couple of bullet clips; an envelope stuffed with letters; two passports, one Israeli, one American, both bearing the photo of the woman in the car. Each carried a different name: Dinah Levi and Elizabeth Teal. He looked at them, then shook out the envelope. Letters and postcards spilled across the bed. And, also, a smaller envelope. Inside, photos done up with an elastic band. He held them up, staring at the top one. It was of a woman cradling a baby. A young woman, plump, curly-haired and heavy-boned, sitting in what looked like a hospital armchair. Time had taken its toll, but he recognized her instantly. Just as he had done in the shot of the uniformed women back in her apartment in Jerusalem. Rivka Kleinberg.

'Fuck me,' he murmured.

'You move even one millimetre,' came a voice from the door, 'and trust me, that's exactly what I'll do.'

For a moment she thought he might try something, his eyes flicking from her Glock to Gidi's Uzi and back again, assessing the situation. Then, accepting he was outgunned, he shook his head and lifted his arms. Gidi covering, she went over and relieved him of his pistol. And, also, the photos, which she snatched away and dropped on to the bed, not wanting his fingers on them.

They took him outside, frisked him, found car keys and a cell phone. She kept the keys and threw the phone to Faz, who disappeared with it into the tech room. Then they marched him over to his car and cuffed him – right wrist to the steering wheel, left ankle to the brake pedal.

347

'You're her daughter, aren't you?' he said as she leant in to check the cuffs were secure. 'You're Rivka Kleinberg's daughter. She was your mother.'

'Whatever.'

She patted round the inside of the car to make sure he didn't have any concealed firearms, tore the car phone off its lead, then, with a last tug on the cuffs, she and Gidi headed back to the compound. Gidi aimed for one of the store sheds to get the explosives and timers; she made for the other one to get the jerrycans.

They'd rehearsed this numerous times, with variations depending on how long they'd have to get out: an immediate getaway, leaving everything; a two-minute scramble, gathering just the essentials; a more ordered departure, with sufficient leeway to gather their stuff and cover their tracks. There was no word from Tamar up on the hill, which suggested that in this instance they had time to play with. She was glad of that. Of all the many places she'd lived in her life, this was the only one that had felt anything like home. She'd always known they'd have to leave at some point, but at least they'd be able to say a proper goodbye.

Opening the shed, she lugged five cans out into the centre of the yard, then went to her room to gather her stuff. There wasn't much of it: some clothes, the letters from her mother, the photos.

The past was a different life, one she deliberately kept buried. The letters and the photos were the only reminders, the only shafts down into the dark. Those and the dreams, of course. In the dreams, the past was always rising to haunt her.

She threw everything into a holdall, along with a couple of paper-filled files and the Barren laptop. The passports went in last. Dinah Levi, Elizabeth Teal – just two of the many names she'd adopted over the years. Dinah, Elizabeth, Sally, Carrie, Mary-Jane – there'd been so many of them. Alter-egos to hide behind, disguises with which to cover herself. With Dinah perhaps the most appropriate of them all, what with its connotations not only of justice and judgement, but, in the Biblical story of Dinah and Shechem, of rape and revenge.

So many different names. So many different masks. So many different hers.

But only Rachel's really true.

She zipped the bag, took a last look around and went outside into the yard. Gidi was moving from building to building laying the charges; a mobile call out to Tamar on the hill confirmed that the highway was clear, there was no one else coming. She told her to get back to the compound, threw her holdall into the Land Cruiser, then went to check on the cop. As soon as he saw her he started in again with all the mother stuff. She didn't bother explaining.

'She was working with you, wasn't she?' he pushed, tugging vainly at the cuffs, the metal biting into his wrist and ankle. 'Rivka Kleinberg was part of the Nemesis Agenda. That's why she kept coming down here.'

Despite herself she smiled. Not just because his shots were so wide of the mark, but because he was shooting at all. Shackled to a car in a hundred-degree heat with no idea whether they were going to live out the next hour, most people would have been whimpering for mercy. But here this guy was, still trying to work the angles. Credit to him for that, even if he had got it completely wrong.

'She had nothing to do with the Nemesis Agenda,' she said, figuring he deserved at least a partial explanation. 'She came down to visit, nothing more.'

'Spend some time with her daughter.'

She didn't rise to that.

'Did she know what you were doing?' he asked, rattling the wrist cuff.

'Of course she knew. I trusted her.'

'Not enough to give her her interview,' he said. 'Three years ago. When she wanted to write a piece for her magazine.'

More credit to him. He'd done his homework.

'She jumped the gun on that one,' she replied. 'Told her editor she could get the interview without clearing it with us. She was in a bad space at the time, had lost her job, wasn't thinking straight. I told her it was too risky – that there was a lot of heat on us, and the moment she did an article like that there'd be a lot of heat on her too. That we'd have to stop meeting. She understood the situation. After that, the Agenda was never mentioned again.'

'Even on her last visit? Four days before she was killed?'

She hesitated. Credit or no credit he was still a cop and she didn't want to get drawn into a conversation with him. Keep quiet, never tell, our little secret – that was a lesson she'd learnt the hard way. At the same time there was part of her that did want to talk. Enough at least to set the record straight. He sensed her uncertainty and pressed her.

'She wanted you to hack Barren, didn't she? That's why she came down here that last time. She wanted your help to find out what Barren were doing in Egypt.'

Her stomach clenched, as it always did at the mention of Barren. She stared at him, trying to figure how to play things, calculate what course would best serve her purposes. Then, coming to a decision, she slid the Glock from the back of her jeans. He stiffened, straining at the cuffs.

'Relax,' she said. 'We're not cop-killers.'

Glancing at her watch, she dropped on to a rock at the side of the track and settled the Glock on her knee. He slumped back and massaged his wrist, which had turned an angry red.

'Am I right?'

A pause, then she nodded.

'She told us she'd found a link between Barren and an article she was doing on sex-trafficking. She knew we kept tabs on Barren, had ways of hacking into their system. She wanted us to go in, see if we could find anything about a gold mine in Egypt. And, also, the port of Rosetta.'

His eyes flickered. 'Did she say why? What she thought she was on to?'

She shook her head. 'I don't think she fully knew herself. Or if she did, she didn't let on. She could be like that – played her cards close to her chest. We were about to head off somewhere, but I said we'd look into it as soon as we got back. By the time we did, she'd been killed.'

She dipped her head – it didn't do to show you were hurting, not to strangers, not to anyone – then looked up again.

'We've been trawling Barren ever since, but we've drawn a complete blank. No Rosetta, no gold mine, nothing. Whatever's going on, they're keeping it well under wraps.'

The cop was still rubbing at his wrist, his forehead crumpled as he worked all this through.

'Do you know if she contacted Barren? Put any of this to them?'

She shrugged. 'I doubt it. It wasn't her style to confront people till she had solid evidence.'

'Do you think Barren killed her?'

She laughed at that, at the naïve obviousness of the question.

'Of course they killed her! That's the sort of thing they do. She found out something about them, they butchered her for it. That's how they operate. They're dirty as shit.'

'And yet you lot have never managed to pin anything on them.'

Another shrug. 'They're clever. We'll get them.'

Along the track, Tamar was approaching, coming at a jog. Enough talking, time to clear out. She stood.

'You're out of your depth,' she told him. 'You have absolutely no concept how powerful these people are, how ... disgusting. A hick policeman like you, sticking to the rules, working within the law – you haven't got a hope in hell of nailing Barren. The only way you bring down a company like that – bring down any of these companies – is to play as dirty as they play. That's why the Nemesis Agenda exists. To do what the law can't and won't do.'

'So help me,' he said. 'Feed me what you find.'

She shook her head. 'That's not the way it works, lover-boy. You may be the straightest cop in the world, but you're still just a cog in the machine. And the machine always looks after the likes of Barren. They're too valuable. Too embedded. You're wasting your time. But good luck anyway.'

'At least tell me what you have found out about them,' he pushed, fighting to keep the conversation alive. 'How do you *know* they killed her? What do you mean "disgusting"?'

She waved the questions away. She'd said all she wanted to. She stared down at him – a picture of frustrated impotence with his cuffed joints and sweat-stained armpits – then Tamar came up and the two of them headed back to the compound. Faz was loading tech gear into the second Land Cruiser; Gidi had just finished laying the charges. While he and Tamar headed off to gather their stuff, she went from building to building sloshing petrol and setting the timers. Once she was done she took a final walk around. Then, on a whim, she unzipped her holdall, flicked through one of the files and pulled out a sheet of paper. By the time she'd folded it and slipped it into her pocket, the Land Cruisers were loaded and they were ready to go.

Gidi and Faz set off immediately. She and Tamar rolled out to the cop's car and stopped. They left him a couple of bottles of water and an empty jerrycan to urinate into. His mobile, car keys and the keys to the cuffs they threw into the boot. They wet-wiped everything, cuffs included, to ensure they left no prints.

'We'll give ourselves a couple of hours to get clear,' she told him, 'then call the police in Mitzpe, let them know you're here.'

'Very kind,' he muttered.

'We've rigged explosives in all the buildings,' she went on. 'Nothing too heavy, but if I were you, around four p.m. I'd get my head down. Just in case.'

He grumbled something. He seemed to have given up on the mother stuff.

'Don't bother trying to trace the number plates because we're going to change them. And don't bother trying to trace us. We're too clever for you.'

With his free hand he flicked her a finger, which made her smile. Reaching into her pocket, she pulled out the folded sheet of paper and dropped it in his lap.

'That's all the help you're going to get from us. It's a list of the companies Barren have links to in Egypt. There might be something there. There might be nothing. You're the detective. You find out.'

She turned for the Land Cruiser. He called after her.

'What is it with you and Barren? Why the grudge?'

She slowed. How could she tell him? How could she tell anyone? Even her crew didn't know the truth. Some motivations were best kept secret. Some identities too. It was her mission, that was all that mattered. Explanations were superfluous.

'They hurt someone close to me,' she murmured, too low for him to hear. He called again, repeated the question, but she ignored him. With a final look back at the compound, she climbed into the Land Cruiser, slammed the door and, with a nod at Tamar, they roared off in a cloud of dust.

In the end it was the best part of four hours before a patrol car from Mitzpe Ramon eventually arrived to release Ben-Roi, by which point the sun was dipping below the horizon, the cluster of buildings had been reduced to heaps of smouldering rubble and he was in the mother of all bad moods.

'I need a phone,' he snapped as he struggled out of the Toyota, hobbling on his swollen ankle. 'One that actually works out here.'

'In our car,' said one of the uniforms, an attractive girl with dark skin and a model's figure. Which somehow made the whole thing even more humiliating.

'Get over there and see if you can find anything,' he ordered, waving them across the remains of the buildings. Less because he thought they *would* find something than because he wanted a bit of privacy. 'And take that smirk off your face!'

He glowered at her, then limped over to the patrol vehicle, snatched up the car phone and dialled. A quick one to Sarah first, just to check in. She sounded pleased to hear from him, asked if he wanted to come over for a meal the following night, just the two of them. In other circumstances he would have been delighted by the offer – she hadn't cooked him dinner since they'd split. Right at the moment, romantic candlelits were the last thing on his mind. He said great, he'd love to come, his voice sounding way less enthusiastic than he was trying to make it, and got her off the line. Second call to Dov Zisky.

'Where the hell have you been?' asked Zisky. 'I've been trying to contact you all afternoon.'

'Tied up,' said Ben-Roi curtly, the pun unintended. 'Did you speak to Barren?'

Zisky had. A meeting had been set up for later that evening – 9 p.m., to allow high-ups in Houston to join in.

'But if you're still down in Mitzpe there's no way you'll—'

'I'll be there,' cut in Ben-Roi, glancing at his watch. 'Anything on Prospecto?'

Not much. The company had been a subsidiary of Barren, established in the 1990s to explore possible gold-mining opportunities in Egypt. It had been wound up after only a couple of years. William Barren had been CEO, which was interesting.

Ben-Roi listened, then told Zisky to get over to Rivka Kleinberg's flat.

'I was actually just leaving the office,' said Zisky. 'I'm meeting—'

'Cancel it and get over there,' growled Ben-Roi, not in the mood for playing Mr Understanding. 'There's a photo in the bedroom. A girl. I think it's Kleinberg's daughter. Currently going under the names Dinah Levi and Elizabeth Teal. I need you to find out everything you can about her. And take a look at the other photo as well, the one of Kleinberg on her National Service. We should have done all this ten days ago.'

Meaning 'I' should have done all this. He'd screwed up, not been as thorough as he should have been. Which, if he was honest, was as much a cause of his bad mood as the fact that he'd been chained up in a car for the last four hours pissing into a jerrycan.

He told Zisky to text him details of the Barren meeting and rang off. Calling over the two uniforms, he gave them the number plates of the Land Cruisers and descriptions of their four occupants, told them to get them circulated. Almost certainly a waste of time, but you had to go through the motions. Once that was done he stomped back to his Toyota, started the engine and sped off in a shower of dust and gravel. Two hundred metres along the track he slewed to a halt, threw open the passenger door and lobbed out the jerrycan. The mother of all bad moods.

LUXOR

'And you've not seen anything unusual out there? Buildings, machinery, lorries . . . ?'

A man's voice echoed down the line, informing Khalifa that no, he had seen nothing out of the ordinary. Just rock, sand and more rock – exactly what you'd expect to find in the middle of a desert.

'Although to be fair, the landscape's so twisted and mountainous, you could pass within a hundred metres of a football stadium and not clock it was there.'

'People?'

Definitely no people. No fauna of any description aside from the occasional ibex and desert hare. The region was so remote even the Bedouin didn't go there.

'Have you *heard* anything unusual?'

'Like what?'

'I don't know. Mining sort of noises? Digging, drilling, hammering?'

'Can't say I have.'

'Sure?'

'Positive.'

Sighing, Khalifa thanked the guy for his time, hung up and wandered over to the window, a Cleopatra dangling disconsolately from the corner of his mouth. The man ran a small desert safari company based out of Hurghada, one of the few such outfits to venture anywhere near the central uplands of the Eastern Desert. Over the course of the day, Khalifa had spoken to every one of them. None had seen or heard anything that might suggest an active gold-mining operation. None had seen or heard anything that might suggest an *inactive* gold-mining operation. Same story with the air companies who ran flights across the desert from Luxor to Hurghada and Port Safaga, and the various balloon-ride outfits who took tourists up to watch the sunrise over the Red Sea mountains. The Ministry of Petroleum and Mineral Resources could add nothing to what they'd already told him; he was still waiting on a call back from the Raissoulis, although he wasn't holding out much hope – if they'd seen anything untoward he would have expected them to mention it during their conversation the previous night.

There had been just two possible hints that he wasn't on a complete wild-goose chase. One of the adventure safari companies he'd spoken to had reported coming across lines of heavy tyre tracks in one of the remote *wadis* running down off the Gebel el-Shalul. In itself that didn't tell him much – in the immutable stillness of the desert, where nothing moved and nothing changed, such tracks could have been laid down decades ago. Then, however, just on the off-chance, he had spoken to the team at Helwan University who were conducting the aerial survey of the hydro-conductive cracks his friend Omar had mentioned. Although they had seen nothing that might suggest the presence of a working gold mine, a few months back one of their pilots *had* spotted what looked like a convoy of trucks moving west across the wilderness between the central uplands and the Nile Valley. Where they were coming from or going to the pilot hadn't been able to say, but there had been a lot of them. At least twenty, maybe more. Something? Nothing? Khalifa had no idea. One thing was for sure – if Barren *had* found the Labyrinth and started working it again, they were keeping the whole operation miraculously well disguised.

He let out another sigh, wondering why he should have got himself so damned obsessed with this case – a case that wasn't even his to obsess about. Then, dragging off the last of his cigarette, he leant his arms against the window pane and gazed out. Five hundred metres away across an expanse of rubbish-strewn scrubland, he could see his apartment block: shabby, whitewashed, half screened by a row of dusty casuarina trees. Beyond that the town's eastern fringes petered away into fields, which in turn gave way to the drab yellow nothing of the desert. A jet had just taken off from Luxor airport and was climbing steeply towards the south, presumably on its way to Aswan, or maybe Abu Simbel; way out to the east, right on the edge of sight, the desert mountains seemed to hover in the air like a rising brown mist. And somewhere beneath those mountains . . .

'Where are you?' he said out loud. 'Where the bloody hell are you?'

'Standing right behind you!'

He turned. Mohammed Sariya was in the doorway, holding a paper plate with two slices of *basboussa* on it.

'Working late?' he asked.

'Just following something up,' said Khalifa. 'I was about to leave.'

'Well, before you do you can help me with these.'

Sariya held up the *basboussa* slices. Khalifa protested, said he wasn't hungry, but his deputy insisted.

'You'll be saving me from myself,' he chuckled. 'I'm getting fat enough as it is.'

Khalifa relented and the two men sat.

'Who's "you", then?' asked Sariya, handing over one of the slices and biting into the other one.

'Hmmn?'

'Where the bloody hell are you?'

'Oh, right. Long story.'

'As in one you don't want to tell me?'

'As in one whose plot doesn't seem to be making a whole lot of sense,' replied Khalifa, nibbling on a corner of his own pastry. For a moment his thoughts veered off to a morning in the distant past when he and Ali had eaten *basboussa* at Groppi's in Cairo. Ali had insisted on having a second slice, had got halfway through it, then had to rush off to the toilet to be violently sick. Khalifa stayed with the memory a moment, cherishing it, then, pushing it away, filled Sariya in on what he'd discovered these last twenty-four hours. Just a basic outline – the mine, the poisoned wells, the water analysis results. He didn't mention Ben-Roi or the Kleinberg woman. Although Sariya was one of the more mellow people on the force, even he would have frowned on the idea of doing spadework for the Israelis.

'Have you told the Attias about this?' he asked when Khalifa had finished.

'Not yet. I was hoping to clarify a few more details first.'

'You want me to take a run out there? I'm off tomorrow, and we should probably let them know. Put their minds at rest that it's not an anti-Christian thing after all.'

'Would you do that?'

'It would be my pleasure. Any excuse not to spend a morning with the mother-in-law. She told me a story the other day that was so boring I thought I was going to pass out.'

Khalifa smiled at that.

'Do you want me to drop into Bir Hashfa as well?' asked Sariya.

'Leave that for the moment. I don't want to be getting people into a panic. Let me try and track down the mine, then we can go out and speak to them when we've got some hard facts.'

Sariya nodded and took another hefty bite of his pastry. There was a silence, then:

'I found that family, by the way.'

Khalifa didn't know what his deputy was talking about.

'You know, the one from Old Qurna. The El-Badris.'

Of course. The family of the girl Pinsker had raped. He'd asked Sariya to check up on them. It no longer seemed particularly relevant now that he'd found out about the gold mine.

'And?' he asked, more out of politeness than interest – he wouldn't want Sariya to feel that he'd wasted his time.

'And not very much,' replied the sergeant through a mouthful of pastry. 'Like you said, most of them got moved up to El-Tarif when Old Qurna got bulldozed. Although the sister had already left.'

'Sister?'

'The one you mentioned. She's down in a village near Edfu. Been there thirty years or more.'

Khalifa was confused.

'Three brothers and a sister,' Sariya reminded him, his tone that of a father explaining something to a forgetful child. 'The brothers are all long buried, but the sister's living down near Edfu.'

'Iman el-Badri?'

'Exactly.'

Khalifa shook his head. 'I think someone's got their wires crossed, Mohammed. Iman el-Badri died years ago. This must be a different one.'

'Not what I was told,' said Sariya. 'There were three brothers – Mohammed, Said and another one whose name I can't remember. Ahmed, I think it was. And the sister Iman. And she's living just outside Edfu. Some sort of holy woman, apparently. Spends her time doling out blessings to expectant mothers.'

Khalifa started to object, to tell Sariya that he had to be mistaken, only to fall silent. Now that he thought about it, no one had actually told him the woman Pinsker had raped was dead.

'But it's not possible,' he murmured. 'She must be well over a hundred.'

'A hundred on the dot, actually. And still going strong, by all accounts.'

From being not especially interested, Khalifa's mind was suddenly fully engaged.

'You're sure about this?'

Sariya gave him an admonishing look.

'Do you know the name of the village?'

Sucking honey off his fingertips, Sariya picked up a pen and scribbled on a sheet of paper. Khalifa examined the sheet, then folded it and slipped it into his pocket.

'Near Edfu, you say?'

'About five kilometres north.'

Khalifa looked at his watch, calculating. Then, giving Sariya a slap on the shoulder, he stood and headed for the stairs, cramming the rest of the *basboussa* slice into his mouth as he went. It was at least an hour's drive either way down to Edfu, and that was most likely going to be the only dinner he got.

ROAD TO JERUSALEM

Earlier that day Ben-Roi had put his foot to the floor for the journey from Jerusalem down to Mitzpe Ramon.

On the way back he practically put his foot *through* the floor, covering the distance twenty minutes faster than he had on the outward trip, his siren raging all the way, which pretty much reflected his mood.

As he drove he ran and reran the afternoon's events in his head, trying to splice them into the framework of the case he'd already built up.

The Nemesis woman being Kleinberg's daughter certainly explained a few things. At the same time, it raised a whole tangle of new questions, not the least of them why the hell Kleinberg should have wanted to keep the fact she had a daughter so quiet (although hadn't her editor said something about her keeping her life rigidly compartmentalized?).

With a bit of luck Zisky would dig up some answers. Ben-Roi's more immediate concern lay with what the Dinah woman had told him about Barren Corporation. Specifically, her insistence that it was Barren, or someone working for them, who had killed Kleinberg.

It wasn't like the idea had come as a bolt from the blue – Barren had been looming over the case almost from the word go. What had struck him was the absolute conviction with which she had pointed the finger. For Dinah Levi, Elizabeth Teal, whatever the hell her real name was, Barren were guilty. Not possibly. Not probably. Definitely.

How could she be so sure? Was she keeping something back, not giving him the full story? Had the Nemesis Agenda turned up some sort of concrete evidence? But then why not reveal it – if not to him, then on the Nemesis website. Given their history with Barren, you would have thought they'd have gone public the instant they found anything even remotely incriminating.

No, he reckoned, she'd been telling the truth – at least so far as what they'd found out about the murder was concerned. Evidence-wise they were as empty-handed as he was. So the question remained: how could she be so certain Barren were responsible? Was it that her loathing for the company – whatever its root cause – was such that she simply couldn't imagine them *not* being guilty? Was she playing some sort of elaborate game with him, sending him off on false angles for reasons only she understood?

Or was it rather that she knew something else about Barren – something so damning, so bad ('disgusting', that's the word she'd used to describe them), that Kleinberg's murder was somehow an inevitable corollary of it? Which once again raised the issue of why, if they had such knowledge, Nemesis hadn't gone public with it.

It didn't make sense. None of it did. Although one thing at least was clear – whoever she was, Dinah Levi had some personal issue with Barren. Something that stretched way beyond the mere dislike of an anti-capitalist campaigner for a global megacorporation. He'd seen it in her eyes; in her body language; in the way her face had seemed to tighten whenever the name Barren was mentioned, as though someone was winding a screw deep inside her skull.

For Rivka Kleinberg's daughter – if that's indeed who she was – Barren Corporation were the Devil.

And now he was rushing back to Jerusalem to meet the Devil. Like he'd said to Zisky before he'd set out that morning: it was high time they found out what these people had got to say for themselves.

Barren's representatives had requested that the interview take place at the King David, Jerusalem's most famous, and most exclusive, hotel. The corporation kept a suite there, apparently, used it as a sort of informal Jerusalem office, with a ready-installed conferencing hook-up with the organization's headquarters in Houston. Normally interviews around a murder investigation would be conducted in a police station, but Ben-Roi had gone with the flow. At the end of the day talking was talking, wherever you did it. So long as they answered his questions he would have met them in a public toilet.

He arrived with two minutes to spare. In 1946 much of the hotel's southern wing had been destroyed in an Irgun bombing – the largest single terrorist atrocity in the history of the region. You wouldn't know it today. The place was a testament to opulent tranquillity, its lavish décor and rich furnishings about as far removed from the cares of the real world as it was possible to get. Ben-Roi had been here a few times over the years and never felt at ease, and he did so even less tonight, given the reason for his visit. With barely a glance at his surroundings he marched across the carpeted foyer and took a lift up to the fourth floor, sharing the carriage with an elderly couple over from England for their grandson's Bar Mitzvah.

The Barren suite was at the back of the building, at the end of a long, softly lit corridor. He paused a moment outside, gathering himself, swiftly running through his plan of attack, then knocked. The door opened immediately and he was ushered in.

The room was a duplex – huge lounge, stairs up to a bedroom area, windows affording spectacular views east across the Hinnom Valley to Mount Zion and the floodlit jumble of the Old City. There were five people waiting inside, which struck him as slight overkill: two men in suits – Barren executives – and, side by side on a sofa, a man and woman whose sharp features and icy stares marked them straight out as legals.

Those were the extras, the supporting cast. It was the fifth person who immediately grabbed Ben-Roi's attention and who was clearly the one in overall charge, his presence dominating the space even though he wasn't physically there. Instead, his face loomed on a giant

TV screen at the suite's far end – bearded, bloated, grizzled, like some glowering Old Testament prophet. Nathaniel Barren.

'You're late, sir.'

The voice was a rasping growl. The sort of sound you could imagine issuing from the faces on Mount Rushmore.

'I don't appreciate being kept waiting. We were due to start at one o'clock Houston time.'

It was now two minutes past. Hardly an outrageous delay, but Ben-Roi apologized nonetheless, not wanting to raise hackles before the interview had even started. Plenty of time for that later. The old man eyed him out of the screen – a disconcerting experience, like being watched by a character in a TV programme. Then, with a shunt of the hand, he motioned the detective to sit.

'When I said we wanted to speak to someone in authority, I wasn't expecting to get the head of the company,' said Ben-Roi as he lowered himself into the only vacant chair.

Eleven thousand kilometres away, Nathaniel Barren's shoulders pulled back slightly, his jacket rucking beneath the armpits.

'When *I* am informed that the good name of Barren Corporation has been dragged into a homicide inquiry,' he growled, 'that is not an issue I care to delegate. I might have taken a step back from the day-to-day running of the company, but it is still *my* company. And *my* family name. I trust you appreciate what I'm saying, Mr . . . ?'

'Ben-Roi,' chipped in one of the executives.

'Senior Detective Ben-Roi,' said Ben-Roi. And yes, he could appreciate it.

'I'm glad we understand each other.'

The conferencing technology was clearly top-of-the-range, because despite the distances involved there wasn't even a fractional time delay on the old man's voice, his image so clear you could make out the individual liver spots on his giant hands. The left one, Ben-Roi noticed, was clasping a plastic oxygen mask.

'Would you care for refreshments, Mr Ben-Roi?'

Ben-Roi said he was fine.

'In that case I suggest we get straight down to business. Ask what you need to ask.'

The fingers of Barren's right hand drummed a slow beat on the surface of the desk at which he was sitting. Although it was still early afternoon in Houston, the room around him – some sort of study or library – appeared sunk in gloom. Even viewing it through a television screen from a third of the way around the world, Ben-Roi could sense the oppressiveness of the place. He rubbed at his wrist, which was still sore from the cuff, flipped through his notebook to a blank page and got going.

'Twelve days ago a journalist named Rivka Kleinberg was murdered in Jerusalem,' he began. 'In the Armenian Cathedral. She was garrotted.'

The statement brought no visible reaction from Barren. He just drummed his fingers and stared out at Ben-Roi through eyes that were at once both rheumy and piercing. The others were staring at him as well – five pairs of eyes boring into him from all directions. Not exactly threatening, but not particularly comfortable either. He was going to have to play this carefully.

'Would you happen to know if there was any recent contact between Mrs Kleinberg and your company?' he asked.

On the screen, Barren's eyes angled towards the two executives, both of whom shook their heads.

'You obviously believe there's a reason for there to have been contact.'

'During the course of our inquiries, it has emerged that shortly before her death Mrs Kleinberg was doing some research into Barren Corporation,' explained Ben-Roi.

One of the lawyers asked what sort of research. Ben-Roi filled them in on the article about the Romanian gold mine.

'She was also looking into a man named Samuel Pinsker. In 1931 it appears this Samuel Pinsker discovered the whereabouts of a long-lost ancient Egyptian gold mine known as the Labyrinth of Osiris.'

The legal was straight in, asking what possible relevance this could have to Barren Corporation. Nathaniel Barren silenced her with a sweep of the fingertips. Much the same gesture Genady Kremenko had used to silence *his* lawyer. Two men who were used to being obeyed without question.

'Continue, Mr Ben-Roi.'

Ben-Roi shifted in his seat.

'It seems this ancient gold mine was located somewhere in the middle of Egypt's Eastern Desert. Not so long ago a Barren subsidiary named Prospecto Egypt were doing survey work in precisely that region.'

The other legal dived in, asking what on earth any of this had to do with a murder inquiry in Jerusalem. Again, Barren waved him quiet.

'Could you tell me a bit about Prospecto?' asked Ben-Roi.

'Mickey?'

Barren motioned to one of the suited executives, a slick young man with neatly razored sideburns and a chunky designer watch.

'They were a small subsidiary operation,' explained the man, his voice clipped and precise, like his appearance. 'Oversaw a two-year exploration licence in the central Red Sea mountains. When the licence lapsed, the company was wound up.'

Pretty much what Zisky had told Ben-Roi earlier.

'It was run as a separate entity?' he asked.

No, replied the man, it had been managed directly out of Houston, with a sub-office in Cairo.

'Did it find anything?'

Some limited emerald deposits, apparently. Very poor quality, way too low grade to make extraction viable. And a couple of phosphate beds. Again, far too limited to warrant further development. 'Other than that, a lot of sand and rock.'

'No gold?'

'No gold.'

'No labyrinths either,' quipped the other executive, drawing a ripple of laughter. Ben-Roi smiled, going with it, then switched the conversation.

'I understand gold-mining produces a significant amount of toxic waste.'

Yet again the legals swooped, yet again Barren waved them quiet, which made Ben-Roi wonder why he'd bothered having them there in the first place. Raising the oxygen mask, the old man took a series of deep, grating breaths, his eyes never leaving the detective. Once he was done he lowered the mask and sat back.

'I have to confess, Mr Ben-Roi,' he wheezed, 'that it is not immediately evident – either to me or to my colleagues – how an understanding of the technical intricacies of gold-mining will assist you in bringing a murderer to justice. On the basis that it *will* assist you, however, and also on the basis that we have always enjoyed excellent relations with the State of Israel, I am happy to give you the benefit of my fifty years experience in the industry.'

He didn't *sound* especially happy, but Ben-Roi wasn't about to labour the point.

'So, to answer your question: yes, gold-mining does produce substantial levels of toxic overspill. The processes have improved over the years, but whichever way you cut it, it's still a dirty business. Always has been, always will be. Like all beautiful things, gold has its downside.'

'Is arsenic part of the downside?'

He watched Barren closely as he said this, scanning for any discernible reaction. As before, there was none.

'It can be,' replied the old man. 'Cyanide's the main off-product, but if the gold's being broken out of arsenopyrite, then yes, you'll get a lot of arsenic residue as well. Which in the long run ends up being more damaging because the degradation rate of arsenic is so much slower than cyanide. Would you care for me to go into more detail?'

Something in his tone seemed to dare Ben-Roi to say yes. He didn't, not wanting to get pulled into a chemistry lecture. After the day's events he could feel tiredness gathering around the margins of his brain and he wanted to get as much ground covered as possible while his mind was still sharp. He changed angle again.

'According to the newspaper article I mentioned, the waste from your Romanian mine is taken back to the US.'

There was a pause as Barren eyed him, then:

'That is correct.'

'You do this with the waste from all your mines?'

The question drew a dismissive snort.

'Do we hell. The tailings from our other operations are disposed of on site. Subject, of course, to the laws of whatever country the site happens to be in. We only go to the trouble with Drăgeș because it was a stipulation of getting the concession. A goddamn expensive stipulation, I might add, what with the cost of shipping, immobilizing, and filling. But then it's such a rich deposit we can absorb the cost. Forty million ounces of gold at concentrations of 35 grams per tonne – take it from me, Mr Ben-Roi, in gold-mining terms that's the mother lode.'

'And of course at Barren Corporation we're delighted to play our part in safeguarding the environment,' chipped in the second of the two executives, a balding man with heavily bagged eyes and a distinct paunch overhanging the trousers of his Armani suit. 'We take our green responsibilities extremely seriously.'

'Extremely seriously,' echoed Barren, his tone suggesting he thought quite the opposite. Ben-Roi shuffled his feet, staring at the old man, sensing he was somehow missing a trick, not asking the questions he ought to be asking. Maybe he *should* have put the interview off, left it till tomorrow when he would be less weary. He was here now, though, doubted he'd get the opportunity again, so pushed on.

'Does your company have any links with the port of Rosetta?' he asked. 'On the north Egyptian coast.'

Barren's finger-drumming started up again.

'Not that I'm aware of,' he replied. 'And since nothing happens in this company *without* me being aware of it, that would be a no.'

Smiles from his employees.

'What about a man named Genady Kremenko?'

'Never heard of him.'

'Dinah Levi?'

A fractional pause, too fleeting for Ben-Roi to tell if it signified anything, then:

'Never heard of him either.'

'It's a her.'

Barren shrugged. Ben-Roi stared at him, trying to read his face, work out if he was telling the truth or was just extremely adept at lying. He couldn't decide – the latter, he sensed, although he'd yet to see any evidence for it – and after a brief pause he changed tack yet again, dancing round like a boxer trying to work an opening.

'Going back to Prospecto a moment,' he said. 'I understand the company was headed by your son, Mr Barren.'

The old man's gaze hardened fractionally, as if he didn't welcome mention of his offspring. The first reaction since the start of the interview.

'We still with your investigation here?' he growled, his hand tightening around the oxygen mask. 'Or just general interest in the way I structure my business?'

Ben-Roi ignored the barb, assured him it was very much to do with his inquiry. Barren peered out from the screen, his massive head seeming to tremble slightly like a rock about to topple and start rolling. Then, with a grunt, he clasped his hands.

'Your understanding is correct,' he said, thumb playing round the curve of his thin gold wedding band. 'We were bringing William on board at the time, getting him familiar with the organization. Running Prospecto was part of that process.'

Ben-Roi hesitated, doodling on his pad, then:

'He's quite a colourful character, your son.'

It was deliberately provocative, and he braced himself as he said it, anticipating a sharp retort. The legals sat forward, like Dobermanns straining at the leash, but again Barren didn't loose them. Instead he sat in silence a moment, then, unexpectedly, smiled. An unsettling expression, like a wound opening up across the bottom of his face.

'I'm a plain-talking man, Mr Ben-Roi,' he growled, 'so let's you and me talk plainly here. As you are obviously aware, my son has a . . . history. Thanks to the gutter press, it's not exactly privileged information. And on the basis of that history you're thinking perhaps under his direction Prospecto – what? Went rogue? Discovered some sort of lost Aladdin's cave and started working it behind our backs? Then maybe bumped off a journalist because she found out about it? Am I hitting any chords here?'

A couple, acknowledged Ben-Roi, although he wouldn't have put it quite that bluntly.

'Well, I like blunt, sir. Blunt leaves no room for doubt. And I'm telling you bluntly that you're way out of line. Way out of line and way off the mark. Firstly, because as I've already told you, nothing happens in this company – *nothing* – that I don't know about. Secondly, because even if it's the remotest goddamn desert on the planet, you don't operate something as big as a gold mine without people finding out about it. And thirdly, and most importantly –' he leant right into the camera as he said this, his face filling the screen – 'because whatever the hell else he is, for good or ill, my son is most certainly *not* some sort of Al Capone figure running around calling hits on anyone who happens to get on the wrong side of him. That's fantasy land, Mr Ben-Roi, and frankly I would have expected better from a representative of one of the world's great police forces. I trust that settles the point.'

Ben-Roi acknowledged that it did.

'Good. You bring my family into this again and the interview's over. Your career too, if I have anything to do with it. Just there please, Stephen.'

This to the figure who had leant into frame from Barren's left. Some sort of valet or manservant to judge by his dark uniform and deferential manner. He remained in shot long enough to place a glass of water on the desk in front of the old man, then backed out and disappeared. Lifting the glass, Barren sipped, his forehead rucked into a concertina of angry wrinkles.

'That it?' he muttered, eyes looming over the glass's rim like a pair of bluebottles. 'Or are there any other crackpot theories you want to run by me?'

Ben-Roi held the stare, refusing to be intimidated. There were other bases he would have liked to have covered – Barren's Egyptian gas field tender for one, and also the list of companies the Dinah woman had given him earlier. He could sense that he was now on borrowed time, and anyway, the comment about ending his career had riled him. Rather than continuing to jab around the margins, therefore, he went straight in with a roundhouse right.

'Mr Barren, do you have any idea why the Nemesis Agenda believe your company murdered Rivka Kleinberg?'

The comment brought an immediate and furious dressing down from the legals, who on this occasion weren't reined in by their employer. Ben-Roi let it wash over him, his attention focused unswervingly on Barren's face, analysing the effects of his words in much the same way as a geologist will analyse earthquake readings on a seismograph. The old man was angry, no question about it, his jaw thrusting out, his mouth clamped into a threatening scowl. At the same time there was something in his eyes that didn't quite tally with the rest of his expression. Difficult to define what exactly – although his screen image was crystal clear, the fact that he wasn't actually there in person somehow made it harder to interpret such tiny pointers. It certainly wasn't fear. Nor guilt either. More a sort of knowing wariness, as if the comment hadn't come as quite as much of a surprise to him as it had to everyone else in the interview.

'Explain yourself, sir,' he snarled.

'With pleasure,' said Ben-Roi. 'Earlier today I was held at gunpoint by Dinah Levi, the woman I mentioned earlier, who I have reason to believe is Rivka Kleinberg's daughter. She is also a member of the Nemesis Agenda.'

Barren said nothing, just glared at him, still with that curious disconnect between his face and his eyes, as if the former was registering one thing, the latter something completely different.

'You've heard of the Nemesis Agenda, I believe.'

The oxygen mask crumpled under the force of the old man's grip.

'You're goddamn right I've heard of them. Only two days ago they brutalized one of my employees in Cairo. If you have a description of this woman I sincerely hope it's been passed over to the relevant authorities.'

'I *am* the relevant authorities,' said Ben-Roi. 'And yes, a description has been circulated.'

Suddenly he was feeling very awake, very clear-headed.

'Four days before she was killed,' he continued, 'Rivka Kleinberg met with this woman. She asked the Nemesis Agenda to hack into your company's computer system to look for information about a gold mine in Egypt and the port of Rosetta.'

He gave it a couple of seconds, allowing that to sink in, then:

'It was Dinah Levi's belief that her mother was pursuing a story that had potential to damage Barren Corporation. It was also her belief – her *firm* belief – that to prevent that story getting out, Barren Corporation, or someone associated with it, killed Rivka Kleinberg. So I repeat the question: do you have any idea why she might think that?'

Ben-Roi had had bad looks in his time – as an Israeli policeman in Jerusalem, rarely a day went by when he didn't get bad looks – but nothing even remotely approaching the one that was currently emanating from the conferencing screen. Such was its malign intensity that even the legals were reduced to silence, the room around Ben-Roi seeming to narrow and recede so that it was just him and Barren alone in the ring together. There was a pause, the only sounds the angry grate of the old man's breath and, from the corridor outside the suite, the muted rattle of a room-service trolley. Then, slowly, Barren sat back, his suited bulk spreading and filling the chair like a flow of hardening magma.

'I can tell you exactly why she thinks that, Mr Ben-Roi,' he said, his voice a guttural rasp, as if his throat was clogged with sandpaper. 'She thinks it for precisely the same reason that people who oppose the State of Israel choose to believe its policemen go about deliberately shooting Arab kids, and anti-Semites get off on the idea that Jews drink babies' blood. Because she and her psycho friends hate us. Not for anything we've done, mind you, not for any laws we've broken, but because of what we represent. And what we represent is the triumph of capitalism. Money – that's what we're about, Mr Ben-Roi, and I make no bones about it, and no apologies for it. We obey the law, we pay our taxes, we lend our support to an array of worthwhile causes, but the bottom line is: we make money. And they can't stand that. Can't stand the fact that I sleep well at night and don't wake up in a cold sweat agonizing about the fact that some fucking tree fell down in the middle of the Amazon. They've been hounding us for the best part of seven years and have never once managed to turn up any evidence of wrongdoing, so frankly it's no surprise whatsoever to me they're now trying to pin a murder on us. I'm just amazed they haven't accused us of the Kennedy assassination yet.'

He broke off, heaving for breath, his face a bruised shade of purple, bubbles of spittle popping at the corners of his mouth. He took another series of pulls on the oxygen mask, his eyes dilating with each in-breath and contracting again as he exhaled, then lowered the mask and accepted the handkerchief that was handed into frame from his left, presumably by the manservant who was still standing there.

'I have been happy to indulge you, Mr Ben-Roi,' he growled, dabbing at his mouth, 'but since we now appear to have moved from the realm of policing into that of slander and insinuation, I am not prepared to continue with this interview. I wish you the best of luck in tracking down your killer, but feel bound to say that on the basis of what I've been hearing these last twenty minutes, you're not going to be doing that any time soon. And trust me, I'll be making my views known to your superiors. Good day, sir.'

His hand came up, ready to cut the video link. Ben-Roi called out: 'One last question, Mr Barren.'

The old man hesitated. So did Ben-Roi, undecided as to what the question should be. Maybe he should ask about Rosetta again. Or push Barren harder on the sex-trafficking angle. Or maybe challenge him about the list of Egyptian companies sitting folded in his pocket. Instead, without really knowing why, he threw out a curveball.

'Do you think the Nemesis Agenda had anything to do with your wife's death?'

Two days ago a similar left-fielder from Dov Zisky had caught Genady Kremenko unawares. No such luck with Barren. The old man glared at the screen, his face contorting with fury, his chest heaving. Then, with a muttered 'Get him out of here,' he reached forward and the screen went blank.

As Ben-Roi was being ushered out of his meeting with Nathaniel Barren, Khalifa was being called into his with Iman el-Badri, the woman who eighty years previously had been so brutally violated by Samuel Pinsker.

He'd arrived at her village over two hours before and had hoped to be well on his way back to Luxor by now, if not already home. As he'd pulled up outside her house, however – a low, mud-brick dwelling with a pigeon tower tacked on to the side and a donkey braying some-where round the back – he'd discovered a dozen black-robed women sitting in a line along the front of the building. Sariya had told him that Pinsker's victim was now some sort of holy figure, and it turned out the women were queuing for her blessing.

In other circumstances he would have flashed his badge and gone straight in. Instinct told him that in this case such a peremptory approach was not appropriate. Calling Zenab to let her know he'd be even later home than expected, he'd taken up his place at the end of the queue and waited his turn, studiously avoiding the supplicants' eyes so as not to compromise their modesty. In these out-of-the-way areas such things were important.

And now, finally, two hours and ten Cleopatras later, a woman's voice was summoning him inside, the last person in the line. Standing, he brushed down his trousers and smoothed his hair, mindful of his appearance even though the person he was visiting was blind. Then he stepped through the bead curtain into the building.

The interior was about as far removed as it was possible to get from the suite in which Ben-Roi had just conducted *his* interview. No electricity, no carpets, no decoration, no fancy furnishings. Instead, Khalifa found himself in a room with a beaten-earth floor, bare mud-brick walls and a smoke-darkened wooden ceiling. A door on the far side led through to the living quarters at the back of the house; a single kerosene lamp gave off just enough light to render the room visible without troubling the shadows bunched in its corners. Furniture-wise the place was bare save for a pair of simple wooden couches pushed up against the side walls. On the right-hand one, an ancient, doll-like woman was sitting cross-legged with her back against the mud-brick. Everything except her heavily wrinkled face was swathed in a *djellaba suda* so that it wasn't immediately obvious where her body ended and the shadows began.

'It is said my blessings give comfort to those who are with child,' she said, her voice croaky yet at the same time curiously gentle. Soothing. Like palm fronds crackling in the breeze. 'Sadly, sir, I fear there is no blessing I can offer that will help you with *your* pregnancy.'

She smiled at her joke and motioned Khalifa on to the couch opposite. How she'd known he was a man he couldn't say – probably she'd caught something in the sound of his breathing, or the weight of his footfall. Crossing to the left-hand couch, he sat.

'You are not from these parts,' she said, canting her head in his direction.

'Luxor.' He paused, then added: 'I'm a policeman.'

She gave a slow nod, as if she had already somehow divined this. Other blind people he'd met had had a dullness to their eyes, a clouding of the irises that gave their condition away. Hers were a brilliant emerald green, almost unnaturally bright, as if her blindness manifested itself not so much in a lack of colour as a surfeit of it.

'Can I get you something to drink?' she asked. 'The night is hot, and you have come a long way.'

Khalifa was thirsty, but declined the offer, not wanting to put her to any trouble. She smiled again, as if understanding the reason for his refusal. Easing herself off the seat, she shuffled into the living quarters at the back of the house, her movements slow but assured – if he hadn't already known it, he would never have guessed she was blind. She returned a couple of minutes later with a glass of tea.

'I have a girl who helps with the household chores,' she explained, handing him the glass and returning to her couch, never once having to fumble for direction, 'but simple things I can manage for myself. Please, drink.'

Khalifa did as she asked, not mentioning the fact that he always took his tea with sugar. It had already been sweetened. Two spoons, he guessed. Just as he liked it.

'*Lazeez*,' he mumbled.

'*Afwan*,' she replied.

A silence, then:

'I am sorry for your loss.'

He thanked her for her commiseration and took another sip, only to realize with a start that he hadn't mentioned Ali.

'How did you . . . ?'

'Some things you can see even without eyes,' she said quietly. 'Your grief is all around you. It hangs off you like a cloak.'

He didn't know what to say. 'It was my son,' was all he managed to get out.

'I am so very sorry.'

She stared at him, or at least seemed to, her eyes twinkling in the uncertain glow of the kerosene lamp, shadows pressing in all around. Then, clasping her withered hands in her lap, she settled back against the wall.

'Something is troubling you,' she said. 'Something that makes you uneasy in my presence. Please, tell me why you are here.'

Khalifa shifted in his seat, unsettled. He'd heard that blind people had heightened senses, could pick up things that were missed by those with perfect vision, but this was something else. It was like she could see right into him, knew exactly what he was thinking and feeling. He hunched forward, swirling the tea around his glass, reluctant, suddenly, to ask the questions he'd come to ask.

'Come,' she pressed, 'it cannot be that bad. Say what you need to say. You will feel better for it. Maybe we both will.'

She opened out her hands, indicating that he should talk. There was a silence, the shadows in the room seeming to deepen and thicken, as if in expectation. Then, drawing a breath:

'Like I said, I'm with the Luxor Police,' he began. 'I'm working on a case ... helping with a case ... a woman was murdered, in Jerusalem. I won't go into details. There seems to be a connection with a man I think you ... knew. A *hawaga*, an *ingileezi* named ... Samuel Pinsker.'

Her head lifted, then dropped.

'Ah,' she murmured.

It was her only reaction.

'I know what happened,' he continued, keeping his tone as gentle as he could, trying to convey not only that he understood what she must be feeling, but also that she had no cause for shame. 'Please, forgive me for reminding you of it.'

'You do not remind me,' she murmured. 'Remind implies it is something I have put from my mind. Not a day goes by when I do not think of that night. Not a minute of a day. It lives with me always. Eighty years and it might have been yesterday.'

She brought up a hand and touched her fingertips to her temples.

Khalifa stared at the floor. Only a few minutes ago the visit had seemed a good idea. Now that he was actually here in her presence . . .

'Forgive me,' he repeated. 'I didn't want to . . .'

'You have no need to apologize. They did what they did. I have learnt to live with it.'

He must have been tired because, as with the Ali comment, it took him a moment to properly register her words. He looked up, frowning.

'They?'

'The ones who committed the crime.'

His frown deepened. 'I don't understand, *Ya Omm*. I thought . . .'

'What?'

'That it was Samuel Pinsker who –' he didn't like to use the word 'rape', to humiliate her – 'was responsible.'

She lowered her hand. Her eyes seemed to burn in the shadowy half-light.

'There were three of them.'

Khalifa's throat tightened.

'Three criminals who were never brought to justice. Three monsters who died peacefully in their beds while their victim . . .'

She dipped her head, her face disappearing into shadow so that it was impossible to catch her expression. Khalifa sat there, cursing himself for his selfishness, for raking it all up again, making an old woman relive an event that appeared to have been even more traumatic than he had imagined, if such a thing was possible. A few seconds passed, then he stood.

'I shouldn't have come. It was a long time ago, it's none of my business. Please, *Ya Omm*, forgive me. I'll leave now.'

He turned for the door. Her voice pulled him back, unexpectedly firm: 'You will stay.'

Her head came up, her face angling towards him. It was so deeply striated there seemed to be more wrinkles than skin.

'Eighty years I have born this secret. It is time the truth was told. God help me, I would have done it sooner if I'd thought anyone would listen. But to be a woman in Egypt, especially a *fellaha* – you do not speak of such things. You do not speak at all if you know what is good for you. Even if I had, it would have made no difference. They were clever, my brothers.'

Khalifa's throat tightened further. His stomach too.

'*Allah-u-akhbar*, you're saying your own brothers were involved in the rape!'

This time he came right out with the word, too shocked to worry about semantic niceties. To his surprise the old woman smiled, although never in his life had he seen a smile with less humour in it.

'There was never any rape,' she whispered, her voice not much louder than the hiss of the kerosene lamp. 'No one laid a finger on me. Least of all Samuel Pinsker.'

She pronounced it *Sam-oo-el Peens-ka*, the name freighted with none of the bitterness you might have expected had it belonged to some-one who had attacked her. Quite the opposite. Her tone suggested a tenderness bordering on reverence. Khalifa came forward a step.

'But there was a witness. A young boy. He saw . . .'

'What? What did he see?'

'Pinsker attacking you.' Khalifa could hear Chief Sadeq describing the assault. 'You were crying, struggling . . .'

She sighed, her head shaking slowly.

'To see is not always to understand, Inspector. Especially when it is done through the eyes of a child. When a child sees tears it does not occur to him they can be tears of joy. When he sees a man clutching a woman he assumes it must be an assault. What the boy saw was not what he thought he saw.'

There was no rancour in her voice, no hint of blame. Just sadness. Infinite sadness. Khalifa stood a moment. Then, crossing the room, he dropped to his haunches in front of her. She was so small and shrunken, the couch so low, that even squatting he was still a head taller than her.

'What happened that night, *Ya Omm?*'

The question brought another smile. Genuine this time.

'What happened? A wonderful thing. The man I loved asked me to marry him. And I said yes. It was the happiest night of my life. For a while, at least.'

She sighed and tilted her head, her gaze, such as it was, angling over Khalifa's shoulder towards the shadows in the top corner of the room. Khalifa's thoughts were spinning, trying to make sense of it all, to readjust. Everything he'd heard about Pinsker, everything he'd assumed these last few days, it all seemed to crumble away from him, like a photograph turning to ash beneath his fingertips. Shuffling closer, he dropped to his knees and took her hands in his.

374

'Tell me,' he said. 'Please, *Ya Omm*. I want to understand.'

Outside the donkey had started braying again, a pained adenoidal honk that somehow seemed to be part of a separate reality. Inside the room the silence was so intense you could almost taste it. Seconds went by – or maybe minutes; from the moment he'd stepped into her presence, Khalifa seemed to have lost all sense of time. Then, slowly, she slipped her hands from his and brought them up to his face. Her fingertips ran back and forth – mouth, nose, cheeks, eyelids, forehead – tracing his features as though they were lines of Braille.

'You are a good man,' she whispered. 'A kind man. I heard it in your voice, now I read it in your face. I read pain too, and anger, much anger, but goodness prevails over all. Just as it did with *Sam-oo-el*. He was a *very* good man. The best I have ever known. So maybe it is fitting you should be the one to hear the truth.'

She held his face a moment longer. Then, lowering her hands, she sat back, closed her eyes and told him the story.

Pinsker had saved her from her brothers. That's how it had started.

He was working in a tomb in the hills above Old Qurna, was walking back through the village one evening, saw her being slapped about, intervened. In the ensuing brawl he had punched one brother so hard he had knocked him out (Mary Dufresne's voice echoed in Khalifa's head, as clear as if she was sitting there beside him: *he got in a fight with some Qurnawis once, laid one of them out cold*). Later the girl discovered Pinsker had been watching her for over a year, too ashamed of his appearance to make any sort of approach.

'Foolish man!' she chuckled. 'What difference could it have made to me? What I see is inside. And inside he was the handsomest man in the world. Never has anyone treated me with such respect. With such dignity.'

The two of them had started to meet – the blind peasant girl and the faceless Englishman. Snatched moments of togetherness in which friendship had swiftly blossomed into romance. All in utmost secrecy, of course. Even today a relationship between a *hawaga* and *fellaha* would be frowned upon, if not condemned outright. In 1931 it was unthinkable. On several occasions Pinsker had said it must end, fearful for her safety. Their feelings were too strong, though, their love too great, and the meetings had continued.

'He was in his thirties, I was nineteen,' she said. 'But this was no young girl's flirtation. I was wise for my years, knew exactly what I was doing. He may have been my elder, but here –' she touched a hand to her head – 'and here –' the hand came down to her heart – 'we were equals. Here too, in the burdens God had seen fit to lay upon us.' She touched her eyes and her face, the gesture speaking for her blindness and Pinsker's deformity.

'It hurt him so much the way he looked,' she said sadly. 'He was strong, but sometimes strength is not enough. The whispers, the looks, the comments. It wore him down. Once a little girl, a *hawagaya*, saw him in Medinet Habu. She screamed and ran away, like he was some sort of monster. He cried when he told me about it. Curled up in my arms and howled like a baby.' (Mary Dufresne's voice again: *I remember him suddenly appearing, me screaming and running away, him following me in that horrible mask of his. I had nightmares about it for weeks.*)

Sometimes Pinsker would go away, out into the desert, disappearing for weeks on end (Khalifa wanted to push for more information on this, but held his counsel). Always he would return, though, and the two of them would pick up exactly as they had left off.

'He was so kind. So gentle. Never took advantage of me. Had he wanted to I would have allowed him, but he was too decent. Said it would not be right. I felt so safe in his presence. So . . . complete. As though for my whole life up to that point I had not even been half a person.'

The courtship had continued for a year. Clandestine trysts in fields and among the ancient ruins strung along the base of the Theban massif. Then, one night, after an even longer absence than usual (how Khalifa wanted to push!), the lovers had met at their favourite spot on the banks of the Nile, and Pinsker had asked her to be his wife.

'I could not believe such happiness was possible. I thought he must be teasing, begged him not to hurt me, not to play with my emotions, but he just laughed, told me not to be so foolish. Even now I can hear his voice, smell the leather of his coat as he held me, the oil on his hands. I wept with joy.'

She had wanted to elope there and then, but Pinsker had insisted on doing things properly. He would go to see her father the next morning, he told her, ask for her hand officially. Until then she must keep their betrothal a secret, tell no one of it.

'I was scared,' she said. 'I knew what my family were like, knew there would be trouble. But he was honourable. The most honourable man I ever met. Had he been less so, he might have lived.'

376

That night she had returned home and laid out her finest *djellaba* in preparation for the following morning. Then, elated, she had gone to bed and dreamt of *Sam-oo-el Peens-ka* and the joyous life they would now share together.

In the still hour before dawn she had woken with a start, a terrible pain in her chest.

'I knew immediately something had happened to him,' she said. 'Something dreadful. It was like my heart was screaming.'

Shortly afterwards her brothers had rattled home in their donkey cart. She had confronted them, demanded to know where they had been, what they had done. The *hawaga* had been dealt with, was all they would tell her. She would never see him again. No one would ever see him again. The will of Allah had been enacted, justice served.

'Justice!' she spat. 'They knew he hadn't raped me. Knew it full well, even before I screamed the truth at them. It was just their excuse. For a year they had bided their time, waited for an opportunity to avenge themselves on him for standing up to them that day. When the boy came running with his story, they seized their chance. Evil men, they were. Cruel. Venomous as snakes.'

She had wept, cursed her brothers, threatened to go to the police. For which they had dragged her inside by her hair and beaten her. Beaten her so badly it had been a month before she was able to walk again.

'I was glad of the pain. Grateful for it. It allowed me to share something of what *Sam-oo-el* had gone through. In pain we were together.'

She had been kept a virtual prisoner for the next forty years, rarely venturing from the family house, rarely speaking. Like the living dead. And then they had found Pinsker's body and she had died all over again.

'Why Holy Allah should allow such a thing to happen I cannot begin to understand,' she said. 'Such a terrible crime, such unbearable cruelty. And for my brothers to get away with it. Although a sort of justice *was* done, for none of them were able to sire offspring. All three died childless. Such is the mystery of His ways. It brings me little consolation.'

With the passing of her last brother she had left the village, moved south, started a new life. Worked to bring others the happiness that had been denied to her.

'I have never visited his grave,' she said. 'Have never wanted to. He still lives here –' she touched her heart. 'And for me, that is all that matters. His name is on my lips when I wake in the morning, and when I go to bed at night, and a million times in between. The most beautiful name in the world. My husband. My darling husband. The finest man I ever knew.'

She ran a withered knuckle beneath her eyes as if to wipe away tears, although the eyes were dry.

'Such,' she said, 'is the story of Iman and *Sam-oo-el*.'

Beside her Khalifa's head had dropped. He didn't know what to feel, let alone what to say. All he could think of was the image of Pinsker's mummified body lying slumped at the back of the tomb. And, also, his son Ali, pale and still on the hospital bed after they had turned off his life support. The ways of Allah were indeed mysterious. So mysterious that not for the first time these last nine months he found himself wondering . . . not if Allah existed, that was beyond dispute, but rather what sort of Being He was. So much pain, so much tragedy, the balance seemingly weighted so heavily away from light towards darkness . . .

'It's about the mine, isn't it?'

He looked up.

'The reason you're here.' Her eyes rolled towards him. 'The woman in Jerusalem. The connection with *Sam-oo-el*. It's the mine, isn't it? The gold mine he found.'

Yet again she seemed to be way ahead of him.

'We think so,' he replied.

'*Sam-oo-el* always said no good would come of it. If word got out. For him, the gold meant nothing, but to others . . . There is much greed in the world.'

A cat came stalking into the room from the rear of the house. It leapt on to the couch beside the old woman and curled up against her leg.

'He was so excited,' she said, reaching out and running a hand along the cat's spine. 'That last night, when he came back. Years, he'd been looking for it. Month after month, alone out in the desert. And then, finally, on that last trip . . . Three months he was down there and he told me he hadn't even explored a half of it. Like an underground city, he said. An underground *world*. He was so happy. We were both so happy.'

She smiled sadly and fell silent. There were so many questions Khalifa wanted to ask, so much he needed to know, but after everything he'd heard tonight he couldn't seem to find his voice. The cat purred; the kerosene lamp hissed; almost a minute went by.

'What was her name?' she asked eventually. 'The woman who was killed.'

Khalifa told her.

'She was a good person?'

He confessed he didn't know much about her. 'I think she was. I believe she tried to help people. Expose wrongdoing.'

'And the mine – it is important? Knowing about it will help you achieve justice for her?'

Again, Khalifa couldn't say for certain. 'I think so,' he repeated.

There was another silence, the old woman's eyes seeming to pull back into themselves as if she was pondering something. Then, slowly, she withdrew her hand from the cat's back. Feeling within the folds of her *djellaba*, she pulled something out. In the darkness it wasn't immediately obvious what it was. Only when she handed it up to Khalifa did he realize that it was a notebook. An old notebook, its leather cover creased and stained, its pages dog-eared and yellowed with age.

'*Sam-oo-el* gave it to me,' she said. 'That last night, the night he proposed. He told me he hadn't had time to buy a ring, so instead was leaving me the most valuable thing he possessed as a plight of his troth. It is his notes from the mine. Eighty years it has rested beside my heart. No one has ever seen it. Myself included.'

Khalifa looked down at the book, his pulse pumping suddenly, his breath coming in short excited bursts. Then, standing, he crossed to the kerosene lamp and thrust the book into its light. Carefully he started to turn the pages.

There was writing – faded, spidery – and lists of numbers, which he guessed must be measurements, and drawings. Page after page of drawings: sketches of ancient tools and votive objects; copies of inscriptions and hieratic graffiti; an elaborate fold-out plan of the layout of the mine, or at least that part of it that Pinsker had managed to navigate. A bewildering matrix of tunnels and corridors and chambers and ventilation shafts, all fanning out from a broad central gallery like some vast subterranean vascular system.

And right at the back of the book, glued to the inside of its rear cover, another fold-out sheet. This one a map. Of the Eastern Desert. Not as detailed as the one his friend Omar had shown him that morning, but detailed enough: Nile, Red Sea, *wadis*, mountains. And there, in a small, sickle-shaped *wadi* tucked under the western flank of the Gebel el-Shalul, a tiny pencilled cross, with beside it the legend: *L of O.*

'*Hamdulillah*,' Khalifa whispered.

He folded the map back and closed the book.

'It is a lot to ask, *Ya Omm*, but would it be possible . . .'

'Take it,' said the old woman. 'With my blessing. And with *Sam-oo-el*'s as well. It is what he would have wanted. Justice was important to him. As it is to me.'

'I'll guard it with my life,' said Khalifa. 'Bring it back as soon as we have finished with it.'

She nodded. He weighed the notebook in his hands. Then, going over to her, he bent and kissed her on each cheek.

'*Shukran giddan, Ya Omm.*'

'*Afwan.*'

He started to straighten, but she took his hand. Her face turned up to him. A face that, despite her great age, still carried echoes of an earlier self beneath the lines, like a young woman dimly glimpsed through a sheet of crumpled baking parchment.

'He is at peace,' she said. 'There is a golden light, and Ali is at peace within it. Never forget that.'

She released his hand and motioned him towards the door. Khalifa just about made it outside before the tears started to come.

RAS AL-SHAITAN, GULF OF AQABA, EGYPT

'Which one is it?'

'That one. At the end.'

'I don't believe you.'

'See for yourself. They're secret agents. I'm telling you.'

The boys flitted along the row of chalets, feet sinking soundlessly into the sand. Waves hissed and slapped on to the beach to their right; behind them a faint hum of music was just about audible from the resort's main building. Otherwise everything was quiet. A huge orange moon dangled above the sea like a medallion.

They reached the last chalet in line – the only one at this end of the holiday village that was occupied – and crept round to the back. Two Land Cruisers were sitting side by side on the concrete parking bay.

'They arrived this evening. Four of them. They've got loads of spy stuff. Look.'

The chalet's windows were tightly curtained. By climbing on to the air-conditioning outlet, however – carefully, so as not to make any noise – they were able to peek through a narrow gap between the top corner of one of the curtains and the window frame. Inside, through the cramped triangle of uncurtained glass, they could see a bed, some bags, a pile of metallic cases and a table. Two people were sitting there, a man and a woman, staring at an opened laptop. Both wore headphones. Another man was kneeling on the floor, fiddling with some sort of electronic device. A fourth person – a woman – was lying on the bed reading a magazine. A handgun lay on the pillow beside her.

'What did I tell you?' whispered the boy. 'Spies.'

His voice was louder than he intended. The woman on the bed looked up, said something. Her companions swung. Terrified, the boys leapt down from the unit and sprinted away among the chalets, too scared to look back.

When they returned an hour later, their inquisitiveness getting the better of them, the Land Cruisers were gone and the chalet was empty, as if no one had ever been there. They debated whether to tell the resort management what they'd seen, but decided against it. Tourism was down as it was, and they'd just get blamed for driving away customers. And anyway, they probably wouldn't be believed. So they kept it to themselves. Their secret.

J E R U S A L E M

When Ben-Roi arrived at Kishle at 7 a.m. on Tuesday, he was in a good mood. Better, certainly, than he'd been in the previous day. He'd slept well, it was a beautiful morning, and that night he was going over for dinner at Sarah's, the first time she'd cooked for him since they'd split, which had to be a good sign.

The mood soured the moment he walked into the station.

First he bumped into Yigal Dorfmann, the investigator on the *yeshiva* student stabbing. Short, weaselly, snide, Dorfmann was an insufferable twat at the best of times. He was even more so this morning when he threw an arm round Ben-Roi's shoulder and cheerfully informed him that the student murder was now case closed.

'Arab kid confessed a couple of hours ago,' he boasted, chomping on a celebratory cigar. 'Iron-clad forensics. Commissioner a happy chappie. Back-slaps all round. But enough of that: how's *your* case going?'

The none-too-subtle subtext being: not half as well as ours.

A few minutes later, still smarting, Ben-Roi had been summoned into Chief Gal's office and given a fierce dressing-down for his handling of Nathaniel Barren the previous night. Barren's representatives had been on to both the Justice Ministry and the Prime Minister's office the moment the interview was over, and lodged a formal complaint about the tenor of Ben-Roi's questioning.

'You can't just bulldoze in and insult these sorts of people,' Gal stormed.

'But Barren are dodgy, sir. The company *and* the family. They're all over this case.'

'They're also best buddies with half the bloody Knesset! You got any evidence? *Real* evidence?'

Ben-Roi admitted that he hadn't.

'Then lay off till you have. Understand? I've taken a lot of heat for this and don't expect any more. Now get out.'

When Khalifa called just before eight, Ben-Roi's good mood was a distant memory.

'Please tell me you've got something for me,' he said, swivelling on his chair so as not to have to look at fellow detectives Yoni Zelba and Shimon Lutzisch, both of whom were supping Goldstars and crowing at the successful conclusion of their own investigation.

'OK,' came Khalifa's voice. 'I've tracked down your mine.'

Ben-Roi had been slumped in the seat. At the mention of the mine, he jerked bolt upright.

'You're joking.'

'The Egyptian police never joke.'

The Israeli smiled at that. Suddenly he could feel the mood-tide turning again.

'How did you find it?'

Khalifa filled him in on the meeting with Iman el-Badri.

'I've been up half the night going through Pinsker's notebook,' he said. 'It's incredible, absolutely incredible. The mine's main gallery is almost a mile deep. And there are literally hundreds of shafts and tunnels and sub-tunnels running off that. And that's just the part of the mine Pinsker managed to explore. "Labyrinth" doesn't even get close to describing it.'

'Any gold?'

Annoyingly, that was the one question Pinsker's notes didn't answer. He'd recorded taking some rock samples from the mine, but obviously he'd been murdered before he'd had a chance to get the samples properly analysed. Other than that, there was no mention of the stuff.

'Which doesn't mean there isn't any down there,' said Khalifa. 'The guy I spoke to on the boat a couple of days ago, the Englishman, he told me Pinsker wasn't interested in gold, he just wanted to find out about the ancient workers. So it's possible the mine's still full of the stuff. We won't know till we actually get out there.'

'Today?'

Unfortunately not.

'A find as big as this, there are a lot of bureaucratic hoops to jump through,' explained Khalifa. 'I've informed the ministry and they're sending someone down tomorrow to look at the notebook. And I've got a meeting this afternoon with a Supreme Council of Antiquities representative. Realistically it's going to be the end of the week at the earliest before everyone gets their act together.'

'You can't move any faster?'

'Trust me, by Egyptian standards the end of the week would be the speed of light.'

Ben-Roi grunted. It was frustrating, but couldn't be helped. At least they'd actually found the mine. That was a big step in the right direction. In the meantime, there was plenty of other stuff to keep him and Zisky occupied. The whole Vosgi thing still needed to be resolved, and William Barren could probably do with a closer look. And there was that list of Egyptian companies the Nemesis woman had given him – that might throw up some new angles. In fact, while he had him on the phone . . .

'Listen, Khalifa, you've already done more than enough, but could I pick your brains on just one more thing?'

'Of course. Anything.'

Ben-Roi told the Egyptian about his experiences the previous after-noon.

'This woman gave me a list of companies in Egypt that Barren have dealings with. We can do all the spadework at this end, but I was wondering if any of these leapt out at you. Just to try and narrow the field down a bit.'

Pulling the sheet from his pocket, he swivelled and flattened it on the desk. There were about forty names, arranged in alphabetical order.

'Ready?'

'Fire away.'

'Adarah Trading.'

'Never heard of them.'

'Amsco.'

'Nope.'

'Bank Misr.'

'Of course. They're one of our biggest banks.'

'Above board?'

'So far as I know. The service is notoriously slow.'

Ben-Roi smiled, pushed on.

'Delta Systems?'

'Nope.'

'Durabi.'

'Nope.'

'EGAS.'

'That's the Egyptian Natural Gas Holding Company,' said Khalifa. 'They're a big state-owned conglomerate, control all our gas reserves.'

That would tie in with Barren's Saharan gas field tender. Ben-Roi scribbled an asterisk beside the name, thinking it might be worth a delve.

'Fawzer Electronics.'

'Nope.'

'Fuzki Metals.'

'Nope.'

'Gemali Ltd.'

'Nope.'

And so it went on down the list. A few names Khalifa had heard of, most he hadn't. None of them rang any bells in terms of dodgy dealings.

EGAS remained the only one against which Ben-Roi put an asterisk.

He reached the bottom of the page and turned over. There were three more names on the other side.

'Ummara Concrete,' he read.

'No.'

'Wasti Logistics.'

'No.'

'Zoser Freight.'

Silence.

'Zoser Freight,' he repeated.

'Yes.'

'Yes, what?'

'Yes, I have heard of them.'

The Egyptian's voice seemed suddenly distant. Like his mind had veered off in another direction and he was no longer fully engaged in the conversation.

'And?' asked Ben-Roi.

Again, he had to repeat the question before he got a response.

'They're a transport company,' mumbled Khalifa. 'Big. Very big. Road, rail, river, that sort of thing. Lot of government connections.'

'That it?'

'Pretty much. Although there's one thing.'

'Go on.'

The sound of a breath being drawn.

'It was a Zoser Freight barge that killed my son Ali.'

LUXOR

Once Ben-Roi was off the line, Khalifa sat for a long time gazing into space, tapping his cigarette pack on the desk.

It was a coincidence, of course. Zoser were a huge company, there was nothing unusual about them having dealings with another huge company. And yet . . . and yet . . .

From the outset, he'd felt something about the Rivka Kleinberg case, some aspect of it that was calling to him, drawing him in. Something beyond the mere desire to help a friend, or get to the heart

385

of an intriguing mystery. Something that had made him stick with the investigation, keep digging, not let go. Something . . . inescapable. And now, suddenly, this.

He flipped the pack lid, pulled a cigarette out with his teeth, left it dangling unlit.

He'd never consciously blamed Zoser for the accident. Not out-right, at least. Yes, the barge had been out of its river lane, the forward watch not doing his job properly. But then Ali and his friends should never have been on the river in the first place. There was no clearly attributable burden of culpability.

And yet now he thought about it – and curiously he hadn't thought much about it; had just accepted it, like Egyptians accept so many inequities and injustices, as if unfairness was somehow hardwired into their DNA – now that he thought about it, it struck Khalifa that he *did* blame Zoser. Blamed them in the same way he blamed the local governorate for bulldozing half of Luxor, and the whole system for turn-ing its back on people like the Attias and the crippled boy at Demiana Barakat's children's home. Not for the accident per se, but rather for their arrogance. For not caring. For the fact that five boys had died beneath one of their barges and the company hadn't even seen fit to hold an internal inquiry into the collision. Had shrugged the whole thing off and carried on as normal, in the way the rich and powerful always seemed to shrug off the wider human impact of their actions.

And now, suddenly, their name had pipped up on the radar of a murder investigation.

Did it mean something, he wondered, this unexpected interface between two apparently separate stories? Did it have some wider relevance?

Or was he simply trying to wring significance from a situation where there was none?

He had no idea. His thoughts were muddled, confused.

All he could say for sure was that – coincidence or no coincidence – he suddenly felt an intense personal connection with Ben-Roi's case. As if he had been dangling his feet in the margins of a whirlpool only to be sucked right into the heart of it. And, also, for reasons he couldn't begin to explain or rationalize, a sense that helping Ben-Roi solve his case would in some way help him. If not to get over his son's death, at least move forward from it.

The path back to daylight, it seemed, lay through the Labyrinth.

He sat back, lit the Cleopatra, smoked it all the way down to the filter, tangles of smoke drifting and weaving above him. Then, stubbing out the butt, he picked up the phone and called down to the station car pool.

Yesterday he'd borrowed an ailing Fiat Uno to get him out to Iman el-Badri's village.

For the journey he was about to undertake, he was going to need something rather more sturdy.

* * *

I have been thinking hard about the forthcoming cleansing. The cleansing of cleansings, if you like. So hard that the news of my failure affected me less than it might otherwise have done. It shook me, of course, to hear that the family were now implicated, to receive words of admonishment. It was not unexpected, though. From the first I had my doubts about the cathedral. I knew I shouldn't have done it sooner than planned.

That is as it is. The past cannot be rewritten. My energies are now focused on the task in hand. Respect the past, but do not be distracted by it – that was another lesson I learnt from my parents. I am looking to the future. Mine, and the family's.

Potassium chloride is a possibility. As is insulin. Subtlety is key, and both are untraceable. Although with so little time, procurement could be a problem.

I shall give it more consideration. As things stand, I am leaning towards simplicity. No needles, no baggage, use just what they have in the room. I have put in some practice, testing my wrists and arms, calibrating the best posture to adopt so as to exert force, but not so much of it as to leave bruises. It's a fine balance, but I should be able to achieve it. And it *would* save me having to look at the face. Ordinarily I have no qualms about such things, but then this is no ordinary cleansing. It is, as I believe they say, a watershed.

Talking of which, I hope I don't cry. I'm not an overtly emotional person – it doesn't do in my line of work – but such is the magnitude of the step I am about to take that I cannot discount the possibility. Whatever the outward dynamic, there's still a bond. And severing it won't be easy, however necessary the severance.

I shall add tissues to my packing list. Hopefully I won't need them, but you never know. These are uncertain times. And in uncertain times, preparation is all.

Road to the Eastern Desert

As the crow flies it was less than 140 kilometres from Luxor to the Gebel el-Shalul. Had there been a direct road Khalifa could have been there in an hour.

There was no direct road. There were precious few tracks – just a vast, heat-seared wilderness of mountains, escarpments, gravel pans and *wadis*. A daunting natural labyrinth protecting the man-made labyrinth of the *shemut net wesir*. Even in a Landrover Defender, a vehicle specifically designed for challenging off-road terrain, it was going to be a tough drive. A risky one too, breaking as it did the first rule of desert travel: never, ever go out there on your own.

He had to give it a try, though. Couldn't wait for Egyptian bureaucracy to wind its interminable course. He wanted to know what was happening at the mine. *Needed* to know. If things got too difficult he could always turn back. And he'd borrowed one of the station satellite phones in case he got into real trouble. It would be fine, he told himself. Difficult, but fine.

Before setting out he stopped off at his apartment, explained to Zenab that he had to drive over to Marsa Alam for work, probably wouldn't be home till late – a lie, but he didn't want to worry her. Satellite phone or no satellite phone, people still died out in the Eastern Desert. And she'd already lost a son.

Another couple of stops to pick up supplies – extra fuel, water, a torch, cigarettes, cheese, *taamiya*, *aish baladi* – and he was on his way. On the seat beside him was his friend Omar's map of the desert's central highlands. And, also, Samuel Pinsker's notebook.

Locating the mine wasn't the problem. It was getting there that was going to be a challenge.

Such as he had one, his plan was to cover as much ground as possible on blacktop. Therefore, although it more than doubled the distance he needed to drive, he headed south first, all the way back down to Edfu, where he picked up Highway 212 east towards Marsa Alam and the Red Sea coast. Halfway along its length, 212 looped sharply to the north. By striking out from the apex of that loop, he calculated he would have less than fifty kilometres of desert to navigate before reaching the environs of the mine. Still a long way, given the extreme hostility of the terrain, but every kilometre he saved increased his chances of making it to his destination.

There were two other reasons for choosing that particular route. According to his notebook, it was the direction from which Samuel Pinsker had approached the mine. And the convoy of trucks that the Helwan University surveying team had spotted from the air had been moving across precisely that part of the desert. Whether the convoy had anything to do with the Labyrinth he had no idea, but its presence suggested that the area was at least partially driveable.

The traffic on Route 2 was heavier than it had been the previous evening and it took him almost two hours to reach Edfu. Once he'd turned east on to 212, however, there was nothing, either on the highway or off it. Just a shimmering thread of black tarmac winding through a sun-bleached wasteland of sand and rock. He passed a police checkpoint just outside Edfu, and a couple of small settlements at El Kannayis and Barramiya – forlorn clusters of concrete and mud-brick clamped to the side of the highway as though clinging on for dear life. Otherwise there were no signs of human intrusion. In the hour it took him to reach the highway's northward loop, he en-countered only one other vehicle – an Isuzu pick-up truck crammed with sheep. He might as well have been on Mars.

Eventually, shortly after eleven, he slowed and pulled over. According to Omar's map, he was now at the road's closest point to the Gebel el-Shalul. He got out and looked north, shielding his eyes against the sun. In front of him a swathe of gravelly sand lifted into a confusion of low hills which in turn erupted into rearing slopes of yellow-brown rock. The slopes grew higher and steeper the further north you looked, climbing and climbing until eventually they merged into the forbidding mountainous haze of the central highlands.

He lit a cigarette, wondering if this was a bad idea. *Knowing* it was a bad idea. Then, fearful that the more he thought about it the less likely he was to do it, he topped up the tank with diesel, let a little air out of each of the Landrover's tyres to improve traction and bumped off the highway into the unknown. Someone had left a Mohammed Mounir cassette in the car stereo and he played that over and over to keep his spirits up.

For the first ten kilometres the going was unexpectedly easy. He wound his way through the gravelly foothills, keeping his speed low, staying in second and third, before picking up a broad *wadi* that took him in exactly the direction he needed to go. The hills rose around him, imposing waves of stone boxing him in to either side.

The *wadi* bed remained relatively flat, however, and he made good progress.

It didn't last. Omar's map showed the *wadi* feeding into an even larger valley that curved to the west before once again pushing north. What it didn't show was the scatter of huge boulders strung across the *wadi*'s upper end, blocking his progress as effectively as a row of bollards. He tried to move a couple, but he couldn't budge them, and with the *wadi* slopes way too sheer for him to be able to creep the Landrover round the side of the blockage, he had no choice but to backtrack and try to find a different way forward.

Four hours later he was still trying. Time and again he'd find himself in a *wadi* that seemed to be taking him in the right direction, only for it to suddenly funnel into an impenetrable cleft, or slam up against a vertical rock wall, or curve a hundred and eighty degrees so that he was now driving away from where he needed to get to. At one point his tyres got bogged in a sand drift and he had to spend thirty minutes digging himself out; twice he went all the way back to the highway so as to come at the problem from a different starting point. Pinsker's notebook was no help -- it merely indicated that he'd reached the mine from the south – and for all its topographic detail, Omar's map seemed to be constantly contradicted by facts on the ground. As the afternoon wore on and the landscape continued to tease and obstruct him, he found himself thinking that maybe he should just call the whole thing off and head home. Leave it to the experts.

Around three o'clock, having pushed fifteen kilometres up yet another apparently promising corridor only for it to peter out at the foot of an impassable, forty-metre-high sand dune, Khalifa stopped the Landrover, cut the engine and got out. He stretched and kicked his legs, took a long glug of water. Then, fetching some binoculars and the bag of food he'd bought back in Luxor, he trudged up to the top of the nearest ridge to get a look at the lie of the land.

He was now well west of the point at which he'd first ventured into the desert. To the south the tarmacked ribbon of Route 212 wound off towards the coast; to the north the central highlands bulged lumpily in the distance – a shimmering fortress of hazy brown rock that was no nearer now than it had been four hours ago. In between, as though he was gazing out across the top of some gigantic maze, spread a churning sea of ridges and scarps and slopes and hilltops, with no obvious passage through to the high *gebel* beyond.

'Bloody dammit,' he muttered.

He surveyed the scene despondently. Then, sitting cross-legged on the ground, he draped a *shaal* over his head against the sun and started unpacking his food. He'd give it another couple of hours, he reckoned, try coming in from yet another direction, then call it quits. Night descended fast in the desert, and although the Landrover was fitted with a pair of A-bar mounted spotlights in addition to its regular lights, he didn't fancy the idea of being stuck out here after dark.

He folded some cheese into a piece of *aish baladi* and bit into it, his gaze tracking across the arid nothingness before dropping down into the *wadi* on the other side of the ridge. It ran parallel to the one in which he'd left the jeep, although it was wider and, rather than continuing directly north, curved round towards the east. There was a tree down there, an acacia, its trunk gnarled and twisted, its dish-shaped canopy tilting at a precarious angle as though exhausted by the heat. It was the first sign of life he'd seen out here and he found himself staring at it as he munched his sandwich, grateful to have something to focus on other than dust and rock. He became quite absorbed, wondering how old the tree was, how on earth it survived in such merciless conditions, and it was only after several minutes that he became aware of the marks running along the ground on the opposite side of the *wadi*. A lot of marks. Deep, compacted, straight, as if someone had scratched a giant fork through the sand.

Tyre tracks.

He stood and lifted the binoculars. The land was so folded it was impossible to tell where the *wadi* came from or went to. He scanned the ridge-top, looking for a way through from the *wadi* in which he'd left the Landrover. He couldn't see one. Like two roads separated by a high wall, with no linking spur between them. He homed in on the tracks. They were wide – way too wide for a 4x4 or a pick-up – and noticeably ridged, as though the tyres that made them had a particularly thick tread. Trucks, no question. Large ones, by the look of it. The same trucks the Helwan surveying team had spotted? He had no idea, but it was definitely worth taking a look where they led. Descending to the Landrover, he started the engine, turned the vehicle round and headed back down the *wadi*, searching for a gap in the wall.

He had to go almost four kilometres before he found one. The ridge dropped suddenly at this point, bowing down into a deep saddle before rising again and continuing on its way. A dune had blown up against the side of the saddle, creating a smooth incline up which he was able to gun the Landrover. It took him four goes to get to the top, the wheels sliding and churning on the sand, but he made it eventually and was able to bump down the rocky slope on the far side and into the adjacent *wadi*.

After that the going improved dramatically. Whatever they were doing out there, the trucks seemed to have been using the *wadi* frequently, for their tracks were densely compacted. Slotting the Landrover's wheels into the grooves gave him almost as good a driving surface as if he was on a proper road. He was able to get his speed up to fifty and in places sixty kilometres an hour, shunting back and forth through the gears, the mellifluous strains of Mohammed Mounir wafting from the car stereo. Ten kilometres on, the *wadi* linked into another *wadi*, and then another, and then others beyond that, drawing Khalifa into an increasingly complex spider's web of dried-up watercourses within which he would soon have become hopelessly lost had he not had the tracks to guide him. Each successive *wadi* was slightly narrower than its predecessor, the slopes rising ever steeper to either side, the landscape wrapping ever tighter around him. Sometimes he found himself bearing towards the west, sometimes the east. Always, however, the overall direction was north, deeper and deeper into the secret heart of the massif, closer and closer to his goal, further and further from what now felt like the relative populousness of the highway. He felt increasingly small, and increasingly alone. And, also, increasingly nervous. If the tracks *were* leading to the mine – and with every passing kilometre it seemed less and less likely they could be going anywhere else – and if the mine *was* being worked illegally, the remoteness of the locale was going to be the very least of his worries. He cut the stereo, made sure the satellite phone was ready beside him. And, also, his Helwan 9mm, its safety disengaged.

On and on he drove, the daylight ebbing away around him, the shadows lengthening, until eventually, after a long, slow climb up yet another meandering valley, the tyre tracks veered to the right and disappeared into a defile between high cliffs. He slowed, stopped and killed the engine. Reaching for Samuel Pinsker's notebook, he flicked through until he came to a faded pencil drawing. Beneath it was the legend: *The approach to the Labyrinth*. He held the book up, comparing the drawing to the view in front of him. The two were a perfect match. He'd made it.

For a minute he sat there listening, head cocked, trying to pick up any sounds. There was nothing, unless silence itself can be thought of as a sound. Satisfied, he restarted the Landrover and drove a hundred metres further up the *wadi* where he parked out of sight in a bay beneath a rocky overhang. He got out and called Ben-Roi. Voicemail.

'I'm at the mine,' he said, not wasting time with explanations. 'I'm going to take a look. I'll come back to you in thirty minutes.'

He threw the phone back into the car – no point taking it, there'd be no signal underground – and grabbed the torch from the boot. Then, Helwan at the ready, he walked back down the *wadi* and picked up the tracks again.

The defile into which they led was narrow, little more than ten metres across, barely wide enough to accommodate a single truck. Rock walls towered above him – bulging, sail-like sheets of limestone billowing upwards towards a pale blue ribbon of sky high above. Swifts skimmed to and fro; despite the lateness of the hour, the air was still dense with heat. He cupped his hands around his mouth and shouted.

'*Salaam-alaam-alaam-alaam-alaam.*'

His voice echoed down the canyon, bouncing from wall to wall, repeating for an improbable length of time before fading into silence. He called again, and again, then started walking, his finger curled tight round the Helwan's trigger. The defile curved left, then right, then sharp left again. As it did so its walls suddenly fell away and he found himself standing on the edge of a huge open space ringed by cliffs – a vast natural amphitheatre tucked under the southern flank of the Gebel el-Shalul.

'*Allah-u-akhbar,*' he murmured.

High above, the *gebel* tops still glowed a warm orange in the late afternoon sun. Down here twilight was already firmly established, the colours bled to a dull yellowy-grey, the cracks and fissures plugged with shadow. Heaps of shattered rock and gravel lay piled against the base of the cliffs – the detritus, he guessed, of five centuries of mining. Directly to his left a vaguely symmetrical scatter of stone blocks suggested the remains of ancient huts. Other than that, and a lot of pottery sherds mixed with the sand of the amphitheatre floor, there was nothing – no buildings, no machinery, no equipment, no indication whatsoever that there had been any sort of industrial activity here recently.

No mine either, so far as he could see. The tracks emerged from the defile behind him, wound themselves into a tangled spaghetti across the amphitheatre floor – presumably as the vehicles that had made them turned around – then exited again. There was no obvious reason for their presence.

He surveyed the scene, trying to figure out what was going on, then walked forward, minuscule as an ant in a football stadium. He reached the centre of the space. For a brief instant he thought he caught a distant hum of machinery, a barely audible growl right out at the very edge of hearing. It was gone the moment he tried to tune into it. He dipped his head, listening. He couldn't pick it up again and assumed he must have imagined it. Raising his eyes, he scanned the rock faces. Nothing. No doorways, no caves, no openings of any description. Just bare stone.

He rotated through 360 degrees, then trudged to the far side of the space and clambered up one of the rock heaps to give himself a better view of the ground. With the greater elevation he could see that although there were tyre marks everywhere, they seemed to be particularly concentrated around the cliff face on the northern side of the amphitheatre. He stared in that direction, peering into the thickening gloom. Still he could see nothing to explain why the trucks should be out here. A minute passed and he was about to turn away when a sudden breeze wafted across his face, funnelling in through the gorge. He caught a flicker of movement. Or at least thought he did. It only lasted a fraction of a second and then everything was still. He leant forward, eyes straining. Another waft, another flicker, right at the base of the cliff, as if the rock was shifting. Rippling.

'What the . . .?'

He came down off the slope and started towards it, still not certain if he had actually seen anything or it was merely the twilight playing tricks. Thirty metres from the cliff he stopped and called out.

'*Salaam-alaam-alaam-alaam!*'

His voice ricocheted around the amphitheatre. It drew no response. No more movement either, although now he was close he did notice that a rectangular-shaped section of wall down at the foot of the cliff seemed to have a slightly different hue to the rest of the stone. A slightly different texture as well. As if someone . . .

'Clever. *Very* clever.'

Slipping the Helwan into the back of his trousers, he marched over. He surveyed the cliff. Then, reaching up, he closed his hands around the rock and yanked. There was a heavy fluttering sound as a canvas tarpaulin detached from its mounts and tumbled to the ground at his feet. Behind, crudely but effectively concealed – viewed from anywhere other than up close, the yellowish material would have been indistinguishable from the surrounding rock – was a pair of large steel doors secured with a chain and padlock. On the rock face above, deeply incised, was a single-word inscription. Khalifa's hieroglyphs weren't what they had once been, but this wasn't too difficult. Particularly with the god determinative.

Wesir. Osiris.

'Gotcha,' he whispered.

He gave the doors a tug, then pulled out his gun, aimed and shot the lock off. The retort thundered around the rock walls, causing half a dozen swifts to lift skywards in alarm. For a brief moment he thought he caught the sound of machinery again. Or a motor. Something mechanical. It was impossible to tell where it was coming from, if indeed it *was* coming from anywhere and wasn't just his imagination playing games with him. He listened, but couldn't pick it up again. Imagination. Had to be. He shook his head, grasped one of the door handles and pulled.

The steel panel rolled back and the Labyrinth opened before him.

JERUSALEM

Ben-Roi had been on the phone to Sarah when Khalifa called, asking if she wanted him to pick anything up on the way over for dinner.

The moment he got the Egyptian's message, he hit callback. Now it was Khalifa's phone that was on voicemail. The greeting was in Arabic, a female voice – Khalifa must have borrowed the handset. A satellite phone, Ben-Roi guessed, if it was getting a signal in the middle of the desert. He left a message of his own, expressing concern that Khalifa had gone out to the mine alone, urging him to be careful and not take any unnecessary risks.

'Call me as soon as you get this,' he concluded. 'As *soon* as you get this. I'll be waiting.'

He rang off. Across the room Dov Zisky had broken from his inquiries into Dinah Levi and swivelled to face him.

'What was all that about?'

Ben-Roi explained. Zisky's eyebrows lifted.

'You think he'll be all right?'

'I hope so. He's a good friend and I'd hate to think . . .'

Ben-Roi didn't say what he'd hate to think. He glanced at the wall clock – just past six – and folded his arms. He wasn't due at Sarah's for another hour and a half, and was expecting to hear back from Khalifa long before then.

Across the room Zisky turned away, reached for his cell and started thumbing in a text.

GEBEL EL-SHALUL

Khalifa stepped into the mine. Clicking on his torch, he played the beam around.

He was in a large chamber. An *enormous* chamber, deep and cave-like, although the tell-tale ripples of ancient chisel marks on the ceiling and walls indicated that the space was man-made rather than natural. Bat guano caked the floor; there was a strong smell of ammonia. Pulling a handkerchief from his pocket, he held it to his nose and walked forward a few paces.

Tunnels opened to left and right, half a dozen on each side – forbidding tubes of blackness fanning out from the central core of the chamber as though gigantic maggots had gone burrowing off into the rock in search of food. Some were at ground level, others higher up. Beneath one of the upper tunnels, an ancient access ladder was still propped against the wall. Khalifa ran the torch across its leather-bound rungs. They looked as sturdy as the day three millennia previously when the last feet had trod them. Dropping the beam, he speared the passage below. There were doorways in there, a lot of doorways – he counted nine before the beam was swallowed by the gloom. According to Pinsker's diagrams, they gave into a warren of rooms and cells where the mine's slave workforce had been housed. A nightmarish troglodytic existence where life expectancy would have been numbered in months, if not weeks. Khalifa circled the torch, picking out scrawls of ancient graffiti on the walls, a row of earthenware storage jars, an upturned wicker basket. Then, withdrawing the beam, he aimed it across the chamber towards the gaping rectangular hole on the far side.

The entrance to the mine's main gallery.

Aside from the sliding doors, he had so far seen nothing to suggest any modern activity in the mine. Here at the gallery mouth, there was clear evidence, although not the sort he was expecting. Still with the handkerchief pressed against his face, he walked across the chamber, the torch held out in front of him, puffs of guano lifting around his feet.

Most of the opening was taken up by a large steel platform. Some sort of loading dock was his immediate thought, since it was about the height of the back of a lorry, and the tyre marks ran through the mine doors and right up to it. Bolted to the top of the platform, a couple of metres apart, was a pair of L-shaped tracks. They sloped down on to the gallery floor – like a slide without a bottom – and from there ran off into blackness.

Khalifa swayed the torch beam around, then ducked underneath the platform into the gallery itself, standing in the gap between the tracks, which ran close to the gallery walls. Something, it seemed, was being brought up from below. Rolled or winched along the rails on to the platform, and then loaded on to lorries and driven away. Ore? Gold? He had no idea. He went forward a few paces. Blackness smothered him – a blackness so dense he could actually feel it, as though he was pushing his way through cobwebs. Shapes skimmed and fluttered below – bats, startled by the sudden illumination. The tracks kept on going. He took another few paces. Still the tracks went on. Pinsker had paced the gallery and estimated it went down almost a mile. Did the tracks go all the way to the bottom? He had no idea, although something told him they did. That whatever was being brought up was coming from the mine's deepest levels. And to find out what it was, he was going to have to go down there.

He backed up. His heart was pounding, his breath coming in short, fast gasps.

He didn't spook easily. Darkness, confined spaces – they'd never fazed him. Numerous times he'd gone off on his own exploring the more obscure tombs in the hills around the Valley of the Kings – tombs that no tourists ever visited and that you had to go down on your hands and knees, if not your belly, to get into. He enjoyed the excitement.

Not today. Today he was badly spooked. As spooked as he'd ever been. There was something forbidding about the blackness, about the weight of rock all around, the bewildering catacomb of tunnels with their lingering air of human misery. More than forbidding. Threatening. The whole mine felt . . . malevolent.

He backed away further, right out of the gallery and into the mine's entrance chamber. And then all the way across to the doors.

In the ten minutes he'd been inside it had grown noticeably darker outside. It still felt bright compared to the blackness he'd just experienced. He gulped air.

He couldn't do it. Couldn't go down there. Not on his own. Five metres had been bad enough. To descend a mile – impossible. He'd go home, return another day. With colleagues, backup. He knew where the mine was now, knew how to get here. Rivka Kleinberg, Barren Corporation, Zoser Freight – the answers could wait. Would have to wait because there was no way on God's earth . . .

He went back in. Crossing to the platform, he ducked underneath and into the gallery again. If anything the darkness felt even more malign, as if the air itself was warning him away. He swished the torch back and forth, slashing at the gloom, wondering how the hell Samuel Pinsker had coped – what sort of obsessive madness it was that had not only drawn the Englishman into the mine, but kept him down here alone for weeks on end, creeping round in pitch blackness painstakingly mapping and recording the place. The idea of it made Khalifa feel sick.

He swished the torch some more. Slices of wall and ceiling momentarily revealed themselves before sinking back into impenetrable shadow. A minute went by, two, the only sounds the laboured rasp of his breathing and the occasional flutter of bat wings below. Then, wincing, as if he was about to thrust his hand into the middle of a flame, he pocketed the handkerchief, pulled his gun from the back of his trousers and started forward between the tracks.

'Allah protect me,' he chanted, 'Allah watch over me, Allah be my light.'

He went cautiously to start with, taking it a few steps at a time, shuffling reluctantly down the gallery's sloping incline. He turned frequently, looking back up at the barely discernible whisper of light coming in from the mine entrance. Every cell in his body urged him to turn and sprint back up to it. He fought the urge and kept going. When, after a couple of hundred metres, the light disappeared, he upped his pace, anxious to get to wherever the tracks were leading and out again as quickly as possible.

'Allah protect me, Allah watch over me, Allah be my light.'

Other tunnels and passages opened off to either side. He tried to count them, but there were so many he soon abandoned the attempt. Some sloped up, some down, some were almost as large as the main gallery, others barely wide enough to accommodate a single person. According to Pinsker's notebook they branched and divided into other tunnels and passages, which then branched and divided in their turn as the Labyrinth fingered its way outward through the rock, growing and spreading and multiplying like some monstrous self-replicating organism. The thought of it made him shudder. It was bad enough here in the gallery, which at least held a straight line. The idea of venturing off that line, losing his bearings in the impossibly tangled web of passages all around . . . he forced the scenario out of his head. Pinsker might have been fool enough to go exploring, but he, Khalifa, would not be deviating a single centimetre from his current path. Down, up, out again. The faster the better.

'Allah protect me, Allah watch over me, Allah be my light.'

Several times the tracks cut through cavernous chambers like the one at the entrance to the mine – vast subterranean rooms with pillars chiselled out of the bare rock and ceilings that still bore the smoke stains of ancient torches. Once, passing a deep side-gallery, he glimpsed a hole in the ground like a pool of black ink (Pinsker had noted just such a hole – he had lowered a rope and weight down it, but after two hundred feet still hadn't managed to locate the bottom).

On more than one occasion he thought he was going to have to go back, such was the sense of dread he felt building inside him. There was something bad down there, he could feel it. Something wicked. Something he absolutely shouldn't be walking towards. Twice he actually turned on his heel and started back towards the surface, only to force himself round and continue his descent.

And always the dark enveloped him, and the rock pressed in, and the tracks went down, deeper and deeper into the bowels of the earth.

'Allah protect me, Allah watch over me, Allah be my light.'

The gallery began to slope more steeply. The air became hotter, odd drips and trickles of water appeared on the walls. A vague odour of rusting metal insinuated itself alongside the acrid ammonia of bat droppings.

And, also, another odour, one that he couldn't immediately place. Only as it grew stronger did he realize what it was – garlic. It intensified the further he descended, filling his nostrils, overpowering everything else. As a child, growing up in the shadow of the Pyramids, his mother used to hang garlic over their front door to ward off the djinns that lurked around the ancient monuments. And now he could smell it down here. In a mine. Where there was absolutely no reason for it to be. Its presence spooked him even more than the blackness and the bewildering maze of passages and tunnels.

Disoriented him too. Made him wonder if perhaps his mind was starting to turn. If there was no such smell and it was simply a phantom odour conjured up by the suggestive power of terror.

And the moment he started to doubt himself on this point, other doubts began to creep in. Was that a faint tap-tapping he could hear down in the depths, or just the echo of his footsteps? Whispers in the dark, or simply the rush of his own breath? He thought he caught the sound of machinery again; several times he was absolutely certain he saw figures moving in the side-tunnels. Shadowy, indeterminate shapes flitting on the margins of sight. The moment he tried to catch them in his torch beam they were gone. The same when he tried to focus on the sounds. Only the smell of garlic withstood scrutiny. It was definitely there. He wasn't imagining it. And getting stronger. As was the pounding in his temples. And the thudding of his heart. And the conviction that something dreadful was waiting for him down there in the dark.

Still he kept going, fighting himself every inch of the way, his desire to know what was going on only just outweighing the raging terror he felt. Down and down into the pit until eventually, after what felt like hours but was, according to his watch, less than thirty minutes, his torch suddenly picked out something ahead.

The gallery was now sloping so steeply that runs of steps had been cut into the rock to aid descent. He stopped and squatted. Holding out the torch, he swayed the beam, trying to make out what was down there. Whatever it was, it was right at the very limit of the torch's reach and he couldn't see it clearly.

'Hello!'

His voice sounded dull, heavy. As if something was blocking the passage, preventing any echo.

'Hello!'

Nothing.

He shuffled down another two steps. The garlic smell had become so intense he was finding it hard to breathe. It would have been more comfortable with the handkerchief over his mouth and nose, but he couldn't hold the handkerchief while at the same time keeping his gun pointed, and he wasn't going to leave himself defenceless, so he put up with the stench.

'Hello!'

Still he couldn't get a clear sense of what was down there, although there seemed to be shapes of some sort, curved edges looming in the murk. It looked like they filled the entire gallery, from floor to ceiling. And the tracks ran right into them. A rock fall? He descended one more step, really having to force himself, the blackness seeming to push him back. The beam picked out something round, like a wheel, and the outline of some sort of crumpled rim or hoop. Unmistakably man-made.

'What the . . . ?'

He reached his foot on to the next step. Tentatively, as if dipping a toe into icy water. At the same time he arched his body back, fearful that something was going to come flying up at him. It didn't. Reassured, he started to lean forward only to tense suddenly. Spinning, he dropped to one knee and aimed his gun into the dark.

Somewhere above, way in the distance, he could hear machinery. Or a motor. Something mechanical.

He'd clocked strange sounds down here before, but they'd evaporated the moment he tried to home in on them. This time, having started, the sound continued – an eerie puttering growl that seemed to float on the air as if the Labyrinth itself was groaning. He listened, ears straining, the torch beam juddering from the trembling of his hand. It was impossible to pinpoint the sound's origin. Above, that was all he could say for certain. Back the way he had come. He

401

gave it a minute, his breath a succession of heaving, arrhythmic gasps. Then, no longer caring what was causing the blockage down below, no longer caring about anything other than getting out of the mine, he stood and started back up the gallery.

He covered twenty metres and stopped. The growl was still there, no louder, no softer. He went on, stopped again. Still he could hear it, although now it was accompanied by another sound. A sort of muted, rumbling clatter, as of distant wheels on rails. He jabbed his torch beam at the darkness, freaked, trying to figure out what was going on, cursing himself for ever having come down here. The clatter seemed to grow louder. Not dramatically so, but definitely louder. For a moment he stood rooted to the spot, his nerves so stretched he felt like his entire body was going to snap. Then, stepping to the right, he put his foot on the track. A faint vibration echoed up his leg. He did the same on the other track. Here too the metal seemed to buzz beneath his shoe. Something was coming towards him. Something big, to judge by the steadily increasing volume of its approach. He backed up, aimed his gun, put his foot on the track again. In five seconds the vibration had grown appreciably stronger. Whatever it was was coming down fast.

'Allah-u-akhbar,' he hissed.

He wheeled the torch. To his left, a wall of rock. To his right, a side-passage, one of the narrow ones, little more than a metre wide and not much taller than he himself was. He wondered if he should duck into it, but it looked so cramped, so claustrophobic, so malevolent, that he couldn't bring himself to do it. Couldn't bring himself to do anything other than stand there between the rails with the gun and the torch held out in front of him, frozen like a rabbit in a set of car headlights. Beside him the tracks started to tremble.

'Stop!' he shouted. And then, louder: 'Stop! Police!'

It was a ludicrous command, comic in its impotence. The clattering was now so loud he could barely hear his own voice. If there were people riding whatever it was that was descending – some sort of mine wagon was his best guess – they wouldn't have had a hope in hell of hearing him. And even if they did, what were they going to do? Stop and hold their hands up? Say sorry and let him arrest them? Crazy. But then terror makes you do crazy things. He shouted again, and again, waving the torch in the hope that the beam would be spotted, that they would clock there was someone down here.

'The tunnel's blocked!' he bellowed. 'Stop now! Police! It's blocked!'

Nothing. The clattering grew louder, and then louder still. Deafeningly loud, like an entire freight train was barrelling down the slope towards him. The tracks heaved, straining at the bolts securing them to the gallery floor. It was close now. Very close. He shouted yet again, really screaming. Then, in desperation, he closed his finger around the Helwan's trigger and shot into the darkness, aiming low. Still the thing kept coming. He loosed off another shot. No effect. The entire gallery shook. The darkness in front of him seemed to bulge like a rising wave. Two more shots and suddenly there was movement at the limit of his torch beam. Hurtling movement. He had a split second to register what looked like a large cylinder or roller careering down the tracks towards him before he leapt sideways into the narrow tunnel.

He misjudged the distance. The tip of his shoe snagged on the right-hand track. He stumbled, sprawled, fell forward into the tunnel mouth. Instinctively he threw out a hand to break his fall. The torch clattered from his grasp and went out, plunging him into blackness. Frantically he fumbled for it, pawing the ground while a few centimetres behind him whatever the thing was tore past with a thunderous roar.

Except that it didn't go past. It kept on coming. Or else more of them kept on coming – in the blackness he couldn't tell whether it was a single entity or a whole succession of objects, one behind the other. For a brief, confused moment he found himself thinking that maybe it was some sort of gigantic earth-moving apparatus that had been sent down to clear the obstruction below. If it was, it wasn't up to the task because four seconds later there was a booming, ear-splitting percussion of crumpling metal as the thing, or things, slammed head-on into the blockage and, by the sound of it, came to a jarring halt. The whole mine seemed to lurch. Showers of dust and rock fragments rained down on him. The noise continued, increasing in volume and violence as more and more of whatever it was surged past behind him and crashed into the pile-up further down the gallery. Panic-stricken, he flailed for the torch, furiously sweeping his hand back and forth across the floor, pleading with Allah to let him find it. His prayers went unanswered, and with the sounds of collision slowly backing up towards him he had no choice but to leave the light and drag himself deeper into the tunnel out of harm's way.

A couple of metres in he rolled over and scrambled on to his feet. Blackness enveloped him. He fumbled out a hand and pressed it against the tunnel wall to steady himself, stood there listening as all around him the mine reverberated to the clatter of descent, and the crunch and thud of impacting metal. He had no concept what was going on, was as blind as Iman el-Badri. Something – a lot of things – was coming down from above and crashing, that's all he could say for sure. And, also, the point of collision was moving in his direction as the gallery rapidly filled with wreckage. Closer and closer it came, louder and louder, stronger and stronger the vibrations of the rock beneath his feet, as though he was standing blindfold beside a highway while in front of him the mother of all car pile-ups unfolded.

And then, suddenly, the sounds became more muffled and moved away to his right, further up the gallery. The vibrations gradually diminished, the noise dwindled, although it was still there.

For almost a minute he stood rooted to the spot, mummified in blackness. Then, trembling, choking at the stench of garlic, which was now so overpowering it made his eyes water, he inched forward a few paces and reached out a hand.

It touched metal.

'Oh God.'

He felt up, and then down. More of the same. Bulges and edges. And, also, some sort of fine, powdery dust spilling out through cracks in the metal.

Barrels, that's what it was. Huge barrels. They'd rolled down from above, slammed into each other, crumpled, split, spilled their contents.

More to the point, they'd filled the tunnel mouth. Top to bottom, side to side, with not even a crack to squeeze his fingers through. As solid as a cell door. A locked cell door. In a maximum security prison.

He was alone, and frightened, and incarcerated in the blackness of the Labyrinth.

JERUSALEM

By 6.45 Ben-Roi was getting worried.

He called Khalifa, got voicemail, left a message. He called again

404

fifteen minutes later, and again twenty minutes after that. Messages both times. No response.

By the time he pitched up at Sarah's at 7.45 he was seriously worried.

'Something smells good,' he said as she led him into the flat, sneaking a look at his mobile.

'Lamb *cholent*.'

'On a Tuesday?'

'If you're going to get all *frumm* about it, I'll call out for pizza.'

He took her arm, turned her towards him, kissed her on the nose. Lamb *cholent* was his favourite. She'd made an effort. And not just with the cooking. She looked fabulous. Hair brushed long, hint of perfume, baby bump curving through the material of her dress – as good as he'd ever seen her. He'd been intending to make an effort himself – she'd bought him a Ted Baker shirt for his last birthday and he'd planned to wear that. Splash on a bit of his best aftershave as well. What with the whole Khalifa thing he hadn't had time to go home and change. Hadn't even had time to buy her flowers. He threw another glance down at his phone . Nothing. What the hell was going on?

'There's beer in the fridge,' she said as they went through into the kitchen. 'Or wine if you prefer.'

'Beer's great.'

He opened the fridge, pulled out a bottle.

'You want one?'

She shot him a look, pointed at the bump.

'Of course. Sorry.'

He popped the lid and took a swig. Sarah bustled around the stove. There was music playing in the living room. Joni Mitchell. *Blue*. The first CD he'd ever bought her. She really was making an effort. He tried to focus.

'Bubu OK?' he asked.

'All good. You want to . . .'

She turned her tummy towards him. He came over and pressed a hand against it.

'The more I think about that name you came up with, the more I like it,' she said.

'Me too.'

'How about Iris if it's a girl?'

He cringed. Iris had been the name of the hooker he'd talked to down in Neve Sha'anan.

'Maybe not,' she said, reading his expression. 'I'll keep thinking.'

She pressed her hand against his. Their eyes met and she smiled.

'It's good to have you here, Arieh.'

'It's good to be here. Really good.'

They stood a moment, Ben-Roi's hand involuntarily closing around the mobile in his jeans pocket. Then she came up on tiptoe and kissed him. Just a quick peck, but on the lips. Tweaking his earlobe, she turned back to the stove and stirred a pot.

'Why don't you go out on the balcony? I'm almost done here. You can light the candles while you're out there.'

She threw him a box of matches. He caught them, told her again how good it was to be here – hoping the repetition would make up for the fact that he hadn't even bothered to put on clean clothes – and took himself outside. There was a neatly laid table with flowers and candles, napkins, a bowl of olives, a basket of pitta breads. By the look of it he wasn't the only one who was thinking about the two of them starting over.

He snaffled a couple of olives, lit the candles, swigged his beer. Then, easing the door closed with his foot, he pulled out his mobile and belled Khalifa again.

'I'm getting worried here. Seriously worried. Call me as soon as you get this. OK?'

He rang off. Sarah came out.

'You're looking guilty,' she said.

'Only 'cos I'm having inappropriate thoughts about you,' he lied, sliding the mobile into his back pocket.

She laughed and threw her arms round his neck.

'I think it's going to be a good evening.'

'Me too. A really good evening.'

He returned the embrace, pulling her close, telling her how beautiful she looked.

And all the while he was thinking about the Labyrinth and willing his mobile to ring.

THE LABYRINTH

Khalifa spent thirty minutes heaving and kicking at the barrels blocking the tunnel entrance. He didn't move them an inch. The force of the collision had driven them into one another, as good as fusing them. Even if by some miracle he *had* managed to get one loose, it wouldn't have made much difference. The ongoing whump and thud of colliding metal – still audible, although barely – told him that the mine's main gallery must now be blocked to a distance of at least a hundred metres from where he was, if not more. Hundreds, perhaps thousands of barrels walling him in. He would have had more chance of clawing his way out through the bare rock. He was going to have to find a different way.

If there was one.

'Help!' he screamed, throat burning from the acrid stench of garlic, which seemed to be coming from the dust inside the barrels. 'Help! Please, help! Help!'

Futile. But then desperate people do futile things. And the idea of fumbling his way blindly through the Labyrinth was just so unbearable . . .

He turned, facing down the tunnel. The darkness was so dense, so impenetrable, it was somehow beyond colour. An absolute void against which even the deepest shade of black would have looked pale. He flailed out a hand. Once, twice, three times. Then, slowly, he started shuffling forward, the distant, metronomic thud of colliding barrels seeming to echo the pounding of his heart.

So deep are its shafts, so numerous its galleries, so bewildering its complexity, that to step through its doorway is to be lost entirely and Daedalus himself would be confounded.

He went a step at a time, dabbing at the floor with his foot, fearful there might be another hole like the one he'd seen way back up the gallery. The tunnel was narrow, somewhere between a metre and a metre and a half wide and just over a couple of metres high. He swept his left hand in front of him, gripped the Helwan with his right. Pointless, given that he couldn't see a damn thing, but the feel of the gun at least gave him a crumb of comfort. And in his current predicament he needed all the crumbs he could get.

The passage ran dead straight. The floor was flat, the walls felt neatly chiselled, like the tombs in the Valley of the Kings. There were no side-tunnels, or at least none that he could find. Part of him was relieved. Side-tunnels meant decisions, complexity, the possibility of getting lost, tangled in the Labyrinth's fiendish web.

Part of him was concerned, however. And the concern grew with every faltering step he took. To have any hope of getting out, of navigating his way through the maze, it was crucial that he stayed as close as he could to the line of the main gallery. And the tunnel seemed to be taking him further and further from that line, deeper and deeper into the unknown.

There wasn't much he could do about it, and so he just pushed on, inching his way forward, the only sounds the terrified pull of his breath and, from somewhere in the far distance, the continuing pulse of impacting barrels. Once, his hand brushed some sort of shallow, fist-sized cavity in the otherwise flat wall. A little further on his foot crunched on something, which when he bent down to investigate, he discovered were the fragments of a shattered jar or pot. Other than that he encountered no other features, no other objects. Nothing but the floor, the walls and the suffocating, all-consuming darkness.

And then, suddenly, the tunnel ended.

'Oh God, no.'

Sliding the Helwan into the back of his trousers, he felt with both hands. In front of him was solid rock. He patted left, right, up to the ceiling, down to the floor. There were no gaps, not even a crack. It was a dead end.

He patted again, and again, exploring every inch of the wall. Then, turning, he slumped back against it and slid to the ground. As he did so the muted thump of barrels finally ceased. A deathly, sepulchral silence descended. He brought up his knees and wrapped his arms round them.

He was buried alive.

JERUSALEM

Starters was Sarah's homemade *baba ghanoush*, another of Ben-Roi's favourites. They turned off the living-room lights, sat out on the balcony with just the candles. There were stars in the sky; the scent of magnolia blossom drifted up from the garden beneath. Joni Mitchell had given way to Etti Ankri.

It would have been perfect if he hadn't been so damned worried.

'Looks like the play scheme's shutting down,' she said, picking a pitta from the basket and tearing it in half.

He'd sneaked the cell phone into his hand under the table, was snatching glances at the display. He looked up at this.

'Oh no!'

She swirled the pitta through the dip.

'It's been on the cards for a while. And we heard today our major donor's dropping out.'

'You can't find another one?'

'Not in the current climate. Reconciliation's dropped way down the agenda.'

'I'm so sorry.'

She shrugged, nibbled on the corner of the pitta.

'In a weird sense, part of me's relieved. It's been like watching someone you love slowly die. Kinder to put it out of its misery. We've got maybe a month's grace, then we'll—'

'Hava Nagila' blasted from Ben-Roi's lap. He whipped out his phone, his focus zeroing in on the screen. It was only his friend Shmuel. Across the table Sarah was looking at him. Not angry. Not even annoyed. Just . . . disappointed.

'I'm sorry,' he said, letting the call go to voicemail.

She reached out a hand, twined her fingers with his.

'Just for tonight I thought you might turn it off, Arieh. You did it before. You're strong enough. I know you are. Come on, fight the urge. Resist! Resist!'

She was trying to make a joke of it. Which made him feel even worse. He squeezed her hand.

'Listen, Sarah, I don't want to make a big thing of this, and I don't want it to get in the way of tonight, but I think my friend Khalifa might be in trouble. I'm going to put the phone here . . .'

He made a show of laying it in the middle of the table.

'And if anyone rings but him, *anyone*, I swear to God I won't answer it. And the moment he does ring, the phone's off and you can do whatever you want with the damn thing. Flush it down the toilet, for all I care.'

Something in her eyes said she'd heard it all before, didn't believe him. She blinked it away and pushed a smile across her face.

'Sounds like a fair deal to me.'

He gave her hand another squeeze. Then, half standing, he leant over the table and kissed her head.

'Thanks for being you,' he said.

'Thanks for being *you*. Even if "you" is the most infuriating man I've ever met.'

He chuckled at that and sat back down. As he did so, his gaze jinked towards the phone's display, just to check.

'Eat up,' she said. 'Or the *cholent*'ll need reheating.'

THE LABYRINTH

Khalifa had no idea how long he sat there at the end of the tunnel, his head pressed into his knees, his arms clasped round his legs, despair enveloping him as absolutely as the blackness of the mine. It might have been a couple of minutes, it might have been a couple of hours. It might even have been a couple of days. Down here, time seemed to have no meaning.

Eventually, though, he unwrapped his arms and pulled himself back on to his feet. He stood a moment, a distant snatch of conversation echoing on the margins of his memory, something he had once said to someone in a situation almost as bleak as this (*Trust in God, Miss Mullray. Trust in anything. But never despair*).

Then, turning, he again patted his hands across the rock at the tunnel end. Up, down, side to side. It was as solid as it had been however long ago it was that he'd first banged into it. No cracks, no gaps, no way through. A dead end. In every sense of the word.

He slammed a fist against the stone. If this had been a film, he thought, some sort of concealed doorway would have sprung open at this point. Then he started to feel his way down the side of the tunnel, sweeping his hands methodically from floor to ceiling on the million-to-one chance he'd missed a side-passage on the way down. He knew he hadn't. Even in pitch blackness the walls were too close together for him not to have sensed an opening if there'd been one. Anything, however, was better than just sitting there counting off the minutes and the hours and the days until death eventually stepped in to put him out of his misery. Like Samuel Pinsker must have counted them off. He didn't want to die like Samuel Pinsker. He didn't want to die, period.

He fell into a sort of rhythm. Shuffle a few centimetres, down on his knees, palms against the wall, caress his way up, stand on tiptoes, touch the ceiling, shuffle a few centimetres, down on his knees, palms against the wall, caress his way up . . .

He didn't need to be so thorough, to explore every single millimetre of rock, but there was something vaguely soothing in the action. And, also, by taking it slowly, he was putting off the moment when he had to acknowledge once and for all that he was doomed. While there was wall left to explore, there was still hope. Only the tiniest flicker of it, but hope nonetheless. When he'd covered every inch of the tunnel and still not found a way out – that's when he'd give in to despair.

Shuffle a few centimetres, down on his knees, palms against the wall, caress his way up . . .

He reached the scatter of broken pottery he'd encountered before – thick, chunky shards, presumably from some sort of large storage jar – and then, a few metres past it, creeping his hands up from the floor, a shallow cavity in the stone. He'd come across a similar cavity on his way down the tunnel, although he seemed to remember that one being at shoulder height, and this was only at the level of his knee. Or maybe it was the same cavity and it was just his memory playing tricks on him. In the Stygian blackness it was impossible to be certain of any of his senses. He paused, exploring the hole with his fingertips. It was only a couple of centimetres deep, more an indentation than a hole, and had a rounded, scooped sort of feel to it. He distinctly recalled the other cavity being deeper and more uneven, which confirmed to him they were two different features. He moved his hands further up the wall. They touched another indentation – this one at hip-height – and another (chest-height), and a fourth, about level with his shoulder. This *was* the one he'd touched before, he was sure of it – same depth, same lumpy feel to its lower lip. Four depressions in the otherwise flat, neatly chiselled wall, one above the other. Interesting.

He crept his hands higher, hit the ceiling, felt across it, found . . .

A hole.

Suddenly his pulse was hammering. Standing on tiptoe, he traced the hole's outline with his fingertips. It was square, roughly half a metre by half a metre. Neatly cut. Right in the middle of the ceiling. Like the bottom end of a chimney flue. He must have walked right under it when he came down the tunnel before.

He jumped and thrust a hand up into it. He couldn't touch rock. He fumbled his way back down the passage and returned with a handful of pottery shards. He launched them upwards, one by one. The flue seemed to go up quite a distance. Another dead end? Or an escape route. Either way it was academic because after an initial surge of excitement he realized there was no way he was ever going to be able to get himself up into it.

Unless . . .

Stepping across to the opposite wall he ran his hand across its surface, top to bottom. His fingertips brushed four more cavities. Same size as the ones on the other side, and at pretty much the same height.

Like an explosion of light, a memory burst into his head. Something he'd seen six, seven years ago. In the Valley of the Kings His Antiquities Service friend Ginger had taken him and Ali on a tour of some of the closed tombs. On the way through the centre of the valley, Ginger had stopped to point out the vertical shaft of Tomb KV56, recently cleared by a team of British archaeologists. On either side of the shaft, shallow depressions had been cut into the rock walls.

'Footholds,' Ginger had explained when Khalifa pointed them out. 'The ancient workers would stand astride the shaft and use them to climb down and up. Like spiders in a pipe. Easy if you've got long legs.'

Khalifa didn't have long legs. What he lacked in physique, however, he more than made up for in brute desperation. Jamming the Helwan deeper into the waistband of his trousers, he shuffled himself astride until his feet were touching the passage walls. It was a stretch, but he could just about do it – had the tunnel been even a few centimetres wider it would have been too much for him. He settled the tip of his left shoe into the lowest of the left-hand slots. Then, pressing his fingers against the rock for balance, he murmured a quick prayer and hopped his right foot up. He missed the corresponding cavity and stumbled forward. He tried again, and again, finally made it on the fourth attempt. For a moment he stood there, his legs bridging the tunnel, the muscles of his groin screaming in protest at the unaccustomed posture. Then he inched his left foot up to the next depression. He hit it, got his right foot up, lost his balance, fell.

'Yalla!' he hissed, knowing this was realistically his only chance of getting out of the tunnel and if he didn't take it he was dead. 'Yalla!

On the next go he got up slightly higher before falling. The go after that he actually managed to get his arms and head into the hole before his legs gave and he crashed back down. Refusing to accept defeat, he launched yet another attempt, ignoring the agony in his thighs, the scouring stench of garlic, the trickle of blood running down his temple from where he'd cut it in his last fall – channelling his entire being into the task of getting up those four depressions and into the shaft.

And this time he made it. He reached the uppermost of the footholds, found a slot cut into the shaft wall, heaved himself up. He found another slot, and then another, heaved and scrambled. And then he was out of the tunnel and into the flue.

'*Hamdulillah, hamdulillah, hamdulillah.*'

He gave himself a moment, legs braced against the flue wall. Then he started to climb. Deep foot- and hand-holds had been cut into the wall at regular intervals and he was able to ascend without too much trouble, moving from one slot to the next as though mounting a ladder. Always at the back of his mind was the fear that the shaft would be another dead end. He didn't dwell on it, just kept going through the blackness, taking it slowly, testing each hold before transferring his weight to it, aware that a fall would mean broken limbs and certain death. Once a bat fluttered down from above and straight into his face. Once he found himself pushing through something soft and gauzy which he assumed must be a spider's web. Otherwise the shaft was mercifully clear and, after a climb of some twenty metres, the walls suddenly fell away and he was clambering out of the hole into some sort of open space. Crawling forward a metre, he slumped face down on to a flat, dusty floor, his relief at escaping from the passage tempered by the knowledge that he was still very much a prisoner of the Labyrinth.

JERUSALEM

Ben-Roi tried. He really did. She meant so much to him, she'd made such an effort to make the evening special. To give the two of them another chance. The three of them.

All his thoughts, however, were on Khalifa. Sarah would be talking, telling him something about the baby, something intimate, and his gaze would keep wandering down to the phone display, willing it to light up. She'd disappear into the kitchen to fetch something and the moment her back was turned the mobile would be in his hand and he'd be leaving Khalifa yet another message, pleading with him to get in touch.

He tried. He really did. But his attention was elsewhere. And Sarah could see it. See it as clearly as if it was flashing from a neon hoarding above his head. She didn't say anything. She didn't make a scene about it. Around 9.30, however, as she was clearing away the remains of the almond cake she'd baked for dessert – yet another of Ben-Roi's favourite dishes – she called time on the evening.

'Go home, Arieh,' she said. 'Or go to the office, go for a walk – go somewhere you can concentrate on what you need to concentrate on.'

'But it's still early. I thought we could . . .'

'You're not here, Arieh. If your friend's in trouble, I think you should be somewhere you can focus on that. Not sitting around making small talk with me.'

He tried to remonstrate, to persuade her to at least let him stay long enough to help wash up, but she was adamant. Not angry adamant, or bitter adamant. Sad adamant. The saddest he'd ever seen her. The chance had gone. The last chance, something told him.

He pocketed his phone and accompanied her to the front door. As she showed him out he tried to kiss her. She angled her face, offering him her cheek.

'I'm sorry,' he said.

'Me too.'

'I had a good time.'

She didn't match that. She allowed him to kiss the curve of her stomach, voiced a hope that Khalifa was OK. Then stepping back, she closed the door.

'I'll call,' he shouted.

No response. He couldn't be sure, but he thought he caught a muffled sob.

THE LABYRINTH

'Salaam!'

Khalifa's voice echoed. By the sound of it, he was in some sort of large cave or chamber. Like the ones he'd passed through on his way

414

down the mine's main gallery. He dipped his head, trying to recall anything similar in Samuel Pinsker's diagrams. He couldn't. He shuffled a few paces forward, arms stretched in front of him like a blind man, then shuffled back. Fumbling in his pocket, he pulled out his handkerchief and spread it on the floor beside the rim of the shaft. When he'd climbed up from below, he'd been facing towards the gallery and he positioned the handkerchief against the shaft edge pointing in that direction. In the tunnel, with two straight walls to either side, it had been easy to keep track of where he was in relation to the mine's primary axis. Here, with no immediate features to guide him, it was going to be a lot harder. The handkerchief would at least provide a point of reference.

He patted the material down, making sure there could be no confusion as to which side of the shaft it was on. Then, straightening, he started forward again, swirling his hands through the darkness, following the line of the passage beneath, back in the direction of the main gallery.

After twenty paces he hit rock.

He felt up and down, started shuffling to the right. The walls were solid. He kept going, inching his way around the chamber, cave, whatever the hell it was. So intense was the black that within a matter of steps he'd lost all sense of where he was relative to the shaft opening. He hit a pile of rocks, picked up one of the smaller ones, threw it into the void above. A dull clack echoed overhead. High overhead, although how high he couldn't tell. He launched another rock across the chamber. Another clack. Ten metres away? Twenty? It was impossible to judge. He threw four more stones to give himself some vague sense of the dimensions of the space – it was big, that was about as precise as he could get – and continued his progress round the walls. He encountered two large earthenware pots – very large, the height of his waist. A little further on his feet crunched something that on closer investigation turned out to be bones of some small animal.

He found no doorways or openings, no exit from the place, and he was just starting to panic, to think that maybe the tunnel, the shaft and the chamber were all part of the same dead end, when he bumped into something propped against the wall.

A ladder.

He ran his hands over it. Vertical stiles, rungs, leather bindings. Solid, by the feel of it. He tested the bottom rung. Firm. He started to climb, carefully, one step at a time. Six rungs up he discovered a large opening in the wall. Just like the ones he'd seen back in the mine's entrance chamber.

'*Salaam!*'

Echoes. It was another tunnel. A way out. But which way was the way out going? And was it the only one, or were there other options?

He clambered back down. Continuing to the right, he shuffled on round the chamber walls, eventually reaching the rock pile again. There were no openings at ground level. No corners either, which told him the space was roughly circular. He felt his way back to the ladder. Dropping to his knees, he crawled across the chamber, aiming as straight as he could, sweeping his hands back and forth, searching for the top of the shaft. After a couple of minutes he hit rock. Dammit! Missed! He stood, felt his way round to the ladder again, knelt, crawled, angling slightly to the left of his previous line. This time he found the opening. The handkerchief was on its far side. Which told him that the tunnel was pointing roughly away from the main gallery. He repeated the process to make sure he'd got his bearings correct, then returned to the ladder. Removing a shoe, he placed it against the wall to mark the ladder's position. Then, hobbling in one socked foot, he started to shunt the ladder around the chamber, climbing and descending, searching for any other openings. There were none. Or at least none that he could discover. He went all the way round, reached the shoe again, put it back on. The decision had been made for him. He climbed the ladder, clambered into the tunnel and started along it, flailing his hand in front of him, keeping his head low to avoid banging it on the ceiling.

Twenty metres in – maybe more, maybe less; he was caught in a netherworld where everything was hopelessly vague and indeterminate – the ceiling lifted and he was able to stand upright. A similar distance beyond that the tunnel branched. The left fork sloped down, the right one up. He chose left, making sure he memorized the split in case he needed to retrace his steps. He descended a way, hit a set of stairs that took him up again, came to a sort of crossroads with other tunnels leading off to left and right. Again, he went left, calculating that he must now be moving roughly parallel to the main gallery, although well above it. This new tunnel ran straight before suddenly sloping steeply down and curling back on itself so that by his calculations – and with every step he was becoming less and less sure of those calculations – he was now heading further into the mine rather than back towards the entrance. A passage opened to his right. He took it, came into what felt like a room full of pillars. Doorways in each of its walls. More passages, more decisions, more complexity, more confusion.

'Oh God help me,' he choked. 'Please God help me. Please. Please.'

And all the while the blackness in his eyes, and the silence in his ears, and the slow, inexorable embrace of the Labyrinth as it coiled itself around him.

JERUSALEM

Ben-Roi went home, tried to work out what to do. About Khalifa *and* Sarah.

He'd call her tomorrow, take round flowers, plead for another chance. *Yet* another chance. Something told him it wasn't going to happen. That he'd blown it once and for all. Sure, he had an excuse for being so distracted. But then he always had excuses. There was always something, some reason why he couldn't give completely of himself. If it wasn't Khalifa it would just be some other crisis. Such was the nature of being a front-line cop. And short of stepping back from the front line and getting a desk job somewhere, or resigning from the force altogether, there was no gesture he could make that was going to resolve the impasse. She needed more from him, deserved more, and he couldn't give it. Stalemate.

He allowed himself a few moments of regretful introspection. Then, accepting that there was nothing he could do about it tonight, he pushed Sarah and the baby out of his head and focused on his immediate priority – Khalifa.

Something had happened to his friend. Something bad. He was sure of it. There was no other explanation for his silence. And he, Ben-Roi, was responsible. It was he who'd got the Egyptian involved in the case. It was on his conscience.

Pacing around his apartment, he put in yet another call to the satellite phone, left yet another message. He called Khalifa's regular cell phone as well, just on the off-chance. And then he booted his laptop and sent him an e-mail too. Just to cover all the bases.

417

What else? He didn't have the Egyptian's home number -- they'd always communicated by mobile or e-mail. Even if he *did* have it, he wasn't sure how much use it would have been. He hardly spoke any Arabic, and although it was possible there was someone in the family who spoke English, what was he going to say to them? *Sorry to trouble you, I just wanted to make sure your husband/father isn't dead?* They already had enough grief to contend with. He didn't want to be adding to their woes. He could track down the number, would call if and when he'd exhausted every other avenue. For the moment, he didn't want to be upsetting them.

He thought about contacting Barren, but dismissed the idea out of hand. They were hardly going to help him find someone who'd gone to investigate a mine of whose existence they denied all knowledge.

Instead he belled Danny Perlmann, a friend of his who worked in Inter-Force Liaison over at National Police Headquarters on Mount Scopus. A fluent Arabic-speaker, Perlmann owed him a favour – several favours actually – and tonight Ben-Roi called them in. Perlmann grouched and grumbled, asked if it couldn't wait till tomorrow, but Ben-Roi pressed him, and in the end he agreed to contact his contacts in the Egyptian Police, get some names and numbers in Luxor, see what he could find out.

'I'll call you if and when I hear anything,' he said, 'but don't be holding your breath. The Egyptians are a bloody nightmare.'

Ben-Roi stressed the urgency, thanked him, rang off.

He switched on the TV, watched two minutes of a documentary about, of all things, a group of men trapped in a mine in Chile, switched it off again. He checked his e-mail. He called Khalifa. Then, with nothing else he could do, he took Sarah's advice and went out for a walk.

Anything, frankly, was better than sitting alone in his apartment contemplating the fact that not only had he killed a relationship, but very possibly a friend as well.

THE LABYRINTH

The crucial thing, the one nano-thread upon which any hope of survival dangled, was for Khalifa never, ever to lose track of his position relative to the mine's main gallery. So long as he could keep a fix on that, knew which direction he was facing, then even with only his touch to guide him there was still the slimmest of chances that he might find his way out.

Within twenty minutes of leaving the cavernous chamber the thread had snapped and the chance was gone.

He was lost. Hopelessly, absolutely, irretrievably lost.

He tried to retrace his steps, fumble his way back to the chamber, but the route map of his memory had become hopelessly tangled. Left or right here? Up or down? Second or third passage? It would have been hard enough if the entire Labyrinth was floodlit. In pitch blackness it was impossible.

He stumbled on – blind, helpless, desperate. Several times he came to places that he thought felt familiar: a steep run of steps; a particularly narrow passage; a floor covered in broken pottery, a line of dirt-filled baskets. The context of the familiarity was lost to him: when he'd been there, what had come before, where he'd gone afterwards. Or if indeed he *had* been there and wasn't just confusing them with some other similar part of the mine. Everything seemed to merge into everything else, all points of reference to dissolve in the darkness like paper in acid, leaving nothing but a featureless black sludge.

He crossed some sort of wooden bridge over some sort of deep pit – from below he heard hissing, and the slap and swirl of slithering bodies. A little later – or perhaps a lot later, or possibly before; time had long ago ceased to have any meaning down here – he found himself pushing through what he at first, in his confusion, took to be heavy bead curtains. Only when he examined them more closely did he realize they were skeletons strung from a beam across the ceiling.

Before or after that he caught the sound of running water. He tried to locate its source, but it was lost in the void.

Or maybe all of it was just in his head. He had no way of telling, no way of distinguishing between what was real and what was imagined. Like the worst nightmare he'd ever had, even the strangest scenarios seemed plausible. The difference being that you woke up from nightmares.

He thought about his family – Zenab, Batah, Yusuf. How would they cope with losing him? With never knowing how or why they'd lost him? (*Please God, don't let them think I ran away and abandoned them!*) Samuel Pinsker too, and Ben-Roi, and Iman el-Badri, and Digby Girling, and the Attias, and all the rest of the cast of characters in the narrative that was set to culminate in his death down here.

Mostly he thought about his son Ali. His beloved boy. Alone and helpless, flailing in the black depths of the Nile.

Just as he himself was now flailing. Funny the way things repeated themselves.

On and on he shuffled, exhausted, thirsty, screaming for help, pleading with God, someone, anyone to save him. Until eventually his voice gave out and all there was was silence.

JERUSALEM

'I'm turning in.'

'OK.'

'You coming?'

'I'll be a little while yet.'

Heaving himself off the sofa, Joel Regev crossed the room and leant over Dov Zisky's shoulder. Papers and photographs littered the desk in front of him; on the computer screen was a page with the star, sword and olive branch logo of the IDF. The page was headed: *Conscription Records 1972.*

'Looks exciting.'

Zisky grunted.

'Still the cathedral case?'

'Always the cathedral case.'

'Getting anywhere?'

'Maybe.'

Regev hovered a moment. Then, squeezing Zisky's shoulder, he turned and padded out of the room.

'Don't overdo it, eh,' he called from the hallway.

Zisky didn't respond. He was leaning forward, staring at the computer screen. There were names and dates of birth, listed in four columns across the page. Lifting his hand, he ran a finger down each of the columns in turn. Midway down the fourth one he stopped. He frowned, fingered through the papers on the desk, pulled out a photo

– a group of women in IDF army fatigues and bush hats. He turned it over, read the dedication on the reverse. Out loud. 'To darling Rivka – Happy Days! Lx'

He looked back at the screen, back at the photo, double checking. Then he broke into a smile.

Somewhere outside there was the screech of tyres and a loud hooting.

The screech and the hoot came from Ben-Roi's Toyota Corolla, which had been forced to swerve when a motorcycle shot out from a side-street without signalling. Instinctively he reached for the siren jack, intending to pull the guy over and give him a stern talking to. He didn't plug it in. Instead he just bellowed '*Kus emek!*', gave another hoot and continued on his way.

It was past midnight. He'd walked for almost two hours, wandering aimlessly through Rehaviya, across Rehaviya Park, up past the Israel Museum and the Knesset, through the Sacher Garden. He'd heard nothing from either Khalifa or his friend Danny Perlmann. Eventually he'd headed back to the apartment, accepting that there was nothing more he could do that night and he was just going to have to sweat it out till the morning.

He'd stripped to his boxers and climbed into bed. For twenty minutes he'd lain there in the dark, gazing up at the ceiling, his cell phone still clutched in his hand. Then, suddenly, the thought had struck him that there *was* one more thing he could do. A long shot, but from the outset he'd known she was going to be the key that would unlock every other aspect of the case. He'd pulled his clothes back on, hurried downstairs to the car, sped off towards the Old City.

Fifteen minutes after his near-collision with the motorcycle, having left the Toyota in the Kishle car park, Ben-Roi was standing outside the heavy wooden gates of the Armenian compound. Where the whole damn thing had started.

He reached up and hammered.

There was a pause, then a door within the gate swung open. A large man in a flat-cap and cardigan was standing there, a cigarette dangling from the corner of his mouth. One of the caretakers Ben-Roi had seen when he'd come here to view Kleinberg's body.

'Compound's closed,' he grumbled.

Ben-Roi showed his badge. 'I need to speak with Archbishop Petrossian.'

'His Eminence has retired for the night. You'll have to come back.'

The man started to close the door. Ben-Roi reached out a hand to prevent it shutting.

'I need to speak to Archbishop Petrossian,' he repeated. Then, aware of the animosity the archbishop's arrest must have caused within the community, he added: 'Please. I need his help. It's urgent. Very urgent.'

The man eyed him, lips clamping and unclamping round the cigarette end, tendrils of smoke drifting from his nostrils. Then, holding up a finger to indicate Ben-Roi should wait, he closed the door and disappeared. A couple of minutes went by, the Old City completely silent, like a ghost town. Then the door opened again and the caretaker ushered him inside.

'His Eminence will see you.'

He closed and locked the door, led Ben-Roi along the vaulted entrance passage and out into the small cobbled courtyard fronting the St James Cathedral. He motioned towards a doorway on the right.

'There. He's at the top.'

Ben-Roi thanked him and crossed to the door. Inside a steep set of stone stairs flanked by the rails of a stairlift took him up to a long, tiled vestibule on the first floor. A glass chandelier hung from the ceiling; large oil paintings hung on the walls. Archbishop Petrossian was standing in a doorway about halfway down, dressed in a plain black cassock. Ben-Roi walked up to him, his trainers squeaking on the polished tiles.

'I'm sorry if I woke you.'

Petrossian lifted a hand, dismissing the apology.

'I am an old man. I do not sleep much. Please.'

He stood back, ushering Ben-Roi through the door into a small office. Unlike what he'd seen of the rest of the compound, the room was plain and spartan – no ornate decoration, no fancy furnishings. There was a desk, a phone, a computer terminal, a couple of leather chairs, shelves with box files and framed photographs. One of them, he noticed, was of Petrossian shaking hands with Pope Benedict. The archbishop motioned him to sit, and took up position behind the desk.

'Mardig told me it was urgent,' he said, folding his hands on the desktop, his amethyst ring of office glinting in the lamplight. 'Tell me, how can I be of assistance?'

His tone was level, soft. If he felt any anger about the way he'd been treated in custody, he didn't show it. Ben-Roi gripped the arms of the chair. Straight in. No pussyfooting.

'I need to find the girl Vosgi.'

Petrossian gave an apologetic smile.

'As I told you yesterday morning, I'm afraid I don't know her.'

'And as *I* told *you* yesterday morning, I think you're lying.'

The old man tilted his head, opened out his hands as if to say 'What can I say?'. Ben-Roi sat forward. He wasn't interrogating now. He was pleading.

'I need to speak to her,' he said, fighting to keep his own tone level. 'I don't know what you've got going on, I don't know why you're lying. Frankly I don't care. What I *do* know is that you know where she is. Like you know about everything that happens in this community. And I need you to tell me. A man's life depends on it. A good man's life.'

Petrossian was still smiling, although something about the expression suddenly looked forced, as if he was having to work to hold it.

'The girl told Rivka Kleinberg something,' Ben-Roi pushed. 'They met, she told her something. About a gold mine, a company called Barren Corporation. Because of that information, Rivka Kleinberg was murdered. And now the same's about to happen to an innocent man. A friend of mine. Might already have happened, God forbid. I have to find out what's going on. It's the only hope I've got of saving him. Please, tell me where Vosgi is. Help me.'

Still Petrossian said nothing, betrayed nothing. Despite that, Ben-Roi could see that he was troubled, was wrestling with himself. It was there in the flickering of his eyelids, the way his thumb and index finger had clamped tight around the ring's purple amethyst. Ben-Roi leaned right forward, resting his hands on the desk, crowding the old man.

'This isn't about a dead woman any more,' he pressed. 'A murder that's already happened, something that can't be changed. This is about *preventing* a murder. Saving a life. A Muslim Egyptian life, in case you're worried about saving an Israeli.'

For the first time this drew a visible reaction. Petrossian tutted, shook his head.

'A life is a life, Detective. They are all equally precious. Religion and nationality have nothing to do with it.'

He was wavering, Ben-Roi could sense it. Whatever he was hiding, and why ever he was hiding it, the cracks were starting to appear. Where interrogation had failed, a direct plea to his humanity seemed to be working. Ben-Roi gave it a final push.

'Please, help me to help my friend. Tell me where Vosgi is. Let me speak to her. I give you my word there'll be no comeback to you.'

Petrossian contemplated this, joining his fingertips and gazing at Ben-Roi over the tops of them. There was a silence, then:

'And if I have done her harm? Still no comeback?'

The question was unexpected. Ben-Roi hesitated, hands gripping the edge of the desk.

'Have you done her harm?'

The archbishop's eyes twinkled. Now it was him who could read doubt in Ben-Roi's expression.

'Difficult, isn't it?' he said. 'As I told you when we spoke yesterday, conscience is a tricky master. Here you are, asking me to betray *my* conscience, and yet when I present you with a similar dilemma – whether to trade justice for information – then you are not quite so assured. So I ask you again: do I have your guarantee that should the girl have been harmed, no action will be taken against either myself or any of my colleagues?'

Ben-Roi shifted, sat back. A moment ago he'd thought he was on top of the situation. Now, suddenly, he'd been wrong-footed.

'I can't give you that guarantee,' he said

Petrossian eyed him, his gaze really boring into Ben-Roi. Somewhere outside a bell started tolling. There was another pause. Then the old man nodded.

'I am pleased to hear it. As you will be aware, my experiences with the Israel Police have not been entirely positive, but you, I sense, are a man of decency and honour. Before tonight is out, those qualities will be put to the test. And just to reassure you, no harm of any sort has come to the child.'

'You'll take me to her?'

'In case you have forgotten, I am under house arrest. I am not permitted to leave the compound.'

'I'll vouch for you.'

Petrossian mulled this. Then, with a nod, he picked up the phone and dialled. He spoke rapidly, in a language that Ben-Roi presumed was Armenian. Replacing the phone, he stood and motioned the detective to follow him.

'Come. And please, bear in mind what has just been said about decency and honour.'

They left the office and headed downstairs.

She'd turned up at the compound five weeks ago. Out of the blue. Terrified. Traumatized. The Israeli government were about to deport her. Send her back to Armenia and straight into the hands of the people who'd trafficked her in the first place. She was desperate, had pleaded for sanctuary.

'We are a family here. We look after our own. She had already suffered beyond endurance. We could not turn her away. It was our duty to help her.'

The archbishop was explaining it all to Ben-Roi as the two of them strode down through the Armenian Quarter, the narrow, deserted streets echoing to the slap of their footsteps.

They'd taken Vosgi to a safe house, he continued, protected her. From the Israeli authorities initially. Then, after the murder in the cathedral, from whoever had killed Rivka Kleinberg.

'Mrs Kleinberg had guessed that if the girl would run anywhere, she would run to her own people,' he said. 'She called me, asked if I had seen Vosgi, knew where she might be able to find her. Had I told her the truth, it might have prevented her death. But I didn't tell her. I denied all knowledge. So she started turning up at the cathedral, hanging around, hoping she might spot the girl herself. Her death, as I said, is on my conscience, but I had no choice. She wasn't part of our community; I had no idea if I could trust her.'

They came to the crossroads at the end of St James, turned right on to Ararat. There was a scuffling sound above them as a cat scrabbled over a wall, startled by their presence.

'Did you recognize Kleinberg's name when she called?' asked Ben-Roi. 'That she was the one who did the article on you back in the seventies? Ruined your career.'

Petrossian's shoulders hunched. 'Of course I remembered her. Please believe me when I say I bore her no ill-will. I had sinned, the fault was mine and mine alone. She was merely the messenger who proclaimed the fault. I have grieved terribly for her death.'

They reached the bottom of Ararat, turned again, this time into a narrow alley. At the end was a wooden door. They walked up to it. There was a video intercom, and a ceramic plaque carrying the name Saharkian. The archbishop pressed the intercom.

'She is just a child,' he said, turning to Ben-Roi as the sound of drawing bolts echoed from within. 'A child who has suffered unimaginable horrors. There is still a chance she can heal, make a life for herself. But if she is deported, if the traffickers find her again . . .'

The door swung back. A man was standing there, a pistol tucked into his belt.

'Just a child,' repeated Petrossian. 'I ask you not to forget that. And also not to go into the particulars of Mrs Kleinberg's murder. Vosgi knows she is dead, but we have kept the more upsetting details from her. She is frightened enough as it is.'

He held Ben-Roi's eyes, making sure he understood, then stepped inside. Ben-Roi followed. The door was closed behind them and the bolts drawn. They were in a large, whitewashed room with a spartan scatter of furniture. Another man was sitting at a table nursing a shotgun; on the far side of the room a set of wooden stairs led up to a low gallery with four closed doors giving on to it. Petrossian walked across the room, looked up, called softly. Ben-Roi didn't understand what he was saying, although he caught something that sounded like Vosgi.

There was a pause, and then the furthest of the doors opened. A dark-haired, elfin figure stepped out on to the gallery. Ben-Roi's jaw tightened and his fingers made an involuntary clenching motion.

As though he was turning a key.

At a word from Petrossian, the Armenian guards disappeared into a side-room. Crossing to the foot of the stairs, the archbishop held out a hand. Hesitantly, the girl descended.

She was slighter than Ben-Roi would have guessed from the head-shots he'd seen of her. Not much more than five feet tall, if that. Prettier, too, in the flesh. Huge almond-shaped eyes, features that were somehow both delicate and tomboyish at the same time. Impossible to guess her age, although the dominant impression was young. Very young. The meeting with the hooker in Neve Sha'anan flashed into his head, what she'd told him about her and Vosgi being made to do shows together – mature and young, teacher and pupil. He felt his gorge rising, shut his mind to the conversation. To the thought, too, that in his own way he was just another a punter. Another man who wanted something from her. He stood with his hands dangling by his sides, offering what he hoped was a sympathetic expression.

The girl reached the bottom of the stairs. Her eyes flicked across to Ben-Roi, then to the archbishop, looking for reassurance. The old man took her hand in his, bowed towards her, said something. Again her eyes lifted towards Ben-Roi, then she nodded. Gently, Petrossian led her across to a sofa, sat down beside her. Ben-Roi took the armchair opposite, trying not to stare at the girl's wrists, both of which bore the trace lines of heavy scarring. She noticed the direction of his gaze and folded her arms tight across her chest, pressing the wrists into the material of her baggy grey T-shirt. Her left thumb-tip played across the silver crucifix hanging at her neck.

'Vosgi understands Hebrew,' began the archbishop, 'but she doesn't speak it very well. If it is acceptable, I will translate for her.'

'Of course,' said Ben-Roi.

Petrossian whispered to the girl. She mumbled a reply. Her gaze was now fixed firmly on the tiled floor.

'In your own time,' said the old man. 'And please, remember what I said as we came in. Try to be –' he made a soothing motion with his hand.

'Of course,' repeated Ben-Roi.

He leant forward, resting his elbows on his knees. He'd conducted hundreds of interviews over the years, but never had he felt quite the degree of anxious expectation he did at this moment. The Kleinberg case, possibly Khalifa's life – everything, it seemed to him, had distilled down to this particular meeting, this particular point. It was like he was standing in front of a door, and opening it would change everything. *Take it gently*, he told himself. *Don't yank the handle too hard in your eagerness to find out what's on the other side.*

'Hello, Vosgi,' he said.

The girl stared at the floor.

'My name is Arieh Ben-Roi. I'm a detective with the Jerusalem Police. You can call me Arieh, if you like. Or even Ari.'

His attempt at softening the mood drew no visible reaction. Probably because despite his best efforts to moderate it, his voice still sounded gruffly formal, like he was talking to her in a police interview room. Not for the first time on this case, he was reminded of his complete inability to do compassionate. Typical bloody *sabra*.

427

'Thank you for agreeing to talk to me,' he went on. 'And let me assure you from the outset this meeting has nothing to do with your residency application. You have my word on that. You have no need to be frightened. Do you understand that?'

She gave a barely discernible nod.

'I need to talk to you about a woman named Rivka Kleinberg. I think you remember her. She visited the Hofesh Shelter a few weeks ago.'

Her gaze lifted, then dropped again. She said something.

'She asks if you've found the people who killed Mrs Kleinberg,' translated Petrossian.

'We're getting close,' said Ben-Roi. 'Very close. You might be able to help us get even closer. Will you help us, Vosgi?'

Her hand closed round the silver crucifix, clutching it as though it was some sort of lifeline. She spoke again. Her voice was slightly louder than before, slightly faster, hinting at rising distress. Petrossian laid a hand on her knee, calming her.

'She says she doesn't want to testify,' he translated.

'No one's asking you to testify, Vosgi. I just need you to answer a few questions. Do you think you can do that?'

She was still gripping the crucifix. A pause, then she drew a breath and nodded.

'Thank you,' said Ben-Roi. 'I'll make this as quick as I possibly can.'

He sounded like a doctor about to administer an injection. He clasped his hands, threw her what he hoped was a reassuring smile.

'When Mrs Kleinberg came to the shelter, you spoke with her. Do you remember?'

'*Ken*,' she mumbled.

'Did you say anything to her about a gold mine?'

The girl shook her head.

'A gold mine in Egypt?'

Another shake.

'You're sure? Take your time.'

Mumbled words.

'She's sure,' conveyed the archbishop.

'How about a company called Barren Corporation. A big American company.'

No.

He repeated the name, slowing it down and spelling it out in case she wasn't getting his pronunciation. Same reaction. He worked to keep his expression neutral, not show his disappointment. He'd been hoping to hit the bull's-eye straight out. Save himself some time, spare her a long interview. It wasn't happening. He was going to have to widen his aim.

'Can you tell me what you *did* talk about, Vosgi?' he asked.

She drew in her shoulders, tucked her right foot under her left knee. More mumbled words.

'She says she told Mrs Kleinberg about where she came from,' came the translation. 'Her village, her family. And then about . . . what had happened to her.'

Ben-Roi opened out a hand, asking for more detail. The girl fumbled with the crucifix. When she answered, her voice had dropped even lower, forcing the archbishop to tilt his head to catch her words.

'She says she was fourteen when they took her,' he translated. 'She was walking home from school. They snatched her off the road. Men. Two of them. She doesn't know who they were. Azerbaijani, possibly – her village was right on the frontier.'

A connection sparked in Ben-Roi's mind. Something Zisky had dug up earlier in the investigation. About Barren. A gold mine they'd been operating in eastern Armenia. Near the border with Azerbaijan. He put it to Vosgi, asked if she knew of it. She didn't. There were no mines where she'd lived. Nothing much at all except mountains and rivers and a chicken-processing factory where her father and brothers used to work. Ben-Roi let it go, motioned her to continue. Petrossian took her free hand, held it.

'*They drove me to a house,*' he translated as she started speaking again. '*And then to other houses. There were other girls. They made us . . .* I think we can take it as read what they made her do.'

The archbishop's eyes met the detective's and Ben-Roi nodded, indicating it wasn't necessary for Vosgi to relive the precise details of what she'd been through.

'Do you know where you were?' he asked.

'*I was moved around a lot,*' relayed Petrossian. '*I know I was in Turkey. I could hear voices outside the window. I recognized the accent. And then I was sold to other people and they took me on a boat to a place with –*' Petrossian broke off, queried something. The girl explained.

'*Tourists,*' he resumed. '*Young people. Different countries. German*

429

maybe. English. She can't be sure. *Then Turkey again. A big city. I was in a basement. It was dark.*'

The girl's voice had grown slightly louder as she relaxed into the narrative. At the same time the tone had become blank, detached, as if she was describing someone other than herself. Ben-Roi remembered what Maya Hillel had told him at the Hofesh Shelter, about the girls using assumed names: *It helps distance themselves from what they're being made to do. Allows them to think it's someone else who's doing it, not the real them.*

'*I think I was in the city for almost a year,*' Petrossian's translation continued. '*And then a group of us went in another boat. And then some Arab people took us across a desert and that's how I came to Israel. There were three, four of us in a flat. We were watched all the time.*'

Ben-Roi held up a hand, motioning her to stop. The story was running ahead of him. His mind had snagged on something further back.

'Can you rewind a moment,' he said. 'You say you were in Turkey, in a city . . .'

Vosgi nodded.

'And then you were taken on a boat?'

Another nod.

'To a port?'

She frowned, turned to the archbishop, said something. He listened, then nodded.

'*Not a big port,*' he said. '*Small. Just single dock. It was night. There were cranes.*'

Without him being aware of it, Ben-Roi's foot had started tapping on the floor.

'This place,' he said, 'this dock – you told Rivka Kleinberg about it?'

She nodded.

'Was it in a town called Rosetta?'

She shrugged, uncertain.

'Egypt? Was it in Egypt?'

Another shrug.

'*I never knew where we were,*' Petrossian translated. '*They told us to look at the ground. So we couldn't see.*'

'But after you got to this dock – then you were taken across a desert into Israel.'

She shook her head.

'*They put us in a van first*' – Petrossian's voice shadowed hers – '*drove us till dawn. Then we were in a house. With Arab men. They . . .*'

From the way her fist clenched round the crucifix it was clear what the men had done. Ben-Roi waved a hand to show she didn't need to dwell on it.

'*The next night they took us in jeeps. Then we had to walk. For about five hours. It was cold. One of the girls tried to run and they shot her. And then other cars picked us up. That's when we were in Israel.*'

Ben-Roi's foot was tapping faster as his mind worked backwards. She'd been brought into Israel across a desert. That had to be the Sinai. And she'd been driven into the Sinai from a port, dock, whatever she wanted to call it. That *had* to be Rosetta. Where Rivka Kleinberg had been going on the night of her murder. And she'd been trafficked into Rosetta on a boat. He could sense the pieces moving, slotting into place, although he was still struggling to make a link with the two main elements of his case: Barren and the Labyrinth. *Take it slowly*, he told himself. *Cover the angles.*

'Do you know who trafficked you?' he asked.

She didn't. Men, that's all she could say. Violent men.

'Genady Kremenko? Have you ever heard of him?'

Lo.

He repeated the question, got the same answer. And again when he threw out the name Zoser Freight. He was close to something, he could feel it. Very close. But he wasn't getting there.

'Can you tell me more about the boat you were on?' he asked, trying another angle. 'The one that brought you from Turkey.'

She bit her lip, her hand clenching and unclenching around the silver crucifix. Almost a minute passed before she eventually found her voice. Ben-Roi could tell from the creasing of the old man's forehead that he was shocked by what he was hearing. More shocked than he had been by anything so far.

'Dear God in heaven,' he whispered. Then: 'They were kept in a container. A shipping container. Thirteen of them. For four days. There was a grille to let in air. Mattresses, blankets, a bucket to relieve themselves. Each night some of them would be removed, taken to cabins so the sailors . . .'

The girl choked. Petrossian let go her hand and wrapped an arm round her shoulders, comforting her. At the same he caught Ben-Roi's

431

eye, lifted his brow to ask if the line of questioning was really necessary. Ben-Roi gave an apologetic half-nod to indicate that it was. Somewhere in Vosgi's story, embedded like a needle in a haystack, was the information he needed, the piece that would complete the jigsaw and finally reveal the picture. And to find that piece he needed to sift the whole stack. Even if it meant forcing the girl back into the nightmare of her captivity.

'Can you tell me about the ship itself?' he asked, trying to help her, narrowing things down a bit. 'Was it big, small . . . ?'

She hesitated, then spread her arms. Big.

'A passenger ship? Fishing? Cargo?'

Fishing, she thought. Or maybe cargo. She hadn't seen much of it. Just the ship's side as they were taken on board, and then the container, and the cabin where they'd raped her.

'What about the crew? Were they Egyptian? Arabic? Dark-skinned?'

Not the ones she'd seen – the ones who'd brought them food, and been with her in the cabin. They'd been pale-skinned. Russian, she thought. Rough. Very rough.

The monotone of her voice was starting to break up, chokes of emotion slipping through. Her body language, too, spoke of increasing distress: the intensity of her grip round the crucifix, the way her free hand had wrapped tight round her stomach as though to protect it. If there'd been any other way of getting the information, Ben-Roi would gladly have taken it. But there wasn't another way. The girl knew something. And he had to get it out of her. Now. Tonight. Again, the thought struck him that he was little better than the men who'd used her. He pushed it from his head, ploughed on.

'The people who put you on the boat in Turkey,' he said. 'Can you tell me anything about them?'

She couldn't, beyond the fact that they'd been Turkish. She'd been driven to the ship, handed over to the crew, pushed into the container. There were already eight girls there. Another four had come later. That was all she could remember.'

'What about when you got off the ship. At this dock place. What happened then?'

Her breathing was coming in rapid, fluttering gasps.

'What happened at the dock, Vosgi?'

The reply was a tearful mumble, her chin pressing right down on her chest as if she was trying to hide. Petrossian translated, reluctantly, his expression signalling to Ben-Roi that he wouldn't allow this to continue for much longer.

'*They made us line up. They told us to take off our clothes. Everything. So that we were naked. Then to put our hands on our heads.* Detective, I really must—'

'Just tell me what she's saying,' snapped Ben-Roi.

The old man drew the girl to him, whispered words of comfort.

'*There was a car,*' he continued. '*A big car. Black. There was a man inside. In the back. He said things. Gave orders. I didn't understand. Then we got dressed again. There were three minibuses. They drove us away. All night. To the house—*'

'The man in the car,' cut in Ben-Roi, his tone sharp, insistent. 'Tell me about the man in the car. What did he look like?'

She was weeping now, rocking back and forth. Ben-Roi repeated the question, hating himself for it, but sensing that this was it, this was the piece he needed.

'*I couldn't see him properly,*' translated Petrossian, the words coming out in short bursts between the girl's sobs. '*It was dark. There were lights pointing at us. He was sitting in the middle of the seat. Away from the window.*'

'You must have seen something.'

She shook her head.

'Something! There must be something!'

'I see nothing,' she cried, breaking into faltering, heavily accented Hebrew. 'He not sit in window. I not see.'

'What language was he speaking?'

'I not know. I say you. I not know!'

Petrossian raised a hand to Ben-Roi, palm out, signalling him to stop. He ignored it.

'Think, Vosgi! Please, think! There must be something you remember.'

'No. Please. I tell truth!'

'Think!'

'Detective, this has gone far—'

'Think, Vosgi! The man in the car. What did he look like?'

'Detective!'

'I not see face,' she screamed. 'I tell you! I tell you! All I see is arm. When he throw out cigarette from window. For one second I see arm with . . . with . . .'

433

She flapped her hands, keening, struggling to find the word she wanted.

'With what, Vosgi? An arm with what?'

'With . . . with . . .'

Her fists were clenching and unclenching. She lurched round, gazed wildly up at Petrossian, cried something in Armenian.

'What?' Ben-Roi shouted, his eyes blazing. 'An arm with what? What did she just say?'

'Tattoo,' translated Petrossian. 'The man had a tattoo on his arm. And that is all I am going to allow, Detective. I specifically asked you not to . . .'

His voice faded out as Ben-Roi's mind zeroed in on something he'd seen four days ago. A prison, a cell, gold bling, jowly face, a man they called *Ha-Menahel* – the Schoolmaster. And on his forearm, in green and pink ink . . .

He came right forward on to the edge of the seat, his pulse racing, his body tense as a bowstring.

'The tattoo, Vosgi. Was it of a –' he curved his hands through the air, outlining a female form.

She hesitated, shivering, then nodded.

'And was the woman –' he levered open his hands, like a pair of spread legs.

A second nod.

Genady Kremenko all along.

'Thank you, Vosgi,' he said. 'That's everything I need. I don't need to trouble you any more.'

She curled into Petrossian's arms, trembling uncontrollably. Ben-Roi thought about going over to her, laying a hand on her shoulder, telling her he was sorry for what he'd just put her through. He sensed it wouldn't do much good. That the last thing she needed right now was a bumbled apology from some bad-ass Jew cop. Instead, he stood, checked his mobile – still no message from Khalifa – and crossed to the front door.

'I think you should stay here with her,' he said as he started to draw the bolts. 'I'll let the station know you're out, clear it with them. You can go back to the compound in your own time.'

He turned to Petrossian. The old man was staring at him. Hard to read his expression. Protective, maybe. Fatherly, even. Not angry, which was a surprise, given how far Ben-Roi had overstepped the

434

mark. Their eyes held a moment. Then, with a tilt of the head – part thank you, part apology – Ben-Roi slid the last of the bolts and opened the door. He was about to step through when something occurred to him and he swung.

'One last question, Vosgi. The picture you were drawing with Rivka Kleinberg. The woman with the blonde hair. Who was that? Someone you were trafficked with?'

The girl looked up. For a moment she was silent. Then she spoke to Petrossian in Armenian. He listened, nodded, conveyed her answer to Ben-Roi.

'It wasn't a real person. It was a picture. On the side of the boat she was taken on. A picture of a mermaid.'

'Ah,' said Ben-Roi.

He turned to the door. The archbishop's voice called him back.

'A last question for you too, Detective. You know where she is now. And you know her situation. May I ask what you intend to do?'

'Right now, go straight down to Tel-Aviv to talk to a man named Genady Kremenko.'

'You know what I mean. About Vosgi.'

Ben-Roi held the old man's gaze, then shrugged. 'I'm afraid you must be mistaken. I don't know anyone called Vosgi.'

He winked, nodded and left the house.

THE LABYRINTH

There was a child crying somewhere. Khalifa was absolutely certain of it. Somewhere in the mine a child was lost like him. It wasn't in his imagination. It wasn't a fantasy conjured up by the blackness. A child was in trouble.

'Stay still!' he croaked, his voice hoarse with thirst and exhaustion. 'Stay still and I'll find you. Don't be scared. We'll get out, I promise!'

He stumbled blindly, feeling his way along the stone walls, trying to get closer to the sound. It kept shifting. Sometimes it was ahead of him, sometimes behind, sometimes a long way off, sometimes tantalizingly close.

'Please, stay still! If you move we'll miss each other. Stay still and I'll find you!'

Now it was coming from a tunnel to his right. A keening, terrified sob. Impossible to tell if it was a boy or a girl. A child, that's all he knew. A lost child. And he had to find them. Because if *he* was scared, what must they be feeling? Poor kid. Poor helpless little kid.

'I'm coming! Don't be afraid! I'm coming!'

He fumbled his way down to the end of the tunnel, descended a set of steps, found himself in some sort of low room. Bats smacked into his face, shrieking; something was scurrying around the floor. A lot of things. Over his shoes, on to the hem of his trousers. He windmilled his arms and kicked his legs, drove forward through the black. He came to a wall, patted along it, found the mouth of yet another passage. A big one, by the feel of it. The child was somewhere down there.

'Stay where you are! I'm coming. It's going to be OK. I'm coming.'

He started along the passage. The sobs were clearly audible in the darkness ahead, although they were growing fainter.

'Please!' he pleaded. 'Stay still. If you move I'll never find you.'

He went faster, his desperation to get to the child overriding his fear that he might trip or smash into something. The passage was broad and high, its floor as flat as smoothed concrete. He broke into a stride and then a jog, powering heedlessly into the void, all else forgotten in the race to reach the little boy or girl before their voice was lost again. Now he was running, his limbs alive with a furious energy, a final frantic push as the voice faded in the distance, a last demented effort to get to—

His foot hit something. He stumbled, flailed his arms as if he was thrashing in water, half regained his balance, tripped on something else – the floor seemed to be scattered with small rocks or stones – sprawled and fell flat on his face. For a brief moment the child's cries echoed in the far distance, and then they were gone.

Silence.

He lay for a while, his head and arms dangling over the edge of some sort of step, his ears straining. There were no more cries. No sounds of any description aside from the rasp of his own breath. Perhaps he had imagined it after all. Perhaps he was going mad.

'God help me,' he groaned.

He heaved himself on to his knees. Patting, he tried to find the next step down, get a sense of what was in front of him. He couldn't feel one. Couldn't feel anything. Just blank space. He leant forward, reached down, stretched out his arm. Nothing. He pulled back, felt along the tunnel floor, from wall to wall. It was the same all the way across. The floor just ended. In some sort of shaft. He swept his arm over the ground, found one of the stones on which he'd tripped (round, heavy, a hammer stone, maybe). He dropped it into the hole. There was a long pause before a distant clunk echoed back up to him as the stone hit the bottom. A very long pause. So long he'd started to wonder if there actually was a bottom. He winced, realizing how close he'd come to falling into it. Shivered too. Maybe the child's cries had been a demon trying to lure him to his death.

'Please God help me,' he repeated.

He dropped another couple of rocks down, then threw one forward, trying to find out how wide the shaft was. There was a clack as it hit something solid – presumably the shaft's opposite wall – and sometime later the echo of it hitting the shaft bottom. He threw another one, harder. This time there was a clattering sound as the rock skittered along a floor. The tunnel must continue on the other side of the shaft. Another throw, another clattering echo. A broad tunnel with a hole in the middle of it . . .

Suddenly he felt his head clearing, his pulse starting to race. Maybe it hadn't been a demon after all. Maybe, just maybe, it had been an angel.

Fumbling around, he gathered a small heap of stones. One by one he started throwing them as hard as he could across the top of the shaft and into the continuation of the passage opposite. Clatter, clatter, clatter, clatter, clatter . . .

Clank.

There was something down there. Just as he'd hoped there would be.

He launched three more rocks, got three more clanks. Not the sound of rock on rock. This was rock against metal. Echoing metal. Humming metal. Vibrating metal. Like some kind of . . .

Rail or track.

And unless there was more than one set of tracks in the mine, it meant somehow, against all the odds, he'd made it back to the main gallery.

He let out a croaking bark of joy. The sound had barely left his mouth before it faded and died.

Because he wasn't back. Not quite. Between him and the way out was a hole. A big hole. The one he'd briefly glimpsed on his way down the gallery. The hole into which Samuel Pinsker had lowered two hundred feet of weighted rope and still not found the bottom.

He brought his hands up to his head, closed his eyes, tried to picture Pinsker's notebook. What had he said about the hole? It was in a side-gallery about halfway down the main gallery. It was square, extended right across the passage – like the well shafts in some of the tombs in the Valley of the Kings. The Englishman had made measurements. Try as he did, Khalifa couldn't remember the crucial one: the distance across the shaft. He thought and thought, clawed at his memory. It wasn't there. He opened his eyes -- for all the good that did – and started launching rocks again, trying to judge how far it was by sound. Somewhere between three and five metres was his best guess. Which was a big margin of error. Three metres he could probably just about jump. Five he couldn't. The margin between life and death.

He turned and shuffled back the way he had come, searching for a side-passage, a way round the shaft. There were none. He reached the room with the bats, went through it, up some stairs, along another passage, further and further from the line of the gallery. He came to a crossways, had a choice of left, right or straight ahead. He chose right. After twenty metres he hit a three-way fork. He stopped, thought about it, then turned on his heel and retraced his steps. He simply couldn't risk getting lost again. He'd been offered a way out. He was going to have to take it.

The Labyrinth, he suspected, did not give second chances.

Back at the shaft, he threw more stones, trying to build up an echo-picture of the leap he was about to make. Then, crawling, he worked his way back along the passage feeling for rocks and moving them out of the way.

If he was going to have any hope of making the jump, he was going to need a long run-up, and a clear one.

TEL-AVIV

It was past 4 a.m. when Ben-Roi pulled up outside Abu Kabir Prison. His warder friend Adam Heber met him at the gate.

'This is on your head, Arieh,' he said, leading the way across to the cell block. 'OK? I had no idea what you were going to do.'

'My head,' said Ben-Roi.

They entered the block. The place was completely silent. Heber took them down a corridor and up two sets of stairs to the top floor. Halfway down another corridor he stopped in front of a metal door. He produced a set of keys, slipped one carefully into the lock, eased the door open.

'How long?'

'Twenty minutes. Call it thirty to be sure.'

'Make sure you keep the noise down. And remember, I had no idea. Right?'

'Right.'

He stood aside and let Ben-Roi through.

'Give him one from me. From all of us.'

The door clicked shut, the lock turned and Heber's footsteps disappeared down the corridor.

Ben-Roi looked round the cell. There was a table, a chair, a basin, a lavatory, a fold-down bed. And lying on the bed – his eyes covered by a satin sleep-mask against the light from the floodlamps outside – Genady Kremenko. He was snoring loudly.

Moving carefully so as not to wake him, Ben-Roi approached the head of the bed. The pimp's left arm had slipped from beneath the covers and was dangling with the fingertips touching the floor, a slat of light cutting right across the tattoo on his forearm. Ben-Roi stared at the image, thinking of Vosgi and what she'd been through. Of what all Kremenko's victims had been through. Then, reaching over to the table, he picked up a plastic water jug. Tipping the lid with his thumb, he emptied its contents over Kremenko's face.

The pimp jack-knifed awake, a roar of protest erupting from his lungs. Ben-Roi cut the roar short with a sharp, hard rabbit-punch to the prisoner's solar plexus. He punched him again, in the jaw this time, then locked an arm round his neck and dragged him across to the toilet. Forcing his face into the bowl, he hit the flush with his knee. Water swirled around the pimp's balding head, immersing it. He bucked and fought, but Ben-Roi was a large, fit, angry cop and more than up to the struggle. He flushed again, and again, screwing Kremenko's face right down to the bottom of the bowl. Then, as he felt him start to slump and go limp, he heaved him away, flipped him on to his back, clamped a hand around his fleshy throat and pressed him hard into the floor. Sweeping his Jericho from his jeans, he gave the pimp a good hard smack on the side of the head with it and aimed the barrel directly between his bulging eyes.

'That's the introductions over with, you fat cunt,' he hissed. 'You're now going to tell me everything you know about Barren Corporation, Rivka Kleinberg and the ship with the mermaid on it. And if you breathe a word of this to anyone I'll cut your fucking eyes out. Got it?'

'Yes, sir,' choked Kremenko.

'Right, I'm listening.'

THE LABYRINTH

Khalifa knew that if he thought too much about it – about how heavy the odds were against him making the jump in pitch darkness, with no clear idea how much distance he had to cover and in a state of complete physical and mental exhaustion – he would never have found the courage to do it, however grim his predicament.

He didn't think about it. Once he'd cleared the passage floor of rocks and obstructions, he spent fifteen minutes pacing and re-pacing his run-up to the shaft edge to make sure he had it exact to the centimetre – take off too short and he wouldn't get across, too long and he'd be plummeting headlong into the abyss.

Then, having thrown his Helwan across to minimize his weight, and performed a quick round of prayers, he took up position at his start point and went for it.

He aborted the first run halfway through, some sixth sense warning him his stride-pattern was fractionally off what it needed to be. Same with his second run. His third one felt good and he kept on going, counting each footfall out loud, building up speed, accelerating all the time, barrelling crazily through the blackness. He had twenty-nine strides to reach maximum velocity before jumping on thirty. At twenty-six an alarm bell went off in his head telling him he was off-stride again. He had built up too much momentum, was too close to the edge to do anything about it. He had just enough time to think *God help me!* and then his foot slammed down on thirty and with a hopeless, despairing howl of '*Allah-u-akhbar!*', he launched himself into the void.

He knew straight away he was doomed. Even in the blackness he could sense he was well short of the shaft edge, hadn't achieved anything close to the amount of lift he needed to carry himself over. For a fleeting instant it was as if he had crossed into a separate reality, an alternative dimension comprised of nothing but blank space – no light, no form, no weight, no time.

Then he crossed back and collided with something solid.

He scrabbled frantically, his hands and arms on a flat surface, his legs and feet against a vertical one, which told him he'd hit the shaft's opposite rim. His foot found some sort of protrusion, he put his weight on it, the protrusion gave, his leg kicked into empty space. He clawed and slapped, searching for a hand-hold, something to grip on to. There was nothing, just flat, dusty floor. He felt himself slipping.

'Please God, please God!'

He drove his elbows and forearms into the ground, tried to lever himself up. He didn't have the strength. He tried to swing his leg on to the rim. He couldn't reach it. His nails scraped on bare rock; his feet kicked at the shaft wall. He felt himself sliding.

I'm dead, he thought. *This is it. I'm dead.*

He continued to rake at the wall, his breath a helpless choke, his grip weakening all the time. With a final, desperate effort, he splayed his leg out to the left. His foot hit something solid. Something metal. A pinion? A spike? He had no idea what it was. He didn't care what it was. All he cared was that it was a foothold, could take his weight. He pushed against it, muscles screaming, his arms and fingers just moments from giving out, somehow heaved, clawed, dragged and fought his way up over the edge of the shaft and on to flat ground. He rolled away from the hole and slumped face down on the tunnel floor, gasping for air.

'Thank you, God,' he gasped. 'Thank you, thank you, thank you.'

For a couple of minutes he just lay there, allowing his heart to settle, at once both traumatized and euphoric. Then, not wishing to remain in the mine a moment longer than he had to, he felt around for his Helwan, stood and fumbled his way down the tunnel. After thirty metres he felt the walls disappear to either side of him. At the same moment his ankle hit metal track and his nose caught a distant hint of garlic.

He was back in the main gallery.

He stepped over the track, turned right, started to climb. When he'd come down this way before – it seemed like days ago, weeks, an entire lifetime – he'd felt dread growing with every step. Now he felt it diminishing. Up and up he went, closer and closer to the entrance, further and further from the horrors below until eventually the floor flattened out and his fingers brushed one of the legs of the metal loading platform. He passed beneath it, shuffled his way across the cavernous chamber at the top of the mine, banged up against the sliding metal doors.

When he had entered the mine he had left them open. Now they were shut tight, presumably by whoever had sent the barrels rolling down the tracks. He worked his fingers into the gap between the panels and heaved, not caring if there was anyone out there, not caring about anything other than seeing the sky and breathing fresh air.

The panels parted an inch. Suddenly there was light. Dim, muffled, brown. At first he was confused. Then he realized the canvas tarpaulin must have been put back in place to cover the doors. He poked at it, felt it billow. And with the billow, a waft of clean air. He poked again. Then, standing back, he aimed the Helwan through the gap and shot away the new padlock with which the doors had been secured. He tugged off the chain, heaved the doors open, bent and pulled up the hem of the tarpaulin. Light exploded into his face, dazzling him.

He stumbled out, dropped to his knees, lifted his arms to the sky and praised Allah for his life.

Then, standing again, he stumbled towards his car.

Between Jerusalem and Tel-Aviv

Ben-Roi was halfway back to Jerusalem, still digesting what Genady Kremenko had told him, when his cell phone rang. When he saw the caller's number he damn nearly swerved off the highway.

'Khalifa!' he cried, slamming the phone to his ear. 'Is that you?'

It was.

'*Toda la'El!* Thank God! Where the fuck have you been?'

'Long story,' came the Egyptian's voice. It sounded rough, croaky. 'I'll fill you in later. Listen, I know what's going on. I've been in the mine. They're not working it. They're—'

'Dumping.'

A fractional pause. 'You know?'

'Long story at this end too.' Ben-Roi angled into the slow lane and dropped his speed right down. 'I only found out forty minutes ago. Barren are using the Labyrinth as a toxic dump. They're running a gold mine in Romania. They're supposed to be transporting all the waste back to the US. But they're cutting corners and ditching it instead. Shipping it to Egypt, transferring it on to Zoser barges, taking it up the Nile, then trucking it out to the mine. They've been doing it for years.'

Even as he described it, Ben-Roi was still struggling to get his head round the scale of the scandal.

'The captain of the tanker that's bringing the waste in – his brother's a big Tel-Aviv pimp. Guy called Genady Kremenko. The two of them were running a sideline in sex-trafficking. Piggy-backing their own operation off Barren's one. They'd load girls on to the ship on the way down from Romania, offload them with the waste in Rosetta, smuggle them across the border into Israel . . .'

'God Almighty.'

'The whole operation was mothballed after Kremenko got arrested a couple of months back, but Rivka Kleinberg met one of the girls who'd already been trafficked and picked up on the whole story. Barren are on the verge of securing a multi-billion-dollar gas field deal with the Egyptian government. If Kleinberg had gone public, it would have fucked the deal, fucked Barren's image, fucked everything. So they killed her. There's still a lot of gaps to fill in, but that's the basic picture. Now tell me what the hell happened to you? I've been—'

'We can get them, Ben-Roi.'

'What?'

'You and me. Barren and Zoser. We can get them. I know where the mine is, I've seen it. There're a million barrels down there. We can get the bastards!'

Suddenly there was an edge to Khalifa's voice. A manic edge. Like he was strung out. Or drunk.

'We can talk it through later,' said Ben-Roi. 'I can tell you're tired—'

'I'm not tired!' The handset seemed to jump at the sharpness of the Egyptian's retort. 'I've never felt less tired in my life. They killed my son and now we can bring them to justice.'

'Come on, Khalifa, we don't know—'

443

'Of course we know! My son was killed by a barge carrying Barren's toxic waste. And now we can get them. For the first time in nine months I actually feel like I'm awake!'

He was gabbling, his voice jittery with a sort of breathless euphoria. Ben-Roi started to tell him to calm down, but Khalifa cut him short again.

'I have to phone Zenab. And then get back to Luxor. I'll call you this afternoon and we can work out what to do. We can get them, Ben-Roi. You and me. Working together. The A-Team. Just like old times!'

There was a brief burst of what sounded like laughter, and then the line went dead. From behind Ben-Roi there was a furious honking as a lorry driver warned him he was drifting out of his lane.

THE EASTERN DESERT

Maybe it was the exhaustion. Maybe the dehydration. Maybe the cumulative trauma of everything he'd been through in the mine. Khalifa didn't analyse it. Didn't see there *was* anything to analyse. His boy had been killed by a Zoser river barge. And it now turned out those same river barges were being used to run toxic waste up the Nile and illegally dump it. Ergo, his son had been killed by a barge loaded with barrels of contaminated dust. It was obvious, clear as daylight. That's why Zoser had stymied any investigation into the accident. Maybe it hadn't even *been* an accident. Maybe the boys had been killed deliberately, to stop them finding out what the barge was carrying. It was all meshing in Khalifa's head. All falling into place. They'd murdered Ali. Barren and Zoser. And now he and Ben-Roi were going to blow the whole scandal wide open. Right a terrible wrong. His son's death would not have been in vain.

He called Zenab, spun her a line about having broken down in the desert.

'I'm on my way back now,' he assured her, his voice sounding strangely unfamiliar to him, like it was someone else talking. 'It's all going to be OK. Everything's going to be just fine.'

She tried to question him, ask why he couldn't at least have called – 'I've been so worried, Yusuf!' – but he cut the conversation short. A little sharply, perhaps, but there were things to do, wheels to set in motion. He glugged an entire bottle of Baraka, crammed some cheese and *aish baladi* into his mouth. Then, firing up the Landrover, he sped away through the desert, back along the tyre tracks towards Highway 212 and civilization.

Nine months of torment, and now, finally, justice was going to be done. He felt good. Really good.

JERUSALEM

It was still only 8 a.m. when Ben-Roi made it back to Jerusalem. He thought about going into the station – he would have liked to corner Baum and Dorfmann, tell them he'd solved the case, see the look on their faces. He decided it could wait. He was knackered, couldn't face the prospect of an extended debrief. Instead he went home, booted his desktop and spent an hour writing the whole thing up: Barren, the Romanian mine, the Labyrinth, Vosgi, Rivka Kleinberg.

There were gaps: things Kremenko hadn't been able to tell him, parts of the story that remained vague. While it seemed pretty certain Barren had stumbled on the Labyrinth when they'd been doing survey work in that part of the desert, for instance, Ben-Roi couldn't say for sure when they'd decided to start using it as a toxic dump, nor who had actually taken that decision. Likewise the precise steps by which Rivka Kleinberg had unravelled the mystery were far from clear. And how the hell had she found out about Samuel Pinsker?

Three questions in particular remained unresolved. First, how had Barren discovered Kleinberg was on to them? Ben-Roi had assumed Kremenko had tipped them off following Kleinberg's prison visit, but the pimp had insisted it wasn't him (how could he have tipped them off, he had argued, when he and his brother had themselves been diddling Barren by trafficking girls on one of their ships?).

Second, who had given the order to kill the journalist? Nathaniel Barren? William Barren? Some third party within the company acting on their own initiative?

Third, and most important, who had actually carried out the order? Who was the shrouded figure who had tailed Kleinberg through the Old City and into the cathedral and there looped a garrotte around her neck and yanked? Who was their murderer?

445

There were still a lot of ends to tie up, and, as a side-issue, there was the Nemesis Agenda to deal with – they'd held him at gunpoint, made an idiot of him and he wasn't about to just shrug that off.

For the moment, however, he'd taken a giant stride towards resolving the whole thing. He banged out a five-page report, checked it, e-mailed copies to Leah Shalev, Chief Gal and, just to piss him off, Chief Superintendent Baum as well. Then, padding through into the bedroom, he kicked off his trainers and collapsed face down on to the bed.

Thirty seconds later he was fast asleep.

THE EASTERN DESERT

Lies have a curious habit of coming true.

So it proved with the one Khalifa told his wife about his car breaking down. He was careering through the desert, his feet and hands dancing a frenetic jig across the Landrover's controls, the speedometer hovering around 70km per hour as he made the most of the compacted lorry tracks, when he misjudged a corner and skidded. He fought the steering, struggling to regain control. He was going too fast. The Landrover slewed, hit some unseen obstruction, lurched, spun and came to rest sideways-on in a deep, ditch-like depression, tilting at 45 degrees.

'Dammit! Dammit!'

He clambered out. Steam was pouring from beneath the bonnet; the rear left tyre was blown and protruding at an unnatural angle, telling him the axle was bent. Whatever else he was going to be doing that morning, he wasn't going to be driving any further.

'Bloody dammit!'

He kicked the bumper. Then, with nothing else for it, he gathered everything he needed to take with him: water, phone, gun, Samuel Pinsker's notebook. Improvising a makeshift bag out of a blanket he found in the back of the Landrover, he tied it all up and set off on foot. A day ago the prospect of walking twenty kilometres through the empty desert would have been a daunting one. After what he'd been through in the mine, it felt like a Friday afternoon stroll in the park.

Ben-Roi had only been asleep for a few minutes when his cell phone went off. Rolling groggily on to his back, he dragged the handset from his pocket and answered. Leah Shalev.

'What the hell's going on, Arieh? Where have you been?'

'Unh? What?' Ben-Roi rubbed his eyes, confused.

'I've been trying to get you all afternoon.'

Levering up an arm, he looked at his watch. It was past 4 p.m. What he'd thought had been just a few minutes had in fact been seven hours.

'Fuck. Sorry, Leah. Long night.'

He struggled into a sitting position, swung his feet on to the floor. His head throbbed; his mouth felt like it was full of brick dust.

'You get my report?' he asked.

'I did. We need to talk.'

Now that his senses were coming back online, he clocked that she didn't sound her normal self. There was a curtness to her tone, a flatness.

'Everything OK?'

'We need to talk,' she repeated, ducking the question. 'Get into the station. Now. My office.'

'What's going—'

The line went dead. He sat a moment massaging his temples, a vague sense of unease nagging in the pit of his stomach. Then, standing, he went through into the bathroom and stuck his head under a cold shower.

He reached Kishle twenty minutes later. As per instructions, he parked up in the compound at the back of the building and went straight through to Leah Shalev's room. She was sitting behind her desk, her fingers playing with a small packet done up in white tissue paper. When she saw him she smiled, although the expression was forced. She looked uneasy, pale. So pale he thought she might be ill.

'You OK, Leah?'

'Just shut the door and sit, Arieh.'

He did as he was told.

'So what's cooking?' he asked.

Her eyes met his briefly before fleeing to the other side of the room.

'A big load of shit,' she muttered.

'My report?'

She nodded. 'It probably wasn't a good idea to copy Baum in on it. Not before me and the chief had had a chance to work through our position.'

He shrugged. 'Couldn't resist it. He needed a lesson teaching. In proper police work. Sanctimonious little turd.'

Normally Shalev would chuckle at his Baum insults, just as he would at hers – their little conspiracy of insubordination. Today she didn't join in the fun. Just sat there fiddling with the paper packet.

'So?' he asked.

'So the sanctimonious little turd forwarded it to his contacts in the ministry and they sent it up the chain. Right up the chain.'

Ben-Roi tipped his head. 'Nice to have an audience.'

'Oh you've got an audience, Arieh, believe me. Suddenly there are a lot of people in a lot of powerful positions showing a lot of interest in this case. A *lot* of interest.'

He might have expected her to be pleased at the attention – she was leading the case, after all. She looked anything but.

'So?' he repeated.

Again her eyes momentarily snagged on his before rolling away again.

'So it's being kicked upstairs. To Special Investigations.'

It took a moment for that to sink in. 'You're joking me.'

'Does this look like my joking face, Arieh?'

It didn't. It looked like the face of someone who was seriously pissed off. And seriously rattled. Ben-Roi was incredulous.

'But we've practically solved the bloody thing. We know why she was killed, we know who was behind it, we know they've illegally dumped a million tonnes of toxic shit in a mine in Egypt –' he snapped a finger up on each point, his voice rising – 'we've put in all the legwork, Leah. There's nothing left to do bar hammer out the fine detail. Why the hell's it going to Special Investigations to finish?'

Her eyes still couldn't meet his. There was a silence, the atmosphere in the room tense, charged. Then, suddenly, Ben-Roi's fist clenched as realization dawned.

'They're not going to finish it, are they? It's being parked. Shelved.'

She didn't say anything. Which was as good as a yes.

'You have to be kidding me, Leah! Tell me you're kidding!'

Her mouth was tight, her fingers trembling. She looked shell-shocked.

'Like I said, I've not got my joking face on.'

'But why? Why?' He was on his feet now. 'We know they did it, Leah! We know why they did it – we could practically take it to court as it is!'

'It's not going anywhere, Arieh. We're off the investigation.'

'But why? Tell me why?' He couldn't stop asking the question. 'We've got an open-and-shut case and now it's just being dropped! I want to know why!'

'Because they're powerful.' Her eyes rolled up. Now that he looked he noticed a redness to them, like she'd been crying at some point. 'They own the system, Arieh. Or at least they own the people who run the system, which is the same thing. They tweak the strings, the puppets dance. And to mix my metaphors, these puppets are right at the top. The order's come down. Barren are off-limits. We're stepping away.'

Ben-Roi's fists were balled so tight the knuckles looked like they were going to split right through the skin.

'You're telling me we can prosecute Katsav, our own president, but not some fat-wallet multinational?'

Again, the answer was in her silence.

'I don't believe I'm hearing this! I thought you told me we still abide by the rule of law in this country.'

'It appears that some people are above the law,' she said quietly. 'Barren have got a lot of friends.'

'God Almighty! God Al-fucking-mighty!'

He dropped back down into the chair. He felt like he'd been punched in the gut. Shalev fiddled with the paper packet; Ben-Roi opened out his hand and rubbed his neck. There was another silence.

'You're just going to let this go?' he asked eventually.

'Trust me, I'm as sick as you are.'

'But you *are* just going to let it go.'

Her face flushed. With shame, it struck him, not anger. Impotent shame.

'This is coming from the very top, Arieh. Like I told you the other day, I've worked hard to get where I am. I can't just throw it all away.'

'The chief?'

She let out a breath. 'Gal retires in five months. His wife's not well, his son's moving up the Justice Ministry. He's not going to rock the boat.'

'I can't believe I'm hearing this!'

Shalev gave a weak shrug.

'I'll take it to the press then.'

'I wouldn't do that.'

'What do you mean, you wouldn't do that?'

'You go public, you'll be pissing off an awful lot of people you don't want to piss off. You've got a baby on the way—'

Ben-Roi flared. 'Are you threatening me, Leah?'

'I'm just telling you—'

'Suddenly you're their little messenger girl?'

Now it was Shalev's turn to erupt.

'Don't you dare patronize me, Arieh Ben-Roi. Do you hear? This is hard enough as it is without your snide insinuations. We're letting a murderer off the hook, you think I feel good about that? I feel about as shit as I've ever felt about anything in my life. But that's the way it is. We're drones, we take orders. And this is the order. Maybe further down the line the guard'll change and justice'll be done – please God it'll be done – but for the moment we bite the bullet and do as we're told. If not for your own sake, then for the sake of the ones you love. Because believe you me, you step out of the box on this and they will go for you like jackals round a fucking carcass.'

She glared at him, breathing hard, the liner on her left eye streaked as if someone had smudged charcoal beneath her eyelid. Then, sitting forward, she dropped her face into her hands. In the five years they'd worked together, it was the first time she'd ever launched at him like that.

'I'm sorry, Arieh,' she mumbled. 'I didn't mean to . . .'

'No, I'm sorry. I shouldn't have said that.'

For a moment she just sat there, her face buried. Then, coming up, she threw the paper packet across to him.

'From the commissioner. Just so you know your efforts haven't gone unnoticed.'

Ben-Roi opened the packet. It contained a nickel medal with a blue and white ribbon. The Israel Police Service Medal.

'I believe the citation goes: "For outstanding contribution to the achievement of the goals of the Police",' she said. 'Or some such bullshit.'

'I'll treasure it,' muttered Ben-Roi.

'There's something else.'

'I'm all ears.'

She hesitated, as if steeling herself to say something she didn't want to, then:

'There's a post come up at the academy. A lectureship. In advanced investigation. I don't know all the details but apparently it's double the wage you're getting at the moment for only four days a week. Plus a subsidized house and early retirement on full pension. I'm told if you applied you'd be a shoo-in.'

He snorted. 'A bribe. To keep me quiet.'

'I think the precise wording was "a recognition of Detective Ben-Roi's unique investigative abilities". But yes – cutting away the crap, it's a pay-off.'

'And you? What are you getting?'

She flushed again. 'A bump up to chief superintendent.'

He shook his head. 'Fucking hell, Leah, I never thought I'd see the day.'

'Me neither,' she mumbled. 'Not in my wildest nightmares.'

There was a silence, neither of them quite certain where to take the conversation. Then a knock at the door.

'Later!' called Shalev.

She sought out Ben-Roi's eyes, held them.

'Think about it, Arieh. Please. Think hard. Not for me, not for you. For Sarah. And the baby. It's checkmate here. You might as well try to salvage something.'

'And feel crap about it for the rest of my life?'

'At least there'll *be* a rest of your life.'

They looked at each other, tight-lipped, shoulders slumped, like players on a team that has just suffered a particularly humiliating defeat. Then Ben-Roi stood and made for the door. She called after him.

'I always had a bad feeling about this case.'

He stopped and turned. A beat, then, as one:

'Craptangle.'

He shook his head, threw open the door and pushed past a uniform out into the corridor.

'Are you trying to kill me, Khalifa? Are you? Because I've got the Valley of the Kings opening in twenty-four hours, the phone's ringing off the hook, and now I find out you've been moonlighting for the fucking Israelis!'

Khalifa shuffled his feet, his hands clenched around the spine of Samuel Pinsker's notebook. After a five-hour trudge through the desert, followed by hitched lifts with, respectively, a police pick-up, a Menatel phone van and – irony of ironies – a Zoser freight lorry loaded with concrete piping, he'd arrived back in Luxor forty minutes ago. He'd swung home, showered and changed, levelled things with Zenab. Then, anxious to speak to Ben-Roi, to waste no time in preparing a case to put to his superiors, he'd gone into the station.

Which was when Hassani had spotted him on the staircase and ordered him straight up to his office.

'They called me at home!' he ranted, his face glowing the colour of pickled beetroot. 'Some pushy *yehoodi* from Israel Police headquarters! In the middle of the night. My private number!'

No tiptoeing around his subordinate this afternoon. No first-name terms or restrained language. This was the Hassani of old – hectoring, belligerent, volcanic.

'He wanted to know if I knew where you were. I said, no offence, matey, but what the fuck is it to you where one of my officers is? He said you'd been helping a colleague of his with an investigation and there was a possibility you were in danger. What the hell's going on, Khalifa? I demand to know what's going on!'

Khalifa stared down at the notebook. He hadn't slept for thirty-six hours and was shattered. At the same time, as if his body was inhabited by two separate people, he felt curiously energized. His boy – he was going to get justice for his boy!

'I'll be doing a report,' he began.

'Too damn right you'll be doing a report!' The room echoed as Hassani's fist hammered down on the table. 'And before that you'll be *telling* me – here, now, face to face. What's going on, Khalifa? Why am I getting calls from Jews on my private number?'

'It's to do with the well-poisonings, sir.'

'What?'

'The ones I told you about. In the Eastern Desert.'

'Oh not the bloody Coptic waterholes again! I thought we'd agreed to put that one on the back burner.'

'There's a gold mine, sir. Out by the Gebel el-Shalul. An ancient—'

'There it is!' cried Hassani. 'There it is! *Ancient!* Funny, but I just knew that word was going to come into it somehow. God forbid you should ever work on a case that has any contemptuous relevance!'

Khalifa resisted the temptation to correct the adjective. When Hassani was in this sort of mood, playing smart-alec was never a good idea. Instead, slowly, carefully, he outlined the situation – Rivka Kleinberg, Barren Corporation, Zoser, mine, toxic dumping – going easy on the Israeli end of things, emphasizing the Egyptian connection. He would have liked to talk to Ben-Roi first, clarified the evidence, marshalled his thoughts, but if Hassani wanted to know now, he wasn't going to hold back. Maybe it was for the best. The sooner his boss was in the loop, the sooner they could start moving against the culprits.

In front of him the chief listened, his expression stony, his fists clenched tight on the desktop as if he was some pharaonic statue. When Khalifa had finished, he levered himself to his feet, went over to the window and stared out at the rear of the Interior Ministry building ten metres away. Almost a minute passed before he turned back to the room.

'So?' he asked.

'I'm sorry?'

'So,' repeated Hassani, his tone unexpectedly light, as if Khalifa had just told him a cheery anecdote. Not at all the reaction he'd been anticipating. He sat forward.

'So an American multinational, aided and abetted by one of our biggest companies, has been illegally dumping contaminated waste on Egyptian territory. Said waste leaching into the water system and causing widespread environmental damage.'

He tried to spell it out without sounding like he was patronizing Hassani. Again, the reaction was not what he was expecting, or hoping for. The chief merely gave an exaggerated shrug and held up his hands as if to say: 'Is this supposed to mean anything to me?' Khalifa could feel his temper rising.

'Sir, this is a major criminal scandal. We're talking thousands, possibly tens of thousands of barrels of toxic waste. I've been down there. I've seen it.'

Recollections of the mine flashed through his mind: the darkness, the claustrophobia, the eerie stench of garlic, which he assumed must be something to do with the arsenic contamination.'These people have broken the law,' he picked up, shaking the memory away. 'We've got the evidence, we need to start moving—'

Hassani held up a finger, silencing him. A stiff, threatening finger, brandished at Khalifa like a cudgel.

'Let me just spell out a few home truths, sonny boy,' he said, each word seeming to quiver under the force of his suppressed anger. 'We are the Luxor Police. The *Luxor* police. We have a patch, we deal with crimes committed on that patch. A Jew woman gets herself killed in Jerusalem – that is of no concern to us whatsoever, beyond the fact that any Zionist death is a cause for celebration. An abandoned mine out in the arse-end of nowhere – that is of no concern either, whatever may or may not be inside it. A poisoned well on the very edge of our beat – that *might* be of interest, and as I have already told you, we'll give the matter more thought once the museum opening is out of the way. As for prossies in Rosetta, mines in Romania and all the other cock-and-bull malarkey, it is nothing, I repeat, nothing, to do with us.'

'I don't believe I'm hearing this,' murmured Khalifa, unbeknown to him echoing almost precisely what Ben-Roi was at that same moment saying to his boss 700 kilometres away in Jerusalem. Then, out loud:

'Sir, I simply cannot allow—'

Hassani ignited. 'What? Cannot allow what? Me explaining the basics of Egyptian policing to you!'

'Barren and Zoser—'

'Are, respectively, an American-based corporation over whom we have absolutely fuck-all jurisdiction, and one of the best-connected, most powerful companies in Egypt.'

'Who just happen to have helped dump a hundred thousand barrels of contaminated dust—'

'A minute ago it was a thousand barrels.'

'A hundred, a thousand, a hundred thousand, it doesn't matter – Zoser have broken the law!'

'They can have broken the nose off the bloody Sphinx for all I care!' Hassani's fist slammed back against the window, the whole room seeming to vibrate to the force of the blow. 'Neither of them have committed a crime on our patch, Khalifa, and if there's been no crime, there's no cause for us to get involved. God Almighty, next you'll be asking me to open a case file because some kid had his bike stolen in Australia.'

Khalifa's own fist had clenched into a flint-like ball as he struggled to hold back his fury. 'So you're just going to turn a blind eye?'

'I'm not going to turn any sort of eye. It's not our business. You understand? Not our patch, not our business!'

'I'll take it off our patch, then. I'll go above you. To the Director of Police.'

He braced himself for another explosion. Instead Hassani let out a guffaw of laughter.

'You be my guest,' he cried. 'Hell, I'll even give you the director's private number. In fact, why stop there? Why not go all the way to the top? To the Interior Minister himself. That being the same Interior Minister whose brother is chairman of Zoser, and who tomorrow night is going to be here in the Valley of the Kings glad-handing the head of Barren Corporation. The *same* Barren Corporation who are currently pumping tens of millions of dollars into the local economy. So you go right ahead and call him, Khalifa. But don't come crying to me when *you* get kicked off the force and your family get kicked out of their new apartment.'

Khalifa launched to his feet, all control lost.

'Is that a threat?' he shouted, again echoing almost verbatim the confrontation between Ben-Roi and Leah Shalev. 'Are you threatening me?'

Hassani came forward a couple of steps, his shoulders tense, his arms cocked at the elbows, like a boxer about to launch at an opponent. There was a pause as the two men fronted up to each other. Then, suddenly, the fight seemed to drain out of the chief. His arms dropped and he stomped back to his desk.

'No, I'm not threatening you,' he said, dropping into his seat. 'I'm reminding you how things are in this country. And how they are is that, revolution or no revolution, there are people you don't touch. If the Israelis want to put in an official governmental request for cooperation, then maybe some wheels will turn. Although given what we all think of the Israelis, even that probably won't have much effect unless it's backed up by the Americans. So why don't you trot off and have a chat with your little Jew-boy buddy? And if the order comes down to investigate, we investigate. Until that point I'm not touching it with a fucking bargepole. And if you know what's good for you, you won't either. Now, if you don't mind, I've got things to attend to. And make sure you shut the door behind you.'

He snatched up the phone and swivelled, turning his back on Khalifa. For a moment the detective stood where he was, fighting the urge to run up and hammer his fists on Hassani's outsized buffalo shoulders, screaming: 'They killed my son! They killed my son!' He knew it wouldn't do any good. Gathering himself, he stalked from the room, making the point of slamming the door in his wake. If Hassani wanted an official request from the Israelis, that's exactly what he'd get. Ben-Roi would know what to do. Ben-Roi wasn't just a good detective – a bloody good detective – he was a friend. A bloody good friend. Together they'd crack it. Make sure justice was done. The A-Team. Just like old times.

He headed down to his office, taking the stairs two at a time.

JERUSALEM

The thing that Ben-Roi found most troubling was not that he'd been offered an official bribe to drop a murder case, but that as he made his way back to the Kishle detectives' suite, he found himself giving the offer serious consideration.

He should have dismissed it out of hand. It went against every moral he possessed, everything he'd ever stood for and fought against. OK, maybe he didn't always play things by the book, was a bit too free with his fists and a bit too loose in his interpretation of what was strictly permissible in the name of law enforcement. He knew right from wrong, though; knew that even if you bent the line at times – as he had last night with Genady Kremenko – there still *was* a line. A clear demarcation between the good guys and the bad guys. And for all his faults, he'd always been on the right side of that line, had never stepped across it. Had always battled to ensure that justice was done.

And now he was being asked to take an eraser and scrub the line. Pretend it didn't exist. Turn his back on everything he'd ever believed in.

He should have told them to go fuck themselves. Passed everything over to Natan Tirat and let him splash it across the front of *Ha'aretz*.

And yet, and yet . . .

He reached the detectives' suite, went through to his office. There was no one there. The whole place felt unnaturally quiet and still. He made himself a coffee, turned off his mobile, flopped into his chair.

He wasn't afraid. It wasn't that. He was a tough guy, was more than capable of standing up for himself. Barren didn't scare him and neither did the politicians.

He wasn't an idiot either, though. Barren carried clout. Serious clout. And going up against them was going to cause trouble. Serious trouble. Not just for him, but potentially for Sarah as well. And the baby. They'd already killed one person. Maybe a whole lot more. *You step out of the box on this and they will go for you like jackals round a fucking carcass.* This wasn't just about him. There were wider considerations here.

He slurped at his cup, tapped the cell phone on his thigh.

Say he did go public, what would it achieve? He'd be screwing his career, putting himself and the people he loved in the firing line, and for what? Sure they had Barren for toxic dumping, but there was no direct link between the company and Rivka Kleinberg's murder, just circumstantial evidence. And with the sort of lawyers Barren would throw at it, circumstantial evidence was as good as no evidence. Hell, they might even twist it in such a way as to pin the dumping charge on a third party, or dodge it altogether. At best it would be a fine and a hit to their reputation. Maybe the loss of their Egyptian gas field tender. Irritating, but hardly catastrophic – not to a company as large as Barren Corporation. For him, on the other hand . . . He was perched on a set of scales and they weren't balancing. Far from it, things were tipping very much against him.

It's checkmate here. You might as well try to salvage something.

He blew on his coffee, took another sip, gazed distractedly across the office at the map on the opposite wall.

It was a good offer, no question. Bribe, pay-off, whatever you wanted to call it. A bloody good offer if you could deal with the moral downside. Life-changing. Double-money, less work, low-rent house, early retirement. And with Sarah's play scheme closing, it meant she was no longer tied to Jerusalem. They could move up north to Kiryat Ata where the academy was based, maybe get a place near the sea, start over. Give their kid – kids, perhaps – a better life than they would ever have in the warping pressure cooker of the Holy City. They'd be nearer their families as well – his just north of Hadera on the Sharon

Plain, hers over near Galilee ... the more he thought about it, the more attractive it seemed.

If he could deal with the moral downside. With the fact that he would be letting a killer off the hook.

Except that, would he be? Shelving a case, after all, wasn't the same as binning it. Like Leah Shalev had said, circumstances change. Barren's influence might wane – maybe it was simply a matter of delaying justice rather than forgoing it. To extend the hook analogy, some fish you reeled in the moment you felt them bite, others you allowed a bit of line, let it run for a while before landing them. The end result was the same. You still had trout for dinner. It was just about timing.

Or perhaps he was just kidding himself. Trying to sweeten the fact that he was contemplating doing a Faustus and selling his soul to the Devil.

He didn't know, he just didn't know. He turned it round, exploring the angles, weighing things up. And all the while he could hear Sarah's voice at the back of his head, something she'd said to him the day they split: *Something has to give, Arieh.* Never had that assessment seemed more true. Something fundamental was going to have to give here, some essential part of him be let go. It was the dilemma of the last four years reduced to the starkest of binary equations: prioritize the ones he loved, or the demands of his conscience. Black or white. Heads or tails. No alternative options. A straight flip of the coin.

Still he couldn't decide, still he felt tugged in different directions, leaning first this way, then that, unable to give himself up fully to one side or the other. Until eventually, as if tired of his dithering, his hand took the initiative. Seemingly of its own volition, it lifted the cell phone and switched it back on. There were messages, but rather than activating voicemail, his fingers instead tapped in a number. The phone came up to Ben-Roi's ear and rang. Answerphone. Sarah's voice. His eyebrows lifted, as if he was somehow surprised, had been handed the phone unexpectedly.

'Sarah,' he said after the beeps had gone. 'Hi. It's me. I ... um ... um ... I'm sorry about last night ... I wanted to ... um ...'

He bumbled on a while, apologizing again, saying how much he'd enjoyed dinner, how beautiful she'd looked. Until suddenly something clicked and the logjam broke.

'Listen, Sarah, I need to talk. Not on the phone, face to face.

There's something I want to run by you. A job I've been offered. A good job. A really good job. Up in Haifa. It would get me off the front line, mean a new start for us. All three of us. I think I'm going to take it. I want to be with you, Sarah. More than anything in the world. With you and Bubu. A proper family. Nothing else matters to me. Nothing. Can I come round later?'

He hesitated, then added, 'I love you so much,' and rang off.

It was the right thing to do. He knew it now. Part of him would always feel bad, but that was the pay-off. Boil it all down and Sarah and the baby were what mattered. He'd just have to deal with the guilt. Hopefully they'd get Barren one day. Just not today. Like Leah Shalev had said: *We're drones, we take orders. And this is the order.* When all was said and done, he was just doing what he was told.

He sat back, feeling curiously calm, as if a weight had been lifted from his shoulders. Almost immediately he sat forward as his phone went off. Assuming it was Sarah, he answered without even looking at the display. It wasn't Sarah.

'Ben-Roi, it's me. I've been trying to get hold of you. We need to talk.'

Suddenly the weight descended again. Right at the moment, this was a conversation he could do without.

LUXOR

Khalifa was sitting perched on the edge of his desk, a dynamo of nervous energy.

'So that's the situation at this end,' he explained, tamping out one Cleopatra and immediately firing up another. 'If we're going to move against these companies, you're going to have to put in a formal request for cooperation. If you can get the American authorities involved, so much the better.'

At the other end of the line Ben-Roi was silent.

'I know it's crazy,' continued Khalifa, misinterpreting the Israeli's lack of response, 'but that's just the way things work in this country. Barren, Zoser – they've got a lot of connections. We need to . . . how do you say . . . attack with two prongs. So: any idea how long it will take to get the request?'

Still no response. Khalifa repeated the question, thinking maybe Ben-Roi was being distracted by something. There was a breath – midway between a sigh and a groan – then:

'We need to talk about this.'

'I know we need to talk about it. That's why I called!'

Khalifa laughed, something faintly manic about the sound. There was no corresponding indication of amusement from the other end.

'Ben-Roi?'

'Listen, my friend, there have been certain complications . . .'

The Egyptian's brows knitted. '*Compillycashions?* How do you mean?'

'Just that . . .' Another breath, as if Ben-Roi was choosing his words. 'Well, to cut a long story short, the case is being taken over by another department, because of Barren being American and all that. They've got a lot of connections here too so we're having to tread carefully.'

Something about his tone set alarm bells ringing in Khalifa's head. 'I don't understand what you're saying.'

'Basically, I'm off the case. I'm not involved any more.'

Khalifa slipped off the desk, cigarette ash raining down on to the floor. The bells were ringing louder now. Much louder.

'Is this a joke you're telling me?'

Ben-Roi grunted. 'Like my boss says, I'm not wearing my joking face.'

'Just like that, you're moved off a case?'

'Looks that way.'

'But why? Why would they do this? You told me this morning you'd practically solved the thing.'

Ben-Roi mumbled something.

'What?'

'I said: these things happen.'

'You're not bothered about it?'

'Of course I'm bothered.'

'You don't sound bothered.'

'Trust me, Khalifa, I'm bothered. There's just not a lot I can do about it. Now look, I'll always be grateful for—'

'So you tell this other department to put in the request.'

'Sorry?'

'Tell this other department to put in the request. I can't do anything without a formal request for assistance from your side.'

'Unfortunately it's not as simple as that.'

'What's not simple? You call them, explain the situation—'

'It's not as simple as that,' repeated Ben-Roi, a hint of annoyance creeping into his voice. Something else as well. Although Khalifa couldn't be sure, it sounded distinctly like embarrassment. He pulled hard on his cigarette, his brow rucking into a concertina of suspicious wrinkles.

'What's going on?' he asked.

'Nothing's going on.'

'You've just been moved off a murder case, and you're telling me nothing's going on.'

Silence.

'Did someone get to you? Is that it?'

'I don't know what you mean.'

'Did someone warn you off?'

'No one warned me to do anything.'

'So why's the case been moved to another department?'

'I just fucking told you!' Unmistakable annoyance now. 'Barren are an American company, they have a lot of connections here, there are certain ways of approaching—'

'So give me a name and a contact number and I'll speak to this other department direct.'

'It doesn't work like that. You can't just call up out of the blue—'

'Like you called me? Remember? That's how all this started. You called me out of the blue and asked for my help. And now I'm asking for your help. I have a mine full of toxic waste, wells being poisoned, barges going up and down the Nile . . . I can't move against the people responsible unless your government asks my government—'

'Don't raise your voice to me, Khalifa.'

'I'm not raising my voice!'

'You are raising your voice! And I don't appreciate it. I don't know what happened to you last night . . .'

'What happened to me last night, my *friend*, is that I nearly died inside a mine because you asked—'

'I didn't ask you to do anything!'

'You asked me to help you with a murder case! I did help you. I *am* helping you. Barren killed a woman in Jerusalem—'

'We don't know they killed her.'

'Of course they killed her. You told me they did this morning.'

461

'*Maybe* they killed her.'

'They killed her! You know they killed her. She found out what they were doing in the mine—'

'We have no direct evidence—'

'What the hell are you talking about? I've got a mine full of evidence! A million barrels of evidence! I've never worked on a case where there was so much!'

'This isn't your case!'

'It *is* my case! If it wasn't for me you'd know nothing about Samuel Pinsker, the mine, Zoser . . .'

'And I'm grateful for that, I've told you. But now the ball's in our court. It's an Israeli case. And I am telling you your help is no longer required.'

'It *is* required!' Khalifa took a furious snatch on his cigarette, his hand trembling. 'It's required because you're clearly not man enough—'

'What? What did you just say to me?'

'You're not man enough to see the investigation through, to go after the criminals.'

'How dare you!'

'Someone got to you, Ben-Roi.'

'I am not going to sit here—'

'Barren got to you.'

'You don't know what the hell—'

'Barren got to you! That's why the investigation's being moved. I helped you, Ben-Roi. I solved the case for you. I risked my life. And now, like the scheming Jew you are—'

'What? What? How dare you, you filthy little rag-head—'

'They killed my son!'

'Don't be bloody—'

'They killed my little boy!' Khalifa was bellowing now. 'A Zoser barge loaded with Barren's toxic waste. They killed Ali. They killed me. They killed Zenab. And now you won't help me bring them to justice because you're too afraid. You bastard! You bastard Jew coward!'

He lashed a foot at the waste-paper basket beside his desk, sending it tumbling across the room. At the other end of the line he could hear Ben-Roi breathing heavily. There was a silence, then the Israeli's voice. He was clearly struggling to keep it under control.

'I'm sorry for what happened to your son, Khalifa. I truly am. And I'm grateful for everything you've done. But this is going no further. It's over. You understand? It's over.'

Another silence. Then, from nowhere, another voice. Not Ben-Roi's. A female voice.

'No, it's not. It's not over at all. In fact, it's only just beginning.'

JERUSALEM

'What the . . .'

Ben-Roi held the phone away from his ear, horrified, then slammed it back. He'd recognized the voice instantly. The woman from the Nemesis Agenda, Rivka Kleinberg's daughter. Dinah Levi or whatever the hell name she was going by now. And she was on the line. Breaking into their conversation. Like the two of them had been talking privately in a room and she had suddenly jumped out of a cupboard.

'How the . . . ?'

'We bugged your phone,' she cut in, anticipating the question. 'Back in Mitzpe Ramon. Clever little device. Allows us to listen not just to your calls but to everything within a five-metre radius of the handset.'

It took a moment for the full implications of this to sink in. When it did, Ben-Roi's face went black.

'Get off the line, Khalifa. Get off now.'

The Egyptian ignored him. 'Who are you?' he snapped. 'What do you mean, it's not over?'

Ben-Roi repeated his demand, but no one was talking any notice. Like the kid who'd been kicked out of the gang, all he could do was sit there listening helplessly while the woman filled Khalifa in on the Nemesis Agenda and what they did.

'Barren have pulled strings,' she explained. 'The Israelis are burying the investigation. Your friend's taken a bribe to drop it.'

'That's a fucking lie! Don't listen—'

'Like I told him when we met a few days back, the law doesn't touch companies like Barren. Or Zoser. Any of them. The only way to bring them down is to play as dirty as they play.'

'So tell me how!' Suddenly Khalifa's voice was excited. Urgent. 'Tell me what I can do!'

'Are you mad, Khalifa? Don't even think—'

'Tell me what I can do!'

'You can help us,' came the woman's voice.

'Yes. I'll do it. Anything.'

'For God's sake, Khalifa!'

'There's a waste shipment arriving tonight. We've hacked the Zoser mainframe, got all the details. They're running a deep-water dock north of Rosetta, right at the mouth of the Nile. The ship's due in around midnight. We're on our way there now. We're going to film the whole thing, maybe interrogate a couple of the crew. Then we need to go to the mine. Can you take us there?'

'Of course!'

'Khalifa!'

'We're going to text you a secure number. Call us back on it and we'll arrange where to—'

'I'm coming to Rosetta!' cried Khalifa. 'They killed my son. I want to be involved.'

'Sorry, but we don't work—'

'I'm coming to Rosetta! That's the deal. I want to see it for myself. I come to Rosetta, then I take you to the mine. It's that or nothing.'

There was a sound of muffled whispering, as if the woman was conferring with someone else, then, reluctantly:

'OK. Rosetta it is. Have you got the notebook? The one about the mine?'

Yes, came the reply.

'Bring it with you. We might be able to use it. We're texting you now.'

'For God's sake listen to me, Khalifa, these people are—'

'What? What are these people?'

It was the first time in two minutes anyone had acknowledged Ben-Roi's presence.

'Tell me what they are, Ben-Roi?'

'They're lunatics! Terrorists!'

'And you're a liar and a coward! And I know who I'd rather be working with right now. You had your chance, Ben-Roi, and you chose to take the bribe and walk away. It's none of your business any more. I'll call you as soon as I get the text.'

This to the woman. Ben-Roi shouted, told Khalifa not to do it, that it was crazy, that they were never going to get Barren and he might as well just accept the fact. He was talking to himself. The line was already dead. He hurled the mobile across the room. As he did so he caught sight of a figure standing in the doorway. Half in, half out. His jaw tightened.

'You been eavesdropping, Dov?'

LUXOR

The text was waiting for Khalifa as soon as he got off the line. A mobile number. Egyptian, by the look of it. He called. The woman answered. They were about two hours out of Rosetta, she told him. Could he get himself up to the coast? No problem, he said. There were regular flights from Luxor to Alexandria via Cairo.

'Although I can't take a gun on the plane. Even with a police badge.'

'Forget it,' she said. 'We've got more than enough firepower to go round. Text us on this number as soon as you know what flight you're on. And don't even think of trying to double-cross us.'

Khalifa didn't know what the phrase meant, but he got the gist. He started to tell her nothing could be further from his mind, but she'd already rung off. For a moment he sat, a tiny warning light blipping somewhere inside his head. He was too pumped up to pay it any mind, too swept away by the current of his emotions. Justice, that was all he cared about. Justice for his son. And he didn't care how he got it. He pushed all doubts aside, snatched up the phone and called EgyptAir to book his flight north.

JERUSALEM

'You been eavesdropping?' Ben-Roi repeated, unable to hide the barb of accusation in the question. Dov Zisky didn't reply, just stood there peering unblinkingly from behind his circular spectacles, a sheaf of papers clutched in his hand.

465

'Dov?'

'We're letting Barren go?'

'So you *were* eavesdropping.'

'I was waiting to give you this.' Zisky lifted the papers. 'You were shouting.'

There was an awkward silence. Then, not wanting to get into another argument, Ben-Roi grunted and waved a hand.

'My fault. I should learn to keep my voice down.'

If he was hoping to defuse the situation, it didn't work. Zisky came forward a step.

'Why?' he asked. 'I thought we were—'

'Leah Shalev'll fill you in,' said Ben-Roi, cutting him off. 'The case is going up to Special Investigations and that's the end of it. These things happen. Now, what have you got there?'

Zisky wasn't going to be put off. 'But we can't just—'

'Don't tell me what we can and cannot do, Dov.' His tone was harsher than he intended, but he was wound up after his confrontation with Khalifa and wasn't in the mood for going through it all again. *Liar. Coward. Not man enough.* The Egyptian's words were still ringing in his ears, all the more crushing because deep down he knew they were true. Yes, he was acting for Sarah and the baby rather than because he himself was afraid, but the fact remained that he was dropping a case and taking a sweetener to do it. Twenty minutes ago he'd imagined he could deal with the guilt. Now he wasn't so sure. And he didn't need Zisky adding to his doubts.

In front of him the kid came forward another step.

'Arieh, listen—'

'It's "sir" to you.'

'But I've found something about Barren that I think—'

Ben-Roi snapped. 'I don't want to hear about Barren. You understand? We're off the case, it's gone upstairs, end of story. Whatever you've got, just leave it on the desk. And then piss off. I'd like a bit of privacy.'

Zisky stood tight-lipped, his expression such that Ben-Roi got the impression it was now *him* who was being accused. Then, stalking forward, he slapped the sheaf on the edge of the desk, turned and walked out.

Before Ben-Roi could reach them, the papers spilled off and scattered all over the floor.

'Fuck it!' he hissed. 'Fuck it!'

He sat a moment, his fist clenching and unclenching, mortified by how much like Chief Superintendent Baum the 'sir' comment had made him sound. Then, standing, he went after Zisky, meaning to apologize for his outburst. He couldn't find him and after trawling the station for five minutes he returned to the office. His mobile was lying in pieces in the far corner of the room. He had no idea what the bug looked like, didn't bother searching for it. Salvaging the SIM card, he took the rest of the pieces through to the rest room and dropped them into the toilet. Back in the office he rifled his colleague Yoni Zelba's desk, fished out the old Nokia he kept there, slotted in the card and put the phone on charge. Then he started collecting the spilled papers. They were all over the floor and under the desk, and he had to get down on his knees to reach the further ones, which struck him as somehow appropriate. He gathered them up, shuffled them into a pile and was just sliding them into his in-tray, sick of the whole bloody thing, when something came out at him off the page. A name. In bold type. Dinah Levi. He remembered asking Zisky to look into her, a couple of days ago, after the Nemesis people had held him prisoner. Presumably this was his report. Although hadn't he just said . . .

Frowning, he sat. The sheets were all out of sequence, and without numbers on the pages it took him a while to get them in order. There was something with the IDF logo on top, a copy of an e-mail from the Israeli Embassy in the US, a printout of a newspaper article about a girl getting arrested at an anti-globalization rally in Houston (wasn't that where Barren's headquarters were?). Quite a collection of stuff. Zisky had clearly been working hard. Which made him feel even worse about the way he'd just spoken to him. He got the pages sorted, tapped them into a neat pile, sat back and started reading through from the beginning. Slowly at first. Then, suddenly, more urgently as the pieces started to fall into place and the overall picture revealed itself. By the time he reached the end his face was ashen and a rash of sweat had pricked up across his forehead.

'Oh my God,' he whispered. And then, out loud: 'Khalifa!'

EgyptAir had no available economy seats that night. No business class, either. Which left Khalifa no choice but to empty out the family's meagre bank account buying a first-class ticket. In any other circumstances he would have been crushed with guilt. Tonight he didn't give it a second thought. His murdered son – that's all he cared about.

He confirmed the flights – 7.05 p.m. up to Cairo, with an 8.20 connection on to Alexandria, arriving at 8.50. As instructed, he texted the details to the Nemesis people. The response came back immediately: *Call when you're on the ground & we'll tell you what to do.* Again the warning light blipped somewhere deep inside his head. Again, he didn't pay it any attention. He phoned home and fobbed Zenab off with another story about having to work late. Then, still with a bit of time to kill before he was due at the airport, he looked up a map of the delta and spent fifteen minutes acquainting himself with the lie of the land he was about to venture into.

Rosetta, or Rashid as it was more commonly known, sat near the mouth of the westernmost of the two arms into which the Nile branched as it approached the coast. There was the town itself, clustered along the river's western shore, and a few kilometres down-river the medieval fort of Qaitbay, where in 1799 Napoleon's invading forces had discovered the famous Rosetta Stone. None of that concerned Khalifa. His interest was in the bare, sandy promontory just north of Qaitbay, where the Nile finally ended its 6,700-kilometre journey and issued into the Mediterranean. The area was marked as both a nature reserve and a militarized zone, which meant only those with authorization could enter. That's where the Zoser dock would be – well away from prying eyes. And there was only one approach road. Either they were going to have to go in on foot, or he'd have to blag it with his police badge. The final decision could wait till they were on the ground. For the moment he just needed to know what they were up against.

Four times while he was studying the map he got calls from Ben-Roi. Each time he let the calls go to voicemail and then wiped the message without listening to it. The Israeli was clearly working to an ulterior agenda and he wasn't interested in hearing more of his lies and excuses. He'd had his chance. What he'd started and bottled out of, he, Khalifa, was going to finish. With the help of the Nemesis Agenda. Ben-Roi could go screw himself. Scheming Jew coward.

He gave the map a final once-over and, just before 6 p.m., headed downstairs, taking Samuel Pinsker's notebook with him. Halfway down he heard Chief Hassani's voice in the foyer below, berating someone about the arrangements for the Valley of the Kings opening the following night. Not wanting a rerun of their earlier encounter, he was forced to hover for five minutes on the first-floor landing until eventually the voice faded as the chief left the building. He gave it another thirty seconds just to be sure. Then, by now behind time for his flight, he hurried outside. He was just turning left on to Medina al-Minawra, ready to flag down a taxi to take him out to the airport, when he heard a voice calling his name. A familiar voice.

Zenab.

She was standing on the opposite side of the street, beside the expanse of scrub-covered waste ground that fronted the police station. He glanced at his watch – 6.10, well behind time – and jogged over to her.

'What are you doing here?'

Her *hijab* had dropped back over her hair; there was sweat on her forehead. Like she'd been running.

'Zenab?'

'You said you were working late.'

'I am. I'm . . . just popping out to get something.'

Twenty years they'd been married and he'd never once lied to her. These last thirty-six hours he seemed to have done little else. She reached out a hand and touched his arm, her gaze rolling up to meet his. There was no need for her to say anything. It was all in her eyes. She knew he wasn't telling the truth. A couple of seconds passed. Then, withdrawing her hand, she stepped back and dropped her eyes to the ground.

'Is she beautiful?'

It took Khalifa a moment to get what she meant.

'Oh, Zenab!' His voice was caught between horror and black amusement. 'Zenab!'

He came up to her, took her arm, guided her a few metres out on to the waste ground, away from the scatter of people lined along the side of the street.

'How could you think such a thing?'

'I know I haven't been a good wife, Yusuf. These last nine months. Since . . .' She blinked away tears. 'I don't blame you. Really I don't.'

'Stop this, Zenab. Stop it now.'

He slid the notebook into the inner pocket of his jacket and took her hands in his. Her beautiful, long-fingered hands. Hands that as long as he lived he would never tire of holding.

'You are the love of my life. In all the years we have been together I have never once looked at another woman. Why would I when the most beautiful woman in the world is right here at my side?'

'Then why, Yusuf? Why are you lying to me like this? I hear it in your voice, I see it on your face. I know you too well.'

Now it was Khalifa's eyes that dropped.

'Where were you last night?' she pressed. 'You don't call. When you come home your clothes are filthy, you haven't slept, there is blood on your arm, you look like a ghost.' Her hands were trembling. 'What is happening, Yusuf? Tell me.'

'Just . . . station stuff,' he mumbled, shuffling his feet, twisting his wrist fractionally to shoot a glance at his watch. 'The Valley of the Kings thing, Chief Hassani . . .'

She snatched her hands away, brought them up to his face.

'Please, Yusuf! Enough lies. I know how much I have leant on you since we lost Ali, how much you have had to bear on top of your own grief, how much of a burden—'

'Don't say that, Zenab! You've never been a burden! Never! You are my wife—'

'Then tell your wife what is happening! Please, I beg you! I beg you!' Tears were gathering on her eyelashes, dropping on to her cheeks. 'These last few days, for the first time I have felt . . . thought maybe there is some light at the end of the tunnel. But I cannot do it without you, Yusuf. There is something wrong, I feel it. I need to know. Because to lose a husband on top of . . . on top of . . .'

She couldn't finish the sentence. Khalifa grasped her shoulders, sneaking another glance at his watch as he did so, hating himself for it, but there was so little time, so much riding on him making the flight . . .

'You're not going to lose a husband, Zenab. I love you, I'm here for you. Always. Always. It's just that tonight . . . tonight I have to go to Alexandria.'

'Alexandria!'

'It's nothing to worry—'

She whipped her hands from his face, stepped away from him again. 'What are you not telling me, Yusuf?'

'Nothing . . .'

'What are you not telling me!'

'It's complicated.'

'So explain it!'

'There's something I have to . . . some people . . . it's a case Ben-Roi . . .'

'Tell me!'

'Ali! It's about Ali!'

It came out louder than he intended, just short of a shout. On the street behind them people turned to see what the commotion was about. Khalifa ignored them.

'It's about our son,' he repeated, struggling to keep his voice level. 'Our boy. I haven't got time to go into details, the details don't matter. All you need to know is that I am going to get justice for Ali.'

She didn't say anything, just stared at him, her hand at her throat, her brown eyes watery with fear.

'They killed him, Zenab. Zoser. And another company like them. They murdered Ali. And I'm going to get them. Punish them. There are people who are going to help me. Good people. There's nothing for you to be afraid of. It's all going to be OK. We're going to have justice for our boy. We're going to get the bastards!'

She was shaking her head. 'I don't recognize you,' she whispered. 'Twenty years and suddenly I no longer recognize my husband.'

'What don't you recognize?' His voice shot up again, something flaring inside him. 'They killed our son and I want justice! What don't you recognize about that?'

'This anger. This . . . this . . . madness.'

'It's madness to want justice?'

'To leave your wife, your family, while you go off on some fool's mission—'

'It's not a fool's mission! Don't say that! The law won't touch them so I have to do it myself! You should be thanking me! You hear? Thanking me, you ungrateful—'

He broke off, abruptly, gazing in horror at the fist he'd raised into his wife's face, the first time in all their years together he'd ever done such a thing. A couple of seconds passed, Khalifa contemplating the

471

fist as if it had somehow materialized out of thin air. Then his hand dropped like a stone.

'Oh God, I'm sorry,' he said. 'Please, I didn't mean . . . I'm so sorry.'

Zenab stared at him, shell-shocked, the amplified call to evening prayer echoing from the minaret of the Elnas Mosque further down the street. Then she did something *she* had never done in all their years together. Coming forward she dropped to her knees in front of Khalifa and clasped her hands in a gesture of supplication.

'My husband,' she whispered, 'my love, my light, my life. Never, ever have I stood in your way. Never have I made demands of you. But tonight I am pleading, pleading: whatever it is you are thinking of doing, let it go. I beg you, let it go.'

He stooped, tried to lift her, aware that people were looking, pointing. She shrugged his hand away, shuffled even closer, right up against him, tears spilling across her cheeks.

'If you could somehow bring our boy back then you would go with every blessing I could give,' she choked. 'I would go with you. To the end of the earth and beyond. But this is not to bring Ali back. This is to seek vengeance for something that was a terrible accident—'

'It wasn't an accident, Zenab! They murdered him, you don't know the story.'

'I know that my son is dead! And if he leaves here tonight, my husband will be too! Is there not enough pain in this family? If not for me, for your children – for Yusuf and Batah. Already they have lost a brother. Please, please, do not add a father to the list!'

'They're not going to lose—'

'They are, Yusuf! I know it, I feel it! All the crazy, dangerous things you have done in our years together – always I have stood by you because you are the finest man in the world and I have known that what you do comes from the goodness in your heart –' she slammed a hand against her chest. 'But this, Yusuf, this . . . whatever it is you are planning, it does not come from goodness. I see it in your eyes. It comes from anger, and hatred, and pain, and nothing can come of that but more pain. If what you say is true, Allah will be these people's judge. It is with Him that their punishment lies, not you. It will end in tragedy, Yusuf, I know it, I know it! And I cannot take more tragedy in my life. None of us can.' She was sobbing now, clinging to his legs. 'I beg you, Yusuf – wife to husband, mother to father, friend to friend: do not go tonight. I beg you. Do not go. Do not leave me. Stay! Stay!'

Ten metres away a small crowd had gathered at the side of the street, watching the unfolding drama. Someone was even holding up a mobile phone, filming the scene. Khalifa paid them no mind. Easing Zenab's arms away, he dropped to his knees and held her.

'It's OK,' he whispered, 'it's OK, my darling. Everything's going to be OK.'

Slowly she calmed. He pulled back, tilted her face up, took a handkerchief from his pocket and wiped the tears from her cheeks. Another few moments passed, the two of them just kneeling there, holding each other, everything beyond their immediate world seeming to fade and disappear so that it was just the pair of them alone in their own private bubble. Then, gently, he helped her to her feet. She started to smile, assuming he had relented. Then she saw him look at his watch.

'Oh God, Yusuf, I thought—'

He lifted a finger and touched it to her lips, silencing her. At any other time these last twenty years, if she'd implored him like that he would have backed down without question. Done whatever she wanted. Jumped off a cliff, if that's what she asked. Something had happened to him in the mine. Something had changed inside. Shifted. Hardened. He was not the person he used to be.

'I love you, Zenab,' he said, his voice suddenly dull and emotionless. 'More than anything in the world. And the kids. You are everything to me. But I have to do this. For Ali. And nothing you or anyone else says is going to stop me. I'll be back tomorrow morning. That's a promise.'

He leant forward and kissed her forehead. Then, with another look at his watch – 6.28; he was cutting this very fine – he pulled Pinsker's notebook from his shirt and set off at a jog. Behind him the man with the mobile phone stretched out his arm and zoomed in, filming as Zenab dropped back to her knees and buried her face in her hands.

BEN-GURION INTERNATIONAL AIRPORT, JERUSALEM

'Hi, Arieh. Got your message. I'm promised for dinner at Rinat's but you can come round later if you want to talk. Or else we could do breakfast. If you're serious about this new job, moving up to Haifa . . . well, let's discuss it. I'll wait to hear from you. *Shalom.*'

Ben-Roi heard the voicemail through, clutching the phone in his left hand while with his right he fished his red police number plates from the Toyota's boot, then played the follow-up message.

'P.S. *Gam ani ohevet ot'cha.* I love you too, big man. Despite my best efforts not to.'

He slammed the boot, locked the car, slapped one of the magnetic plates on to the rear panel, all the while trying to figure out how best to respond to the messages – to convey the fact that although he loved Sarah more than anything, he was, yet again, about to let her down. He couldn't think how to word it, make it sound anything other than what it was – another brush-off. With time evaporating, he decided to leave it till he'd got himself on board. He gave Khalifa one last try, then pocketed the phone, attached the front number plate and ran full tilt into the departures hall of Ben-Gurion International Airport.

It was a crazy thing to do, insane, but it was the only plan he could come up with at such short notice. The Egyptian wasn't answering his calls. Same with his friend Danny Perlmann in Inter-Force Liaison, which meant he had no direct line to the Egyptian authorities. And even if he did get a line, what was he going to tell them? That a bunch of anti-capitalist headbangers was about to launch an attack on Egyptian soil? Aided and abetted by one of their own police officers? He couldn't see that playing particularly well for Khalifa. Even if it did save his life.

In the end, desperate, unable to see any other alternative, he'd called El-Al. They ran a once-weekly service into Alexandria – the one Rivka Kleinberg had been booked on. It didn't fly till the following night, however, by which point the trap would almost certainly have sprung and Khalifa would be lying face down with a bullet through his head. The only other option was an Egyptian carrier, Air Sinai, a subsidiary of EgyptAir. He'd contacted them, not holding out much hope. His pessimism was misplaced. They had a service that night. At 7.10 p.m. Arriving Alexandria at 8.45 p.m. He'd stalled, frantically trying to think of some easier way of helping his friend. Short of heading down to the Western Wall and praying, he couldn't come up with one, and with the clock ticking he had booked his seat. He'd spun home to get his passport, then driven like a maniac down to Lod, arriving seventeen minutes before take-off. The rush was

474

probably a good thing. Like Khalifa's jump in the mine, if he'd really taken the time to think through what he was doing, he would never have done it.

The Air Sinai check-in desks were all empty, the flight's last call having long since gone out. That close to take-off, a civilian would never have made it on to the plane. With his police ID he was able to skip the red tape and sprint straight through to the gate. He had a stand-up row with the girl checking the boarding passes, who didn't want to let him on. His details were on the computer, however, and matched his passport, and eventually he managed to hector her into submission. He was still strapping himself into his seat – between an elderly Arab woman and an overweight man with his arm in a sling – as the plane backed away from its stand and started its taxi out to the runway.

He retrieved his mobile. Things were likely to get hectic once he landed in Egypt and he didn't want distractions. If he was going to respond to Sarah's messages, he should do it now. He ducked his head and started to dial her number, quickly, hoping the cabin crew wouldn't spot him, only to change his mind and switch to text. For no reason he could explain – the stress of the situation, most likely – the wording of the message suddenly assumed huge importance to him. He spent the entire length of the taxi thinking it through, and it wasn't until the plane had wheeled on to the runway and the engines begun to power up for take-off that he finally started to dab at the keypad.

Love U both. More than anything in world. Promise will always B there 4 you. Will call tomorrow. We'll B the happiest family ever.

He just had time to add kisses and press send as the plane roared down the runway. And then they were off the ground and he was leaving his homeland.

'You shouldn't have that on,' admonished the man in the sling. 'It can interfere with the controls.'

'Right,' said Ben-Roi. 'Sorry.'

He killed the phone. Easing his seat back, he stared up at the ceiling, his eyes inexplicably pricked with tears.

William Barren was also staring at an aeroplane ceiling, although in his case it was one of the company's Gulfstream G650s, and his eyes most certainly weren't pricked with tears. Far from it. He was feeling about as good as he'd ever felt in his life. The climax was fast approaching. All the years of planning and scheming, manoeuvring and ground-laying . . . boy, was it going to be a climax! Better than anything he'd achieved with those underage nigger whores in downtown Houston. Talk about delayed gratification!

He swirled his bourbon round the tumbler.

It had been a spontaneous decision to fly out. Although his presence wasn't strictly required, he had felt a sudden need to be close to the action. Not in the middle of it – others were doing the dirty work – but close. A few hours ago he'd been lounging in his pent-house. Now he was well on his way. It was what the company had long needed, a bit of spontaneity. His father's decision processes were glacial. He didn't do spur-of-the-moment. That would all be changing when he, William, was in charge. A bit more gut-instinct, a bit more flexibility. Under him, Barren would be a very different company. Although still a top predator. Some things didn't change. Some things were hardwired.

He sipped the bourbon and tapped his mobile on the seat's armrest. One of the crew came through and gave him an update on their progress. They were ahead of time, would be landing twenty minutes earlier than planned. William thanked him and sank back into the white leather, gazing at the phone. The special phone. The one on which he'd soon be getting the call.

Forty-eight hours and all family business would be settled. He smiled and took another sip, the cabin vibrating gently around him. As good as he'd ever felt in his life.

ALEXANDRIA

Had Khalifa looked up as he strode into the arrivals terminal of Alexandria Nozha just after 9 p.m., he would have seen a familiar figure remonstrating with security officials on the far side of the hall. And had he gone over and spoken to that figure, much subsequent heartache might have been avoided.

He didn't look up. He was too busy on his mobile, listening as the Nemesis woman relayed details of where they were going to meet him. By the time she was off the line he was already pushing through

476

the airport exit doors, and the one fleeting chance of averting tragedy had been missed.

Outside the terminal he waved down a taxi and, as instructed, told the driver to take him east towards Rosetta. The man tried to engage him in conversation, asking about his family, what he was doing in this part of the world, what he thought of the new government. Khalifa's answers were grudging mumbles, and after a few kilometres, tiring of the man's questions, he pulled out his police badge and flashed it. Thereafter they drove in silence.

It took a while for them to get out of the city. Only when they had crossed a long causeway over a reed-fringed lake did the tenements and factories and oil refineries finally drop off behind them, giving way to a patchwork landscape of sandy scrub, cotton fields and palm and citrus groves. Khalifa smoked, and stared out of the window, and thought about his son.

Halfway to Rosetta – just as the Nemesis woman had described – they passed a neon-lit Mobil petrol station followed by two giant road-side hoardings: one advertising Pierre Cardin shoes, the other KFC. Ordering the driver to pull over, Khalifa counted out the fare, got out, walked fifty metres further down the road and took up position beside a wigwam-shaped stack of cut reeds. Thirty minutes passed. Then, from nowhere, a white Toyota Land Cruiser swerved off the highway and skidded to a halt in front of him. At the same moment there was a crunch of footsteps in the palm grove behind and a young woman emerged from the shadows.

'In,' she said, chopping a hand towards the Land Cruiser's open rear door.

Khalifa did as he was told. The woman slid into the front passenger seat and the driver – a slim, Arab-looking man with a cigarette dangling from the corner of his mouth – took them back on to the highway.

'I was starting to think you weren't coming,' said Khalifa as they picked up speed.

'We needed to watch a while,' explained the woman, swivelling to face him. 'Make sure you weren't being tailed.'

She flipped out a hand.

'Dinah. And this is Faz. Glad you could join us.'

Khalifa took the hand.

'Yusuf Khalifa.'

'I know,' she said. 'We've been listening to your calls, remember. That the notebook you were talking about?'

She indicated the leather-bound volume peeping out of Khalifa's jacket. He nodded.

'Keep it safe. We'll decide what to do with it later.'

'It's just the two of you?'

'The others are up at the coast. Reccying the dock.'

'What's the plan?'

She gave a noncommittal shrug.

'Right at the moment there isn't one. The ship's due in at midnight. From what we picked up on the Zoser system, it comes in once a month, offloads the waste then goes to get more while Zoser barges work in relays ferrying what's already been delivered up the Nile. What the whole operation actually looks like on the ground, though...' Another shrug. 'We're making this one up as we go along.'

Turning, she fumbled in the glove compartment and passed a gun back to Khalifa.

'You know how to use one of these?'

'Of course.'

'I'm hoping it won't be needed, but we can't take any chances. We don't know what we're going to run into up there.'

Khalifa weighed the gun in his hand. A Glock, by the look of it. She watched him, her pale, intense face looming in and out of shadow as lights came and went alongside the highway. There was a silence, then:

'You're taking quite a risk coming here. Throwing in your lot with us. Like your friend said, we're dangerous. Lunatics.'

'Ex-friend,' corrected Khalifa, laying the gun aside and pulling out his Cleopatras. 'And I'll take my chances.'

For a moment their eyes held. Then, with a nod, she turned and faced forward. Khalifa dropped his window and lit a cigarette. Nothing more was said for the rest of the journey.

They came into Rosetta twenty minutes later, just after 10.30. Faz the driver seemed to know where he was going, navigating confidently through a tangle of noisy, brightly lit streets and out the other side of town, where they picked up a narrow tarmac road north to the coast. The Nile tracked them to their right – broad and black and dotted with boats and the pontoons of floating fish farms. There were scattered houses and barns, and, strung along the shoreline, a succession of brickworks, their smoke-darkened chimney stacks silhouetted against the night sky like the remains of some blasted forest. Once they were past the village of Qaitbay the buildings disappeared, leaving nothing but maize fields, the odd palm grove and, ahead in the distance, a fuzzy, dome-shaped glow that suggested a concentration of light somewhere near the mouth of the Nile. The Zoser dock, guessed Khalifa. His pulse quickened.

They continued for another few kilometres, watchful now, cutting the lights, keeping the speed right down, the glow growing brighter all the time. Then, as some sort of illuminated security point loomed into view ahead, they turned off the road on to a narrow track. After a couple of hundred metres it petered out in a clearing in the middle of a palm grove. The spot seemed to have been prearranged because another Land Cruiser was waiting for them. Two people were standing beside it: a fit-looking man and a crop-haired woman. They pulled up behind and got out. Introductions were made.

'So how are we looking?' asked the Dinah woman.

'Not as bad as it could be,' said the man, 'although we could really do with more time.'

'We haven't got more time. It's either tonight or we have to wait another month.'

The man acknowledged the point and waved them over to a laptop sitting on the bonnet of the second Land Cruiser. On the screen was a mosaic of some forty photographs, presumably the fruit of the reccying mission he and the short-haired woman had undertaken. He enlarged the first image: the security point they'd just seen. A high chain-link fence stretched off to either side of it, topped with loops of razor wire. In the background, facing towards the river, were what looked like a row of warehouses, crane-tops peeping above them.

'The fence goes right the way round the site,' he began, 'three guards on the gate . . .'

'Army?' asked Khalifa.

The man nodded.

'They'll be conscripts. Just going through the motions.'

'That's certainly the way it looked. One of them was asleep, the others were watching TV. There's a couple of guys patrolling inside, but they didn't seem particularly interested and there's a lot of distance between them. The fence isn't electrified, and there are no security cameras we could see. We cut through without any problem.'

'How far from there to the dock?' asked the Dinah woman.

'About seven hundred and fifty metres. It's open ground, but there are dunes and scrub which provide decent cover. We got across without any trouble.'

He called up another photo. A long expanse of concrete wharf, bounded on one side by warehouses, on the other by a vista of choppy, moonlit water where the Nile issued into the sea. A hundred metres offshore a ridge of enormous concrete cubes had been sunk to create a protective breakwater. On the dock itself there were three huge gantry cranes with cantilevered jibs projecting out over the water.

'As you can see it's brightly lit, and there are people around. Dock workers mainly, although there's some security.'

He clicked on the laptop again. A telephoto image came up of a burly man in a leather jacket, toting a Heckler & Koch MP5 sub-machine gun.

'Private contractor, by the look of it. Nothing we can't handle. There are good filming positions here, at the near end of the dock --' he returned to the previous image – 'and here, from between these warehouses.' Three more photos: a long shot of a pile of crates stacked in the gap between two warehouse buildings; a close-up of the crates; a shot taken from behind the crates, looking across the centre of the dock towards the water.

'It's all perfectly doable. The problem's going to be getting anywhere close to the ship. We can film from a distance, but actually getting on board, maybe nabbing one of the crew – that's going to be tough given the amount of light and how exposed it is. There might be a way, but we're not going to know for sure till the ship's actually in and we can see how it all plays out. Until then we're just guessing.'

The Dinah woman nodded. Glancing at her watch, she leant forward on to the bonnet and started working through the images, bringing them up one by one, familiarizing herself. Her friends joined her. Khalifa hung back a step. They were the experts. He was just along for the ride.

Several minutes passed, a momentary breeze rattling the palm fronds above them, a distinct salt tang in the air. Then, as one, they came up straight.

'OK, let's do it,' said Dinah.

She turned to Khalifa.

'We're going to need someone to hang near the fence, cover our backs in case it all kicks off. You up for it?'

'I'm coming to the dock,' said Khalifa, aware that he sounded like a petulant child, but wanting to be at the heart of the action. *Needing* to be at the heart of the action. To his surprise she smiled.

'Somehow I thought you'd say that. OK, Faz, you're backstop. Gidi, Tamar, you set up at the end of the dock. Me and our new recruit will take the warehouse position. That's about as much as we can plan for the moment. Beyond that, we're going to have to play it by ear.'

They unloaded their equipment – cameras, walkie-talkies, a couple of Uzi sub-machine guns – and divvied it up. Then, each with a knapsack on their back, their hands and face smeared with a rudimentary camouflage of dampened soil to make them less visible – Khalifa would have laughed at himself had the stakes not been so high – they locked the cars and set off on foot. Somewhere out on the river a barge horn sounded. He curled his finger around the Glock's trigger and gritted his teeth, knowing he was doing the right thing.

Twenty minutes later they were in position. They'd got through the fence without any trouble, come round the warehouses from the rear, climbed on to the crate stack, set up the camcorder. In front of them the dock was awash with light. The crates themselves were set back and sunk in shadow. Khalifa felt curiously secure. Like he wasn't actually there, was watching the whole scene on television. The other pair radioed in to say that they were also in position, down at the far end of the dock. According to Khalifa's watch it was 11.42. All they had to do now was wait.

'You really think we can get them?' he asked, gazing out across the wharf. 'That all this will have any effect?'

'I wouldn't be doing it if I didn't.'

They ducked as a gigantic forklift truck whirred past in front of them. As they came up again he felt her hand on his arm.

'I should have said earlier: I'm sorry about your son.'

For a moment her face seemed to soften, although her eyes remained cold and unyielding. Then she removed her hand and looked away.

Out in the river mouth, mist was starting to gather, drifting over the water like wafts of steam.

A tunnel of light. That's what it's like when I approach a cleansing. A long tunnel of light with me at one end and the target at the other and everything else on the outside. Total focus. Total concentration. Until the job is done and I can step out of the tunnel and back into the daily run of things.

Of course there are differences this time around. I am not alone for a start, as I normally am. And the mess to be cleansed is closer to home. *At* home, in a sense, despite the distances involved. And naturally I have duties to perform, distractions, which is never usually the case.

Despite that, inside my head, I am in the tunnel. No more doubts, no more questions, no more worries. I see my target clearly -- how could I not, it's right beside me! – and I am moving steadily towards it. Soon it will be cleansed and I will be safe out the other side. Although what is *on* the other side remains to be seen. A different order, that's for sure. Who knows, maybe there will even be children. The patter of tiny feet. I hope so. I have always loved children. They appeal to my sense of . . . goodness.

For a little while longer, though, I must continue to play the part. Keep up the charade. From my face you would never know what I am shortly to do. Never in a million years. I am, and always have been, the consummate performer.

The ship eventually came in shortly before 1 p.m. There was a series of distant horn blasts and the activity on the dock suddenly intensified. A klaxon sounded, motors burst into life, dock workers hurried to and fro.

Offshore, the mist had been steadily thickening. The river mouth was now shrouded in a dense, gauze-like veil of impenetrable grey. They'd been watching its progress anxiously, fearful it would swamp the dock and make filming impossible. To their relief it had held back, sending out a few lazy tendrils on to the land, fingering the quayside, curling round the base of one of the cranes, but otherwise confining itself to the water. If the wind came up it would be a different story, but for the moment their view was clear. Khalifa's companion brought the walkie-talkie to her mouth and depressed the speak button.

'Everyone ready?'

Ready, came the reply.

'Faz?'

A surly voice announced that a convoy of diesel tankers had just passed through the main gate, but that otherwise everything was quiet behind them.

'OK, here we go.'

The horn blasts continued – an eerie plaintive bellow emanating from within the fog like the call of some primordial sea monster. Five minutes went by. Then, suddenly, as if it had been cleaved by a giant axe, the mist tore open and the prow of a huge ship loomed into sight away to their left. Slowly it glided towards the dock front, a towering wall of black steel whose stern-end remained lost in the murk even as its prow came level with the shore. On and on it came, more and more of it, impossibly large and threatening until eventually its bridge tower slipped from the mist and the whole vessel was revealed. Three hundred metres long and tall as an apartment block, it dwarfed everything below, making the bustling stevedores look no larger than ants. On its bow was a picture of a mermaid, her blonde hair streaming out as though pulled by the wind. Beside it, in white lettering, was the ship's name: *Maid of the Ocean*.

The camcorder pinged as his companion started recording the scene.

The vessel drew in flush with the dock, chivvied into place by a pair of tugs. Engines were thrown into full reverse; ropes were flung down and secured; stepped gangways descended fore and aft; there was a roar of hydraulics as giant hatches lifted and retracted. Crane hoists moved into position and dropped.

Another few minutes went by. Then, slowly, metal barrels started to emerge, neatly arranged on huge steel pallets, a hundred to a pallet. They lifted into the night, hovered, then retreated gracefully shoreward where they were lowered on to the giant forklifts and transported down the dock.

'You getting this?' crackled the walkie-talkie.

'Certainly am,' replied Khalifa's companion, pressing the handset right against her mouth to be heard above the commotion. 'All we need is for the fog to hold off a bit longer, then come in strong and blanket the whole place. That way we might have a chance of actually getting on board.'

Even as she spoke, Khalifa felt a sudden whisper of breeze brush across his face. It died, then came back, harder, ruffling his hair, causing the mist in front of them to bulge and drift like a billowing curtain. It started to creep over the ship.

'Just a few more minutes,' whispered Khalifa's companion. 'Just a few more minutes and then we can—'

She didn't finish the sentence. One moment she was there beside him, the next she was flying backwards off the crate on which they were standing. He wheeled. The ground behind the stack was black with shadow and he couldn't immediately see what was happening, just that there were two figures down there: the woman, and someone much larger who appeared to be pinning her to the floor. Leaping down he lifted the butt of his Glock ready to slam it into the attacker's head only to freeze as a familiar voice rang out.

'Back off, Khalifa. It's me.'

A craggy, square-jawed face turned up to him. A face he hadn't seen for four years but recognized instantly. A beat, then it looked back down at the woman.

'Now, *Rachel*, I think it's time we told our friend what you're really doing here.'

Ben-Roi's plan, such as he had a plan, had been to get to the docks as quickly as possible, locate Khalifa and pull him out before anyone harm could come to him.

Security at Alexandria airport had had other ideas. They'd detained him for over two hours, suspicious about the fact that he was Israeli, that his return flight was the next day, that he had no hotel reservation and above all that he didn't have an official visa. He could have told them the truth, that he was a policeman here to help one of their own policemen who was at that moment walking blindly into a trap. He sensed that to do so would only complicate matters, tangle him up in an interminable web of explanation. Instead he'd played dumb and stuck to his story: he was meeting an old friend from Luxor, the whole thing had been arranged last minute, the friend was organizing accommodation, he'd been assured he could obtain a temporary visa on arrival. It was flimsy in the extreme, and he had feared they wouldn't buy it, would take him for some sort of spy. His one hope was that they'd just check on 'Yusuf Khalifa' and find that someone with that name had indeed flown down from Luxor that night, thereby corroborating his story. Which was what, after an agonizing wait, they seemed to have done. There had been suspicious muttering and dark looks – a small insight into how it was for Arab travellers coming into Israel – but in the end they'd stamped his passport and waved him on his way.

'Make sure you're on that flight tomorrow,' one of the security officials had told him menacingly.

'Trust me, the sooner I'm out of here the better,' had been Ben-Roi's muttered reply.

He'd withdrawn a wad of money from a Bank of Alexandria cashpoint, taken a taxi out to Rosetta and from there north towards the mouth of the Nile, which was where the Nemesis woman had said the dock was located. As they approached the coast the driver had started jabbering at him in Arabic, signing that the road was a dead end, didn't lead anywhere, that they ought to turn round and go back. Ben-Roi had brandished a fistful of cash and told him to continue. They'd reached the point where the army security post had loomed into view ahead, whereupon the driver had stopped and refused to go any further.

'End,' he said. 'Soldier. No good.'

Ben-Roi had paid him off and got out. As the taxi had reversed around, the driver shaking his head as if he'd just been dealing with some sort of madman, the headlights had picked out narrow tracks heading towards a palm grove. And, within the grove, a flash of white. Ben-Roi had gone towards it, discovered two Toyota Land Cruisers parked up beneath the trees. The same Toyota Land Cruisers he'd seen back in Mitzpe Ramon, although now carrying Egyptian number plates.

Nemesis were here.

'Please God don't let me be too late,' he'd murmured.

He'd worked his way through the grove, came out twenty metres short of a high chain-link fence. Tubes of razor wire across the top, which was going to make climbing it a big ask. The Nemesis people would almost certainly have cut their way through, but he could spend an age searching for the opening, and time was already stretched to snapping point. He'd followed the edge of the grove back towards the security point, keeping low, thinking maybe he could try to slip through unnoticed. As he'd done so there'd been a rumble of engines and a convoy of ten diesel tankers had come chugging along the road, pulling up in front of the gate. The last one stopped almost level with him and he'd taken his chance. Sticking to the shadows he'd skirted round behind the tanker, scaled the ladder on the back of it and flattened himself on the curve of the tank's surface. There was a honk and the convoy started to move.

He was through.

A couple of minutes later they'd pulled up behind a line of

warehouses. Ben-Roi slipped down the ladder and melted into the shadow. The whole place was much bigger than he'd anticipated, and he'd feared it would take hours to locate Khalifa, by which point it would almost certainly be too late.

As it was it took him less than twenty minutes. He'd been to one end of the docks, watched the ship coming in from behind a hillock of metal containers, then doubled back the other way. He found a door in the rear of one of the warehouses, opened it, glanced inside – pitch black with a heavy smell of engine oil. Closing the door, he'd moved on to the end of the warehouse. The next warehouse was five metres away. Between the two buildings a broad grassy alley ran down to the dock, its end blocked with a stack of crates. And there, standing on the crates, facing away from him, two figures. It was hard to be a hundred per cent certain at that distance because the lights from the dock had thrown them into silhouette, but something told him he'd run down his quarry. He thought about shouting out, warning Khalifa from where he was standing, but he knew she'd be armed and the risk was too great. Treading carefully, therefore, the clank and roar of machinery covering the sound of his footfalls, he had moved towards them. Twenty metres away one of the figures had turned to the other and he had seen for sure that it was her. He'd frozen, pressing himself back against the side of one of the warehouses. She'd turned away again and he'd continued forward, creeping right up behind them. No fancy stuff. No grand speeches. No heroics. He had reached out, grabbed her belt and yanked the murdering bitch backwards off the crates and on to the ground.

'What in God's name are you doing, Ben-Roi? Get off her! Get out of here!'

Khalifa clawed at the Israeli's face. Ben-Roi butted his hand away. Wresting the gun from the woman's grasp, he threw it behind him, hauled her to her feet and propelled her down the alley between the warehouses, away from the dock and deeper into shadow. Khalifa came after them, tried to grab Ben-Roi's arms. Ben-Roi lashed with his foot, catching the Egyptian in the knee, knocking him over.

'Back off, you fucking idiot. I'll explain it all. Just back off.'

The woman was fighting and kicking, but he held her firm, one hand around her collar, the other jamming her right arm tight up behind her back. He pushed her twenty metres, then forced her down again, driving her into the ground. Khalifa was back on his feet.

Stumbling up behind Ben-Roi, he shoved the muzzle of his Glock hard into the nape of his neck.

'Get off her!' he snarled. 'You hear me? Get off her or so help me God, I'll shoot!'

'She's not what you think she is, Khalifa!'

'Get off her!'

'She's working for Barren!'

Beneath him the woman was bucking and lashing.

'Kill him!' she choked. 'For God's sake. He'll give us away!'

'I'm not warning you again, Ben-Roi!'

'Listen to me!' hissed the Israeli. 'She's duped everybody! You, the Nemesis people . . . she's a plant. She's Barren's person on the inside!'

'He's fucking crazy!'

She heaved furiously, trying to free herself. Ben-Roi was too strong. Leaning his full weight to hold her flat, breathing hard, he cranked his face round. The Glock's muzzle trailed along the line of his jaw as it turned, coming to rest on the tip of his chin. His eyes burned in the darkness.

'We've been here before, Khalifa,' he growled. 'Remember? Germany? You were going to kill me then too. And who was right that time?' He glared up at the Egyptian. 'Hear me out. That's all I ask. Hear me out for one minute. Because you need to know what she is. *Who* she is. If you want to shoot me after that, go right ahead.'

Khalifa's hand was trembling. He made no move to pull the gun away, but neither did he push it harder into Ben-Roi's face. He didn't trust the Israeli, didn't trust him an inch. He'd dropped the investigation, taken a bribe to step away. At the same time there was something in his tone, in the expression on that craggy, out-of-proportion face that gave him pause. And he *had* called it right before. There was a silence, the three of them locked together as though they had been freeze-framed – Ben-Roi holding the woman, Khalifa covering Ben-Roi. Then, with the faintest of nods, Khalifa indicated he would listen.

'It's all about families, you see,' began Ben-Roi, looking down and up again. 'Thing is, I've been barking up the wrong family tree. I got it in my head she was Rivka Kleinberg's daughter. Took a better detective than I'll ever be to find out the truth. Turns out she's not her daughter at all. She's Rivka Kleinberg's *god-daughter*. Isn't that the case, eh, *Rachel?*'

He gave her a shove, again emphasizing the name, his eyes never leaving Khalifa.

'Her mother and Kleinberg were best friends. Did their national service together. Stayed in touch. Even when her mother got a job abroad. At the Israeli Embassy. In Washington. Cultural Affairs department. Which is how she caught the eye of a certain billionaire American industrialist. A rather unpleasant man by the name of –' he let it hang a beat – 'Nathaniel Barren.'

Beneath him the woman tensed, then went limp. Khalifa stood with his finger tight around the trigger, mind whirring, trying to compute what he'd just heard.

'She's . . .'

'Exactly. Barren's daughter. Rachel Ann Barren, to give her her full name, although like her brother she was schooled under a pseudonym, kept well out of the limelight. Still a Barren, though. The dutiful daughter. And like all dutiful daughters, it seems she's been looking out for family interests.'

The woman's fists, Khalifa noticed, were knotted tight as flints.

'Is this true?' he croaked.

No answer. Which was all the answer he needed. Suddenly his throat was very dry. His finger eased off the trigger. Ben-Roi gave the gun a shunt with his chin, moving it away from his face. Khalifa allowed him to do it. The roar and clang of the dockyard seemed to fade as though a door had been eased shut between them.

'It's a curious thing, don't you think?' continued the Israeli, addressing himself as much to the woman as to Khalifa. 'All those dodgy multinationals the Nemesis Agenda's exposed over the years, all those high-tech hacking attacks, all those daring guerrilla raids, and the one company they've never once managed to dig any dirt on is Barren Corporation. Why do you think that is? Not because there isn't any dirt to dig, we know that for sure. So why? How come Barren's the one company that always comes up smelling of roses? Has always managed to keep itself one step ahead?'

No response. It was like there were three actors on stage and two of them had forgotten their lines.

'OK, here's another one for you,' said Ben-Roi. 'How did Barren find out Rivka Kleinberg was on to them? It's something that's been bugging me for a while now. She didn't contact Barren, she was keeping a low profile, gathering her evidence on the quiet. Only two people knew she was starting to make the connections. One was the pimp I told you about, Genady Kremenko, and he swears blind he didn't say anything. Which given that he had a gun halfway down his throat at the time, I'm inclined to believe. Which just leaves—' he gave the figure beneath him another shove. 'She's in it up to her neck, Khalifa. I haven't joined all the dots yet, haven't worked out the full story, but somehow Barren have got her into the Nemesis Agenda, and she's been protecting the company from the inside ever since. That's why she was so keen to meet up with you. That's why she wanted you to bring Samuel Pinsker's notebook. Because without you and the notebook no one's ever going to know where the mine is. And without the mine no one's ever going to know what Barren have been doing down there. She was going to waste you, Khalifa. Just like she wasted her own godmother. Isn't that true, Rachel? You killed her. You killed Rivka Kleinberg.'

On the ground the woman somehow managed to crane her head round so that she was half looking up at him.

'You really are a fucking idiot,' she spat. 'Even more of an idiot than I thought you were. When they killed Rivka I was two and a half thousand miles away in the middle of the Congo. And if I'd wanted to kill him –' she jerked a shoulder towards Khalifa – 'I could have done it any time in the last three hours. Just as I could have put a bullet through *your* head back in Mitzpe Ramon. No wonder companies like Barren get away with it when the best the law can throw at them is fuckwits like you.'

Above her, a transient flicker of doubt passed across Ben-Roi's face. Shaking it away, he hauled her back on to her feet.

'Like I said, I haven't got all the answers. The answers can wait. For the moment, we're getting out of here. And you're coming—'

He was cut short by a sudden burst of static from the walkie-talkie they'd left lying on the crates. There was what sounded like a crack of gunfire, and then a voice. A female voice. Frantic, hoarse with alarm.

'Get out, Dinah! It's a trap. They were waiting for us! Get out! Get out! They know we're—'

The voice was swallowed by another crackle of gunfire. Startled, uncertain what was going on, Ben-Roi's grip momentarily slackened. It was enough. His prisoner's foot kicked viciously back into his ankle while in the same movement she squirmed from his grasp. Swinging round, she slammed a knee up into his crotch, doubling him, then smashed the base of her palm hard into the underside of his jaw, snapping his head back, knocking him off his feet. Khalifa started to reach for her, but she was already running, back down the alley towards the crates at the end.

'Shoot her,' choked Ben-Roi, clawing himself up on to his knees, blood pumping from his mouth. 'Shoot the bitch!'

Instinctively Khalifa brought the Glock up, clasping his right wrist with his left hand to steady his aim. It was an easy shot despite the shadows, the sides of the warehouses narrowing her range of movement, the dock illumination back-lighting her to provide a clear target. He sighted down the barrel, tracking her, finger curled round the trigger. He couldn't bring himself to pull it. She reached the mouth of the alley, snatched up her Glock from the ground where Ben-Roi had thrown it, leapt up the crates as though hopping a set of stairs. At the top she stopped and turned. For a brief instant her eyes met Khalifa's. He couldn't be certain, but he thought she shook her head, although what it signified if she did he couldn't say. Then, scooping up the walkie-talkie and the camcorder, she jumped off the crates and was gone. He lowered the gun.

Beside him, Ben-Roi was back on his feet.

'Why the fuck didn't you shoot her?' he coughed, his voice thick and mushy, as though someone had stuffed a wet sponge in his mouth.

'Couldn't,' Khalifa mumbled. 'Not a woman. Not in the back.'

For several seconds he stood there, too dazed to move, his mind churning. Then there was another crack of gunfire, behind them this time, out by the perimeter fence, and he felt the Israeli's hand on his shoulder.

'We've got to get out of here.'

Khalifa turned. He had no idea what was going on, who was shooting, why they were shooting, whether Ben-Roi was right about the woman or not. What he did know was that the Israeli had come a long way and put himself in a lot of danger to help him, and that at least deserved some acknowledgement. He started to say something, broke off, unable to find the words he wanted. Instead, lifting his arm, he dabbed a sleeve against the big man's bloodied mouth.

'You look a mess, you arrogant Jew bastard.'

Ben-Roi grunted. 'And you look exactly what you are – a cheeky Muslim cunt.'

They nodded at each other, clasped hands and started down the alley away from the dock. They'd only gone a few metres when dark figures suddenly loomed in front of them. An explosion of bullets chewed up the ground at their feet.

'Gun down and hands on heads!' ordered a gruff voice. American accent. 'I'll only tell you once.'

The gun went down and the hands went up.

They were pushed along the back of the warehouse and round on to the dock.

The fog had come in noticeably over the past twenty minutes. In front of them the ship was now shrouded in a dense veil of white, rendering its outline blurred and indistinct, as if 60,000 tons of steel were in the process of slowly dematerializing. Wafts of vapour were rolling across the surface of the dock like dry-ice; the giant squares of the gantry cranes were receding into obscurity. It lent the whole scene a strangely unreal, dreamlike feel. A feel that was amplified when a klaxon sounded and the unloading work suddenly stopped. Engines died, dock workers melted away, lights dimmed. Everything became eerily silent and still.

Ben-Roi and Khalifa glanced at each other, but didn't say anything.

They were led across the dock to the ship's stern. A large black limousine was parked there at the foot of the boarding gangway. Beside it stood three muscular, stern-faced figures dressed similarly to the ones who were guarding the detectives: jeans, desert boots, flak jackets. They were armed with Heckler & Koch MP5s and Sig Sauer handguns. Their faces registered no discernible interest as the detectives were pushed past them on to the ship's gangway.

They climbed up the side of the vessel, the metal steps clanking beneath their feet. At the top they issued on to a narrow corridor of deck running round the ship's bridge tower. The mist was much denser up here, as though they had climbed into a cloud, and the top of the tower was lost in the murk above them. Somewhere overhead they could hear voices talking in a language they didn't understand. *Russian*, thought Ben-Roi. He felt something brush across his face, realized it was cigarette ash raining down. He didn't bother voicing a complaint.

With a wave of their guns, their captors motioned the two detectives to the right, around the base of the tower to its forward side. Sitting there, right at the back of the deck, was a rectangular storage container. The one Vosgi and those other poor girls must have been trafficked in, thought Ben-Roi. Its steel doors were open. It was too dark to see much of the interior beyond some foam mattresses laid on the floor. There was a sharp smell of urine and rusting metal.

They were waved up against the side of the container, into a dim pool of light thrown by a lamp on the tower above. In front of them a narrow gantry ran away into the mist, providing a walkway across the open cargo holds. The guards stepped back, covering them with their Hecklers.

A couple of minutes passed, the guards just standing there, Khalifa and Ben-Roi exchanging the occasional look, but otherwise silent, uncertain what was going on. Then, suddenly, they tensed. There was a sound. Faint, but audible. In front of them. Somewhere in the mist along the gantry. A sort of ghostly, rhythmic squeak. Instinctively their fists clenched, eyes straining into the gloom, trying to work out what was causing it. The sound continued, drawing closer. There was something unsettling about it, malevolent, the way it echoed out of the gloom as though something predatory was creeping towards them, snuffling its way along the gantry with evil intent.

'I've got a bad feeling about this,' murmured Khalifa, pressing himself back against the side of the container.

'You don't say,' was Ben-Roi's response.

Closer and closer came the sound, louder and louder. It was accompanied by footsteps now – slow slaps thudding on the latticed metal of the walkway. And, also, a shape. An indistinct blur of shadow looming within the mist. It bulged and deepened, as if forming itself before their eyes, its outline slowly solidifying until eventually it had resolved itself into the figure of a man. A huge, grizzled, overweight man shuffling along behind a three-wheeled walking frame.

Nathaniel Barren.

He came forward into the circle of light.

'Good evening to you, gentlemen.'

His voice was a deep, rasping growl. There was a pause as he eyed them up, then:

'She's a mighty impressive ship, don't you think? Just been for a turn along the deck. Need to get this wheel looked at.' He indicated one of the frame's castors. 'Little bit of oil should do the job.'

He grunted and lifted a hand, motioning the guards back. They retreated to the edge of the mist – far enough to take them out of the scene, near enough to keep the prisoners covered with their Hecklers.

'Normally we leave security matters to our Egyptian colleagues,' said the old man, adjusting his weight on the walking frame, 'but for tonight I thought it best to bring in some of our own people as well. Just to beef things up a bit. And a very good job they're doing.'

He gave an approving nod. A plastic mask was hanging on a cord around his neck. A thin tube dropped from it to an oxygen cylinder nestling in a sling below the walking frame.

'I was due out in Egypt anyway,' he went on, pulling a handkerchief from his pocket and dabbing at his mouth. 'Got this damned museum opening tomorrow night down in Luxor. Seemed reasonable to stop by here as well. Kill two birds with one stone, so to speak.'

In front of him Khalifa and Ben-Roi were backed up against the side of the shipping container. Khalifa's eyes were locked on Barren, alight with hatred. Ben-Roi's expression was more quizzical. Inside his head cogs were turning, trying to weave together all the strands, work out exactly what was going on.

'We just met your daughter,' he said, touching a hand to his swollen mouth.

'Did you now?' Barren smiled. 'An extraordinary young lady, don't you think?'

'She was working for you all along?'

The smile widened. 'Like I say, an extraordinary young lady. And a gutsy one. I'm very proud of her.'

'She set all this up?' asked Khalifa, his face white, his voice curiously blank. 'Brought Nemesis out here so you could kill them?'

Barren shuffled his feet and rolled his shoulders, adjusting his weight on the walking frame.

'Let's just say it's a great comfort to know that when I'm gone both the family and the company will be in safe hands.'

He chuckled, a dry, unpleasant sound, like a dog panting. Dabbing at his mouth again, he pocketed the handkerchief. Inside Ben-Roi's mind the cogs were still turning. Somehow the strands weren't quite weaving. There were dangling ends. Things that didn't fit.

'These people . . . they were only a part of it,' he said. 'A splinter group, a cell. The Nemesis Agenda still exists. You haven't got rid of it.'

Another chuckle.

'Bit by bit, Detective. Step by step. Trust me: we're on top of the situation.'

'And what about Rivka Kleinberg?' Ben-Roi thought he might as well get as much of the picture as he could before the inevitable happened. 'Who killed her? Rachel?'

Barren waved the question away. 'Someone who has the company's best interests at heart,' he said. 'In the circumstances I don't think there's much point in being any more specific than that. Although credit where credit's due – you worked the rest of it out pretty well. I saw a copy of the report you wrote. A very fine piece of detective work.'

He lifted a swollen, liver-spotted hand and tipped Ben-Roi an ironic salute.

'Like you surmised, we stumbled on the mine when we were prospecting in that part of the world. Didn't really think a great deal of it at the time. It was only when we landed the Drăgeş concession that it struck us we had a ready-made storage facility for some of the waste we were being obliged to ship.'

A gust of wind came up, momentarily blurring his huge pumpkin face behind a veil of mist.

'That was the only major detail you got wrong,' he continued as the mist cleared. 'We're not actually dumping *all* the waste. Only about a quarter of it. The rest of the stuff does indeed go back to the US for reprocessing and landfill. Damned expensive business, as I told you when we spoke the other night. Cuts our margins way down. Even offloading just twenty-five per cent of it is saving us hundreds of millions of dollars. Which is to say, *making* us hundreds of millions of dollars. And ultimately that's what it's all about, isn't it? Increasing the margins. Making money.'

His bushy grey eyebrows arched as if he was expecting Ben-Roi and Khalifa to express their agreement with this analysis. They didn't, just stood there in silence. Barren didn't seem especially put out by the lack of response.

'I met her a few times, by the way,' he added. 'The Kleinberg woman. She was a friend of my dear departed wife. Can't say I ever took to her. Don't think she did to me either. Funny, the little coincidences life throws up.'

He grinned, the expression almost immediately crumpling as he broke into a fit of coughing. His shoulders heaved, his rheumy eyeballs bulged as his lungs contorted, fighting for air. In front of him, Ben-Roi's eyes were flicking towards the guards as he tried to figure their chances of overpowering them. Slim, he decided. Very slim.

'So what now?' he asked when Barren had finally recovered himself.

'Now?' The old man's hands opened and closed around the walker's rubber grips. 'Now I believe we're going to wait for this mist to lift and finish the unloading. And then Captain Kremenko and his crew are going to start making amends for all the trouble they've caused with their little whore-smuggling operation by taking you gentlemen out into the middle of the ocean, chopping you up into bits and throwing you to the fish. Same with the bodies of those Nemesis hoodlums, which I believe are being gathered even as we speak. Them I can't say I'll be shedding any tears for, but if it's any consolation, killing police-men has never been something that sits easy with my conscience. But what can I do?'

He gave a helpless shrug, as if the whole thing had somehow been forced upon him.

'You should have taken the bribe, Detective. Primary rule of business: if you're offered a good deal, leap on it.'

He broke into a renewed fit of coughing. Beside Ben-Roi, Khalifa too was weighing the chances of rushing the guards. Like the Israeli, he was figuring them to be slim bordering on non-existent. In front of him, just a few metres away, stood the man he considered responsible for his son's death. The centre of the wheel on which his entire world had been broken. And he couldn't get to him. His chest felt hollow with the frustration of it.

'Anyway, gentlemen,' resumed Barren eventually. 'Enough talking. I'm a straight-down-the-line sort of guy, and I wanted to stand here in front of you and look you in the eye, clear up any questions you might have. Now that I've done that, I see little point in prolonging the meeting, so if you wouldn't mind . . .'

He tipped his head towards the guards. They came forward a couple of steps, Hecklers levelled, faces robotically impassive. With a sweep of their guns they motioned the two detectives into the shipping container.

'I've never been a great one for theatre,' said Barren as they stepped into the foetid interior and turned, 'but you have to admit there's a certain . . . what's the word? . . . synchronicity to the whole thing. Our problems started with this container, and that's exactly where they're going to end. If nothing else, it appeals to my sense of neatness.'

He smiled and signalled the guards. They started to close the container. Khalifa put out a foot, blocking one of the doors, holding it open.

'You killed my son,' he said, staring out at Barren. 'You killed my son, and I'm going to kill you.'

The old man's jaw pushed out. 'Are you now? Well –' he lifted his arm and examined his watch – 'you've got about four hours to do it. After which you're going to be way down on the bottom of the ocean with crabs chewing at your eyes. So if I were you I'd get a move on.'

Another of those wheezing chuckles, and Khalifa was shoved backwards and the container door slammed shut in his face. There was a metallic clunk as a padlock was secured – the second time in twenty-four hours he'd found himself trapped in impenetrable blackness – and the squeak of Barren's walker as he shuffled away along the deck. After a few seconds it stopped. There was a silence, then:

'Hello, Daddy. It's been a long time.'

Clenching a fist, Khalifa slammed it against the inside of the door.

'Liar!' he cried. 'Liar, liar, liar!'

RACHEL

The moment she'd heard Tamar's screams on the walkie-talkie – 'Get out! It's a trap!' – she'd known he was there at the dock. She couldn't explain it, she couldn't rationalize it. She'd just known. Had suddenly felt his presence. Inside her bones, way down deep in the pit of her stomach. Inside her insides. Just as she'd used to feel it as a child. Brooding in his library up at the top of the mansion; approaching like a storm cloud along the dimly lit corridors. All these years and now he was close again. Daddy dearest. Come to fetch his little girl. As she'd always known he would. The family always gathers up its own. The Labyrinth always draws you back into its heart.

She'd dealt with the Israeli cop, got herself over the crates, started sprinting down the dock, ignoring the shouts of the longshoremen, brandishing the gun at anyone who came too close. It was like she'd tumbled into a dream – everything vague and indeterminate from the mist, the way all the motors had suddenly stopped and silence descended. She'd called into the walkie-talkie, over and over, shouting their names – 'Gidi! Tamar! Faz!' – but she knew it was pointless and eventually she'd cast the handset aside. The camcorder too. She didn't even know why she'd bothered picking it up. Didn't know anything except that the others were dead and she was running and Daddy was here and it had all finally caught up with her, just as she'd been waiting for it to catch up these last eleven years. There's only so long you can hold the past at bay; only so much of yourself you can bury.

Keep me hidden, let no one see.

And now the past had become present. It was all unravelling.

Twice men had appeared from nowhere and seized her, twice she'd heard voices ordering her release.

'That's the one. Let her go.'

You're the one, Rachel. You've always been the one.

She'd shoved them away, kept on running.

At the end of the dock the fog was thick as milk. She'd clambered off the concrete down on to the rocks below, fumbled around where Tamar and Gidi had set up their camera, searching for them. There was nothing she could do to change what had happened, but she needed to see it with her own eyes. At least try to say goodbye before she went to find him. Particularly to Tamar. With Tamar she'd broken the golden rule. Got close. Just as she'd broken it with Rivka. And her mother too. And always when you broke the rule bad things happened.

'It's not my fault,' she choked. 'It's not my fault. It's not my fault.'

Although deep down, even after all these years, there was still a part of her that wondered if maybe it *was* her fault. If she could have done more to resist. If Rachel really was a whore.

'I'm sorry. I'm so sorry.'

She'd fumbled a while. Then an engine had started up somewhere ahead and to her right, away from the river. A truck engine. Lights through the mist. She'd stumbled towards them, found herself on gravelly sand, some sort of track. None of it seemed real. The fog had torn. In front of her, five metres away, the back of a pick-up truck. Two men sitting on the sides, dressed like the ones who had seized her up on the dock – jeans, desert boots, flak jackets. And lying at their feet in the truck's bed, like hunting trophies, three bodies. Two male, one female. Eyes open. A lot of blood. She'd heard screaming, had taken a moment to realize it was coming from her own mouth. She'd reached out but the truck was already moving away. One of the men had chopped a hand back towards the ship, mouthed something that might have been, 'He's there.' And then the fog had gathered again and the truck was gone.

She was alone. Like she'd always been. Alone in the mist. The murk of her own shame.

On autopilot, she had retraced her steps. Back across the rocks, back on to the dock, back towards the ship, the Glock still dangling in her hand. It all seemed to be happening in slow motion, like she was a character in a film spooling at half speed. She'd reached the gangway at the prow of the vessel, climbed on to the deck, followed the gantry down the middle of the ship, cargo holds gaping to either side like black pools.

Stronger, his presence had grown stronger with every step. A dark gravity inexorably drawing her in.

And then, suddenly, there he was in front of her. Shuffling along on a walker past the end of a large shipping container. A bloated, lumbering shadow looming through the mist. Just as she remembered him.

He must have felt her too, because he'd stopped and turned. Their eyes had met. The grizzled, ursine face had broken into a smile. As it did so the film cranked up to regular speed and it was no longer like a dream. Suddenly it was all very immediate and very real. Her heart had lurched, her stomach clenched. That ache between her legs again.

'Hello, Daddy. It's been a long time.'

To Ben-Roi and Khalifa it sounded like the greeting of a loving daughter. The return of the prodigal.

What they couldn't see – locked in the darkness of the container, separated by a wall of steel – was the expression on her face.

The expression of pure, unadulterated loathing. A loathing bordering on the demented, as if she was confronting something so disgusting, so utterly abhorrent, it was as much as she could do not to drop to her knees and vomit.

For a moment she stood there, frozen, the deck echoing to the pounding of fists from within the container, the cries of 'Liar!' Then, finger tight round the Glock's trigger, she came forward a couple of steps, into the circle of light. In front of her Barren shuffled the walker around and also came forward, waving the guards off the deck so that it was just the two of them standing there. Face to face. Father and daughter. After all this time.

'Hello, my darling Rachel.' His rheumy eyes were moist and twinkling, his mouth curved into an adoring smile. 'It has indeed been a long time. I've missed you. More than I can possibly say.'

He extended a trembling hand, reaching for her. She didn't move. All these years and the horror was as intense as it had ever been.

'You look wonderful,' he wheezed, his gaze moving admiringly up and down. 'All grown up. A beautiful woman now. I see your mother in you. A lot of your mother. You make me so proud.'

He made to shuffle forward some more, but she lifted the gun.

'Don't.'

He stopped, chest heaving as the breaths fought their way up through his diseased lungs. For a fraction of a second his features hardened. Almost immediately they relaxed.

'I'm sorry about your friends,' he said, the smile rearranging itself into an expression of sympathy. 'Truly I am. I know it must be upsetting for you. But it had to be done. It's time, you see. Time for you to come home. Your daddy needs you. Your *family* needs you.'

She just stared at him, her face pale as the mist. She could smell his aftershave – dense, oily, vaguely metallic. A smell that brought so many other things with it. Sounds – feet on carpet, creak of door handle – sensations: weight, pressure, entry. The things of her nightmares. The things she'd been running from her whole life.

'It's not been easy,' he was saying. 'Not having you there. The house so empty. Especially since your dear mother passed away . . .'

'She didn't "pass away".' Her voice was curiously blank, toneless. 'She killed herself. You know that.'

In front of her Barren leant forward on the walker, head shaking sorrowfully.

'I do know that, Rachel, I do, although I try—'

'Killed herself because she found out the truth. Because I told her what happened.'

Again the momentary tightening of the old man's features. It lasted longer this time.

'It's in the past, Rachel. We shouldn't dwell on it. It's the present that matters. And the future. The future of our family. That's why it was time to put a stop to all this –' he circled an arm – 'fetch you home. I've given you your freedom. Allowed you to get it all out of your system. Now it's time for you to come back where you belong. Take up your responsibilities.'

He stared at her a moment, then dropped his head as a succession of coughs tore through his chest. Fumbling for the oxygen mask, he clamped it to his mouth. It was a while before he was able to recover himself.

'Your daddy's not a well man, Rachel,' he rasped, eyes swelling over the mask's rim, his voice muffled by the transparent plastic. 'Doctors are giving me six months. Twelve at the outside. I have to think about the succession. Who's going to lead the family. Front-up the business. William –'

The name provoked a renewed fit of coughing, his whole body shaking, his eyes bulging so forcefully it looked like they were going to pop right out of their sockets.

'William . . . well, we all know what your brother is. A useless drug-addled, whore-mongering fantasist. Lives in a goddamn dream world. Thinks he's the big man. Thinks he's going to take control. Lead some sort of hostile takeover. Some sort of coup d'état. In here! All of it in here –' his fingertips hammered derisively against the side of his head. 'He's a runt. Always has been, always will be. Knew it the moment I saw him. No spine. No intelligence. You, on the other hand –' he lowered the mask, chest pumping beneath his tweed jacket – 'you, Rachel, are the real thing. A true Barren. More guts and brains than that shit-stick sibling of yours will ever have. You've proved it these last years. Over and over. You're the one. The true heir. The rightful heir. It's yours, Rachel. All of it. And now I need you to start taking up the reins. Need you to come home and do what you were born to do.'

His hand reached out again, beckoning to her. She stared at it, head shaking, face twisted into a rictus of disbelief.

'You're mad,' she murmured. Then, louder: 'You're mad.'

The old man's shoulders swelled, like a cobra puffing out its hood.

'I know you're hurting, Rachel—'

She erupted. 'You're fucking mad!' Suddenly her voice was flooded with emotion. 'Come home! After what you've done! After what you *did*! Why do you think I got out in the first place? Got as far away as I could. Changed my name, my identity, spent my every waking hour fighting people like you? Did everything I could to screw Barren? Just like you screwed—'

'Rachel—'

Her head flew back. 'I was a child, you fucking animal!' Screaming now, her eyes wild, flecks of spittle firing from her mouth. 'Ten years old! Every night! Our little secret! Daddy's special love! Just to show how much I care. Don't worry if it hurts a little! It's natural, perfectly natural! You vile, vile—'

'Enough, Rachel!'

'Come home! Take up the reins! After that? After Rivka? After tonight? You mad, deluded fucking –' Her voice was breaking up, the words snagging in her throat, her breath coming in short, desperate gasps. 'I will never come back! Do you understand me? Never. Never. I will never be involved in any of it. Never work for Barren. Never be part of your loathsome, twisted . . .'

Her left hand had started clawing at her scalp. Just like it used to do when she was young. When he had been inside her. Yanking at her hair as if she was desperately trying to drag herself away from him.

In the same motion her other hand lifted and levelled the Glock at his head. Which was what she'd come up here to do in the first place. What she should have done a long time ago. Had simply been projecting these last eleven years, what with all the marches and protests and riots and Nemesis actions. Transferring. Substituting. Whatever you wanted to call it. Putting off the inevitable.

And now it was time. Like Daddy said.

Time for the real thing.

Punishment time.

In front of her Barren had clamped the mask to his face again. He drew a series of slow, grating breaths, eyes never leaving her, the plastic misting around his mouth. Then, slowly, the mask came down.

'Oh my Rachel,' he said. 'My darling, darling Rachel.'

No guilt in his voice, although she wouldn't have expected it – her father was not a man who did self-reproach. Did any sort of moral accounting. No fear either, even though he had a gun aimed directly between his eyes. Instead a sort of ghastly, reproachful indulgence. Like a parent whose child has misbehaved, but who loves that child too much to be overly upset about it.

She felt her stomach turning.

'I know how difficult this is for you, Rachel. How much of a burden it can be. Duty. Destiny. You always were a free spirit. It was never going to be easy. But you have to understand that this *is* your destiny. To lead the family. The company. You can no more escape it than you can the blood in your own veins. You're a Barren. Like it or not, you're part of it. Involved. It's who you are. As for working for us –' he smiled – 'well, you're already doing that, so it's not so great a leap.'

Her eyes flickered, uncertain what he meant. He craned towards her over the walker, eyes gleaming.

'Message received,' he said softly. 'Offer accepted. We fight together.'

Already pale, her face seemed to assume an even more deathly pallor. Her mouth had to work a while before she could get any words out. 'What do you . . . how did you . . .'

'Oh, Rachel, don't you see?' Again, that tone of reproachful indulgence. '*We're* the Nemesis Agenda. Barren Corporation. It's us. We run it.'

A brief, horrified silence. Then her legs seemed to go from beneath her. She stumbled backwards, a breathy gurgle echoing up from inside her: part groan, part choke.

'No,' she whispered. 'You're lying. You're lying.'

Although she could see from his face that he wasn't. The loose fleshy grin. The triumphant hardness in his eyes. Just like when he used to come into her room at night, pull away her covers, absolute mastery . . .

'Oh God, no,' she whispered. 'Oh please God, no.'

He opened out his hands. Blotched, leathery hands, huge as baseball gloves. 'We own it all, Rachel. Control it all. Everything. That's what Barren is. In control.'

'Oh God, no.'

'Never imagined for a moment it would get this big. It was only supposed to be a small thing. A one-off. A little ploy to undermine a couple of our competitors. One of our in-house guys suggested creating a website, digging some dirt, putting it out there for the world to see under the guise of one of these crackpot anti-capitalist groups.' He shook his head. 'The whole thing just took off. Tapped into some sort of cockamamie zeitgeist. We've got a pair of supergeeks co-ordinating the whole thing back in Houston. And an international network of activists feeding us material in the mistaken belief they're somehow helping bring down the system. We're having to pay our guys a goddamn fortune to keep their mouths shut, but trust me, it's been worth it. With Nemesis, we can screw any rival we want to at the push of a button. Like shooting fish in a barrel. Un-be-fucking-lievable!'

Another shake of the head. The lottery winner struggling to come to terms with the immensity of his good fortune.

'Obviously we've had to be careful. Not *just* target rivals. That would leave way too clear a trail. And obviously we've targeted ourselves a few times. Nothing too heavy, just enough to throw people off the scent. Irony is, the Agenda's evolved into some sort of warped yardstick of corporate probity. Nobody trusts the fuckwit regulators any more, but the Nemesis Agenda – they're on the side of the angels! If they say it, it surely must be true. And the fact that the Agenda's never managed to dig up anything about Barren – jumping Christ, it's like getting an endorsement from God Himself! Never realized what a force for good the internet could be!'

His laugh was a sandpapery caw. Her head was shaking, her expression broken.

'And then what do you know? Out of the blue a message comes into the Nemesis site from my own little girl. My Princess Rachel. Asking if she can join forces. Work with the Agenda. Couldn't have been more perfect if I'd scripted it myself. The dream scenario. You get to blow off some steam, have your little adventures, fight the good fight and all the while you're really working for the corporation. Back in the fold again. Back where you belong.'

She was trembling, ashen-faced, the Glock now dropped to her side as though she no longer had the strength to support it. It was like she was in the mansion again. Curled in her bed. Small, weak, helpless, her father pressing down on her, impossible to resist.

'Although of course the reality is that whatever you might like to think, you've never actually been out of the fold,' he continued, moving the walker forward half a step, its wheel squeaking as it revolved. 'Truth is, we've always been watching you, Rachel. From the moment you left home there hasn't been a single moment of a single day when I haven't known exactly where you are and what you're doing and who you've been talking too. All those groups you joined, those marches you went on – every one of them, I had people around you keeping a close eye. Your little Nemesis adventures –

always there were specialists on hand ready to step in in case things went wrong. Your hideaway in the Negev – bugged and camera-ed from top to bottom. That's how we found out about Rivka Kleinberg. There's not a single thing you've said or done that I haven't heard or seen. All of it, Rachel. *All* of it. You and your little dyke friend . . .'

His chest heaved, his eyelids seemed to flutter.

'Christ, you're so beautiful. So beautiful, my darling. You have no concept how much I want to hold . . .'

She doubled up, gagging, vomit pattering from her mouth on to the steel of the deck. He made to shuffle forward again, but she got the gun up, flailed it at him.

'Keep away!' she howled. 'Keep away, you vile fucking—' Another spurt of sick.

'Let me help you, Rachel, please.'

'Keep away!'

He shook his head, grotesque parody of the pained parent.

'I know it's hard, my darling. But it's just the way things are. Like I said, we own it all. We control it all. There's no point fighting it. No point resisting. It's your destiny. There's no way out. You're coming home, Rachel. Please, don't make it hard on yourself. Accept what you are. Embrace it.'

In front of him she gave a final retch and came up straight, wiping a sleeve across her mouth. For a moment the two of them stood facing each other, Barren smiling benignly, his daughter broken and hollow-faced. Then, with a nod, she lifted the gun, aimed and fired.

There was an explosion of metal as the padlock securing the container blew apart.

'What the . . .' Barren started to shuffle the walker around, trying to see what was going on. She circled him, came up to the container, jerked the shattered lock away and heaved open the doors. In front of her Ben-Roi and Khalifa were standing side by side. They looked bewildered.

'Out!' she ordered.

They hesitated, uncertain.

'Out!'

They did as she said.

'Rachel, what do you think you're . . . ?'

A hammer of footfalls as the two guards came running back round the bridge tower, alerted by the gunshot. She moved sideways, aimed towards the sound, shot the men in turn as they burst from the mist. One in the forehead, the other through the eye. Shockingly accurate. Their bodies crashed. Stepping over, she yanked the Hecklers out of their hands and threw them to the detectives. There were shouts below now, the scramble of booted feet as men came running up the gangway.

'Get out of here,' she hissed. 'That way. No guards.'

She gesticulated down the side of the ship towards the prow. Again the detectives hesitated, again she repeated the order.

'Come with us,' cried Ben-Roi.

'Go, you fucking idiot!'

She grabbed his shirt and propelled him across the deck. Khalifa followed. As he passed Barren, his Heckler instinctively levelled at the old man. She clocked what he was thinking and pushed the muzzle away.

'My business,' she said. 'Go. Now.'

Their eyes met for a fraction of a second. Then, with a nod and a muttered, 'Thank you,' he set off after the Israeli. She watched until the two of them were swallowed by the mist, then turned to her father.

'Rachel, you really shouldn't have—'

'Shut up.'

She approached him, gun arm extended. The rush of feet was getting closer. It meant nothing to her. She came right up to him, touched the Glock's muzzle to his ogreish forehead. He just stood there, leaning on his walker, his expression more amused than fearful.

'Oh Rachel, Rachel, is this really what you want?'

That soft, soothing voice. The voice he used to use when he was violating her. The soundtrack of abuse.

'Is it, Rachel? Then, please, go ahead. If it'll make you feel better, my darling. Help make up for whatever sins you believe I might have committed. It doesn't matter to me. Doesn't matter a jot. Like I told you, I've not long left anyway. The family, that's what matters. And with you I know the family's in good hands. The best hands. The very best. So go right ahead, Rachel. Ease your aching heart. Exorcize your demons. And for myself, I'll die happy in the knowledge that in you I am bequeathing a fine future to the glorious name of Barren. God, you make me proud.'

He beamed at her.

A pause as she steeled herself. Accepted that there was no other way out. Then, unexpectedly, she beamed back at him.

A shadow of doubt in his eyes. 'Rachel. What . . . ?'

'Goodbye, Daddy dearest.'

For a moment he looked confused. Then, suddenly, his eyes widened in horror as she withdrew the gun from his forehead, bent her arm and jammed the muzzle into the roof of her mouth.

'Oh my God, Rachel, don't you dare—'

A deafening blast and the old man's grizzled face was spattered in a vapour of bone and blood.

Her body toppled away from him and thudded to the deck.

BEN-ROI AND KHALIFA

They were halfway along the ship, enveloped in fog, when the shot rang out behind them. There was a howl of 'Rachel!' followed by an agonized, guttural bellow, like the roar of some mortally wounded animal.

Ben-Roi and Khalifa stopped and looked at each other, uncertain what had happened. Another bellow, and then, echoing around the dock as though broadcast through a loudspeaker, a raging cry of 'Find them! Find the murdering animals!'

They started running.

They reached the ship's bow and fumbled their way on to the forward gangplank. Barely had they started down it when there were shouts below and a clatter of footsteps. The woman had got it wrong. There *were* guards down there. Lots of them, by the sound of it. And they were coming up.

They retreated, pulling back into the triangle of deck formed by the ship's prow and the furthermost of the raised cargo hatches. Visibility in the fog was little more than a couple of metres, but they didn't need to see to know they were trapped. Shouts and footsteps to their left, ascending. Similar sounds ahead of them, approaching along the sides of the ship.

'Find them! Butcher them!'

They looked wildly at each other. Then, instinctively, without saying anything, they split. Ben-Roi moved left, covering the top of the gangway and the narrow channel of deck between the ship's side-rail and the open cargo holds. Khalifa took the port-side channel.

They peered into the murk, Hecklers levelled, heads cocked, listening. Twenty seconds passed. Tense, harrowing seconds, the sounds of their hunters' approach drawing closer all the time, the net inexorably tightening. Then figures loomed at the top of the gangway. Two of them. Ben-Roi fired, point-blank, dropping them. Khalifa also saw movement and unleashed a volley of shots. Return fire raged all around, the air vibrating to the ping and clank of bullets hitting metal, crackles of white light slashing through the fog shroud. The detectives pressed themselves behind the protective steel wall of the raised cargo hatch, swinging out to fire before ducking back again. With Barren's men only able to approach along the sides of the ship and up the gangway, the two of them were able to hold their position despite being heavily outnumbered. Only so long as their ammunition lasted, however. And that was fast diminishing.

'Cover me!' cried Ben-Roi.

Loosing a final burst into the whiteness along his side of the ship, Khalifa shifted to Ben-Roi's side and resumed firing. Dropping to his knees, the Israeli rolled across the deck to the top of the gangway, grasped one of the bodies that was lying there and hauled it back behind the cargo hatch. He repeated the process with the second body, bullets clanging all around like metal hail. Khalifa rolled across to cover the right-side channel again; Ben-Roi patted the bodies down. Jackpot. Each was clasping an MP5 and had a belt holster with a Sig Sauer handgun, plus spare Heckler magazines tucked into the pockets of their flak jackets. Thirty-bullet, by the look of it. Quite the miniature arsenal. He slid one of the Hecklers over to Khalifa along with a couple of clips, grabbed spare clips for himself, unleashed another volley of bullets.

For the moment at least they could hold out while they tried to figure out how to get off the ship.

The firefight continued for another few minutes, the detectives cornered, Barren's men unable to get close to them. Then shouts and the sound of withdrawing feet. An eerie silence descended.

'What are they doing?' hissed Khalifa.

Ben-Roi had no idea. 'Not letting us go, that's for sure.'

They stayed flattened against the metal of the cargo hatch, ears straining, hearts thudding, both desperately trying to come up with a plan. The bottom of the gangplank would be covered; likewise the narrow strips of deck running beside the cargo holds.

'You think we could jump?' asked Ben-Roi.

'Are you crazy? It's a forty-metre drop. Dock on one side, rocks on the other and a tug at the front. We'd be lucky if we just broke our backs.'

Ben-Roi didn't bother arguing the point.

'We're in trouble,' was his only assessment.

The silence continued for almost ten minutes, presumably as their pursuers also worked through their options. Then, suddenly, echoing across the dock, that raging voice again. Barren's voice.

'I don't care! I want them killed now! Now, do you hear! Do it! Take it out! Now! Take it out! That's an order!'

The two of them exchanged a look, uncertain what he meant. The answer came almost immediately. There was a deep, ominous throbbing sound, and beneath their feet the steel of the deck started to vibrate as the ship's engines roused themselves into life. Almost simultaneously hydraulics purred and the cargo hatch that had been protecting them started to lower, as did the other hatches along the length of the deck, folding down over the holds like a row of collapsing dominoes. The two of them pulled back, crouching in the scant cover offered by the satellite navigation mast right at the prow of the ship. Between them and the bridge tower, where Barren's men were gathered, there were now two football-pitch lengths of empty space, with nothing to shield them but the fog.

'They're taking us out to sea,' said Ben-Roi. 'The moment the air clears we'll be sitting ducks. They'll just pick us off from the bridge. It'll be a fucking turkey shoot. We have to risk it! We have to get down the steps!'

He started to edge towards the starboard rail. Even as he moved there were shouts and the roar of an engine down on the dock below, and then a deafening crash and squeal of shearing metal. Something – it was impossible to see what exactly – had torn the gangplank off the side of the ship, cutting off their only line of escape.

'We're screwed,' said Ben-Roi, downgrading his previous assessment of their situation.

The volume of the engines built, as did the trembling of the deck beneath their feet. Such was the thickness of the fog that it was only when the dim, ghostly radiance of the dock lights started to fade that they realized they were already moving, sliding backwards away from their mooring and out into the open sea. The gunfire started up again, a steady stream of bullets raging down the length of the open deck. Random rather than accurate, it nonetheless kept the two of them pinned tight in their narrow sanctuary behind the satellite mast. Pinned until the air cleared and Barren's men could pick them off at their ease.

'How far out do you think the fog goes?' asked Ben-Roi.

'How should I know!'

Khalifa fired off a couple of volleys from the Heckler. They could sense the ship starting to undulate, subtle heaves that told them they were moving further from shore into larger waves. Judging by the sound of the engines, they were picking up speed all the time. Still reversing – Barren's men weren't going to waste time turning the vessel. They had a few minutes maybe. Probably less.

'We have to jump,' said Ben-Roi.

Khalifa didn't reply, just raked the control tower with his Heckler.

'We have to jump,' repeated the Israeli. 'It's our only chance.'

'It's too far! We'll be killed!'

'We'll be killed if we stay here! We have to do it.'

'No way! We'll fight it out.'

'We can't fight it out, you idiot! There are too many of them. They've got too much firepower. We have to jump before we come out of the fog. Come on!'

He grabbed Khalifa's jacket, but the Egyptian swept his hand away.

'You jump if you want. I'll take my chances here.'

'Khalifa!'

'I'm not jumping!'

'We have to!'

'No!'

'We're not even a mile offshore yet. We'll be—'

'No! No!'

'We can just swim—'

'Dammit, I can't swim! Do you hear me? I can't bloody swim. I'm scared of the water.'

He threw a furious, humiliated look at Ben-Roi, then turned away and emptied out the Heckler clip.

'You go, I'll stay,' he muttered, breaking out the used magazine and clicking in a new one. 'Don't worry about me. Go on, off you go.'

For a moment Ben-Roi stared at him. Then, snatching the Heckler from the Egyptian's grasp, he threw it over the side.

'What in God's name—!'

The Israeli seized his jacket, tight, yanking his face close.

'We're jumping, Khalifa. You understand? I'm a good swimmer. You do as I say, we'll be fine. If we stay here we're dead. No question. At least in the sea we've got a fighting chance.'

Khalifa opened his mouth, ready to protest, then closed it again. A bullet ricocheted off the satellite mast a centimetre from his head. Several seconds passed, then:

'You'll hold me?'

'Like I was making love to you.'

Khalifa shot him a none-too-enthusiastic look. A couple of beats, then, reaching into his jacket, he pulled out Samuel Pinsker's notebook, which had been sitting there all the time, in the inside pocket.

'Take this. Just in case I don't ... you know ... It shows where—'

Ben-Roi took the notebook and shoved it back inside Khalifa's jacket.

'We're going to live, Khalifa. Trust me. We're both going home. Now when we hit the water, don't fight, OK? Just relax and let me guide you. Shoes off.'

They kicked off their shoes. There was a sudden lull in the firing from the other end of the ship. Taking advantage of it, they stood and clambered over the bow rail. Beneath them was a void of fog, with somewhere inside it the roar and bubble of churning water.

Ben-Roi dropped his own Heckler and grasped the back of Khalifa's jacket.

'Count of three. Jump as far out as you can. OK?'

'OK.'

'One ...'

'*Allah-u-akhbar!*'

'Two.'

The gunfire started up again.

'Three!'

They leapt. As they left the deck, Ben-Roi felt a sharp, burning thud in the back of his left leg, between his groin and the underside of his buttock. For a confused instant he thought maybe he'd been stung by some large insect. He didn't have time to work the thought through because already they were falling, plummeting downwards through the murk towards the sea beneath. As they dropped, Khalifa experienced his own fleeting fantasy: that he was actually still in the mine. That he had missed the jump and was hurtling down the shaft and everything that had happened since – the dock, the ship, the Nemesis woman, Barren – had all simply been a dream. A last chaotic surge of imagination before he slammed into the shaft bottom and his lights went out for ever.

As with Ben-Roi, the thought didn't have time or space to take root. There was an interim of chaos, everything – the fog, the churning of water, the rumble of engines, the crackle of gunfire, the wind in their faces – seeming to blur into everything else so that it was impossible to unpick the individual strands.

And then, with a bone-jarring, stomach-lurching thwack, they hit the water and went under.

The force of the impact tore them apart, ripping Ben-Roi one way, Khalifa another. For a brief, bewildered moment the Egyptian allowed the sea to take him, his body spearing down to what felt like an immense depth, water enveloping him, wrapping his face and mouth and eyes, swirling his hair, sucking at his clothes, seeming to push and pull him all at the same time. Then, despite what Ben-Roi had said, instinct kicked in and he started to fight. He flailed his arms and legs, kicking and punching at the water, grabbing and clawing at it, frantically trying to get it away from him, to drag himself up towards the surface. Bubbles exploded from his mouth, his lungs started to heave, panic surged through him. He could hear himself screaming – a muffled boom that filled his ears and head – could feel the strength flooding out of him with every sweep of his limbs so that barely had he started to struggle when his movements began to slow. Still he battled, pawing at the void, twisting and turning so that he lost all sense of which way he needed to go to reach air, until eventually his strength was gone and a curious calm descended. Seawater leached into his throat and windpipe; his mind fuzzed; his eyes filled with surges of colour; he felt his hands and feet drifting away from him as if he was slowly dissolving and breaking apart.

'This is what it was like for Ali,' he found himself thinking. 'What my son went through, I too am now experiencing. I am going to my little boy. We're going to be together again.'

The thought brought him a strange feeling of satisfaction, and he was giving himself up to it, when he felt something grasp his collar. There was a jarring yank as if he was being torn from a comfortable sleep, and suddenly his head was out of the water and he was coughing and spluttering and choking for air.

'Don't fight me, Khalifa!' Ben-Roi's voice sounded strangely distant, like it was coming from a long way away. 'Relax. Just relax. You're OK. I've got you.'

Somehow the Israeli got an arm underneath him and buoyed him up, keeping his head above the surface as he gagged and gasped, water vomiting from his mouth and nostrils.

'Ease back. Let me take your weight. Trust me. I've got you. You're safe.'

The voice sounded closer now. He was managing to get some breaths into him. Things were coming back into focus. 'Hold me, Ben-Roi. Please, hold me!'

He grasped at the Israeli, not caring how pathetic he sounded, just desperate not to be under the water again.

'Relax, for fuck's sake! Please, you have to relax and help me, otherwise I can't do this. Just ease back. I've got you. You're safe.'

Turning him around, Ben-Roi curled an arm underneath his throat, the two of them floating on their backs, the Israeli's legs moving beneath him. There was something reassuring about the big man's size and strength and Khalifa started to calm, allowing Ben-Roi to hold and guide him.

'That's good. Just take it easy. Keep breathing.'

They could still hear the rumble of the ship's engine and occasional crackles of gunfire. The sounds were growing more distant all the time. Ben-Roi moved them in the opposite direction. The water was cool, but not too cold, the swell high but not rough. Strangely, the fog helped. Had Khalifa been able to see the lights on the shore, how far out to sea they were, he would have panicked. As it was, visibility was little more than a few metres in any direction and he was able to soothe himself with the illusion that safety was not that far away.

'I think we might be able to do this,' he said.

'Sure we can. You and me. The A-Team.'

'I hope the ship doesn't come back and run over us.'

'One problem at a time, eh?'

They paddled for a few minutes, then Ben-Roi slowed and stopped, treading water, struggling to keep Khalifa afloat.

'You OK?' asked the Egyptian.

'Just a little out of breath. If you could kick your legs a bit, that might help to carry some of the weight.'

Khalifa tried, ended up thrashing and driving them both under the surface.

'Don't worry,' coughed Ben-Roi, getting them back above water. 'It's probably easier if you just let me do it.'

He resumed paddling, pulling Khalifa with him, his legs kicking, although it seemed to Khalifa that one of the legs was working harder than the other. Another few minutes went by, then the Israeli slowed and stopped again. His breath was coming in gasps now.

'Ben-Roi?'

'I think a bullet might have nicked me when we jumped. Nothing to worry about. It's just causing a bit of pain. If I can take it slowly . . .'

He bobbed a moment, grunting, fighting to hold himself and Khalifa above the surface, then went back to paddling. This time he only managed a minute's worth before his strength gave out.

'I'm sorry, Khalifa, I just need to—'

His head dipped under the water, came back up again. Khalifa tried to help him, to kick his legs, but it only made things worse. They coughed and spluttered, somehow got on to their backs again, splashed on for another thirty seconds before Ben-Roi called yet another halt. He was struggling. Struggling badly.

'Let me go,' said Khalifa. 'Save yourself. Just let me go.'

'Don't be ridiculous.'

'It's no good, Ben-Roi. We're too far out. At least save yourself.'

'I'm fine, if we can just . . .'

Khalifa started to push him away, trying to force the point, but Ben-Roi wouldn't let him. For a moment they struggled, rising and falling on the swell, gasping and thrashing. Then, suddenly, Ben-Roi stiffened.

'What the fuck's that!'

Something was looming out of the fog. Something large and dark. Very large. Gliding towards them on the surface of the water. For a terrified instant Khalifa thought it must be a shark or a whale and he drew up his legs to kick it. As he did so, the thing lifted on a wave and came right up against them.

'*Ward-i-nil!*' he cried, terror turning to joy. '*Hamdulillah, ward-i-nil!*'

Ben-Roi had no idea what that meant. He didn't care what it meant. All he cared about was the huge, floating mat of vegetation that from nowhere had miraculously appeared beside them. A dense tangle of roots and stalks and leaves that when he slapped a hand on top of it proved to be remarkably buoyant. Almost like a raft. Heaving and splashing and gasping, spasms of pain shooting down his injured leg, he somehow managed to get Khalifa up on to it, the Egyptian shunting his way forward until his entire body from the knees up was supported. Working his way round to the other side, Ben-Roi got himself up as well, clawing and scrambling until he was out of the water to the level of his waist.

'*Toda la'El.*'

'*Hamdulillah.*'

For a while they just lay there, catching their breaths, the vegetation undulating gently beneath them like some enormous lilo, the rumble of the ship still just audible in the distance, although the gunfire seemed to have stopped. Then, straining round, Ben-Roi felt the back of his thigh. There was a hole in his jeans, and he could feel blood pumping. Not too heavily, which was a relief. No exit wound he could find.

'You OK?' asked Khalifa.

'A lot better now the swimming lesson's over.'

'Are you definitely hit?'

Ben-Roi confirmed that he was, but that it didn't seem to be too serious.

'I think the bullet might still be in there, but I'm not losing too much blood and it doesn't hurt as much as it did. If I can just get a tourniquet round it . . .'

Fumbling, his face sinking into the mat of leaves, he managed to get his belt off and wind it round the upper part of his thigh. There'd been a moment back there when he'd thought they were goners. Now they were out of the water – halfway out of it in his case – he was feeling a lot more assured. They couldn't be that far offshore, and once the fog had cleared they could either try to kick their way back on the raft, or else wait till they were picked up. His only real concern was that the ship would come back and run over them, but it was a big sea and hopefully they'd be all right. Like he'd said to Khalifa, one problem at a time. They were safe for the moment. He felt curiously relaxed. Drained, but relaxed. Light-headed almost. He yanked the belt tight.

'That Nemesis Agenda thing was bit of an eye-opener, eh?' he grunted, tying it off. 'Couldn't have got that more wrong if I'd tried. Not exactly a recommendation for teaching advanced investigation!'

Khalifa didn't know what he was talking about, didn't bother asking. Instead, bellying himself forward, he reached out and took the Israeli's hand.

'Thank you,' he said. 'For saving my life. Again.'

Ben-Roi waved it away. 'Bill's in the post.'

They bobbed a while, their hands clasped, the fog wrapping them like a blanket, the only sounds now the plop and glug of water. Then:

'I said some things, Ben-Roi. Before. On the phone. Some bad things. Please . . .'

'We both said some bad things. It's forgotten.'

A beat, then:

'Cunt.'

'Bastard.'

They laughed. Deep belly laughs. The laughs of two old mates out on the town.

Ben-Roi's leg had started throbbing again, really throbbing, but it didn't seem to matter. He felt happy. How crazy was that?

'I'll do whatever I can to help,' he said. 'With Barren, Zoser. We'll get them. Together. I promise. For Ali.'

The Egyptian's grip tightened, squeezing Ben-Roi's hand. 'Thank you, Arieh. You're a good friend.'

'You too, Yusuf. The best.'

In the four years they'd known each other, it was the first time they'd used first names. They didn't even notice.

There was another long silence, a breath of wind coming up and stirring the fog. Then, struck by a sudden thought, Ben-Roi lifted his head.

'Hey, listen, it's probably not the right time, but there was something I wanted to ask you. A bit of a favour. To do with the baby. I don't know if you'd be . . .' He didn't finish the sentence. In front of him there was a soft snoring. The Egyptian was asleep.

'For God's sake,' muttered Ben-Roi.

Shaking his head, he gave his companion a playful slap on the cheek, then wriggled himself over so that he was lying on his back, his legs dangling in the water, his arms thrown out to either side. He thought he could sense the bleeding getting stronger, even with the tourniquet, but he let it go. Why worry himself? He was on the raft, and his friend was there, and they were both alive, and the water wasn't too cold, and the movement of the sea just felt so good beneath him. Why spoil the moment?

More minutes went by – or maybe hours, he had no idea, didn't care. And then there was another breath of wind, harder this time, and he laughed out loud because directly above him a gap opened in the fog and he could see stars. Joyous, magical clusters of twinkling blue stars, fat as fireflies. The most beautiful thing he'd ever seen. He lifted a hand towards them.

'I'll be there,' he whispered. 'I promise. I'll always be there for you. My little boy. Or little girl. I'll never let you down. I promise.'

He smiled as above him more and more of the sky came clear and more and more stars revealed themselves, shimmering and twinkling, a pathway of lights calling him home to the ones he loved.

He started humming.

It was late the following morning when Khalifa eventually made it back to Luxor.

Ben-Roi had flown straight on to Houston to start things moving against Barren, but he had wanted to be with his family and had told the Israeli he'd get a later flight.

As soon as he saw Zenab standing outside their apartment block, he knew something had happened in his absence. He tried to ask her what was going on, but she shushed him quiet and waved him upstairs.

'Come quick,' she said. 'You have to see.'

He followed her into the apartment. Ali's *Mary Poppins* DVD was playing in the living room. Full volume. 'Let's Go Fly A Kite'. With those terrible subtitles. *We're launching our kite into the sky*. He started to tell her to turn it down in case they upset the woman in the flat below, but again she shushed him quiet.

'You have to see,' she repeated. 'You won't believe it.'

They came up to the door of the bathroom. Inside he could hear running water.

'Come on, Zenab, enough mucking around. What's—'

The words caught in his mouth as she threw open the door. The shower was running, splashing water across the concrete floor. And there underneath the shower, glistening wet, his head thrown back, laughing . . .

'Ali,' choked Khalifa, reeling against the door frame. 'My son! My boy!'

With a wild, ecstatic bellow, he charged across the room and leapt underneath the shower, fully clothed, wrapping his son in a euphoric embrace, sobbing with joy. Water cascaded down across his hair and face, soaking him, getting into his eyes and nose and mouth, making him cough and splutter, but he didn't care.

'Ali!' he cried. 'Ali! Ali!'

He woke up.

It was daylight. His mouth tasted of salt. His clothes were sodden. All around him a vista of green-blue sea stretched off in every direction. He lay for a couple of seconds, flummoxed. Then, as it all came back to him, he shifted and craned his head. As he did so the *ward-i-nil* rose on a swell and he caught sight of a line of yellow shore. About a kilometre away. Maybe nearer. No sign of the ship. Or the dock either. They must have drifted down the coast during the night, although which way down the coast he had no idea.

'Hey, Arieh.'

He turned to the Israeli.

He wasn't there.

'Arieh?'

No response.

Assuming his friend was merely tangled somewhere in the leaves of the *ward-i-nil*, like Ali had been tangled, he heaved himself up a couple of inches, running his eyes back and forth across the mat of vegetation.

No sign of him. He felt a shudder of panic.

'Arieh! Ben-Roi!'

Nothing.

He tried to heave himself up further but the added weight pushed his arms right through the weave of stems and he slapped face forward, water filling his mouth. Maybe the Israeli had made a swim for shore? Gone to get help now the fog had cleared. Yes, that must be it. He'd left him sleeping and swum for shore. Crazy idiot! Again he tried to crank himself up, again his arms pushed right through the raft into the sea beneath. At the same moment the *ward-i-nil* lifted and he caught sight of something off to his right. About twenty metres away. At first he couldn't see what it was and it was only with the next swell that he recognized Ben-Roi's jeans and jacket. He appeared to be floating there, arms spread out to either side, face down, gazing into the depths.

Khalifa must still have been groggy from sleep because the first thought that came to mind was that the Israeli was looking for fish. It took a couple of seconds for realization to dawn. Then it did he let out a howl of despair.

'Oh God, no! Oh please God, no! Arieh! Arieh!'

He tried to kick his legs and splash with one of his arms, to drive the *ward-i-nil* closer, but to no effect. All he could do was lie there watching as his friend's body hove in and out of sight, calling his name over and over.

'Arieh! Arieh!'

His son's name as well, the two of them weaving together in a single strand of unbearable grief.

'Arieh! Ali! Arieh! Ali!'

For almost an hour he floated like that, crying himself hoarse. Then there was a particularly heavy swell and Ben-Roi's body suddenly came a lot closer, to within a couple of metres. For a moment it floated there, one of the arms seeming to reach for Khalifa – 'Like he was saying goodbye,' the Egyptian would later describe it – before slowly, peacefully, his friend slid beneath the waves and was gone for ever.

'Arieh! Ali! Arieh! Ali!'

He was picked up eight hours later, early in the afternoon, by a small fishing boat out of Rosetta. The fishermen were full of questions about what he was doing out there clinging to an island of *ward-i-nil*. By way of an answer, he pulled out his sodden wallet and flashed his police ID.

They found him some dry clothes and left him alone.

The current had pulled him well to the west, and it took them almost an hour to reach the mouth of the Nile. He sat on a pile of nets, chain-smoking cadged cigarettes, gazing at the shoreline, cradling Samuel Pinsker's ruined notebook in his lap, its pages reduced to an indecipherable pulp by the seawater. He should have felt guilty about it. He should have felt a lot of things. He didn't. Just empty Like someone had taken a wire brush and scoured out his insides.

Only one thing remained. An absolute, unwavering certainty of what had to be done.

I'm reminding you how things are in this country, Khalifa. Revolution or no revolution, there are people you don't touch.

He'd be seeing about that.

They reached the Nile estuary and turned south, holding a line up the middle of the river. The Zoser dock was clearly visible on its promontory on the western shore. No sign of the cargo ship. Instead a pair of Nile barges were now pulled up along the wharf front, the giant gantry cranes slowly loading them with barrels. He watched a moment, curiously detached from the whole thing – Luxor, that's where he needed to be. He borrowed one of the crew's mobiles and made three calls.

Zenab first, to let her know he was OK. Her voice conveyed both fury at the way he had treated her, and relief that he was safe. He couldn't tell which was the dominant narrative, didn't bother finding out. He told her he'd be home later that evening and rang off.

Second call, anonymous, to the Israeli Embassy. One of their nationals had died in an accident, he informed them. A policeman by the name of Arieh Ben-Roi. From Jerusalem. He'd left it at that, would call back at a later date to furnish more details.

Third and final call to Corporal Ahmed Mehti at the Luxor Police shooting range. He explained what he needed, said he'd drop by as close to 7 p.m. as he could make it. If Mehti could supply some sort of carry bag, all the better.

After that he sat in silence running everything through in his head, trying to picture the maps Chief Hassani had been showing them these last few weeks, the precise deployments. There was a blind spot, he was sure of it. Up by Tuthmosis III. And a way to it as well, coming round from the south end of the massif. It was possible things had been tightened last minute, the gap closed, but he'd just have to risk it.

The law doesn't touch companies like Barren. Or Zoser. Any of them. The only way to bring them down is to play as dirty as they play.

Bring it on.

They docked in Rosetta shortly before 3 p.m. Keeping just the shoes they'd lent him, he exchanged his borrowed clothes for his old ones, now dry, and went ashore, not even bothering to thank the crew. Running on autopilot. He bought Cleopatras from a street vendor, marched into the centre of town, picked up a service taxi into Alexandria. An hour later he was at the airport. Three hours after that his return ticket had got him back to Luxor.

All the way he thought about Ali, and Ben-Roi, and the mine full of arsenic waste, and the blind spot up near Tuthmosis III. The pivot on which his entire world now seemed to balance.

He was at the police firing range by 7.20.

'Strictly speaking this shouldn't be leaving here without official authorization,' admonished Corporal Mehti, handing over a bulky canvas carrier. 'But seeing as it's you . . .'

Khalifa accepted the carrier, slipped Pinsker's notebook into one of the zip pockets, signed the relevant release forms. He didn't offer an explanation, Mehti didn't ask for one. They'd known each other long enough; the corporal trusted him. Khalifa hoped it wouldn't get the old trooper into trouble, but if it did . . . well, it couldn't be helped. Nothing could be helped any more. Nothing mattered any more. Except the blind spot. Please God, don't let them have tightened the cordon.

Clutching the carrier, he took a taxi down the river, then a motor-boat across to the West Bank, then another taxi up to the base of the Theban hills. On the far side of those hills, curving into the massif as though gouged with some enormous fork, the Valley of the Kings. With tonight's VIP museum opening, every path over to the valley was floodlit and closely policed. By tracking south along the foot of the range, however, out past Medinet Habu, the pottery-strewn ruin-field of Malqata, the Deir el-Muharrib monastery with its beehive domes and mud-brick walls, he calculated he should be able to flank the cordon. As proved to be the case. He picked up a little-known track on to the back of the hills, circled around, crept his way through the net and down towards the cliffs at the head of the valley. Towards the cleft in which was secreted the tomb of Tuthmosis III. And just to the left of that cleft, jutting out from the cliffs like some enormous stomping elephant's leg, a high, flat-topped promontory with a direct and unimpeded view down the valley to the museum at its centre. The weak point. The blind spot. The place no one had thought to worry about because with all the paths over the hills covered, no one could get to it. But he had got to it. And now he was going to make use of it.

He held back a moment, surveying the slopes, satisfying himself the promontory wasn't being watched, then moved forward. A low rock-wall curved around the promontory's rim – a three-thousand-year-old windbreak used by the ancient valley guards. He crouched down behind it. In front of him, less than three hundred metres away, an array of floodlights illuminated the glass and stone front of the new museum. The Barren Museum of the Theban Necropolis.

And in front of the museum, clearly visible, the wooden platform on which the assembled dignitaries were gathered to witness the building's inauguration ceremony.

And somewhere among those dignitaries . . .

Ducking down, he unzipped the carrier and eased out the rifle. The Dragunov SVD 7.62mm sniper rifle. Russian-designed, Egyptian-made. Effective range of 1,300 metres. A thousand more than he needed. Mechanically he slotted in the ten-round magazine – nine more than he needed – came up again and found his position, left arm resting on top of the wall, the gun's skeletonized wooden stock settled firmly into his right shoulder. Curling a finger round the trigger, he pressed an eye to the sight. Suddenly the intervening distance was gone and he was right there with the dignitaries on the platform.

Chief Hassani, that was the first person he saw. Bullish and sweating, perched on a seat at the back of the platform, his neck rolling out over the collar of an overly tight white shirt. With a humourless grunt Khalifa wondered if perhaps he should pop him off as well, while he had the opportunity. He eased the rifle to the right, scanning the platform. He recognized a few faces from the Antiquities Service – Moustapha Amine, Head of the Supreme Council of Antiquities; Dr Masri al-Masri, the long-time Director of Antiquities for Western Thebes. A few local government officials as well. It was the front row that really interested him, and that's where he allowed the sight to settle, tracking down the line of faces. The Interior Minister; the Regional Governor; the Mayor of Luxor; the ubiquitous Zahi Hawass; a couple of foreigners, one of whom he thought might be the American Ambassador.

And there in the middle of the row, huge and glowering and hunched over, dressed in a heavy tweed suit despite the evening heat, his oxygen mask clamped limpet-like to his face, Nathaniel Barren.

Fixing the white-haired head in the cross-hairs, Khalifa tightened his finger, drawing the trigger back.

He'd be caught. No question about it. The moment the gunshot sounded, a four-hundred-strong ring of policemen would draw tight around him like an executioner's noose. If they didn't shoot him on sight, he'd be dragged away and shot or hanged later. Either that or sentenced to a lifetime breaking rocks in the Tura quarries, which amounted to the same thing. His family too – Zenab, Batah, little Yusuf – they'd catch the blowback full-on. Thrown out of their apartment, ostracized, their lives blighted as the relatives of a high-profile murderer.

He didn't care. He wasn't even thinking about it. All he was thinking about was killing the man who'd killed his son. And his friend. And himself, too, in a way. The man who had come to stand for all men of his sort – the oblivious rich, the corrupt untouchables, the privileged abusers, the generators of misery. Like a drug-addict about to shoot up his next fix, the prospect of comedown meant nothing to him. Didn't even register. All his focus was on the moment of release – the pull of the trigger, the prick of the needle, the moment when the blackness would be gone and everything in the world would be all right again.

This, Yusuf, this ... It comes from anger, and hatred, and pain, and nothing can come of that but more pain.

But there couldn't be any more pain. He was in so much of it already. A labyrinth of pain. And this was the only way out.

... play as dirty as they play.

His finger tightened another half-notch, cajoling the trigger back, the cross-hairs centred bang in the middle of the Barren's oversized head. He could hear music playing, 'Biladi Biladi Biladi', the Egyptian national anthem. And from the front of the platform, someone speaking into a microphone, praising Barren Corporation, extolling the company's virtues, thanking them for their wonderful generosity to the people of *Misr*.

Allah will be their judge. It is with Him that their punishment lies, not you.

It wasn't true. It was a lie. Even Almighty Allah was powerless in the face of the likes of Barren. The law certainly was. The Barrens of this world always came out on top. Trod the Khalifas and the Ben-Rois and the Rivka Kleinbergs – the Attias and the Helmis and the Samuel Pinskers and the Iman el-Badris – into the shit, while they marched on regardless. What else could he do? How else could he make things right?

I'll fight if I have to. I might be poor, but I am still a man.

He blinked away a bead of sweat, took the trigger another quarter millimetre, right to the very brink of firing. It was like he was standing before a wall of paper-thin glass, and the slightest breath would shatter it.

Now Barren himself was standing, cranking himself up on to bloated legs, shuffling forward to the front of the stage with the aid of his walker. There was applause, a rasp and a cough as the old man lowered the oxygen mask, a screech of static as he adjusted the microphone. And then he was speaking.

Except that he wasn't speaking. Or at least it wasn't Barren's voice that Khalifa heard. Kneeling there with the gun pressed against his shoulder and his finger tight round the trigger and the cross-hairs filling his eye and his entire world condensed to the three-hundred-metre thread between gun and target, a fraction of an instant away from loosing the bullet, it was suddenly another voice that rang clear in his ears.

Catch me, Dad! Throw me up and catch me!

His eyes closed, sprang open again.

Swing me! Swing me round!

He shook his head, trying to block the voice out, hold his focus.

I'll be in goal, Dad. You kick.

The voice wouldn't be silenced.

Please can we go to McDonald's? Please! Please!

His head dropped, his finger unwound. He gave himself a moment, sweat stinging his eyes, his heart thudding, his breath coming in shallow, rapid bursts. Then, looking up again, he re-engaged the trigger and re-sighted.

I won a prize at school!

His body seemed to spasm.

You're the best detective in Egypt, Dad!

There was something in his chest and throat. A sound, coming up from deep inside. Not a sob, or a choke. Something deeper. Rising from right down in his very core. He fought it back, dragged his head up, locked on to Barren again. But now there were other voices. Crowding his head. Calling out to him.

I don't recognize you. Twenty years and suddenly I no longer recognize my husband.

To protect my family, my children. It is a man's greatest duty.

You're the best, Dad.

523

My love, my light, my life.
Catch me!
The finest man in the world.
Swing me!
What you do comes from the goodness in your heart.
I can eat two whole Big Macs!

And then, loudest of all, cutting clear through the cacophony:

He is at peace. There is a golden light, and Ali is at peace within it. Never forget that.

Something lurched up from inside him. That sound again? Except that now it wasn't just a sound. It was as much a . . . vapour. A blackness. As black as the inside of the Labyrinth. Surging up through him. His body heaved, his mouth levered open as though he was vomiting, although nothing tangible came out. At the same time, it felt like everything was coming out. On and on, more and more of it, an unstoppable flood of pitchy black, welling up like oil from a well.

And then, as suddenly as it had started, it was over. He was kneeling there with the gun in his hand and his finger round the trigger and the cross-hairs centred on Barren's boulder-like head. Everything as it had been. And yet at the same time nothing as it had been. Something had drained. Easing his finger away from the trigger, he carefully swung the gun around and laid it on the ground, blinking rapidly, like he had just woken from a particularly vivid dream, uncertain whether what he thought had happened *had* happened.

For several moments he knelt there, the fuzzy, amplified growl of Barren's voice drifting up from the valley below, the moon seeming to balance on the peak of the Qurn high above. Then, slowly, he unscrewed the gun sight, clicked out the magazine and returned them and the rifle to the canvas holder. Zipping it, he stood.

Terrible crimes had been committed. Justice was unlikely ever to be done, unless Allah pulled something spectacular out of the hat. The world was as dark a place as it had ever been.

And yet from nowhere, like the raft of *ward-i-nil* that had bobbed up to save his life – although not that of his dear friend – it struck him that there *was* a glimmer of light. Of hope. A beacon to guide him through the night. And he knew where to look for it, too.

Hefting the carrier on to his shoulder, he turned his back on the valley and set off on the long walk home.

Joel Regev sat forward as the recovery program threw up the password he needed. Menorah3. Not even weak, which was why the program had delivered in less than five minutes. You'd have thought a policeman would be a bit more cautious about these things, but that wasn't his concern. None of it was his concern. He was only doing it because Dov had begged him, said it was important. He typed the password into the log-in field and hit OK.

'You're in business,' he called as the screen came up.

Zisky walked through from the kitchen where he was making coffee. Regev vacated the chair for him.

'I don't need to tell you this is seriously illegal, hacking a police computer.'

'It's only for a few minutes. I just need to check something.'

'Well, check it quickly. I've bounced us around so we can't be traced, but I still don't want to take any chances.'

Zisky gave him a thumbs-up and leant into the screen, his glasses glowing in the ambient light. Regev left him to it.

Ben-Roi was dead. The news had come into the station late that afternoon. No absolute confirmation, no details except that an anonymous call had been received from someone in Egypt. Zisky didn't need details. It was to do with the Kleinberg case. No question. The case that had had Egypt written all over it and that yesterday afternoon had been mysteriously bumped upstairs. Why exactly it had been bumped upstairs no one was saying, although he could take an educated guess. What he did know was that a rumour had been doing the rounds about Ben-Roi sending an e-mail. He'd sent an e-mail, the shit had hit the fan, and that's when the investigation had been kicked into touch.

He needed to see that mail. Which was why he'd inveigled Joel into deploying his cyber security skills to hack Ben-Roi's account. Circling the mouse, he clicked on the mail icon, followed by the Sent box. It was the first thing listed. The last message Ben-Roi had ever sent. To Leah Shalev, copied into Chief Gal and Chief Superintendent Baum. Heading: Case Solved.

Tweaking the clips holding his *yarmulke*, he sat back and read.

He'd been hurt by the way Ben-Roi had spoken to him at their last meeting – 'It's "sir" to you!' – but that didn't in any way diminish his admiration for the man. In a force with more than its fair share of bigots and arseholes, Ben-Roi had proved himself one of the good guys. The best. That's why he'd got such a buzz out of partnering him these two weeks ('Although not in *that* sense!' He could almost hear Ben-Roi's voice).

And that's why, also, he had a curious feeling that Ben-Roi would approve of what he was now doing. Was somehow, somewhere, egging him on. Like him, the big man had had his own take on things. They'd made a good team. Could have made a great one.

He read through to the end of the report, his amazement growing with each page. And, also, his admiration at the way Ben-Roi had tied it all together. Then, reaching up and fingering the silver *Magen David* at his neck, he tried to work out what to do. Because he *had* to do something. He couldn't just let it lie. He owed that to Ben-Roi. And to his mother as well.

'I'll be a good policeman,' he'd promised her that last time in the hospital, holding her hand, stroking her prematurely bald head. 'Always try to do the right thing, bring the wrongdoers to justice.'

He thought for a couple of minutes, twirling the pendant. Then, with a nod and a smile, he Googled two names. Clicking on the e-mail's Forward button, he copied over the relevant addresses: natan-tirat@haaretz.co.il, mordechaiyaron@gmail.com. He changed the subject heading to SCOOP, pressed send, waited till he was sure it had gone, then shut everything down and went through into the kitchen, wondering what sort of bomb he'd set off.

'Fancy a beer?' he asked.

LUXOR

Nathaniel Barren stood on the balcony of his suite in the Winter Palace Hotel, leaning his dropsied hulk against the stone balustrade, gazing out across the Nile towards the distant looming humpback of the Theban hills.

He'd done what was necessary in the Valley of the Kings, returned to the hotel, dined alone. If he was grieving you would never have known it from his expression. Only his hands hinted at some deeper torment, some more tempestuous internal dialogue. His hands were curled into claws, the yellowed nails digging into the surface of the parapet like butcher's hooks into a carcass.

He stood for almost thirty minutes, rocking back and forth, the incessant beep of taxis and cars blaring up from below, the chatter of families promenading along the Corniche. Then, with a sigh, he turned and shuffled back into the room.

'I'll turn in now, Stephen.'

His manservant stepped from the shadows and with a deferential nod started to prepare his master for bed. He helped him undress and get into his nightclothes, held his arm as he settled his bulk on to the mattress, brought across the tray with his medication – an array of different coloured pills neatly arranged in a line and washed down one after the other with a glass of lightly warmed milk. Once they had been taken, the tray was removed and the manservant eased Barren back on to the hillock of pillows. He drew the sheets up to the middle of his chest, handed him his oxygen mask, examined the dial on the tank to ensure the flow was good. Then, extinguishing all but the night lamp on the bedside table, he wished his master a good night and withdrew.

Alone, Barren stared up at the ceiling. His chest heaved like a blacksmith's bellows; the room echoed to the gurgle and rasp of his breath. A minute passed, then his eyes started to close, the mucousy lids sliding slowly down over the irises. When all that was left was a thin line of white, his hands suddenly clamped tight around the material of the sheets and he whispered something, a single word, muffled by the misted rubber of the oxygen mask. It sounded like 'racial'.

And then his eyes closed and he was asleep.

I allow half an hour before returning to the suite. As anticipated, he is completely out. The sedative I added to the milk was most likely not necessary – he has always been a heavy sleeper – but in this instance I must employ even greater caution than usual. I could not abide the thought of him waking mid-cleansing. Fixing me with one of those looks of his. That would be most off-putting. Wouldn't do at all.

I stand watching him a while. I experience less emotion than I feared I would. I have served for the best part of thirty years, just as my father served before me. You might have thought such a length of time – almost half my life – would provoke greater feeling. As it is, I feel very little. All my agonizing is done. All doubts behind me. Now I am in the tunnel. The tunnel of light. All that concerns me is the cleansing, and doing my job to the very best of my ability.

I cross to the cupboard and remove one of the spare pillows. Lovely pillows they have here, plump and firm. Then, going over to the bed, I ease off the oxygen mask. I lay the mask aside, ensure a firm, grip on the material at each end of the pillow and, without further ado, flatten it over his face, applying sufficient pressure to smother, but not enough to leave discernible marks.

The family have always used us for the special cleansings. The ones that require particular delicacy and discretion. That are of particular significance to the well-being of the family (and they don't come much more significant than this!). My father, I am told, was a master cleanser. So, too, am I in my own way. I have lost track of the number of times I have been called upon to eradicate a potentially damaging mess.

I have another little job for you, Stephen. The details are in the envelope.

Actually I haven't lost track at all. The tally stands at thirty-two. Thirty-three, if you count tonight. Which of course I will. Family business is family business, irrespective of who gives the order.

He struggles less than I imagined. Barely struggles at all, in fact. There is one attempted arch of the back, and a certain amount of shuddering, but after twenty seconds he is still. I take no chances and maintain the pressure for a count of two hundred, just to be sure. Then I remove the pillow. His expression I would describe as surprised bordering on vexed, although that is mostly down to the fact that his eyes and mouth are open. I close them and he is transformed. Restful now. Serene even. Just as you'd expect from an unwell man who has died peacefully in his sleep.

I feel no sorrow of any description. No regret, no sadness. The baton has passed. And with it, my loyalty. The tissues, it seems, were not needed after all.

I replace the oxygen mask, smooth the pillows beneath his head, brush down the cleansing pillow and return it to the cupboard. A final check, then I take out the cellular telephone, dial the number and convey the good news.

I always saw something in Master William. Something his father appeared to wilfully ignore. A talent. A potential. Mistress Rachel was a fine woman in her own way, but she was never going to be the future. In my mind, Master William was the only viable way forward.

Which is why, when he approached me, explained it was time to open up a new chapter, asked for my assistance, it was not really that difficult a decision. The family, you see, is everything. Much more than the sum of its individual parts. That's what my father taught me. And such is the creed I have lived my life by. With Master Nathaniel ailing, the succession had to be assured. The family's future protected. And Master William is the future.

Not a difficult decision at all. A no-brainer, as I believe the saying goes.

When I tell him it is done, the Master – the *new* Master – is effusive in his praise. I should not crave such affirmation – it is my job, after all – but I cannot help but feel a certain thrill of satisfaction. He suggests that I treat myself to a holiday, wherever in the world I wish to go, all expenses paid, but why would I wish to do that? My place is with the family. At the heart of the family. Serving in whatever way I can.

I take a last look around – where cleansings are concerned you can never be too careful – then retire to my own room. I am not an extravagant sort of person, but on this occasion I think I might order something from room service. A nice cup of tea, perhaps. With a biscuit to help it down.

The future, it seems to me, is looking bright.

EPILOGUE

THREE MONTHS LATER

Senior Detective Arieh Ben-Roi of the Jerusalem Police kept his promise.

How he did it, no one would ever know. The currents in that part of the Mediterranean should have pulled him in completely the opposite direction. Maybe he was carried by a freak wave. Maybe he became tangled in a trawler net. Maybe – and this was what Khalifa always chose to believe – Allah, God, Yahwe gave the big man a helping hand. Because despite the prickly exterior, he had at heart been a good person, and a righteous one, and one of the best friends Khalifa had ever had. Allah saw these things.

Allah saw everything.

Whatever the truth – wave, net, God, some other agency – at around 6.30 a.m. on a clear, warm morning, as screams rang out in the delivery suite of Jerusalem's Hadassah Hospital, a man walking his dog on the beach just south of Bat Yam saw something floating in the water. Approaching the tide line, he watched as the waves nudged it towards the shore. Closer and closer it came, louder and louder rang the screams, until with a guttural, exhausted cry of release, a healthy baby boy was delivered safe into the world and drew his first breath. At almost precisely the same moment a body lifted on a wave and was laid gently on to the sand. Despite its long immersion it was, by all accounts, perfectly preserved. And had a broad smile on its face.

Arieh Ben-Roi was home.

Khalifa knew all this because out of the blue he'd received a call from Ben-Roi's partner Sarah. They'd had some contact in the intervening months, Khalifa having written to explain the circumstances of Ben-Roi's death. In this instance, with a baby to care for, she hadn't talked for long. Had just filled him in on developments, and asked two favours. Would he be there for Ben-Roi's funeral? And, also, would he be godfather to their newborn son?

Of course, Khalifa had replied. It would be an honour. On both counts.

Which was why flights and hotels had swiftly been booked (despite Khalifa's protests he had not been allowed to pay for a thing).

And why he and his family were now standing on a hillside overlooking the Old City of Jerusalem while a simple wooden coffin was lowered into the ground and a rich-voiced rabbi slowly intoned the Jewish burial *kaddish.*

'*Yisgadal v'yiskaddash sh'mey rabboh.*'

As he listened, head bowed, one hand holding Zenab's, the other wrapped protectively around Batah and Yusuf, Khalifa found himself reflecting on all that had happened these last three months. All that had changed.

The whole Barren/toxic dumping story had broken in the press, starting in Israel and rapidly spreading to front pages around the world. Unusually in such cases, there had been no attempt at denial or buck-passing. On the contrary, the new head of the company, William Barren, had delivered a very public condemnation of, and apology for, his late father's running of the corporation. Things would be different under his leadership, he had promised. Starting with the establishment of a fund to clear up the mess his father had bequeathed. The barrels would be removed, the aquifer flushed, compensation paid to all those who had suffered as a result of the pollution. Substantial compensation. Whether the contrition was genuine, or merely a cynical move to shore up the company's battered reputation, Khalifa had no idea. What he did know was that the Attia family wouldn't be having to worry about money for a while.

For its part in the scandal, Zoser Freight had been hit with a record fine and the entire board placed under criminal investigation, including the Interior Minister's brother. Khalifa would never know for certain if the barge that had killed his son had been one of the ones carrying toxic waste, but he took some small comfort in the knowledge that if a company as large and connected as Zoser could be brought low, then there was indeed hope for the new Egypt.

He and Zenab were still grieving deeply for their boy. Always would be. At the same time – and it was hard to explain to anyone who had not themselves experienced such things – their lives had somehow

opened up these last few months. The sorrow was as acute as ever, but there seemed to be an ever-widening circle around it. Space for other things to take root and flourish. Pain no longer dominated. There was even talk of trying for another child, although nothing had yet happened. *Inshallah* the time would come.

One of his priorities after the night on the ship had been to return Samuel Pinsker's ruined notebook, and at the first opportunity that presented itself he had driven south to visit Iman el-Badri. He had done so with a heavy heart, knowing he had broken his promise to her. On arrival, he had been informed that the old woman had died peacefully in her sleep a week previously. The very same night he had come to see her. Almost as if she had held on long enough to perform that last duty of sharing the notebook, and only then allowed herself to rest. He had gone out to her grave, recited the *Salat al-Janazah* and, when no one was looking, scooped a hole in the ground and laid the notebook with her. A week after that he had tracked down Samuel Pinsker's tomb in Cairo and emptied out a handkerchief of dust from Iman el-Badri's burial. It was a small gesture, but one that he hoped would mean something to the two of them. As Zenab never ceased to remind him, he was soft like that.

What else?

Barren's Saharan gas field tender had been quietly dropped; the Nemesis Agenda website had, for no reason anyone could explain, mysteriously disappeared. There was much speculation in chat rooms about CIA involvement, Mossad, international capitalist conspiracy. None of it was ever proved. Nor, in the long run, did it matter. The Agenda had been a beacon, had fired the imagination of all those who believed in a more equitable world. Other groups would carry on its work. The abusers *would* be held to account.

Of Rachel Barren's tragic story, nothing was ever made public. Or at least nothing Khalifa ever heard about. He hoped and prayed that she was at peace, wherever she was.

Two final things.

Within a day of each other, Khalifa had received two e-mails. One from his childhood friend Mohammed Abdullah, who was now something big in the dotcom industry; the other from Katherine Taylor, a millionaire American crime novelist with whom he had struck up a loose friendship a few years back when she was in Luxor researching a new book. He had completely forgotten the e-mails he himself had

sent them, so it came as a very pleasant surprise when both declared themselves delighted to help fund Demiana Barakat's children's home. Mohammed Abdullah had gone further and offered the children an all-expenses-paid trip to Cairo to visit Dreampark and the Puppet Theatre and Dr Ragab's Pharaonic Village. Khalifa had always considered the village rather tacky, but in the circumstances he thought it would have been churlish to say so.

And Rivka Kleinberg? Her murder was an Israeli matter, so Khalifa only knew what he picked up on the internet. While Barren's involvement was beyond dispute, the Israelis were no nearer to catching the actual killer. The last time he looked, the investigation was focusing on a new lead concerning a Turkish hitman. He awaited developments with interest.

A murmur of '*omeyn*' signalled the ending of prayers and pulled him from his reverie. In front of him the menfolk were forming into a line, stepping forward one by one to empty a shovelful of earth into the grave. As a Muslim, Khalifa wasn't sure if he should take part, but there was some sort of priest in the line – a short plump man in a black cassock with a purple ring on his finger and a flat silver cross around his neck – so he decided it was probably OK. He joined the queue, taking up position behind a slim young man wearing circular glasses and a knitted blue skullcap.

'*Ma'a salaam, sahebi,*' he whispered as he emptied his own shovelful.

As the funeral ended and the crowd started to disperse – and it was a big crowd, very big – a woman holding a baby came up to the Khalifas and introduced herself. Their flight had been delayed and they'd only just got to the cemetery on time, so it was the first chance he'd had to speak to Ben-Roi's partner Sarah.

'Say hello to your godson,' she said, handing him the baby. Zenab, Batah and Yusuf crowded in as he cradled the child.

'He's so handsome,' he said.

And it was true. There was a fineness to his features, a brightness to his eyes that suggested, looks-wise, he had inherited more from his mother than his father. Which Ben-Roi himself would have been the first to admit was no bad thing.

'I don't even know his name.'

'We've called him Eli,' said Sarah. 'Eli Ben-Roi.'

Khalifa's throat tightened.

'But this is a wonderful coincidence! My son . . . we lost our son . . . his name was Ali. Eli, Ali. They are almost the same.'

Sarah smiled and laid a hand on his wrist. The gesture said: *It was no coincidence.*

Khalifa blinked and had to look away. A silence, then Zenab leant over and whispered in his ear.

'Of course, of course.'

Recovering himself, he kissed the baby's forehead and handed him back to his mother. He then dipped into his pocket and pulled out a small plastic box.

'A few years ago, when I first met Arieh, he gave me this,' he said. 'I have treasured it ever since. Now I think there is maybe a better place for it.'

He opened the box. Inside, on a bed of tissue, was a small silver menorah on a chain. The menorah Arieh Ben-Roi himself used to wear. Taking it out, Khalifa gently placed it over the baby's head.

'There. Just like his father.'

The baby started howling.

'*Just* like his father,' said Sarah.

They stood a moment as she settled the child. Then, sensing she needed to be alone for a while, just herself, her baby and Ben-Roi, they excused themselves and moved away. There was a road running up beside the cemetery and they decided to follow it, up on to the top of the hill with its spectacular view across to the Old City. Batah and Yusuf stopped to gaze down into a garden with an aviary full of fluttering birds. Khalifa and Zenab walked on a bit further before sitting down on a wall. In front of them the Dome of the Rock burned gold in the morning sun; around it, corralled by the city's giant stone-block walls, roofs and domes and towers and the occasional cypress tree were all crammed together so tightly it was impossible to tell where one ended and the next began.

There was tension down there, Khalifa knew it. Anger and resentment and bitterness and hatred. He had his own opinions on the rights and the wrongs of the situation. Seen from up here, however, it all looked quiet and peaceful. No more troubled than toys in a children's play-box.

And whatever the rights and the wrongs, Ben-Roi had been a friend. A good friend. There was a lesson in that. And hope too.

For several minutes they just sat there in silence, legs dangling,

watching as directly beneath them a group of black-coated figures bowed back and forth in front of a tomb. Then Khalifa curled an arm round his wife's waist and drew her close.

'I miss him,' he said quietly. 'Ali. I loved him so much.'

'Love him,' she corrected, nestling into him. 'He's here. He'll always be here.'

Khalifa nodded and pulled her even closer.

'We're OK, aren't we?'

'Of course we are. We're Team Khalifa.'

He smiled at that and turned to kiss her, but was interrupted by movement behind them as Batah and Yusuf came up. He satisfied himself with blowing in Zenab's ear. The children joined them on the wall and they all linked hands. There was another silence, none of them feeling the need to speak, all of them just happy to be there with each other. With their family. Then, lifting a hand, Yusuf pointed.

'Look, Daddy. Someone's flying a kite.'

Over in the Old City a tiny red triangle was fluttering and pulling above the jumble of rooftops. They watched it a while. Then, as one, they started singing.

> *We're launching our kite into the sky,*
> *We're making it go up really high.*

It was such an inept translation they only managed half a verse before the four of them burst into fits of laughter.

GLOSSARY

Abu Kabir   A neighbourhood in the south of Tel-Aviv.

Afwan   'You're welcome'.

Agatharchides   Ancient Greek historian and geographer. Lived in the second century BC, although almost nothing is known about his life.

Ahhotep jewellery   Fabulous collection of gold funerary equipment belonging to Eighteenth-Dynasty Queen Ahhotep (*c.*1550BC). Discovered in 1859 at Dra Abu el-Naga.

Ahl el-kitab   Literally, 'People of the Book'. Muslim term for Jews and Christians, whose scriptures were incorporated into Islam.

Aish baladi   Pitta-type bread made from wholemeal flour.

Akhenaten   Eighteenth-Dynasty pharaoh. Ruled *c.*1353–1335BC. Father of Tutankhamun.

Al-Gama'a al-Islamiyya   Literally, 'the Islamic Group'. A militant Egyptian Islamic movement.

Aliya   Literally, 'Going up'. Emigration to the land of Israel.

Allah-u-Akhbar   Literally, 'God is greater' or 'God is greatest'.

Al-Masry al-Youm   Egyptian daily newspaper.

Al-Quds   Arabic name for Jerusalem.

Amenemhat III   Middle Kingdom pharaoh (Twelfth Dynasty). Ruled *c.*1844–1797BC. The mortuary temple attached to his pyramid at Hawwara in the Fayoum was so complex that ancient writers referred to it as a labyrinth.

Amenhotep I   Eighteenth-Dynasty pharaoh. Ruled *c.*1525–1504BC.

Amenhotep III   Eighteenth-Dynasty pharaoh. Ruled *c.*1391–1353BC. Father of Akhenaten, grandfather of Tutankhamun.

Amenhotep Colossi   Also known as the Colossi of Memnon: two giant seated statues that once stood in the mortuary complex of the pharaoh

Amenhotep III (*c.*1391–1353) on the West Bank of the Nile at Luxor.

Amr Diab   Hugely popular Egyptian musician.

Amrekanee (**f.** *Amrekanaya*)   American.

Amun   Ancient Egyptian god, often depicted with the head of a ram. The patron deity of ancient Waset (modern Luxor). In the New Kingdom he was merged with Ra to form the composite deity Amun-Ra. His name means 'the hidden one'.

Ardon, Mordechai   One of Israel's greatest artists. Created the stained-glass windows for the National Library of Israel in Jerusalem. Lived 1896–1992.

Ay   Eighteenth-Dynasty pharaoh. Ruled *c.*1323–1319BC. Succeeded Tutankhamun.

Baba ghanoush   Middle Eastern dish made from tahini and mashed aubergine.

Balash   'Detective'.

Banana Island   A Luxor beauty spot.

Bar Refaeli   Israeli supermodel.

Basboussa   Egyptian sweet pastry made with semolina, nuts and honey.

Bassatine Cemetery   A Jewish cemetery in Cairo.

Begin, Menachem   Israeli politician. Served as Prime Minister 1977–1983. Signed the Camp David Peace Treaty with Egypt in 1979. As leader of the Irgun (*qv*), he ordered the 1946 bombing of Jerusalem's King David Hotel in which ninety-one people were killed. Lived 1913–1992.

Ben Ali, Zine el Abidine   Former President of Tunisia, ousted by the Jasmine Revolution of December 2010/January 2011. Currently in exile in Saudi Arabia.

Ben-Gurion, David   Founding father of the State of Israel. Served as Prime Minister 1948–1954 and 1955–1963. Lived 1886–1973.

Bersiim   A type of clover used as cattle feed in Egypt.

Bezeq   Israel's national telecommunications company.

BFST   'Brigade des Forces Spéciales Terre': the French equivalent of the SAS.

Bhopal   Indian town, capital of the state of Madya Pradesh. On 3 December 1984, a toxic leak at a pesticide plant owned by Union Carbide India Limited killed thousands and injured tens of thousands.

Blintzes   Israeli dish: thin pancakes, similar to crepes.

Bris   Yiddish rendering of *Brit Milah*, the Jewish ceremony of circumcision.

Bruyère, Bernard French archaeologist. Excavated the ancient workers' village of Deir el-Medina on the West Bank of the Nile at Luxor. Lived 1879–1971.

Bulti Arabic name for the Nile tilapia fish.

Bureka Israeli dish: a triangle of puff pastry stuffed with cheese, spinach or potatoes.

Burton, Henry (Harry) English Egyptologist and archaeologist. Served as photographer on the Tutankhamun excavation. Lived 1879–1940.

Cachette Court A courtyard in the great temple complex at Karnak, so called because a huge cache of buried statues was discovered there in the early twentieth century.

Callender, Arthur R. English architect and engineer. A close friend of Howard Carter, who worked with him on the Tutankhamun excavation. Nicknamed 'Pecky'. Died 1936.

Carter, Howard English archaeologist, discoverer, in 1922, of the tomb of Tutankhamun. Lived 1874–1939.

Cartouche An oval loop with a horizontal line at the bottom within which a pharaoh's name was written in hieroglyphs.

Černý, Jaroslav Czech Egyptologist. Lived 1898–1970.

Challah A plaited loaf eaten by Jews on the Sabbath.

Chevrier, Henri French Egyptologist and archaeologist, best known for his work at Karnak in the 1920s.

Cholent A traditional Jewish slow-cooked stew, usually eaten on the Sabbath.

Copt An Egyptian Christian. The Copts are one of the oldest Christian communities in the world, dating back to the first century AD when St Mark brought the Gospel to Egypt. They account for approximately 10 per cent of the population of modern Egypt.

Daedalus A figure from Greek mythology. The creator of the labyrinth for King Minos.

Dafook Hebrew for 'moron'.

Dana International Transsexual Israeli pop singer.

Danishaway Village in the Delta region of northern Egypt. Scene of an infamous incident in 1906 in which four innocent Egyptians were executed after an altercation with a group of British soldiers.

Deir el-Bahri Site of the mortuary temple of Queen Hatshepsut (ruled *c.*1473–1458BC). On the West Bank of the Nile at Luxor.

Deir el-Medina   Ancient village on the West Bank of the Nile at Luxor, home to the workers who dug and decorated the tombs of the Valley of the Kings.

Deir el-Muharrib monastery   The 'Monastery of the Warrior'. A small Coptic monastery at the base of the Theban massif, near the ancient site of Malqata.

Diodorus Siculus   Greek historian who lived in the first century BC. His *Bibliotheca Historica* provides one of the earliest accounts of gold-mining in Nubia and eastern Egypt.

Djehuty burial   Collection of gold funerary objects from the tomb of Eighteenth-Dynasty general Djehuty. Discovered at Saqqara in 1824.

Djellaba   Traditional robe worn by Egyptian men and women.

Djellaba suda   A black robe worn by Egyptian peasant women.

Dra Abu el-Naga   Village (and ancient burial ground) on the West Bank of the Nile at Luxor.

Dr Ragab's Pharaonic Village   A Cairo theme park based around life in ancient Egypt. Founded in 1974 by Dr Hassan Ragab.

Druze   A monotheistic religious sect incorporating elements of Judaism, Christianity and Islam. They are found mainly in Syria, Lebanon, Israel and Jordan.

Dynasty   The ancient historian Manetho divided Egyptian history into thirty ruling Dynasties, and these remain the basic building blocks of ancient Egyptian chronology. The Dynasties have subsequently been grouped into Kingdoms and Periods.

Egged   Israeli intercity bus company.

Eighteenth Dynasty   Ancient Egyptian history is divided into Kingdoms (Old, Middle and New), which are in turn subdivided into Dynasties. The Eighteenth Dynasty comprised fourteen rulers and covered the period *c.*1550–1307BC. It was the first of the three Dynasties of the New Kingdom (*c.*1550–1070BC).

Ein Karem   A village near Jerusalem. Has a large artistic community.

El-Awamaia   District of Luxor, at the south end of the town.

Elohim adirim   'God Almighty!'

Elwat el-Diban   Literally 'Mound of the Flies'. Small hill beside the road to the Valley of the Kings, site of Howard Carter's dig house. Now a museum.

Eretz Nehederet   Literally 'Wonderful Country'. Popular Israeli satirical TV show.

Etti Ankri   Popular Israeli singer/songwriter.

Fayoum   A large oasis in Egypt's Western Desert, about 130km south-west of Cairo.

Fellaha (pl. *fellaheen*)   'Peasant'.

Frumm/frummer   An extremely devout Jew.

Gadaffi, Muammar   Former Libyan leader and dictator, killed in 2011 by revolutionary fighters. Born 1942.

Gatro, Yahonathan   Openly gay Israeli musician and actor.

Gebel   'Mountain'.

Gehinnom   A valley outside the Old City of Jerusalem. According to Rabbinic literature it is the place where the wicked are punished and is thus synonymous with hell.

Gezira   A district of central Cairo occupying the southern part of Gezira Island in the Nile.

Goldstar   A make of Israeli beer.

Goldstein, Baruch   Jewish extremist. Shot dead twenty-nine Muslim worshippers in Hebron in 1994 before he himself was beaten to death. Regarded as a hero by right-wing Jewish settlers.

Goneim, Muhammed Zakaria   Pioneering Egyptian archaeologist. Lived 1905–1959.

Goy (pl. *Goyim*)   Derogatory Yiddish term for a non-Jew.

Graeco-Roman   The final period of ancient Egyptian history, inaugurated with Alexander the Great's conquest of the country in 332BC, and lasting until AD395.

Gush Shalom   Literally, the 'Peace Bloc': Israeli peace group.

Gut Shabbas   Traditional Yiddish Sabbath greeting.

Ha'aretz   Israeli daily newspaper.

Hadash   Left-wing Israeli political party.

Hajj   Pilgrimage to Mecca, one of the five 'pillars' of the Muslim faith.

Halva   Popular Israeli/Middle Eastern confectionery made from sesame paste and sugar.

Hamas   Militant Palestinian nationalist Islamic movement, founded in 1987. Hamas is both the Arabic for 'zeal' and a reverse acronym for the 'Islamic Resistance Movement'.

Ha-matzav   Hebrew for 'the situation'. Generally used by Israelis to refer to the conflict with the Palestinians.

Hamdulillah   Literally, 'Praise be to Allah'.

Hapo-el Tel-Aviv   Israeli football club based in Tel-Aviv.

Haram Al-Sharif   Literally, 'the Noble Sanctuary'. The enclosure in

Old Jerusalem containing the Al-Aqsa Mosque and the Dome of the Rock, the third holiest site in the Islamic world. Overlies the remains of the ancient Jewish temple.

Haredi **(pl.** *Haredim*)   Ultra-Orthodox Jew.

Hasfari, Shmuel   Israeli playwright. Born 1954.

Ha-Shem   Hebrew for 'the Name': God.

Hatshepsut   Eighteenth-Dynasty (New Kingdom) queen, who ruled Egypt *c.*1473–1458BC as joint pharaoh with her stepson Tuthmosis lll. Her mortuary temple at Luxor is one of the most spectacular monuments in Egypt.

Hauser, Walter   American architect, draughtsman and archaeologist. Worked with Howard Carter on the clearance of Tutankhamun's tomb.

'Hava Nagila'   Traditional Hebrew folk song.

Hawass, Zahi   Egypt's best-known archaeologist. Former Minister of State for Antiquities, and head of the Supreme Council of Antiquities 2002–2011.

Hawaga **(f.** *hawagaya*)   Egyptian term for a foreigner.

Herodotus   Ancient Greek historian, known as 'the father of history'. Lived *c.*485–425BC.

Hijab   A headscarf worn by observant Muslim women.

Horemheb   Last pharaoh of the Eighteenth Dynasty. Ruled *c.*1319–1307.

Huppah   The ceremonial canopy beneath which a Jewish marriage takes place.

IDF   Israel Defence Force: the Israeli army.

Imbaba riots   An outbreak of murderous sectarian violence in the Imbaba district of Cairo in 2011, sparked when Muslims attacked a Coptic Christian church.

Imma **(pl.** *immam*)   Headscarf or turban. Worn by men throughout Egypt.

Ingileezi **(f.** *ingileezaya*)   English man/woman.

Inshallah   Literally, 'God willing'.

Irgun   Full name Irgun Zvai Leumi (National Military Organization). Zionist right-wing paramilitary group operating in Mandate-era Palestine.

Jabotinsky, Ze'ev (Vladimir)   Right-wing Zionist leader and thinker. Lived 1880–1940.

Justine   Famous Cairo restaurant.

Kaddish   A prayer recited by Jewish mourners.

Kadima   A centrist Israeli political party, established in 2005 by Ariel Sharon. Literally, 'Forward'.

Kahane, Meir   Brooklyn-born Jewish extremist. Advocated forcible removal of all Arabs from the biblical land of Israel. Born 1932. Assassinated 1990.

Karkady   A drink made from an infusion of hibiscus petals, popular throughout Egypt.

Ken   'Yes' in Hebrew.

Kharga   A large oasis in Egypt's Western Desert.

Kingdom   The history of ancient Egypt covers almost 3,000 years, during which time there were three extended periods of national unity and powerful central government: the Old, Middle and New Kingdoms.

Kom Lolah   A village on the West Bank of the Nile at Luxor, near the temple of Medinet Habu.

Knesset   Literally, 'assembly'. The Israeli parliament.

Krav Maga   An aggressive self-defence system developed in Israel by former boxer and wrestler Imi Lichtenfeld. Widely used by the Israeli security services.

Kubbeh   An Armenian dish: a deep-fried, sausage-shaped croquette stuffed with minced beef or lamb.

Kufr   Name given to those who do not follow Islam; 'unbelievers'.

Labor   Centre-left, social democratic Israeli political party.

Late Period   Final period of ancient Egyptian history in which the country was governed by native rulers. Comprised Dynasties 25 to 30. Lasted 712–332BC, when Egypt was conquered by Alexander the Great.

Latke   Potato pancake/patty.

Lazeez   'Delicious' in Arabic.

Lider, Ivri   Gay Israeli pop singer.

Lieberman, Avigdor   Right-wing, nationalist Israeli politician. Founder of the Yisrael Beiteinu Party.

Likud   Literally, 'Consolidation'. Centre-right Israeli political party; founded in 1973 by Menachem Begin.

Livni, Tzipi   Israeli (female) politician. Former leader of the Kadima Party. Born 1958.

Lo   Hebrew for 'no'.

Lucas, Alfred   English Egyptologist and conservator, member of the team responsible for the clearing of Tutankhamun's tomb. Lived 1867–1945.

Maasiyahu   Prison in Ramle, central Israel.

Mabruk   Arabic for 'Congratulations'.

Maccabi Tel-Aviv   Hugely successful Israeli basketball and football club.

Mahata   Arabic for 'maze'.

Mahmoud, Karem   Popular Egyptian singer. Known as the 'Melodious Knight'. Lived 1922–1965.

Mallory, George   English explorer and mountaineer who disappeared in 1924 while climbing Mount Everest. His body was discovered on the mountain in 1999.

Mandate era   Period from the end of World War One to 1948 when Palestine was governed by the British under a mandate from the League of Nations.

Maniak   Hebrew for 'arsehole'.

Magen David   Literally, 'Shield of David'. A six-pointed star, one of the most recognizable symbols of Jewish identity.

Mahane Yehuda   Neighbourhood of Jerusalem with a famous covered market.

Malqata   Archaeological site on the West Bank of the Nile at Luxor. Formerly the palace of Eighteenth-Dynasty pharaoh Amenhotep III.

Manjet **Barque**   Also known as the 'Barque of Millions of Years'. The boat in which the sun god Ra crossed the sky once a day.

Matkot   Popular ball game played in Israel, similar to beach tennis, in which two people hit a ball using wooden paddles. The word means 'rackets'.

Mauristan   An area in the Christian Quarter of Jerusalem's Old City.

Mazel tov   Hebrew for 'good luck'. Used to express congratulations.

Mea Sharim   Neighbourhood in central Jerusalem. Home to a large ultra-Orthodox *Haredi* (*qv*) community.

Medinet Habu   Village on the West Bank of the Nile at Luxor. Site of the mortuary temple of Ramesses III.

Meir, Golda   Israeli politician and stateswoman. Served as Prime Minister 1969–1974. Lived 1898–1978.

Menatel   Egyptian telecommunications company.

Menorah   A seven-branched lamp used in the ancient temple of Jerusalem. One of the defining symbols of Judaism.

Merenptah   Nineteenth-Dynasty pharaoh. Ruled 1224–1214BC. Son of Ramesses II.

Meretz   Israeli left-wing political party.

Meshugganah   Yiddish for 'crazy', 'mad'.

Mezuzah   Literally, 'doorpost'. A small case containing verses from the biblical book of Deuteronomy. Attached to the doorways of Jewish homes.

Middle Kingdom   One of the three great Kingdoms of ancient Egypt. Comprising Dynasties 11 to 14, it lasted *c.*2040–1640BC.

Mishteret   Hebrew for 'police'.

Misr   Arabic for Egypt. The full name is Junhuriyah Misr al-Arabiyah – the Arab Republic of Egypt.

Molocchia   Green leafy plant similar to spinach.

Moshav   An Israeli cooperative farm or agricultural community. Similar to a kibbutz.

Mossad   Also known as the Institute for Intelligence and Special Operations; Israel's national intelligence agency. Renowned for its skill and ruthlessness.

Moulid   Literally, 'birthday'. A traditional Egyptian festival celebrating the birth and life of a holy person.

Mounir, Mohammed   Egyptian singer and actor. Born 1954.

Mr Zol   Israeli supermarket.

Mubarak, Hosni   Former President of Egypt (1981–2011). Resigned following the Revolution of January 2011. Born 1928.

Muslim Brotherhood   Egyptian Islamist movement founded in 1928 by Hassan al-Banna. Its political arm, the Freedom and Justice Party, became the dominant force in Egyptian politics after winning 47 per cent of the seats in the Parliamentary elections of January 2012.

Nectanebo I   Thirtieth-Dynasty pharaoh. Ruled *c.*380–362BC.

Naqba   Arabic for 'disaster', 'catastrophe'. The word used by Palestinians to describe the impact of the creation of the State of Israel in 1948.

Netanyahu, Benjamin ('Bibi')   Right-wing Israeli politician. Prime Minister since 2009 (he served an earlier term 1996–99).

Newberry, Percy Edward   English Egyptologist. Part of the team responsible for the clearance of Tutankhamun's tomb. Lived 1869–1949.

New Kingdom   The last of the three great Kingdoms of ancient Egypt. Comprising the Eighteenth to the Twentieth Dynasties, it lasted *c.*1550–1070BC, and included some of the most famous pharaohs of Egyptian history, such as Tutankhamun and Ramesses II.

Noshech kariot   Literally, 'pillow biter'. Derogatory Hebrew term for a gay man.

Nu be'emet   Hebrew for 'Come on!', as in, 'Come on, you can't be serious!'

Opet Festival   Ancient Egyptian religious festival in which statues of Amun, Mut and Khonsu, the three patron deities of Thebes, were ceremonially paraded in a boat from Karnak to Luxor Temple.

Oslo Accords   Set of peace proposals between Israelis and Palestinians, negotiated in secret in Oslo and signed in Washington in 1993.

Park Heights   Upmarket district of Tel-Aviv.

Pendlebury, John Devitt Stringfellow   British Egyptologist and archaeologist. He excavated at Amarna. Shot by the Germans on Crete during World War Two.

Pe'ot   Sidelocks worn by ultra-Orthodox Jewish men.

Peres, Shimon   Israeli politician and statesman. Has twice served as Prime Minister of Israel (1984–1986 and 1995–1996) and in 2007 was elected President.

Petrie, William Matthew Flinders   Influential British Egyptologist and archaeologist. Established many of the basic ground rules of modern archaeology. Nicknamed 'the father of pots'. Lived 1853–1942.

Petrie Museum   Attached to University College London. Contains some 80,000 objects from Egypt and the Sudan, one of the most important collections of such material in the world. Named after Egyptologist Flinders Petrie.

Pylon   Massive entrance or gateway standing in front of a temple.

Qa'ba   Cube-shaped shrine in Mecca, the holiest site in the Muslim world. It contains a stone believed to have been given by the Angel Gabriel to Abraham. All Muslims turn towards it when praying.

Qurnawis   Inhabitants of the village of Shaykh Abd al-Qurna on the West Bank of the Nile at Luxor.

Qurn   Literally, 'the horn'. Pyramid-shaped peak overlooking the Valley of the Kings.

Ramadan War   Arab name for the Yom Kippur war of 1973.

Ramesses I   First pharaoh of the Nineteenth Dynasty. Ruled c.1307–1306BC.

Ramesses II   Nineteenth-Dynasty pharaoh. One of the greatest of all Egyptian rulers. Ruled c.1290–1224BC.

Ramesses III   Twentieth-Dynasty pharaoh. Ruled *c.*1194–1163BC. His mortuary temple at Medinet Habu is one of the most beautiful monuments in Egypt.

Ramesses VII   Twentieth-Dynasty pharaoh. Ruled *c.*1143–1136BC.

Ramesses IX   Twentieth-Dynasty pharaoh. Ruled *c.*1112–1100BC.

Rehaviya   Upmarket neighbourhood of Jerusalem.

River Oaks   Upmarket suburb of Houston.

Romema   A neighbourhood of Jerusalem.

Rosetta Stone   An ancient Egyptian stone stele inscribed with the same text in three different scripts: hieroglyphs, demotic (a cursive form of hieroglyphs) and Greek. Discovered near the town of Rosetta (Al-Rashid) in 1799, it provided the key to the deciphering of hieroglyphs. It has been on display in the British Museum since 1802.

Sabah el-khir   Arabic for 'Good morning'.

Sabra   Nickname for a native Israeli. The *sabra* is a cactus plant and, like the cactus, Israelis are supposed to be prickly on the outside with a soft centre.

Safra Square   A square in central Jerusalem. Home to Jerusalem's City Hall.

Saheb/Sahebi   Arabic for 'friend'/'my friend'.

Saidee   A native of Upper (or southern) Egypt. Saidees tend to be darker-skinned than those from Lower (northern) Egypt.

Salafists   Ultra-conservative Islamic movement.

Salat   Islamic daily prayers.

Salat al-Janazah   An Islamic funeral prayer.

Schwartze   Yiddish word for a black person.

Seer limoon   'Lemonade'.

Seminary   A religious school or college.

Sephardi   Literally, 'Spanish'. A descendant of the Jews who were expelled from the Iberian Peninsula in the fifteenth century.

Seti I   Nineteenth-Dynasty pharaoh, father of Ramesses II. Ruled *c.*1306–1290BC.

Sgan nitzav   Chief Superintendent.

Shaal   Cloth shawl or wrap.

Shabbat   Hebrew word for the Jewish Sabbath.

Shabbat Shalom   Traditional Sabbath greeting.

Shabas   Acronym for the Israeli Prison Service.

Shaykh Abd al-Qurna   A village on the West Bank of the Nile at Luxor, located at the base of the Theban massif.

Shas   Ultra-Orthodox Israeli political party.

Shebab   Literally, 'youth'. Young Palestinians.

Sherut   Shared taxi, usually a seven-seater Mercedes. Ubiquitous throughout Israel.

Shikunim   Residential housing blocks or tenements.

Shisha   A water pipe. Smoked throughout the Middle East.

Shivah   Literally, 'seven'. The seven-day mourning period observed by Jews on the death of a close relative. It is customary for mourners to sit on low stools.

Shoter   Constable. Lowest rank in the Israel Police.

Shuk   Market.

Shukran   'Thank you'.

Shul   Yiddish word for a synagogue.

Shuma   A staff or walking stick.

Siga   An Egyptian board game, also known as *Tab-es-siga*. Similar to draughts.

Sofgania (pl. *sofganiot*)   An Israeli dish: doughnuts.

Soujuk   Traditional Armenian dish of spicy sausages.

Supreme Council of Antiquities   The government body overseeing all Egypt's archaeological sites and museums. Now renamed the Ministry of Antiquities.

St Pachomius   Coptic saint, one of the founders of monasticism. Lived *c*.292–346AD.

Taamiya   Deep-fried chickpea patty, like *falafel*.

Talatat   Standardized blocks of decorated stone used in the temple-building programme of the pharaoh Akhenaten (*c*.1353–1335BC). Later pharaohs tore down Akhenaten's temples and reused the constituent blocks in their own monuments. Almost 40,000 *talatat* have been recovered from inside the pylons and beneath the floors of the temple complex at Karnak.

Talmid hakham   Literally, 'disciple of the wise'. Someone devoted to the study of Jewish law.

Tanach   The Hebrew Bible. Equivalent to the Old Testament.

Tawla   Backgammon.

Tell Basta hoard   Collection of Nineteenth Dynasty (*c*.1307–1196BC) jewellery and drinking vessels, discovered in 1906 at Tell Basta (ancient Bubastis) in the Delta region of northern Egypt.

Termous   Type of bean. Popular snack in Egypt.

Thebes   The Greek name for ancient Egyptian Waset, modern Luxor.

Theban massif   Range of hills on the West Bank of the river Nile at Luxor.

Theban Necropolis   The ancient burial grounds and mortuary temples on the West Bank of the Nile at Luxor.

The Wall   Also known as the West Bank Barrier and the Separation Fence. A controversial barrier comprising sections of fencing and concrete wall designed to separate Israel from the Palestinian-controlled West Bank. Construction began in 2002 and is still ongoing. In 2004 the International Court of Justice ruled that the barrier was illegal.

Toda   Hebrew for 'thank you'.

Torshi   A mixture of pickled vegetables. Popular Egyptian snack.

Touria   'Hoe'. Used extensively in Egyptian agriculture.

Trafigura   A multinational metals, energy and oil trading company. Accused of illegally dumping toxic waste in Côte d'Ivoire in 2006.

Tufah   'Apple'. Apple-flavoured tobacco is popular among *shisha* smokers.

Tura   A large prison just outside Cairo.

Tuthmosis I   Eighteenth-Dynasty (New Kingdom) pharaoh. Ruled *c*.1504–1492BC.

Tuthmosis II   Eighteenth-Dynasty (New Kingdom) pharaoh. Ruled *c*.1492–1479BC.

Tuthmosis III   Eighteenth-Dynasty (New Kingdom) pharaoh. Ruled *c*.1479–1425BC. Regarded as one of Egypt's greatest warrior pharaohs.

Tzadik   A Jewish person considered especially righteous and holy.

Vanunu, Mordechai   A former Israeli nuclear technician who revealed details of Israel's nuclear programme to the British press in 1986. He was subsequently kidnapped by Mossad, returned to Israel and spent eighteen years in prison, over half of them in solitary confinement. Since his release he has been rearrested on a number of occasions for violating his draconian probation terms. His treatment has become a cause célèbre for human rights groups.

Wadi   Arabic word for a valley or a dried-up river course.

Ward-i-nil   Literally, 'Nile flower'. Common Egyptian water plant. Large clumps of it can be seen floating down the Nile.

Winlock, Herbert Eustis   American Egyptologist and archaeologist. Worked under the auspices of the Metropolitan Museum of Art. Lived 1884–1950.

Women in Black   A worldwide anti-war and human rights campaigning movement founded in Israel in 1988.

Ya kalb   Arabic for 'You dog'.

Yalla   Arabic for 'Come on!' or 'Go!'.

Ya Omm   Literally, 'Oh, Mother'. Respectful term used when addressing an old lady.

Yarkon   A river in northern Tel-Aviv.

Yarmulke   Skullcap worn by Jews during prayer. Orthodox Jews wear one all the time.

Yedioth Ahronoth   Highest circulation Israeli daily newspaper.

***Yehood* (pl. *Yehoodi*)**   Arabic word for 'Jew'.

Yeshiva   A Jewish religious school.

Yiddish   A language fusing elements of German and Hebrew. Widely spoken in Orthodox Jewish communities.

Yisrael Beiteinu   A hard-line, right-wing, nationalist Israeli political party. The name means 'Israel is our home'.

***Zikhrono livrakha* (f. *Zikhrona livrakha*)**   Literally, 'May his/her name be a blessing'. Hebrew phrase used when referring to someone who has died.

Zikr   A group of devout Muslims, usually belonging to one of the mystic Sufi brotherhoods, who perform a trance-inducing devotional dance.

ACKNOWLEDGEMENTS

Although getting words out of your head and on to the page can be a solitary business, writing a novel is ultimately a collaborative effort, drawing on the support, skills, knowledge and generosity of a wide range of people. This book is no exception. Without the following I would never have made it through the labyrinth:

First and foremost Alicky, my wife, my life, without whom nothing is possible, and whose patience, advice and insightful comments were central to the creation of this story. As with all my books, I owe her a greater debt than I could ever repay.

Likewise my amazing agent, Laura Susijn, who has gone way beyond the call of duty in offering support and encouragement; and Simon Taylor, who has been not simply a great editor, but a good friend as well.

Professor Stephen Quirke and Dr Nicholas Reeves offered crucial advice on aspects of ancient Egyptian history and language; Stuart Hamilton and Simon Mitchell did the same for, respectively, the sciences of pathology and computer security. Professor Jan Cilliers proved – excuse the pun – a rich seam of knowledge on all aspects of the gold mining industry; Rasha Abdullah corrected my woeful Egyptian Arabic; Nava Mizrahi and Iris Maor helped with my even more woeful Hebrew.

Thanks also to First Sergeant Moeen Saad of the David Police Station, Jerusalem; Rachel Steiner and Asher Kupchik of the National Library of Israel; the staff of the Good Samaritan Society for Handicapped People, Luxor; the management and staff of the Winter Palace Hotel, Luxor; David Pratt, Jorge Pullin, David Blasco, Lisa Chaikin, Leah Gruenpeter-Gold, George Hintalian, Kevin Taverner and Rishi Arora.

Three particular thank-yous:

Firstly, to Dr Avi Zelba of the Israel Police, for advice, access and hospitality.

Secondly, to His Eminence Archbishop Aris Shirvanian of the Armenian Patriarchate, Jerusalem, for sharing his knowledge and experience of the Armenian community.

Thirdly, to Rinat Davidovich and the staff and residents of the Ma'agan Shelter, Petah Tikva. The issue of sex trafficking is a deeply distressing one, and the Shelter does an extraordinary and courageous job in supporting its victims. Without their advice and help this book could never have been written. You can find out more about their work at: http://www.maagan-shelter.org.il/English.html

A GLOBAL AFFAIR

In northern Afghanistan, 1990.

A GLOBAL AFFAIR

An Inside Look at the United Nations

Edited by Amy Janello and Brennon Jones
Introduction by Brian Urquhart

Jones & Janello

UPI/Bettmann

UN headquarters under
construction, September 1949.

Contents

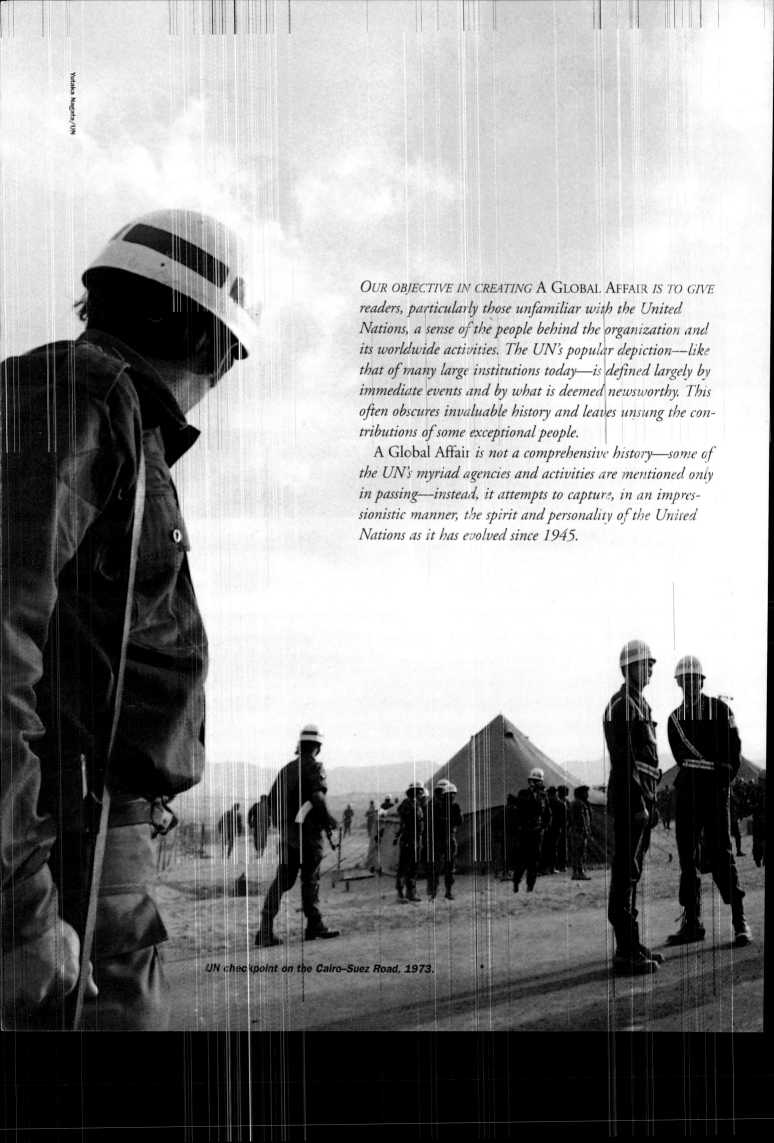

OUR OBJECTIVE IN CREATING A GLOBAL AFFAIR IS TO GIVE
readers, particularly those unfamiliar with the United
Nations, a sense of the people behind the organization and
its worldwide activities. The UN's popular depiction—like
that of many large institutions today—is defined largely by
immediate events and by what is deemed newsworthy. This
often obscures invaluable history and leaves unsung the con-
tributions of some exceptional people.

A Global Affair is not a comprehensive history—some of
the UN's myriad agencies and activities are mentioned only
in passing—instead, it attempts to capture, in an impres-
sionistic manner, the spirit and personality of the United
Nations as it has evolved since 1945.

UN checkpoint on the Cairo–Suez Road, 1973.

In 1970 the journalist Richard Hudson wrote in
The New York Times, *"Every time I walk into the United
Nations, I am struck by the fact I am leaving the United
States….the swirl of international politics here would
always give me this strange, exhilarating feeling of being in
a uniquely cosmopolitan atmosphere."*

We hope A Global Affair *conveys that sense of energy, a
hallmark of the United Nations for most of its history, and
brings to life those UN involvements that are far from headquarters but from which the world organization's ultimate
successes and failures can be most clearly gauged.*

The Editors

Introduction

Brian Urquhart

I WAS 14 YEARS OLD WHEN ADOLF HITLER CAME TO POWER IN 1933. The Japanese were already in Manchuria. The free nations of the world failed to use the League of Nations to stop this international banditry. Two years later Mussolini invaded Abyssinia, and the humiliating descent to World War II began. As a teenager I, along with many others, felt that something should be done to stop the slide to disaster. Our governments, however, sat on their hands.

It was this bitter early experience that gave me a passionate desire to work for a world organization dedicated not only to peace, but to resisting evil. Six years' service in the British Army during the war, and especially the spectacle of the rape, ruin and disgrace of Europe under the Nazis, only strengthened this ambition. To this day, working for the United Nations seems to me the most interesting job—and the highest privilege—that a reasonable person could ask for. It is, of course, a frustrating and often disappointing vocation, but who ever expected working for a better world to be easy?

The United Nations and its galaxy of specialized organizations were created in a fervent reaction to the human race's greatest collective disaster, the Second World War. The system was set up by national leaders who had experienced that disaster firsthand and were determined that nothing like it should ever happen again. The UN Charter was their blueprint for a more just and peaceful world and, at the beginning at any rate, they all seemed determined to make it work.

It was not long, however, before nations began to re-arm and to threaten one another all over again. Even worse, the growing enmity of the UN's two most powerful members, the United States and the Soviet Union, caused the world to be divided into two hostile, nuclear-armed camps for more than 40 years. Despite the chilling international climate, the organization forged ahead. Having presided over a surprisingly peaceful process of worldwide decolonization, the UN developed the technique of peacekeeping—using soldiers as intermediaries between hostile forces—to fill dangerous power vacuums and contain regional conflicts. The organization provided a sort of safety net to prevent a sudden lurch to nuclear war. Although there were many small wars in the first 50 years of the UN, there was no third *world* war.

In other fields as well the UN did pioneering work, again despite the Cold War. It put human rights on the international map as a criterion for national and international behavior, and turned its attention to a new generation of global problems—development, the environment, women's rights, population, poverty, to name a few—that will help determine the future of the human race. It moved into virtually all major fields of human activity and made substantial progress in many of them.

"*L'ONU, c'est quelle tribu?*"—(The UN, what tribe is that?)—a provincial Congolese administrator inquired when we arrived in the chaos of the Congo in 1960, shortly after the nation had won its independence. His question is not as odd as it might seem. The United Nations—the largest collection of foreigners in the world (currently comprising 185 member states), yet with no sovereign power of its own—is often viewed with suspicion and a good deal of skepticism. Its true value is best seen in great international crises, when it can provide an acceptable escape from a major calamity. History, however, may well judge as more significant its less spectacular, longer-term work in international law, in economic development and on social issues.

Only a few of the men and women who do the real work of the UN and its agencies are well known, or known at all. The young people saving lives and caring for children in a refugee camp in Rwanda, the soldiers sheltering civilians under fire in Sarajevo, may be glimpsed on the television screen, but none will be known by name. Their colleagues who devote their lives to developing international law, devising development programs or engaging in the endless exchanges of preventive diplomacy will remain invisible and anonymous. And yet, without them, the best-laid plans of governments and international organizations would remain nothing but brave phrases in diplomatic documents.

Few people now remember the veteran foot soldiers of the international world, the people who represented the true spirit of the United Nations as it was conceived 50 years ago. Even Ralph Bunche, the world's champion mediator and the father of peacekeeping, is almost forgotten. Who remembers Maurice Pate, the American investment banker who founded UNICEF; or General E.L.M. Burns of Canada, the first commander of a peacekeeping force; or René Cassin of France, Eleanor Roosevelt's partner in establishing the Universal Declaration of Human Rights; or Robert Jackson of Australia, the greatest of humanitarian relief operators; or Colonel S. S. Maitra of India, who, 35 years ago in the Congo, provided a perfect example of the peacekeeper as humanitarian and military man combined; or David Owen of Britain, who masterminded and built the UN Development Programme; or Raúl Prebisch of Argentina, the great economist of Latin America? Even less remembered are the countless faithful workers who served them.

I remember a difficult evening in Africa in November 1961. I was then the head of the UN operation in Katanga, the Congo, and I had been rather forcefully kidnapped from a dinner party in Elizabethville, the capital of Katanga, by the thugs of the secessionist regime. As I sat, in considerable anxiety and discomfort, in some godforsaken camp in the bush, I asked myself what on earth I thought I was doing. The answer, curiously enough, was comforting and invigorating. I was trying, as an objective and disinterested civil servant, to sort out a particularly messy and violent episode in the short history of a newly independent nation. That is what I had been sent to do, and maybe the idea would eventually get through to my captors. Fortunately, it did. I am sure that this experience has been shared many times in different ways by those who have chosen to serve the United Nations.

This book commemorates some of the dedicated civil servants and national representatives who have striven to make the United Nations work in its tumultuous first 50 years. It gives vivid glimpses of them at various stages of what Dag Hammarskjöld once described as "a venture in progress towards an international community living in peace under the laws of justice."

CHAPTER ONE
The Early Years

The Early Years

Kathleen Teltsch

T HE MOOD IN SAN FRANCISCO'S WAR MEMORIAL OPERA HOUSE
was one of high hopes and exhilaration. President Harry S.
Truman, preparing to address the delegates who had gathered for the
signing of the United Nations Charter on June 26, 1945, summed
up the mood when he raised his hands and spontaneously exclaimed,
"Oh, what a great day this can be in history!"

The delegates had spent more than two months drafting the charter. On the day of the signing, newspapers carried reports of ground
battles and air strikes against enemy targets in the Pacific; the war in
Europe had been over for less than two months. The world was weary of
war. Many of the delegates had lived for years with blackouts, rationing
and other privations; some bore the scars of war. For them, the birth of
the United Nations seemed to mark the beginning of a shining new era,
a time in which wartime allies would work together to preserve the peace.

There was reason to be optimistic. Whereas a quarter of a century
before, the United States had held itself aloof from the League of
Nations, thus spelling the organization's doom, now it was committed
to making sure that the United Nations—a name proposed by President
Franklin D. Roosevelt—worked and endured. The Allies, who had
fought so hard together, would surely now work equally hard to preserve
the peace.

The first threat to the new charter came not from a recalcitrant government but from the hordes of eager photographers who rushed toward
the document. A UN official, moving quickly, wrapped his arms protectively around the charter while yelling for guards to keep back the press.

The actual signing of the charter took many hours. It was delayed
a bit, among other reasons, because the members of the Chinese delegation needed time to grind a stick of dry ink in a mortar backstage before
Foreign Minister Wellington Koo, using a calligrapher's brush, affixed
the first signature. Fifty governments were signatories; Poland had to be

PREVIOUS SPREAD *Escorted by New York's finest, outgoing UN Secretary-General Trygve Lie (center left) welcomes Dag Hammarskjöld, the newly appointed UN secretary-general, at Idlewild Airport in April 1953. Hammarskjöld, a Swede, had flown in from Stockholm.*

ABOVE *Elated Russian delegates at the San Francisco conference savor war's end in May 1945.*

RIGHT *Arriving at the San Francisco conference, US President Harry S. Truman greets spectators and the press. In a radio address to the nation, Truman said of conference delegates, "[You] are to be the architects of the better world. In your hands rests our future."*

TOP *Delegates from the League of Nations listen to Hitler's envoy defend Germany's militarization of the Rhineland in 1936. The promises and failures of the League, the first international organization—formed in the aftermath of World War I and dissolved in 1946—were a constant reminder to the architects of the United Nations.*

ABOVE LEFT *Roosevelt and Churchill sign the Atlantic Charter aboard the USS Augusta in 1941.*

ABOVE *Churchill, Roosevelt and Stalin agreed on the voting formula for the UN Security Council at Yalta in 1945.*

LEFT *US, Chinese and British delegates at the Dumbarton Oaks conference, where the outline of the UN Charter was agreed upon, have an informal lunch in September 1944.*

It seems to us that the President's death, instead of weakening the structure at San Francisco, will strengthen it. Death almost always reactivates the household in some curious manner, and the death of Franklin Roosevelt recalls and refurnishes the terrible emotions and the bright meaning of the times he brought us through. By the simple fact of dying, he has again attacked in strength. He now personifies, as no one else could, all the American dead—those whose absence we shall soon attempt to justify. The President was always a lover of strategy: he even died strategically, as though he had chosen the right moment to inherit the great legacy of light that Death leaves to the great. He will arrive in San Francisco quite on schedule, and in hundredfold capacity, to inspire the nations that he named United.

The delegates to San Francisco have the most astonishing job that has ever been dumped into the laps of a few individuals. On what sort of rabbit they pull from the hat hang the lives of most of us, and of our sons and daughters. If they put on their spectacles and look down their noses and come up with the same old bunny, we shall very likely all hang separately—nation against nation, power against power, defense against defense, people (reluctantly) against people (reluctantly). If they manage to bring the United Nations out of the bag, full blown, with constitutional authority and a federal structure having popular meaning, popular backing, and an over-all authority greater than the authority of any one member or any combination of members, we might well be started up a new road.

The pattern of life is plain enough. The world shrinks. It will eventually be unified. What remains to be seen (through eyes that now bug out with mortal terror) is whether the last chapter will be written in blood or in Quink.

—E. B. White, excerpts from *The New Yorker*, 1945

added later, after it was decided which political faction was the real Poland.

Then the charter—encased in a container, secured with four straps and provided with its own parachute—was flown to Washington in the custody of Alger Hiss, the conference's secretary-general.

The conference produced an enduring symbol: the United Nations emblem, a graphic rendering of a map of the world clasped by two laurel branches, signifying peace. The design, intended only as an identifying badge to be worn by authorized participants, was subsequently adopted as the official

"...and in conclusion, Mr. President, I say that if after this great war we are to have a federation of all nations of the earth, where would it be more fitting to have the seat of government of this great brotherhood of free and friendly peoples than right here in God's country?"

From a cartoon US Senate, one representative gives President Roosevelt his views on the future United Nations in June 1944.

insignia. The first model used San Francisco as its focal point; this was changed later to the Greenwich meridian, supposedly at the suggestion of a British representative.

The charter-drafting sessions had not been free of bickering: The Soviets and the West accused each other of reneging on an agreement between President Roosevelt and Soviet Premier Stalin about limiting the veto's use. Even small issues proved thorny. The French, who were told that there were not enough French interpreters, surprised the American hosts by ingeniously placing their own people around a conference room. As a result, US Secretary of State Edward R. Stettinius, Jr., had to speak against an annoying murmur of whispered translations.

Although Trygve Lie was a participant at the San Francisco conference as foreign minister of Norway's government-in-exile, he was not one of its stars, either as a speaker or as a particularly skilled negotiator. He left early, rushing home after news came of Germany's surrender, on May 7, and thus missed the signing ceremony. Then, in London—where the General Assembly held its first session in January 1946—the Big Powers picked Lie as their compromise choice for UN secretary-general.

Lie's immediate preoccupation was getting "this machine," as he sometimes called the organization, into working order. The hastily

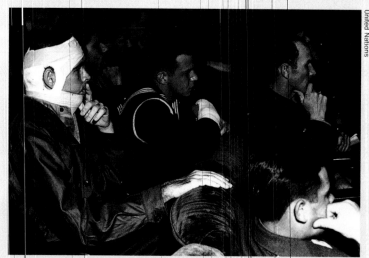

TOP *South African delegate H. T. Andrews (left), and Viscount Cranborne of the United Kingdom (right) wrestle with wording on a draft of the UN Charter.*

ABOVE *Bearing the wounds of the Second World War, uniformed veterans were among the most intent spectators at the UN founding conference.*

RIGHT *Leaving the rostrum at the UN founding conference, President Truman, accompanied by US Secretary of State Edward R. Stettinius, Jr., acknowledges the conference secretary-general, Alger Hiss.*

BELOW While taking in the San Francisco sights, Prince Faisal ibn Abdul Aziz, head of the Saudi Arabian delegation to the UN conference, attracts the attention of a four-year-old aspiring sailor.

BOTTOM LEFT Dr. Mary McCleod Bethune of the National Association for the Advancement of Colored People represented just one of the 42 nongovernmental organizations from the United States invited to San Francisco as consultants.

BOTTOM RIGHT In the plush seats of the San Francisco Opera House, delegates debated the precise language of the UN Charter for hours at a time.

BELOW Lester Pearson of Canada, who went on to win the Nobel Peace Prize in 1957 for his peacekeeping efforts during the Suez Canal crisis, addresses a meeting during the conference. Seated at his left is Bertha Lutz of Brazil, one of just four women delegates at the conference.

United Nations

AP/Wide World Photos

United Nations

UPI/Bettmann

19

ABOVE *It's a long queue for spectators anxious to enter Central Hall for the UN's first session.*

BELOW *The ornate Central Hall at Westminster in London was chosen as the meeting place for the first session of the General Assembly, held in January 1946.*

TOP RIGHT *A final touch-up in preparation for the tide of international delegates attending the third UN General Assembly at the Palais de Chaillot in Paris in 1948. A devaluation of the franc made France the economical choice to host the Assembly that year.*

BOTTOM RIGHT *Norwegian statesman Trygve Lie was secretary-general for the UN's first eight years.*

In 1946 the British Government was looking for a building situated close to the Houses of Parliament for the inaugural meeting of the United Nations. Few areas of London had been left unscathed by the bombing of the Second World War, but Westminster Central Hall had sustained only minor damage, and so was chosen to be the venue for this historic event.

Built at the turn of the century, Central Hall is UK headquarters for the Methodist Church and stands opposite Westminster Abbey. In addition to the Great Hall, which seats more than 2,300 people, the building houses extensive exhibition space and smaller conference rooms.

Westminster Central Hall underwent a transformation for the Assembly. Approximately half of the seating was removed, glass-fronted cabinets for the translation services were installed, and wall-to-wall carpeting laid down. The church sanctuary was boarded up and boxed in to create a modern square appearance and, outside, a great striped awning was erected bearing the flags of the participating nations.

And the church? The church moved out for the only time in its history, first to the Victoria Palace Theatre and then, when that proved too small, to the 2,500-seat London Coliseum, now the home of the English National Opera.

The leaders of the Methodist Church were honored to allow the Hall to be used to launch the UN organization. As Reverend W. E. Sangster, the superintendent minister of Central Hall, commented at the time: divine providence had preserved the building for the establishment of world peace, for in 1946 it was rare to find a hall still intact in the center of London.

---Peter Tudor, general manager, Westminster Central Hall

Bill Bruce and I met in November 1945 at Church House in London where we worked on the conference staff preparing for the first session of the UN General Assembly in London in February 1946. Bill was on loan from the US State Department. I was hired from the staff of the Royal Institute of International Affairs (Chatham House) which for the duration of the Second World War was absorbed into the Foreign Office as the Foreign Office Research Department. We both began our UN careers in November 1945...

In 1942, Bill had been hired by the War Relocation Authority to assist in the administration of a relocation camp at Manzanar, California, where Japanese were interned after the attack on Pearl Harbor. Disturbed by the internment of the American-born Japanese, Bill went to Washington attempting to secure their release and reinstatement in American society. He was hired by the US State Department where he served two years, before attending the founding conference of the UN in 1945...

I came to the UN in part because of my experience living in London during the war, but primarily because of what I had seen and heard during brief visits to Nazi Germany as a teenager. These visits, which included staying with a family where the mother was Jewish, and another in which the son was a member of the SS, and the Munich crisis period of 1938, convinced me that war was inevitable to deter Hitler, and that the atrocities of the Nazi regime, some of which I had witnessed firsthand, should not be permitted to recur.

Bill and I believe that our shared sense about injustices committed, albeit to a very different degree and in very different circumstances, brought us together in London in 1945, and ultimately led to our marriage which continues into the fiftieth anniversary year of the United Nations and hopefully many years beyond.

—Margaret Bruce

recruited staff was an odd mix: Some were veterans of the League of Nations; many more came out of governments or the armed services. Several interpreters had served in underground resistance movements. One declared that he would fight again just for the privilege of being present.

UNTIL 1952, WHEN IT settled in its permanent headquarters on the East River, the United Nations was a transient in search of a home. In its first few years, it moved from temporary quarters in a midtown Manhattan hotel to quarters at Hunter College in the Bronx, then settled for four years in the former Sperry Gyroscope plant on Long Island. Those who put stock in omens should have been pleased with the symbolism: the peace organization occupying a site that had housed a supplier of war material and whose postal address was Lake Success. Assembly sessions were held in a converted indoor skating rink at Flushing Meadow, with diplomats and staff members shuttling between the two sites.

Big Power relations were deteriorating ominously. Still, there was a heady excitement about the United Nations. At least in the early years, New York was pleased to be looked on as the world's capital, especially during the fall 1946 Assembly session, which brought thousands of foreign dignitaries to the city. Crowds would gather outside the Waldorf-Astoria for a glimpse of the Saudi princes in their robes and the motorcades whipping through midtown.

The converted plant was an ugly, sprawling collection of jerry-built offices and miles of corridors. There was a cafeteria, which everybody used at times, and a diplomats' lounge, which was more than a mere watering hole. Here diplomacy was conducted in quiet corners. Meeting rooms and offices were all on one floor, creating a certain intimacy—and a chance for a close-up look at men and women engaged in a historic adventure.

Where the United Nations would make its permanent home was a major preoccupation for the delegates and for Lie and his staff. A search committee toured Westchester towns and found that some were downright hostile to the notion of playing host to the organization. The members considered San Francisco fondly. Too far for the Soviets. Philadelphia? "How can you put the capital of the world in a town that has both baseball clubs in last place?" quipped Herbert Evatt, the Australian foreign minister. A proffered gift from John D. Rockefeller, Jr., of

Objects to Selection: Prescott Bush acted as moderator of a stormy two-hour meeting in Greenwich [Connecticut], as a wave of protests arose today from the area tentatively picked as headquarters of the United Nations Organization. Bush said his neighbors "feel the site might be better in an area where it is wanted."

—*New York Journal-American*, 1946

The Secretariat is a masterly example of the power of architecture to express monumentality by the use of the rectangle alone. It is a triumph of unadorned proportion.

—George Howe, *Architectural Forum*, 1950

I will say that the Secretariat building seems to me a superficial aesthetic triumph and an architectural failure....Whereas modern architecture began with the true precept that form follows function, and that an organic form must respect every human function, this new office building is based on the theory that even if no symbolic purpose is served, function should be sacrificed to form.

—Lewis Mumford, *The New Yorker*, 1951

TOP LEFT *A 1946 drawing by Hugh Ferriss of Walter K. Harrison's concept for X-City, a development William Zeckendorf of Webb and Knapp was planning for the East River site prior to the UN purchase. Elements of the self-contained city—though not the futuristic airstrip and dock—were incorporated into the UN headquarter's final design.*

BOTTOM LEFT *Members of the UN site selection commit-tee for the permanent headquarters survey the Blue Hills reservation near Boston, one of 16 US sites considered before New York City was chosen in December 1946.*

ABOVE *An international team of renowned architects, who considered more than 50 designs, shows its final model for the new UN headquarters. From left to right: G. A. Soilleux, Australia; Howard Robertson, United Kingdom; Gaston Brunfaut, Belgium; Jean Antoniades, Greece; Wallace K. Harrison, director of planning, Unit-ed States; Ernest Cormier, Canada; Julio Vilamajo, Uruguay; Oscar Niemeyer, Brazil; and Josef Havlicek, Czechoslovakia. Charles Le Corbusier of France is not pictured.*

RIGHT *A 1946 sketch by Charles Le Corbusier for New York headquarters hints at the final design.*

This memorandum sets forth the terms and conditions of the offer made by me in my letter to you dated December 10, 1946. I have acquired a firm offer from Webb and Knapp, Inc. to sell to the United Nations within thirty days from December 10, 1946 at $8,500,000, the following property between First Avenue and Franklin D. Roosevelt Drive: 1) The western portion of the block between 42nd and 43rd Streets. 2) All of the four blocks between 43rd and 47th Streets. 3) Two small parcels in the block between 47th and 48th Streets.

In addition representatives of the City of New York have assured me of the desire and willingness of the City to acquire and give to the United Nations the balance of the block between 47th and 48th Streets.

To make possible the acquisition of this property by the United Nations, should they decide to accept said offer and to make it the site of their permanent headquarters, I hereby offer to give to the UN the sum of $8,500,000 on the following terms and conditions: a) That the gift shall be made at the time of the closing of the purchase of said property. b) That the City of New York shall agree to give to the UN 43rd, 44th, 45th, 46th and 47th Streets between First Ave and Franklin D. Roosevelt Drive upon terms which shall permit the UN to close any or all thereof to passage and otherwise to use them for its own purposes without restriction or limitation. c) That the City of New York shall agree to acquire to give absolutely to the UN all the balance of that city block bounded by First Ave, 47th, 48th Streets and Franklin D. Roosevelt Drive not covered by the firm offer of Webb and Knapp, Inc. d) That the City of New York shall agree to give to the UN all rights to bulkheads and piers along the river frontage of the East River between 42nd and 48th Streets. e) That each of the said agreements of the City of New York shall have been concluded in form satisfactory to the parties in interest at or prior to the time of the making of my said gift. f) That prior to the making of my said gift, assurances satisfactory to my attorneys shall have been given to me that the said gift from me will be free and clear of all taxes of the United States, the State of New York, or any other taxing authority having jurisdiction with respect thereto.

—John D. Rockefeller, Jr.

$8.5 million to purchase an 18-acre site on Manhattan's East side resolved the issue.

Designing the structures was another matter. For months speculation ran riot. There were reports that the theme would be Mayan. An Egyptian artist offered a design for a capitol with its own riverside dock, and sketched in a few feluccas. Wallace K. Harrison, the architect in charge of planning, drew a rough pen sketch on a tablecloth. A newsman whipped the cloth off and photographed the drawing, and the picture ran in *The New York Times*. The soaring Secretariat building, flanked by a low-lying domed Assembly, was recognizable in the crude sketch.

LEFT *Clearing the way for construction of the 39-story headquarters meant tearing down old slaughterhouses on the Turtle Bay site. To close the purchase deal, UN officials had to sign a clause promising not to kill cattle at their new location.*

BOTTOM LEFT *A simple, typewritten letter from John D. Rockefeller, Jr., completed an $8.5-million deal for title to the UN headquarters site in New York.*

ABOVE *New York City Mayor William O'Dwyer (right) presents UN Secretary-General Trygve Lie with the deed for seven acres of land that completed the future site of UN headquarters. New York power-brokers Robert Moses (second from left) and Francis Cardinal Spellman (fourth from left) are among those looking on.*

RIGHT *After depositing copies of the UN Charter and the Universal Declaration of Human Rights inside, Secretary-General Trygve Lie (left) and chief architect Wallace K. Harrison seal the cornerstone at the new UN headquarters during a ceremony marking the fourth anniversary of the United Nations in October 1949.*

SOMETIMES THE UNITED NATIONS SEEMED LESS ABOUT GOVERNMENTS and issues than about people. And what personalities they were! What a thrill to watch Eleanor Roosevelt hurrying along, usually trailed by two young State Department advisers.

When foreign diplomats addressed her in formal sessions, they frequently spoke of the United Nations as her late husband's legacy to the world, and she would acknowledge the tribute with a nod. But she was very much her own person—sometimes too much so for the American delegation of which she was a member.

There was the day she made the impromptu observation, in a small committee discussion, that aid to Chiang Kai-shek was "water down the

drain." The press, which had been covering more important sessions or just dozing, caught up with her in a corridor. While American advisers tried to explain away this seeming break with Washington policy, she stood listening and then said quietly, "If I said it, I guess I said it."

She also took on a Soviet spokesman who, during a debate on freedom of information, attacked the "war-mongering American press" and demanded a treaty to curb their evil ways. When he had finished talking, she leaned across the conference table to explain to her "young Soviet friend" that, while the free press might have its failings, "the controlled press is like an egg—part bad, all bad."

On another occasion, she was compelled to explain Washington's view that the United Nations International Children's Emergency Fund, which had done admirable work in relieving suffering, was no longer in an "emergency" situation and should begin winding up its work. The position infuriated Pakistani diplomat Ahmed Bokhari, who retorted angrily that, with the European war over, the United States was willing to see Asian children die of malnutrition.

Mrs. Roosevelt looked shaken and conveyed her dismay to Washington; reports had it that she threatened to resign. In any event, the United States backed away from its demands, and the organization known as UNICEF remains one of the gems in the international aid system. Mrs. Roosevelt's personal contribution was the unanimous approval of the Universal Declaration of Human Rights, which she had seen through committee, at an Assembly session in Paris in 1948.

There were many others who made their impact in those early years. Pakistan's Bokhari, a professional dancer in his youth, went on to become an under secretary-general, a rather unconventional one, who could make brilliant conversation but also enjoyed shocking his listeners. Often, after a long meeting, he would turn up at a dinner party wearing a rough peasant's cloak pulled over his head and spend an hour sitting on the floor, reciting verse or playing tunes on a shepherd's pipe.

The Philippines for years was represented at Assembly openings by its ebullient foreign minister, Carlos P. Romulo, who had more friends in the press than any other diplomat. (One American newsman named his son in Romulo's honor.) Informal and gregarious, General Romulo on occasion didn't mince words. Once, after a meeting with Latino delegates whose conduct he thought had been less than statesmanlike, he wagged his finger at them and admonished them to shape up. "Other-

You know why they built it that way, like a match box on end"? said a taxi driver approaching the UN building in New York, "They did it so that, when they want to, they can strike a match down its side and the whole thing will go up in smoke."

The UN building does resemble a match box. And, unfortunately, many Americans *would* like to see the whole organization go up in smoke. But if they knew it as I do, if they could see its accomplishments with their own eyes, I think they would feel differently....

[T]he UN *is* a sounding board for communist propaganda, and for anticommunist propaganda, too. That is what it was designed to be: a place where political opinions of all kinds could be expressed in words, rather than bullets. The hope was that differences among nations could be resolved by words, rather than bullets.

Possibly there are "spies and foreign agents" in the Secretariat and the delegations, although an astute intelligence office could surely think of more useful tasks for its operatives....

Each member nation is allowed a certain number of permanent employees on the UN staff. The number assigned to Russia is between 120 and 130. But the actual number of Russian representatives employed in the UN secretariat is *twenty!*

Despite repeated requests, the UN has been unable to inveigle more "spies and foreign agents" out of Moscow. During World War II, the USSR lost so many experts of various sorts that it cannot spare any more for the UN.

—Eleanor Roosevelt, *See,* **1952**

TOP LEFT *Soviet Premier Nikita S. Khrushchev's appearance at the 15th UN General Assembly in 1960—with his fist-pounding, shoe-banging antics—is one of the best-remembered moments in UN history.*